ERCHIE,
MY DROLL FRIEND

ERCHIE,
MY DROLL FRIEND

NEIL MUNRO
(HUGH FOULIS)

Edited by
BRIAN D. OSBORNE
&
RONALD ARMSTRONG

Birlinn

This edition first published in 2002 by
Birlinn Limited
West Newington House
10 Newington Road
Edinburgh
EH9 1QS

www.birlinn.co.uk

Reprinted 2005

First published in book form in 1993
by Birlinn Limited as
Erchie & Jimmy Swan

Introductory material and notes
copyright © Brian D. Osborne and
Ronald Armstrong 1993 and 2002

ISBN 10: 1 84158 202 6
ISBN 13: 978 1 84158 202 3

British Library Cataloguing-in-Publication Data
A catalogue record for this book is available
from the British Library

The publisher acknowledges subsidy from

THE SCOTTISH ARTS COUNCIL

towards the publication of this book

Typeset by Koinonia, Manchester
Printed and bound by Antony Rowe Ltd, Chippenham

Contents

NOTE

Stories 1–29 are those printed in book form by William Blackwood &
Sons in Munro's lifetime. Their order of appearance in book form bears
no relation to their original order of newspaper appearance and four
stories (nos. 15, 24, 26 and 29) were specially written for the book. Munro
presumably approved the sequence used by Blackwood and we have not
felt it appropriate to interfere with the order of these 29 stories.

The following stories are those that first appeared in book form in
the 1993 Birlinn edition, or are now appearing for the first time in book
form and they have been arranged in one chronological sequence of
appearance in the *News*. The date of each story is shown in the notes for
that story at the end of the book.

Neil Munro

NEIL MUNRO was born on 3rd June 1863 in Inveraray on Loch Fyneside, Argyll into a Gaelic-speaking family from a crofting background. His mother, Anne Munro, was an unmarried kitchen maid; no father's name was recorded on his birth certificate, which also registers the birth of a stillborn twin sister. In an age when the stigma of illegitimacy was still considerable such a start in life was not propitious.

One of the minor mysteries of Munro's biography is that he consistently provided an alternative, but entirely false birth date, to works of reference such as *Who's Who*. This alternative date, 3rd June 1864, was diligently copied by every standard reference work and is still given wide currency despite evidence for the correct date appearing in the present editors' editions of *Para Handy* in 1992 and *Erchie and Jimmy Swan* in 1993. Even more surprising is the fact that the monument to Munro in Glen Aray, unveiled in 1935, bears the correct birth date while his gravestone in Kilmalieu Cemetery, Inveraray, perpetuates the false date, but this inconsistency does not ever seem to have entered into the consciousness of literary historians, librarians and compilers of reference works.

Another mystery is the identity of his father. Persistent legend suggests that a member of the ducal House of Argyll was Munro's father. While such stories are hard to prove, and equally hard to disprove, one later incident in the young Munro's life does tend to suggest a certain degree of well-placed patronage being shown in his favour.

In the 1871 census returns for Inveraray a one-roomed dwelling at McVicar's Land, Ark Lane, Inveraray was shown as being occupied by Angus McArthur Munro, a 66-year-old former crofter, his daughter, Agnes an un-married domestic servant aged 38 and his grandson, Neil, aged seven. In 1875 Neil's mother Ann married Malcolm Thomson, the governor of Inveraray Jail. In the 1881 Census returns Neil is shown living in Crombie's Land, Inveraray, with his great-aunt Bell McArthur, a 77-year-old retired field worker, and Bell's daughter Lilly McDougall, a 44-year-old laundress, while Munro's mother, then fifty-one, was living with her 76-year-old husband Malcolm Thomson and his 41-year-old son Malcolm Jnr.

From about 1869 to 1876 Munro attended Inveraray Burgh School, where he was taught by Henry Dunn Smith, a significant influence on the young Munro and later a friend.

After leaving school at the age of thirteen or fourteen he was, to quote his own later words: "insinuated, without any regard for my own desires, into a country lawyer's office, wherefrom I withdrew myself as soon as I arrived at years of discretion and revolt." (*The Brave Days*)

Munro's comment glosses over much that is significant. The lawyer's office in Inveraray into which he was 'insinuated' was that of William Douglas. Douglas was an extremely well established lawyer in the county and had been clerk to the Commissioners of Supply since 1864 and was appointed clerk to the Lieutenancy of Argyll in 1873. These posts brought Douglas into close contact with official Argyll and when one recollects that the lord lieutenant of Argyll was the duke one may legitimately speculate about the source of the influence that placed a youth from such a disadvantaged, poor, working-class background in a position which would normally be eagerly competed for by the sons of the middle classes. Munro's fellow clerks in Douglas's office included the son of the local doctor, and the son of Douglas's managing clerk.

Munro seems to have found the work uncongenial and, as he wrote later, was dismayed to find: "I could earn in an afternoon for my employer far more than the £5 per annum I was getting as salary." In the 1881 Census Munro is described as law clerk (apprentice), but there is no evidence of his actually completing indenture papers as an apprentice. Munro was to leave Inveraray, more or less on his eighteenth birthday, in June 1881. It seems quite probable that the timing of his decision to move to Glasgow, with the eventual aim of taking up a career in journalism, was motivated by a desire to avoid committing himself to a five-year apprenticeship. Inveraray was however to remain central to his life and writings — he later had holiday homes there and in 1903 became the tenant of the house in the High Street once lived in by William Douglas, his former employer. He said on one occasion that "he never apparently could keep Inveraray and the romantic district of Argyll out of any story of his, and possibly he never would."

He and a friend, Archie McKellar, sailed on the Glasgow & Inveraray Steamboat Company's *Lord of the Isles* for Glasgow. Here he worked for two years as a clerk in a wholesale potato merchant and in an ironmonger's store, occupying some of his spare time improving his shorthand, a vital prerequisite for a career in journalism.

While at home in Inveraray he had read widely and had written essays for local publications. In the early years in Glasgow he developed his literary skills, submitting material to various publications. His first documented poem "The Phantom Smack: A Lochfyne Fisher's 'Bar'," appeared, under the pen name of Bealach-an-Uaran (a place-name near Inveraray), in the widely circulated *Oban Times*, on 3rd February 1883. Other poems have been traced in *The Lennox Herald* in June 1883 and the *Oban Times* in July 1884. By the time of this last publication Munro had found a place on the *Greenock Advertiser*, which however closed a few weeks after he joined it. He then got a place on a morning daily paper, the *Glasgow News* (not to be confused with the *Glasgow Evening News* with which he was so long associated. The *Glasgow Evening News* was re-titled the *Glasgow News* in 1905).

In July 1884 Munro married Jessie Ewing Adam, the daughter of Hugh Adam, a mechanic living in Braid Street,

Glasgow. Jessie was the same age as Munro and is described in the 1881 census as a clothfolder. In November of that year they moved to Falkirk, where Munro took up a post on the *Falkirk Herald*. Their first child, Annie, was born there, but died of meningitis aged two and a half.

In April 1887 the Munros returned to Glasgow and Neil resumed work as a reporter on the *Glasgow News*. In February 1888 the *Glasgow Evening News* absorbed the *News* and Munro became a sub-editor, very swiftly becoming chief reporter. Over the next few years Munro worked hard at journalism, submitting articles to a wide range of newspapers and magazines in Scotland and England; his activities included such curious and diverse tasks as reporting sermons for the *Scottish Pulpit* at fifteen shillings a time. In the early 1890s he was having sensational thriller fiction published in English newspapers and articles accepted by increasingly prestigious national magazines. By 1892 he had written a short story, a West Highland sketch, "Anapla's Boy", and submitted it to *Blackwood's Magazine*. Although this was rejected, a later submission, "Shudderman Soldier", was accepted, and over the next couple of years further "sheiling tales" based on West Highland themes were accepted by Blackwood until 1896, when they were able to bring out a small volume of eleven short stories under the title of *The Lost Pibroch*. This was enthusiastically reviewed and seen as the work of a new and fresh Scottish voice.

In 1897 Munro's career took a major move forward when *John Splendid*, his first historical novel, a work of broader appeal than *The Lost Pibroch*, was accepted for serialisation in *Blackwood's Magazine* and subsequent publication in book form by William Blackwood & Son. In October of that year, having sold his next novel, *Gilian the Dreamer* for serialisation in *Good Words* and subsequent book publication by the London publishing house Isbister, he felt secure enough to resign his staff appointment on the *Evening News*, while retaining the Thursday literary column *Views and Reviews* and the Monday column *The Looker-On*.

Munro's career, despite his abandoning the security of full-time journalism, flourished. A steady production of fiction, his *Evening News* work, regular columns for various other newspapers and magazines, occasional features and reports for London newspapers all made for a very considerable income and a substantial reputation. A rival newspaper, the *Glasgow Herald,* wrote in its obituary tribute to Munro: "No man exercised a more subtle literary influence on the West of Scotland than Neil Munro. His discriminating praise was sufficient to set aglow the heart of the young writer."

Nor was Munro's influence and literary connections confined to the West of Scotland. His diary and correspondence show links with such major literary figures of the period as Joseph Conrad, J. M. Barrie, John Buchan, Arnold Bennett, Andrew Lang, John Galsworthy, and R. B. Cunninghame Graham.

His income, although suffering the inevitable variability of the freelance author, was very substantial. In 1901, for example, his diary records earnings for the year of £1,243 — equivalent in modern terms to around £77,000. By this time the Munro's and their five surviving children had moved out of Glasgow, first of all to a house at Waterside, near Busby, Renfrewshire and then in 1902 to a house in Gourock. So successful had Munro become that he was able to send his eldest daughter Effie, aged seventeen, to finishing school in Switzerland in 1907. A final move, in 1918, brought him to an elegant Regency villa in Helensburgh, which he promptly renamed Cromalt, after a stream in his native Inveraray.

The theme of much of Munro's serious fiction was process of change and the decline of the old order in the Highlands. His continuing reputation centres on the three most famous historical novels, *John Splendid, Doom Castle* and *The New Road. The New Road,* published in 1914, confirmed his position as the pre-eminent historical novelist of his day. A review of it by John Buchan for the *Glasgow News* enthused, "It is a privilege to be allowed to express my humble admiration of what seems to me one of the finest romances written in our time. Mr Neil Munro is beyond question the foremost of living Scottish novelists, both in regard to the scope and variety of his work and its rare quality."

Sadly *The New Road* was to be the last great work of fiction from Munro's pen. During the First World War he was recalled to work on the *Glasgow News* and edited it for a number of years during and after the war, as well as going to France as a war correspondent on three occasions. Munro lost his eldest son, a medical student turned infantry subaltern in the Argyll & Sutherland Highlanders, on the Western Front in 1915 and felt the loss keenly.

A sequel to *The New Road* featuring the enigmatic central character Ninian Macgregor Campbell and set in the aftermath of the '45 was planned. It was first mentioned to Blackwood in 1915 and in 1918 he was able to say that he had made a start on it — but as late as October 1928 George Blackwood was still patiently enquiring after it: "a real Munro novel for 1929 would be the very thing..." It never materialised, although eleven intriguing chapters remain among Munro's papers in the National Library of Scotland and are being published by Birlinn in a Munro Anthology prepared by the present editors. Munro's post-1914 work consisted of *Jimmy Swan: the Joy Traveller* (1917), a 1918 short story collection, *Jaunty Jock*, which collected together various short stories he had published in various places over the previous decade, a third collection of Para Handy stories, *Hurricane Jack of the Vital Spark* (1923), to follow the two earlier collections in 1906 and 1911, and, rather bizarrely, a *History of the Royal Bank of Scotland 1727–1927*.

After Munro's death all his humorous fiction appeared in an omnibus edition under his own name and his friend and protégé George Blake edited two delightful collections of his journalism, *The Brave Days* (1931) and *The Looker-On* (1933) — these collections suggest the charm and variety of his newspaper columns and also afford some valuable biographical details. Munro never wrote an autobiography, although among his papers in the National Library of Scotland is what is described as his diary. This was probably started around 1905, with the aim of retrospectively recording the principal events and developments in his life and was presumably intended as an aid to biography or autobiography.

Munro was honoured in his lifetime by the award of the freedom of his native burgh of Inveraray in 1909 and the honorary degree of Doctor of Laws from Glasgow University in 1908. In 1930, two months before his death, Edinburgh University, as part of the installation ceremonies for their new chancellor, J. M. Barrie, also conferred a Doctorate of Laws on him.

Munro died at Helensburgh on 22nd December 1930 and was buried at Kilmalieu Cemetery, Inveraray. A memorial service was held in Glasgow Cathedral, attended by his many Glasgow friends, representatives of the university and the Church.

His own old newspaper made his death their lead story under the triple-decker headline:

DEATH OF NEIL MUNRO
PASSING OF A GREAT NOVELIST
GENIUS IN JOURNALISM

and the *Glasgow Herald* obituarist observed that although in later years he had published but little: "he had already accomplished his life's work — of taking up and wearing the mantle of R.L.S."

The connection with Stevenson was frequently made in tributes. The Rev. Lauchlan MacLean Watt, a noted literary authority of the period, and minister of Glasgow Cathedral, implicitly placed him above Stevenson when he described Munro as "the greatest Scottish novelist since Sir Walter Scott, and in the matter of Celtic story and character he excelled Sir Walter because of his more deeply intimate knowledge of that elusive mystery."

Five years after his death a monument was erected to him on a hillside in Glen Aray, overlooking the home of his ancestors. The initiative for the erection of the monument was taken by An Comunn Gàidhealach and it takes the form of a pyramid of local stone crowned with a Celtic book-shrine and bears Munro's name, the correct date of his birth and death, and the Gaelic inscription *Sar Litreachas* — " matchless literature".

Introduction

THE GLASGOW of 1902 into which Neil Munro's engaging character Erchie MacPherson appeared was a city of enormous energy, vitality and character. Self-confidently describing itself as the "Second City of the Empire" and with its dominant heavy engineering industries it was indeed the "Workshop of the World." Neil Munro knew this Glasgow well, he had been a journalist in and around the city since 1884 and had worked on the city's leading evening paper, *The Glasgow Evening News*, since 1887 and in 1888 had been appointed its chief reporter.

In 1897 he gave up his full-time post with the *News* to concentrate on his literary career. However the two commitments to the paper that he maintained were a weekly column of literary news, criticism and comment: "Views and Reviews" and a Monday column: "The Looker-On." Munro would maintain these influential and widely respected columns throughout most of the rest of his life — only giving them up in 1927. "The Looker-On" was an attractively eclectic mixture of reportage, comment and fiction and in its columns first appeared Munro's three great comic creations — Erchie, Para Handy and Jimmy Swan, the Joy Traveller.

Erchie MacPherson is a Kirk beadle: a term which has sadly gone out of fashion and is now replaced in Scottish Church usage by the more anodyne "church officer." In either form it denotes a post which broadly equates to the English verger: the incumbent had responsibility for the heating, cleaning and security of the church, and usually carried the Bible into church and escorted the minister to the pulpit. The beadle, sometimes known as "the minister's

man," is a stock character in Scottish literature, his privileged position giving him opportunity to observe and comment on a wide range of matters. Munro's beadle
combines his ecclesiastical duties with casual work as a
waiter at civic functions — a useful device for widening his
contacts and enlarging the range of matters on which he
can credibly comment.

What will inevitably strike any reader of the Erchie
stories is that they are almost all topical— they are, with
very few exceptions, inspired by news headlines, current
events, a fashion, a social trend, or even by natural phenomena. Munro, despite his protestations to the contrary,
was a journalist to his fingertips and a natural satirist of a
gentle and kindly type and used Erchie, as he would later
use Para Handy, and to an extent Jimmy Swan, as vehicles
for comment on the great and small issues of the day. Para
Handy famously reflects on such topics as spy scares and
German–British naval rivalry. Erchie certainly does not
avoid such geopolitical issues but as a Glaswegian: as, in
the title of one of the stories, "A Son of the City", he is more
often used to comment on domestic topics such as Edward
VII's visit to Glasgow's George Square. His Majesty on
entering George Square looks at the assembly of statues
and asks: "Whitna graveyaird's this?" and is promptly told
"It's no' a graveyaird; it's a square, and that's the Municeepal Buildin'."

Slum clearance, tramcars, the volunteer movement, the
Free Church dispute, the coming of the cinema, early
aviation, all feature in the Erchie stories and these specific
references to people and events, all entirely familiar to the
original early twentieth century newspaper reader, are now
often somewhat opaque and the editors of this edition have
attempted to enlighten the twenty-first century reader by
providing explanatory notes and comments.

The language of the stories is a rich Glaswegian dialect
of Scots — remarkably effective and remarkably authentic
when it is remembered that the author was born into a
Gaelic-speaking community in Argyllshire and only came

to Glasgow to find work just before his eighteenth birthday. We have not attempted to gloss every Scottish word
or phrase in the stories — this already large volume would
have become impossibly unwieldy. In most cases the sense
is clear enough from the context and in case of doubt
recourse can always be had to a Scots dictionary. We have
explained a few, particularly dated, particularly obscure or
particularly interesting terms, but most of our notes deal
with biographical and historical topics.

Indeed, reading the Erchie stories provides a remarkably
good insight into most of the history of the first quarter of
the twentieth century and the diligent reader will be instructed on such diverse and seemingly unlikely topics as
the controversial result of the marathon at the 1908 London
Olympics, the dispute between Peary and Cook over their
claims to have been the first man to reach the North Pole,
the post-war transfer market in footballers and the result of
the 1921 Carpentier/Dempsey heavyweight championship
of the world.

The warm reception that the Erchie stories received on
their appearance in the *Evening News* led William Blackwood to write to Munro in October 1903:

> My nephew George is very keen about your publishing
> the "Erchie sketches" in a popular form if you care to
> consider such a thing. If you thought it might clash with
> your more dignified works of fiction, it would always be
> possible for you to make use of a *nom de plume* or issue
> anonymously. Perhaps you will think it over.

Munro was by this time a well-established and critically
acclaimed short-story writer and novelist. His collection of
Highland stories *The Lost Pibroch* had been published
serially in *Blackwood's Magazine* and in volume form by
Blackwoods in 1896. Historical novels like *John Splendid*
(1898), *Doom Castle* (1901) and *Children of Tempest* (1903)
had been published by Blackwoods and had developed
Munro's reputation.

He was clearly worried by the damage to his reputation

that might ensue from the publication of these light-hearted pieces of journalism under his own name. His newspaper column was unattributed and although most of the literary world knew perfectly well who "The Looker-On" was and who produced "Views and Reviews" Munro still felt it would be wise to maintain a distance between the two parts of his life, between journalism and "dignified works of fiction".

He replied to William Blackwood's suggestion:

… as to *Erchie,* I have every reason to believe a collection of the philosophical utterances of that gentleman would be secure of a certain degree of popularity; I should not care to publish them with my name, however, and in any case I think it would be a mistake to consider their publication till next Spring at least as the market for that sort of material is very much glutted at present.

J. J. Bell's *Wee Macgreegor* was possibly on Munro's mind — he had reviewed it favourably for the *News* and helped set it on its way to huge sales.

Munro settled on the pen-name of "Hugh Foulis", and this was used for the book editions of all his comic series" — Erchie, the three volumes of Para Handy tales and Jimmy Swan. The first name was doubtless taken from the Christian name of his eldest son, Hugh Adam Munro, born in 1893, while the Foulis element is a knowing reference to his own surname, and confirmation that no very serious attempt was being made to conceal the identity of the *Erchie* author — the chief of the clan Munro is Munro of Foulis, and resides at Foulis Castle, in Easter Ross.

Blackwoods were remarkably committed to the publication of *Erchie* and were convinced that they had a potential major best-seller on their hands. Their print run for the one shilling paperback was a truly remarkable 107,000 copies, which would have made Munro around £1000 in royalties — an enormous sum at 1904 prices and equivalent in purchasing power to over £60,000 at 2002 prices. With this investment, Blackwoods energetically promoted the book, which was unusually produced with a number of photographic plates showing somewhat stagy representations of Erchie in a number of characteristic poses. As William Blackwood wrote to Munro:

> We should I think send a copy of the book to every editor and reviewer in the country, and enclose with it a sheet of extracts giving some characteristic passages likely to attract attention and be quoted. We should also send out a good blaze of advertisements at the very outset, and in the repeats and show bills keep introducing continually some topical feature until the desired result is obtained.

With such enthusiasm from the publishing house it is sad to report that *Erchie*, though very successful, did not quite manage to live up to Blackwood's remarkable expectations. First year sales were over 47,000 (earning Munro over £474 in royalties — about £24,000 at modern values) but thereafter sales declined sharply and the firm was obliged to relaunch it as a 6d cheap edition — with a marked decline in Munro's royalties.

Bookman, the leading book trade magazine of the day, in its Scottish wholesale trade report for July 1904 noted: "The shilling book of the month was unquestionably *Erchie,* by Hugh Foulis — a book of real Scots humour — well-known to have been written by one of our leading Scottish novelists."

The same column in August commented: "The remarkable success of *Erchie,* by Hugh Foulis, still continued, and although of special interest to Glasgow readers, it obtained ready purchasers in all parts of the country." Even the *Bookman*'s English wholesale report for the same month noted *Erchie* as one of the books most in demand. The suggestion of a particularly heavy Glasgow demand is perhaps what could have been expected.

Two clues as to why *Erchie* had not quite lived up to the publisher's high expectations come from Munro's correspondence with Blackwood. In September 1904 William

Blackwood wrote that "It has been sticking rather of late and sales in England have been very disappointing, but it has run well in the West [of Scotland] and here [Edinburgh], and we hope sales may yet revive."

The next year Munro was writing to Blackwood trying to interest him in a collection of the Para Handy stories, which had been running for a few months in the *News:*

> Since the retirement of *Erchie* I have been fortnightly writing in the *Glasgow News* a series of somewhat analogous articles and stories round about the title *The Vital Spark* ... I have not the slightest doubt that if you care to undertake their publication this Winter in the shilling form of *Erchie* they would exceed that gentleman's popularity. The dialect, for one thing, is reduced to a minimum and the articles are quite within the comprehension of the English reader without any glossary.

The conclusion is clear — the language of the *Erchie* stories proved just too great a barrier to their widespread success in England and abroad. Although their sales were by all standards, other than Blackwood's somewhat inflated expectations, remarkable, this seems to have been substantially due to good Scottish sales. When Blackwood's first print run of 107,000 copies sold out, in full price, cheap and colonial editions, *Erchie* was allowed to go out of print and did not make a renewed appearance until the posthumous collection of humorous short fiction — *Para Handy and other tales* published in 1931. Interestingly enough Blackwood, despite the author's assurance that *Para Handy* would be more accessible for the wider market only ordered an initial print run of 19,800 — although high demand meant that a reprint of 10,000 copies was called for within a month. A 1911 and a 1923 collection of new Para Handy stories followed — but Erchie was never revived, even though Munro continued to delight readers of the *Glasgow News* (as the *Evening News* was re-titled in 1905) with tales of his Kirk beadle until 1926.

In 1993 the present editors, having discovered 52

previously uncollected stories published in the *News* at dates ranging from January 1910 to June 1926, produced an edition combining the 29 original stories from the Blackwood edition, the newly discovered stories — making a total of 81 Erchie tales, the 30 Jimmy Swan stories published in 1917 and 7 newly discovered Jimmy Swan stories, together with notes and introduction. At that time it was assumed that all the Erchie stories had been found. However re-checking of the *News* archive revealed that there was a considerable body of Erchie stories dating from 1902 to 1904, which had been previously overlooked — largely because the assumption had been that all Munro's early *News* stories had been used for the 1904 Blackwood's edition. Another group of stories dating from 1908 to 1909 were also discovered. Ten of these represent an attempt by the *News* to use the Erchie stories in their weekend supplement rather than in the Monday "Looker-On" column. The stories appeared on a Saturday under the heading "Odd Hours with Erchie" and this change was announced in "The Looker-On" column accompanied by one of the very few public statements in the author's lifetime that Neil Munro was the author of the Erchie and Para Handy stories. This experiment only lasted from April to August 1908 and in September the traditional placing was resumed — Munro may well have been glad enough to regain these popular regular features for his Monday column.

Inevitably the question will be asked — why reprint material that Munro was happy enough to leave buried in the files of the *News*? The only possible answer is that the quality of the uncollected material is every bit as high as the 29 stories published by Blackwood.

In any collection, whether of 29, 81 or 142 stories, there are obviously peaks and troughs — but for comic brilliance and inventiveness one would be hard put to better the 1923 tale, "The Grand Old Man Comes Down." Inspired by a rearrangement of the statues in Glasgow's George Square, occasioned by the building of the Cenotaph, Erchie spins a marvellous fantasy about a council scheme to move the city's statues, because "Statues nooadays are like comic songs; they go awfu' quick oot o' fashion." He goes on to tell his slightly naïve and credulous friend Duffy that "Under the new movement for brightenin' up Gleska the authorities is gaun to put a' the statues on wheels and hurl them to different sites in the city twice a year. The priceless gift o' Art is to be brung hame to the toilers o' Brigton Cross and Maryhill."

The vein of shrewd observation and sentiment that pervades many of the stories, for example "The Prodigal Son" and "The Prodigal Returns" from the original collection, is mirrored in many of the uncollected stories, such as the 1908 story in praise of Glasgow tenement life "Erchie's Great Wee Close."

While these stories range widely there is no doubt that they provide a fascinating and vivid picture of a vanished Glasgow — and a picture which is valuable corrective to the often polarised representation of the city which would suggest that there was nothing in Glasgow between the artistic life of the Glasgow Boys and Charles Rennie Mackintosh and the razor gangs of the Gorbals and the Gallowgate. Art tea-rooms and slums certainly come into the Erchie stories, but they form part of a matrix of an entirely credible Glasgow of smoking concerts, Fair Holidays, "skoosh-caurs", flittings, Burns suppers, football matches and international exhibitions. The stories are peopled with figures representative of the great majority of the city's population, characters living lives of quiet obscurity, intermittent absurdity, and occasional splendour and generosity of spirit in the myriad replicas of "Erchie's Great Wee Close" across Glasgow.

That Munro knew the value of what he had created, and how little he really cared for the illusory pseudonym afford by the "Hugh Foulis" persona, is suggested by his re-using the character of Erchie in his play *Macpherson*, which was performed with considerable success by the Repertory Theatre in Glasgow in 1909. The *Glasgow Herald* noted that "his Macpherson is neither more nor less than 'jist Erchie', and Erchie on the boards bids fair to be the fashion in Glasgow." The stage Erchie, although transformed from beadle and waiter to butler, capitalised on the enormous affection created by the newspaper character. The *Herald*'s reviewer observed of Munro the playwright: "He achieves strong national comedy with an under-current of serious-ness and sentiment, expressed in perfectly natural conver-sation." Much the same could be said of Munro the short story writer.

Neil Munro suffered a not-uncommon posthumous decline in reputation. From being seen as one of the key figures in Scottish letters — as the heir of Scott and Steven-son in Highland historical fiction — he became an increasingly marginalized figure, patronised when he was not ignored. With an irony which might perhaps have appealed to him the historical novels on which his reputa-tion was based (rightly, as three or four of them are clearly of the first rank) went out of print and for a time the only work of Munro which was available anywhere outside the second-hand book trade was an incomplete edition of *Para Handy*. Fortunately the position is now infinitely healthier with all the great novels, two collections of "literary" short stories and complete editions of the humorous fiction available; even the final accolades of academic attention and a literary society devoted to his work have been accorded to him.

Perhaps it is now possible to examine Munro's work in the round and at last to move away from the false dicho-tomy between Neil Munro, author of what William Black-wood called "dignified works of fiction" and the journal-istic "Hugh Foulis," author of comic fiction. The same brain was behind all the works, the same artistic imagin-ation informed and inspired all the works, the same love of language, the same delight in words and ideas shines through *Erchie* as shines through *John Splendid* and *The New Road*. Because Munro worried about his name being associated with the newspaper fiction, though quite how

worried he was must be very debatable, does not mean that
we need to make the same distinction, or to assume, on the
basis of a title page apartheid that there are two classes of
Munro: the essential unity of the author's creative imagination needs to be asserted.

The stories of Erchie are not just a humorous joy and
delight, not just a splendid insight into the great and
vibrant city of Glasgow at the height of its prosperity; they
are splendidly crafted miniature works of art — often pushing the boundaries of the absurd in an astonishing way. In
the 1922 story *Glasgow in 1942* Erchie paints a dystopian
view of a future city where traffic will have increased to
such an extent that:

> "Aboot 1942, if I'm no' mistaken, everybody in Gleska
> 'll have his jackets made wi' a ring in the middle o' the
> back."
>
> "What for?" asked Duffy.
>
> "To cross the streets wi'. They'll sling him across on
> overhead wires, and the ring's 'jll be needed to hook him
> on wi'. The Dalrymple Patent Safety-First Slinger. Ball
> bearin's. No jerk at the start and no jar on landin'."

1. *Introductory to an Odd Character*

ON SUNDAYS he is the beadle[1] of our church; at other times he waits. In his ecclesiastical character there is a solemn dignity about his deportment that compels most of us to call him Mr MacPherson; in his secular hours, when passing the fruit at a city banquet, or when at the close of the repast he sweeps away the fragments of the dinner-rolls, and whisperingly expresses in your left ear a fervent hope that "ye've enjoyed your dinner," he is simply Erchie.

Once I forgot, deluded a moment into a Sunday train of thought by his reverent way of laying down a bottle of Pommery, and called him Mr MacPherson. He reproved me with a glance of his eye.

"There's nae Mr MacPhersons here," he said afterwards; "At whit ye might call the social board I'm jist Erchie, or whiles Easy-gaun Erchie wi' them that kens me langest. There's sae mony folks in this world don't like to hurt your feelings that if I was kent as Mr MacPherson on this kind o' job I wadna mak' enough to pay for starchin' my shirts."

I suppose Mr MacPherson has been snibbing-in preachers in St Kentigern's Kirk pulpit and then going for twenty minutes' sleep in the vestry since the Disruption;[2] and the more privileged citizens of Glasgow during two or three generations of public dinners have experienced the kindly ministrations of Erchie, whose proud motto is "A flet fit but a warm hert."[3] I think, however, I was the first to discover his long pent-up and precious strain of philosophy.

On Saturday nights, in his office as beadle of St Kentigern's he lights the furnaces that takes the chill off the Sunday devotions. I found him stoking the kirk fires one Saturday, not very much like a beadle in appearance, and much less like a waiter. It was what, in England, they call the festive season.

"There's mair nor guid preachin' wanted to keep a kirk gaun," said he; "if I was puttin' as muckle dross on my fires as the Doctor whiles puts in his sermons, efter a Setturday at the gowf, ye wad see a bonny difference on the plate. But it's nae odds — a beadle gets sma' credit, though it's him that keeps the kirk tosh and warm, and jist at that nice easy-osy temperature whaur even a gey cauldrife[4] member o' the congregation can tak' his nap and no' let his lozenge slip doon his throat for chitterin' wi' the cauld."

There was a remarkably small congregation at St Kentigern's on the following day, and when the worthy beadle had locked the door after dismissal and joined me on the pavement:

"Man," he said, "it was a puir turn-oot yon — hardly worth puttin' on fires for. It's aye the wye; when I mak' the kirk a wee bit fancy, and jalouse[5] there's shair to be twa pound ten in the plate, on comes a blash o' rain, and there's hardly whit wid pay for the starchin' o' the Doctor's bands.

"Christmas! They ca't Christmas, but I could gie anither name for't. I looked it up in the penny almanac, and it said, 'Keen frost; probably snow,' and I declare – to if I hadna nearly to soom frae the hoose.

"The almanacs is no' whit they used to be; the auld chaps that used to mak' them maun be deid.

"They used to could do't wi' the least wee bit touch, and tell ye in January whit kind o' day it wad be at Hallowe'en, besides lettin' ye ken the places whaur the Fair days and the 'ool-markets was, and when they were to tak' place — a' kind o' information that maist o' us that bocht the almanacs couldna sleep at nicht wantin'. I've seen me get up at three on a cauld winter's mornin' and strikin' a licht to turn up Orr's Penny Commercial and see whit day was the Fair at Dunse. I never was at Dunse in a' my days, and hae nae intention o' gaun, but it's a grand thing knowledge, and it's no' ill to cairry. It's like poetry — 'The Star o' Rabbie Burns' and that kind o' thing — ye can aye be givin' it a ca' roond in your mind when ye hae naething better to dae.

"Oh, ay! A puir turn-oot the day for Kentigern's; that's the drawback o' a genteel congregation like oors — mair nor half o' them's sufferin' frae Christmas turkey and puttin' the blame on the weather.

"The bubblyjock[6] is the symbol o' Scotland's decline and fa'; we maybe bate the English at Bannockburn, but noo they're haein' their revenge and underminin' oor constitution wi' the aid o' a bird that has neither a braw plumage nor a bonny sang, and costs mair nor the price o' three or four ducks. England gave us her bubblyjock and took oor barley-bree.[7]

"But it's a' richt; Ne'erday's comin'; it's begun this year gey early, for I saw Duffy gaun up his close last nicht wi' his nose peeled.

"'Am I gaun hame, or am I comin' frae't, can ye tell me?' says he, and he was carryin' something roondshaped in his pocket-naipkin.

"'Whit's wrang wi' ye, puir cratur?' I says to him.

"'I was struck wi' a sheet o' lichtnin','' says he, and by that I kent he had been doon drinkin' at the Mull of Kintyre Vaults, and that the season o' peace on earth, guid-will to men was fairly started.

"'MacPherson,' he says, wi' the tear at his e'e, 'I canna help it, but I'm a guid man.'

"'Ye are that, Duffy,' I says, 'when ye're in your bed sleepin'; at ither times ye're like the rest o' us, and that's gey middlin'. Whit hae ye in the naipkin?'

"He gied a dazed look at it, and says, 'I'm no shair, but I think it's a curlin'-stane, and me maybe gaun to a bonspiel[8] at Carsbreck.'

"He opened it oot, and found it was a wee, roond, red cheese.

"'That's me, a' ower,' says he — 'a Christmas for the wife,' and I declare there was as much drink jaupin' in him as wad hae done for a water-shute.

"Scotland's last stand in the way o' national customs is bein' made at the Mull o' Kintyre Vaults, whaur the flet half-mutchkin, wrapped up in magenta tissue paper so that it'll look tidy, is retreatin' doggedly, and fechtin' every fit o' the way, before the invadin' English Christmas caird.

Ten years ago the like o' you and me couldna prove to a
freen' that we liked him fine unless we took him at this
time o' the year into five or six public-hooses, leaned him
up against the coonter, and grat on his dickie.[9] Whit dae
we dae noo? We send wee Jennie oot for a shilling box o'
the year afore last's patterns in Christmas cairds, and show
oor continued affection and esteem at the ha'penny
postage rate.

"Instead o' takin' Duffy roon' the toon on Ne'erday,
and hurtin' my heid wi' tryin' to be jolly, I send him a
Christmas caird, wi' the picture o' a hayfield on the ootside
and 'Wishin' you the Old, Old Wish, Dear,' on the inside,
and stay in the hoose till the thing blaws bye.

"The shilling box o' Christmas cairds is the great peace-
maker; a gross or twa should hae been sent oot to Russia
and Japan,[10] and it wad hae stopped the war. Ye may hae
thocht for a twelvemonth the MacTurks were a disgrace to
the tenement, wi' their lassie learnin' the mandolin, and
them haein' their gas cut off at the meter for no' payin' the
last quarter; but let them send a comic caird to your lassie
— 'Wee Wullie to Wee Jennie,' and they would get the len'
o' your wife's best jeely-pan.

"No' but whit there's trouble wi' the Christmas caird.
It's only when ye buy a shillin' box and sit doon wi' the
wife and weans to consider wha ye'll send them to that ye
fin' oot whit an awfu' lot o' freen's ye hae. A score o'
shillin' boxes wadna gae ower half the kizzens I hae, wi' my
grandfaither belangin' to the Hielan's, so Jinnet an' me jist
lets on to some o' them we're no' sendin' ony cairds oot
this year because it's no' the kin' o' society go ony langer.
And ye have aye to keep pairt o' the box till Ne'erday to
send to some o' the mair parteecular anes ye forgot a'
thegither were freen's o' yours till they sent ye a caird.

"Anither fau't I hae to the Christmas cairds is that the
writin' on them's generally fair rideeculous.

"'May Christmas Day be Blythe and Gay, and bring
your household Peace and Joy,' is on the only caird left
ower to send to Mrs Maclure; and when ye're shearin' aff

the selvedges o't to mak' it fit a wee envelope, ye canna but think that it's a droll message for a hoose wi' five weans lyin' ill wi' the whoopin'-cough, and the man cairryin' on the wye Maclure does.

"'Old friends, old favourites, Joy be with you at this Season,' says the caird for the MacTurks, and ye canna but mind that every third week there's a row wi' Mrs MacTurk and your wife aboot the key o' the washin'-hoose[11] and lettin' the boiler rust that bad a' the salts o' sorrel in the Apothecaries 'll no tak' the stains aff your shirts.

"Whit's wanted is a kin' o' slidin' scale o' sentiment on Christmas cairds, so that they'll taper doon frae a herty greetin' ye can truthfully send to a dacent auld freen' and the kind o' cool 'here's to ye!' suited for an acquaintance that borrowed five shillin's frae ye at the Term,[12] and hasna much chance o' ever payin't back again.

"If it wasna for the Christmas cairds a lot o' us wad maybe never jalouse there was onything parteecular merry aboot the season. Every man that ye're owin' an accoont to sends it to ye then, thinkin' your hert's warm and your pouches rattlin'. On Christmas Day itsel' ye're aye expectin' something; ye canna richt tell whit it is, but there's ae thing certain — that it never comes. Jinnet, my wife, made a breenge for the door every time the post knocked on Thursday, and a' she had for't at the end o' the day was an ashet[13] fu' o' whit she ca's valenteens, a' written on so that they'll no even dae for next year.

"I used to wonder whit the banks shut for at Christmas, but I ken noo; they're feart that their customers, cairried awa' wi' their feelin' o' guid-will to men, wad be makin' a rush on them to draw money for presents, and maybe create a panic.

"Sae far as I can judge there's been nae panic at the banks this year.

"Every Ne'erday for the past fifty years I hae made up my mind I was gaun to be a guid man," he went on. "It jist wants a start, they tell me that's tried it, and I'm no' that auld. Naething bates a trial.

"I'm gaun to begin at twelve o'clock on Hogmanay, and mak' a wee note o't in my penny diary, and put a knot in my hankie to keep me in mind. Maist o' us would be as guid's there's ony need for if we had naething else to think o'. It's like a man that's hen-taed — he could walk fine if he hadna a train to catch, or the rent to rin wi' at the last meenute, or somethin' else to bother him. I'm gey faur wrang if I dinna dae the trick this year, though.

"Oh! ay. I'm gaun to be a guid man. No' that awfu' guid that auld freen's 'll rin up a close to hide when they see me comin', but jist dacent — jist guid enough to please mysel', like Duffy's singin'. I'm no' makin' a breenge at the thing and sprainin' my leg ower't. I'm startin' canny till I get into the wye o't. Efter this Erchie MacPherson's gaun to flype[14] his ain socks and no' leave his claes reel-rall aboot the hoose at night for his wife Jinnet to lay oot richt in the mornin'. I've lost money by that up till noo, for there was aye bound to be an odd sixpence droppin' oot and me no' lookin'. I'm gaun to stop skliffin'[15] wi' my feet; it's sair on the boots. I'm gaun to save preens by puttin' my collar stud in a bowl and a flet-iron on the top o't to keep it frae jinkin' under the chevalier[16] and book-case when I'm sleepin'. I'm gaun to wear oot a' my auld waistcoats in the hoose. I'm — "

"My dear Erchie," I interrupted, "these seem very harmless reforms."

"Are they?" said he. "They'll dae to be gaun on wi' the noo, for I'm nae phenomena; I'm jist Nature; jist the Rale Oreeginal."

2. *Erchie's Flitting*

HE CAME down the street in the gloaming on Tuesday night with a bird-cage in one hand and a potato-masher in the other, and I knew at once, by these symptoms, that Erchie was flitting.[1]

"On the long trail, the old trail, the trail that is always

new, Erchie?" said I, as he tried to push the handle of the masher as far up his coat sleeve as possible, and so divert attention from a utensil so ridiculously domestic and undignified.

"Oh, we're no' that bad!" said he. "Six times in the four-and-forty year. We've been thirty years in the hoose we're leavin' the morn, and I'm fair oot o' the wye o' flittin'. I micht as weel start the dancin' again."

"Thirty years! Your household gods plant a very firm foot, Erchie."

"Man, ay! If it wisna for Jinnet and her new fandangles, I wad nae mair think o' flittin' than o' buyin' a balloon to mysel'; but ye ken women! They're aye gaun to be better aff onywhaur else than whaur they are. I ken different, but I havena time to mak' it plain to Jinnet."

On the following day I met Erchie taking the air in the neighbourhood of his new domicile, and smoking a very magnificent meerschaum pipe.

"I was presented wi' this pipe twenty years ago," said he, "by a man that went to California, and I lost it a week or twa efter that. It turned up at the flittin'. That's ane o' the advantages o' flittin's; ye find things ye havena seen for years."

"I hope the great trek came off all right, Erchie?"

"Oh, ay! no' that bad, considerin' we were sae much oot o' practice. It's no' sae serious when ye're only gaun roond the corner to the next street. I cairried a lot o' the mair particular wee things roond mysel' last nicht — the bird-cage and Gledstane's picture and the room vawses[2] and that sort o' thing — but at the hinder-end Jinnet made me tak' the maist o' them back again."

"Back again, Erchie?"

"Ay. She made oot that I had cairried ower sae muckle that the flittin' wad hae nae appearance on Duffy's cairt, and haein' her mind set on the twa rakes,[3] and a' the fancy things lying at the close-mooth o' the new hoose till the plain stuff was taken in, I had just to cairry back a guid part o' whit I took ower last nicht. It's a rale divert the pride o' women! But I'm thinkin' she's vext for't the day, because yin o' the things I took back was a mirror, and it was broke in Duffy's cairt. It's a gey unlucky thing to break a lookin'gless."

"A mere superstition, Erchie."

"Dod ! I'm no' sae shair o' that. I kent a lookin' gless broke at a flittin' afore this, and the man took to drink a year efter't, and has been that wye since."

"How came you to remove at all?"

"It wad never hae happened if I hadna gane to a sale and seen a coal-scuttle. It's a dangerous thing to introduce a new coal-scuttle into the bosom o' your faimily. This was ane o' thae coal-scuttles wi' a pentin' o' the Falls o' Clyde and Tillitudlem Castle on the lid. I got it for three-and-tuppence; but it cost me a guid dale mair nor I bargained for. The wife was rale ta'en wi't, but efter a week or twa she made oot that it gar'd the auld room grate we had look shabby, and afore ye could say knife she had in a new grate wi' wally[4] sides till't, and an ash-pan I couldna get spittin' on. Then the mantelpiece wanted a bed pawn[5] on't to gie the grate a dacent look, and she pit on a plush yin. Ye wadna hinder her efter that to get plush-covered chairs instead o' the auld hair-cloth we got when we were mairried. Her mither's chist-o'-drawers didna gae very weel wi' the plush chairs, she found oot in a while efter that, and they were swapped wi' twa pound for a chevalier and book-case, though the only books I hae in the hoose is the Family Bible, Buchan's *Domestic Medicine*, and the *Tales o' the Borders*. It wad hae been a' richt if things had gane nae further, but when she went to a sale hersel' and bought a Brussels carpet a yaird ower lang for the room, she made oot there was naethin' for't but to flit to a hoose wi' a bigger room. And a' that happened because a pented coal-scuttle took ma e'e."

"It's an old story, Erchie; 'c'est le premier pas qui coûte,' as the French say."

"The French is the boys!" says Erchie, who never gives himself away. "Weel, we're flittin' onywye, and a bonny trauchle it is. I'll no' be able to find my razor for a week or twa."

"It's a costly process, and three flittin's are worse than a fire, they say."

"It's worse nor that; it's worse nor twa Irish lodgers.

"'It'll cost jist next to naethin',' says Jinnet. 'Duffy'll tak' ower the furniture in his lorry for freen'ship's sake, an' there's naethin' 'll need to be done to the new hoose.'

"But if ye ever flitted yersel', ye'll ken the funny wyes o' the waxcloth that's never cut the same wye in twa hooses; and I'll need to be gey thrang at my tred for the next month or twa to pay for the odds and ends that Jinnet never thought o'.

"Duffy flitted us for naethin', but ye couldna but gie the men a dram. A flittin' dram's by-ordinar;[6] ye daurna be scrimp wi't, or they'll break your delf for spite, and ye canna be ower free wi't either, or they'll break everything else oot o' fair guid-natur. I tried to dae the thing judeecious, but I forgot to hide the bottle, and Duffy's heid man and his mate found it when I wasna there, and that's the wye the lookin'-gless was broken. Thae cairters divna ken their ain strength.

"It's a humblin' sicht your ain flittin' when ye see't on the tap o' a coal-lorry."

"Quite so, Erchie; chiffoniers[7] are like a good many reputations — they look all right so long as you don't get seeing the back of them."

"And cairters hae nane o' the finer feelin's, I think. In spite o' a' that Jinnet could dae, they left the pots and pans a' efternoon on the pavement, and hurried the plush chairs up the stair at the first gae-aff. A thing like that's disheartenin' to ony weel-daein' woman.

"'Hoots!' says I to her, 'whit's the odds? There's naebody heedin' you nor your flittin'.'

"'Are they no'?' said Jinnet, keekin' up at the front o' the new land. 'A' the venetian blinds is doon, and I'll guarantee there's een behind them.'

"We werena half-an-oor in the new hoose when the

woman on the same stairheid chappet at the door and tellt us it was oor week o' washin' oot the close.[8] It wasna weel meant, but it did Jinnet a lot o' guid, for she was sitting in her braw new hoose greetin'."

"Greetin', Erchie? Why?"

"Ask that! Ye'll maybe ken better nor I dae."

"Well, you have earned your evening pipe at least, Erchie," said I.

He knocked out its ashes on his palm with a sigh.

"I hiv that! Man, it's a gey dauntenin' thing a flittin', efter a'. I've a flet fit, but a warm hert, and efter thirty years o' the auld hoose I was sweart to leave't. I brocht up a family in't, and I wish Jinnet's carpet had been a fit or twa shorter, or that I had never seen yon coal-scuttle wi' the Falls o' Clyde and Tillitudlem Castle."

3. *Degenerate Days*

"THE TRED's done," said Erchie.

"What! beadling?" I asked him.

"Oh! there's naethin' wrang wi' beadlin'," said he; "there's nae ups and doons there except to put the books on the pulpit desk, and they canna put ye aff the job if ye're no jist a fair wreck. I'm a' richt for the beadlin' as lang's I keep my health and hae Jinnet to button my collar, and it's generally allo'ed — though maybe I shouldna say't mysel' — that I'm the kind o' don at it roond aboot Gleska. I michtna be, if I wasna gey carefu'. Efter waitin' at a Setturday nicht spree, I aye tak' care to gie the bell an extra fancy ca' or twa on the Sunday mornin' jist to save clash and mak' them ken MacPherson's there himsel', and no' some puir pick-up that never ca'd the handle o' a kirk bell in his life afore.

"There's no' a man gangs to oor kirk wi' better brushed boots than mysel', as Jinnet 'll tell ye, and if I hae ae gift mair nor anither it's discretioncy. A beadle that's a waiter has to gae through life like the puir troot they caught in the

Clyde the other day — wi' his mooth shut, and he's worse aff because he hasna ony gills — at least no' the kind ye pronounce that way.

"Beadlin's an art, jist like pentin' photograph pictures, or playin' the drum, and if it's no' in ye, naethin' 'll put it there. I whiles see wee skinamalink[1] craturs dottin' up the passages in UF kirks carryin' the books as if they were MCs at a dancin'-schule ball gaun to tack up the programme in front o' the band; they lack thon rale releegious glide; they havena the feet for't.

"Waitin' is whit I mean; it's fair done!

"When I began the tred forty-five year syne in the auld Saracen Heid Inn,[2] a waiter was looked up to, and was well kent by the best folk in the toon, wha aye ca'd him by his first name when they wanted the pletform box o' cigaurs handed doon instead o' the Non Plus Ultras.

"Nooadays they stick a wally door-knob wi' a number on't in the lapelle o' his coat, and it's, 'Hey, No. 9, you wi' the flet feet, dae ye ca' this ham?'

"As if ye hadna been dacently christened and brocht up an honest faimily!

"In the auld days they didna drag a halflin callan'[3] in frae Stra'ven, cut his nails wi' a hatchet, wash his face, put a dickie and a hired suit on him, and gie him the heave into a banquet-room, whaur he disna ken the difference between a finger-bowl and a box o' fuzuvian lichts.[4]

"I was speakin' aboot that the ither nicht to Duffy, the coalman, and he says, 'Whit's the odds, MacPherson? Wha the bleezes couldna sling roon' blue-mange at the richt time if he had the time-table, or the menu, or whatever ye ca't, to keep him richt?'

"'Wha couldna sell coal,' said I, 'if he had the jaw for't? Man, Duffy,' says I, 'I never see ye openin' your mooth to roar coal up a close[5] but I wonder whit wye there should be sae much talk in the Gleska Toon Cooncil aboot the want o' vacant spaces.'

"Duffy's failin'; there's nae doot o't. He has a hump on him wi' carryin' bags o' chape coal and dross up thae new,

genteel, tiled stairs, and he let's on it's jist a knot in his
gallowses, but I ken better. I'm as straucht as a wand
mysel' — faith, I micht weel be, for a' that I get to cairry
hame frae ony o' the dinners nooadays. I've seen the day,
when Blythswood Square[6] and roond aboot it was a' the
go, that it was coonted kind o' scrimp to let a waiter hame
withoot a heel on him like yin o' thae Clyde steamers gaun
oot o' Rothesay quay on a Fair Setturday.

"Noo they'll ripe your very hip pooches for fear ye may
be takin' awa' a daud o' custard, or the toasted crumbs frae
a dish o' pheasant.

"They needna' be sae awfu' feart, some o' them. I ken
their dinners — cauld, clear, bane juice, wi' some strings o'
vermicelli in't; ling-fish hash; a spoonfu' o' red-currant
jeely, wi' a piece o' mutton the size o' a domino in't, if ye
had time to find it, only ye're no' playin' kee-hoi[7]; game
croquette that's jist a flaff o' windy paste; twa cheese
straws; four green grapes, and a wee lend o' a pair o' silver
nut-crackers the wife o' the hoose got at her silver weddin'.

"Man! it's a rale divert! I see big, strong, healthy Bylies[8]
and members o' the Treds' Hoose and the Wine, Speerit,
and Beer Tred risin' frae dinners like that, wi their big,
braw, gold watch-chains hingin' doon to their knees.

"As I tell Jinnet mony a time, it's women that hae fair
ruined dinner-parties in oor generation. They tak' the
measure o' the appetites o' mankind by their ain, which
hae been a'thegether spoiled wi' efternoon tea, and they
think a man can mak' up wi' music in the drawin'-room for
whit he didna get at the dinner-table.

"I'm a temperate man mysel', and hae to be, me bein' a
beadle, but I whiles wish we had back the auld days I hae
read aboot, when a laddie was kept under the table to lowse
the grauvats[9] o' the gentlemen that fell under't, in case
they should choke themsel's. Scotland was Scotland then!

"If they choked noo, in some places I've been in, it wad
be wi' thirst.

"The last whisk o' the petticoat's no roon' the stair-
landin' when the man o' the hoose puts the half o' his

cigarette bye for again, and says, 'The ladies will be wonderin' if we've forgotten them,' and troosh a' the puir deluded craturs afore him up the stair into the drawin'-room where his wife Eliza's maskin' tea,[10] and a lady wi' tousy hair's kittlin' the piano till it's sair.

"'Whit's your opinion about Tschaikovski?' I heard a wumman ask a Bylie at a dinner o' this sort the ither nicht.

"'I never heard o' him,' said the Bylie, wi' a gant,[11] 'but if he's in the proveesion tred, there'll be an awfu' run on his shop the morn's morn'.'

"Anither thing that has helped to spoil oor tred is the smokin' concerts.[12] I tak' a draw o' the pipe mysel' whiles, but I never cared to mak' a meal o't. Noo and then when I'm no' very busy other ways I gie a hand at a smoker, and it mak's me that gled I got ower my growth afore the thing cam' into fashion; but it's gey sair on an auld man to hear 'Queen o' the Earth' five or six nichts in the week, and the man at the piano aye tryin' to guess the richt key, or to get done first, so that the company 'll no' rin awa' when he's no' lookin' withoot paying him his five shillin's.

"I've done the waitin' at a' kinds o' jobs in my time — Easy-gaun Erchie they ca' me sometimes in the tred — a flet fit but a warm hert; I've even handed roond seed-cake and a wee drap o' spirits at a burial, wi' a bereaved and mournfu' mainner that greatly consoled the weedow; but there's nae depths in the business so low as poo'in' corks for a smokin' concert. And the tips get smaller and smaller every ane I gang to. At first we used to get them in a schooner gless; then it cam' doon to a wee tumbler; and the last I was at I got the bawbees in an egg-cup."

4. *The Burial of Big Macphee*

ERCHIE LOOKED pityingly at Big Macphee staggering down the street. "Puir sowl!" said he, "whit's the maitter wi' ye noo?"

Big Macphee looked up, and caught his questioner by

the coat collar to steady himself. "Beer," said he; "jist beer. Plain beer, if ye want to ken. It's no' ham and eggs, I'll bate ye. Beer, beer, glorious beer, I'm shair I've perished three gallons this very day. Three gallons hiv I in me, I'll wager."

"Ye wad be far better to cairry it hame in a pail," said Erchie. "Man, I'm rale vexed to see a fine, big, smert chap like you gaun hame like this, takin' the breadth o' the street."

"Hiv I no' a richt to tak' the breadth o' the street if I want it?" said Big Macphee. "Am I no' a ratepayer? I hiv a ludger's vote,[1] and I'm gaun to vote against Joe Chamberlain and the dear loaf."[2]

"Och! ye needna fash aboot the loaf for a' the difference a tax on't 'll mak' to you," said Erchie.

"If ye gang on the wye ye're daein' wi' the beer, it's the Death Duties yer freends 'll be bothered aboot afore lang."

And he led the erring one home.

Big Macphee was the man who for some months back had done the shouting for Duffy's lorry No. 2. He sustained the vibrant penetrating quality of a voice like the Cloch fog-horn on a regimen consisting of beer and the casual hard-boiled egg of the Mull of Kintyre Vaults. He had no relatives except a cousin "oot aboot Fintry", and when he justified Erchie's gloomy prediction about the Death Duties by dying of pneumonia a week afterwards, there was none to lament him, save in a mild, philosophical way, except Erchie's wife, Jinnet.

Jinnet, who could never sleep at night till she heard Macphee go up the stairs to his lodgings, thought the funeral would be scandalously cold and heartless lacking the customary "tousy tea"[3] to finish up with, and as Duffy, that particular day, was not in a position to provide this solace for the mourners on their return from Sighthill Cemetery, she invited them to her house. There were Duffy and a man Macphee owed money to; the cousin from "oot aboot Fintry" and his wife, who was, from the outset, jealous of the genteel way tea was served in Jinnet's parlour, and suspicious of a "stuckupness" that was only in her own imagination.

"It's been a nesty, wat, mochy, melancholy day for a burial," said Duffy at the second helping of Jinnet's cold boiled ham; "Macphee was jist as weel oot o't. He aye hated to hae to change his jaicket afore the last rake, him no' haein' ony richt wumman buddy aboot him to dry't."

"Och, the puir cratur!" said Jinnet. "It's like enough he had a disappointment ance upon a time. He was a cheery chap."

"He was a' that," said Duffy. "See's the haud o' the cream-poorie."

The cousin's wife felt Jinnet's home-baked seed-cake was a deliberate taunt at her own inefficiency in the baking line. She sniffed as she nibbled it with a studied appearance of inappreciation. "It wasna a very cheery burial he had, onyway," was her astounding comment, and at that Erchie winked to himself, realising the whole situation.

"Ye're richt there, Mistress Grant," said he. "Burials are no' whit they used to be. Perhaps — perhaps ye were expectin' a brass band?" And at that the cousin's wife saw this was a different man from her husband, and that there was a kind of back-chat they have in Glasgow quite unknown in Fintry.

"Oh! I wasna sayin' onything aboot brass bands," she retorted, very red-faced, and looking over to her husband for his support. He, however, was too replete with tea and cold boiled ham for any severe intellectual exercise, and was starting to fill his pipe. "I wasna saying onything aboot brass bands; we're no' used to thae kind o' operatics at burials whaur I come frae. But I think oor ain wye o' funerals is better than the Gleska wye."

Erchie (fearful for a moment that something might have been overlooked) glanced at the fragments of the feast, and at the spirit-bottle that had discreetly circulated somewhat earlier. "We're daein' the best we can," said he. "As shair as death your kizzen — peace be wi' him! — 's jist as nicely buried as if ye paid for it yersel' instead o' Duffy and — and Jinnet; if ye'll no' believe me ye can ask your man. Nae doot Big Macphee deserved as fine a funeral as onybody, wi' a wheen coaches, and a service at the kirk, wi' the organ playin' and a' that, but that wasna the kind o' man your kizzen was when he was livin'. He hated a' kinds o' falderals."[4]

"He was a cheery chap," said Jinnet again, nervously, perceiving some electricity in the air.

"And he micht hae had a nicer burial," said the cousin's wife, with firmness.

"Preserve us!" cried Erchie. "Whit wad ye like? — Flags maybe? Or champagne wine at the liftin'? Or maybe wreaths o' floo'ers? If it was cheeriness ye were wantin' wi' puir Macphee, ye should hae come a month ago and he micht hae ta'en ye himsel' to the Britannia Music-ha'.[5]"

"Haud yer tongue, Erchie," said Jinnet; and the cousin's wife, as fast as she could, took all the pins out of her hair and put them in again. "They think we're that faur back in Fintry," she said with fine irrelevance.

"Not at all," said Erchie, who saw his innocent wife was getting all the cousin's wife's fierce glances. "Not at all, mem. There's naething wrang wi' Fintry; mony a yin I've sent there. I'm rale chawed we didna hae a Fintry kind o' funeral, to please ye. Whit's the patent thing aboot a Fintry funeral?"

"For wan thing," said the cousin's wife, "it's aye a rale hearse we hae at Fintry and no' a box under a machine, like thon. It was jist a disgrace. Little did his mither think it wad come to thon. Ye wad think it was coals."

"And whit's the maitter wi' coals?" cried Duffy, his professional pride aroused. "Coals was his tred. Ye're shairly awfu' toffs in Fintry aboot yer funerals."

The cousin's wife stabbed her head all over again with her hair-pins, and paid no heed to him. Her husband evaded her eyes with great determination. "No' that great toffs either," she retorted, "but we can aye afford a bit crape. There wasna a sowl that left this close behind the corp the day had crape in his hat except my ain man."

Then the man to whom Big Macphee owed money laughed.

"Crape's oot o' date, mistress," Erchie assured her.

"It's no' the go noo at a' in Gleska; ye micht as weel expect to see the auld saulies.[6]"

"Weel, it's the go enough in Fintry," said the cousin's wife. "And there was anither thing; I didna expect to see onybody else but my man in weepers,[7] him bein' the only freen' puir Macphee had but — "

"I havena seen weepers worn since the year o' the Tay Bridge," said Erchie, "and that was oot at the Mearns."

"Weel, we aye hae them at Fintry," insisted the cousin's wife.

"A cheery chap," said Jinnet again, at her wits' end to put an end to this restrained wrangling, and the man Big Macphee owed money to laughed again.

"Whit's mair," went on the cousin's wife, "my man was the only wan there wi' a dacent shirt wi' tucks on the breist o't; the rest o' ye had that sma' respect for the deid ye went wi' shirt-breists as flet as a sheet o' paper. It was showin' awfu' sma' respect for puir Macphee," and she broke down with her handkerchief at her eyes.

"Och! to bleezes! Jessic, ye're spilin' a' the fun," her husband remonstrated.

Erchie pushed back his chair and made an explanation. "Tucks is no' the go naither, mistress," said he, "and if ye kent whit the laundries were in Gleska ye wadna wonder at it. A laundry's a place whaur they'll no stand ony o' yer tucks, or ony nonsense o' that kind. Tucks wad spoil the teeth o' the curry-combs they use in the laundry for scoorin' the cuffs and collars; they're no' gaun awa' to waste the vitriol they use for bleachin' on a wheen tucks. They couldna dae't at the money; it's only threepence ha'penny a shirt, ye ken, and oot o' that they hae to pay for the machines that tak's the buttons aff, and the button-hole bursters — that's a tred by itsel'. No, mem, tucked breists are oot o' date; ye'll no' see such a thing in Gleska; I'm shair puir Macphee himsel' hadna ane. The man's as weel buried as if we had a' put on the kilts, and had a piper in front playin' 'Lochaber no More.' If ye'll no believe us,

Duffy can show ye the receipted accoonts for the undertaker and the lair; can ye no', Duffy?"

"Smert!" said Duffy.

But the cousin's wife was not at all anxious to see
accounts of any kind, so she became more prostrate with
annoyance and grief than ever.

"Oot Fintry way," said Erchie, exasperated, "it's a' richt
to keep up tucked shirt-breists, and crape, and weepers,
and mort-cloths, and the like, for there canna be an awfu'
lot o' gaiety in the place, but we have aye plenty o' ither
things to amuse us in Gleska. There's the Kelvingrove
Museum, and the Waxworks. If ye're no' pleased wi' the
wye Macphee was buried, ye needna gie us the chance
again wi' ony o' yer freen's."

The cousin's wife addressed herself to her husband.
"Whit was yon ye were gaun to ask?" she said to him. He
got very red, and shifted uneasily in his chair.

"Me!" said he. "I forget."

"No ye dinna; ye mind fine."

"Och, it's a' richt. Are we no' haein' a fine time?"
protested the husband.

"No, nor a' richt, Rubbert Grant." She turned to the others.
"Whit my man was gaun to ask, if he wasna such a sumph,[8]
was whether oor kizzen hadna ony money put by him."

"If ye kent him better, ye wadna need to ask," said
Duffy.

"He was a cheery chap," said Jinnet.

"But was he no' in the Shepherds,[9] or the Oddfellows,
or the Masons, or onything that wye?"

"No, nor in the Good Templars nor the Rechabites,"
said Erchie. "The only thing the puir sowl was ever in was
the Mull o' Kintyre Vaults."

"Did I no' tell ye?" said her husband.

"Good-bye and thenky the noo," said the cousin's wife,
as she went down the stair. "I've spent a rale nice day."

"It's the only thing ye did spend," said Erchie when she
was out of hearing. "Funerals are managed gey chape in
Fintry."

"Oh ye rascal, ye've the sherp tongue!" said Jinnet.

"Ay, and there's some needs it! A flet fit, too, but a warm hert," said Erchie.

5. *The Prodigal Son*

Jinnet, like a wise housewife, aye shops early on Saturday, but she always leaves some errand — some trifle overlooked, as it were — till the evening, for, true daughter of the city, she loves at times the evening throng of the streets. That of itself, perhaps, would not send her out with her door-key in her hand and a peering, eager look like that of one expecting something long of coming: the truth is she cherishes a hope that some Saturday to Erchie and her will come what comes often to her in her dreams, sometimes with terror and tears, sometimes with delight.

"I declare, Erchie, if I havena forgotten some sweeties for the kirk the morn," she says; "put on yer kep and come awa' oot wi' me; ye'll be nane the waur o' a breath o' fresh air."

Erchie puts down his *Weekly Mail*, stifling a sigh and pocketing his spectacles. The night may be raw and wet, the streets full of mire, the kitchen more snug and clean and warm than any palace, but he never on such occasion says her nay. "You and your sweeties!" he exclaims, lacing his boots; "I'm shair ye never eat ony, in the kirk or onywhere else."

"And whit dae ye think I wad be buyin' them for if it wasna to keep me frae gantin' in the kirk when the sermon's dreich?"

"Maybe for pappin' at the cats in the back coort,"[1] he retorts. "There's ae thing certain shair, I never see ye eatin' them."

"Indeed, and ye're richt," she confesses. "I havena the teeth for them nooadays."

"There's naething wrang wi' yer teeth, nor onything else aboot ye that I can see," her husband replies.

"Ye auld haver!" Jinnet will then cry, smiling.

"It's you that's lost yer sicht, I'm thinkin'. I'm a done auld buddy, that's whit I am, and that's tellin' ye. But haste ye and come awa' for the sweeties wi' me: whit'll thae wee Wilson weans in the close say the morn if Mrs MacPherson hasna ony sweeties for them?"

They went along New City Road[2] together, Erchie tall, lean, and a little round at the shoulders; his wife a little wee body, not reaching his shoulder, dressed by-ordinar for her station and "ower young for her years", as a few jealous neighbours say.

An unceasing drizzle blurred the street lamps, the pavement was slippery with mud; a night for the hearthside and slippered feet on the fender; yet the shops were thronged, and men and women crowded the thoroughfare or stood entranced before the windows.

"It's a wonnerfu' place, Gleska," said Erchie. "There's such diversion in't if ye're in the key for't. If ye hae yer health and yer wark, and the weans is weel, ye can be as happy as a lord, and far happier. It's the folk that live in the terraces where the nae stairs is, and sittin' in their paurlours readin' as hard's onything to keep up wi' the times, and naething to see oot the window but a plot o' grass that's no' richt green, that gets tired o' everything. The like o' us, that stay up closes and hae nae servants, and can come oot for a daunder efter turnin' the key in the door, hae the best o't. Lord! there's sae muckle to see — the cheeny-shops and the drapers, and the neighbours gaun for paraffin oil wi' a bottle, and Duffy wi' a new shepherd tartan-grauvit, and Lord Macdonald singin' awa' like a' that at the Normal School,[3] and — "

"Oh, Erchie! dae ye mind when Willie was at the Normal?" said Jinnet.

"Oh, my! here it is already," thought Erchie. "If that laddie o' oors kent the hertbrek he was to his mither, I wonder wad he bide sae lang awa'."

"Yes, I mind, Jinnet; I mind fine. Whit for need ye be askin'? As I was sayin', it's aye in the common streets that things is happenin' that's worth lookin' at, if ye're game for fun. It's like travellin' on the railway; if ye gang first-class, the way I did yince to Yoker by mistake, ye micht as weel be in a hearse for a' ye see or hear; but gang third and ye'll aye find something to keep ye cheery if it's only fifteen chaps standin' on yer corns gaun to a fitba'-match, or a man in the corner o' the cairriage wi' a mooth-harmonium playin' a' the wye."

"Oh! Erchie, look at the puir wean," said Jinnet, turning to glace after a woman with an infant in her arms. "Whit a shame bringin' oot weans on a nicht like this! Its face is blae wi' the cauld."

"Och! never mind the weans," said her husband; "if we were to mind a' the weans ye see in Gleska, ye wad hae a bonnie job o't."

"But jist think on the puir wee smout, Erchie. Oh, dear me! There's anither yin no' three months auld, I'll wager. It's a black burnin' shame. It should be hame snug and soond in its wee bed. Does 't no' mind ye o' Willie when I took him first to his grannie's?"

Her husband growled to himself, and hurried his step; but that night there seemed to be a procession of women with infants in arms in New City Road, and Jinnet's heart was wrung at every crossing.

"I thocht it was pan-drops[4] ye cam' oot for, or conversation-losengers," he protested at last; "and here ye're greetin' even-on aboot a wheen weans that's no' oor fault."

"Ye're a hard-herted monster, so ye are," said his wife indignantly.

"Of course I am," he confessed blythely. "I'll throw aff a' disguise and admit my rale name's Bluebeard, but don't tell the polis on me. Hard-herted monster — I wad need to be wi' a wife like you, that canna see a wean oot in the street at nicht withoot the drap at yer e'e. The weans is maybe no' that bad aff: the nicht air's no' waur nor the day air: maybe when they're oot here they'll no' mind they're hungry."

"Oh, Erchie! see that puir wee lame yin! God peety him!
— I maun gie him a penny," whispered Jinnet, as a child in
rags stopped before a jeweller's window to look in on a
magic world of silver cruet-stands and diamond rings and
gold watches.

"Ye'll dae naething o' the kind!" said Erchie. "It wad jist
be wastin' yer money; I'll bate ye onything his mither
drinks." He pushed his wife on her way past the boy, and,
unobserved by her, slipped twopence in the latter's hand.

"I've seen the day ye werena sae mean, Erchie
MacPherson," said his wife, vexatiously. "Ye aye brag o'
yer flet fit and yer warm hert."

"It's jist a sayin'; I'm as mooly's⁵ onything," said Erchie,
and winked to himself.

It was not the children of the city alone that engaged
Jinnet's attention; they came to a street where now and
then a young man would come from a public-house
staggering; she always scanned the young fool's face with
something of expectancy and fear.

"Jist aboot his age, Erchie," she whispered. "Oh, dear! I
wonder if that puir callan' has a mither," and she stopped
to look after the young man in his cups.

Erchie looked too, a little wistfully. "I'll wager ye he
has," said he. "And like enough a guid yin, that's no' forgettin' him, though he may gang on the ran-dan,⁶ but in her
bed at nicht no' sleepin', wonderin' whit's come o' him,
and never mindin' onything that was bad in him, but jist a
kind o' bein' easy-led, but mindin' hoo smert he was when
he was but a laddie, and hoo he won the prize for composeetion in the school, and hoo prood he was when he
brocht hame the first wage he got on a Setturday. If God
Almichty has the same kind o' memory as a mither, Jinnet,
there'll be a chance at the hinderend for the warst o' us."

They had gone at least a mile from home; the night grew
wetter and more bitter, the crowds more squalid, Jinnet's
interest in errant belated youth more keen. And never a
word of the sweets she had made-believe to come out
particularly for. They had reached the harbour side; the

ships lay black and vacant along the wharfs, noisy seamen and women debauched passed in groups or turned into the public-houses. Far west into the drizzling night the river lamps stretched, showing the drumly[7] water of the highway of the world. Jinnet stopped and looked and listened. "I think we're far enough, Erchie; I think we'll jist gang hame," said she.

"Right!" said Erchie, patiently; and they turned, but not without one sad glance from his wife before they lost sight of the black ships, the noisy wharves, the rolling seamen on the pavement, the lamplights of the watery way that reaches to the world's end.

"Oh! Erchie," she said piteously, "I wonder if he's still on the ships."

"Like enough," said her husband. "I'm shair he's no' in Gleska at onyrate without comin' to see us. I'll bate ye he's a mate or a captain or a purser or something, and that thrang somewhere abroad he hasna time the noo; but we'll hear frae him by-and-by. The wee deevil! I'll gie him't when I see him, to be givin' us such a fricht."

"No' that wee, Erchie," said Jinnet. "He's bigger than yersel'."

"So he is, the rascal! Am I no' aye thinkin' o' him jist aboot the age he was when he was at the Sunday school."

"Hoo lang is't since we heard o' him, Erchie?"

"Three or four years, or maybe five," said Erchie, quickly. "Man! The wye time slips bye! It doesna look like mair nor a twelvemonth."

"It looks to me like twenty year," said Jinnet, "and it's naething less than seeven, for it was the year o' Annie's weddin', and her wee Alick's six at Mertinmas. Seeven years! Oh, Erchie, where can he be? Whit can be wrang wi' him? No' to write a scrape o' a pen a' that time! Maybe I'll no' be spared to see him again."

"I'll bate ye whit ye like ye will," said her husband.

"And if he doesna bring ye hame a lot o' nice things — shells and parrots, and bottles of scent, and Riga Balsam for hacked hands, and the rale Cheena cheeny, and ostrich feathers and a' that, I'll — I'll be awfu' wild at him. But the first thing I'll dae 'll be to stand behind the door and catch him when he comes in, and tak' the strap to him for the rideeculous wye he didna write to us."

"Seeven years," said Jinnet. "Oh, that weary sea, a puir trade to be followin' for ony mither's son. It was Australia he wrote frae last; whiles I'm feared the blecks catched him oot there and killed him in the Bush."

"No! nor the Bush! Jist let them try it wi' oor Willie! Dod! he would put the hems[8] on them; he could wrastle a score o' blecks wi' his least wee bit touch."

"Erchie."

"Weel, Jinnet?"

"Ye'll no' be angry wi' me; but wha was it tellt ye they saw him twa years syne carryin' on near the quay, and that he was stayin' at the Sailors' Home?"

"It was Duffy," said Erchie, hurriedly. "I have a guid mind to — to kick him for sayin' onything o' the kind. I wad hae kicked him for't afore this if — if I wasna a beadle in the kirk."

"I'm shair it wasna oor Willie at a'," said Jinnet.

"Oor Willie! Dae ye think the laddie's daft, to be in Gleska and no' come to see his mither?"

"I canna believe he wad dae't," said Jinnet, but always looked intently in the face of every young man who passed them.

"Weel, that's ower for anither Setturday," said Erchie to himself, resuming his slippers and his spectacles.

"I declare, wife," said he, "ye've forgotten something."

"Whit is't?" she asked.

"The sweeties ye went oot for," said Erchie, solemnly.

"Oh, dear me! amn't I the silly yin? Thinkin' on that Willie o' oors put everything oot o' my heid."

Erchie took a paper bag from his pocket and handed it to her. "There ye are," said he. "I had them in my pooch since dinner-time. I kent ye wad be needin' them."

"And ye never let on, but put on your boots and cam' awa' oot wi' me."

"Of coorse I did; I'm shairly no' that auld but I can be gled on an excuse for a walk oot wi' my lass?"

"Oh, Erchie! Erchie!" she cried, "when will ye be wise? I think I'll put on the kettle and mak' a cup o' tea to ye."

6. *Mrs Duffy Deserts Her Man*

"THEY'RE yatterin' awa' in the papers there like sweetie wives aboot Carlyle and his wife,"[1] said Erchie. "It's no' the thing at a' makin' an exposure. I kent Carlyle fine; he had a wee baker's shop in Balmano Brae,[2] and his wife made potted heid.[3] It was quite clean; there was naething wrang wi't. If they quarrelled it was naebody's business but their ain.

"It's a gey droll hoose whaur there's no' whiles a rippit. Though my fit's flet my hert's warm; but even me and Jinnet hae a cast-oot noo and then. I'm aye the mair angry if I ken I'm wrang, and I've seen me that bleezin' bad-tempered that I couldna light my pipe, and we wadna speak to ane anither for oors and oors.

"It'll come the nicht, and me wi' a job at waitin' to gang to, and my collar that hard to button I nearly break my thoombs.

"For a while Jinnet 'll say naethin', and then she'll cry, 'See's a haud o't, ye auld fuiter!'

"I'll be glowerin' awfu' solemn up at the corner o' the ceilin' when she's workin' at the button, lettin' on I'm fair ferocious yet, and she'll say, 'Whit are ye glowerin' at? Dae ye see ony spiders' webs?'

"'No, nor spiders' webs,' I says, as gruff as onything. 'I never saw a spider's web in this hoose.'

"At that she gets red in the face and tries no' to laugh. 'There ye are laughin'! Ye're bate!' I says.

"'So are you laughin',' says she; 'and I saw ye first. Awa', ye're daft! Will I buy onything tasty for your supper?'

"Duffy's different. I'm no' blamin' him, for his wife's

different too. When they quarrel it scandalises the close and gies the land a bad name. The wife washes even-on, and greets into her washin'-byne till she mak's the water cauld, and Duffy sits a' nicht wi' his feet on the kitchen-hobs singin' 'Boyne Water,' because her mither was a Bark,[4] called M'Ginty, and cam' frae Connaught. The folk in the flet abin them hae to rap doon[5] at them wi' a poker afore they'll get their nicht's sleep, and the broken delf that gangs oot to the ash-pit in the mornin' wad fill a crate.

"I'm no' sayin', mind ye, that Duffy doesna like her; it's jist his wye, for he hasna ony edication. He was awfu' vexed the time she broke her leg; it pit him aff his wark for three days, and he spent the time lamentin' aboot her doon in the Mull o' Kintyre Vaults.

"The biggest row they ever had that I can mind o' was aboot the time the weemen wore the dolmans.[6] Duffy's wife took the notion o' a dolman, and told him that seein' there was a bawbee up in the bag o' coal that week, she thocht he could very weel afford it.

"'There's a lot o' things we'll hae to get afore the dolman,' says he; 'I'm needin' a new kep mysel', and I'm in a menoj[7] for a bicycle.'

"'I'm fair affronted wi' my claes,' says she; 'I havena had onything new for a year or twa, and there's Carmichael's wife wi' her sealskin jaicket.'

"'Let her!' says Duffy; 'wi' a face like thon she's no' oot the need o't.'

"They started wi' that and kept it up till the neighbours near brocht doon the ceilin' on them.

"'That's the worst o' leevin' in a close,' said Duffy, 'ye daurna show ye're the maister in yer ain hoose withoot a lot o' nyafs[8] above ye spilin' a' the plaister.'

"Duffy's wife left him the very next day, and went hame to her mither's. She left oot clean sox for him and a bowl o' mulk on the dresser in case he micht be hungry afore he could mak' his ain tea.

"When Duffy cam' hame and found whit had happened, he was awfu' vexed for himsel' and begood to greet.

"I heard aboot the thing, and went in to see him, and found him drinkin' the mulk and eatin' shaves o' breid at twa bites to the shave the same as if it was for a wager.

"'Isn't this an awfu' thing that's come on me, Mac-Pherson?' says he; 'I'm nae better nor a weedower except for the mournin's.'

"'It hasna pit ye aff yer meat onywye,' says I.

"'Oh!' he says, 'ye may think I'm callous, but I hae been greetin' for twa oors afore I could tak' a bite, and I'm gaun to start again as soon as I'm done wi' this mulk.'

"'Ye should gang oot,' I tells him, 'and buy the mistress a poke o' grapes and gang roond wi't to her mither's and tell her ye're an eediot and canna help it.'

"But wad he? No fears o' him!

"'Oh! I can dae fine withoot her,' he tells me quite cocky. 'I could keep a hoose wi' my least wee bit touch.'

"'Ye puir deluded crature,' I tell't him, 'ye micht as well try to keep a hyena. It looks gey like a collie-dug, but it'll no' sup saps, and a hoose looks an awfu' simple thing till ye try't; I ken fine because Jinnet aften tellt me.'

"He begood to soop the floor wi' a whitenin'-brush, and put the stour under the bed.

"'Go on,' says I, 'ye're daein' fine for a start. A' ye want's a week or twa at the nicht-schools, where they learn ye laundry-work and cookin', and when ye're at it ye should tak' lessons in scientific dressmakin'. I'll look for ye comin' up the street next week wi' the charts under your oxter and your lad wi' ye.'

"For a hale week Duffy kept his ain hoose.

"He aye forgot to buy sticks for the fire at nicht, and had to mak' it in the mornin' wi' a dizzen or twa o' claes-pins. He didna mak' tea, for he couldna tak' tea withoot cream till't, and he couldna get cream because he didna ken the wye to wash a poorie,[9] so he made his breakfast o' cocoa and his tea o' cocoa till he was gaun aboot wi' a broon taste in his mooth.

"On the Sunday he tried to mak' a dinner, and biled the plates wi' soap and soda to get the creesh aff them when he found it wadna come aff wi' cauld water and a washin'-clout.

"'Hoo are ye gettin' on in yer ain bonny wee hoose noo?' I asks him ae dirty, wet, cauld day, takin' in a bowl o' broth to him frae Jinnet.

"'Fine,' says he, quite brazen; 'it's like haein' a yacht. I could be daein' first-rate if it was the summertime.'

"He wore them long kahootchy[10] boots up to your knees on wet days at his wark, and he couldna get them aff him withoot a hand frae his wife, so he had just to gang to his bed wi' them on. He ordered pipeclay by the hunderwicht and soap by the yard; he blackleaded his boots, and didna gang to the kirk because he couldna get on his ain collar.

"'Duffy,' I says, 'ye'll mak' an awfu' nice auld wife if ye leeve lang enough. I'll hae to get Jinnet started to knit ye a Shetland shawl.'

"Efter a week it begood to tell awfu' bad on Duffy's health. He got that thin, and so wake in the voice he lost orders, for a wheen o' his auldest customers didna ken him when he cried, and gave a' their tred to MacTurk, the coalman, that had a wife and twa sisters-in-law to coother him up wi' beef-tea on wet days and a' his orders.

"Duffy's mind was affected too; he gave the richt wicht,[11] and lost twa chances in ae day o' pittin' a ha'penny on the bag wi' auld blin' weemen that couldna read his board.

"Then he ca'd on a doctor. The doctor tell't him he couldna mak' it oot at a', but thocht it was appen —what d'ye ca't?—the same trouble as the King had,[12] and that Duffy had it in five or six different places. There was naething for him but carefu' dietin' and a voyage to the Cape.

"That very day Duffy, gaun hame frae his wark gey shauchly, wi' a tin o' salmon in his pooch for his tea, saw his wife comin' doon the street. When she saw him she turned and ran awa', and him efter her as hard's he could pelt. She thocht he was that wild he was gaun to gie her a clourin'; and she was jist fair bate wi' the runnin' when he caught up on her in a back coort.

"'Tig!' says Duffy, touchin' her; 'You're het!'[13]

"'Oh, Jimmy!' she says, 'are ye in wi' me?'[14]

"'Am I no'?' says Duffy, and they went hame thegither.

"'There was a stranger in my tea this mornin',' says Duffy: 'I kent fine somebody wad be comin'.'

"His wife tellt Jinnet a while efter that that she was a great dale the better o' the rest she got the time she went hame to her mither's; it was jist the very thing she was needin'; and, forbye, she got the dolman."

7. *Carnegie's Wee Lassie*

ERCHIE SOUGHT me out on Saturday with a copy of that day's *News* containing a portrait of Carnegie's[1] little daughter Margaret.

"Man, isn't she the rale wee divert?" said he, glowing. "That like her faither, and sae weel-put-on! She minds me terrible o' oor wee Teenie when she was jist her age."

"She has been born into an enviable state, Erchie," I said.

"Oh, I'm no' sae shair aboot that," said Erchie. "It's a gey hard thing, whiles, bein' a millionaire's only wean. She canna hae mony wee lassies like hersel' to play the peever wi', or lift things oot o' the stanks o' Skibo Castle[2] wi' a bit o' clye and a string. I'm shair it must be a hard job for the auld man, her paw, to provide diversions for the puir wee smout. And she'll hae that mony things that she'll no' can say whit she wants next. I ken fine the wye it'll be up yonder at Skibo.

"It'll be, 'Paw, I'm wantin' something.'

"'Whit is't, my dawtie, and ye'll get it to break?' Mr Carnegie 'll say, and lift her on his knee, and let her play wi' the works o' his twa thoosand pound repeater watch.

"'I dinna ken,' says the wee lassie, 'but I want it awfu' fast.'

"'Whit wad ye be sayin' to an electric doll wi' a phonograph inside it to mak' it speak?' asks Mr Carnegie.

"'I'm tired o' dolls,' says the wee yin, 'and, besides, I wad rather dae the speakin' mysel'.'

"'Ye're a rale wee woman there, Maggie,' says her paw.

"'Weel, whit dae ye say to a wee totey motor-car a' for your ain sel', and jewelled in four-and-twenty holes?' says he efter that, takin' the hands o' his watch frae her in case she micht swallow them.

"'Oh! A motor-car,' says the wee lassie. "No, I'm no carin' for ony mair motor-cars; I canna get takin' them to my bed wi' me.'

"'Ye're weel aff there,' says he. 'I've had the hale o' the Pittsburg[3] works to my bed wi' me,' he says.

"'They were in my heid a' the time when I couldna sleep, and they were on my chest a' the time when I was sleepin'.'

"'Whit wye that, paw?' says the wee lassie.

"'I was feart something wad gae wrang, and I wad lose a' the tred, and be puir again.'

"'But I thocht ye wanted to die puir, paw?' says the wee lassie.

"'Ay, but I never had ony notion o' leevin' puir,' says Mr Carnegie as smert's ye like, 'and that mak's a' the difference. If ye're no' for anither motor carriage, wad ye no' tak' a new watch?'

"'No, paw,' says the wee lassie, 'I'm no' for anither watch. The only thing a watch tells ye is when it's time to gang to bed, and then I'm no wantin' to gang onywye. Whit I wad like wad be ane o' thae watches that has haunds that dinna move when ye're haein' awfu' fine fun.'

"'Oh, ay!' says her paw at that; 'That's the kind we're a' wantin', but they're no' makin' them, and I'm no' shair that I wad hae muckle use for yin nooadays even if they were. If ye'll no hae a watch, will ye hae a yacht, or a brass band, or a fleein'-machine,[4] or a piebald pony?'

"'I wad raither mak' mud-pies,' says the wee innocent.

"'Mud-pies!' cries her faither in horror, lookin' roond to see that naebody heard her. 'Wheesh! Maggie, it wadna look nice to see the like o' you makin' mud-pies. Ye havena the claes for't. Beside, I'm tellt they're no' the go nooadays at a'.'

"'Weel,' says she at that, 'I think I'll hae a hairy-heided lion.'

"'Hairy-heided lion. Right!' says Mr Carnegie. 'Ye'll get that, my wee lassie,' and cries doon the turret stair to the kitchen for his No. 9 secretary.

"The No. 9 secretary comes up in his shirt sleeves, chewin' blot-sheet and dichting the ink aff his elbows.

"'Whit are ye thrang at the noo?' asks Mr Carnegie as nice as onything to him, though he's only a kind o' a workin' man.

"'Sendin' aff the week's orders for new kirk organs,' says the No. 9 secretary, 'and it'll tak' us till Wednesday.'

"'Where's a' the rest o' my secretaries?' asks Mr Carnegie.

"'Half o' them's makin' oot cheques for new leebraries[5] up and doon the country, and the ither half's oot in the back-coort burning letters frae weedows wi' nineteen weans, nane o' them daein' for themsel's, and frae men that were dacent and steady a' their days, but had awfu' bad luck.'

"'If it gangs on like this we'll hae to put ye on the night-shift,' says Mr Carnegie. 'It's comin' to't when I hae to write ma ain letters. I'll be expected to write my ain books next. But I'll no' dae onything o' the kind. Jist you telegraph to India, or Africa, or Japan, or wherever the hairy-heided lions comes frae, and tell them to send wee Maggie ane o' the very best at 50 per cent aff for cash.'

"Early ae mornin' some weeks efter that, when the steam-hooter for wakenin' the secretaries starts howlin' at five o'clock, Mr Carnegie comes doon stair and sees the hairy-heided lion in a crate bein' pit aff a lorry. He has it wheeled in to the wee lassie when she's at her breakfast.

"'Let it oot,' she says; 'I want to play wi't.'

"'Ye wee fuiter!' he says, lauchin' like onything, 'ye canna get playin' wi't oot o' the cage, but ye'll can get feedin't wi' sultana-cake.'

"But that disna suit wee Maggie, and she jist tells him to send it awa' to the Bronx Zoo in New York.

"'Bronx Zoo. Right!' says her paw, and cries on his No.
22 secretary to send it aff wi' the parcel post at yince.

"'That minds me,' he says, 'there's a cryin' need for
hairy-heided lions all over Europe and the United States.
The moral and educative influence o' the common or bald-
heided lion is of no account. Noo that maist o' the kirks has
twa organs apiece, and there's a leebrary in every clachan
in the country, I must think o' some ither wye o' gettin' rid
o' this cursed wealth. It was rale 'cute o' you, Maggie, to
think o't; I'll pay half the price o' a hairy-heided lion for
every toon in the country wi' a population o' over five hundred that can mak' up the ither half by public subscription.'

"And then the wee lassie says she canna tak' her
parridge.

"'Whit for no'?' he asks her, anxious-like. 'Are they no
guid?'

"'Oh, they're maybe guid enough,' she says, 'but I wad
raither hae toffie.'

"'Toffie. Right!' says her paw, and orders up the chef to
mak' toffie in a hurry.

"'Whit's he gaun to mak' it wi'?' asks the wee yin.

"'Oh, jist in the ordinar' wye—wi' butter and sugar,'
says her paw.

"'That's jist common toffie,' says the wee lassie; 'I want
some ither kind.'

"'As shair's death, Maggie,' he says, 'there's only the ae
wye o' makin' toffie.'

"'Then whit's the use o' haein' a millionaire for a paw?'
she asks.

"'True for you,' he says, and thinks hard. 'I could mak'
the chef put in champed rubies or a di'mond or twa grated
doon.'

"'Wad it mak' the toffie taste ony better?' asks the wee
cratur'.

"'No' a bit better,' he says. 'It wadna taste sae guid as
the ordinary toffie, but it wad be nice and dear.'

"'Then I'll jist hae to hae the plain, chape toffie,' says
wee Maggie.

"'That's jist whit I hae to hae mysel' wi' a great mony things,' says her paw. 'Being a millionaire's nice enough some wyes, but there's a wheen things money canna buy, and paupers wi' three or four thoosand paltry pounds a-year is able to get jist as guid toffie and ither things as I can. I canna even dress mysel' different frae ither folks, for it wad look rideeculous to see me gaun aboot wi' gold cloth waistcoats and a hat wi' strings o' pearls on it, so' a' I can dae is to get my nickerbocker suits made wi' an extra big check. I hae the pattern that big noo there's only a check-and-a-half to the suit; but if it wasna for the honour o't I wad just as soon be wearin' Harris tweed.'"

"Upon my word, Erchie," I said, "you make me sorry for our philanthropic friend, and particularly for his little girl."

"Oh, there's no occasion!" protested Erchie. "There's no condeetion in life that hasna its compensations, and even Mr Carnegie's wee lassie has them. I hae nae doot the best fun her and her paw gets is when they're playin' at bein' puir. The auld man 'll nae doot whiles hide his pocket-money in the press, and sit doon readin' his newspaper, wi' his feet on the chimney-piece, and she'll come in and ask for a bawbee.

"'I declare to ye I havena a farden, Maggie,' he'll say; 'but I'll gie ye a penny on Setturday when I get my pay.'

"'I dinna believe ye,' she'll say.

"'Then ye can ripe me,'[6] says her paw, and the wee tot'll feel in a' his pooches, and find half a sovereign in his waistcoat. They'll let on it's jist a bawbee (the wee thing never saw a rale bawbee in her life, I'll warrant), and he'll wonner whit wye he forgot aboot it, and tell her to keep it and buy jujubes[7] wi't, and she'll be awa' like a whitteruck[8] and come back in a while wi' her face a' sticky for a kiss, jist like rale.

"Fine I ken the wee smouts; it was that wye wi' oor ain Teenie.

"Other whiles she'll hae a wee tin bank wi' a beeskep on't, and she'll hae't fu' o' sovereigns her faither's veesitors slip't in her haund when they were gaun awa', and she'll put it on the mantelpiece and gang out. Then her paw'll get up lauchin' like onything to himsel', and tak' doon the wee bank and rattle awa' at it, lettin' on he's robbin't for a schooner o' beer, and at that she'll come rinnin' in and catch him at it, and they'll hae great fun wi' that game. I have nae doot her faither and mither get mony a laugh at her playin' at wee washin's, too, and lettin' on she's fair trauchled aff the face o' the earth wi' a family o' nine dolls, an' three o' them doon wi' the hoopin'-cough. Oh! they're no that bad aff for fine fun even in Skibo Castle."

8. *A Son of the City*

MY OLD friend came daundering down the street with what might have been a bag of cherries, if cherries were in season, and what I surmised were really the twopenny pies with which Jinnet and he sometimes made the Saturday evenings festive. When we met he displayed a blue hyacinth in a flower-pot.

"Saw't in a fruiterer's window," said he, "and took the notion. Ninepence; dod! I dinna ken hoo they mak' them for the money. I thocht it wad please the wife, and min' her o' Dunoon and the Lairgs and a' thae places that's doon the watter in the summer-time.

"Ye may say whit ye like, I'm shair they shut up a' thae coast toons when us bonny wee Gleska buddies is no' comin' doon wi' oor tin boxes,[1] and cheerin' them up wi' a clog-wallop on the quay.[2]

"It's a fine thing a flooer; no' dear to buy at the start, and chaper to keep than a canary. It's Nature — the Rale Oreeginal. Ninepence! And the smell o't! Jist a fair phenomena!"

"A sign of spring, Erchie," I said; "Thank heaven! the primrose is in the wood, and the buds bursting on the hedge in the country, though you and I are not there to see it."

"I daursay," said he, "I'll hae to mak' a perusal doon the length o' Yoker on the skoosh car[3] when the floods is ower. I'm that used to them noo, as shair's death I canna get my naitural sleep on dry nichts unless Jinnet gangs oot to the back and throws chuckies at the window, lettin' on it's rain and hailstanes. When I hear the gravel on the window I cod mysel' it's the genuine auld Caledonian climate, say my wee 'Noo I lay me,' and gang to sleep as balmy as a nicht polisman.

"There's a great cry the noo aboot folks comin' frae the country and croodin' into the toons and livin' in slums and degenerating the bone and muscle o' Britain wi' eatin' kippered herrin' and ice-cream. Thoosands o' them's gaun aboot Gleska daein' their bit turns the best way they can, and no' kennin', puir craturs, there's a Commission sittin' on them as hard's it can.

"'Whit's wanted,' says the Inspectors o' Poor, "is to hustle them aboot frae place to place till the soles o' their feet gets red-hot wi' the speed they're gaun at; then gie them a bar o' carbolic soap and a keg o' Keatin's poother,[4] and put them on the first train for Edinburgh.'

"'Tear doon the rookeries,'[5] says anither man, 'and pit up rooms and kitchens wi' wally jawboxes[6] and tiled closes at a rent o' eighteenpence a-week when ye get it.'

"'That's a' very fine,' says the economists, 'but if ye let guid wally jawbox hooses at ten shillin's a year less than the auld-established and justly-popular slum hoose, will't no' tempt mair puir folk frae the country into Gleska and conjest the Gorbals worse than ever?' The puir economists thinks the folks oot aboot Skye and Kamerhashinjoo's[7] waitin' for telegrams tellin' them the single apairtment hoose in Lyon Street, Garscube Road, 's doon ten shillin's a year, afore they pack their carpet-bags and start on the *Clansman*[8] for the Broomielaw. But they're no'. They divna ken onything aboot the rent o' hooses in Gleska, and they're no' carin', for maybe they'll no' pay't onywye. They jist come awa' to Gleska when the wife tells them, and Hughie's auld enough for a polisman.

"Slums! Wha wants to abolish slums? It's no' the like o' me nor Duffy. If there werena folk leevin' in slums I couldna buy chape shirts, and the celebrated Stand Fast Craigroyston serge breeks at 2s. 11³/4d. the pair, bespoke, guaranteed, shrunk, and wan hip-pocket.

"When they're proposin' the toast o' the 'Army, Navy, and Reserve Forces,' they ought to add the Force that Live in Slums. They're the men and women that's aye ready to sweat for their country — when their money's done. A man that wants the chapest kind o' chape labour kens he'll aye can get it in the slums; if it wasna for that, my Stand Fast Craigroyston breeks wad maybe cost 7s. 6d., and some of the elders in the kirk I'm beadle for wad hae to smoke tuppenny cigars instead o' sixpenny yins.

"The slums 'll no' touch ye if ye don't gang near them.

"Whit a lot o' folk want to dae 's to run the skoosh cars away oot into the country whaur the clegs and the midges and the nae gas is, and coup them oot at Deid Slow⁹ on the Clyde, and leave them there wander't. Hoo wad they like it themsel's? The idea is that Duffy, when he's done wi' his last rake o' coals, 'll mak' the breenge for Deid Slow, and tak' his tea and wash his face wi' watter that hard it stots aff his face like a kahootchy ba', and spend a joyous and invigoratin' evenin' sheuchin' leeks and prunin' cauli-flooer-bushes in the front plot o' his cottage home.

"I think I see him! He wad faur sooner pay twelve pounds rent in Grove Street, and hae the cheery lowe o' the Mull o' Kintyre Vaults forenent his paurlor window, than get his boots a' glaur wi' plantin' syboes¹⁰ roond his cottage home at £6. 10s.

"The country's a' richt for folks that havena their health and dinna want to wear a collar to their wark, and Deid Slow and places like that may be fine for gaun to if ye want to get ower the dregs o' the measles, but they're nae places for ony man that loves his fellow-men.

"And still there's mony a phenomena! I ken a man that says he wad stay in the country a' the year roond if he hadna to bide in Gleska and keep his eye on ither men in the same tred's himsel', to see they're no' risin' early in the mornin' and gettin' the better o' him.

"It wadna suit Easy-gaun Erchie. Fine I ken whit the country is; did I no' leeve a hale winter aboot Dalry when I was a halflin'?

"It's maybe a' richt in summer, when you and me gangs oot on an excursion, and cheers them up wi' our melodeon wi' bell accompaniment; but the puir sowls havena much diversion at the time o' year the V-shaped depression's[11] cleckin' on Ben Nevis, and the weather prophets in the evening papers is promisin' a welcome change o' weather every Setturday. All ye can dae when your wark's done and ye've ta'en your tea's to put on a pair o' top-boots and a waterproof, and gang oot in the dark. There's no' even a close to coort in,[12] and if ye want to walk along a country road at nicht thinkin' hoo much money ye hae in the bank, ye must be gey smert no' to fa' into a ditch. Stars? Wha wants to bother glowerin' at stars? There's never ony change in the programme wi' them in the country. If I want stars I gang to the Britannia.[13]

"Na, na, Gleska's the place, and it's nae wonder a' the country-folks is croodin' into't as fast's they can get their cottage homes sublet.

"This is the place for intellect and the big pennyworth of skim-milk.

"I declare I'm that ta'en wi' Gleska I get up sometimes afore the fire's lichted to look oot at the window and see if it's still to the fore.

"Fifteen public-hooses within forty yairds o' the close-mooth; a guttapercha works at the tap o' the street, and twa cab-stances at the foot. My mornin' 'oors are made merry wi' the delightfu' strains o' factory hooters and the sound o' the dust-cart man kickin' his horse like onything whaur it 'll dae maist guid.

"I can get onywhere I want to gang on the skoosh cars for a bawbee or a penny, but the only place I hae to gang to generally is my wark, and I wad jist as soon walk it, for I'm no' in ony hurry.

"When the rain's blashin' doon at nicht on the puir miserable craturs workin' at their front plots in Deid Slow, or trippin' ower hens that 'll no' lay ony eggs, I can be improvin' my mind wi' Duffy at the Mull o' Kintyre Vaults, or daunderin' alang the Coocaddens[14] wi' my hand tight on my watch-pocket, lookin' at the shop windows and jinkin' the members o' the Sons of Toil Social Club (Limited), as they tak' the breadth o' the pavement.

"Gleska! Some day when I'm in the key for't I'll mak' a song aboot her. Here the triumphs o' civilisation meet ye at the stair-fit, and three bawbee mornin' rolls can be had efter six o'clock at nicht for a penny.

"There's libraries scattered a' ower the place; I ken, for I've seen them often, and the brass plate at the door tellin' ye whit they are.

"Art's a' the go in Gleska, too; there's something aboot it every ither nicht in the papers, when Lord Somebody-or-ither's no' divorcin' his wife, and takin' up the space; and I hear there's hunders o' pictures oot in yon place at Kelvingrove.

"Theatres, concerts, balls, swarees, lectures — ony mortal thing ye like that'll keep ye oot o' your bed, ye'll get in Gleska if ye have the money to pay for't."

"It's true, Erchie."

"Whit's true?" said the old man, wrapping the paper more carefully round his flower-pot. "Man, I'm only coddin'. Toon or country, it doesna muckle maitter if, like me, ye stay in yer ain hoose. I don't stay in Gleska; not me! It's only the place I mak' my money in; I stay wi' Jinnet."

9. *Erchie on the King's Cruise*

I DELIBERATELY sought out Erchie one day in order to elicit his views upon the Royal progress[1] through the Western Isles, and found him full of the subject, with the happiest disposition to eloquence thereon.

"Man! I'm that gled I'm to the fore to see this prood day for Scotland," said he. "I'm daein' hardly onything but read the mornin' and evenin' papers, and if the Royal yacht comes up the length o' Yoker I'm gaun doon mysel' to wave a hanky.'His Majesty in Arran. Great Reception,' says they. 'His Majesty in Glorious Health. Waves his hand to a Wee Lassie, and Nearly Shoots a Deer,' says they. 'His Majesty's Yacht Surrounded by the Natives. Escape round the Mull. Vexation of Campbeltown, and Vote of Censure by the Golfers of Machrihanish,' says they. Then the telegrams frae 'Oor Special Correspondent': 'OBAN, 1 P.M. — It is confidently expected that the Royal yacht will come into the bay this evenin' in time for tea. The esplanade is being washed with eau-de-cologne, and a' the magistrates is up at Rankine's barber shop gettin' a dry shampoo.' 'OBAN, 1.30 P.M. — A wire frae Colonsay says the Royal yacht is about to set sail for Oban. Tremendous excitement prevails here, and the price o' hotel bedrooms is raised 200 per cent. It is decided to mobilise the local Boys' Brigade, and engage Johnny M'Coll to play the pipes afore the King when he's comin' ashore.' '6 P.M. — The Royal yacht has just passed Kerrera, and it is now certain that Oban will not be visited by the Royal party. All the flags have been taken down, and scathing comments on the extraordinary affair are anticipated from the local Press.'

"Maybe ye wadna think it, but his Majesty's gaun roond the West Coast for the sake o' his health.

"'Ye'll hae to tak' a month o' the rest cure,' the doctors tellt him, 'a drap o' claret wine to dinner, and nae worry aboot business.'

"'Can I afford it?' said his Majesty, that vexed-like, for he was pullin' aff his coat and rollin' up his sleeves to start work for the day.

"'There's nae choice in the maitter,' said the doctors; 'we order it.'

"'But can I afford it?' again said his Majesty. 'Ye ken yoursel's, doctors, I have had a lot o' expense lately, wi' trouble in the hoose, and wi' the Coronation and aething and another. Could I no' be doin' the noo wi' Setturday-to-Monday trips doon the watter?'

"But no; the doctors said there was naethin' for him but rest. So his Majesty had to buy a new topcoat and a yachtin' bunnet, and start oot on the *Victoria and Albert*[2].

"It's a twa-funnelled boat, but I'm tellt that, bein' Government built, yin o' the funnels has a blaw-doon, and they daurna light the furnace below't if the win's no' in a certain airt.

"The yacht made first for the Isle o' Man, and wasna five meenutes in the place when the great novelist, Hall Corelli or Mary Caine,[3] or whichever it is, was aboard o' her distributin' hand-bills advertisin' the latest novel, and the King took fright, and left the place as soon as he could.

"I'm tellin' ye it's a gey sair trauchle[4] bein' a King. The puir sowl thought the Hielan's wad be a nice quate place where naebody wad bother him, and so he set sail then for Arran.

"'What is that I see afore me?' said he, comin' up past Pladda.

"The captain put his spy-gless to his e'e, and got as white's a cloot.

"'It's your Majesty's joyous and expectant subjects,' says he. 'They've sixty-seven Gleska steamers oot yonder waitin' on us, and every skipper has his hand on the string o' the steam-hooter.'

"'My God!' groaned the puir King, 'I thought I was sent awa' here for the guid o' my health.'

"Before he could say knife, a' the Gleska steamers and ten thoosan' wee rowin'-boats were scrapin' the pent aff the sides o' the *Victoria and Albert*, and half a million Scottish taxpayers were cheerin' their beloved Sovereign, Edward VII, every mortal yin o' them sayin', 'Yon's him yonder!' and p'intin' at him.

"'Will I hae to shoogle hands wi' a' that crood?' he asked the captain o' the *Victoria and Albert*, and was told it wad dae if he jist took aff his kep noo and then.

"And so, takin' aff his kep noo and then, wi' a' the Gleska steamers and the ten thoosan' wee rowin'-boats hingin' on to the side o' the yacht, and half a million devoted subjects takin' turn aboot at keekin' in through the port-holes to see what he had for dinner, his Majesty sailed into Brodick Bay.

"'The doctors were right,' says he; 'efter a', there's naething like a rest cure; it's a mercy we're a' spared.'

"The following day his Majesty hunted the deer in Arran. I see frae the papers that he was intelligently and actively assisted in this by the well-known ghillies, Dugald M'Fadyen, Donald Campbell, Sandy M'Neill, and Peter M'Phedran.

"They went up the hill and picked oot a nice, quate he-deer, and drove it doon in front o' where his Majesty sat beside a stack o' loaded guns.

"His Majesty was graciously pleased to tak' up yin o' the guns, and let bang at the deer.

"'Weel done! That wass gey near him,' said Dugald M'Fadyen, strikin' the deer wi' his stick to mak' it stop eatin' the gress.

"His Majesty fired a second time, and the deer couldna stand it ony langer, but went aff wi' a breenge.[5]

"'Weel, it's a fine day to be oot on the hull onywye,' says M'Phedran, resigned-like, and the things that the heid ghillie Campbell didna say was terrible.

"The papers a' said the deer was shot, and a bloody business too; but it wasna till lang efter the cauld-clye corpse o't was found on the hill.

"'Here it is!' said M'Fadyen.

"'I daursay it is,' said M'Neill.

"'It'll hae to be it onywye,' said the heid man, and they had it weighed.

"If it was sold in Gleska the day it would fetch ten shillin's a pound.

"If there's ae thing I've noticed mair nor anither aboot Hielan' ghillies, it's that they'll no' hurt your feelin's if they can help it. I'm Hielan' mysel'; my name's MacPherson; a flet fit but a warm hert, and I ken.

"Meanwhile Campbeltoon washed its face, put a clove in its mooth, and tried to look as spruce as it could for a place that has mair distilleries than kirks.[6] The Royal veesit was generally regairded as providential, because the supremacy o' Speyside whiskies over Campbeltoon whiskies o' recent years wad hae a chance o' being overcome if his Majesty could be prevailed on to gang through a' the distilleries and hae a sample frae each o' them.

"It was to be a gala day, and the bellman went roon the toon orderin' every loyal ceetizen to put oot a flag, cheer like onything when the King was gaun to the distilleries, and bide inside their hooses when he was comin' back frae them. But ye'll no' believe't — THE YACHT PASSED CAMPBELTOON!

"The Provost and Magistrates and the hale community was doon on the quay to cairry the Royal pairty shouther-high if necessary, and when they saw the *Victoria and Albert* they cheered sae lood they could be heard the length o' Larne.

"'Whit's that?' said his Majesty.

"'By the smell o't I wad say Campbeltoon,' said his skipper, 'and that's mair o' your Majesty's subjects, awfu' interested in your recovery.'

"'Oh man!' said the puir King, nearly greetin', 'we divna ken whit health is, ony o' us, till we lose it. Steam as far aff frae the shore as ye can, and it'll maybe no' be sae bad.'

"So the yacht ran bye Campbeltoon.

"The folk couldna believe't at first.

"'They must hae made a mistake,' says they; 'Perhaps they didna notice the distillery lums,' and the polis sergeant birled his whustle by order of the Provost, to ca' the King's attention, but it was o' no avail. A rale divert!

"The yacht went on to Colonsay.

"That's the droll thing aboot this trip o' his Majesty's; it's no' ony nice, cheery sort o' places he gangs to at a', but oot-o'-the-wye wee places wi' naethin' aboot them but hills and things — wee trashy places wi' nae nice braw new villas aboot them, and nae minstrels or banjo-singers on the esplanade singin' 'O! Lucky Jim!' and clautin' in the bawbees.[7] I divna suppose they had half a dizzen flags in a' Colonsay, and ye wad fancy the King's een's no' that sair lookin' at flags but whit he wad be pleased to see mair o' them.

"Colonsay! Man, it's fair peetifu'! No' a Provost or a Bylie in't to hear a bit speech frae; nae steamboat trips to gang roond the Royal yacht and keek in the port-holes; but everything as quate as a kirk on a Setturday mornin'.

"A' the rest o' Scotland wanted to wag flags at his Majesty Edward VII, and here he maun put up at Colonsay! The thing was awfu' badly managed.

"If Campbeltoon was chawed at the yacht passin' withoot giein' a cry in, whit's to describe the vexation o' Oban?

"Oban had its hert set on't. It never occurred to the mind o' Oban for wan meenute that the King could pass the 'Charin' Cross o' the Hielans'[8] withoot spendin' a week there at the very least, and everything was arranged to mak' the Royal convalescent comfortable.

"The bay was fair jammed wi' yachts, and a' the steam-whustles were oiled. The hotels were packed to the roof wi' English tourists, some o' them sleepin' under the slates, wi' their feet in the cisterns, and gled to pay gey dear for the preevilege o' breathin' the same air as Edward VII.

"Early in the day somebody sent the alarmin' tidin's frae Colonsay that the *Victoria and Albert* micht pass Oban efter a', and to prevent this, herrin'-nets were stretched aff Kerrera to catch her if ony such dastardly move was made.

"But it was nae use; Oban's in sackcloth and ashes.

"'Where are we noo?' asked the Royal voyager, aff Kerrera. 'Is this Shingleton-on-the-Sea?'

"'No, your Majesty,' says the skipper of the Royal yacht, 'it's Oban, the place whaur the German waiters get their education.'

"'Heavens!' cried his Majesty, shudderin'; 'we're terrible

close; put a fire under the aft funnel at a' costs and get past as quick as we can.'

"It was pointed oot to his Majesty that the toon was evidently expectin' him, and so, to mak' things pleasant, he ordered the steam pinnace to land the week's washin' at the Charin' Cross o' the Hielan's — while the *Victoria and Albert* went on her way to Ballachulish."

10. *How Jinnet saw the King*

"I SAW him and her on Thursday,"[1] said Erchie, "as nate's ye like, and it didna cost me mair nor havin' my hair cut. They gaed past oor kirk, and the session put up a stand, and chairges ten shillin's a sate.

"'Not for Joe,' says I; 'I'd sooner buy mysel' a new pair o' boots'; and I went to Duffy and says I, 'Duffy, are ye no' gaun to hae oot yer bonny wee lorry at the heid o' Gairbraid Street[2] and ask the wife and Jinnet and me to stand on't?'

"'Right,' says Duffy, 'bring you Jinnet and I'll tak' my wife, and we'll hae a rale pant.'

"So there was the four o' us standin' five mortal 'oors on Duffy's coal-lorry. I was that gled when it was a' bye. But I'll wager there was naebody gledder nor the King himsel', puir sowl! Frae the time he cam' into Gleska at Queen Street Station till the time he left Maryhill, he lifted his hat three million seven hundred and sixty-eight thousand and sixty-three times.

"Talk aboot it bein' a fine job bein' a King! I can tell ye the money's gey hard earned. Afore he starts oot to see his beloved people, he has to practise for a week wi' the dumb-bells, and feed himsel' up on Force, Grape-nuts, Plasmon, Pianolio, and a' thae strengthenin' diets that Sunny Jim eats.[3]

"I thocht first Jinnet maybe wadna gang, her bein' in the Co-operative Store[4] and no' awfu' ta'en up wi' Royalty, but, dod! she jumped at the chance.

"'The Queen's a rale nice buddy,' she says; 'no' that I'm personally acquainted wi' her, but I hear them sayin'. And she used to mak' a' her ain claes afore she mairried the King.'

"So Jinnet and me were oot on Duffy's lorry, sittin' on auld copies o' *Reynolds' News*,[5] and hurrayin' awa' like a pair o' young yins.

"The first thing Jinnet saw was a woman wi' a wean and its face no' richt washed.

"'Fancy her bringin' oot her wean to see the King wi' a face like that,' says Jinnet, and gies the puir wee smout a sweetie.

"Frae that till it was time for us to gang hame Jinnet saw naething but weans, and her and Duffy's wife talked aboot weans even on. Ye wad think it was a baby-show we were at and no' a King's procession.

"Duffy sat wi' a tontine face[6] on him maist o' the time, but every noo and then gaun up the street at the back o' us to buy himsel' a bottle o' broon robin,[7] for he couldna get near a pub; and I sat tryin' as hard's I could to think hoo I wad like to be a King, and what kind o' waistcoats I wad wear if I had the job. On every hand the flags were wavin', and the folk were eatin' Abernaithy biscuits.

"At aboot twelve o'clock cannons begood to bang.

"'Oh my! I hope there's nae weans near thae cannons or they micht get hurt,' says Jinnet.

"Little did she think that at that parteecular meenute the King was comin' doon the tunnel frae Cowlairs,[8] and tellin' her Majesty no' to be frichted.

"When the King set foot in the Queen Street Station he gied the wan look roond him, and says he, 'Is this Gleska, can ony o' ye tell me?'

"'It is that, wi' your Majesty's gracious permission,' says the porter; 'sees a haud o' yer bag.'

"'I mind fine o' bein' here yince afore,' says the King, and gangs oot into George Square.

"'Whitna graveyaird's this?'[9] he asks, lookin' at the statues.

"'It's no' a graveyaird; it's a square, and that's the Muni-ceepal Buildin',' somebody tells him. His Majesty then laid a foundation-stone as smert's ye like wi' his least wee bit touch, and then went into the Municeepal Buildin's and had a snack.

"He cam' oot feelin' fine. 'The Second City o' the Empire!'[10] he says. 'I can weel believ't. If it wasna for my business bein' in London I wad hae a hoose here. Whit am I to dae next?'

"They took his Majesty doon Buchanan Street.

"'No bad!' says he.

"Then he cam' to Argyle Street, and gaed west, past the Hielan'man's Cross[11] at the heid o' Jamaica Street. He sees a lot o' chaps there wi' the heather stickin' oot o' their ears, and a tartan brogue that thick it nearly spiled the procession.

"'The Hielan'man's Cross,' says he; 'Man, ay! I've heard o't. Kamerhashendoo. If I had thocht o't I wad hae brocht my kilts and my pibroch and a' that.'

"A' the wey doon the Dumbarton Road the folk were fair hingin' oot o' their windows, wavin' onything at a' they could get a haud o', and the Royal carriage was bump-bump-bumpin' like a' that ower the granite setts.[12]

"'Whit's wrang wi' the streets o' Gleska?' says the King, him bein' used to wud streets in London, whaur he works.

"'It's granite, if ye please,' says they.

"'Oh ay!' says the King; 'Man, it mak's a fine noise. Will we soon be there? I like this fine, but I wadna like to keep onybody waitin'.'

"At Finnieston the folk cam' up frae the side streets and fair grat wi' patriotic fervour. Forbye, a' the pubs were shut for an 'oor or twa.

"'Whit I want to see's the poor,' says the King. 'I'm tired lookin' at the folk that's weel aff; they're faur ower common.'

"'Them's the poor,' he was tellt; 'it's the best we can dae for your Majesty.'

"'But they're awfu' bien-lookin' and weel put on,' says he.

"'Oh ay!' they tells him, 'that's their Sunday claes.'

"And so the Royal procession passed on its way, the King being supplied wi' a new hat every ten minutes, to mak' up for the yins he spiled liftin' them to his frantic and patriotic subjects.

"In ten to fifteen minutes he examined the pictures in the Art Galleries — the Dutch, the English, the Italian, and the Gleska schools o' painters;[13] the stuffed birds, and the sugaraully hats[14] the polis used to hae when you and me was jinkin' them.

"'Och, it's fine,' says he; 'there's naething wrang wi' the place. Are we no' near Maryhill noo?'

"Ye see his Majesty had on a bate he could see the hale o' Gleska in five 'oors or less, an' be oot sooner nor ony ither king that ever set a fit in it. They wanted him to mak' a circular tour o't, and come back to the Municeepal Buildin's for his tea.

"'Catch me,' says he. 'I'm gaun back to Dalkeith.'[15]

"A' this time we were standin' on Duffy's lorry, flanked on the left by the Boys' Brigade, lookin' awfu' fierce, and the riflemen frae Dunoon on the richt. Every noo an' then a sodger went bye on a horse, or a lassie nearly fainted and had to be led alang the line by a polisman, and him no' awfu' carin' for the job. Duffy was gaun up the street to buy broon robin that aften he was gettin' sunburnt, and my wife Jinnet nearly hurt her een lookin' for weans.

"'Look at thon wee wean, Erchie,' she wad aye be tellin' me, 'does't no' put ye in mind o' Rubbert's wee Hughie? Oh, the cratur!'

"'Wumman,' I tellt her, 'this is no' a kinderspiel[16] ye're at; it's a Royal procession. I wonder to me ye wad be wastin' yer e'esicht lookin' at weans when there's sae mony braw sodgers.'

"'Oh, Erchie!' says she, 'I'm bye wi' the sodgers'; and jist wi' that the procession cam' up the street. First the Lancers wi' their dickies stickin' ootside their waistcoats.

"'Man, them's fine horses,' says Duffy, wi' a professional eye on the beasts. 'Chaps me that broon yin wi' the white feet.'

"'Then cam' the King and Queen.

"'Whaur's their croons?' asks Duffy's wife. 'I divna believe that's them at a'.'

"'That's them, I'll bate ony money,' I says. 'Ye can tell by the hurry they're in.'

"'Oh, the craturs!' says Jinnet, and then says she, 'Oh, Erchie! Look at the wean hanging ower that window. I'm feart it'll fa' ower.'

"Afore she could get her een aff the wean the King's cairrage was past, and the rest o' the Lancers cam' clatterin' after them.

"'Noo for the brass bands!' says Duffy, lookin' doon the street. But there was nae brass bands. The show was bye.

"'If I had kent that was to be a' that was in't, I wad never hae ta'en oot my lorry,' says Duffy, as angry as onything, and made a breenge for anither bottle o' broon robin.

"'Och, it was fine,' says Jinnet. 'I never saw sae mony weans in a' my days.'

"And the crood began to scale.

"His Majesty reached Maryhill Station exact to the minute, wi' his eye on his watch.

"'Weel, that's bye onywye,' says he, and somebody cries for a speech.

"'People o' Gleska,' he says, 'I have seen your toon. It's fine — there's naething wrang wi't,' and then the gaird blew his whustle, and the train went aff.

"The great event was ower, the rain begood to fa' again; the Gilmorehill student hurried hame to blacken his face and put on his sister's frock.[17] The coloured ping-pong balls strung ower Sauchieha' Street was lighted, the illuminated skoosh cars began to skoosh up and doon the street, the public-hooses did a fine tred.

"'I'm gled it's a' bye,' says Jinnet, when we got hame to oor ain hoose.

"'Indeed, and so am I,' says I. 'There wad be fine fun in this warld a' the time if we werena trying for't.'"

11. *Erchie Returns*

FOR WEEKS I had not seen Erchie. He was not to be met on the accustomed streets, and, St Kentigern's Kirk having been closed since July for alterations and repairs, it was useless to go there in search of its beadle. Once I met Duffy, and asked him what had become of the old man.

"Alloo you[1] Erchie!" was all the information he would vouchsafe; "If he's keepin' oot o' sicht, he'll hae his ain reason for't. Mind, I'm no' sayin' onything against the cratur, though him and me's had mony a row. He's a' richt if ye tak' him the richt wye. But sly! He's that sly, the auld yin, ye can whiles see him winkin' awa' to himsel' ower something he kens that naebody else kens, and that he's no gaun to tell to them. I havena seen the auld fuiter since the Fair week; perhaps he's gotten genteel and bidin' doon at Rothesay till the summer steamboats stop. There's yin thing sure — it's no' a casc o' wife-desertion, for Jinnet's wi' him. I can tell by the venetian blinds and the handle o' their door. Sly! Did ye say sly? Man, it's no' the word for't. Erchie MacPherson's fair lost at the waitin'; he should hae been a poet, or a statesman, or something in the fancy line like that."

It was with the joy of a man who has made up his mind he has lost a sovereign and finds it weeks after in the lining of his waistcoat, I unexpectedly met Erchie on Saturday.

"Upon my word, old friend," I said, "I thought you were dead."

"No, nor deid!" retorted Erchie. "Catch me! I'm nane o' the deein' kind. But I micht nearly as weel be deid, for I've been thae twa months in Edinburgh. Yon's the place for a man in a decline; it's that slow he wad hae a chance o' livin' to a grand auld age. There's mair o' a bustle on the road to Sichthill Cemetery ony day in the week than there is in Princes Street on a Setturday nicht. I had a bit job there for the last ten weeks, and the only pleesure I had was gaun doon noo and then to the Waverley Station to see the bonny wee trains frae Gleska. They're a' richt for scenery and the like o' that in Edinburgh, but they're no' smert."

"But it's an old saying, Erchie, that all the wise men in Glasgow come from the East — that's to say, they come from Edinburgh."

"Yes, and the wiser they are the quicker they come," said Erchie. "Man! and it's only an 'oor's journey, and to see the wye some o' them gae on bidin' ower yonder ye wad think they had the Atlantic Ocean to cross. There should be missionaries sent ower to Edinburgh explainin' things to the puir deluded craturs. Ony folk that wad put thon big humplock o' a hill they ca' the Castle in the middle o' the street, spilin' the view, and hing their washin's on hay-rakes[2] stuck oot at their windows, hae muckle to learn."

"Still, I have no doubt Edinburgh's doing its best, Erchie," I said.

"Maybe, but they're no' smert; ye wad hae yer pouch picked half a dizzen times in Gleska in the time an Edinburgh polisman tak's to rub his een to waken himsel' when ye ask him the road to Leith.

"Did ye ever hear tell o' the Edinburgh man that ance ventured to Gleska and saw the hopper dredgers clawtin' up the glaur[3] frae the Clyde at Broomielaw?

"'Whit are ye standin' here for? Come awa' and hae a gless o' milk,' said a freen' to him.

"'No, nor awa',' said he, glowerin' like onything; 'I've coonted 364 o' thae wee buckets comin' oot the watter, and I'll no move a step oot o' here till I see the last o' them!'

"The puir cratur never saw a rale river in his life afore. Och! but Edinburgh's no' that bad; ye can aye be sure o' gettin' yer nicht's sleep in't at ony 'oor o' the day, it's that quate. They're aye braggin' that it's cleaner than Gleska, as if there was onything smert aboot that.

"'There's naething dirtier nor a dirty Gleska man,' said yin o' them to me ae day.

"'There is,' says I.

"'Whit?' says he.

"'Twa clean Edinburgh yins,' says I.

"Och! but I'm only in fun. Edinburgh's a' richt; there's naething wrang wi' the place ance ye're in it if ye hae a book to read. I hate to hear the wye Duffy and some o' them speak aboot Edinburgh, the same as if it was shut up a' thegither; hoo wad we like it oorsel's? I hae maybe a flet fit, but I hae a warm hert, and I'll aye stick up for Edinburgh. I had an uncle that near got the jyle there for running ower yin o' their tramway caurs. They've no skoosh cars in Edinburgh;[4] they're thon ither kin' that's pu'ed wi' a rope, and whiles the rope breaks; but it doesna maitter, naebody's in ony hurry gaun to ony place in Edinburgh, and the passengers jist sit where they are till it's mended."

"Well, anyhow, Erchie, we're glad to see you back," I said.

"Gled to see me back!" he cried. "I'll wager ye didna ken I was awa', and the only folk that kent we werena in Gleska for the past twa or three months was the dairy and the wee shop we get oor vegetables frae.

"When I was in Edinburgh yonder, skliffin' alang the streets as fast's I could, and nippin' mysel' every noo and then to keep mysel' frae fa'in' asleep, I wad be thinkin' to mysel', 'Hoo are they gettin' on in Gleska wantin' Erchie MacPherson? Noo that they've lost me, they'll ken the worth o' me.' I made shair that, at least, the skoosh cars wad hae to stop runnin' when I was awa', and that the polis band wad come doon to the station to meet me when I cam' hame.

"Dod! ye wad hardly believe it, but ever since I cam' back I meet naebody but folk that never ken't I was awa'. It's a gey hertless place Gleska that way. Noo, in Edinburgh it's different. They're gey sweart to lose ye in Edinburgh ance they get haud o' ye; that's the way they keep up the price o' the railway ticket to Gleska.

"I was tellin' Duffy aboot Edinburgh, and he's gaun through wi' a trip to see't on Monday. It'll be a puir holiday for the cratur, but let him jist tak' it. He'll be better there than wastin' his money in a toon. When Duffy goes onywhere on ony o' the Gleska holidays, it's generally to Airdrie, or Coatbrig, or Clydebank he goes, and walks aboot the streets till the polis put him on the last train hame for Gleska, and him singin' 'Dark Lochnagar' wi' the tears in his een.

"He'll say to me next mornin', 'Man! Erchie, thon's a thrivin' place, Coatbrig, but awfu' bad whisky.'

"There's a lot like him aboot a Gleska holiday. They'll be gettin' up to a late breakfast wi' no parridge till't on Monday mornin', and sayin', 'Man! it's a grand day for Dunoon,' and then start druggin' themsel's wi' drams. Ye wad think they were gaun to get twa teeth ta'en oot instead o' gaun on a holiday.

"That's no' my notion o' a holiday, either in the autumn or the spring. I'm takin' Jinnet oot on Monday to Milliken Park[5] to see her kizzen that keeps a gairden. We'll hae an awfu' wrastle in the mornin' catchin' the train, and it'll be that crooded we'll hae to stand a' the way. The wife's kizzen 'll be that gled to see us she'll mak' tea for us every half-'oor and send oot each time to the grocer's for mair o' thon biled ham ye aye get at burials. I'll get my feet a' sair walkin' up and doon the gairden coontin' the wife's kizzen's aipples that's no' richt ripe yet, and Jinnet and me 'll hae to cairry hame a big poke o' rhuburb or greens, or some ither stuff we're no wantin', and the train 'll be an 'oor late o' gettin' into Gleska.

"That's a holiday. The only time ye enjoy a holiday is when it's a' bye."

12. *Duffy's First Family*

MORE THAN a year after the King's visit Erchie and I one day passed a piano-organ in the street playing 'Dark Lochnagar.' The air attracted him; he hummed it very much out of tune for some minutes after.

"Do ye hear that?" said he, "'Dark Lochnagar'; I used ance to could nearly play't on the mooth harmonium. I learned it aff Duffy. Him and me was mairried aboot the same time. We lived in the same close up in the Coocaddens — him on the top flet, and Jinnet and me in the flet below. Oor wifes had turn aboot o' the same credle — and it was kept gey throng, I'm tellin' ye. If it wasna Duffy up the stair at nicht, efter his wark was done, rockin' awa' wi' a grudge to the tune o' 'Dark Lochnagar,' it was me below at no' 'Auld Lang Syne,' but yon ither yin ye ken fine. I daresay it was rockin' the credle helped to mak' my feet flet, and it micht hae happened in a far waur cause.

"It was Duffy's first wife; she dee'd, I think, to get rid o' him — the cratur! Duffy's yin o' thae men wi' a great big lump o' a hert that brocht the tear to his ain een when he was singin' 'Bonny Annie Laurie' doon in the Mull o' Kintyre Vaults, but wad see his wife to bleezes afore he wad brush his ain boots for Sunday, and her no' weel. She fair adored him, too. She thocht Duffy was jist the ordinar' kind o' man, and that I was a kind o' eccentric peely-wally sowl, because I sometimes dried the dishes, and didna noo' an then gie Jinnet a beltin'.

"'His looks is the best o' him,' she wad tell Jinnet.

"'Then he's gey hard up!' I wad say to Jinnet when she tellt me this.

"'He's no very strong,' — that was aye her cry, when she was fryin' anither pun' o' ham and a pair o' kippers for his breakfast.

"Duffy's first wean was Wullie John. Ye wad think, to hear Duffy brag aboot him, that it was a new patent kind o' wean, and there wasna anither in Coocaddens, whaur, I'm tellin' ye, weans is that rife ye hae to walk to yer work skliffin' yer feet in case ye tramp on them.

"Duffy's notion was to rear a race o' kind o' gladiators, and he rubbed him a' ower every nicht wi' olive-oil to mak' him soople. Nane o' your fancy foods for weans for Wullie John. It was rale auld Caledonia — parridge and soor dook,[1] that soor the puir wee smout went aboot grewin' wi' its mooth a' slewed to the side, as if it was practising the wye the women haud their hairpins.

"Mony a time I've seen oor Jinnet sneak him into oor hoose to gie him curds and cream; he said he liked them fine, because they were sae slippy.

"'Show your temper, Wullie John,' Duffy wad tell him when onybody was in the hoose; and the wee cratur was trained at that to put on a fearfu' face and haud up his claws.

"'See that!' Duffy wad say as prood as onything; 'the game's there, I'm tellin' ye.'

"Then Duffy began to harden him. He wad haud him up by the lug to see if he was game, and if he grat that was coonted wan to Duffy, and Wullie John got nae jeely on his piece. He was washed every mornin', winter and summer, in cauld watter in the jaw-box, and rubbed wi' a tooel as coorse as a carrot-grater till the skin was peelin' aff his back.

"'Ye need to bring oot the glow,' Duffy wad say to me.

"'If it gangs on much further,' I tellt him, 'I'll bring oot thc polis.'

"Wullie John was fair on the road for bein' an A1 gladi-ator, but he went and dee'd on Duffy, and I never saw a man mair chawed.

"Duffy's next was a laddie too — they ca'd him Alexan-der. There was gaun to be nane o' their hardenin' dydoes wi' Alexander.

"It was aboot the time Duffy took to politics, and said the thing the Democratic Pairty[2] wanted was educated men wi' brains. He made up his mind that Alexander wad never cairry a coalpoke, but get the best o' learnin' if it cost a pound.

"He wasna very strong, was Alexander, and Duffy fed him maist o' the time on Gregory's mixture,[3] cod-ile, and ony ither stuff he could buy by word o' mooth at the apothe-cary's withoot a doctor's line. Alexander was getting medicine poored into him that often he was feared to gant in case he wad jar his teeth on a table-spoon when his een was shut. He wore hot-water bottles to his feet in the deid o' summer, and if he had a sair heid in the mornin' afore he started for the school on the geography days he was put to his bed and fed on tapioca. Everything went wrang wi' puir wee Alexander. The hives[4] went in wi' him, and the dregs o' the measles cam' oot. He took every trouble that was gaun aboot except gymnastics; Duffy took him to Professor Coats,[5] the bump-man, and had his heid examined; the Professor said it was as fine a heid o' its kind as ever he saw, and Duffy put a bawbee on the bag o' coals richt aff, and began to put the money bye for Alexander's college fees.

"Alexander's a man noo, and daein' fine. He's in the gas office; the only time he went to college was to read the meter there.

"Ye canna tell whit laddies 'll turn oot, and it's no' ony better wi' lassies. Duffy had a wheen o' lassies; I forget hoo mony there was a'thegither, but when they were coortin' ye wad think ye were gaun doon the middle o' the Hay-makers' country dance when ye cam' up the close at nicht.

"The auldest — she was Annie — was naething parti-cular fancy; she jist nursed the rest, and made their peenies, and washed for them, and trimmed her ain hats, and made Duffy's auld waistcoats into suits for the wee yins, and never got to the dancin', so naebody married her, and she's there yet.

"A' the chaps cam' efter her sisters.

"The sisters never let on aboot the coal-ree and Duffy's lorry, but said their paw was in the coal tred — a kind o' a coal-maister. It was a bonny sicht to see them merchin' oot to their cookery lessons in the efternoons, their hair as curly's onything, and their beds no' made.

"The days they tried new dishes frae the cookery lessons at hame, Duffy took his meat in the Western Cookin' Depot, and cam' hame when it was dark. Yin o' them played the mandolin. The mandolin's a noble instrument; it cheers the workman's hame; a lassie gaun alang the street wi' a nice print dress, and a case wi' a mandolin, is jist the sort I wad fancy mysel' if I was a young yin and there wasna Jinnet.

"A fruiterer married the mandolin. The nicht she was merrit, Duffy sang 'Dark Lochnagar,' and winked at me like a' that.

"'Learn your dochters the mandolin Erchie,' says he in my lug, 'and they'll gang aff your haunds like snaw aff a dyke. That's the advice I wad gie ye if ye had ony dochters left. I wad hae made it the piano, but we couldna get a piano up past the bend on the stair.'

"Efter the mandolin went, the boys begood to scramble for Duffy's dochters as if they were bowl-money,[6] The close-mooth was never clear o' cabs, and the rice was always up to your ankles on the stair. Duffy sang 'Dark Lochnagar' even-on and aye kept winkin' at me.

"'That's the mandolin awa',' says he, 'and the scientific dressmakin', and the shorthand, and the 'Curfew Must Not Ring To-night,' and the revival meetin's, and the no' very weel yin that needs a nice quate hame; they're a' gane, Erchie, and I'm no' gien jeely-dishes awa' wi' them either. I'm my lee-lane, me and Annie; if ony o' the chaps cam' efter Annie, I wad chase him doon the stair.'

"'Man! Duffy,' I says till him, 'ye're selfish enough workin' aff a' them ornamental dochters on the young men o' Gleska that did ye nae hairm, and keepin' the best o' the hale jingbang in the hoose a' the time in case they see her.'

"'Let them tak' it !' says Duffy, 'I'm no' a bit vexed for them,' and he started to sing 'Dark Lochnagar' as lood as ever, while Annie was puttin' on his boots.

"That was in Duffy's auld days. He married a second wife, and it was a fair tak'-in, for he thocht a wee greengrocer's shop she had was her ain, and a' the time it was her brither's.

"'That's the mandolin for you, Duffy,' says I, when he tellt me.

"But that yin died on him too; she died last Mertinmas; Duffy's kind o' oot o' wifes the noo. And the warst o't is that his dochter Annie's gettin' married."

13. *Erchie goes to a Bazaar*

THERE WAS a very self-conscious look on Erchie's face on Saturday when I met him with a hand-painted drainpipe of the most generous proportions under his arm.

"It's aye the way," said he. "Did ye ever hae ony o' yer parteecular freen's meet ye when ye were takin' hame a brace o' grouse? No' a bit o' ye! But if it's a poke o' onything, or a parcel frae the country, whaur they havena ony broon paper, but jist *The Weekly Mail*, and nae richt twine, ye'll no' can gang the length o' the street without comin' across everybody that gangs to yer kirk."

He put the drain-pipe down on the pavement — it was the evening — and sat on the end of it.

"So you are the latest victim to the art movement,[1] Erchie?" I said. "You will be putting away your haircloth chairs and introducing the sticky plush variety; I was suspicious of that new dado in your parlour the day we had the tousy tea after Big Macphee's burial."

"Catch me!" said Erchie. "Them and their art! I wadna be encouragin' the deevils. If ye want to ken the way I'm gaun hame wi' this wally umbrella-staun', I'll tell ye the rale truth. It's jist this, that Jinnet's doon yonder at the Freemasons' Bazaar wi' red-hot money in her pooch, and canna get awa' till it's done. She's bocht a tea-cosy besides this drain-pipe, and a toaster wi' puce ribbons on't for haudin' letters and papers, and she'll be in luck for yince if she disna win the raffle for the lady's bicycle that she had twa tickets for. Fancy me oot in Grove Street in the early mornin' learnin' Jinnet the bicycle, and her the granny o' seeven!

"Of course, Jinnet's no' needin' ony bicycle ony mair than she's needin' a bassinette,[2] but she has a saft hert and canna say no unless she's awfu' angry, and a young chap, speakin' awfu' Englified, wi' his hair a' Vaseline, got roond her. She's waitin' behin' there to see if she wins the raffle, and to pick up ony bargains just a wee while afore the place shuts up — the rale time for bazaar bargains if ye divna get yer leg broken in the crush. I only went there mysel' to see if I could get her to come hame as lang as she had enough left to pay her fare on the skoosh car, but I micht as weel speak to the wind. She was fair raised ower a bargain in rabbits. It's an awfu' thing when yer wife tak's to bazaars; it's waur nor drink.

"It's a female complaint; ye'll no' find mony men bothered wi't unless they happen to be ministers. Ye'll no' see Duffy sittin' late at nicht knittin' wee bootees for weans they'll never in this warld fit, nor crochetin' doyleys, to aid the funds o' the Celtic Fitba' Club.[3] Ye micht watch a lang while afore ye wad see me makin' tinsey 'ool ornaments wi' paste-heided preens for hingin' up in the best room o' dacent folk that never did me ony hairm.

"There wad be nae such thing as bazaars if there werena ony weemen. In thoosands o' weel-daein' hames in this Christian toon o' Gleska there's weemen at this very meenute neglectin' their men's suppers to sit doon and think as hard's they can whit they can mak' wi' a cut and a half o' three-ply fingerin' worsted, that'll no' be ony use to ony body, but 'll look worth eighteenpence in a bazaar. If ye miss your lum hat,[4] and canna find it to gang to a funeral, ye may be shair it was cut in scollops a' roond the rim, and covered wi' velvet, and that wee Jeenie pented flooers on't in her ain time to gie't the richt feenish for bein' an Art work-basket at yer wife's stall in some bazaar.

"Maist weemen start it withoot meanin' ony hairm, maybe wi' a table-centre, or a lamp-shade, or a pair o' bedroom slippers. There's no' much wrang wi' that; but it's a beginnin', and the habit grows on them till they're scoorin' the country lookin' for a chance to contribute whit they ca' Work to kirk bazaars and ony ither kinds o' bazaars that's handy. It mak's my hert sair sometimes to see weel-put-on weemen wi' men o' their ain and dacent faimilies, comin' hame through back-streets staggerin' wi' parcels o' remnants for dressin' dolls or makin' cushions wi'. They'll hide it frae their men as long as they can, and then, when they're found oot, they'll brazen it oot and deny that it's ony great hairm.

"That's wan way the trouble shows itsel'.

"There's ither weemen — maistly younger and no' mairried — that's dyin' for a chance to be assistant stall-keepers, and wear white keps and aiprons, jist like table-maids.

"That's the kind I'm feared for, and I'm nae chicken.

"When they see a man come into the bazaar and nae wife wi' him to tak' care o' him, they come swoopin' doon on him, gie him ony amount o' cleck, jist in fun, and ripe his pooches before he can button his jaicket.

"'I'm no' sayin' they put their hands in his pooches, but jist as bad; they look that nice, and sae fond o' his tie and the way he has o' wearin' his moustache, that he's kittley doon to the soles o' his feet, and wad buy a steam road-roller frae them if he had the money for't. But they're no' sellin' steam road-rollers, the craturs! They're sellin' shillin' dolls at twa-and-six that can open and shut their een, and say 'Maw' and 'Paw.' They're sellin' carpet slippers, or bonny wee bunches o' flooers, or raffle tickets for a rale heliotrope Persian cat. It's the flyest game I ken. When that puir sowl gets oot o' the place wi' naething in his pooches but his hands, and a dazed look in his een, the only thing he can mind is that she said her name was Maud, and that her hair was crimp, and that she didna put a preen in his coat-lapelle when she was puttin' the shillin' rose there, because she said a preen wad cut love. She said that to every customer she had for her flooers that day, wi' a quick look up in their face, and then droppin' her eyes confused like, and her face red, and a' the time her, as like as no', engaged to a man in India.

"I wonder hoo it wad dae to hae a man's bazaar? They ocht to have made the Freemasons' bazaar a man's yin, seein' the Freemasons 'll no tell the weemen their secrets nor let them into their lodges.

"A man's bazaar wad be a rale divert: naethin' to be sold in't but things for use, like meerschaum pipes, and kahootchy collars, and sox the richt size, and chairs, and tables, and concertinas — everything guaranteed to be made by men and them tryin'.

"The stalls wad be kept by a' the baronets that could be scraped thegither and could be trusted withoot cash registers, and the stall assistants wad be the pick o' the best-lookin' men in the toon — if ye could get them sober enough. If Jinnet wad let me, I wad be willin' to gie a hand mysel'; for though I've a flet fit I've a warm hert, I'm tellin' ye.

"I think I see Duffy walkin' roond the St Andrew's Hall,[5] and it got up to look like the Fall o' Babylon, tryin' to sell bunches o' flooers. Dae ye think he wad sell mony to the young chaps like whit Maud riped? Nae fears! He wad hae to tak' every customer oot and stand him a drink afore he wad get a flooer aff his hands.

"Can ye fancy Duffy gaun roond tryin' to sell tickets for a raffle o' a canary in a cage?

"'Here ye are, chaps and cairters! The chance o' yer lives for a graund whustler, and no' ill to feed !'

"Na, na! a man o' the Duffy stamp wad be nae use for a bazaar, even wi' a dress suit on and his face washed. It wad need young stockbrokers, and chaps wi' the richt kind o' claes, wi' a crease doon the front o' their breeks — Grosvenor Restaurant chaps,[6] wi' the smell o' cigars aff their topcoats, and either ca'd Fred or Vincent. Then ye micht see that the ither sex that hiv a' the best o't wi' bazaars, the wye they're managed noo, wad flock to the man's bazaar and buy like onything. And maybe no'.'"

Erchie rose off the drain-pipe, and prepared to resume his way home with that ingenious object that proves how the lowliest things of life may be made dignified and beautiful — if fashion says they are so.

"Well, good night, old friend," I said. "I hope Mrs MacPherson will be lucky and get the bicycle."

"Dae ye, indeed?" said he. "Then ye're nae freen' o' mine. We're faur mair in the need o' a mangle."

"Then you can exchange for one."

"I'm no' that shair. Did I ever tell ye I ance won a powney in a raffle? It was at the bazaar oor kirk had in Dr Jardine's time when they got the organ. I was helpin' at the buffet, and I think they micht hae left me alane, me no' bein' there for fun, but at my tred, but wha cam' cravin' me to buy a ticket aff her but the doctor's guid-sister.

"'There's three prizes,' says she; 'a powney wi' broon harness, a marble nock, and a dizzen knifes and forks.'

"'I wad maybe risk it if it wisna for the powney,' I tellt her; 'I havena kep' a coachman for years, and I'm oot o' the way o' drivin' mysel'.'

"'Oh! ye needna be that feared, ye'll maybe no' get the powney,' said she, and I went awa' like a fool and took the ticket.

"The draw took place jist when the bazaar was shuttin' on the Setturday nicht. And I won the powney wi' the broon harness.

"I tore my ticket and threeped[7] it was a mistake, but I couldna get oot o't; they a' kent the powney was mine.

"It was stabled behind the bazaar, and had to be ta'en awa' that nicht. I offered it to onybody that wanted it for naething, but naebody wad tak' it aff my hands because they a' said they had to tak' the car hame, and they wadna be allooed to tak' a powney into a car wi' them. So they left me wi' a bonny-like prize.

"I put its claes on the best way I could, fanklin' a' the straps, and dragged it hame. We lived in the close at the time, and I thocht maybe Jinnet wad let me keep it in the lobby till the Monday mornin' till I could see whit I could dae. But she wadna hear tell o't. She said it wad scrape a' the waxcloth wi' its airn buits,[8] and wad be a bonny-like thing to be nicherrin' a' Sunday, scandalisin' the neebours, forbye there bein' nae gress in the hoose to feed it on. I said I wad rise early in the mornin' and gaither dentylions[9] for't oot at the Three-Tree Well, but she wadna let me nor the powney inside the door.

"It wasna an awfu' big broad powney, but a wee smout o' a thing they ca' a Shetland-shawl powney, and its harness didna fit it ony place at a'. It looked at the twa o' us, kind o' dazed like.

"'Ye're no' gaun to turn my hoose into a stable, and me jist cleaned it this very day,' said Jinnet.

"'And am I gaun to walk the streets a' nicht wi't?' I asked, near greetin'.

"'Put it oot in the ash-pit, and the scavengers 'll tak' it awa' in the mornin',' she said; and I did that, forgettin' that the mornin' was the Sunday.

"But it didna maitter; the powney wasna there in the mornin', and I took guid care no' to ask for't."

14. *Holidays*

"WELL, ERCHIE; not away on the Fair holidays?" I asked the old man one July day on meeting him as he came out of a little grocer's shop in the New City Road. The dignity of his profession is ever dear to Erchie; he kept his purchase behind his back, but I saw later it was kindling material for the morning fire.

"Not me!" said he. "There's nae Fair holidays for puir auld Erchie, no' even on the Sunday, or I might hae ta'en the skoosh car doon the wye o' Yoker, noo that a hurl on Sunday's no' that awfu' sair looked doon on, or the 'Mornin' Star' 'bus to Paisley. But Jinnet went awa' on Setturday wi' her guid-sister to Dunoon, and I'm my lee-lane in the hoose till the morn's mornin'. It's nae divert, I'm tellin' ye; there's a lot o' things to mind forbye the windin' o' the nock on Setturday and watering the fuchsia. I can wait a municeepal banquet wi' ony man in my tred, but I'm no' great hand at cookin' for mysel'.

"Did I ever tell ye aboot the time the wife was awa' afore at a Fair, and I took a notion o' a seed-cake Duffy's first wife had to the tea she trated me to on the Sawbath?

"'It's as easy to mak' as boilin' an egg,' says Mrs Duffy, and gied me the receipt for't on condeetion that when I made it I was to bring her a sample. Something went wrang, and I brought her the sample next day in a bottle. It was a gey damp seed-cake thon!

"I havena been awa' at a Fair mysel' since aboot the time Wullie was in the Foondry Boys,[1] and used to gang to the Hielan's. I mind o't fine. Nooadays, in oor hoose, ye wad never jalouse it was the Fair at a' if it wasna for the nae parridge in the mornin's.

"Ye'll hae noticed, maybe, that though we're a' fearfu' fond o' oor parridge[2] in Scotland, and some men mak' a brag o' takin' them every mornin' just as they were a cauld bath, we're gey gled to skip them at a holiday and just be daein' wi' ham and eggs.

"But in thae days, as I was sayin', the Fair was something like the thing. There was Mumford's and Glenroy's shows, and if ye hadna the money to get in, ye could aye pap eggs at the musicianers playing on the ootside, and the thing was as broad as it was lang. Forbye ye didna get the name o' bein' keen on the theatricals if your faither was parteecular.

"I mind ance I hit a skeely-e'ed trombone, or maybe it was an awfuclyde,[3] wi' an egg at Vinegar Hill.[4] The glee pairty[5] — as ye might ca' him if ye were funny — chased me as far doon as the Wee Doo Hill.[6] I could rin in thae days; noo I've ower flet feet, though I've a warm hert too, I'm tellin' ye.

"If ye werena at the Shows in thae days ye went a trip wi' the steamer *Bonnie Doon*,[7] and ye had an awfu' fine time o't on the Setturday if ye could jist mind aboot it on the Sunday mornin'. Duffy's gey coorse, bein' in the retail coal tred and cryin' for himsel'; I'm no' like that at a' mysel'; it widna dae, and me in the poseetion, but I mind aince o' Duffy tellin' me he could never fa' asleep at the Fair Time till his wife gave him the idea o' lyin' on his left side, and coontin' yin by yin a' the drams he had the night afore. He said it worked on him like chloryform.

"I hope ye'll no' mind me speakin' aboot drink; it's awfu' vulgar coonted noo, I hear, to let on ye ever heard that folk tak' it, but in thae days there was an awfu' lot o't partaken o' aboot Gleska. I'm tellt noo it's gaen clean oot o' fashion, and stane ginger's a' the go, and I see in the papers every Monday efter the Fair Setturday that 'there has been a gratifying decrease in the number o' cases at the Central Police Court compared wi' last year.' I'm that gled! I have been seein' that bit o' news in the papers for the last thirty years, and I hae nae doot that in a year or twa drunks and disorderlies 'll be sae scarce in Gleska at the Fair, the polis 'll hae to gang huntin' for them wi' bloodhounds.

"It's a fine thing the Press. It's aye keen to keep oor herts up. Ye'll notice, perhaps, that at every Gleska holiday the papers aye say the croods that left the stations were unprecedented. They were never kent to be ony ither wye.

"I daursay it's true enough. I went doon to the Broomielaw on Setturday to see Jinnet aff, and the croods on the Irish and Hielan' boats was that awfu', the men at the steerage end hadna room to pu' oot their pocket-hankies if they needed them. It's lucky they could dae withoot. When the butter-and-egg boats for Belfast and Derry left the quay, the pursers had a' to have on twa watches — at least they had the twa watch-chains, ane on each side, for fear the steamer wad capsize. I says to mysel', 'It's a peety a lot o' thae folk for Clachnacudden and County Doon dinna lose their return tickets and bide awa' when they're at it, for Gleska's a fine toon, but jist a wee bit ower crooded nooadays.'

"I hae nae great notion for doon the watter mysel' at the Fair. Jinnet jist goes and says she'll tell me whit it's like. Whit she likes it for is that ye're never lonely.

"And it's that homely doon aboot Rothesay and Dunoon, wi' the Gleska wifes hangin' ower the windows tryin' as hard as they can to see the scenery, between the whiles they're fryin' herrin' for Wull. And then there's wee Hughie awfu' ill wi' eatin' ower mony hairy grossets.[8]

"But it's fine for the weans, too, to be gaun sclimbin' aboot the braes pu'in' the daisies and the dockens and the dentylions and — and — and a' thae kin' o' flooers ye'll can touch withoot onybody findin' fau't wi' ye. It's better for the puir wee smouts nor moshy[9] in the back-coort, and puttin' bunnets doon the stanks. They'll mind it a' their days — the flooers and the dulse for naething, and the grossets and the Gregory's mixture. It's Nature; it's the Rale Oreeginal.

"It does the wife a lot o' guid to gae doon the watter at the Fair. She's that thrang when she's at hame she hasna had time yet to try a new shooglin'-chair we got at the flittin'; but 'it's a rest,' she'll say when she comes back a' moth-eaten wi' the midges. And then she'll say 'I'm that gled it's ower for the year.'

"That's the droll thing aboot the Fair and the New Year; ye're aye in the notion that somethin' awfu' nice is gaun to happen, and naethin' happens at a', unless it's that ye get your hand awfu' sair hashed pu'in' the cork oot o' a bottle o' beer."

"You'll be glad, I'm sure, to have the goodwife back, Erchie?" I said, with an eye on the fire-kindlers. He betrayed some confusion at being discovered, and then laughed.

"Ye see I've been for sticks," said he. "That's a sample o' my hoose-keepin'. I kent there was something partee-cular to get on the Setturday night, and thought it was pipeclye. The grocer in there wad be thinkin' I was awa' on the ping-pong if he didna ken I was a beadle. Will ye be puttin' ony o' this bit crack in the papers?"

"Well, I don't know, Erchie; I hope you won't mind if I do."

"Oh! I'm no heedin'; it's a' yin to Erchie, and does nae hairm to my repitation, though I think sometimes your spellin's a wee aff the plumb. Ye can say that I said keepin' a hoose is like ridin' the bicycle; ye think it's awfu' easy till ye try't."

"That's a very old discovery, Erchie; I fail to understand why you should be anxious to have it published now."

Erchie winked. "I ken fine whit I'm aboot," said he. "It'll please the leddies to ken that Erchie said it, and I like fine to be popular. My private opeenion is that a man could keep a hoose as weel as a woman ony day if he could only bring his mind doon to't."

15. *The Student Lodger*

IT WAS with genuine astonishment Erchie one day had his wife come to him with a proposal that she should keep a lodger.

"A ludger!" he cried. "It wad be mair like the thing if ye keepit a servant lassie, for whiles I think ye're fair wrocht aff yer feet."

"Oh, I'm no' sae faur done as a' that," said Jinnet. "I'm shair I'm jist as smert on my feet as ever I was, and I could be daein' wi' a ludger fine. It wad keep me frae wearyin'."

"Wearyin'!" said her husband. "It's comin' to't when my ain wife tells me I'm no' company for her. Whit is't ye're wantin', and I'll see whit I can dae. If it's music ye're for, I'll buy a melodian and play't every nicht efter my tea. If it's improvin' conversation ye feel the want o', I'll ask Duffy up every ither nicht and we'll can argue on Fore Ordination[1] and the chance o' the Celtic Fitba' Club to win the League Championship the time ye're darnin' stockin's. 'Wearyin',' says she! Perhaps ye wad like to jine a dancin' school; weel, I'll no' hinder ye, I'm shair, but I'll no' promise to walk to the hall wi' ye every nicht cairryin' yer slippers. Start a ludger! I'm shair we're no' that hard up!"

"No, we're no' that hard up," Jinnet confessed, "but for a' the use we mak' o' the room we micht hae somebody in it, and it wad jist be found money. I was jist thinkin' it wad be kind o' cheery to have a dacent young chap gaun oot and in. I'm no' for ony weemen ludgers; they're jist a fair bother, aye hingin' aboot the hoose and puttin' their nose into the kitchen, tellin' ye the richt wye to dae this and that, and burnin' coal and gas the time a man ludger wad be oot takin' the air."

"Takin' drink, mair likely," said Erchie, "and comin' hame singin' 'Sodgers o' the Queen,' and scandalisin' the hale stair."[2]

"And I'm no' for a tredsman," Jinnet went on, with the air of one whose plans were all made.

"Of course no'," said her husband, "tredsmen's low. They're no' cless. It's a peety ye mairried yin. Perhaps ye're thinkin' o' takin' in a chartered accoontant, or maybe a polisman. Weel I'm jist tellin' ye I wadna hae a polisman in my paurlor; his helmet wadna gang richt wi' the furniture, and the blecknin' for his boots wad cost ye mair than whit he pyed for his room."

"No, nor a polisman!" said Jinnet. "I was thinkin' o' maybe a quate lad in a warehouse, or a nice factor's clerk, or something o' that sort. He wad be nae bother. It's just the ae makin' o' parridge in the mornin'. Ye're no' to thraw wi' me aboot this, Erchie; my mind's made up I'm gaun to keep a ludger."

"If your mind's made up," he replied, "then there's nae use o' me argy-bargyin' wi' ye. I'm only your man. It bates me to ken whit ye're gaun to dae wi' the money if it's no' to buy a motor cairrage. Gie me your word ye're no' gaun in for ony sports o' that kind. I wad hate to see ony wife o' mine gaun skooshin' oot the Great Western Road on a machine like a tar-biler, wi' goggles on her e'en and a kahootchy trumpet skriechin' 'pip! pip!'"

"Ye're jist an auld haver," said Jinnet, and turned to her sewing, her point gained.

A fortnight after, as a result of a ticket with the legend 'Apartments' in the parlour window, Jinnet was able to meet her husband's return to tea one night with the annoucement that she had got a lodger. "A rale gentleman!" she explained. "That weel put-on! Wi' twa Gledstone bags, yin o' them carpet, and an alerm clock for waukenin' him in the mornin'. He cam' this efternoon in a cab, and I think he'll be easy put up wi' and tak' jist whit we tak' oorsel's."

"I hope he's no' a theatrical," said Erchie. "Me bein' a beadle in a kirk it wadna be becomin' to hae a theatrical for a ludger. Forbye, they never rise oot o' their beds on the Sunday, but lie there drinkin' porter and readin' whit the papers say aboot their play-actin'."

"No, nor a theatrical!" cried Jinnet. "I wadna mak' a show o' my hoose for ony o' them! It's a rale nice wee fair-heided student."

Erchie threw up his hands in amazement. "Michty me!" said he, "a student. Ye micht as weel hae taen in a brass baun' or the Cairter's Trip[3] when ye were at it. Dae ye ken whit students is, Jinnet? I ken them fine, though I was never at the college mysel', but yince I was engaged to hand roond beer at whit they ca'd a Gaudiamus.[4] Ye have only to tak' the mildest wee laddie that has bad e'e-sicht and subject to sair heids frae the country and mak' a student o' him to rouse the warst passions o' his nature. His mither, far awa' in Clachnacudden, thinks he's hurtin' his health wi' ower muckle study, but the only hairm he's daein' himsel' is to crack his voice cryin' oot impidence to his professors. I'm vexed it's a student, and a fair-heided yin at that: I've noticed that the fair-heided yins were aye the warst."

"Weel, he's there onywye, and we'll jist hae to mak' the best we can wi' him," said Jinnet. "Forbye, I think he's a guid-leevin' lad, Erchie; he tellt me he was comin' oot for a minister."[5]

"Comin' oot for a minister!" said Erchie. "Then that's the last straw! I'm sorry for your chevalier and book-case; he'll be sclimbin' int't some nicht thinkin' it's the concealed bed."

The room door opened, a voice bawled in the lobby, "Mrs MacPherson, hey! Mrs MacPherson," and the student, without waiting his landlady's appearance, walked coolly into the kitchen.

"Hulloo! old chap, how's biz?" he said to Erchie, and seated himself airily on the table, with a pipe in his mouth. He was a lad of twenty, with spectacles.

"I canna complain," said Erchie. "I hope ye're makin' yersel' at hame."

"Allow me for that!" said the student.

"That's nice," said Erchie, blandly. "See and no' be ower blate, and if there's onything ye're wantin' that we havena got, we'll get it for ye. Ye'll no' know whit ye need till ye see whit ye require. It's a prood day for us to hae a diveenity student in oor room. If we had expected it we wad hae had a harmonium."

"Never mind the harmonium," said the student. "For music lean on me, George P. Tod. I sing from morn till dewy eve. When I get up in the morning, jocund day stands on the misty mountain top and I give weight away to the bloomin' lark. Shakespeare, Mr MacPherson. The Swan of Avon. He wrote a fairly good play. What I wanted to know was if by any chance Mrs MacPherson was a weepist?"

"Sir?" said Jinnet.

"Do you, by any chance, let the tear doon fa'?"[6]

"Not me !" said Jinnet, "I'm a cheery wee woman."

"Good!" said Tod. "Then you're lucky to secure a sympathetic and desirable lodger. To be gay is my forte. The last landlady I had was thrice a widow. She shed the tears of unavailing regret into my lacteal nourishment with the aid of a filler, I think, and the milk got thinner and thinner. I was compelled at last to fold my tent like the justly celebrated Arabs of song and silently steal away. 'Why weep ye by the tide, ladye?' I said to her. 'If it were by the pint I should not care so much, but methinks your lachrymal ducts are too much on the hair-trigger.' It was no use, she could not help it, and — in short, here I am."

"I'm shair we'll dae whit we can for ye," said Jinnet. "I never had a ludger before."

"So much the better," said George Tod. "I'm delighted to be the object of experiment — the *corpus vile*, as we say in the classics, Mr MacPherson — and you will learn a good deal with me. I will now proceed to burn the essential midnight oil. Ah, thought, thought! You little know, Mr MacPherson, the weary hours of study —"

"It's no' ile we hae in the room, it's gas," said Erchie. "But if ye wad raither hae ile, say the word and we'll get it for ye."

"Gas will do," said the student; "it is equally conducive to study, and more popular in all great congeries of thought."

"When dae ye rise in the mornin', Mr Tod?" asked Jinnet.
"I wad like to ken when I should hae your breakfast ready."

"Rise !" said Tod. "Oh, any time! 'When the morn, with
russet mantle clad, walks o'er the dew on yon high eastern
hill.'"

"Is't Garnethill or Gilshochill?" said Erchie, anxiously.
"I wad rise mysel', early in the mornin', and gang oot to
whichever o' them it is to see the first meenute the dew
comes, so that ye wadna lose ony time in gettin' up and
started wi' your wark."

The lodger for the first time looked at his landlord with
a suspicious eye. He had a faint fear that the old man might
be chaffing him, but the innocence of Erchie's face
restored his perkiness.

"I was only quoting the bard," he explained, as he left
the kitchen. "Strictly speaking, the morn with russet
mantle clad can go to the deuce for me, for I have an alarm
clock. Do not be startled if you hear it in the morning. It
goes off with incredible animation."

"Oh, Erchie, isn't he nice?" said Jinnet, when the lodger
had withdrawn. "That smert, and aye talks that jovial, wi'
a lot o' words I canna mak' heid nor tail o'."

Erchie filled his pipe and thought a little, "Smert's the
word, Jinnet," said he. "That's whit students is for."

"I don't think he's very strong," said Jinnet. "If he was
in his mither's hoose she wad be giein' him hough soup for
his dinner. I think I'll jist mak' some for him to-morrow,
and put a hot-water bottle in his bed."

"That's richt," said Erchie; "and if ye hae a haddie or a
kippered herrin', or onything else handy, it'll dae for me."

"Ye're jist a haver!" said Jinnet.

For a week George P. Tod was a model lodger.

He came in at early hours of the evening and went to
bed timeously, and was no great trouble to his landlady,
whose cookery exploits in his interest were a great improvement on anything he had ever experienced in lodgings
before.

When he was in his room in the evenings Jinnet insisted on the utmost quietness on the part of her husband. "Mr Tod's at his hame lessons," she would say. "It'll no' dae to disturb him. Oh, that heid wark! that heid wark! It must be an awfu' thing to hae to be thinkin' even-on."

"Heid wark!" said her husband. "I ken the heid wark he's like enough at; he's learnin' the words o' 'Mush, Mush, tu-ral-i-ady' to sing at the students' procession, or he's busy wi' a dictionary writin' hame to his paw to send him a post-office order for twa pounds to jine the YMCA. But he's no' thinkin' o' jinin' the YMCA; he's mair likely to start takin' lessons at a boxin' cless."

But even Erchie was compelled to admit that the lad was no unsatisfactory lodger.

"I declare, Jinnet," he said, "I think he's yin o' the kind o' students ye read aboot but very seldom see. His faither 'll be a wee fairmer up aboot Clachnacudden, hainin' a' the money he can, and no' giein' his wife her richt meat, that he may see his son through the college and waggin' his heid in a pu'pit. Him and his faither's the stuff they mak' the six shillin' Scotch novells oot o' — the kind ye greet at frae the very start — for ye ken the puir lad, that was aye that smert in the school, and won a' the bursaries, is gaun to dee in the last chapter wi' a decline."

"Puir things," said Jinnet.

"Ye divna see ony signs o' decline aboot Mr Tod, do ye?" asked Erchie, anxiously.

"I didna notice," replied Jinnet, "but he tak's his meat weel enough."

"The meat's the main thing! But watch you if he hasna a hoast and thon hectic flush that aye breaks oot in chapter nine jist aboot the time he wins the gold medal."

"Och, ye're jist an auld haver, Erchie," said the wife. "Ye're no' to be frichtenin' me aboot the puir callant, jist the same age as oor ain Willie."

The time of the Rectorial Election approached, and Tod began to display some erratic habits. It was sometimes the small hours of the morning before he came home, and though he had a latch-key, Jinnet could never go to bed until her lodger was in for the night. Sometimes she went out to the close-mouth to look if he might be coming, and the first night that Erchie, coming home late from working at a civic banquet, found her there, Tod narrowly escaped being told to take his two bags and his alarm clock elsewhere.

"I was needin' a moothfu' o' fresh air onywye," was Jinnet's excuse for being out at such an hour. "But I'm feared that puir lad's workin' himsel' to death."

"Whaur dae ye think he's toilin'?" asked her husband.

"At the nicht-school," said Jinnet. "I'm shair the college through the day's plenty for him."

"The nicht-school!" cried Erchie. "Bonny on the nicht-school! He's mair likely to be roond in Gibson Street[7] batterin' in the doors o' the Conservative committee-rooms, for I ken by his specs and his plush weskit he's a Leeberal. Come awa' in to your bed and never mind him. Ye wad be daein' him a better turn maybe if ye chairged the gazogene[8] to be ready for the mornin', when he'll be badly wantin't, if I'm no' faur mistaken."

Erchie was right — the gazogene would have been welcome next morning. As it was, the lodger was indifferent to breakfast, and expressed an ardent desire for Health Salts.

Erchie took them in to him, and found him groaning with a headache.

"The dew's awfu' late on the high eastern hills this mornin', Mr Tod," said Erchie. "Losh, ye're as gash as the Laird o' Garscadden![9] I'm feart ye're studyin' far ower hard; it's no' for the young and growin' to be hurtin' their heids wi' nicht-schools and day-schools; ye should whiles tak' a bit rest to yersel'. And no' a bit o' yer breakfast touched! Mrs MacPherson 'll no' be the pleased woman wi' ye this day, I can tell ye!"

Tod looked up with a lack-lustre eye. "Thought, Mr MacPherson, thought!" said he. "Hard, incessant, brain-corroding thought! In the words of the Bard of Avon, 'He who increaseth knowledge increaseth sorrow.'"

"I aye thocht that was Ecclesiastes, Mr Tod," said

Erchie, meekly.

"In a way, yes," hastily admitted Tod. "It *was* Ecclesiastes, as you say; but Shakespeare had pretty much the same idea. You will find it in — in — in his plays."

That afternoon began the more serious of Jinnet's experiences of divinity students. Nine young gentlemen with thick walking-sticks visited Tod's apartment *en masse;* the strains of 'Mush Mush, tu-ral-i-ady', bellowed inharmoniously by ten voices, and accompanied by the beating of the walking-sticks on the floor, kept a crowd of children round the close-mouth for hours, and somewhat impeded the ordinary traffic of the street.

"There must be a spree on in auld MacPherson's," said the tenement. When Erchie came home he found Jinnet distracted. "Oh, whit a day I've had wi' them students!" she wailed.

"But look at the money ye're makin' aff your room," said her husband. "Wi' whit ye get frae Tod, ye'll soon hae enough for the motor cairrage and a yacht forbye."

"I'm feart to tell ye, Erchie," said Jinnet, "but I havena seen the colour o' his money yet."

"Study! study!" said Erchie. "Ye canna expect the puir lad to be thinkin' even-on aboot his lessons, and learnin' Latin and the rest o't, no' to mention 'Mush Mush', and still keep mind o' your twa or three paltry bawbees."

"I mentioned it to him on Setturday and he was rale annoyed. He yoked on me[10] and said I was jist as bad as the weedow he lodged wi' afore; that he was shair I was gaun to let the tear doon-fa'. He gied me warnin' that if I let the tear doon-fa' he wad leave."

"If I was you I wad start greetin' at yince," said Erchie. "And he'll leave onywye, this very Setturday."

That afternoon the students were having a torchlight procession, when, as usual, most of them marched in masquerade. It was the day of the Rectorial Election, and the dust of far-flung pease-meal — favourite missile of the student — filled the air all over the classic slopes of Gilmorehill. It had been one of Erchie's idle days; he had

been in the house all afternoon, and still was unbedded,
though Jinnet for once had retired without waiting the
home-coming of her lodger.

There came a riotous singing of students along the
street, accompanied by the wheezy strains of a barrel-
organ, and for twenty minutes uproar reigned at the
entrance to the MacPherson's close.

Then Tod came up and opened the door with his latch-
key. He had on part of Erchie's professional habiliments —
the waiter's dress-coat and also Erchie's Sunday silk hat,
both surreptitiously taken from a press in the lobby. They
were foul with pease-meal and the melted rosin from torches.
On his shoulders Tod had strapped a barrel-organ, and the
noise of it, as it thumped against the door-posts on his
entry, brought Erchie out to see what was the matter.

He took in the situation at a glance, though at first he
did not recognise his own clothes.

"It's you, Mr Tod!" said he. "I was jist sittin' here
thinkin' on ye slavin' awa' at your lessons yonder in the
Deveenity Hall. It maun be an awfu' strain on the
intelleck. I'm gled I never went to the college mysel', but
jist got my education, as it were, by word o' mooth."

Tod breathed heavily. He looked very foolish with his
borrowed and begrimed clothes, and the organ on his
back, and he realised the fact himself.

"'S all ri', Mr MacPherson," he said. "Music hath
charms. Not a word! I found this — this instuimet outside,
and just took it home. Thought it might be useful. Music
in the house makes cheerful happy homes — see advertisements — so I borrowed this from old friend, what's
name — Angina Pectoris, Italian virtuoso, leaving him the
monkey. Listen."

He unslung the organ and was starting to play it in the
lobby when Erchie caught him by the arm and restrained
him.

"Canny, man, canny," said he. "Did I no' think it was a
box wi' your bursary. I never kent richt whit a bursary was,
but the lad o' pairts in the novells aye comes hame wi' a

bursary, and hurts the spine o' his back carryin' his prizes frae the college. I jalouse that's the hectic flush on your face; puir laddie, ye're no' lang for this warld."

Erchie stared more closely at his lodger, and for the first time recognised his own swallow-tail coat.

"My goodness!" said he, "my business coat, and my beadlin' hat. It was rale ill done o' ye, Mr Tod, to tak' them oot withoot my leave. It's the first time ever I was ashamed o' them. Jist a puir auld waiter's coat and hat. I wonder whit they wad say if they kent o't up in Clachna-cudden. The auld dominie that was sae prood o' ye wad be black affronted. My business coat! Tak' it aff and gang to your bed like a wise man. Leave the hurdy-gurdy on the stair-heid; ye divna ken whit the other monkey micht hae left aboot it, and Jinnet's awfu' parteecular."

Next day Mr Tod got a week's notice to remove, and went reluctantly, for he knew good lodgings when he got them. He paid his bill when he went, too, "like a gentleman," as Jinnet put it. "He was a rale cheery wee chap," she said.

"I've seen faur worse," Erchie admitted. "Foolish a wee, but Nature, the Rale Oreeginal! I was gey throughither[11] mysel' when I was his age. Ye never tellt me yet whit ye wanted wi' the ludging money."

"I was jist thinkin' I wad like to see ye wi' a gold watch the same as Carmichael's, next door," said Jinnet. "It's a thing a man at your time o' life, and in your poseetion, should hae, and I was ettlin' to gie ye't for your New Year."

"A gold watch!" cried her husband. "Whit nonsense!"

"It's no' nonsense at a'," said Jinnet. "It gies a man a kind o' bien, weel-daein' look, and I thocht I could mak' enough aff ludgers to buy ye yin."

"If it was for that ye wanted the ludger, and no' for a motor cairrage," said Erchie, "I'm gled Tod's awa'. You and your watch! I wad be a bonny like la-di-da wi' a watch at the waitin'; the folks wad be feared to tip me in case I wad be angry wi' them."

And so Erchie has not yet got a gold watch.

16. *Jinnet's Tea-Party*

ERCHIE'S GOODWIFE came to him one day full of thrilling news from the dairy, where she had been for twopence worth of sticks.

"Oh, Erchie, dae ye ken the latest?" said she. "The big fat yin in the dairy's gaun to mairry Duffy!"

"Lord peety Duffy! Somebody should tell the puir sowl she has her e'en on him. I'll bate ye he disna ken onything aboot it," said Erchie.

"Havers!" said Jinnet. "It's him that's wantin' her, and I'm shair it's a guid thing, for his hoose is a' gaun to wreck and ruin since his last wife dee'd. Every time he comes hame to dry his claes on a wet day he's doon in the dairy for anither bawbee's worth o' mulk. The man's fair hoved up[1] wi' drinkin' mulk he's no needin'. I hae catched him there that aften that he's kind o' affronted to see me. 'I'm here again, Mrs MacPherson,' says he to me yesterday when I went doon and found him leanin' ower the coonter wi' a tumbler in his haund. He was that ta'en he nearly dropped the gless."

"It wasna for the want o' practice — I'll wager ye that!" said Erchie. "He could haud a schooner a hale nicht and him hauf sleepin'."

"'I'm here again,' says he, onywye; 'the doctor tellt me yon time I had the illness I was to keep up my strength. There's a lot o' nourishment in mulk.' And the big yin's face was as red as her short-goon.

"'It's a blessin' the health, Mr Duffy,' says I; 'we divna ken whit a mercy it is till we lose it,' and I never said anither word, but took my bit sticks and cam' awa'."

"And is that a' ye hae to gang on to be blamin' the chap?" said Erchie. "Mony's a man 'll tak' a gless o' mulk and no' go ower faur wi't. But I think mysel' ye're maybe richt aboot the big yin, for I see Duffy's shaved aff his Paisley whiskers, and wears a tie on the Sundays."

Less than a week later the girl in the dairy gave in her

notice, and Duffy put up the price of coals another ha'penny. He came up the stair with two bags for Jinnet, who was one of his customers.

"Whit wye are they up a bawbee the day?" says she.

"It's because o' the Americans dumpin'," said Duffy. "They're takin' a' the tred frae us, and there's a kind o' tariff war.[2]"

"Bless me! is there anither war?" said Jinnet. "Weel, they're gettin' a fine day for't onywye. I hope it'll no put up the price o' the mulk."

Duffy looked at her and laughed uneasily. "I'm kind o' aff the mulk diet the noo," he said, seeing disguise was useless. "Ye're gey gleg,[3] you weemen. I needna be tellin' ye me and big Leezie's sort o' chief this while back."

"Man! dae ye tell me?" said Jinnet, innocently. "A rale dacent lassie, and bakes a bonny scone. And she's to be the new mistress, is she? We'll hae to be savin' up for the jeely-pan. I'm shair I aye tellt Erchie a wife was sair wanted in your hoose since Maggie dee'd."

"Jist at the very time I was thrangest," said Duffy, with regret. "I was awfu' chawed at her."

"Ye'll hae to bring yer lass up to see me and Erchie some nicht," said Jinnet. "It's a tryin' time the mairryin'."

"There faur ower mony palavers aboot it," confided the coalman. "I wish it was ower and done wi', and I could get wearin' my grauvit at nicht again. Leezie's awfu' pernick-etty aboot me haein' on a collar when we gang for a walk."

"Oh, ye rascal!" said Jinnet, roguishly. "You men! you men! Ah, the coortin' time's the best time."

"Ach! it's richt enough, I daursay; but there's a lot o' nonsense aboot it. Ye get awfu' cauld feet standin' in the close. And it's aye in yer mind. I went to Leezie's close-mooth the ither nicht to whistle on her, and did I no' forget, and cry oot 'Coal!' thinkin' I was on business."

And thus it was that Jinnet's tea-party came about. The tender pair of pigeons were the guests of honour, and Jinnet's niece, and Macrae the night policeman, were likewise invited. Macrae was there because Jinnet thought

her niece at thirty-five was old enough to marry. Jinnet did
not know that he had drunk milk in Leezie's dairy before
Duffy had gone there, and he himself had come quite
unsuspicious of whom he should meet. In all innocence
Jinnet had brought together the elements of tragedy.

There was something cold in the atmosphere of the
party. Erchie noticed it. "Ye wad think it was a Quaker's
meetin'," he said to himself, as all his wife's efforts to
encourage an airy conversation dismally failed.

"See and mak' yer tea o't, Mr Macrae," she said to the
night policeman. "And you, Sarah, I wish ye would tak' yin
o' thae penny things, and pass the plate to Mr Duffy. Ye'll
excuse there bein' nae scones, Mr Duffy; there hasna been
a nice scone baked in the dairy since Leezie left. There's
wan thing ye'll can be shair o' haein' when ye're mairret till
her, and that's guid bakin'."

Macrae snorted. "What's the maitter wi' dough-feet, I
wonder?" thought Erchie, as innocent as his wife was of
any complication. "That's the worst o' askin' the polis to
yer pairties — they're no' cless; and I'm shair, wi' a'
Jinnet's contrivance, Sarah wadna be made up wi' him."

"A wee tate mair tea, Mr Macrae? Leezie, gie me Mr
Macrae's cup if it's oot."

Macrae snorted again. "I'll not pe puttin' her to the
bother, Mrs MacPherson," said he, "Murdo Macrae can
pe passin' his own teacups wisout botherin' anybody."

"Dough-feet's in the dods,"[4] thought Erchie, to whom
the whole situation was now, for the first time, revealed
like a flash.

"I think, Jinnet," said he, "ye wad hae been nane the
waur o' a pun' or twa o' conversation-losengers."

They ate oranges after tea, but still a depression hung
upon the company like a cloud, till Erchie asked Macrae if
he would sing.

"Onything ye like," said he, "as lang's it's no' yin o' yer
tartan chants that has a hunder verses, and that needs ye to
tramp time wi' yer feet till't. I've a flet fit mysel', though
my hert's warm, and I'm nae use at batin' time."

Macrae looked at Leezie, who had all night studiously evaded his eye, cleared his throat, and started to sing a song with the chorus:

'Fause Maggie Jurdan
She made my life a burden;
I don't want to live,
And I'm gcy sweart to dee.
She's left me a' forlorn,
And I wish I'd ne'er been born,
Since fause Maggie Jurdan
Went and jilted me.'

Leezie only heard one verse, and then began hysterically to cry.

"Look you here, Mac," broke in Erchie, "could ye no' mak' it the sword dance, or the Hoolichan, or something that wadna harrow oor feelin's this way?"

"Onything that'll gie us a rest," said Duffy, soothing his fiancée. "The nicht air's evidently no' very guid for the voice."

"Coals!" cried the policeman, in a very good imitation of Duffy's business wail; and at that Leezie had to be assisted into the kitchen by the other two women.

Duffy glared at his jealous and defeated rival, thought hard of something withering to hurl at him, and then said, "Saps!"

"What iss that you are saying?" asked Macrae.

"Saps! Big Saps! That's jist what ye are," said Duffy. "If I wasna engaged I wad gie ye yin in the ear."

Jinnet's tea-party broke up as quickly as possible after that. When her guests had gone, and she found herself alone in the kitchen with Erchie and the tea dishes he carried in for her, she fell into a chair and wept.

"I'll never hae anither tea-pairty, and that's tellin' ye," she exclaimed between her sobs. "Fancy a' that cairry-on ower a big, fat, cat-witted cratur like thon! Her and her lads!"

"It's a' richt, Jinnet," said Erchie; "you syne oot[5] the dishes and I'll dry them if ye'll feenish yer greetin'. It's no'

the last tea-pairty we'll hae if we hae oor health, but the
next yin ye hae see and pick the company better."

17. *The Natives of Clachnacudden*

"YOU ARE looking somewhat tired, Erchie," I said to the
old man on Saturday. "I suppose you were waiter at some
dinner last night?"

"Not me!" said he promptly. "I wasna at my tred at a'
last nicht; I was wi' Jinnet at the Clachnacudden conversashion. My! but we're gettin' grand. You should hae seen
the twa o' us sittin' as hard as onything in a corner o' the
hall watchin' the young yins dancin', and wishin' we were
hame. Och, it's a fine thing a conversashion; there's naething wrang wi't; it's better nor standin' aboot the street
corners, or haudin' up the coonter at the Mull o' Kintyre
Vaults. But I'll tell ye whit, it's no' much o' a game for an
auld couple weel ower sixty, though no' compleenin', and
haein' their health, and able to read the smallest type
withoot specs. I wadna hae been there at a', but Macrae,
the nicht polisman that's efter Jinnet's niece, cam' cravin'
me to buy tickets.

"'I'm no' a Clachnacudden native,' says I till him. 'If it
was a reunion o' the natives o' Gorbals and district, it
micht be a' richt, for that's the place I belang to; and if a'
the auld natives cam' to a Gorbals swaree I micht get some
o' the money some o' them's owin' me. But Clachnacudden! — I never saw the place; I aye thocht it was jist yin
o' thae comic names they put on the labels o' the whisky
bottles to mak' them look fancy.'

"Ye'll no' believe't, but Macrae, bein' Hielan' and no
haein' richt English, was that angry for me sayin' that
aboot Clachnacudden, that he was nearly breakin' the
engagement wi' Jinnet's niece, and I had to tak' the tickets
at the hinder-end jist for peace' sake. Jinnet said it was a
bonny-like thing spilin' Sarah's chances for the sake o' a
shillin' or twa.

"So that's the wye I was wi' the Clachnacudden chats. Dae ye no' feel the smell o' peat-reek aff me? If it wasna that my feet were flet I could gie ye the Hielan' Fling.

"But thae natives' reunions in Gleska's no' whit they used to be. They're gettin' far ower genteel. It'll soon be comin' to't that ye'll no can gang to ony o' them unless ye have a gold watch and chain, a dress suit, and £10 in the Savin's Bank. It used to be in the auld days when I went to natives' gatherin's for fun, and no' to please the nicht polis, that they were ca'd a swaree and ball, and the ticket was four-and-six for yoursel' and your pairtner. If ye didna get the worth o' your money there was something wrang wi' your stomach, or ye werena very smert. Mony a yin I've bin at, either in the wye o' tred, or because some o' Jinnet's Hielan' kizzens cam' up to the hoose in their kilts to sell us tickets. There was nae dress suits nor fal-lals aboot a reunion in thae days. Ye jist put on your Sunday claes and some scent on your hanky, wi' a dram in your pocket (if ye werena in the committee), turned up the feet o' your breeks, and walked doon to the hall in the extra-wide welt shoes ye were gaun to dance in. Your lass — or your wife, if it was your wife — sat up the nicht before, washin' her white shawl and sewin' frillin' on the neck o' her guid frock, and a' the expense ye had wi' her if ye werena merried to her was that ye had to buy her a pair o' white shammy leather gloves, size seeven.

"A' the auld folk frae Clachnacudden in Gleska were at thae swarees, as weel as a' the young folk. Ye were packed in your sates like red herrin' in a barrel, and on every hand ye heard folk tearin' the tartan[1] and misca'in' somebody at hame in Clachnacudden. The natives wi' the dress suits that had got on awfu' weel in Gleska at the speerit tred or keeping banks, sat as dour as onything on the pletform lettin' on they couldna speak the tartan. Ithers o' them — that had the richt kind o' legs for't — wad hae on the kilts, wi' a white goat-skin sporran the size o' a door-bass[2] hung doon to their knees fornent them, haudin' in their breaths in case the minister wad smell drink aff them, and tryin' to feel like Rob Roy or Roderick Dhu.

"In thae days they started oot wi' giein' ye tea and a poke o' fancy breid — penny things like London buns and fruit-cakes; and between the speeches oranges were passed roond, and wee roond hard sweeties, fine for pappin' at the folk in front. Ye aye made a guid tea o't, the same as if ye never saw tea in your life afore, and preferred it weel biled.

"When the tea was bye and the boys were blawin' as much breath as they had left into the empty pokes, and bangin' them aff like cannons, the chairman wad stand up on the pletform and make a speech aboot Clachnacudden. I used to ken that speech by hert; it was the same yin for a' the natives' reunions. He said that Clachnacudden was the bonniest place ever onybody clapped eyes on. That the Clachnacudden men were notorious a' ower the world for their honesty and push, and aye got on like onything if they were tryin', and didna tak' to the drink; and that the Clachnacudden lassies were that braw, and nice, and smert, they were lookit up to every place they went. When he said that the natives o' Clachnacudden kent fine it was the God's truth he was tellin' them, they got on their feet and waved their hankies and cheered for ten meenutes.

"Havin' taken a drink o' watter frae the caraffe at his side — efter makin' a mistake and tryin' to blaw the froth aff the tumbler — the chairman then begood generally to say that Gleska was a gey cauld, sooty, dirty, wicked place for onybody to hae to live in that had been born in the bonny wee glens, and the hulls, and hedges, and things aboot Clachnacudden, but still

'Their herts were true, their herts were Hielan', And they in dreams beheld the Hebrides.'[3]

At that ye wad see the hale o' the Clachnacudden folk puttin' whit was left o' their pastry in their pouches and haudin' their hankies wi' baith hands to their e'en to kep the tears frae rinnin' on their guid waistcoats or their silk weddin' goons. And the droll thing was that for a' they misca'd Gleska, and grat aboot Clachnacudden, ye couldna get yin o' them to gang back to Clachnacudden if ye pyed the train ticket and guaranteed a pension o' a pound a week.

"Clachnacudden bein' Hielan', they aye started the music efter the chairman's speech wi' a sang frae Harry Linn[4] ca'd 'Jock Macraw, the Fattest Man in the Forty-Twa,' or some ither sang that kind o' codded themsel's. Then the minister made a comic speech wi' jokes in't, and tried to look as game as onything; and the folk frae Clachnacudden leaned forrit on their sates and asked the wifes in front if they had mind wen his mither used to work in the tawtie field. 'Fancy him a minister!' says they, 'and tryin' to be comic, wi' his mither jist yin o' the MacTaggarts!' A' the time the puir minister was thinkin' he was daein' fine and wonderin' if *The Oban Times* was takin' doon a' his speech.

"And then a lot o' nyafs in the back sates aye began to heave orange-peelin's at folk that was daein' them nae hairm.

"Efter the swaree was ower, the weemen went into the ladies' room to tak' aff their galoshes, and tak' the preens oot o' their trains, and the men went ower to the Duke o' Wellington Bar, rinnin' like onything, for it was nearly eeleven o'clock. The folk the hall belanged to started to tak' oot the sates for the dancin', and sweep the corks aff the floor; and at eleven prompt the Grand Merch started. Whiles they had Adams' or Iff's band, and whiles they jist had Fitzgerald, the fiddler that used to play on the Lochgoilhead boat. It didna maitter, for a' the Clachnacudden folk were fine strong dancers, and could dance to onything. Man! I aye liked the Grand Merch. The man wi' the reddest kilts aye started it at the Clachnacudden, and when the Grand Merch got a' fankled, they jist started 'Triumph'; and did the best they could.

"That was in the grand auld days afore they got genteel. Nooadays, as I'm tellin' ye, it's a' conversashions, and they work aff their speeches on ye wi' no tea at a' and no pokes o' pastry, nor naething. Ye're no use unless ye hae the lend o' a dress suit, and your pairtner has to hae pipe-clyed shoon, a muslin frock no' richt hooked at the neck, her hair put up at Bamber's,[5] and a cab to tak' her hame in. It's naething but the waltzin'. I'm prood to say I never waltzed in a' my born days, though they say I have the richt kind o' feet for't, me bein' so lang at the waitin'. And a' they auld classic dances, like La-va and the Guaracha Waltz and Circassian Circle's oot o' date; I havena even seen Petronella for mony a day.

"And the music's a' spiled; it's a' fancy music they hae noo, wi' nae tune ye can sing to't as ye gang up the back or doon the middle. Ye'll see them yonder wi' their piano, three fiddles, and a cornet. If I was gaun to hae a cornet I wad hae a cornet and no' a brass feenisher.

"Ye'll no' see ony o' the dacent auld Clachnacudden folk at their modern reunions; the puir sowls has to bide at hame and gang to ther beds early that they may get up in time to mak' a cup o' tea for their dochters that was at the conversashion. No; Jinnet and me's no' keen on Clachnacudden or onything o' the kind nooadays; we wad faur sooner stay at hame and read The Weekly Mail."

18. Mary Ann

"I SEE frae The News," said Erchie, "that Mary Ann's no' gaun to see her kizzen on her nicht oot the noo, but has the kitchen table cleared for action wi' a penny bottle o' Perth ink and a quire o' paper to write letters to the editor, telling him and his readers that the country doesna ken her value.

"If ye're in the habit o' tryin' to keep a general,[1] ye canna be shair but at this very meenute she's doon the stair, wi' her sleeves rowed up and her fingers a' Perth Blue Black, paintin' your wife's photograph as a slave-driver, and givin' your hoose a character that would mak' ye lose your nicht's sleep if ye kent it. Faith, it's comin' to it!

"The servant problem is the only ane that's railly o' ony interest to the country, as far as I can mak' oot frae hearin' things when I'm either beadlin', or waitin' at waddin'-

breakfasts. Twa women canna put their heads thegither ower a cup o' tea withoot gaun ower a list o' a' the lassies they've had since last November; and the notion ye get is that they change frae place to place that often they must hae motor cairrages.

"Mary Ann sails in with her kist and a fine character[2] frae her last place on Monday at 8 p.m., and aboot ten minutes efter that she's on the road again. She is the greatest traveller o' the age; it is estimated by them that kens aboot thae things, that the average domestic, if she keeps her health and gets ony chance at a' gangs 15,000 miles every three years shifting her situation.

"It is the age of the lairge-built, agile, country girl; no ither kind can stand the strain o' humpin' kists up and doon area stairs. An aluminium kist that when packed weighs only fifteen pounds has been invented specially for the 'strong and willing general, early riser, no washin', fond o' weans'; but in spite o' that, she canna get ower mair nor 250 to 263 different situations in the year.

"The Hielan's is the peculiar home o' the maist successful domestic servants, though a very gude strain o' them is said to come frae Ayrshire and roon' aboot Slamannan.

"They are catched young, carefully clipped, curry-combed and shod, and shipped to Gleska at the beginnin' o' the winter, wi' fine characters frae the UF minister. On the day they start their first situation they're generals, that say 'Whit is't?' quite angry, at the door to folk that come to their mistress' efternoon teas; on the Wednesday they're wanting their wages up; and on the Thursday they start in anither place as experienced hoose- and table-maids. At least, that's whit I gaither frae overhearin' the ladies: we have nae servant in oor hoose — Jinnet does everything hersel'.

"When Mary Ann's no' packin' her kist, or haein' confabs wi' the butcher, or trimmin' a frock for the Clachna-cudden natives' swarree and ball, she's lookin' the papers to see the rate o' servants' wages in Kimberley,[3] near whaur the wars were. Some day she's gaun to Kimberley, or

Australia, or ony ither foreign pairt, whaur intelligent cooks get the wages o' cabinet ministers, and can get mairrit jist as easy's onything.

"In the fine auld times servant lassies used to bide wi' ye till they were that auld and frail ye had to have somebody sittin' up wi' them at nicht.

"Yince they got a fit in yer hoose ye couldna get quat o' them: they fastened their kists to the floor wi' big screwnails, and wad scarcely go oot the length o' the kirk for fear ye wad shut up the hoose and rin awa' and leave them. As for the wages they got, they were that small, folks used to toss up a bawbee to see whether they wad keep a servant or a canary.

"But nooadays a man that's in the habit o' payin' ony heed to the servant lassies that opens the door for him or hands him his letters, thinks it's a magic-lantern show he's at, wi' a new picture every twa seconds.

"He doesna see his wife except on the Sundays, for a' the ither days o' the week she's cyclin' roond the registries wi' five pounds o' change in silver, payin' fees.

"'Hoose-tablemaid, ma'am? Certainly, ma'am; we'll see whit we can dae for ye between noo and the next Gleska Exhibeetion,' says the registry, rakin' in the half-croons as hard's she can.

"When there's a rumour gets aboot Dowanhill[4] that a servant lass, oot o' a situation, was seen the week afore last, hundreds o' ladies mak' for the registries, and besiege them in the hope o' catchin' her; and of late, I'm tellt they're engagin' trained detectives for trackin' plain cooks.

"Domestic service is the only profession in Europe the day whaur the supply's less than the demand, and if I had twa or three boys ready to gang oot and work for themselves, I wad sooner mak' them into scullerymaids than apprentice them wi' an electrical engineer.

"In the last ten years wha ever heard o' a servant lassie oot o' a situation ony langer than the time she took to rin frae ae hoose to anither, if she had the richt number o' hands and e'en?

"She disna need to gang onywhere lookin' for a place; the sleuth-hounds o' Dowanhill track her to her lair as soon as she's landed at the Broomielaw or Buchanan Street Station, and mak' a grab at her afore she learns enough o' the language to ask her wye to a registry.

"A new servant in a hoose is like a field-marshal back frae the front — she's trated wi' sae muckle deference. Ye daurna mak' a noise through the day for fear it'll spoil her sleep. Ye pit on the fire for her in the mornin', and brush her golfin' buits afore ye start for the office. Ye pay sixpence a day o' car fares for her to go and see ker kizzens in case she's wearyin', puir thing! And if 'Rob Roy's' on at the theatre ye'll be as weel to let her know and gie her tickets for it, or she'll gie notice when she reads the creeticism in the paper and finds oot she missed it. Mair nor a dizzen societies have been started for giving medals and rewards to servant lassies that have been a lang lang while in the ae situation; they're worked on a graduated scale:

"Hoosemaids, in one situation two months — Bronze medal of the Society and 30s.

"Generals, three months — Silver medal and fountain pen.

"Plain cook, six months — Gold medal, £5, and gramophone.

"Whit the country wants is the municeepilisation[5] o' domestic service. The better hoosin' o' the poor's a thing that there's nae hurry for. Plain cooks and general servants that ken the difference between a cake o' black lead and a scrubbing-brush are a communal needcessity; they can nae mair be done without than gas, water, skoosh cars, or the telephone.

"The Corporations should import and train Mary Anns in bulk, gie them a nate uniform and thirty shillin's a week, and hire them oot 'oorly, daily, weekly, or monthly, as required, reserving for them a' the rights and privileges that belong to them, wi' limitation o' workin' 'oors, strick definition o' duties, stipulated nichts oot, and faceelities

for followers. Look at the polis. Ye can depend on gettin' a
polisman nine times oot o' ten if ye want him; a lassie to
gang oot wi' the pramlater,[6] or a hoose-tablemaid, should
be jist as easy got by every ratepayer when wanted, and
that's only to be secured by the Corporations takin' the
domestic service into their ain haunds."

19. *Duffy's Wedding*

I DID not see Erchie during the New-Year holidays, and so
our greetings on Saturday night when I found him firing
up the church furnace had quite a festive cheerfulness.

"Where have you been for the past week?" I asked him.
"It looks bad for a beadle to be conspicuous by his absence
at this season of the year."

"If ye had been whaur ye ocht to hae been, and that was
in the kirk, last Sunday, ye wad hae found me at my place,"
said Erchie. "Here's a bit bride's-cake," he went on, taking
a little packet from his pocket. "The rale stuff! Put that
below your heid at nicht and ye'll dream aboot the yin
that's gaun to mairry ye. It's a sure tip, for I've kent them
that tried it, and escaped in time."

I took the wedding-cake. To dream of the one I want to
marry is the desire of my days — though, indeed, I don't
need any wedding-cake below my pillow for such a
purpose. "And whose wedding does this — this deadly
comestible — come from, Erchie?" I asked him.

"Wha's wad it be but Duffy's," said Erchie. "'At 5896
Braid Street, on the 31st, by the Rev. J. Macauslane, Eliza-
beth M'Niven Jardine to James K. Duffy, coal merchant.'
Duffy's done for again; ye'll can see him noo hurryin'
hame for his tea when his work's bye and feared ony o' the
regular customers o' the Mull of Kintyre Vaults 'll stop
him on the road and ask him in for something. His wife's
takin' him roond wi' a collar on, and showin' him aff
among a' her freen's and the ither weemen she wants to
vex, and she's him learning to ca' her 'Mrs D' when they're

in company. He wasna twa days at his work efter the thing
happened when she made him stop cryin' his ain coals[1]
and leave yin o' his men to dae't, though there's no' twa o'
them put thegither has the voice o' Duffy. I wadna wonder
if his tred fell aff on accoont o't, and it's tellin' on his
health. 'She says it's no' genteel for me to be cryin' my ain
coals,' he says to me; 'but I think it's jist pride on her part,
jist pride. Whit hairm does it dae onybody for me to gie a
wee bit roar noo and then if it's gaun to help business?' I
heard him tryin' to sing "Dark Lochnagar' on Friday nicht
in his ain hoose, and it wad vex ye to listen, for when he
was trampin' time wi' his feet ye could hardly hear his
voice, it was that much failed. 'Duffy,' I says till him, takin'
him aside, 'never you mind the mistress, but go up a close
noo and then and gie a roar to keep your voice in trim
withoot lettin' on to her onything aboot it.'

"Yes, Duffy was mairried on Hogmanay Nicht, and we
were a' there — Jinnet and me, and her niece Sarah, and
Macrae the nicht polis, and a companion o' Macrae's frae
Ardentinny, that had his pipes wi' him to play on, but
never got them tuned. It was a grand ploy, and the man
frae Ardentinny fell among his pipes comin' doon the stair
in the mornin'. 'Ye had faur ower much drink,' I tellt him,
takin' him oot frae amang the drones and ribbons and
things. 'I'm shair ye've drunk a hale bottle.' 'Whit's a
bottle o' whusky among wan?' says he. If it wasna for him it
wad hae been a rale nice, genteel mairrage.

"Duffy had on a surtoo coat,[2] and looked for a' the
warld like Macmillan, the undertaker, on a chape job. He
got the lend o' the surtoo frae yin o' the men aboot the
Zoo, and he was aye tryin' to put his haunds in the ootside
pooches o' them no' there. 'Oh, Erchie,' he says to me, 'I
wish I had on my jaicket again, this is no' canny. They'll a'
be lookin' at my haunds.' 'No, nor yer feet,' I tellt him;
'they'll be ower busy keepin' their e'e on whit they're gaun
to get to eat.' 'If ye only kent it,' says he, 'my feet's a
torment to me, for my buits is far ower sma'.' And I could
see the puir sowl sweatin' wi' the agony.

"The bride looked fine. Jinnet nearly grat when she saw her comin' in, and said it minded her o' hersel' the day she was mairried. 'Ye're just haverin',' I tellt her, gey snappy. 'She couldna look as nice as you did that day if she was hung wi' jewels.' But I'll no' say Leezie wasna nice enough — a fine, big, sonsy, smert lass, wi' her face as glossy as onything.

"When the operation was by, and the minister had gane awa' hame, us pressin' him like onything to wait a while langer, and almost breakin' his airms wi' jammin' his topcoat on him fast in case he micht change his mind, we a' sat down to a high tea that wad dae credit to F & Fs.[3] If there was wan hen yonder there was haulf a dizzen, for the bride had a hale lot o' country freen's, and this is the time o' the year the hens is no' layin'.

"There were thirty-five folk sat doon in Duffy's hoose that nicht, no' coontin' a wheen o' the neighbours that stood in the lobby and took their chance o' whit was passin' frae the kitchen. Duffy hadna richt started carvin' the No. 6 hen when a messenger cam' to the door to ask for the surtoo coat, because the man in the Zoo had his job changed for that nicht and found he needed the coat for his work; so Duffy was quite gled to get rid of it, and put on his Sunday jaicket. 'Ask him if he wadna like a wee lend o' my new tight boots,' he says to the messenger frae the Zoo; 'If he does, come back as fast's ye can for them, and I'll pay the cab.'

"Efter the high tea was by, the Ardentinny man never asked onybody's leave, but began to tune his pipes, stoppin' every twa or three meenutes to bounce aboot the player he was, and that his name was M'Kay — yin o' the auld clan M'Kays. Macrae, the nicht polis, was awfu' chawed that he brocht him there at a'. Ye couldna hear yersel' speakin' for the tunin' o' the pipes, and they werena nearly half ready for playin' on when the bride's mither took the liberty o' stoppin' him for a wee till we wad get a sang frae somebody.

"'James 'll sing,' says the bride, lookin' as prood's ye like at her new man. 'Will ye no' obleege the company wi' 'Dark Lochnagar'?'

"'I wad be only too willin',' he tellt her, 'if I had on my ither boots and hadna ett thon last cookie.' But we got him to sing 'Dark Lochnagar' a' richt. In the middle o't the man frae Ardentinny said if Duffy wad haud on a wee he wad accompany him on the pipes, and he started to tune them again, but Macrae stopped him by puttin' corks in his drones.

"Jinnet sang the 'Auld Hoose.' Man! I was prood o' her. Yon's the smertest wumman in Gleska. The Rale Oreeginal!"

"Don't you yourself sing, Erchie?"

"Not me! I'm comic enough withoot that. A flet fit and a warm hert, but timmer in the tune.[4] Forbye, I was too busy keepin' doon the man frae Ardentinny. He was determined to hae them pipes o' his tuned if it took him a' nicht. I tried to get him to gang oot into the back-coort to screw them up, but he aye said they were nearly ready noo, they wadna tak' him ten meenutes, and he kept screechin' awa' at them. It was fair reediculous.

"At last the bride's mither got him put into the kitchen, and was clearin' the room for a dance. Duffy was very red in the face, and refused to rise frae the table. 'Whit's the use o' dancin'?' says he; 'are we no' daein' fine the way we are?' And then it was found oot he had slipped his tight boots aff him under the table, and was sittin' there as joco as ye like in his stockin' soles.

"The young yins were dancin' in the room to the playin' o' a whustle, and the rest o' us were smokin' oot on the stairheid, when the man frae Ardentinny cam fleein' oot wi' his bagpipes still gaspin'. He said it was an insult to him to start dancin' to a penny whustle and him there ready to play if he could only get his pipes tuned.

"'Never you heed, Mac,' says I; 'ye'll hae a chance at Macrae's waddin' if ye can get the pipes tuned afore then; he's engaged to oor Sarah.'

"I was that gled when the cat-wutted cratur fell amang

his pipes gaun doon the stair in the mornin'; it served him richt."

"And where did Duffy and his bride spend their honeymoon, Erchie?" I asked.

"They took the skoosh car oot to Paisley; that was a' their honeymoon."

20. *On Corporal Punishment*

"ON THIS question of corporal punishment in the schools, Erchie," I said to my old friend, "what are your views? I've no doubt you're dead against any alteration on use and wont."

"Whiles," said Erchie; "whiles! I buy the paper ae day, and when I read the wye brutal and ignorant schoolmaisters abuse their poseetion, I feel that angry I could fling bricks at the windows o' a' the schools I pass on the wye to my wark; but the next day when I read whit perfect wee deevils a' the weans is nooadays, and hoo they'll a' turn oot a disgrace to their faithers and mithers if they divna get a beltin' twice a-day, I'm sair tempted to gae ower to my guid-dochter's in the Calton[1] and tak' a razor-strop to wee Alick afore he gangs to his bed, jist in case he's bein' negleckit. That's the warst o' the newspapers; they're aye giein' ye the differen' sets o't, and ye read sae much on the ae side and then the ither that ye're fair bate to mak' up your mind. My ain puir auld faither — peace be wi' him! — didna seem to be muckle fashed wi' the different sets o't in the newspapers; he made up his mind awfu' fast, and gied ye his fit-rule ower the back o' the fingers afore ye could gie your wee brither a clip on the nose for clypin' on ye. They may abolish corporal punishment in the Gleska schools, but they'll no' pit an end to't in hooses whaur the faither's a plumber and aye has a fit-rule stuck doon the outside seam o' his breeks."

"Ah yes! Erchie, but these paternal ebullitions of ill-temper — "

"Ill-temper or no'," said Erchie, "it's a' in the scheme o' nature, and an angry man's jist as much the weepon o' nature as a thunderbolt is, or a lichted caundle lookin' for an escape o' gas. If ye dinna get your licks in the school for bein' late in the mornin', ye'll get fined an awfu' lot o' times for sleepin' in when ye're auld enough to work in Dubs';[2] so the thing's as braid as it's wide, as the Hielan'man said."

"Then you seem to think a fit of anger is essential to paternal punishment, Erchie? That's surely contrary to all sober conclusions."

"Sober conclusions hae naethin' to dae wi' skelpin' weans, as I ken fine that brocht up ten o' a family and nearly a' that's spared o' them dacin' weel for themsel's. The auld Doctor in oor kirk talks aboot love and chastisement, but in my experience human nature wad be a' to bleezes lang afore this if faithers and mithers didna whiles lose their tempers and gie their weans whit they deserved. If you're the kind o' man that could thresh a puir wee smout[3] o' a laddie in cauld bluid, I'm no', and I canna help it."

"And did you thrash your ten much, Erchie?" I asked, with a doubt as to that essential ill-temper in his case.

"That has naethin' to dae wi't," said he, quickly. "My private disinclination to hae the wee smouts greetin' disna affect the point at a'. If oor yins needed it, I went oot for a daunder and left the job to Jinnet. A woman's aye the best hand at it, as I ken by my aunty Chirsty. When she had the threshin' o' me, she aye gied me tuppence efter it was done if I grat awfu' sair, and I took guid care I never went wantin' money in thae days. I was only vexed she couldna thresh me threepence-worth the time the shows were roond oor wye, and mony's the time I worked for't.

"When the papers mak' me wonder whether corporal punishment's guid for the young or no', I jist tak' a look at mysel' in Jinnet's new wardrobe looking-gless, and, except for the flet feet — me bein' a waiter — I don't see muckle wrang wi' Erchie MacPherson, and the Lord kens there was nae slackness o' corporal punishment in his days, though then it was simply ca'd a leatherin'. My mither threshed me because it wadna gae wrang onywye — if I wasna need'n't the noo I wad be need'n't some ither time; and my faither threshed me because there was a hard knot in the laces o' his boots, and he couldna lowse't. It didnae dae me ony hairm, because I kent they were fond enough o' me.

"In the school we were weel threshed in the wintertime to keep us warm, and in the summer-time a stirrin'up wi' the tawse a' roond made up for the want o' ventilation. If I never learned much else in the school, I got a fair grup o' naitural history, and yin o' the tips I got was that a horse-hair laid across the loof[4] o' the haund 'll split a cane or cut the fingers aff a tawse,[5] when ye're struck by either the yin or the ither. I made twa or three cairt-horses bald-heided at the tail wi' my experimentin', but somethin' aye went wrang; the maister either let fly ower sudden, or it was the wrang kind o' horse — at onyrate, I never mind o' cuttin' the cane or the tawse.

"Whiles when I'm across at my guid-dochter's, I hear her wee laddie, Alick, greetin' ower his coonts,[6] and fear't the maister 'll cane him because they're no' richt.

"'If a cistern wi' an inlet pipe twa-and-a-half inches in diameter lets in seventy-nine gallons eleeven quarts and seeven pints in twenty-fower and a half 'oors, and an ootlet pipe o' three-quarters o' an inch diameter discharges forty-eight gallons nineteen quarts and five pints in the six 'oors, whit o'clock will the cistern be empty if the ootlet pipe hiz a big leak in't?'

"That's the kind o' staggerer puir wee Alick gets thrashed for if he canna answer't richt. I couldna dae a coont like that mysel', as shair's death, if I was pyed for't, unless I had the cistern aside me, and a len' o' the measures frae the Mull o' Kintyre Vaults, and Jinnet wi' a lump o' chalk keepin' tally. I'm no' shair that it's ony guid to thrash wee Alick for no' can daein' a coont o' that kind, or for no' bein' able to spell 'fuchsia', or for no' mindin' the exact heights o' a' the principal mountains in Asia and Sooth America.

"Noo wad ye like it yoursel'? Ye canna put mathematics

into a callan's heid by thrashin' him ower the fingers, if he's no' made wi' the richt lump in his heid for mathematics; and if Alick's schoolmaister gaes on thinkin' he can, I'll gae oot some day to his school and maybe get the jyle for't."

"Come, come, Erchie," I protested; "you are in quite an inconsistent humour to-day; surely Alick's thrashings are all in the scheme of nature. If he is not punished now for inability to do that interesting proposition in compound proportion, he will be swindled out of part of his just payment when paid for bricklaying by the piece when he has taken to the trade, and the thing — once more as the Highlandman said — is as broad as it's wide."

"Nane o' my guid-dochter's sons is gaun to tak' to treds," said Erchie, coldly; "they're a' gaun to be bankers and electreecians and clerks and genteel things o' that sort. If I'm no' consistent aboot this, it's because o' whit I tellt ye, that I've read ower mony o' thae letters and interviews in the papers, and canna mak' up my mind. I ken fine a' the beltin's I got in the school were for my guid, but — but — but it's different wi' wee Alick."

"But we all have our wee Alicks, Erchie."

"Then we're a' weel aff," said Erchie, glowing, "for yon's the comicalest wee trate! The Rale Oreeginal."

"But the teachers don't understand him?"

"That's the hale p'int," said Erchie, agreeably; "the teachers never dae. They're no' pyed for understandin' a' the wee Alicks: a' that can be expected for the wages the schoolmaisters get in Gleska is that they'll haul the wee cratur by the scruff o' the neck through a' the standards. The schoolmaister and the mither ought to be mair prized and bigger pyed than ony ither class in the country, but they're no', and that's the reason their jobs are often sae badly filled up.

"If education was a' that folk think it is, there wad lang syne hae been nae need for cane nor strap. For mair nor a generation noo, every bairn has had to go to the school — a' the parents o' a' the weans in school the noo have had an education themsel's, so that baith at hame and in the school the young generation of the present day have sae mony advantages ower whit you and I had, they ought to be regular gems o' guid behaviour and intelligence.

"But I canna see that they're ony better than their grand-faithers were at the same age. Except my guid-dochter's boy Alick, I think they're a' worse.

"A' the difference seems to be that they're auld sooner than we were, smoke sooner, and swear sooner, and in a hunner wyes need mair leatherin' than we did. Education o' the heid's no' education o' the hert, and the only thing that comes frae crammin' a callant o' naiturally bad disposeetion with book-learnin' is that he's the better trained for swindlin' his fellow-men when he's auld enough to try his hand at it. I wad be awfu' prood o' every new school that's in Gleska if I didna ken that I had to pye a polis tax for't by-and-bye as well as school tax."

"How glad we ought to be, Erchie, that we were born in a more virtuous age," I said, and Erchie screwed up his face.

"We werena," said he. "It's aye been the same since the start o' things. I've jist been sayin' to ye whit I mind o' hearin' my faither say to mysel'. There'll aye be jist enough rogues in the world to keep guid folk like you and me frae gettin' awfu' sick o' each ither."

21. *The Follies of Fashion*

MY OLD friend has a great repugnance to donning new clothes. His wife Jinnet told me once she had always to let him get into a new suit, as it were, on the instalment system: the first Sunday he reluctantly put on the trousers; the second he ventured the trousers and waistcoat; and on the third he courageously went forth in the garb complete, after looking out at the closemouth first to see that Duffy or any other ribald and critical acquaintance was not looking.

I saw a tell-tale crease down the front of the old man's legs yesterday.[1]

"New sartorial splendour, Erchie?" I said, and pinched him for luck.

He got very red.

"You're awfu' gleg in the e'en," said he; "am I no' daein' my best to let on they're an auld pair cleaned? Blame the wife for't! There's naethin' o' the la-di-da aboot easy-gaun Erchie. But weemen! Claes is their hale concern since the day that Adam's wife got the shape o' a sark frae the deevil, and made it wi' a remender o' fig-leafs.

"There's no much wrang wi' Jinnet, but she's far ower pernicketty[2] aboot whit her and me puts on, and if she has naething else to brag aboot she'll brag I hae aye the best-brushed buits in oor kirk. She took an awfu' thraw yince at yin o' the elders, for she thocht he bate me wi' the polish o' his buits, and she could hardly sleep ower the heid o't till I tellt her they were patent.

"'Och!' says she, 'is that a'? Patent's no' in the game.'

"'Onything's in the game,' says I to her, 'that's chaper nor heeling and soling.'

"It's bad enough," he went on, "to be hurtin' yer knees wi' new breeks, and haein' the folk lookin' at ye, but it's a mercy for you and me we're no weemen. You and me buys a hat, and as lang's the rim and the rest o't stick thegither, it's no' that faur oot the fashion we need to hide oorsel's. The only thing I see changes in is collars, and whether it's the lying-doon kind or the double-breisted chats, they hack yer neck like onything. There's changes in ties, but gie me plain black.

"Noo, Jinnet has to hae the shape o' her hat shifted every month as regular's a penny diary. If it's flet in June, it's cockin' up in July; and if the bash is on the left side in August, it has to be on the right side in September.

"Och! but there's no muckle wrang wi' Jinnet for a' that; she wanted to buy me a gold watch-chain last Fair.

"'A gold watch-chain's a nice, snod,[3] bien-lookin' thing aboot a man,' says she, 'and it's gey usefu'.'

"'No, nor usefu',' says I; 'A watch-chain looks fine on a man, but it's his gallowses[4] dae the serious wark.'"

"Still, Erchie," I said, "our sex can't escape criticism for its eccentricities of costume either. Just fancy our pockets, for instance!"

"Ye're right, there," Erchie agreed; "hae I no' fifteen pouches mysel' when I hae my top-coat on? If I put a tramway ticket into yin o' them I wadna be able to fin' oot which o' them it was in for an 'oor or twa.

"Pockets is a rale divert. Ye canna dae without nine or ten in Gleska if ye try yer best. In the country it's different. Doon aboot Yoker, and Gargunnock, and Deid Slow and them places, a' a man needs in the wye o' pouches is twa trooser yins — yin for each haund when he's leanin' against a byre-door wonderin' whit job he'll start the morn.

"There's a lot o' fancy wee pouches that'll no' haud mair nor a pawn-ticket aboot a Gleska man's claes, but in the country they dae wi' less and dig them deep.

"Sae faur as I can see, the pouch is a new-fashioned thing a'thegither.[5] Look at them auld chaps ye see in pictures wi' the galvanised or black-leaded airn suits on; if yin o' them wanted a pouch he wad need to cut it himsel' wi' a sardine-opener, and then he wad peel a' his knuckles feelin' for his hanky or the price o' a pint. I'm gled I wisna gaun aboot when them galvanised airn suits was the go; it must hae been awfu' sair on the nails scratchin' yersel'. Yer claes were made then in a biler-works. When ye went for the fit-on, the cutter bashed in the slack bits at the back wi' a hammer and made it easier for ye under the oxter wi' a cauld chisel.

"'I want it higher at the neck,' says you.

"'Right!' says he, quite game, and bangs in twa or three extra rivets. And your wife, if ye had yin, had to gie your suits a polish up every Friday when she was daein' the kitchen grate.

"It was the same when the Hielan's was the wye ye read aboot in books, and every Hielan'man wore the kilts.

"There was nae pocket in a pair of kilts.

"I daursay that was because the Hielan'man never had

onything worth while to put in a pocket if he had yin. He hung his snuff-mull and his knife and fork ootside his claes, and kept his skean-dhu in his stockin'.

"It's a proof that weemen's no' richt ceevilised yet that they can be daein', like the men I'm speaking aboot, withoot ony pooches. Jinnet tells me there's nae pooch in a woman's frock nooadays, because it wad spoil her sate on the bicycle. That's the wye ye see weemen gaun aboot wi' their purses in their haunds, and their bawbees for the skoosh car inside their glove, and their bonny wee watches that never gang because they're never rowed up, hingin' just ony place they'll hook on to ootside their claes.

"I was yince gaun doon to Whiteinch on a Clutha[6] to see a kizzen o' the wife's, and Jinnet was wi' me. Me bein' caury-haunded,[7] I got aff by mistake at Govan on the wrang side o' the river, when Jinnet was crackin' awa' like a pengun wi' some auld wife at the sherp end o' the boat, and she didna see me.

"'Oh! Erchie!' she says when she cam' hame, 'the time I've put in! I thocht ye wis drooned.'

"'And ye hurried hame for the Prudential book,[8] I suppose?' says I.

"'No,' says she, 'but I made up my mind to hae a pooch o' my ain efter this, if I merrit again, to haud my ain Clutha fares, and no' be lippenin'[9] to onybody.'"

22. *Erchie in an Art Tea-Room*

"I SAW you and Duffy looking wonderfully smart in Sauchiehall Street on Saturday," I said to Erchie one morning.

"Man, were we no'?" replied the old man, with an amused countenance. "I must tell ye the pant we had. Ye'll no' guess where I had Duffy. Him and me was in thon new tea-room wi' the comic windows.[1] Yin o' his horses dee'd on him, and he was doon the toon liftin' the insurance for't. I met him comin' hame wi' his Sunday claes on, and the three pound ten he got for the horse. He was that prood he was walkin' sae far back on his heels that a waff o' win' wad hae couped him, and whustlin' 'Dark Lochnagar.'

"'Come on in somewhere and hae something,' says he, quite joco.

"'Not me,' says I 'I'm nane o' the kind; a beadle's a public man, and he disna ken wha may be lookin' at him, but I'll tell ye whit I'll dae wi' ye — I'll tak' ye into a tea-room.' 'A' richt,' says Duffy; 'I'm game for a pie or ony-thing.'

"And I took him like a lamb to the new place.

"When we came fornent it, he glowered, and 'Michty!' says he, 'Wha did this?'

"'Miss Cranston,'[2] says I.

"'Was she tryin'?' says Duffy.

"'She took baith hands to't,' I tellt him. 'And a gey smert wumman, too, if ye ask me.'

"He stood five meenutes afore I could get him in, wi' his e'en glued on the fancy doors.

"'Do ye hae to break yer wey in?' says he.

"'No, nor in, I tells him; look slippy in case some o' yer customers sees ye!'

"'Och! I havena claes for a place o' the kind,' says he, and his face red.

"'Man!' I says, 'ye've henned — that's whit's wrang wi' ye: come in jist for the pant; naebody 'll touch ye, and ye'll can come oot if it's sore'

"In we goes, Duffy wi' his kep aff. He gave the wan look roond him, and put his hand in his pooch to feel his money. 'Mind I have only the three flaffers and a half,[3] Erchie,' says he.

"'It'll cost ye nae mair than the Mull o' Kintyre Vaults,' I tellt him, and we began sclimmin' the stairs. Between every rail there was a piece o' gless like the bottom o' a soda-water bottle, hangin' on a wire; Duffy touched every yin o' them for luck.

"'Whit dae ye think o' that, noo?' I asked him.

"'It's gey fancy,' says Duffy; 'Will we be lang?'

"'Ye puir ignorant cratur!' I says, losin' my patience

a'thegither, 'Ye havena a mind in the dietin' line above a sate on the trams o' a lorry[4] wi' a can o' soup in your hand.'

"I may tell ye I was a wee bit put aboot mysel', though I'm a waiter by tred, and seen mony a dydo in my time. There was naething in the hale place was the way I was accustomed to; the very snecks o' the doors were kind o' contrairy.

"'This way for the threepenny cups and the guid bargains,' says I to Duffy, and I lands him into whit they ca' the Room de Looks.[5] Maybe ye havena seen the Room de Looks; it's the colour o' a goon Jinnet use to hae afore we mairried: there's whit Jinnet ca's insertion on the table-cloths, and wee beeds stitched a' ower the wa's the same as if somebody had done it themsel's. The chairs is no' like ony other chairs ever I clapped eyes on, but ye could easy guess they were chairs; and a' roond the place there's a lump o' lookin'-gless wi' purple leeks[6] pented on it every noo and then. The gasalier in the middle was the thing that stunned me. It's hung a' roond wi' hunners o' big gless bools,[7] the size o' yer nief — but ye don't get pappin' onything at them.

"Duffy could only speak in whispers. 'My Jove!' says he, 'ye'll no' get smokin' here, I'll bate.'

"'Smokin'!' says I; 'Ye micht as weel talk o' gowfin'.'

"'I never in a' my life saw the like o't afore. This cows a'!' says he, quite nervous and frichtened lookin'.

"'Och!' says I, "it's no' your fau't; you didna dae't onywye. Sit doon.'

"There was a wheen lassies wi' white frocks and tippets on for waitresses, and every yin o' them wi' a string o' big red beads roond her neck.

"'Ye'll notice, Duffy,' says I, 'that though ye canna get ony drink here, ye can tak' a fine bead[8] onywye,' but he didna see my joke.

"'Chaps me no'!' says he. 'Whit did ye say the name o' this room was?'

"'The Room de Looks,' I tellt him.

"'It'll likely be the Room de Good Looks,' says he,

lookin' at the waitress that cam' for oor order. 'I'm for a pie and a bottle o' Broon Robin.'

"'Ye'll get naething o' the kind. Ye'll jist tak' tea, and stretch yer hand like a Christian for ony pastry ye want,' said I, and Duffy did it like a lamb. Oh! I had the better o' him; the puir sowl never saw onything fancy in his life afore since the time Glenroy's was shut in the New City Road, where the Zoo[9] is. It was a rale divert. It was the first time ever he had a knife and fork to eat cookies wi', and he thocht his teaspoon was a' bashed oot o' its richt shape till I tellt him that was whit made it Art.

"'Art,' says he, 'whit the mischief's Art?'

"'I can easy tell ye whit Art is,' says I, 'for it cost me mony a penny. When I got mairried, Duffy, haircloth chairs was a' the go; the sofas had twa ends to them, and you had to hae six books wi' different coloured batters[10] spread oot on the paurlor table, wi' the tap o' yer weddin'-cake under a gless globe in the middle. Wally dugs[11] on the mantel-piece, worsted things on the chair-backs, a picture o' John Knox ower the kist o' drawers, and 'Heaven Help Our Home' under the kitchen clock — that was whit Jinnet and me started wi'. There's mony a man in Gleska the day buyin' hand-done pictures and wearin' tile hats to their work that begun jist like that. When Art broke oot — '

"'I never took it yet,' says Duffy.

"'I ken that,' says I, 'but it's ragin' a' ower the place; ye'll be a lucky man if ye're no' smit wi't cairryin' coals up thae new tenements they ca' mansions, for that's a hotbed o' Art. But as I say, when Art broke oot, Jinnet took it bad, though she didna ken the name o' the trouble, and the haircloth chairs had to go, and leather yins got, and the sofa wi' the twa ends had to be swapped for yin wi' an end cut aff and no' richt back. The wally dugs, and the worsted things, and the picture o' John Knox, were nae langer whit Jinnet ca'd the fashion, and something else had to tak' their place. That was Art: it's a lingerin' disease; she has the dregs o't yet, and whiles buys shillin' things that's nae use for onything except for dustin'.'

"'Oh! is that it?' says Duffy; 'I wish I had a pie.'

"'Ye'll get a pie then,' I tellt him, 'but ye canna expect it here; a pie's no becomin' enough for the Room de Looks. Them's no' chairs for a coalman to sit on eatin' pies.'

"We went doon the stair then, and I edged him into the solid meat department. There was a lassie sittin' at a desk wi' a wheen o' different coloured bools afore her, and when the waitresses cam' to her for an order for haricot mutton or roast beef or onything like that frae the kitchen, she puts yin o' the bools doon a pipe[12] into the kitchen, and the stuff comes up wi' naething said.

"'Whit dae ye ca' that game?' asks Duffy, lookin' at her pappin' doon the bools; 'It's no' moshy, onywye.'

"'No, nor moshy,' I says to him. 'That's Art. Ye can hae yer pie frae the kitchen withoot them yellin' doon a pipe for't and lettin' a' the ither customers ken whit ye want.'

"When the pie cam' up, it was jist the shape o' an ordinary pie, wi' nae beads nor onything Art aboot it, and Duffy cheered up at that, and said he enjoyed his tea."

"I hope the refining and elevating influence of Miss Cranston's beautiful rooms will have a permanent effect on Duffy's taste," I said.

"Perhaps it will," said Erchie; "but we were nae sooner oot than he was wonderin' where the nearest place wad be for a gless o' beer."

23. *The Hidden Treasure*

"I WISH somebody would leave me some money," said Jinnet, "and the first thing I would dae wi't would be to buy ye a new topcoat. That yin's gettin' gey shabby, and that glazed I can almaist see my face in the back o't."

"Then ye're weel aff," said Erchie, "for there's seldom ye'll see a bonnier yin in a better lookin'-gless."

"Oh, ye auld haver!" cried Jinnet, pushing him. "I wonder ye divna think shame to be talkin' like a laddie to his first lass; and me jist a done auld body! If I could jist get a shape I wad buy a remnant and mak' ye a topcoat mysel'. I could dae't quite easy."

"I ken fine that," said her husband, "but I'll bate ye would put the buttons on the wrang side, the wye ye did wi' yon waistcoat. It's a droll thing aboot weemen's claes that they aye hae their buttons on caurey-handed. It jist lets ye see their contrairiness."

"Oh! it's a peety ye mairried me," said Jinnet; "a contrairy wife must be an awfu' handfu'."

"Weel, so ye are contrairy," said Erchie firmly.

"It tak's twa to be contrairy, jist the same wye as it tak's twa to mak' a quarrel," said Jinnet, picking some fluff off his sleeve. "Whit wye am I contrairy I would like to ken?"

"If ye werena contrairy, ye would be thinkin' o' buyin' something for yersel' instead o' a topcoat for me, and ye're far mair needn't," said Erchie, and with that a knock came to the door.

"There's somebody," said Jinnet hastily; "Put on the kettle."

"Come awa' in, Mr Duffy, and you, Mrs Duffy," said Jinnet; "We're rale gled to see ye, Erchie and me. I was jist puttin' on the kettle to mak' a drap tea."

Duffy and his wife came into the cosy light and warmth of the kitchen, and sat down. There was an elation in the coalman's eye that could not be concealed.

"My jove! I've news for ye the nicht," said he, taking out his pipe and lighting it.

"If it's that the bag o' coals is up anither bawbee," said Erchie, "there's nae hurry for't. It's no' awfu' new news that onywye."

"Ye needna be aye castin' up my tred to me," protested Duffy. "Whaur would ye be wantin' coals?"

"Mr MacPherson's quite richt," said Mrs Duffy; "Everybody kens it's no' an awfu' genteel thing sellin' coals, they're that — that black. I'm aye at him, Mrs MacPherson, to gie up the ree and the lorries and start a eatin'-

house. I could bake and cook for't fine. Noo that this money's comin' to us, we could dae't quite easy. Look at the profit aff mulk itsel'!"

"Dear me! hae ye come into a fortune?" cried Jinnet eagerly. "Isn't that droll? I was jist saying to Erchie that I wisht somebody would leave me something and I would buy him a new topcoat."

"That'll be a' richt," said Duffy. "If he'll gie me a haund wi' this thing I called aboot the nicht, I'll stand him the finest topcoat in Gleska, if it costs a pound."

"If it's ca'in on lawyers and the like o' that ye want me to dae," said Erchie, "I'm nae use to ye. I've a fine wye wi' me for ministers and the like o' that, that's no' aye wantin' to get the better o' ye, but lawyers is different. I yince went to a lawyer that was a member in oor kirk to ask him if he didna think it was time for him to pay his sate-rents. He said he would think it ower, and a week efter that he sent me an account for six-and-eightpence for consultation. But I'm prood to hear ye've come in for something, Duffy, whether I get a topcoat or no'. I never kent ye had ony rich freen's at a'. Faith, ye're weel aff; look at me, I havena a rich freen' in the warld except — except Jinnet."

"Oh, I never kent she was that weel aff," cried Mrs Duffy.

"Is it her!" said Erchie. "She has that much money in the bank that the bank clerks touch their hats to her in the street if she has on her Sunday claes. But that wasna whit I was thinkin' o'; there's ither kinds o' riches besides the sort they keep in banks."

"Never mind him, he's an auld fuiter," said Jinnet, spreading a table cloth on the table and preparing for the tea. "I'm shair I'm gled to hear o' your good luck. It doesna dae to build oorsel's up on money, for money's no everything, as the pickpocket said when he took the watch as weel; but we're a' quite ready to thole't. Ye'll be plannin' whit ye'll dae wi't, Mrs Duffy?"

"First and foremost we're gaun to get rid o' the ree, at onyrate," said Mrs Duffy emphatically. "Then we're gaun to get a piano."

"Can ye play?" asked Erchie.

"No," admitted Mrs Duffy, "but there's nae need tae play sae lang's ye can get a vinolia[1] to play for ye. I think we'll flit at the term to yin o' yon hooses roond the corner, wi' the tiled closes,[2] and maybe keep a wee servant lassie. I'm that nervous at havin' to rise for the mulk in the mornin'. No' an awfu' big servant wi' keps and aiprons, ye understaund, but yin I could train into the thing. I'm no' for nane o' your late dinners: I jist like to tak' something in my hand for my supper."

"Och ay, ye'll can easy get a wee no' awfu' strong yin frae the country, chape," said Erchie. "Ye must tak' care o' yer ain health, Mrs Duffy, and if ye're nervous, risin' in the mornin' to tak' in the mulk's no' for ye. But my! ye'll no' be for speakin' to the like o' us when ye come into your fortune."

"It's no' exactly whit ye wad ca' a fortune," Duffy explained, as they drew in their chairs to the table.

"But it's a heap o' money to get a' at yince withoot daein' onything for't."

"Will ye hae to gang into mournin's for the body that left it?" Jinnet asked Mrs Duffy. "I ken a puir weedow wumman that would come to the hoose to sew for ye."

"Ye're aff it a'thegither," said Duffy. "It's naebody that left it to us — it's a medallion. Whit I wanted to ask ye, Erchie, is this — whit's a medallion?"

"Jist a kind o' a medal," said Erchie.

"My jove!" said Duffy, "the wife was richt efter a'. I thocht it was something for playin' on, like a melodian. Weel, it doesna maitter, ye've heard o' the hidden treasure the newspapers's puttin' here and there roond the country? I ken where yin o' them's hidden. At least I ken where there's a medallion."

"Oh, hoo nice!" said Jinnet. "It's awfu' smert o' ye, Mr Duffy. I was jist readin' aboot them, and was jist hopin' some puir body wad get them."

"No' that poor naither!" said Mrs Duffy, with a little warmth.

"Na, na, I wasna sayin' — I didna mean ony hairm," said poor Jinnet. "Streetch yer hand, and tak' a bit cake. That's a rale nice brooch ye hae gotten."

Erchie looked at Duffy dubiously. For a moment he feared the coalman might be trying on some elaborate new kind of joke, but the complacency of his face put it out of the question.

"Then my advice to you, Duffy, if ye ken where the medallion is," said Erchie, "is to gang and howk it up at yince, or somebody 'll be there afore ye. I warrant it'll no' get time to tak' root if it's within a penny ride on the Gleska skoosh cars. There's thoosands o' people oot wi' lanterns at this very meenute scrapin' dirt in the hunt for that medallion. Hoo do ye ken whaur it is if ye havena seen it?"

"It's there richt enough," said Mrs Duffy; "It's in the paper, and we're gaun to gie up the ree; my mind's made up on that. I hope ye'll come and see us sometime in our new hoose — house."

"It says in the paper," said Duffy, "that the medallion's up a street that has a public-hoose at each end o't, and a wee pawn in the middle, roond the corner o' anither street, where ye can see twa laundries at yince, and a sign ower yin o' them that puts ye in mind o' the battle o' Waterloo, then in a parteecular place twenty yairds to the richt o' a pend-close wi' a barrow in't."

Erchie laughed. "Wi' a barrow in't?" said he.

"They micht as weel hae said wi' a polisman in't; barrows is like bobbies — if ye think ye'll get them where ye want them ye're up a close yersel'. And whit's the parteecular place, Duffy?"

Duffy leaned forward and whispered mysteriously, "MY COAL-REE."

"But we're gaun to gie't up," explained his wife.

"Oh, ay, we're gaun to give the ree up. Ye hae no idea whaur — where — I could get a smert wee lassie that would not eat awfu' much, Mrs MacPherson?"

"I measured it a' aff," Duffy went on. "It's oor street richt enough; the pubs is there — "

"— I could bate ye they are," said Erchie. "If they werena there it wad be a miracle."

" — and the laundries is there. 'Colin Campbell' over yin o' them, him that bate Bonypart, ye ken, and twenty yairds frae the pend-close is richt under twenty ton o' coal I put in last week. It's no' M'Callum's wid-yaird; it's my ree."

"My papa was the sole proprietor of a large widyaird," irrelevantly remarked Mrs Duffy, who was getting more and more Englified as the details of the prospective fortune came out.

"Was he, indeed," said Jinnet. "That was nice!"

"Noo, whit I wanted you to dae for me," Duffy went on, "was to come awa' doon wi' me the nicht and gie's a hand to shift thae coals. I daurna ask ony o' my men to come, for they wad claim halfers."

Erchie toyed with a teaspoon and looked at the coalman, half in pity, half with amusement. "Man, ye're a rale divert," said he at last. "Do ye think the newspapers would be at the bother o' puttin' their medallion under twenty ton o' coal in your coal-ree, or onybody else's? Na, na, they can mak' their money easier nor that. If ye tak' my advice, ye'll put a penny on the bag o' coal and gie short wecht, and ye'll mak' your fortune far shairer than lookin' under't for medallions."

"Then ye're no' game to gie's a hand?" said Duffy, starting another cookie. "See's the sugar."

"Not me!" said Erchie promptly. "I've a flet fit and a warm hert, but I'm no' a'thegither a born idiot to howk coal for medallions that's no' there."

Next day Duffy came up with two bags of coals which Jinnet had ordered.

"Did ye find the medallion?" she asked him.

"I didna need to look for't," he replied. "I heard efter I left here last nicht that a man found it in a back-coort in the Garscube Road. Them sort of dydoes should be put doon by the polis."

"Oh, whit a peety!" said Jinnet. "And hoo's the mistress the day?"

"She's fine," said Duffy. "She's ca'in' me Jimmy again; it was naething but Mr Duffy wi' her as lang's she thocht we were to get rid o' the ree."

24. *The Valenteen*

ON THE night of the last Trades House[1] dinner I walked home with Erchie when his work was done. It was the 13th of February. There are little oil-and-colour shops in New City Road, where at that season the windows become literary and artistic, and display mock valentines. One of these windows caught my old friend's eye, and he stopped to look in.

"My!" he said, "time flies! It was only yesterday we had the last o' oor Ne'erday currant-bun, and here's the valenteens! That minds me I maun buy — " He stopped and looked at me, a little embarrassed.

I could only look inquiry back at him.

"Ye'll think I'm droll," said he, "but it just cam' in my heid to buy a valenteen. To-morrow's Jinnet's birthday, and it would be a rale divert to send her ladyship yin and tak' a kind o' rise oot o' her. Come and gie's a hand to pick a nice yin."

I went into the oil-and-colour shop, but, alas! for the ancient lover, he found there that the day of sentiment was done so far as the 14th of February was concerned.

"Hae ye ony nice valenteens?" he asked a boy behind the counter.

"It's a comic ye mean?" asked the boy, apparently not much amazed at so strange an application from an elderly gentleman.

"A comic!" said my friend in disdain. "Dae I look like the kind o' chap that sends mock valenteens? If ye gie me ony o' your chat I'll tell yer mither, ye wee — ye wee rascal! Ye'll be asking me next if I want a mooth harmonium. Dae ye think I'm angry wi' the cook in some hoose roond in the terraces because she's chief wi' the letter-carrier? I'll comic ye!"

"Weel, it's only comics we hae," said the youthful shopkeeper; "The only ither kind we hae's Christmas cairds, and I think we're oot o' them."

He was a business-like boy — he flung a pile of the mock valentines on the counter before us.

Erchie turned them over with contemptuous fingers. "It's a gey droll age we live in," said he to me. "We're far ower funny, though ye wadna think it to see us. I have a great respect for valenteens, for if it wasna for a valenteen there maybe wadna hae been ony Jinnet — at least in my hoose. I wad gie a shillin' for a rale auld-fashioned valenteen that gaed oot and in like a concertina, wi' lace roond aboot it, and a smell o' scent aff it, and twa silver herts on't skewered through the middle the same as it was for brandering. Ye havena seen mony o' that kind, laddie? Na, I daursay no'; they were oot afore your time, though I thocht ye micht hae some in the back-shop. They were the go when we werena nearly sae smert as we are nooadays. I'm gled I havena to start the coortin' again."

He came on one of the garish sheets that was less vulgar than the others, with the picture of a young lady under an umbrella, and a verse of not unkindly doggerel.

"That'll hae to dae," said he, "although it's onything but fancy."

"I hope," said I dubiously, "that Mrs MacPherson will appreciate it."

"She's the very yin that will," he assured me, as he put it in his pocket. "She's like mysel'; she canna play the piano, but she has better gifts — she has the fear o' God and a sense o' humour. You come up the morn's nicht at eight, afore the post comes, and ye'll see the ploy when she gets her valenteen. I'll be slippin' oot and postin't in the forenoon. Though a young lassie canna get her valenteens ower early in the mornin', a mairried wife's 'll dae very weel after her wark's done for the day."

"It's yersel'?" said Mrs MacPherson when I went to her door. "Come awa' in. I kent there was a stranger comin' — though indeed I wadna be ca'in' you a stranger — for there was a stranger on the ribs o' the grate this mornin', and a knife fell aff the table when we were at oor tea."

"Ay, and who knocked it aff deeliberate?" interposed her husband, rising to welcome me. "Oh, she's the sly yin. She's that fond to see folk come aboot the hoose she whiles knocks a knife aff the table to see if it'll bring them."

"Oh, Erchie MacPherson!" cried his wife.

"I'm no' blamin' ye," he went on; "I ken I'm gey dreich company for onybody. I havena a heid for mindin' ony scandal aboot the folk we ken, and I canna understaund politics noo that Gledstone's no' to the fore, and I canna sing, or play a tune on onything."

"Listen to him!" cried Jinnet. "Isn't he the awfu' man? Did ye ever hear the like o' him for nonsense?"

The kettle was on the fire: I knew from experience that it had been put there when my knock came to the door, for so the good lady's hospitality always manifested itself, so that her kettle was off and on the fire a score of times a day, ready to be brought to the boil if it was a visitor who knocked, and not a beggar or a pedlar of pipeclay.

"Tak' a watter biscuit," Jinnet pressed me as we sat at the table; "They're awfu' nice wi' saut butter."

"Hae ye nae syrup to put on them?" asked her husband with a sly glance.

"Nane o' yer nonsense," she exclaimed, and attempted a diversion in the conversation, but Erchie plainly had a joke to retail.

"I'll tell ye a baur aboot watter biscuits and syrup," said he. "When I was coortin' my first lass I wasna mair nor nineteen years o' age, and jist a thin peelywally callant, mair like playin' moshy at the bools than rinnin' efter lassies. The lassie's faither and mither jist made fun o' us, and when I wad be gaun up to her hoose, lettin' on it was her brither I wanted to see, they used to affront me afore their dochter wi' speakin' aboot the Sunday School and the Band o' Hope I belanged to (because the lassie belanged to them tae), and askin' me if I was fond o' sugar to my parridge, and when I was thinkin' o' startin' the shavin'. I didna like it, but I jist had to put up wi't. But the worst blow ever I got frae them was yince when I gaed up wi' a new pair o' lavender breeks, and the lassie's mither, for the fun o' the thing, asked me if I wad hae a piece and jeely. I tellt her I wasna heedin', that I was jist efter haein' my tea; but she went and spread syrup on a watter biscuit and handed it to me the same as if I was a wee lauddie wi' a grauvit on."

Jinnet laughed softly at the picture.

"Oh, ye may lauch," said her husband.

"There was nae lauchin' in my heid, I'm tellin' ye. For there was the syrup comin' dreepin' through the holes in the watter biscuit, so that I had to haud the biscuit up every noo and then and lick in below't so as to keep the syrup frae gaun on my braw lavender breeks. A bonny object for a lass to look at, and it was jist to mak' me look reediculous her mither did it. She thocht I was faur ower young to be comin' efter her dochter."

"So ye were," said Jinnet. "I'm shair ye hadna muckle sense at the time, or it wadna be yon yin ye went coortin'."

"Maybe no'; but I never rued it," said Erchie.

"She was as glaikit as yersel'," said Jinnet.

"She was the cleverest lass in the place," protested Erchie. "My! the things she could sew, and crochet, and mak' doon, and bake!"

"Her sister Phemie[2] was faur cleverer than she was," said Jinnet. "She couldna haud a candle to her sister Phemie in tambourin'[3] or in gingerbreid."

"And dancin'! She could dance on a cobweb and no' put a toe through't."

"Ye'll need a line wi' that yin Erchie," said his wife, who did not seem remakably jealous of this first love.

"Ye should hear her singin' —"

"She wad hae ben far better mendin' her wee brither's stockin's, and no' leavin' her mither to dae't," said Jinnet.

"She was a gey licht-heided yin."

Erchie seemed merciless in his remniscence — I really felt sorry for his wife.

"Ye may say whit ye like to run her doon, but ye canna deny her looks."

"Her looks dinna concern me," said Jinnet abruptly.

"Ye're jist an auld haver; think shame o' yersel'!"

"Ye ken ye canna deny't," he went on. "It was alooed all over the place she was the belle. I wasna the only yin that was efter her wi' my lavender breeks. She kept the Band o' Hope for nearly twa years frae burstin' up."

"I'll no' listen to anither word," protested Jinnet, now in obvious vexation; and mercifully there came a rapping at the door.

She returned to the kitchen with an envelope and a little parcel. Erchie winked at me, hugging to himself a great delight.

"I wonder wha in the world can be writin' to me," said she, looking at the addresses.

"It'll likely be an accoont for di'mond tararas[4] or dress-making," said Erchie. "Oh you weemen! Ye're a perfect ruination. But if I was you I wad open them and see."

She opened the envelope first. It was Erchie's valentine, and she knew it, for when she read the verse she shook her head at him laughingly, and a little ashamed. "When will ye be wise?" said she.

Then she opened the little parcel: it contained a trivial birthday gift from an anonymous friend in whose confidence only I, of all the three in the room, happened to be. Vainly they speculated about his identity without suspecting me; but I noticed that it was on her valentine Jinnet set most value. She held it long in her hand, thinking, and was about to put it into a chest of drawers without letting me see it.

"Ye needna be hidin' it," said her husband then. "He saw it already. Faith! he helped me to pick it."

"I'm fair affronted," she exclaimed, reddening at this exposure. "You and your valenteens!"

"There's naething wrang wi' valenteens," said her husband. "If it wasna for a valenteen I wad never hae got ye. I could never say to your face but that I liked ye; but the valenteen had a word that's far mair brazen than 'like,' ye mind."

"Oh, Erchie!" I cried, "you must have been blate in those days. The word was — "

He put up his hand in alarm and stopped me. "Wheesht!" said he. "It's a word that need never be mentioned here where we're a' three Scotch!"

"But what came over the first lass, Erchie?" I asked determined to have the end of that romance.

He looked across at his wife and smiled. "She's there hersel'," said he, "and ye better ask her."

"What! Jinnet?" I cried, amazed at my own obtuseness.

"Jinnet of course," said he. "Wha else wad it be if it wasna Jinnet? She's the Rale Oreeginal."

25. *Among the Pictures*

"WHAUR ARE ye gaun the day?" said Erchie to Duffy on Saturday afternoon when he came on the worthy coalman standing at his own close-mouth, looking up and down the street with the hesitation of a man who deliberates how he is to make the most of his Saturday half-holiday.

"I was just switherin'," said Duffy. "Since I got mairried and stopped gaun to the Mull o' Kintyre Vaults, there's no' much choice for a chap. I micht as weel be leevin' in the country for a' the life I see."

"Man, aye!" said Erchie, "that's the warst o' Gleska; there's nae life in't — naethin' daein'. Ye should try yer hand at takin' oot the wife for a walk, jist for the novelty o' the thing."

"Catch me!" said Duffy. "She wad see ower mony things in the shop windows she was needin'. I was jist wonderin' whether I wad buy a *Weekly Mail* or gang to the fitba' match at Parkheid."

Erchie looked pityingly at him. "A fitba' match!" said he. " Whit's the use o' gaun to a fitba' match when ye can see a' aboot it in the late edeetion?[1] Forbye, a fitba' match doesna improve the mind; it's only sport. I'll tell ye whit I'll dae wi' ye if ye're game. I'll tak' ye to the Art Institute;[2] the minister gied me twa tickets. Awa' and put on your collar and I'll wait here on ye."

"Do you need a collar for the gallery?" asked Duffy, who thought the Art Institute was a music-hall. On this point Erchie set him right, and ten minutes later, with a collar whose rough edges rasped his neck and made him unhappy, he was on his way to Sauchiehall Street.

The band was playing a waltz tune as they entered the Institute.

"Mind, I'm no' on for ony dancin'," Duffy explained. "I canna be bothered dancin'."

"There's naebody gaun to ask ye to dance," said Erchie. "Do you think there couldna be a baun' playin' withoot dancin'? It's jist here to cod a lot o' folk into the notion that they can be cheery enough in a place o' the kind in spite o' the pictures. And ye can get aifternoon tea here, too."

"I could be dacin' wi' a gless o' beer," said Duffy.

"No. They're no' that length yet," Erchie explained. "There's only the tea. The mair determined lovers o' the Fine Arts can dae the hale show in an aifternoon wi' the help o' a cup o' tea, so that they needna come back again. It's a great savin'. They used to hae to gang hame for their tea afore, and whiles they never got back. The Institute wasna popular in thae days; it was that quate and secluded that if a chap had done onything wrang and the detectives were efter him he took a season ticket, and spent a' his days here. Noo, ye can see for yersel' the place is gaun like an inn. That's the effect o' the baun' and the aifternoon tea. If they added a baby incubator to the attractions the same's they hae in the East-End Exhibeetion,[3] they would need the Fire Brigade wi' a hose to keep the croods oot. Ye hae nae idea o' the fascination Art has for the people o' Gleska if they're no' driven to't."

"My jove!" exclaimed Duffy, at the sight of the first gallery. "Whit a lot o' pictures! There'll be a pile o' money in a place o' this kind. Hiv they no water-shoot, or a shootin' jungle, or onything lively like that?"

"Man, ye're awfu' common, whiles, Duffy," said Erchie. "I'm fear't I wasted my ticket on ye. This is no' an ordinary show for haein' fun at; it's for enlargin' the mind, openin' the e'en to the beauties o' nature, and sellin' pictures."

"Are they a' for sale?" asked Duffy, looking with great intentness at a foggy impression by Sidaner,[4] the French artist.

"No' the hale o' them; there's some on lend."

"I could hae lent them a topper," said Duffy, "faur aheid o' onything here. It's a drawin' o' a horse I yince had in my first lorry; it was pented for me by a penter that lodged above us, and had a great name for sign-boards. It cost me nearly a pound wan wye or anither, though I provided the pent mysel'."

"Ay, Art's a costly thing," said Erchie. "Ye'll seldom get a good picture under a pound. It's no' a'thegither the pent, it's the layin' o't on by hand."

"This yin's done by hand onywye," said Duffy, pointing to the foggy impression by Sidaner. "It's awfu' like as if somebody had done it themsel's in their spare time."

"You and me's no' judges o' that sort o' thing," said Erchie. "Maybe it's no' near so bad as it looks."

"Ye see," Erchie went on, "Art pentin's a tred by itsel'. There used to be hardly ony picture-penters in Gleska; it was a' shipbuildin' and calanderin',[5] whitever that is, and chemical works that needed big lums. When a Gleska man did a guid stroke o' business on the Stock Exchange, or had money left him in thae days, and his wife wanted a present, he had his photygraph ta'en big size, ile-coloured by hand. It was gey like him, the photygraph, and so everybody kent it wasna the rale Art. Folk got rich that quick in Gleska, and had sae much money to spend, that the photygraphers couldna keep up wi' the demand, and then the hand-pentin' chaps began to open works in different pairts o' the city. Ye'll hardly gang into a hoose noo whaur ye'll no' see the guidman's picture in ile, and it micht be bilin' ile sometimes, judgin' from the agony on his face."

"My jove!" said Duffy, "is it sore to get done that wye?"

"Sore!" replied Erchie; "no, nor sore. At least, no' that awfu' sore. They wadna need to dae't unless they liked. When maistly a' the weel-aff Gleska folk had got their photygraphs done and then de'ed, the penters had to start the landscape brench o' the business. Them's landscapes a' roon' aboot" — and Erchie gave his arm a comprehensive sweep to suggest all the walls.

"They must be pretty smert chaps that does them," said Duffy. "I wish I had gone in for the pentin' mysel'; it's cleaner nor the coals. Dae ye hae to serve your time?"

"No, nor time; ye can see for yersel' that it's jist a kind o' knack like poetry — or waitin'. And the plant doesna cost much; a' ye need to start wi' 's paper, brushes, pent, and a saft hat."

"A saft hat!"

"Ay; a saft hat's the sure sign o' an artist. I ken hunners o' them; Gleska's fair hotchin' wi' artists. If the Cairters' Trip wasna abolished, ye wad see the artists' tred union walkin' oot wi' the rest o' them."

The two friends went conscientiously round the rooms, Erchie expounding on the dimensions, frames, and literary merits of the pictures, Duffy a patient, humble student, sometimes bewildered at the less obvious transcripts of nature and life pointed out to him.

"Is there much mair o' this to see?" he asked at last, after having gone through the fourth gallery. "I'm gettin' dizzy. Could we no' hae something at the tea bar if we gied them a tip? They micht send oot for't. Or we might get a pass-oot check."[6]

"Mair to see!" exclaimed Erchie. "Ye're awfu' easy made dizzy! The like o' you wad faur raither be oot skreichin' yer heid aff at the fitba' match at Parkheid, instead o' improvin' the mind here. Ye canna get onything at the tea place but jist tea, I'm tellin' ye, and there's nae pass-oot checks. They ken better nor to gie ye pass-oot checks; hauf o' your kind wad never come back again if yince ye escaped.

"My jove!" said Duffy, suddenly, "here's a corker!" and he indicated a rather peculiar drawing with a lady artist's name attached to it.

Erchie himself was staggered. "It's ca'd 'The Sleeper'[7] in the catalogue," said he. "It's a wumman, and her dozin'. The leddy that pented it wasna ower lavish wi' her pent. That's whit they ca' New Art, Duffy; it jist shows ye whit weemen can dae if ye let them."

"And dae ye tell me there's weemen penters?" asked Duffy in astonishment.

"Of course there's weemen penters."

"And hoo dae they get up and doon lethers?"[8] asked Duffy.

"I'm tellin' ye Art pentin's a brench by itsel," said Erchie. "The lady Art penters divna pent windows and rhones and hooses; they bash brass, and hack wud, and draw pictures."

"And can they mak' a living at that?"

"Whiles. And whiles their paw helps."

"My jove!" said Duffy, bewildered.

"We'll gang on to the next room noo," said Erchie.

"I wad raither come back some ither day," said Duffy. "I'm enjoyin' this fine, but I promised the wife I wad be hame early for my tea." And together they hastily made an exit into Sauchiehall Street.

"I wonder wha won the semi-final at Parkheid," said Duffy. "We'll awa' doon the toon and see; whit's the use o' hurryin' hame?"

26. *The Probationary Ghost*

ONE DAY I observed Erchie going off the pavement rather than walk under a ladder.

"And are you superstitious too?" I asked him, surprised at this unsuspected trait in a character so generally sensible.

"I don't care whither ye ca't supersteetion or no'," he replied, "but walkin' under lethers is a gey chancy thing; and there's mony a chancy thing, and I'm neither that young nor that weel aff that I can afford to be takin' ony risks."

"Dear me!" I said; "I wouldn't be surprised to learn that you believed in ghosts."

"Do I no'?" he answered. "And guid reason for't! Did I no' yince see yin? It was the time I had the rheumatic fever, when we were stayin' in Garnethill.[1] I was jist gettin' better, and sittin' up a wee while in the evenin' to air the bed, and Jinnet was oot for a message. The nicht was wild and wet, and the win' was daudin' awa' at the window like onything, and I was feelin' gey eerie, and wearyin' for the wife to come back. I was listenin' for her fit on the stair, when the ootside door opens, and in a second there was a chap at the kitchen door.

"'Come in if your feet's clean,' says I, pretty snappy. 'Seein' ye've made sae free wi' the ae door ye needna mak' ony ceremony wi' this ane.' I heard the hinges screechin', but naebody cam' in, and I looks roon' frae where I was sittin' wi' a blanket roond me at the fire, and there was the ghost keekin' in. He was a wee nyaf o' a thing, wi' a Paisley whisker, a face no bigger than a Geneva watch, a nickerbocker suit on, Rab Roy tartan tops to his gowfin' stockings, and potbellied to the bargain. I kent fine he was a ghost at the first gae-aff.

"'It's you,' says I. 'Come in and gies yer crack till Jinnet comes. Losh, it's no' a nicht for stravaigin'.'[2]

"He cam' glidin' in withoot makin' ony soond at a' and sat doon on a chair."

"'Ye're no' feared,' says he, trying to gnash his teeth, and makin' a puir job o't, for they were maistly arteeficial.

"'Feared?' says I. 'No me! I never did onybody ony hairm that wad mak' it worth ony ghost's while to meddle wi' me. A flet fit but a warm hert.'

"'We'll see aboot that,' says he, as cocky as onything. 'I had a fine job findin' oot where ye were. Fancy me gaun awa' doon to Millport on a nicht like this to haunt ye, and findin' that ye had flitted up here last term.' And he begood to gnash his teeth again.

"'Millport!' says I. 'Man! I was never near the place, and I've lived in this hoose for seventeen year, and brocht up a faimily in't.'

"I never seen a ghost mair vexed than he was when I tell't him that. His jaw fell; he was nearly greetin'.

"'Whit's yer name?' he asked.

"'Erchie MacPherson, and I'm no' ashamed o't. It's no' in ony grocers' nor tylers' books that I ken o', and if I ever murdered ony weans or onything o' that sort, it must hae been when I was sleepin'. I doot, my man, ye're up the wrang close.'

"The ghost begood to swear. Oh my! such swearin'. I never listened to the bate o't. There was fancy words in't I never heard in a' my life, and I've kent a wheen o' cairters.

"'That's jist like them,' says he. 'They tellt me Millport; and efter I couldna find the man I was wantin' at Millport, I was tellt it was here, No. 16 Buccleuch Street.[3] Fancy me bungin' awa' through the air on a nicht like this! My nickerbockers is fair stickin' to me knees wi' wet.'

"'Peter,' says I (of course I didna ken his richt name, but I thocht I wad be nice wi' the chap seein' he had made such a mistake), 'Peter,' said I, 'ye're needin' yer specs on. This is no' No. 16, it's No. 18, and I think the man ye maun be lookin' for is Jeckson, that canvasses for the sewin'-machines. He came here last term frae aboot Millport. If he's done ony hairm to onybody in his past life — murdered a wife, and buried her under the hearth-stane,

or ony daft-like thing o' that sort — I'm no' wantin' to hear
onything aboot it, for he's a guid enough neebour, has twa
bonny wee weans, comes hame regular to his tea, and
gangs to the kirk wi' his wife. He's been teetotal ever since
he came here. Gie the chap a chance!'

"'Jeckson!' said the ghost, and whips oot a wee book.
'That's the very man!' said he. 'Man! is't no' aggravatin'?
Here's me skooshin' up and doon the coast wi' my thin
flannels on lookin' for him, and him toastin' his taes at a
fire in Buccleuch Street! Jist you wait. It shows ye the wye
the books in oor place is kept. If the office was richt up-to-
date, Jeckson wadna be flitted ten meenutes when his new
address wad be marked doon. No wonder the Americans is
batin' us!⁴ Weel, it's no' my faut if I'm up the wrang close,
and I'm no' gaun to start the job the nicht. I'm far ower
cauld.'

"There was an empty gless and a teaspoon on the
dresser, for Jinnet had been giein' me a drap toddy afore
she gaed oot. The ghost sat doon on a chair and looked at
the gless.

"'Could ye save a life?' said he.

"'Whit wad be the use o' giein' it to you, Peter?' I asked
him; 'ye havena ony inside, seein' ye're a ghost.'

"'Have I no'?' says he. 'Jist try me.' So I pointed to the
press, and he took oot the decanter as smert's ye like and
helped himsel'.

"He turned oot a rale nice chap in spite o' his tred, and
he gave me a' the oots and ins o't. 'I've nae luck,' he said.
'It's my first job at the hauntin', and I've made a kind o'
botch o't, though it's no' my faut. I'm a probationer; jist
on my trial, like yin o' thae UF ministers. Maybe ye think
it's easy gettin' a haunter's job; but I'm tellin' ye it's no'
that easy, and when ye get it, it's wark that tak's it oot o' ye.
There's mair gangs in for the job there than for the Ceevil
Service here, and the jobs go to competition. Ye hae to
pass an examination, and ye hae nae chance o' gettin' yin if
ye divna mak' mair nor ninety per cent o' points. Mind ye,
there's mair than jist plain ghostwark. It used to be, in the

auld days, that a haunter wad be sent to dae onything — to
rattle chains, or gie ye the clammy hand, or be a blood-
curdler. Nooadays there's half a dizzen different kinds o'
haunters. I'm a blood-curdler mysel',' and he gied a
skreich that nearly broke a' the delf on the dresser.

"'Nane o' that!' says I, no' very weel pleased; 'Ye'll hae
the neebours doon on us. Forbye, there's naething patent
aboot that sort o' skreich. Duffy the coalman could dae
better himsel'. That's no' the wye a dacent ghost should
cairry on in ony hoose whaur he's gettin' a dram.'

"'Excuse me,' he says; 'it's the dram that's ta'en my
heid. Ye see, I'm no' used to't. It's mony a day since I had
yin.'

"'Are they that strict yonder?' I asked.

"'Strict's no' the word for't! If a blood-curdler on
probation was kent to gang to his work wi' the smell o'
drink aff him, he wad lose his job': and he helped himsel'
to anither dram.

"'Weel, ye're no' blate onywye,' says I.

"'Blate! Catch me,' says he. 'I wadna need to be blate
at this tred, I'm tellin' ye. Jist you think o' the kind o'
customers we hae to dale wi'! They wad sooner see a tax-
collector comin' into their hooses than yin o' us chaps.
There's some hooses ye hae to gang to work in where it's
easy. I ken a ghost that's been fifteen years on the same
job, and gettin' fat on't. He has the name o' bein' the best
white-sheet ghost in the Depairtmen', and he's stationed
in an auld castle up aboot the Hielan's, a job he got
because he had the Gaelic. He made it sae hot for the
folk, walkin' aboot their bedrooms at a' 'oors o' the nicht,
that naebody 'll stay in the place but himsel' and an auld
deaf and dumb housekeeper. There's naething for him to
dae, so he can lie in his bed a' nicht and no' bother himsel'
aboot onything. It's a very different thing wi' anither chap
I ken — a chain-clanker in England. He has to drag ten
yairds o' heavy chain up and doon stairs every nicht; and
it's no easy job, I'm tellin' ye, wi' the folk the hoose
belang to pappin' things and shootin' at whaur they think

the soond comes frae. Oh ay! there's a great run on the best jobs. My ain ambeetion is to be in the clammy-hand brench o' the business in some quate wee place at the coast. I hae my e'e on a likely thing at Rothesay. Of course the clammy hand's no' a very nice occupation for the winter, but this is a hoose that's shut up in the winter, and I wad only hae to work it in the fine summer nichts.'

"'Hoo dae ye dae the clammy hand, Peter?' I asked him, and he just winked.

"'If I was tellin' ye that,' says he, 'ye wad be as wise as mysel'. Never you mind, MacPherson; ask me nae questions and I'll tell ye nae lees. Weel, as I was sayin', I aye had a notion o' a quate job at the coast. I couldna stand Gleska; there's such a rush aboot it, and sae mony stairs to sclim,[5] and pianos aye playin' next door. And the accent's awfu'! Gie me a nice wee country hoose whaur somebody hanged himsel', wi' roses on the wa', and dandelions in the front plot. But there's plenty o' us lookin' efter jobs o' that sort — far ower mony; and it's generally them wi' influence that gets them at the hinder-end.'

"'That's whit everybody says aboot the situations here, Peter,' says I. 'If they're nae use at their tred they talk a lot aboot influence. I'm thinkin' ye wad soon get a job at the coast if ye were fit for't.'

"He was the shortest-tempered ghost ever I seen. I had nae sooner said that than he gied anither skreich, and disappeared in a blue lowe wi' an awfu' smell o' brimstone.

"'Come oot o' that!' I says to him; 'I can see the taps o' yer gowfin' stockings'; and at that he gied a kind o' shamed lauch and was sittin' in the chair again, helpin' himsel' to anither dram.

"'I'll tell ye whit I'll dae wi' ye,' said he. 'I'll no' mind aboot Jackson at a', but I'll hing aboot your hoose for a week or a fortnight, and they'll never ken at the office. I canna think to gang into Jackson's hoose if he's a tee-totaler. Teetotalers is aye that — that — that teetotal. I wad never get sittin' doon in Jackson's to a jovial gless like this.'

"'Ye're far ower jovial for me,' says I. 'See's that decanter,' and I took it frae him. 'I'm awfu' prood to see ye, but ye better be slidin' afore her ladyship the wife comes in, or she'll put the hems on ye. She canna stand ghosts.'

"'Michty!' said he. 'Have ye a wife?'

"'The nicest wee wife in Gleska,' said I. 'And I wish to goodness she was hame, for I'm awfu' tired.'

"'Then I'm no' playin',' said the ghost. 'I'll awa' roon' and gie Jeckson a cry afore he gangs to his bed.'

"He grabbed the decanter and emptied it into the tumbler, gied ae gulp, and anither gnash to his teeth, and went awa' withoot sae much as 'thenk ye.'

"Jinnet's step was on the stair. Fine I kent it! Man, that's the smertest wee wumman!

"'There's nae livin' in this hoose wi' ghosts,' says I to her when she cam' in, and she had some grapes for me.

"'Is there no', Erchie?' she said, lookin' at me. 'My ain puir auld man!'

"'Look at that decanter,' says I; 'the rascal emptied it.'

"'Hoots! the decanter's a' richt,' says she, takin't frae the press; and as shair's onything, there wasna a drap oot o't!

"And she put me to my bed there and then."

27. *Jinnet's Christmas Shopping*

JINNET HAD money in the Savings Bank. Erchie used to chuckle when some neighbour had gone out to whom she had casually mentioned the fact and say, "That's it, Jinnet, you be braggin o' your deposits like that, and they'll be thinking I mairried ye for your fortune." But the truth was that when their savings at first were lodged in Erchie's name, they had an unfortunate way of disappearing without Jinnet's knowledge, and it was to protect himself from himself that the husband finally opened the account in the name of his wife.

The first day she went to the bank with money it was with no little trepidation. "Maybe they'll no' tak' sae much as twenty-wan pounds," she suggested; "It's a guid pickle money to hae the responsibility o'."

"Ay, and gled to get it!" he replied. "That's whit they're there for. If it was twice twenty-wan they wad mak' room for't, even if they had to shift forrit the coonter. Ye hae nae idea o' the dacency o' thae banks!"

"But whit if the bank was to burst?" said Jinnet. "Lots o' folk losses their money wi' banks burstin',[1] and hae to go on the Board[2] a' the rest o' their days."

"Burst!" laughed Erchie. "Man! ye wad think it was a kitchen biler ye were talkin' aboot. It'll no' burst wi' a' we'll put into it, I'll warrant ye."

"Will ye hae to pay them much for takin' care o't?" she asked, still dubious of these immense financial operations.

Erchie laughed till the tears ran into his tea.

"Oh, my!" said he, "but ye're the caution! It's them that pays you. If ye leave the twenty-wan pound in for a twelvemonth, they'll gie ye something like twenty-wan pound ten shillin's when ye gang to lift it."

This troubled Jinnet worse than ever. "It's rale nice o' them," said she, "but I'm no' needin' their ten shillin's; we're no' that faur doon in the warld, and it's like enough they wad jist be takin' it aff some ither puir cratur."

But eventually the money was lodged in Jinnet's name. She used to take out her bank-book and examine it once a week, to make sure, as she said, "the money was still there," a proceeding at which Ernie would wink to himself, and with difficulty restrain his laughter.

On Saturday Jinnet expressed a wish that she had some of her money to make purchases for Christmas and the New Year.

"Weel," said her husband, "whit's to hinder ye gaun to the bank and liftin' a pound or twa?"

Her face turned white at the very thought. "Me!" she cried. "I wadna ask for money at that bank if I was stervin'."

"But, bless my sowl! it's yer ain money; they canna keep ye frae gettin' it if ye want it," said her husband.

"I'm no' carin'," Jinnet protested. "I divna like to ask for't, and them maybe busy. Perhaps the puir craturs havena got it to spare the noo."

"Weel, they can jist send oot for a wee lend o't frae somebody they ken," said Erchie. "It's your money, and if ye want ony o't oot they must gie ye't; that's whit banks is for."

"Will you no' gang for the twa pound ten for me, and I'll mak' something nice and tasty for your tea the nicht?" said Jinnet coaxingly; but Erchie had his own way of teaching Jinnet self-confidence, and refused. "They wadna gie't to me withoot a lot o' palaver," he explained; "Ye'll just hae to gang yersel'. Speak nice to them, and they'll no' touch ye. There hasna been a customer murdered in a Gleska bank for years and years." He explained the process she was to follow, and she set out with great misgivings.

"Weel, hoo did ye get on?" Erchie asked her when she returned. "Ye got the money onywye — I can see by the wye yer nief's shut."

"Oh, Erchie!" she cried hysterically, and dropped into a chair. "I wad never mak' a man o' business. My hert's in a palpitation — jist fair stottin'. I peety them that has the bother o' muckle money."

"My jove!" said Erchie in alarm. "Were they no' nice to ye? If they werena nice and ceevil, I'll— I'll tak' oot every penny, and then they'll see whaur they are."

"Oh, they were as nice as they could be," Jinnet hurried to explain. "And I got the money a' richt. But oh! I was that put-aboot. Thon slippy floor aye frichtens me, and the gentlemen inside the coonter in their wee cages like Duffy's goldie — "

"Goldies — ay, that's jist whit they are," said Erchie. "It's a fine bird a goldie if ye get a guid yin; it can whustle better nor a canary."

" — like Duffy's goldie, and that rale weel put-on. Each o' them had as muckle gold and silver aboot him as wad fill a bakie.³ I nearly fented when yin o' them spoke to me awfu' Englified, and askit whit he could dae for me the day. 'Oh,' says I, 'I see ye're throng;'⁴ I'll can come back anither time,' and I was makin' for the door when he cried me back, and said he wasna that throng but that he wad be gled to dae onything he could for me. I thocht he wad gie me the money wi' a grudge when he found I wanted twa pound ten in silver, but he coonted it oot like lichtnin', and bangs it fornent⁵ me. A rale obleegin' lad he was, but no' lookin' awfu' strong; I think I'll knit him a pair o' warm socks or a muffler for his New Year."

"Ye're a rale divert, Jinnet!" said Erchie.

"I jist picked up the money withoot coontin' it and turned to gang awa'. 'Hold on, Mistress MacPherson,' he cries; 'Ye'll be as weel to coont yer siller afore ye leave the bank in case I'm cheatin' ye,' and my face got as red's the fire. 'I wadna hae the cheek to doot ye efter seein' ye coontin't yersel',' I tellt him, and cam' awa'. But I went up a close farther along the street and coonted it."

"I could bate a pound ye did," said Erchie.

And now, having got out her money, Jinnet had to go shopping. Ordinary shopping had no terrors for her; she loved to drop into Lindsay the grocer's, and discourse upon the prices of simple things to eat, and feel important when he offered to send his boy with the goods; she was quite at home in the little side-street shops where they sell trimming, and bolts of tape, and remnants of print; or the oil-and-colour shops where she was known and could spend a pleasant ten minutes' gossip over the purchase of a gallon of paraffin. But Christmas shopping was no ordinary shopping, and was entered on with almost as much apprehension as her expedition to the bank. It had to be done in big warehouses, where the attendants were utter strangers to her, and had ways frigid and unfamiliar.

"Put on your kep and come awa' doon the toon wi' me," she said to Erchie. "I hate gaun into some o' thae big shops mysel'."

"Then whit wye dae ye no' jist gang into the wee yins ye

ken?" he asked her. "If ye're feared they'll eat ye in the big
yins I wadna gang to them."

"Oh, that's a' very weel, but the wee yins havena the
turnover," she explained. "Ye get things far fresher at this
time o' the year doon the toon."

"I'll gang wi' ye, for I ken that if I didna gang they wad
tak' a fair lend o' ye," Erchie agreed at last; "But mind, I'm
no' gaun to stand lookin' in at baby-linen shop-windows or
onything o' that sort. Me bein' a public man in a kind o'
wye, it disna dae."

"I'll no' ask ye to dae onything o' the kind, ye pridefu'
auld thing ye," she promised, and off they set.

She wanted a pair of gloves for a favourite grand-
daughter, an umbrella for a sister of Erchie's, who was a
widow and poor, and something as a wedding-present for
Duffy's fiancée.

There was scarcely a drapery warehouse in Argyle Street
whose window did not attract her. Erchie never looked
into any of them, but patiently stood apart on the edge of
the pavement or walked slowly ahead.

"Come here and see this at seevenpence threefardens,"
she entreated him.

"It's fine, a rale bargain; I wad tak' that," he replied,
looking towards the window from afar off, and quite
ignorant of what she alluded to, but determined not to be
caught by any one, who knew him as waiter or beadle,
looking into a shop-window full of the most delicate
feminine mysteries of attire.

She went into the warehouse, while he walked on to the
next shop — a cutler's — and looked intently in at the
window of it, as if he were contemplating the purchase of a
costly pocket-knife with five blades, a corkscrew, and an
appliance popularly supposed to be for taking stones out of
a horse's hoof. When he was joined by Jinnet, she had
plainly begun to lose her nerve.

"I've got gloves," said she, "and a thing for Duffy's lass,
but they're naither o' them whit I was wantin'."

"Of course they're no'," said Erchie. "Ye've got a grate

consait o' yersel', if ye think a puir auld body like you can
get exactly whit ye want in yin o' them warehooses wi' the
big turnover ye aye talk aboot. Was it a peerie and a fiddle
ye wanted that made ye tak' gloves?"

"Oh! dinna bother me, Erchie; I canna help it; the
lassies that serve ye in there's that Englified and that smert
that when they havena got whit I'm wantin' I jist aye tak'
whit they can gie me."

"I've seen you in a big shop afore noo," said her
husband, "and I ken fine the wye ye aye spile yersel' wi'
them Englified smert yins. Ye gang forrit to the coonter as
if ye were gaun to ask if they had ony windows to clean, or
back-stairs to wash oot, and ye get red in the face and tak'
yer money oot o' yer pocket to show ye have it, and ye
lauch to the lassie as if ye kent her fine, and ye say, 'If you
please' to her, or, 'Oh! it's a bother to ye.' That mak's the
lassie see at yince ye're no' cless; she gets a' the mair
Englified, lettin' on to hersel' she's the Duchess o'
Montrose, and can put the like o' you in your place wi' the
least wee bit touch. That's no' the wye to dae in a shop o'
that kind. Ye should breenge up to the coonter, and cry
'Gloves!' as hard as Duffy cries 'Coals!' then sit doon
withoot askin' on a chair, and wi' a gant noo and then
watch them puttin' oot gloves by the hunderwicht in front
o' ye, and them a' in the shakers in case ye'll no' think
they're smert enough.

"Dinna be blate; that's my advice to ye. Talk Englified
yersel', and sniff wi' yer nose noo and then as if ye felt a
nesty smell in the place, and run doon the goods like dirt.
Never let your e'e rest on the folk that serve ye, unless they
happen to hae a shabby tie on or a button aff somewhere;
glower at that, and it'll mak' them uncomfortable, and — "

"Oh, that's a' richt, Erchie," said Jinnet; "ye'll hae to
come into the next shop I gang to, and show me the wye."

"No fears o' me," said Erchie promptly; "I'm tellin' ye
whit to dae, but I divna say I could dae't mysel'."

But when it came to the purchase of the umbrella he did
go into the shop with her, and she got what she thought

was a bargain, as well as the finest affability and courtesy from the gentleman who sold it.

"That's because I was wi' ye," said Erchie, when they came out.

"I daresay," she agreed; "There's aye some use for a man."

28. *A Bet on Burns*

DUFFY CAME round to Erchie's on Saturday night for the loan of a copy of Burns, which he knew the old man had on the shelves of what he called his chevalier and book-case. "I'm wantin' to learn a sang," said he, "for I'm gaun to the Haggis Club in the Mull o' Kintyre Vaults on Monday if I'm spared."

"Are ye, indeed!" said Erchie, drily. "Ye'll be takin' the new wife wi' ye?"

"No fears o' me," said Duffy. "Wha ever heard o' a wife at a Burns meetin'?"

"Oh! I divna ken onything aboot it," said Erchie; "I thocht maybe the weemen were gaun to thae things nooadays, though they didna go when I was young, and I thocht maybe you bein' sae lately mairried ye wanted to gie her a trate. It's a droll thing aboot Burns that though the weemen were sae ta'en up wi' him when he was leevin', they're no' awfu' keen on him noo that he's deid. There'll be thoosands o' men hurrayin' Burns on Monday nicht in a' pairts o' the warld, and eatin' haggis till they're no' weel, but I'll bate ye their wifes is no' there. No; their wifes is at hame mendin' their men's sox, and chairgin' the gazogene for the morn's mornin', when it'll be sair wanted. And ye're gaun to a Haggis Club, are ye? I didna ken ye were such a keen Burns hand."

"Me!" cried Duffy, "I'm jist daft for Burns. Fifty or mair o' the members tak' their coals frae me. Burns! Man, Erchie, I could gie ye Burns by the yaird — 'Dark Lochnagar,' and 'The Flooers o' the Forest,' 'We're a' Noddin','' and 'Rollin' Hame to Bonnie Scotland' —

'Rollin' hame to Bonnie Scotland,
Rollin' hame across the sea.'"
He sang the lines with gusto.

"Stop!" said Erchie, in alarm, "Stop! There's nae deafenin' in thae ceilin's, and the folk abin 'll think I'm giein' Jinnet a leatherin'. Man! I didna think ye kent sae mony o' Rabbie's sangs. It's a credit to ye. I'm shair ye divna need ony book to learn affa."

"To tell ye the rale sets o't, Erchie," said Duffy, "it's a bate. There's a chap yonder at the coal hill thrieps doon my throat Burns didna write 'Dark Lochnagar'[1] the wye I sing 't, and I want to show him 't in the book."

"Hoo much is the bate?" asked Erchie.

"Hauf-a-croon," said Duffy.

"Then sell yin o' yer horses and pye the money," said Erchie, "for ye've lost the bate. Burns had nae grudge against his countrymen. They did him nae hairm. He didna write 'Dark Lochnagar' the wye you sing it, for Burns never made his sangs wi' a saw; in fact, he never wrote 'Dark Lochnagar' at a'; it was put oot by anither firm in the same tred, ca'd Byron."

"My jove!" said Duffy," I never kent that afore!"

"There's lots o' things ye never kent," said Erchie. "Seein' ye're gaun to eat haggis on Monday nicht, ye micht tell us whit ye ken, no' aboot Burns's sangs, but aboot Burns himsel'."

"There was naething wrang wi' the chap," said Duffy, "if he just had stuck to his wark. When I'm sellin' coal I'm sellin' coal, and no' pentin' pictures. But there was Burns! If he happened to come on a moose's nest in the field when he was plewin', or see a flooer in his road when he was oot workin' at the hye, he wad stop the plew, or lay doon his rake, and tak' the efternoon aff to mak' a sang aboot the moose or the daisy."

"A', and jist wi' his least wee bit touch," said Erchie, admiringly. "He was great, that's whit he was."

"Maybe he was, but it spiled the wark; we wadna aloo that in the coal tred," said Duffy. "He didna ken what compeetition was. I've seen things in my ain tred a knacky chap could mak' a fine sang aboot if he was jist lettin' himsel' go."

"Then for mercy's sake aye keep a grip o' yersel'," said Erchie. "Mind ye hae a wife dependin' on ye!"

"And then," said Duffy, "he was a bit o' the la di-da. There's naething o' the la-di-da aboot me."

"There is not!" admitted Erchie, frankly.

"But Burns, although he was a plewman to tred, went aboot wi' a di'mond ring spilin' folks' windows. If he saw a clean pane o' gless he never lost the chance o' writin' a bit verse on't wi' his di'mond ring. It was gey chawin' to the folk the windows belanged to, but Burns never cared sae lang's he let them see he had a rale di'mond ring that wad scratch gless."

"It was the fashion at the time, Duffy," said Erchie. "Nooadays when a poet has an idea for twa lines he keeps it under the bed till it sproots into a hale poem, and then he sends it to a magazine, and buys his wife, or somebody's else's, a di'mond ring wi' whit he gets for't. Writin' on window-panes is no' the go ony langer. It's oot o' date."

"But I'm no' runnin' doon the chap," said Duffy "Only I aye thocht it was him that wrote 'Dark Lochnagar.' Are ye shair it wasna?"

Erchie nodded. "Nor 'Rollin' Hame to Bonnie Scotland' either. He was far ower busy writin' sangs aboot the Marys, and the Jeans, and the Peggys at the time to write aboot ony o' yer 'Dark Lochnagars.'"

"So he was," admitted Duffy. "Yon's a rare yin aboot Mary — 'Kind, kind, and gentle is she —

... kind is my Mary
The tender blossom on the tree
Is half sae sweet as Mary'."

"Calm yersel', Duffy," said Erchie, in dramatic alarm. "I'm no deaf."

"That was written aboot 'Hielan' Mary'," said Duffy. "He met her at Dunoon[2] the Fair Week, and I've seen her monument."

"It's yonder as nate's ye like," said Erchie. "Faith! it's you that's weel up in Burns, Duffy."

"Oh! I'm no' that faur back in my history," said Duffy, quite pleased with himself. "But I could hae sworn it was him that put thegither 'Rollin' Hame to Bonnie Scotland'; it's his style. He micht be rollin' but he aye got hame. He was a gey wild chap, Burns."

"I'm no' denyin't, Duffy," said Erchie. "But he hadna ony o' the blessin's we have in oor time to keep him tame. There was nae Free Leebrary to provide him wi' books to keep him in the hoose at nicht, nae Good Templar Lodges to help him in keepin' clear o' the horrors o' drink; and Poosy Nancy's public-hoose didna shut at ten o'clock, nor even eleeven. If Burns had thae advantages, there's nae sayin' whit he micht hae risen to; perhaps he might hae become an MP, and dee'd wi' money in the bank."

"Och! there's worse than Burns," said Duffy. "I was gey throughither mysel' when I was a young chap."

"Ah! but ye couldna hae been that awfu' bad, for ye never made ony poetry."

"I never tried," said Duffy; "I was the youngest o' nine, and I was put oot to wark early. So there wasna time for me to try and be fancy in ony wye. But a gey wild chap, Burns!"

"Maybe no' that awfu' wild," said Erchie. "Ye're aye harpin' on the wild. Burns was like a man takin' a daunder oot in a country road on a fine nicht: he kept his e'en sae much on the stars that sometimes he tripped in the sheuch. If it was the like o' you and me, Duffy, we wad be keepin' oor e'e a' the time on the road at oor feet to see if onybody hadna dropped onything, and there wad be nae fears o' us fa'in in the sheuch. Except for his habit o' makin' sangs when he micht be makin' money, Burns wasna very different frae the rest o' us. There was ae thing aboot him — he aye payed his way, and never forgot his freen's. He had a warm hert."

"Man, ye should be doon at the Mull o' Kintyre Vaults Haggis Club on Monday and propose the toast," said Duffy, admiringly.

"I'm better whaur I am," said Erchie; "the best Burns Club a man can hae 's a weel-thumbed copy o' the poems on his chevalier and book-case, and a wife that can sing 'Ye Banks and Braes' like oor Jinnet."

29. *The Prodigal's Return*

A SAILOR-MAN with a thick black beard, and all his belongings apparently on his back — for the dunnage bag[1] he carried was so poorly stuffed it could have held little more than a pair of sea-boots — went into Erchie's close one afternoon, and slowly climbed the stair. He put the bag at his feet when he came to Erchie's door with 'Mac-Pherson' on the name-plate, scratched his head, hitched his waist-belt once or twice, and seemed in a mood to turn and flee rather than to ring or knock. At last he faintly tugged the bell-pull, and leaned against the door-post with the air of one who expected he might have some parley before getting admittance.

There was a step in the lobby, and Erchie himself in his shirt-sleeves came to the door.

"We're no' for onything the day," said he. "We have a sewin'-machine already, and we're a' in the Prudential Insurance, and the staircase windows were cleaned on Setturday, and — "

"Faither," said the sailor-man, "do ye no' ken me?"

Erchie came closer and looked at the bearded face, and put his hand tremblingly upon the young man's shoulder.

"Willie!" said he. "Willie!" he repeated. "Man ye're sair needin' shavin'." He shook his son, and "O, Willie," said he, "whit'll yer mither say? I suppose if I was the rale thing mysel', I should kill the fatted calf or start the greetin'; but as shair's death we havena kept a calf in this hoose since ye left it yoursel', and I was never yin o' the greetin' kind. My goodness! Willie!"

He was so bewildered he forgot his visitor stood on the door-mat, until Willie lifted his dunnage-bag, and then he urged him into the kitchen.

"Where's — where's mother?" said the sailor.

"She micht be deid and in her grave for you," said his father; "but she's no'. She's doon at Lindsay the grocer's for a loaf. Oh, ye rogue! ye rogue! Whit 'll she say to ye? Seeven years, come the fifth o' June! Oh, ye're awfu' needin' shavin'. I hope — I hope the health's fine?"

"Fine," said Willie, and sat in a chair uneasily, like a stranger.

"And whaur in a' the warld did ye come frae?" said his father, putting the kettle on the fire. They had not even shaken hands.

"China and roond aboot there," said the son.

"China!" said his father. "And hoo did ye leave them a' in China? They're throng at the war[2] there the noo, I see. I hope ye werena hurted."

"No, nor hurted," said Willie. "I hope ye're fine yersel' — and mother?"

"Me!" said Erchie. "Jist a fair gladiator! Divna ken my ain strength, and can eat onything, jist like a connoshoor. As for yer mother, she's wonderfu'; a wee frail, but aye able to dae her turns. She'll be the gled wumman this — whit I mean to say is, ye should get a reg'lar leatherin' for your cairry-on. If I hadna my rheumatism in my shoother gey bad, I wad tak' a stick to ye. I'm pretty wild at ye, mind I'm tellin' ye. Whit dae ye think o' yersel', to gang awa' and no' write us for seeven years?"

"No' an awfu' lot," said the son.

"That's hopeful," said his father. "I'm gled ye're no' puttin' the blame on us. And I'm gled ye havena ony brass buttons on your claes."

"Brass buttons?" said Willie.

"Ay! When your mother was wearyin' to hear frae ye, I used to be tellin' her that ye were likely a mate, or a purser, or something o' that sort, and that busy in foreign pairts liftin' the tickets in the fore saloon, where the dram's cheaper and maist o' the passengers go, that ye hadna time to write. Yince I took her doon to the docks and showed

her a big ship gaun awa' to Australia, wi' the Captain on
the tap flet, ca'in a handle[3] and roarin' 'Let go that gangway!' and "Nae smokin' abaft the funnel!' and she was as
pleased as onything to see't. Ever since then she thinks o'
her son Willie as a chap wi' brass buttons ca'in a handle the
same as he was a tramway driver, and that busy he hadna
time to write. I'm gled ye havena brass buttons," concluded
Erchie, looking at his rather shabbily clothed scion. "It's
mair to your credit that ye were jist a fool and no' a rascal."

"Man, ye're jist as great a caution as ever," said Willie,
with the sincerest admiration.

"Duffy the coal-man tellt me he saw ye yince doon
aboot the Broomielaw," said Erchie. "It was three years
ago. I daursay ye were ower throng at the time to come up
and see your mither and me. It's a guid wye up here frae
the Broomielaw; it costs a penny on the skoosh car. Or
maybe it was a wet day."

Willie's face got red. "It wasna only yince I was at the
Broomielaw," he said. "I've been in Gleska four times
since I left it."

"Were ye indeed?" said his father. "Weel, weel, it was
rale considerate o' ye no' to bother your auld mither and
me. I'll wager ye werena needin' ony money."

"I was needin' money gey bad every time," said the son.
"I aye had some when I landed, but it never got past the
Broomielaw wi' me. And that's the wye I never cam near
ye. I was ashamed, as shair's death. Every time I was in the
Clyde I cam up here at nicht, or to the auld hoose afore ye
flitted, and looked at the close or went roond to the back
coort and looked at the kitchen window."

"It's a good thing I didna see ye there, or I wad maybe
hae gien ye a clourin'."[4]

"I wad hae liked it fine if ye had," said the young man.
"A clourin' was the very thing I was needin', and I kent it
mysel'. I was an awfu' fool, faither."

"That's jist whit ye were," Erchie admitted. "It's a
lingerin' disease, and that's the warst o't. I hope ye'll
maybe get ower't."

"If I didna think I had got ower't I wadna hae been here the nicht," said the son. "I'll warrant ye'll no' hae to complain o' me again."

Erchie took his hand. "Willie," said he, "gie me your thoomb on that. I ken the MacPhersons, if their mind's made up, and I think ye're auld enough noo to try your hand at sense. It'll no' hurt ye. Willie, Willie, it wasna mysel' I worried aboot thae seeven years, nor you either; for I kent fine the prodigal wad come back, if it was only to see if his faither de'ed and left him onything. The prodigal son! Awfu' needin' a shave! Your mither 'll be the prood wumman this nicht."

Before Jinnet had come back from the grocer's Erchie put his son into the parlour, so that the returned wanderer might not too abruptly confront his mother. She suspected nothing for a little, going about her ordinary offices in the kitchen till something fidgety in her husband's appearance directed her more close attention to him, and there was seen then an elation in his countenance that made her ask him what the matter was.

"Ye're awfu' joco," said she. "Are ye plannin' some baur for Duffy?"

"Not me," said Erchie. "I'm jist wearyin' for my tea. And, by the wye, Jinnet," he added, "ye micht put doon anither cup for a frien' o' mine I'm expectin' frae abroad."

"Frae abroad!" cried Jinnet, turning pale. "Ye havena heard onything o' — o' —"

"Have I no'?" said Erchie. "There's a chap in the room at this meenute that wad be awfu' like Willie if he had a clean shave."

Ten minutes later Erchie joined his wife and Willie in the room. The dunnage-bag was being emptied before Jinnet by a son who was anxious to make the most of his gifts from foreign parts, though painfully conscious of their value.

"Oh, whit braw shells!" cried his mither. "Jist the very thing I was needin' for the mantelpiece. The Carmichaels say wally dugs is no' the go noo at a'. It was rale thochtfu' o' ye to tak' them a' the wye frae abroad for me."

"And here's a song folio and a pund o' sweet tobacco for you, faither," said Willie.

Erchie took them in his hand. "Man, that's the very thing," said he. "If 'Dark Lochnagar's' in't, I'll be upside wi' Duffy."

"Whit's this?" asked Jinnet, as the sailor brought forth for her a bottle containing some dark thick fluid.

"Riga balsam — whit the sailors use for sair hands," said Willie.

"Oh, it's the very thing Erchie used to say ye wad bring back when ye cam," cried Jinnet in delight. "It'll be awfu' useful. I'm almost vext I havena onything sair aboot me the day."

"No' even a sair hert,"[5] said Erchie, and the son looked contritely at his mother.

30. *Erchie*[1]

ON SUNDAYS he is the beadle[2] of our church; at other times he waits. In his ecclesiastical character there is a solemn grandeur about his deportment that compels most of us to call him Mr MacPherson; in his secular hours, when passing the fruit, or when at the close of the repast he sweeps away the fragments of the dinner-rolls, and whisperingly expresses in your left ear a fervent hope that "ye've enjoyed your dinner," he is simply Erchie. Once I forgot, deluded a moment into a Sunday train of thought by his reverent way of laying down a bottle of Pommery as if it were a sacred volume on the pulpit book-board, and called him Mr MacPherson. He reproved me with a glance of his eye. "There's nae Mr MacPhersons here," said he; "At whit ye might call the social board I'm just Erchie. There's sae mony folks in this world don't like to hurt your feelings that if I was kent as Mr MacPherson on this kind o' job I wadna mak' enough to pay for starchin' my shirts." I suppose Mr MacPherson has been snibbing-in preachers in St. Kentigern's Kirk pulpit and then going for 10 minutes' sleep in the vestry since the Disruption, and the more privileged citizens of Glasgow during two or three generation of public dinners have experienced the kindly ministrations of Erchie, whose proud motto is 'a flet fit but a gey warm he'rt beatin' under't.' I think, however, I am the first to discover his long-pent up and precious strain of philosophy.

"This is a dreadful business about the Chief-Constable's pension," I said to him yesterday.

"Man, ay!" said Erchie. "But it has its consolations. If it hadna happened, we would never have jaloused the lichtnin'-like rapeedity wi' which Glesga's getting' sober and parteecular.[3] I mind when maist foks had the name o' takin' a bit dram whiles, but it's plain noo the thing's gane oot o' fashion. I daurna have the smell o' a glass o' sherry wine aboot mysel' (and it's rare I tak it); but I'm feart Duffy the coalman 'll write a letter to the papers sayin' I should be dragged oot before the public e'e and made a disgracefu' object o' and lose my bit benefit frae the Waiters' Society when I'm too shaunchly to carry a jeely shape withoot jaupin't ower the dish. You and me'll hae to keep gey quate they days, or else we'll be fun oot to be awfu' faur behin' the rest o' the warld in this maitter o' strict sobriety. Forty years gaun' aboot Glasga — nae wonder my feet's flet — and I've seen a wheen very respectable offeecials skliffin' at the aff-'oors o' the day on their way to a pension without ony fraca aboot it, sae lang as they did the wark they were paid for. I've noticed a great change in the last few years since the workin'-man begood to fin' oot that ither folks took a refreshment like himsel'. Public men tak' nae drink noo', but just hae to fly to cloves and rheumatic losenges when they feel yon win' aboot the he'rt.

"I aye hated the polis mysel'. When I was a halflin there was naethin' gied me greater pleesure than to hench a stane at ane o' them and bash in his sugar-awlly hat.[4] I was that young and ignorant then I never thocht hoo much

greater fun there wad be in ha'in a skelp at the head o' a'
the polis himsel'; but there's a guid deal o' the halflin aboot
a great mony auld folks ye wad hae expected to ken better,
and as they canna heave divots noo wi' ony dignity to
themselves or any chance o' hittin' anythin' smaller than
the gable o' a tenement, they fling ink. I saw Duffy, the
coalman, comin' hame stottin fu' o' public spirit on Friday,
and sittin' doon to write the *News* a holy terror o' a letter
proposing that Scott Gibson[5] tak' the Lord Provost's chair,
and put his heel doon on the hydrant-heided monster[6] o'
insobriety and corruption that he heard o' first himsel' frae
a man no' lang oot o' Barlinnie. I'm prood o' Duffy, I'm
prood to see sae mony honest, weel-daein', and I daursay
mair strictly teetotal men than him unitin' in a grand
heroic jump on the chest o' a man wha had the effrontery
to hae nine hunder pound a year, and look like earnin' it
maist o' the time he had it. There a'ething I canna thole
mysel' — it's to see ony suspeecion o' a deeviation frae the
strict path o' righteousness on the pairt o' onybody wi' twa
shillin's a week mair nor mysel'. Naebody wi the reediculous wage o' nine hunder a year should dae onything to
anger Duffy, the coalman."

"Rather a delicate position, Erchie?" I said.

"At least," said Erchie, "he should tak' care and no' be
fun' oot. You and me hasna been fun' oot yet."

"I am a great admirer of Mr Scott Gibson, Erchie," I
said.

"So am I," said Erchie. "He's a rale divert. Puir Glesga
was fair gaun to bleezes till this high-spirited young chap
gave up, in the maist noble and disinterested way, his extraordinar' profitable and arduous professional engagements,
whitever they were, and took aff his jaicket, and spat on his
hands, preparatory to jerkin' us on to the rails again. I'm
sleepin' fine and soon' noo at night. It's a' richt wi' Glesga.
So Duffy says. I'm an auld man — fifty years waitin', and
paid my taxes a' the time, and ten o' a family; a flet fit, but
a gey warm he'rt under't— and I'm prood o' Duffy. He's
the man that's doin' the maist o' the hurrahing for Scott

Gibson. His wife's lookin' efter the ree[7] while he's dampin'-down the inward flames o' revolt against a rotten magistracy wi' schooners o' beer at the Auld Blue Vaults, and whiles goin' over to George Square to say he'll be dawmned afore he'll pay the polis rates if the money's to gang to pension aff Captain Byde.[8] Duffy's polis rates come to aboot three-and-nine (includin' costs), and he has never been kent to pay them, for he's a fine-spirited man, and can spare a clock or a kist-o'-drawers, or the wife's sewing-machine if need be. I whiles tell him the only thing he's no' sparin' o' is his wind — except when he's helpin' his man wi' a rake o' coal. Duffy thinks that noo Scott-Gibson has the whup-hand, the polis 'll be abolished a'thegither, and ye'll can cairry ony sort o' weights ye like on the lorry. Is it no' just horrible to think that afore this gallant young gentleman took things in haund we wis governed in the Cooncil by a lot o' ruffians. I've seen them mysel' at mony a dinner where I waited — auld grey-heided reprobates o' the maist sordid nature that had run successful businesses o' their ain, and looked plausible enough; and sometimes ca'd me Erchie and slippit a shillin' in my han', and four or five cigars in their pouches to be gaun hame wi'. We ken noo whit they are. I'm tellt they're awfu' wild at him. He gaes yap-yapperin' awa' in the Cooncil hall sae that they canna get their naiteral sleep after luncheon.

"Ye'll hae heard," said Erchie after a pause, "that the Lord Provost[9] has invented a new scheme o' a philanthropic kind that'll maybe needcessitate his bein' returned to office for another three years to cairry it oot. He's organisin' a corps o' rale leddies o' leisure to gan roond the slums[10] in a kind o' friendly way to hae a bit crack noo and then wi' the puir folks there. It's a rale divert. The mandolin and ping-pong trade,[11] I'm tellt, is aghast at the prospect. Ruin stares it in the face. On the ither hand, there's a prospect o' a great demand for Keating's Poother,[12] and ane o' the brichtest young authors oot o' Gilmorehill is busy writin' a book o' 'Small Talk for Slummers' and

'Chippy Little Chafing-dish Suppers in Sixty Ways'. It is expected that within a week or twa efter the crusade opens ye'll can go up ony close in Glesga without the least risk to yersel' if ye cairry a club and leave yer watch and purse at home. The folks to be benefited by the scheme is, I'm tellt, makin' hurried preparations ta mak' it a success. Iron bolts are bein' pit on a' the doors, the auld-fashioned widden ane bein' coonted nae langer up to the needcessities o' the time. There's flittin's every day frae the scheduled areas, and mony o' the folk threatened hiv changed a new leaf and promised to lead a better life.

"Ah! Erchie," I said, "we shall have best solved the problem o' the slums when we have got such a garden city[13] outside Glasgow as that gentleman lecturer described the other evening."

"Where wid yo put it?" he asked, curiously. "I wis thinkin' o' Deid Slow[14] mysel'. It wad tak' a year or mair to mak' the place hame-like, though I aloo that the river in the summer-time wad gae a lang way to mak' the atmosphere naitural to folks frae Lyon Street and the Wee Doo Hill.[15] Man canna grow syboes and dahlys without workin', though, and there wad need to be a carefully thocht-out scheme o' wee pawns and shebeens in the garden ceety. Duffy says there's a time o' life when ye canna dae withoot the luxuries o' the ceety, if ye've been brocht up to them, and I daur-say he's richt. Life's a real divert, if ye look at it the richt way."

31. *Erchie is Ambitious*[1]

ERCHIE WAS butler pro tem at a dinner party given in the house of the minister of St. Kentigern's on Friday; I met him gliding home after the function, with a singularly large brown paper parcel, which all unasked for, and with quite uncalled-for candour, he said contained some "orra bits o' things he had gotten in a present." There was a distinctly perceptible odour of cold game, and, at intervals, an inexplicable gurgle of liquids. It was doubtless to distract attention from these curious manifestations that Erchie grew eloquent on public affairs.

"Dod!" said he, "there's a'e guid bit o' news this week."

"What is that?" I asked, thinking he had, perhaps, been engaged as wine hand for the united Cork-Cutters Festival.

"The war's[2] feenished. Jist gaed oot in a flaff like a' thae kin' o' things. Arteelery, horse, fit, and marines, the British Airmy's on its way hame."

"It is the first time I have heard of this."

"Oh, but it's as shair's death; I saw't wi' my ain een, and nae ither body's in the *News* the ither nicht. The hale Airmy's left Sooth Africa, and practicin' the maneepulation o' the bull's-e'e lantern and the oilskin tippet, and seeking to come to Gleska to tak' up the job o' Chief-Constable. I had a notion o' tryin for the place mysel', but there's little chance for Erchie MacPherson, a plain-soled waiter, against Cornels and Majors and Adjutants and the like.

"Whenever Kitchener got word o' Captain Byde's place at a thoosand bein' vacant, he ca'd a' his men thegether, and put it to them if their easy-gaun ke-hoi way wi' De Wet was to staund in the road o' a chance like this. I hinna heard yet whether on the heid o' that they jist smashed a' the Boers to the fore, or spread bird-lime on the veldt and catched them by the feet, or cam' away leavin' the puir craturs wi' nae mair chance o' getting khaki clothes[3] and convoy ammunition and rations; but the thing's shair that they're comin' hame onway. I'm tellt that some o' the best runners in the Airmy, either on horse or fit, is seekin' the thoosand pounds: 'I h'e been informed,' writes ane o' them, 'that steadiness is a signkenone.[4] I'm that steady mysel', on soul and conscience, that if ye put me on a gude horse, I couldna fa' aff't. My wecht is 19½ stane, and I'm a vegetarian.' 'If it's dignity ye want, as is reported,' says anither ane – a Captain o' Macafferty's Flyin' Horse – 'I'm worth mair nor double the salary. I've gone through the hale o' this unfortunate champagne withoot buttonin' on my ain breeks mair nor aince, and I defy onybody to say

they saw me in the very thick o' battle withoot my eye-
gless.' 'Dear Lord Chisholm,' says anither o' the brave
fellows, 'what ye plainly need at this juncture is discipleen;
I've been in a' the guard-rooms o' a' the British garrison
toons, and got sentenced to CB a hundred times, and
though I'm only a Corporal I ken as muckle aboot disci-
pline as'll dae me my lifetime.'

"Oh, aye! the Airmy's rushin' hame; it's a bonny sicht!
I'm no' grudgin' the chaps the chance o' the job, but as I
tellt ye I had an e'e on't mysel'. I could dae't wi' the least
wee bit touch. Perhaps ye think I hinna the qualifications. I
may hae a flet fit, but I've a gey warm he'rt, mind ye. And
I've had a wheen o' advantages nane o' the Airmy lads can
brag o'. Efter forty years beadlin' in a Gleska kirk, and
forty years haundin' roon the wine at Gleska dinner
pairties, its naiteral I should hae an instinct for the maist
delicate kind o' polis wark, which, I tak' it, is to ken yer
rogue when ye see him. Some o' the maist namely em-
bezzlers o' the age hiz come under my observation baith in
kirk and ha'. I've noticed that they wiz aye aften the maist
scrupulous in the ordinances i' the kirk and couldna tak'
Christian elements at the dinner table, but had to be
coothered up wi' gazagone stuff and Appolinaris and
wersh drinks o' that kind. As for the Polis Force itsel', wha
kens't better nor auld Erchie? Mony's the sergeant I've
slipped oot a wing o' a chicken or a daud o' pasty to, no' to
speak o' some human comfort o' a stimulatin' kin' for a
caul winter's nicht. Efter a', there's no' sae muckle differ
atween a polisman and a plain Christian body. It disna need
neither a Field Marshal nor an auld frien' o' his ain to tak'
command o' Constable Cawmill, C062; the main thing,
sae faur as I can see, is to get a gentleman that'll look fairly
weel in the job, shave at least yince a week, be at haund
when the peyday comes roon', put the fear o' death on a'
ranks if need be, and send back ony wine-cases that come
to him frae admirin' frien's i' the licencin' tred. The mistake that's been made mair nor aince in Gleska has been to
put a cairt-horse to dae the work o' a thoroughbred.

"Ay man, it's a rale divert the way the Bylies is palaverin' awa' wi' the licensin' tred. Mr Chisholm, I see, is awfu' pit aboot that the public-hooses shouldna be shut at ten in the Broomielaw and Crosshill, and vext to the he'rt to see hoo the 'schooner'[6] o' beer fluctuates in quantity and sae defrauds the workin' man oot o' his leegitimate measure, sae he wants the 'schooner' abolished a'thegither. Noo I think the schooner is a democratic measure that has its origin in human nature. Furthermair, that it's a measure distinctly moral and temperate in its influence. If ye were a gentleman that took beer yoursel' in thae low haunts o' vice Duffy the coalman and the likes o' him spends his money in, ye wad hae noticed that there's a state o' body when the ordinar' three-bawbee gless jist fa's short by hauf-an-inch o' satisfyin' a raisonable drouth. Indeed, there's some tuppeny glesses in the mair genteel places that fluctuate sae muckle in size ye canna tell when ye order a gless whether ye're gaun to hae luck and get a drink, or jist a damp spot on the palate, and if the uncertainty o' the schooner is the thing that's wrang wi't, whit aboot the uncertainty o' the ordinar' gless? Weel, as I was sayin', a plain gless aften leaves ye where ye were, and drives ye to hae anither, or maybe jist a quart an' be dune wi't. Ye'll hae noticed that there's naething said aboot the powny o' beer. Na, na; the powny's that sma' it's likely the Lord Provost never heard o't.

"An' they're gaun to shut the Broomielaw hooses at ten?[7] It's a rale divert! Ye'll can get as much drink as ye like till eleven on the up side o' Argyle Street, but no' a sup efter ten on the doon. All I can say is they'll hae to run the sparky-caurs[8] a guid dale slower in Argyle Street aboot ten o'clock, or else there'll be a lot o' sudden deaths amang the croods crossin't. But maybe ye'll hae to produce a receipt for yer rent and yer birth certificate to show ye belang to the richt end o' the toon afore ye'll get served anywhere up till eleeven. I wadna won'er at onything. The scheme's a dastardly blow at the interests o' Geordie Geddes;[9] he'll hae to shift the Humane Society hoose and boats and life-buoys up to the Kelvin noo. As for Crosshill, it doesna maiter muckle; I've aye had my doots if there wiz ony such place, though I see the name pented on the tramway caurs."

Erchie's parcel gurgled more eloquently than ever as he 'skliffed' along the pavement. He eyed me apprehensively, and went on rapidly.

"They're doin' reel weel in the Toon Cooncil the noo. Oh, aye! Awfu' weel! They hae a man ower the medical department and anither ane ower the sanitary depairtment that canna 'gree wi' each ither, and instead o' makin them 'gree or gae away and lift their graith,[10] they're gaun to mak' a new job, and app'int a man abin' the twa o' them. It's rale divert! And they've gotten seventy-five thoosand pounds for new hooses to tak' the place o' the yins they're gaun to knock doon in the slums this summer. They're pittin' up some o' thae new hooses already on the ootside o' the toon, seeven meeits' walk frae a caur terminus, and expectin' the people frae the back-lands o' Carrick Street and the like to daunder oot there for the sake o' their healths. Man is't likely?"

32. *Erchie on Windfalls*[1]

"I NOTICED," said Erchie to me this morning, "that there wiz a great wheen o' the folk in oor kirk yesterday[2] wiz neither takin' their naitural sleep nor listenin' to the minister. Fine I kent whit kept them waukened thinkin' — it wiz this money of Gutta-perka[3] Dick's. It's been the only thocht in Gleska this week back. Naebody's been speakin' aboot ony ither thing, and even Jinnet, my wife, that's generally fu' o' the maist divertin' bits o' news regairdin' the Queen's spring bunnets, model mithers in 'Home Chat,' or the cairry-on o' the folk doon the stair, 'll no' gie me peace to read my *News* wi' her yatterin' aboot the hunder thoosand pounds Mr Dick left his wark-people. Sometimes she mak's 't a hunder thoosan', sometimes she mak's 't a hunder million — it's a' ane to Jinnet! Ae thing she's shair o' is that it's a guid pickle money onyway. It's wonnerfu' the effeck an affair like this hiz on people; ye wad hardly believe't, but Jinnet, that's generally gey prood o' me beein' a waiter an' haein' the beadlin' to dae, hiz done naethin' but ca' doon my tred since ever she heard aboot Dick's money. She thinks I made a great mistake when I begood wark that I didna gae into Dick's employ; and it's nae use for me to tell her that there wiz nae Dick when I started; she hauds to the extraordinar' opeenion that I threw awa' a great chance somewye. 'The very labourers in the dacent man's warks is getting a thoosan',' she says, 'and it's gey chawin' for me to be sittin' here even-on darnin' sox.' Puir Jinnet! I micht hae mony a waur wife, but she hisna ony heid for figures.

"I've jist been thinkin' mysel' since the thing wiz reported in the paper, that nae maitter whit a very rich man does wi' his money it's boun' to dae a lot o' hairm. That's the wye I've taken care mysel' never to be a millionaire. I get up at a' 'oors o' the mornin' to think whit I can dae to save mysel' frae an end like that, and the factor o' the hoose I'm in is, I've nae doot, up jist as early wonderin' hoo he can help me. I wonder hoo mony o' the folks that come into this money 'll mak' a guid use o't? There's wheens o' them 'll buy their wives pianos, or tak' bigger hooses, and sae introduce into contented hooseholds the spirit o' ambeetion and display. Ye micht as weel bring a pair o' Bostock's teegurs[4] into yer hoose and try to train them up to ha'e a likin' for parridge and soor mulk. But it's no' only them that gets the money left them this wye that's in danger o' bein' hairmed; there's hairm in't for them that gets naething. My wife Jinnet is jist like a great mony ither folks in Gleska the day; she never thocht she wiz that bad aff either until she begood to think hoo lucky ithers wiz to get sae muckle money for daein' naethin'. And Duffy the coalman tells me he's gaun to pit a bawbee on the bag o' coal jist oot o' spite. When ye hear folk say it wiz rale thochtfu' and nice o' Mr Dick to leave his workers a' this money, ye can be shair that a' the time they're grudgin' that any ither body but themselves should fin' money sae easy. It mak's them discontended wi' their ain lot, and som o' them 'll think efter this that the best wye to get money is to get it withoot workin' for't. Of course there's nae doot in the warld it is the best wye; the like o' you and me kens that brawly; but it's no' guid for some folks' healths to be told o't."

"What do you think of the Tobacco War?"[5] I asked Erchie.

"I havena pit my mind very much into't yet," said he, "for the price o' thick blue's no' affected in ony wye. But I think, seein' the war hiz only to dae wi' cigarettes, it'll be for the guid o' the country in the long run."

"I do not follow, Erchie."

"O! it's simple enough; the Americans and the British cigarette folks is no' trying' to cut each ither's throats jist for the fun o' the thing, and the ane that wins 'll like enough pit up the price o' cigarettes till the time 'll come when ye'll be switherin' whether ye'll can buy yersel' a half-an-ounce o' cigarettes or a pair o' new buits. Whit's wrang wi' cigarettes the noo is that they're ower cheap. I daursay we wad ha'e bate the Boers a year or twa syne if we hadna spoiled oor constitutions wi' takin' the reek o' paper an' hay into oor insides an' pittin't oot again. That's bad for the lungs; its spiles a man's runnin', and the Boers, that disnae smoke cigarettes, can run like stour. I whiles think oor sodgers is wastin' their time on the veldt gaitherin' cigarette photographs and makin' them into competition albums. It's a sair day for the British Airmy when its generals hiz their photographs inside threepenny boxes o' cigarettes as if they wiz play-actresses in tights. I'm no' carin' sae much aboot the Tobacco War, but I'm feared it's jist the beginnin' o' a war in a' treds, and if the thing gaes muckle further we'll be ha'ein' American waiters and beadles in Gleska, and puir Erchie MacPherson 'll ha'e to speak through his nose[6] and wear a billygoat beard afore he'll get a job. It'll be a shoe war next, and the cobblin' tred o' this country 'll be done wi't. Haulf the folk ye meet nooadays is wearin' American buits, and braggin' o't as if it wiz a sign of great genteelity."

"So we are to have no municipal banquet, Erchie, on Coronation Day?"[7]

"No, so I see! Man, it's a rale divert. My views on the thing bein' o' needcessity professional, as ye micht ca' it, they're maybe a wee partial, but I think the Cooncil's gettin' awfu' feart. Ye wad notice in the papers that there's some strong public feelin' in favour o' ha'ein' a banquet, as weel as the conversaziones, so as to gie Lord Provost Chisholm a chance o' proposin' the King's health. Ye'll maybe be wonderin' wha's expressin' this great public feelin' and I'll tell if ye dinna let it gae ony further. It's jist me and some ither waiters, with some assistance frae ane or twa o' the men that made Gleska when the polis wisna watchin', and are in a chronic state of indisjeestion through municipal banquets. It's quite true that the Lord Provost may drink the King's health at ane o' the conversaziones, and do't in kola, as he wad dae't in ony case; but clerit cup's a gey wersh drink to get up a herty response on."

"The idea of a gigantic garden party in the parks is abandoned, however?"

"It wad need to be, my certy! But I canna say the Cooncil hiz a guid idea o' whit wad maist entertain the ceetizens on Coronation Day. We'll no' be all asked to the conversaziones, and some of us are by the age for dancin' in the parks. Faith, I'm no a dancer mysel'; I have flet feet, but a gey warm he'rt. There should be processions."

"Processions, Erchie?"

"Aye, processions, Jist fancy hoo fine it would be te ha'e a' the Volunteers and the Freemasons and the Orangemen and the Guid Templars — a' the Boys Brigades, as weel as a' the treds, marchin' up and doon a' the streets! Everybody wad hae a chance o' seein' something then. But I wad ha'e the Magistrates and Toon Cooncil at the very heid o' the procession, wi' their haund-me-doons on. They're no' hauf enough in the public e'e. That pairt o' the procession could be brawly combined wi' a display frae the Zoo.

Instead o' driving in cairriages, the Lord Provost could lead the van on an elephant, and the Magistrates could follow up on dromedaries, and droll cratures o' that sort. The common riff-raff o' oor representatives might follow in band waggons, wavin' flags and lookin' as smert as they could. It wad be a guid idea to ha'e the notabilities ticketed in plain letters, so that the public could hurrah or itherwise as they thought fit. A display o' that sort wad greatly cheer the ratepayers, and mak' them see that sae faur as looks gang there's no' muckle difference atween the folk ye read aboot in the papers and ordinar' men."

"They're gaun to ha'e the weans in the parks that day. I hope they ken whit they're gaun to dae wi' them! It's mair nor they did when they had them there afore. They merched the puir wee smouts frae the schools to the parks, and stood them in raws and gi'ed them a bun and a big drink o' water, and then merched them hame again. Whiles Bylie W. F. Anderson galloped bye on his horse and looked fine and braw, but that wiz nae great diversion for weans. I hope they'll dae something better nor that for them this time. They should engage somebody that kens the business o' entertainment, and let him get up a scheme for ha'ein' Punch and Judy shows, jugglers, baunds, and things o' that kind. There's to be dancing, but I'm feared the young folks o' Gleska hiz lost skill o' dancin' on the gress or on the gravel; if the tastes o' maist o' them wiz to be considered in the respect o' dancin' they wad rather ha'e a night's clog-walloping at a close-mouth or daein' the glide in La-va[8] alang the flair o' the Moolder's Hall."[9]

"Well, Erchie, those who get to the conversaziones will have ample opportunities for dancing after more genteel fashions."

"Dancin'! Na, na; there's nae dancin' at municipal conversaziones. Ye jist walk roon' at them winnerin' whit wye ye came at a', and wishin' ye wiz on the commytee, and whiles makin' a breenge for the buffet, whaur the gress[10] sandwiches and the claret-cup wiz for nearly fower meenites efter the doors opened. The only advantage o' bein' at a conversazione that ever I seed is that ye can kind o' cast it up to yer frien's that they werna asked. For a' the rest that's in it, it's nae greater sport than gaen doon the watter on the Fusilier[11] on a Fair Seterday."

33. *Erchie on the Cars*[1]

"Man!" said Erchie, 'when I see the wye Gleska's gettin' on, I'm that gled I'm to the fore.'

"Yes," I admitted, "we do bound a bit. But what do you particularly refer to?"

"Oh, it's jist everything; we're gettin' on that fast, ye canna see oor feet for stour. Look at thae skoosh caurs.[2] I was on yin o' the kin' o' room-and-kitchen[3] yins that gangs to Springburn the ither day, and we jinked that many weans on the road ye wad think we were playin' tig. It wasna like that in the auld days, when yon tartan buses was on. It was a gey lang, weary hurl up to Springburn then, and faith it wad need to be, for it cost threepence. The only time ye saw them gaun sort o' gleg[4] oot that wye wi' the tartan buses was when they was trying to bate a Sichthill funeral. And noo I'm tellt the very last horse the Tramway Depairtment had is sellt aff. They should hae stuffed it, and had it ready for the openin' o' the new museum, or made a present o't to Edinburgh, where I'm hearin' they're sae faur back the caurs is pu'd alang the street wi' string.[5] Puir craturs! I daursay they couldna gie them the overheid wire in Edinburgh for fear the folks that hings oot their washin's on the bowsprits o' their windows in the High Street[6] wad want to dry their claes on the wires.

"Oh, aye! we're gettin' on fine, but ye canna please everybody. From some o' the letters I read aboot the Gleska caur service, I can see there's folk that wadna be content if the caurs took them up to their ain stair-heid, and pit them oot on the bass[7] for a bawbee. A chap the ither day wrote Mr Young to see if beecyclists couldna be aloo'ed to pit their machines on the front platform. He was faur ower easy pleased; he didna want to tak' it inside wi' him, and he didna seem to expect a patent dry sate for't; all he wanted was to mak' the job mair interestin' for the man that ca's the haundle[8] in front, and has so little to do the noo wi' jinkin' the weans. Then there's someyin else seekin' to get a' the blin' folk carried for naething. When Duffy the coal-man heard o' this at first he said it wad be grand for Setterday nichts, but he didna understaun' the thing richt. Whit's botherin' me, supposin' the blin' folk is to get free on the caurs, is hoo will the gaird ken whither ye're blin' or no' if ye shut yer e'en and gang forrit wi' a dug in the yae haund and a tinnie in the ither? Will ye hae to tak' an oculist wi' ye to swear that ye're bona-fide? When the blin' folk get for naethin', whit wye should the lame folk no' get for naething too? They're no' sae weel able to walk as the ithers."

"I should not wonder, Erchie, if the philanthropy of the Corporation made them include the deaf and dumb, and so down the whole scale of physical and mental infirmities, until the tram-cars are fitted as ambulance waggons, and a special free line runs out to Gartnavel."

"Oh! I wadna wonder. It's a rale divert. I see they're startin' a store noo in George Square and the Bylie's pittin' on a brattie.[9] We'll be gettin' tokens for a dividend when we gang to pay the gas. 'Will ye co-operate wi' us?' says the Bylie to the puir restaurant-keeper that wants to get his leecence renewed and get hame to his tea wi' the wife. 'Whit for!' says the restaurant man. 'Oh, jist for the fun o' the thing,' says the Bylie. 'It's a new game. A' ye ha'e to dae is to open your mouth and shut your e'en, and if onything hurts ye that coonts wan to me. Try't. A' we ask ye is jist to co-operate.' 'Ha'e ye a dictionary handy?' says the puir restaurant man that hisna much schoolin' except whit he got at the nicht-schule, an' aye thocht afore this that co-operation was a different kind o' thin' a' thigither. 'A dictionary!' says the Bylie. 'Nane o' your hunker-slidin' wi' us; come awa' bonny and co-operate.' 'Whit wye am I to do't?' asks the restaurant man. 'If ye divna say at once ye'll co-operate wi' us,' says the Bylie, 'I'll gie ye a dunt in the lug.' And so the puir restaurant man says he'll dae onything for peace, and gangs awa' dazed."

"I fancy, Erchie, a little co-operation among the Magistrates themselves would obviate a lot of the senseless tearing up of streets by various departments."

"I daursay, but that's no' whit we're playing the noo. It's ane o' the hallowed tradeetions o' the Municeepal Buildin's[10] that an offeecial shouldna ken the name o' the man in the office on the ither side o' the lobby. I used to wait at the Cooncil luncheon afore they took on barmaids to dae the wark, and I learned a lot o' curious things aboot municeepal affairs then. There's no' an offeecial in the place wad be seen speakin' to his neighbour, unless it was to tell him to be shair and shut the door efter him. It's a stately auld exclusiveness that runs frae tap to bottom o' the hale hypothie. When the Toon-Clerk needs to hae ony dealin's wi' the Polis Clerk, though they work on the same stairheid, he hiz to go aboot it in due and ancient form. First he sends for a clerk. 'Is there a Polis Clerk in Gleska nooadays?' he says, says the Toon-Clerk. 'I mind there used to be yin,' says the clerk and gaes oot and asks yin o' the women washin' oot the marble stair. He comes back and tells the Toon-Clerk that he is creditably informed that such an offeecial as a Polis Clerk still exists. Then they look up the 1887 Directory for the address, and when the Toon-Clerk finds oot that the Polis Clerk is jist through the wa' from him, he says it's a gey small world efter a', and sits and writes a letter to him. When the Polis Clerk gets the letter through the post next day he says 'Marwick? Marwick? Wha the bleezes is Marwick, Toon-Clerk? Somebody must hae sent this for a valenteen.'

"We had a swatch o' this fine auld style the ither day when the Medical Officer and the Sanitary Depairtment was tried to be introduced to each ither for the first time. Ye maun understaun' the Magistrates keep a' their snash for the public; they canna be too ceevil wi' their ain offeecials. So when smallpox and plague and a' they kin' o'

things wis making life sae interesting for us, the
Magistrates went to the Sanitary Depairtment and says,
'Oh, jist when you're ready; there's nae hurry. If you're
ower busy the day we'll come back again. Whit we called
aboot was this Medical Officer's Depairtment o' oors.
Ye'll maybe no' ha'e heard o't, for it's only started sixty or
seeventy years ago. Dae ye no' think, without pittin'
yoursel' aboot a great dale, ye could sometimes ha'e a bit
crack wi' the man at the heid o't? The Sanitary Depairtment said it had naething to dae wi' the Medical Officer
nor onybody else, but wad gang on spreadin' chloride o'
lime and smeekin' oot hooses the wye it had aye done,
withoot onybody's interference. The Magistrates said they
was sorry they spoke, and went awa' sair vexed, and so a
guid job was lost for the callan they was thinkin' o'
engaging' to show the Medical Officer the wye to the
Sanitary Depairtment, and the Sanitary Officer the wye to
the Medical Officer's office ance a week or so.

"When the Gas Depairtment or the Statute Labour
Depairtment, or ony ither o' thae depairtments that's for
tearin' the streets up, gangs to dae onything in front o' the
Fire Brigade, they tak' oil-skins and sou-westers wi' them
for fear the Fire Brigade 'll no' be pleased and maybe scoot
watter on them. I think mysel' the Fire Brigade should
scoot every time they see a man wi' a pick an' shovel; it
wad be for the guid o' the ceety. Duffy aften says to me
'They're taking' up Buchanan Street again, Erchie; it's the
third time this efternin; whit does it mean?' I never let on
to the like o' Duffy but I ken fine whit it means. When the
electric light folks hae a job on, the Gas folk staund up a
close watchin' till the job's done and the last bit o' causey's
laid down, and then whustle up their gang, and gar them
tak' up a' the causey again to lay a new pipe. If they're
done afore dark, a hasty meetin' o' the Statute Labour
Committee will be ca'd and hauf-an-'oor after that they'll
be pittin' doon junks of jarrah wud wi' the licht o' hauf-a-
dizzen fizzin' lamps. It wad be ower much to expect co-
operation a' the time frae the folks in George Square, but

whiles I think they micht a' meet thegither at a soirée, or somethin' o' that nature, yince a year, and swap conversation lozenges."

34. *Erchie on the Volunteers*[1]

THERE IS nothing military about Erchie's appearance, and I never suspected him of having any association with the defensive forces of the country till I came upon him, on Saturday, shrewdly reviewing a rifle battalion on its march out. "The season's begood again," said he, "and man! it'll be an anxious time for mithers." "Oh! wars are not perpetual, Erchie," I said; "The period of anxiety is over." "I wizna thinkin' aboot the war at a'," he said, "but the pipeclye and the gun in the hoose. They're givin' medals nooadays to a' the auld Volunteers, but if they did the richt thing they wad gie them to the Volunteers' wifes and guidsisters, that did maist o' the wark cleanin' the belts and the spats, and lost their sleep at nicht for thinkin' the gun wad gae aff itsel' under the bed. When I jined the auld 105th[2] first, the wife widnae let me tak' my gun in ower the doorstep till I stuck a cork in the neb o't."

"Then you, too, have served your Queen and country, Erchie?"

"Hiv I no' jist? I hiv a flet fit noo, but a gey warm hert for the sodgerin'! I wiz in nane o' your stripe-doon-the-leg-and-the-wee-pom-pom-in-the-kep corpses, but in the Gleska Hielanders. Things is changed a lot since then, and dod! they tak' ye at yer word noo afore ye can say knife if ye swear to serve your country. In the days we jined the 105th it wiz done maistly for the sake o' gettin' photygraphed in the uniform. But we wiz alloo'ed to be a grand body o' men. There wizna a reel fit in the regiment, and every ane o' us had braw side whiskers. I think mysel' they hae spiled the guns noo wi' makin' them ower fancy; in oor time ye jist chowed the end aff the cattridge, and rammed in the poother and ball by the neb o' her. If ye had mind, ye took oot the ram-rod afore ye fired. It took a while to load, but it wiz a' gey simple, and there wizna that mony deaths efter a'. The dreel³ wiz different too. Ye cried 'hooray' like onything at the chairge, and spiled yer bits wi' sittin' on the heel to shoot.

"I had to leave the 105th mysel' because I couldna sit mair nor twa meenits on my heel the richt wye, and wiz aye forgettin' to keep my gun at the port when I wiz in the rear rank and we got the word to chairge baignets. They tried makin' me a pioneer, and gied me a hatchet to cairry, but the wife spiled it breakin' sticks and chappin' coals, and I wiz reprimanded by the sergeant, big Mackendrick, that had a leg on him like yin o' the pillars o' the Royal Exchange.⁴ But there's far mair fandangles aboot volunteerin' nooadays. Ye hae to be able to touch you taes without lettin' them see ye bendin' your knees, and when ye gang to the camps noo ye get weel pyed for't but ye daurna get drunk. There's velocipedes noo, and chaps wi' broon bandages on their legs to ride them. The airmy's a' chynged, and whiles I'm gled I'm oot o't."

The rearguard of the 6th VB of the — swung past us very juvenile, indeed. Erchie cast after them the scrutinising glance of the ancient, but not unkindly.

"Puir wee smouts!" said he. "They're a rale divert."

"You'll be very busy next month with Coronation festivities, Erchie," I said as we walked up the street.

"Haud yer tongue! I'm feart to think o't. That's the warst o' oor tred, that it a' comes on ye wi' a breenge like the taxes."

"We are an intensely loyal and patriotic people, Erchie."

"We are that! Jinnet — that's the wife, ye ken — hinna had time to darn a sock for three or fower weeks back; she's that thrang readin' aboot the King's breeks."

"Breeks, Erchie?"

"Aye. The papers is fu' o' them. It tells ye there that His Maist Gracious Majesty buys eight suits o' claes at a time, and never wears a pair o' breeks oftener nor fower times. The suits cost him eight pounds each (no' allooin' for twa

hip-pouches and a spacial pouch for handin' his fit-rule),
and I hae been calculatin' that the tailors 'll hae to be
pittin' the tape ower him yince a fortnight at the very least.
If the King wiz as kittly[5] as me, he wad dee lauchin'. Ye
wad think wi' a' thae breeks thrown aff no' the least wee bit
tashed money could be saved, though there's naebody in
His Majesty's ain family to tak' them up, if they made
them doon for the Prince o' Wales' wee yins. But no; it's
etiquette, accordin' to the papers, that ye daurna cut doon
a royal pair o' breeks. They're pit awa' on shelves, and
that's the wye, I daursay, His Majesty hiz sae mony hooses
up and doon the country.

"It mun be a gey sair trauchle bein' a King, efter a';
when you're no shiftin' your claes you're bein' photygraphed. Jinnet tells me His Majesty hiz to pit on a
different kind o' bunnet every 'oor o' the day, and never
wears ane the second time, but jist bangs it doon on the
lobby table when he gaes in, and a man comes efter him
wi' a basket getherin' up. I daursay the valets 'll mak' a bit
extra to their wages by palmin' aff some o' the auld anes on
His Majesty if he dinna hae them punched wi' ane o' thae
tramway-caur contrivances. A pair o' boots is no' soled
and heeled in Sandringham[6] mair nor yince, and His
Majesty canna be bothered windin' his watch, so he jist lets
it run doon, and then sends a boy oot to buy a new yin."

"These are wonderful details of Royal domesticity,
Archie."

"They are that. Jinnet his them a' by he'rt, puir buddy.
She disna ken that I ken the man that invents them."

"Who is the gifted party?"

"Oh, jist the same lad that adverteezed the Encyclopedia Menoges.[7] Ye mind o' him? He made it oot that if ye
didna buy your weans an Encyclopedia, ye should be taken
up by the Society for Prevention o' Cruelty to Children.
Were ye no' gettin' your sleep? Buy an Encyclopedia —
sixpence the noo and the rest before the Fair — and read
Vol. II. Whit'll we dae wi' oor sons? Turn to page 961, vol.
5 and read the article on Pirates. Are ye thinkin' o' gettin'

married? Buy the Encyclopedia in fifteen volumes and a chevalier and book-case; it's a' the furniture ye need in the up-to-date home. Ay; it's the same man that's writin' the bit stories aboot the King.

"But the Coronation's guid for tred, I daursay; it's gaun to be guid for the waiter, onywye. Clachnacudden and a' thae wee places is gaun to hae cake and wine banquets, and let aff squeebs and hae bonfires. Everything's Coronation noo. Jinnet tells me Duffy the coalman's wife hiz a new Coronation-red goon, and her in a room-and-kitchen hoose, wi' no Venetian blinds on the windows! The printworks is workin' the nicht-shift makin' flags and Union Jack hankies that'll maybe be popular, and mak' a difference on the Gleska pavements; and I saw a man in the Coocaddens on Friday nicht sellin' Coronation oranges. 'Fine Coronation Seville oranges,' says he; 'Nane o' your foreign trash.'"

"Let us hope the war will be ended before the great days come off, Erchie."

"Ended! Dod! is't on yet? I hivna seen a paper for an 'oor or two, and the last yin I saw said peace wiz assured, and Delarey[8] wiz furnishin' a but-an'-ben in Pretoria, a sure sign it wiz a' settled."

"But that was an hour or two ago, Erchie, as you say."

35. *Erchie on Things in General*[1]

ON SATURDAY, in his beadle capacity, Erchie spends the afternoon dusting out the vestry and pulpit of St. Kentigern's Kirk. At intervals he comes out and smokes a contemplative pipe on the steps of the side door, and silently surveys the passing world, or exchanges gems of philosophy with the cab-drivers on the rank. I found him thus engaged on Saturday. "I aye come oot for my bit draw," said he, alluding to the pipe. "I think it's no' richt to smoke in the kirk, even on a Setturday. It's a kin' o' sacrileege, and I wiz brocht up gey strict. Na, na; I wadna think o't. Besides the minister hiz a gey sherp nose, and he micht fin' oot."

"Settled down in the new house[2] all right now, Erchie?"

"Oh! aye. Kin' o'. Jinnet hiz had twa skirmishes aboot the key o' the washin'-house, and the kitchen nock's near gaun again; it jist wants the last wee bit touch noo and then; and the folk up the stair abin us is gettin' into the wye o' chappin' at the door on a Sunday and askin' can Mrs MacPherson oblige wi' a wee tate sulphur and whisky no' mixed, for their ween hiz the hives. I tellt them last Sunday we had naethin' bit beer in the hoose, and they said that wad jist ha'e to dae. But the change o' air hizna done mysel' muckle guid; I'm jist better o' the influenza."[3]

"Influenza, Erchie? That's bad. I thought you looked a little off colour."

"Aff colour! Man, its's nae wonder. I went to my bed on a Monday quite hale and hearty, able to read the smallest print withoot the help o' specs, and a' my faculties aboot me, and on Tuesday mornin' Jinnet had oot the Prudential book,[4] and sat for an 'oor or twa countin' up whether it wiz £12. 10s. and £15 she wad get when I had slipt awa'; no' that the cratur wanted me oot o' the wye, but that she wad be vexed no' to ha'e a nice, genteel funeral. Had ye ever the influenza? It's nae divert, I'll assure ye! When I wakened on the Tuesday I tried to mind if I had been havin' ony argyment wi' onybody the nicht afore, and wha it wiz that carried me hame. I had the toothache in every jynt in my body, and the black squad frae Fairfield yaird[5] wiz inside my heid rivettin' whiles, and whiles ha'ein' a bit holiday and gaun roon' and roon' carryin' flags and cryin' 'Hurrah for Dan!' Twa or three o' the Corporation Depairtments wiz at their auld games puttin' doon pipes and liftin' them again every five minutes a' alang the spine o' my back. First the Water Depairtment gang wad come an' lift a' the causey and put in twa or three lengths o' pipe weel-bedded in hot Archangel tar. When that wiz done, the Electric Light[6] gang wad come wi' dynamite and blast it up again, and a' the time Jinnet yonder coontin' up the Prudential book. I can tell ye I wiz gey vexed for mysel'. A man that comes through the influenza comes through a gey hard fight; the Government should gie medals for't."

"It's this weather Erchie. Did you ever see such a summer?"

"No' since the winter Loch Lomon' wiz bearin'. It's fair redeeculous. I could mak' a better summer mysel' wi' a wee waterin'-can and a pair o' bellows. The only man that agrees wi't is Duffy the coalman; he says it's rale nice, bracin', healthy weather, and he's aye pittin' another bawbee on the bag of coal. If it lasts this week, Mrs Duffy'll be able to tak' a' her weans wi' her to the Coronation in London. There's some says it's ae thing that accoonts for this kin' o' weather, and some say it's the ither thing; but Duffy mak's oot it's the vulcanite explosions awa' in thae foreign places. 'A' the heat's gettin' oot at the ither end,' he says. 'There'll be nae mair straw bashers and nae mair growth in this country,' he says, 'till they sowder a new lid on Mount Peleo and put a tea-cosy ower the tap o't. It's them and their science that's done the hale thing,' says Duffy. 'They werena content wi' sixpenny telegraphs o' the guid, auld-fashioned kind,' says he, 'but they maun be caperin' awa' wi' yins withoot wires, drawin' a' the substance oot o' the atmospheric air and playin' Auld Horney wi' the weather.'[7] That's Duffy's wye o't. But there's folk I meet that's quite pleased to think they ha'e been preevileged to see sic a miraculous summer. Ten years efter this, if they're spared, they'll be braggin' about eighteen ninety-twa, the record bad year, jist as if they had invented it themselves."

"The only two bright spots in the year, so far, are the Peace and the Coronation, Erchie."

"The Peace," said Erchie. "Man, aye! I put oot a wee bit flag mysel', but, so far, it hizna made ony difference on the price o' beef. Am I no' thrang readin' aboot the Boers surrenderin'? 'Gather roon', boys,' says Kitchener[8] to them, and him winkin' at his under-generals; 'gather in, boys; there's a letter from hame.' 'Wha's it from?' says De Wet, wi' his face washed for the first time in three years and a new dicky on. 'It's from King Edward,' says Kitchener, tryin' hard no' to hit him a bash in the ear jist for auld spite. 'His Majesty sends his best respects,' says Kitchener, 'and is prood o' ye a'. Hurry up wi' them guns, like nice lads, and I'll mak' two speeches.' The Boers pack oot a' the roosty auld guns and fling them at Kitchener's feet, till he looks like a man in a broker's store, and when that's done they get their tea. When the Boers hiz had their tea, Kitchener staun's up on a soap-box, and says, 'Gentlemen, and fellow-rate payers, ye're the only frien's I ha'e in this world. I liked ye frae the very first, and the mair I say o' ye the mair I respected ye. Ye're no' beauty to look at, but ye mak' a nice, interestin' fight, and my he'rt went oot to every yin o' ye when I wiz drivin' ye up against the block-hooses. Noo, we're a' Jock Tamson's bairns, and the penny stamp 'll be sold at twelve for a shillin' frae Cape Town to Pretoria. God save the King!'

"The Boers cheer like onything, and sing a verse o' 'Dolly Grey', wi' the Tommies, only in a different key, for the Boer has nae ear for music. Then Botha mak's a speech in reply, and says he's prood to belang to the British Empire, and 'll dae the best he can to merit this confidence and regaird. 'It's been a' a mistake,' says Botha. 'If we had kent ye were sae fond o' us, we wad hiv come in mair nor a year ago, and brocht jugs wi' us. The British sodger is a gallant man, and kens fine when he's no' bate.' 'Don't mention it,' says Kitchener, and passes Botha his cigarette case. 'I'm that gled,' says Botha, 'I'm a British subject noo; I'll can sleep soond at nicht.' Then De Wet staun's up wi' a Coronation button preened on his waistcoat, and says his great grandfaither on his mither's side wiz a MacDougall, and that he himsel' never saw a map o' Britain withoot sheddin' tears o' joy and happiness. 'Excuse me,' says he, 'if I didna call in to see ye a' during the last year or twa, and seemed hurried and discourteous in my movements; the fact is I wiz ordered a lot o' horseback exercise by my medical adviser, and frequent changes o' air suited my complaint. Noo that we're brithers I'm willin' to go to the

Coronation at the expense o' the country, and show the folks there the wye a plain Boer man that couldna translate a line o' Homer to sae his life eluded the unsleepin' vigilance o' the hale British Airmy, and wore oot seven pairs o' 'lastic-sided boots and nine pairs of courderoy ridin' breeks in daen't. 'We'll see aboot that the morn,' says Kitchener; 'In the meantime, tak' the key-note from me, and a' jine in 'Auld Lang Syne." The Britons and the Boers a' staund in a ring on the veldt at that, with their haunds jined, and sing 'Auld Lang Syne,' the Boers daein' as naitural as onything, and no' kennin' the words, jist the very wye we dae at hame in Scotland.

"Oh, aye, it's a grand thing peace, as ony merried man'll tell ye. Twa years ago, the chaps that sends the things to the newspapers couldna find words bad enough to describe the treachery and bloodthirstiness and cowardice o' the Boers. The mair he bate us, the mair o' a blackguard he wiz; but noo that we hiv bate him, he hiz become the boldest, bravest, maist honourable foeman every cocked a gun. Maybe he picked up a' thae virtues between the times he wiz jinkin' us roond the barbed wire fences.[9] Onywye, the Boer and Tommy is noo swapping socks on the veldt like brithers born, and trying to dae each ither in the bargain; and the war correspondents is cablin' hame poems describin' the love which thae twa hae for ane anither noo, and the only folks that's vext the row's a' by is the Irish."

36. *Erchie at the Water Trip*[1]

THERE WAS a very poor attendance at St. Kentigern fore-noon[2] service yesterday, possibly because most of the wives in our part of the city are at present at the coast with the children and under these circumstances the masculine collar-stud is singularly hard to find on a Sunday morning. I was coming out at the tail-end of the congregation when my eye caught a solemn portentous wink from the beadle.

It is a vulgar liberty Erchie, the waiter, would never dream of indulging in, but not to be counted for presumption in Mr MacPherson, the church officer. It was an indication that he had something of importance to communicate, so I loitered in a convenient side street till he came out and was privileged with his company part of my way home.

"A thin house to-day, Mr MacPherson," I said.

"Faith, ye may well say't," said he. "And a gey thin sermon to be upsides wi't. Maist o' oor customers 'll be doon aboot Craidendoran and Cove and them places, that gled it's raining, because they'll no' can gang oot to the kirks there and spoil their shove-ons."

"Chiffons,[3] Erch— Mr MacPherson?"

"Oh, well, maybe that's it; I'm no scholar. Chiffons by name and shove-ons by nature."

He put a hand into his coat breast pocket, gingerly produced something wrapped carefully in a scrap of newspaper and formally presented me with the same. It was a large cigar. (Flor de Grandiose); I identified the Town Council brand.

"Ah! Erch— Mr MacPherson; this speaks of civic junkettings. You have been officially at the gorgeings of Bailies. I accept the votive offering with thanks and no scruples, being a consistent payer of police and other rates."

"I wiz at the Water Trip," said Erchie, "and I thocht ye micht like to ken something aboot it. I hear ye're puttin' bits in the papers[4] whiles aboot me. Oh, it disna maitter, no offence, it's a' the go nooadays to get your name in the paper, and it's daein' me nae harm. Indeed, I daursay I michtna hae been tae'n to the Water Trip[5] if they hadna seen aboot me in the papers, and kent frae that I wiz a judeecious hand for onything like a ploy."

"So you have been officiating at the luncheons and dinners of the Council on their Highland tour? That is interesting. Tell me all about it."

"Is it for the papers?" asked Erchie, cautiously.

"Well, perhaps."

"Oh, then," said he, "ye can say it's changed days wi' the Water Inspection.[6] It used to be a gey expensive kind o' picnic, but noo that economy's the rage it puts me in mind o' the auld carters' trip, only withoot the flit bauns. We started on Thursday, between fifty and sixty o' us, maist o' us takin' the caurs oot the length o' Maryhill, and every man paying his ain wheck. Bylie Paton nodded his heid at the guard o' the yin I wiz in to let him ken it was a'right, and we wiz, as ye micht say, on the committee, but the man took naethin' aff. From Maryhill, efter a call in at Antoni Ferranini's Rale Original where the conveners and sub-conveners had Broon Robin, we begood the walk to Aberfoyle. It's a gey dreich road, let me tell ye, and some o' us no very able. The Lord Provost ran maist o' the wye, keepin' his e'en on the sheuchs and plantin's for fear the Wee B.B. micht be watchin' –"

"The Wee B.B., Mr MacPherson?"

"Aye; that's the bonnie Wee Bounding Boy — Scott Gibson; whit did ye think it meant? Weel, as I wiz sayin', the Lord Provost kept his e'en on the sheuchs and the taps o' the trees for fear the cratur wiz watchin' him, but he got the length o' Aberfoyle withoot seein' onything suspeecious. 'I'm Dr Chisholm though ye michtna think it,' says he to the innkeeper, efter takin' a gless o' limejuice on draught, 'and the hale jingbang o' the Gleska Toon Cooncil's on the road there efter me.'

"'I kent fine it wad come to this at the hinder-end,' says the innkeeper; 'ye canna hide here.'

"'Wha's talkin' aboot hidin'?' says his Lordship; 'We're a' here thegither on the Water Inspection.'

"Wi' that the innkeeper whistles into a kahcotchy tube, 'Jeck, look alive, and pit two hunder bottles o' Pommery on ice, and knock the heid aff a cask of brandy.'

"'Na! na!' says Dr Sam, gey quick; 'nane o' that; there's maybe somebody lookin'. Jist mak' it a bottle o' herb beer and a biscuit and cheese.'

"'If Glesca's doon to that,' says the innkeeper, 'I'll hiv to hae my money forehaunded.'

"The rest o' us wiz late o' reachin' the Clachan, for we saw whit some o' us took to be the Wee B.B. keeking behind a dyke, and we went five miles oot o' the straucht road, and happened to come on a place that kept coos and didna ken the Glesca measure for milk. When we got to the Clachan Inn every man got his biscuit and cheese and bottle o' herb beer, and the Cooncil officer stood bye wi' his red coat on tickin' aff the names in a penny diary, and makin' a carefu' note o' a' the expenses. Mr Battersby wanted a roll sandwich, and a Committee o' Ways and Means sat on't — no' on the sandwich, I mean, but on the subjeck — and decided that a roll sandwich wiz not a needceesity o' life within the strick meaning' o' the Act. Efter that, we inspected the water works."

"An arduous task, I am assured, Mr MacPherson."

"Ye may weel say't. It wiz a dry day to walk sae faur in, and it fair hurt your een to look at sae much cauld water. And it's no' like bein' doon at the Lairgs or Rothesay, for there's neither dulse nor cockles. When we were done wi' that pairt o' oor business, we got a lift in some hay-cairts the length o' Callander. In the auld days o' the water trip, I'm tellt that by the time the Cooncillors reached Callander they didna ken whether they were gaun to the inspection o' the works or comin' hame frae't, but it wasna that wye on Thursday; when we got to the Dreadnought Hotel the folks in't took us for Christian Endeavourers,[7] and said they had no park to let for games.

"'Wha's wantin' your parks?' says the Lord Provost, gey huffy. 'Whit can ye dae us a nice meat tea for?' The innkeeper looked at some o' the Bylies, and said there wiz a No. 1 meat tea and a No. 2 meat tea — the first boys' size, the second three times the size and highly popular wi' gowfers. We had the No. 2 meat tea, and spent the rest o' the nicht makin' speeches as hard as onythin' to keep us frae gettin' hungry afore bed-time.

"We went to bed at half-past nine, efter lookin' under a' the beds to see if the wee B.B. wasna hidin'. I pit my bits under my heid, for I had mind o' hearin' a lot o' stories o' the high jinks that used to be common on thae occasions; but I micht ha'e saved mysel' the trouble — naebody wad ha'e touched them. When it cam' to payin' the bill in the mornin' afore we left, a' them that wiz cyclists produced their tickets and claimed twa-and-a-hauf per cent. discoont. I'm thinkin' the inn didna mak' much aff oor visit unless it wiz by sellin' the empty milk-bottles left in the bedrooms."

"All this does not suggest a very Aldermanic outing, Mr MacPherson, nor do I see where your excellent services as a waiter came in."

Erchie winked again.

"You're wantin't for the papers," said he. "Weel, that's a kind o' offeecial accoont o' the proceedin's. Never you let dab. We're bound to baffle the wee B.B. somewye."

"This cigar is excellent; it is not a Christian Endeavourer's cigar, Erch— Mr MacPherson. This is a brand which must have been singularly out of keeping with the Brown Robin, stone ginger, 'brut', and No. 2 large size high tea."

The face of my beadle-waiter was corrugated by a most eloquent smile.

"Say naethin'!" said he.

"Clearly, Glasgow Corporation has entered upon a period of plain living and high thinking," said I.

"Oh, aye! it's a rale divert," said Erchie. "There's to be nae min-mous in George Square efter this. The wee B.B.'s thrang writin' oot a book o' 'Good Mainners for Muneecipal Meetin's; by One That Does His Best!' 'My Lord Provost, I say, you there,' says he himsel', when he's daein' his best, 'nane o' yer hunker-slidin', but pay attention when I ask ye this — Hoo mony cups o' tea was drunk by the Bylies at Glengyle Cottage last month?' The Lord Provost stands shakin' in his shoon, and says it's a maitter he'll inquire into. 'Coward!' says the B.B. 'Don't you try, you there, to burke[8] the honest investigations o' the only honest man ever to set foot among this gang o' robbers and resurrectionists.' 'Please, I'm no' burking onything,' says the puir Lord Provost, nearly greetin'.' 'Do you call me a liar, you there, whit's-your-name?' cries the B.B., and looks up to the gallery to see if there's onybody there frae Springburn to see hoo fine he's gettin' on. Springburn may weel be prood o' its wee B.B."

37. *Erchie on the Coronation*[1]

MY WORTHY friend the waiter was on duty at the 'light lunch' with which Glasgow Corporation celebrated Our Gracious Majesty's Coronation[2] on Saturday. The menu was a triumph of art, a circumstance which of itself made me suspicious when I took my seat at the table, for I observed that the enterprise and expenditure of many public banquests often exhaust themselves upon the printed bill-of-fare, and that beautifully-executed photographic embellishments upon the same generally mean that the meal is to be more arty than hearty. Erchie confirmed my worst surmises. "Dinna let onything slip past ye," he whispered over my shoulder as he handed me my soup; "or ye'll ha'e a gey sair hert and an awfu' drouth on ye by the time they come to the toasts, and for them I'll see that ye get a guid carafe o' water fornent ye, seein me and you's auld freends."

"Why! what's the matter, Erchie?" I asked. "Because his Lordship and the Bounding Boy are virtuous, are there to be no more cakes and ale?"[3]

"I dinna ken onything aboot cakes and ale," said Erchie; "but ye shouldna ca' them doon, for ye'll maybe be gled o' them afore nicht. This is whit they ca' a 'light lunch', but whit huz yins in the tred ca' a fine-froth-and-a-daunder-roond-dinner. Watch me when I come roond wi' the Chateau Lafitte and the Bollinger '95. Ye'll find that the Chateau Lafitte'll be gey noo-and-then, and that when I froth up the champagne so as to mak' a thimble-fu' look like fair wastry, I aye tak' a daunder doon Buchanan Street and up by Dobbie's Loan[4] afore ye see me comin' back wi' a second helpin'."

Alas for us! Erchie's gloomy vaticinations were quite fulfilled, which was more than we were ourselves, but then

the subsequent orations were so fine that they made up for
the fine-froth-and-a-daunder-roond nature of the
banquet. I confess it was with regret I found myself compelled to drink Long Life to the King in a glass of unadul-
terated Chateau Loch Katrine.[5] Otherwise I was charmed.
"A notable and representative gathering," I whispered to
Erchie at the coffee. "Man, is't no'?" said he. "This is no'
the men that made Gleska when the polis wisna lookin';
they'll be awa' up in London, like enough, or at hame
greasin' their boots for gaun to the grouse shootin', but
everybody else is here that I dinna ken. Weel! weel! Jist let
them tak' it! It serves them richt for ha'ein' a dinner on a
Seterday and keepin' me frae gettin' to clean oot my
vestry." Erchie's vestry was doubtless cleaned out for him
on Saturday by his wife Jinnet, for I came on him late in
the evening looking at the illumination of the Municipal
Buildings from a coign of vantage beside the Scott Monument. "Man! it's no' bad," he said; "It pits ye in mind o' the
Bungalow[6] last year and it aye mak's wark for somebody.

"It's a prood nicht this for Gleska," he went on.
"Thoosands o' big ping-pong balls lichted up and hingin'
ower Renfield Street, and hale three skoosh caurs a'
covered ower wi' lamps and loaded to the mast-heid wi'
brass bauns gaun breengin' up and doon the toon. There's
as mony folk oot watchin' them as if it wiz the King passin'
himsel', and ye daurna venture the length o' Sauchiehall
Street withoot the risk o' ha'ein' your pocket picked in four
places. Jist to mak' it the mair divertin' the Bylies in the
polis coorts this mornin' let aff a' the folks brought afore
them. 'If I had jaloused that,' says Duffy to me, 'I wad
never hae been hame last nicht.' 'This is a great and never-
to-be-forgotten day,' says the Bylies, when the drunks and
disorderlies wiz brocht up, 'and jist to mak' ye keep mind
o't we'll let ye aff withoot ony sentence. Awa' hame, like
guid weans, and wash your faces, and if ye hae ony flags
aboot ye hing them oot at the windows.' I hear that some
of the 'cute, auld haunds wanted to borrow enough money
frae the Bylies to pay for takin' their Sunday claes oot the

pawn in honour o' the occasion. Man, it's wonderfu' the universal interest and pride o' the nation in this great and glorious event.

"We had a flag or two oot oorselves. I'm no' saying I wad hae ta'en the trouble, but Jinnet was fair set on't to be upsides wi' the Duffys. Mrs Duffy was makin' cretonne and turkey red flags for a week past, and braggin' aboot it a' ower the street, and Jinnet made oot we had to dae something, so I was sent trauchlin' roon the wee pipe-clye shops lookin' for Scottish standards. Oh! aye! it had to be Scottish standards or naethin'. Ye maun ken, Jinnet's a rale patriot ever since she saw yon chap they ca' Theodore Napier wi' the kilts,[7] and had an awfu' notion o' the pattern o' his hose. But it seems the Germans is no' makin' Scottish standards. I could get ony ither kin' o' flag ye could mention — Union Jecks, and Irish herps, and yon four-quartered chapes where the greed o' the English gies them hauf-a-dizzen lions for puir auld Scotland's yin. 'Whit I was tellt to get particular,' says I to the last shop I went into, 'was Scottish standards.' 'Whit kin' o' flag's that?' says the man that kept the shop — a man Campbell that had two sons at the front. 'Yon yellow yin wi' the red lion staggerin' hame,' says I. 'Man,' says he, 'I canna mind o' ever seein' that,' says he. 'But I can put ye in thae nice wee tastey Union Jecks at tuppence a piece, and whit mair do ye want?'"

"I took the Union Jecks hame, and Jinnet tacked them on the claes-poles when she found we couldna dae ony better, and ye could see them quite plain if ye put your heid back faur enough and looked up at them. Duffy put twa flags on his lorry, and stuck paper roses on a' the knobs o' his horse, and then put a bawbee extra on the bag o' coals to pay for the decorations. He's a great republican, Duffy, aboot the time o' the year the rent and taxes is to be paid, and reads *Reynolds's Newspaper*[8] and *Modern Society* on Sundays. 'I dinna believe it's the King they hae in the procession at a',' says he, 'but a man dressed up to look like him,' and then he tells me aboot whit he ca's the 'flag incident' oot at Celtic Park the day the neegar troops wiz there. There wiz a Scottish flag on the top o' the pole, accordin' to Duffy, and daein' weel enough, and the Irish flag, of course, wiz there tae, for whit could ye expect ony better at Parkhead? and as mony Union Jecks as wad carpet a room. Up comes the Cornal o' the neegurs, and when he sees the Scottish flag he wiz awfu' angry, and sclimbed the pole and tore it doon wi' his ain haunds. 'Nane o' yer foreign trash here,' says he. At least that's the wye Duffy tells the story, and that seems to be the kin' o' notion of the wee B.B.

"I didna see the Colonial troops mysel'," went on Erchie, "but I see plenty o' oor ain khaki lads in the Yeomanry gaun aboot the streets thae days. The toon's fair hootchin' wi' them. I'm tellt that maist o' them jist got oot the length o' Cape Toon, and wiz turned hame frae there because the war wiz over. It'll be them, I daursay, that gang aboot wi' the fifteen pair o' spurs on their heels and the catstails roon' their hats. Man, whit rare slops[9] they wad mak'! I'm that prood I'm Scotch when I see them, sae finc-lookin' and weel-pit-on an' awfu' weel pleased wi' themsel's; but there's an' auld soger up oor close has ta'en to his bed on accont o' them. He's an auld Forty-twa man, and auld-fashioned ye ken, and never saw rale sogers afore, wi' cats-tails on their hats and mufflers roond their necks and their boots no' brushed. 'The British Airmy's a' to bleezes,' he says."

"Old soldiers have been saying that for a hundred years, Erchie."

"I daursay," said Erchie. "The concate o' mankind's a rale divert."

38. *Erchie on the Preachers*[1]

A MAN is not twenty years beadle of a church without forming some decided opinions regarding the clergy, and Erchie claims that he is "as guid a judge o' a sermon, and can tak' the size o' a minister as wael's ony half-dizzen kirk-sessions." He can adduce reasons for his sagacity. "Ye see," says he, "I've had a' the advantages, wi' me bein' a waiter as weel's a beadle. You're no able to judge whit kin' o' man a minister is till ye see him at a dinner he hisna onything to pay for. I mind I used to be awfu' feart o' the ministers, when I was a halflin callant,[2] and I wad hide up a close if I saw yin comin' alang the street, in case he wad maybe get his e'e on me and mak' me guid. In thae days I didna want to be guid, but just middlin', for it was the time I was gaun to the jiggin' — that's the dancin', ye ken. I thocht if I was awfu' guid I wad lose mony a tare[3] that never did onybody ony hairm, and if I wasna' that bad but jist middlin' I wadna vex my mither. I wisna twelve-months at the beadlin' when I fun' oot that ministers, frae the dugcollar doon, were awfu' like ither folk, and I havena been sair feart for ony o' them since that.

"There's oor ain yin," proceeded my worthy old friend, with a gesture indicating the soaring steeple of St. Kentigern Church, in which he officiates; "There's oor ain yin, the Doctor. Mony a baur[4] him and me hiz in the vestry that I canna but hae a wee bit lauch aboot to mysel' when he's in the pulpit. Sae weel we micht, for I'm thinkin' it's my ringin o' the bell that brings the folks to the kirk as much as his sermons, though I'll no' deny he can gie a rouser whiles. Oh, ay! I've heard a' the maist noted preachers, and at the hinder-end I think oor ain yin's as guid as ony, and he's nae trouble at a' to get on wi' in the beadlin' line. But I doot he's auld-fashioned nooadays, for his name's never in ony o' the newspapers. 'Doctor,' I says to him sometimes, when him and me's ha'ein' a palaver, 'can you and me no' bring them oot better in the forenoon?'

He'll gie a bit lauch at that, and say, 'Whit wad ye suggest, Mr MacPherson?' 'Oh!' I says, 'could ye no' come oot wi' a wee bit book or a pamphlet, or somethin' o' the kin' makin' oot that hell's no' that bad, and that on that accoont it should be spelled wi' yin "l" and a sma' "h."' 'Man, I doot that's no' drastic enough, Mr MacPherson,' he says; 'There's faur ower muckle competition alang that line.'

"'Weel, then,' I says at that, 'could ye no try your haund at a 'Marryin'-the-landlady's-dochter' sermon in the wee Fergus style only gie'n't in the forenoon instead o' the evenin'?' 'Man!' says he, 'I'm a puir comic, and couldna dae that sort o' thing unless I had my face blackened and had the haud o' a tambourine!' 'Oh me! Doctor,' says I, 'ye're a dour yin in your ain wye, but we'll no' be bate yet. Could ye no' slip in a kin' o' altar wi' can'les on't, clap on a wee skull-kep on your heid, and gang bobbin' aboot wi' your back to the congregation.'⁵ 'I'm feart they wadna like that, Mr MacPherson,' says the Doctor, scandaleesed-like; 'It's gaun ower close on the Babylonian Wumman!' 'Hoots!' says I, 'hauf o' them wad never notice; they wad be soond sleepin' onywye. I dinna see that there's onything for't, then, but takin' the opposite wye o't, and gaun stravaigin' roond the country like Mr Primmer, singin' 'Boyne Water'⁶ in a' the kirks. It's plain that naebody'll ever hear much aboot ye, or see your name in the papers, if ye're jist a plain, ordinary auld-fashioned minister than minds his ain business, and gangs plouterin' aboot his ain parishioners, no' hip-hurrahin' at onything. If it wis me, Doctor,' says I, 'I wad send the choir through the toon on a lorry afore the forenoon and evenin' service, singin' hymns an' wavin' a flag wi' "St Kentigern Kirk — The Auld Original; Plain Thoughts for the Workin'-Man; Fancy Religions for the Genteel" printed on't in gold letters.'

"But there's nae use argy-bargyin' wi' the Doctor. I'm thinkin' his day's bye for ony exploits o' that sort, and me an' him'll hae to wauchle awa' at St Kentigern the wye we've been daein' for the last twenty years. It's gey chawin' when ye see the kin' o' craturs that's ha'ein' their names in the papers every ither day. There's Mr Primmer, he hiz nae mair delivery than mysel', and if he contented himsel' wi' preachin' the cardinal doctrines o' oor faith in his ain kirk, and gaun tae funerals, and christenin' weans, and speirin' for a' the auld ill folk in his pairish, his name wadna be kent ootside Dunfermline. But that disna suit Jacob; he maun gang roond the country, as I said already, keekin' into a' the kirks, and wakenin' up dacent folk jist when they're doverin' ower[7] in the middle o' the sermon. It's no' fair horney;[8] hoo wad he like it himsel'? I wis awfu' pleased the ither day to see the wye the Dundee Sheriff gi'ed him his kale through the reek.[9] 'Put me in jyle,' cried Jacob. 'I'm prepared for seven days o' scone and watter!' 'I'm no' saynt, but scone and watter wad be guid enough for ye,' said the Sheriff — a gey pawky yin — 'but I'm no' gaun tae hae oor nice, quate, Christian jyles spoiled; awa' hame wi' ye, and be a guid man.' 'I insist on gaun tae the jyle,' cried Jacob. 'Do ye?' said the Sheriff; 'Then let me tell ye that ye'll no' get gaun; that wad be lettin' the Dunfermline folk aff far ower easy; awa' back to them.'

"And then there's the Boy Preacher that's drawin' croods to the Ceety Hall, the same as if he was the late Signor Foli or a Burns Nicht wi' the Select Choir. He's an American, I'm tellt. It's a great age for the Americans; they're batin' us a' alang the line wi' their tinned salmon, and their champed oat-meal wi' the patent names, and their buits that disna need ony blecknin'. This wee callan' they tell me's rale guid — a fair spell-binder. A spell-binder's a man, ye ken, that holds ye spell-bound. Some folk does it wi' patent medicines, like Sequah; ithers dae't wi' the trance medium sort of thing, like Baldwin, the man that wiz in Hengler's Circus[10] some years syne, and could tell ye where your Uncle Jamie was that followed the sea, and got lost in the Bush in 1873. This young spell-binder's just sixteen years o' age, and he can preach jist like rale. If he had been thirty years o' age nobody wad hae paid ony heed, but the oddity o' the thing drags thoosands to hear the laddie. He has a tutor wi' him, they say, to learn him his geography and the multiplication table between the whiles he's preachin'. It's a grand wye o' plunkin' the school; I wish I had thocht o't mysel' when I was a laddie. And the divert is that them that gangs to hear him think they never heard onything half sae fine afore. It's jist champed meal, as I said — champed meal, or milled meal, or flaked meal, or whitever ye ca't. Plain, auld-fashioned folk like mysel's quite content to mak' oor parridge wi' guid auld Edinburgh oats, but for the novelty o't the younger generation maun hae their parridge made oot o' the champed stuff ye buy a guid deal dearer in fancy pasteboard boxes.

"Nae doot it's a' for oor guid, I'm no' sayin'. But I'm an auld man, and I mind o' mony anither novelty in the preachin' line that did his best for puir ould Gleska, and made a few roar sae lood ye wad think Duke Street Jyle might shut up its doors, the ceety was gaun to be that guid for ever efter. There was Richard Weaver, in the days o' the Auld Wynd, and there was Moody and Sankey[11] and there was oor auld frien' Nero, the black that was sae popular wi' the leddies. Aye! aye! man, they were the days! They worked a great change on us at the time, and noo whaur are we? Some o' us are in Peterhead, and a wheen mair o' us wad be there if we wer'na pretty slippy. And I havena noticed ony great difference on Gleska wi' a' that's come and gane. Jinnet canna leave her bleachin' oot at nicht in the back court, and I hae still to button my jaicket ower my watch-chain when I gae into the Central Station on a Setturday night."

"Oh, Erchie!" I said, "I fear you are a cynical, unregenerate, old rogue."

"Tuts!" says he, "I'm jist auld Erchie, wi' a flet fit, but a warm he'rt, no' that bad, nor no' that guid, but jist middlin' like the majority o' us."

39. *Erchie on the Modern Young Man*[1]

"NOW THAT the winter is coming on, you're likely to be pretty busy in your profession, Erchie," I said to my old friend on Saturday.

"Man, no' sae thrang as ye wad think, either," said he. "The waitin' tred's no' whit it used to be, and nooadays we ha'e to dae a' sorts o' jobs that we wadna think o' takin' in haund when I begood. Yesterday I had to pit on my swallow-tail to haund roond seed-cake and Madeery wine at an auld-fashioned funeral. Waitin', to tell ye the truth, is the last job for an auld man. The Germans ha'e spiled the business in Scotland, and whit's the German waiter, efter a', wi' his three languages and his nae skliff to his feet? But it's no' the foreign competion sae muckle as the smokin' concert and that kin' o' shove-by for the suppers we used to ha'e twenty years syne. The man that invented the smokin' concert was an enemy o' the race; I wadna be astonished if it was ane o' thae heid-stane hewers oot on the road to the Necropolis. If there had been ony smokin' concerts when I was young, I wadna ha'e a flet fit the day, but my shouthers wad be gey sair wi' flyin'.

"It's death onywye ye look at it. There's the cigarettes, and the drink, and the entertainment. The last's the maist fatal o' the hale rickmatick. The smokin' concert sang is eatin' its wye into the hert o' the nation, for a' the time you and me and young Duffy and the rest o' us is sitting afore a pint o' lager beer, reekin' like Tennant's lum, and singing, 'We're boys o' the bulldug breed,' the American is workin' the nicht shift wi' the aid of the lucigen licht, and no' as much as takin' time to spit. The only man I hae ony respect for at a smoking concert is the lad that dunts the dominoes.[2] If he gets the music he can follow't no' that bad, but he wad jist as soon vamp. 'Whit key wad ye like it on?' he says to the puir cratur that gaun to perform. 'Ony key that's no' ower high nor ower low,' says the singer, and clears his throat, and starts 'Queen o' the Earth' in the rale Gallowgait. Oh, ay! 'Queen o' the Earth.' It's a' that kin' o' sang noo, and nae chance at a' for the auld Poet's Box ballads, seeing ye can buy rale music aff the street for tuppence.

"'A skipper am I, all danger scornin',' sings the wee draper wi' the wife that'll bang him ower the heid wi' the besom[3] when he gets hame, and naebody lauchs, though it's well enough kent he has that puir a stomach for the water that he gets sea-sick if he pits a fit on the Jamaica Brig. 'Oh, Genevieve, sweet Genevieve, thou are my only guidin' star,' sings the man wi' the red nose, that disna need ony guidin' star sae lang as he has that in front o' him. 'This is life,' says a' the halflins sittin' roond, wi' their double-breisted collars on, and their chubb-keys chained to their gallowses for fear they'll ha'e their pockets picked o' a' that's in them. There's a guid deal in the name. Thirty years syne se didna ha'e ony smokin' concerts, but jist sat in a beershop drinkin' and smokin' and singin'. It was the same thing, though no' coonted respectable, and the free-and-easy wasna ony better, but a 'smokin' concert' is thocht quite genteel, and they ha'e them even in connection wi' some o' the kirks.

"The Boer war was nearly lost in the smokin' concerts and the tea rooms o' Gleska. The strength o' the nation is bein' sapped wi' the buttered pancake at a penny and the threepenny lairge cup o' tea. Into thae resorts, where the furniture is that fly ye canna tell whether it's a chair ye sit doon on or the case o' an auld piano, flock the bricht young souls o' the country, to trifle wi' the affections o' a lassie that stabs hersel' to the hert every noo and then wi' a keelivine pencil,[4] and answers by the name o' Millie. 'Twa cheese-cakes, a scone and marmalade, and one Russian,' says the hope of Britain's future, feelin' in his pouch for the five-pence and the presentation toothpick frae the *Lord o' the Isles*.[5] As the fair young cratur' extracts the keelivine pencil frae her person, and jots doon the damnin' evidence o' man's gluttony, she mak's up her mind she'll no mairry, and small blame to her. But ye see a man canna bang his sax-pences at smokin' concerts and pay for chops for his dinner.

"The only thing the young man of the day has is an auld-standin' accoont wi' his tailor, twa cigarette cases, and a lodger's vote.[6] I'm creditably informed that in the College and Partick Diveesions o' the ceety, there's 500 000 young men payin' fifteen shillin's a week for a room wi' a piano in't, and every mortal yin o' them has three names at the very least. They're a' Frederick Wilfred Macdougalls, or Dunsmore Macallister Macgees, or George Duff-Duffs. They're that keen on politeecks that they hardly tak' time to feenish their tea at nicht afore they hurry doon to the Empire or the Britannia[7] to cry hip-hurrah when ony o' the serio-comics mentions the name o' Lord Kitchener. 'Whit's the size o' the hoose ye bide in?' asks the Sheriff. 'A room and kitchen,' says the eager young politeecian that has a stake in the country and seventeen shillin's a week (wi' a petty cash-box) in some-body's office. 'Whose hoose is it?' 'My aunty's,' says the brave young chap, awfu' vext he forgot to tak' the paper aff his cuffs afore he left the office. 'Hoo mony live in't?' 'Me and six others,' says the claimant, 'and I pay fifteen shillin's a week for board.' 'Claim aloo'ed, and God help your aunty,' says the Sheriff. 'Next!'"

"Ah! but you do the young man of the day injustice Erchie," I protested. "Remember we have been young ourselves. On the other hand, just think of the thousands of lads who go to the evening classes to finish there a better education than you or I got in our time."

"Imph! Maybe aye! They're awfu' preevileged, nae doot, but it's as braid's it's lang; if there's mair o' them in the nicht schools, there's mair o' them at the street corners. We're a' Jock Tamson's bairns. But I begood by speakin' o' my tred, and the wye smokin' concerts and the like had spiled it. I wish I had been onythin' but a waiter."

"If you could be born again," said I, laughing, "who would you like to be?"

"My wife Jinnet's second man," said my old friend, promptly, and looked as if he meant it.

40. *Erchie on Hooliganism*[1]

"I SEE the Edinburgh students are at their auld capers," said Erchie the other day. "They opened the winter session wi' a display o' that fine auld idiotcy that's coonted awfu' comical in colleges. I was never at the college mysel' except since I was handin' roon' beer at a smoking concert in Gilmorehill, and it was an easy job, but if I dinna ken a' aboot students, it's no' for want o' hearin' them and seein' them. There's twa tame yins lodgin' in oor ain close whiles, sittin' up till a' 'oors wastin' the gas, whiles playin' the melodian and singin' 'Mush Mush Taloora ladity.' My wife Jinnet she's bate to understaun' them, but I say to her, 'My good woman, that's no' a common melodian wi' bell accompaniment same as played by Kier Hardie[2] in the advertisments, and that's no' 'Mush Mush'; it's the gled, high, prood note o' Scottish academic humour and independence. They're practisin' their lessons, puir cratures. To-morrow, Jinnet,' I says, 'ye'll see the newspapers sayin', "Great sermon at Gilmorehill. The reverend Principal bowled down. Fire Brigade turned oot." 'It bates me,' says Jinnet, 'but I'm gled I gave a' oor ain sons a tred.'

"Ye have only to tak' the mildest wee laddie that has bad sight and is subject to sair heids frae the country and mak' a student o' him to rouse a' the latent fury o' the species. His mither far awa' in Clachnacuddin thinks he's hurtin' his health wi' ower muckle wark, but the only hairm he's daein himsel' is to crack his voice cryin' oot impudence to the professor. It's coonted Hooliganism in London if ye mak' yoursel' a conspicuous nuisance, but the chosen home o' Hooliganism, sae faur as I can see, is the Scotch college, where ye pap peas at your teacher and imitate the bray o' the cuddy.[3] They learn everything in colleges, sae faur as I can understaun', except dacent mainners and consideration for the feelings o' ither folk. They're branches o' common elementary education it's likely you're expected to get in the nicht schools, and the students havena been at ony o' the nicht schools sae they missed that bit. Whit I'm feart o' is that, sae faur frae improvin', the Scottish student 'll get worse on account o' Carnegie's[4] generosity; he'll ha'e the money he saves frae his fees to buy peas wi'."

"We can leave the young gentlemen of academic groves to their folly, Erchie," I said; "Tell me now what you think of the Common Good."[5]

"Man! that's a rale divert," said Erchie. "Here we ha'e been staundin' trates for years to a' sorts o' folk frae the British Assocation to the Stamp-Collectin' Society Federation and noo Sir James Marwick[6] ups and tells us we had nae legal right to spend a penny. 'Ye can ask wha ye like to the Municipal Buildin's and entertain them ony wye ye ha'e a notion o', but ye daurna spend a penny o' the Common Good on them,' says Sir James.

"'Could we no' be gi'en them a sma' trifle like a bottle o' Kola and a London bun or onything like that?' asks the Lord Provost.

"'Ye can gi'e whit ye like but ye daurna pay for 't.' Great sensation in the Toon Council. Big, strong men that ha'e eaten three or four commercial dinners every week for the last ten or twelve years turn white at the notion that they'll maybe ha'e to pay for whit they get. It's a' that wee cratur Scott Gibson, the man's a fair torment. If they wad tak' my advice they wad mak' him convener o' some committee or ither, even if they had to invent yin for him and send him on a deputation or twa. It would be a' in the interests o' peace.

"I'm a waiter to tred, and they canna ha'e ower many public dinners for Erchie MacPherson, but between me and you the thing has been cairried to a length that's no' canny. If the East London Branch o' the Bottle-washers Association wanted a change o' air and a nourishing diet, it held its annual conference in Gleska, sae far-famed for its hospitality, and the bottle-washers were aye sure to ha'e a friend in George Square to propose a fittin' reception. 'Bottle-washin',' he wad say, 'is the maist important o' oor national industries; Gleska is closely associated wi' bottle-washin', and must dae honour to its representatives.' So the bottle-washers wad be asked to a Reception and Conversazione, and wad wear holes in the carpet o' the satin-wud salon wi' walkin' in sparabelled boots between the refreshment buffets. The name o' Gleska went abroad through a' the land, as a toon flowin' wi' claret-cup, and nane o' the ratepayers said cheep, for it was kent to come oot o' the Common Good, and naebody kent whit the Common Good was except that there's nae mention o't in the Polis Rates. The only man that didna gang to their banquets was Sir James Marwick; he was a man wi' an awfu' auld-fashioned conscience."

"Well, it's changed days, Erchie. The city that flows with claret cup and honey is experiencing a great deal of adverse criticism from other quarters for its municipal system."

"It'll be somebody that wasna asked to onything; I'll wager it's no the bottle-washers, onywye. When I read thae criticisms I'm ashamed o' the toon I leeve in. I see noo that the skoosh cars, though they're sae nice to sit in, and gang sae fast and chairge sae little, are naething but whited sepulchres. They're paying like onything and they're no' paying, accordin' to the wye ye look at it, and I'm that vexed we ever did awa' wi' Duncan's auld horse-crawlers[7] that pyed a' the time, though ye wadna think it by the look o' them."

41. *Erchie on the Election*[1]

"WHERE AWAY, Erchie?" I asked the old man on meeting him turning out of New City Road on Saturday. "How goes it, old friend?" "Oh, just skliffin'; I canna complain. And I'm awa' to see hoo Duffy is the nicht." "Duffy," said I; "What's the matter with that worthy coal merchant?" "He's no' very weel, ower the head o' an argyment," said Erchie. "He was doon at the Mull o' Kintyre Vaults on Thursday nicht puttin' them a' richt on the election, and

met a man frae Ulster, and his puir wife spent the rest o'
the nicht stickin' jam-pot covers ower the hacks on his
face. He was oot wi' his lorry yesterday, but lost the tred on
haulf-a-dozen regular customers in the backlands because
they didna ken his new-fangled voice. I wish ye could put
an article in your bit paper about the thing! — 'Awful Warnin'
to the Retail Coal Tred. How the Americans Get the Better
o' Us. Sudden Illness o' the Well-known Peter K. Duffy.'"
"But why the unusual heat of Duffy at pet-house argu-
ments, Erchie?" "Oh, jist the election in the Woodside
Ward, ye ken. Duffy's a man that never fashes aboot his
vote since ever they stopped paying fer't in the dacent,
auld-fashioned wye, except the time yin o' the Bylies
bought a truck o' coal aff the bing frae him, and never
asked the price. But this time Duffy's fair aff his heid aboot
the election on Tuesday, and wad sooner be at Chisholm's
and Scott Gibson's meetin's than stay at hame and haud
the weans for his puir wife when she's washin'. He gangs
roon to the Vaults every nicht and argyfies. He could argyfy
twenty-fowr 'oors without a rest if ye paid his drink for him
and let him spit on your buits when he felt the need o't.

"I never gang to the Mull o' Kintyre Vaults mysel', me
bein' a beadle, and the stuff havin' a bad name there; but
whiles Duffy nails me on the street at nicht, and gives me
the hale set o't. I'm that fu' o' knowledge aboot municipal
affairs noo that it gi'es me a sair heid, and I cannot faind
sometimes whaur I put down my kep. He says to me the
ither nicht, 'MacPherson, we must arise, us workin' men,
arise in oor micht.' 'Oh! a' richt,' sais I, 'ye can rise awa',
but I hope when ye dae rise, ye'll mind to put on the fire for
the wife and gie her a cup o' tea afore ye gang oot. As for
me, I'm nane o' the risin' kind; my wark's nicht wark, and
I like to see the day weel aired aince I put a fit oot o' the
bed in the mornin'. 'You're a puir doon-trodden serf,' says
he, 'and it's ignorance that keeps ye like that.' 'You're a
liar,' says I; ' I'm a MacPherson, and as for ignorance, whit
dae you ken aboot the history o' Greece and Rome?'
'Glesga's gone to the bankruptcy courts by leaps and

bounds,' says he. 'Weel,' says I, 'whit for dae ye no' pye yer taxes and gie the puir auld place a chance?' 'I spend 'oors doon the Mull o' Kintyre Vaults rousin' my fellow-workers,' says he. 'It's the only thing ye dae spend there by all accounts,' says I, and he took the huff at that and went awa' and left me. I was that vexed!

"But Duffy wasna done wi' me. He came up last Tuesday to the hoose for the len' o' a white-wash brush, and I said I was gled he was gettin' better. 'There's no better cure,' says I, 'for the trouble you hiv than a spell at puttin' ochre on a kitchen wa', or maybe splittin' sticks for the fire in the mornin'.' 'Whit trouble?' says he. 'Daein' a' your thinkin' wi' your mooth,' says I. 'It's epidemic the noo, and if the disease spreads they'll ha'e to clap a score o' new wards to Belvidere Hospital.'[2] 'Duffy,' I says, 'I ken ye fine. It was you that wrote yon articles on Gleska in the *London Times*. Ye needna deny't. I couldna be mistaken.' But I was oot o' the puir crature's depth there, and he jist glowered at that and said he wanted the white-wash brush to dae some bill-postin' for the cause. 'Man, I've aye noticed,' says I, 'that when the like o' you ha'e a cause to dae ony bill-postin' for, ye aye ha'e to borrow somebody else's white-wash brush.' 'I'm doon on depitations and banquets,' says he, 'and Sam Chisholm's gaun to slide this twist.' 'Man, dae ye tell me?' says I. 'Whit's the matter wi' the puir sowl?' And then Duffy gi'ed me the latest views o' what he ca'd the proletariat on the Lord Provost.

"'Look at the banquets he's aye hivin' at the expenses o' the rates,' says Duffy. 'I canna,' says I, 'they're a' eaten. The big fat men that Mr Nicoll aye invites took guid care o' that. And let me tell ye this, Duffy, that when it comes to banquets I never kent a man that could dae less justice to the guid things o' this life than Lord Provost Chisholm. It wasna him that invented the banquets; they've been goin' on for hunders o' years, and there's a wheen dacent auld burgesses lyin' in the Necropolis that de'ed o' naethin' else.' 'There's a' thae depitations,' says Duffy. 'Just that!' says I; 'But they were the vogue lang afore there was a

Chisholm, and I'm tell't the pavement at Piccadilly corner in London was worn thin twenty years ago wi' honest Scots depitation bylies staun'in' there at nicht enlarging their views o' life.' 'He wanted the King doon the ither day to open the Art Galleries,'[3] says Duffy, 'so that he micht ha'e anither chance o' a title.' 'I wadna put it bye him,' says I. 'And he wadna be the first. We're a' wantin' oor wee bit titles, and it took a bit manoeuvrin' for mysel' to get the beadleship. There's ex-Provosts o' Gleska that ha'e bocht their titles and pyed pretty sweet for them too, and if we didna hear muckle aboot it at the time it was because in thae days we made some allooance for human nature even in Lord Provosts. Dod! it wad be a trate to see the cratur get his title if it was only to prove hoo chape it could be done by a lang-heided man o' business.

"'I'm no sayin', min' ye, Duffy, that his Lordship's perfect; a' the perfect men's in the coal trade like yoursel', or at the waitin', like me, and when we have a Provost to pick, we maun jist dae the best we can wi' the material at oor disposal. I've noticed in his Lordship a singular great respect for the man that wear his Lordship's hat. He's no whit ye wad ca' blate, but in that respeck he's like the maist o' us, only he hisna the sense to hide it. I daursay he would come aff better at the poll next week if he got somebody else to mak' his speeches afore the electors. If it's a blate man ye want in the Woodside Ward, then of course ye canna hae better than the wee yin frae Springburn.[4] I'm tellt he gets red in the face if he has tae speak aboot himsel', and is that modest he hates to see his name in the papers, though in his nomination he's described as a journalist. That's a heavy yin for the chaps that writes newspapers! Let them jist tak' it! The Boundin' Boy wad find it gey hard, I'm thinkin', to describe his occupation since the time he left the school, unless indeed he ca'd himsel' Gentleman that sometimes figures at elections as a tred. But a journalist — faith, ay! it fits weel enough, for there's nae man figurin' aftener in letters to the journals the noo that Mr Scott Gibson.

"'Whit hae ye to say aboot Scott Gibson?' said Duffy, quite sherp at that. 'Naethin' that I wad need to say to ye if ye hadna the disease I spoke o', and did your thinkin' in the acrobatic wye I mentioned. A wheen of ye imagine it's aye the loodest bummer that's the best bummer and the callant kens your wakeness. He's bummin awa like a ship-yard horn, and a' the time he's no' a bee at a', but jist a cleg.[5] The cleg nae doot has its purposes in nature; it's a cheery kin' o' feature in the landscape, and helps to keep the coos awake chewin' their cuds, and makin' milk then they micht be inclined to fa' asleep in the sun, and forget their duty to the dairyman; but nane o' us wi' oor wits aboot us is tempted to put the cleg into a skep expectin' a big increase in the output o' honey. I'm gaun to say naethin' aboot the personal character o' the Boundin' Boy, Duffy; that's a way o' warfare that may be left to the Woodside Ward, that seems to be in the haunds of a' the keelies in Gleska just at present. Besides I ken naethin aboot him. I saw a pamphlet sellin' on the streets the day wi' "Scathin' Exposure o' Scott Gibson" printed on't, and payed my tuppence for't like a fool, expectin' some o' thae scurrilous and scandalous attacks we're a' sae pleased to find made oan ither folks. The thing wasna worth a snuff, Duffy. It didna say he had been a resurrectionist in his early life, or robbed banks, or murdered his great-grandfather for the sake o' his specs. It didna ca' a him a leear, and prove't; it didna say onything worth paying a bawbee for, far less tuppence, and I hae been thinkin' since that maybe the body put it oot himsel.

"'I'm sayin' naething aboot the laddie, Duffy, but just you put him into the Toon Council for the Woodside Ward in place o' Mr Chisholm, and I'll stand by and lauch. He's cocky enough the noo, God knows! but in that case they wad hae to lift the roof o' the Coouncil hall ten or twenty feet to gie him room for his heid. Of course his feet wad be in't a' the time; they're that wye the noo. I hae na doot the men that's backin' him frae Springburn and other mis-guided pairts o' the ceety wad be gled to see the cratur in the provost's chair. That wad be a rale divert, I'm tellin' ye. Lord Provost Scott Gibson! — "His Lordship did the honours o' the ceety to the British Association yesterday, and presided at a genial cup o' cocoa and scones purveyed in their usual excellent and rekerky style[6] by Lookharts" — "His Lordship, as the depitation appointed to inquire into the state o' the water-works, took the tramway caur to Maryhill on Monday, and walked to Mugdock reservoir,[7] takin' a piece in his pocket" — "We are informed that his Lordship Mr Scott Gibson has sold the antiquated and useless chain o' office and applied the proceeds to the purchase o' new keps for the lamplichters"[8] — "It is reported from London that the King, havin' expressed a desire to visit his faithful subjects in Gleska, a communication has been received at Windsor from Lord Provost Scott Gibson refusing any title that it may be in His Majesty's mind to offer him.

"'If it wasna that I was an auld enough man to ken that there's a great deal o' the sheep in human nature, I wad wonder at the ignorance o' you and your like, Duffy,' says I. 'For forty years ye havena had as muckle interest in the toon's affairs as wad mak' ye pye yer polis money in time, or let ye gang to vote. Gleska did very weel withoot your interest, growing bigger and better and mair prosperous every generation, just because ye drank your beer in peace and ignorance and let sensible men look efter the ceety's interests, that were as much theirs as yours. And noo because ye like to see a habble and tek' the bizzin' o' the cleg for the bummin' o' the bee, ye come here for me dacent white-wash brush.'

"'Rax[9] me ower the brush, Jinnet,' says I, 'and dip it in the soap-sapple,[10] and I'll gie't to Duffy here — across the lugs.'

"Ye'll maybe no' believe it," concluded Erchie, "but Duffy took to his heels for 't and wadna serve the wife wi' coals on Wednesday. But I ha'e nae ill-will to the cratur'; a flet fit and a warm hert's auld Erchie's motto, and so I'm just gaun in to ask for him."

42. *Erchie's Resolutions*[1]

"Every Ne'erday for the past fifty years I ha'e made up my mind I was gaun to be a guid man," said Erchie. "It jist wants a start, they tell me that's tried it, and I'm no' that auld. Naething bates a trial. I begood at twal o'clock[2] on Hogmanay, and made a wee note o't in my penny diary, and pit a knot in my hankie to keep me in mind. Maist o' us would be as guid's there's ony need for if we had naething else to think o'; it's like a man that's hen-taed — he could walk fine if he hadna a train to catch or somethin' else to bother him. I'm gey faur wrang if I dinna dae the trick this year, though. Oh! aye. I'm gaun to be a guid man. No' that awfu' guid that auld frien's 'll rin up a close to hide when they see me comin', but jist dacent — jist guid enough to please mysel', like Duffy's singin'. I'm no' makin' a breenge at the thing and sprainin' my leg ower't. I'm startin' canny till I get into the wye o't. Efter this, Erchie MacPherson's gaun to flype his ain socks[3] and no' leave his claes reel-rall aboot the hoose at night for his wife Jinnet to lay oot richt in the mornin'. I've lost money by that up till noo, for there was aye bound to be an odd sixpence droppin' oot and me no' lookin'. I'm gaun to stop skliffin' wi' my feet: it's sair on the boots; I'm gaun to save preens[4] by puttin' my collar stud in a bowl and a flet-iron on the top o't to keep it frae jinkin' under the chevalier and book-case when I'm sleepin'; I'm gaun to wear oot a' my auld waistcoots in the hoose. I'm —"

"My dear Erchie," I interrupted, "these seem very harmless reforms."

"Are they?" said he. "They'll dae to be gaun on wi' the noo. If I can maister them I'll maybe start next New Year, if we're a' spared to see't, with a resolution to tak' nae tips and aye tell the truth aboot Duffy. Perhaps by that time they'll ha'e invented a machine for aye keepin' ye moral and up to the mark. I wadna put it by them, for it's a wunnerfu' age; whiles I canna mak' up my mind whether

I'm gled to be spared to see't or wad be saving money if I wasna to the fore. There's folk lyin' wide awake a' nicht wonderin' what they'll dae next to ameliorate the lot o' their fellow-beings. See at thon chap Marconi[5] that used to ha'e the Original Ice-Cream Saloon in Garscube Road noo makin' his thoosands oot o' telegraphin' withoot ony wires. Ye're no' safe to gang oot at nicht in case ye get a dunt on the lug frae an urgent wireless message o' his bummin' up the wrang street. Duffy swears it's him that's spilin' the climate o' the country wi' takin' a' the sap oot o't for his telegraphs. They're sending telegrams to ships in mid-ocean[6] noo, and when a puir cratur's jist in the middle o' a storm, and writin' oot a few last words to put in a lemonade bottle, he gets a telegram frae Partickhill: 'Where did you leave the key of the wine cellar? Reply paid.'

"They've even started a daily newspaper on the Atlantic liners, wi' a' the news up to the meenute o' gaun to press. Feelin' far frae weel in the fogs aff Newfoundland, the saloon passenger may buy the six o'clock edition o' the *Etruria Evenin' News*, and see that the Celts were dirty bate at Parkhead, or that Cohen's into the Cooncil for Springburn. He'll find the discomforts o' the passage tremendously modified by the knowledge that the price o' his Gympie gold mine shares canna gae doon a p'int withoot his learnin' aboot it afore he goes to bed. I have nae doot they'll mak' thae ship-newspapers jist like rale, wi' advertisements in them, and photograph portraits o' new MPs, that look guilty, but maybe never did onybody ony hairm. 'Great Sale of Marine Curiosities in the Fore Saloon at five o'clock to-morrow: tin basins, 6½d.; sou'-westers marked doon to 2s. 11d.' 'Would the young lady who spoke with the man on the bridge on Monday night please communicate with J.K.S., second mate?' 'Kurasma for the hair; won't wash clothes.'

"Oh, a maist wunderfu' age! There's oor ain skoosh caurs that'll gie ye a hurl for a penny to Whiteinch and Bishopbriggs and a wheen ither places naebody in their senses ever wanted to gang to unless maybe there was a fitba' match at them. The chapest tramways in the kingdom, they're ca'd, and they're that chape a workin'-man spends a shillin' a week on them where afore he wad ha'e walkit. There's turbine steamers[7] that fly sae fast between Gourock and Campbeltown ye miss a' the scenery if ye gang doon the stairs to see the engines twice. There's the cinemato- graph – I never afore kent whit the refinin' influence o' art they talk aboot was till I saw Fitzsimmons jab Corbett[8] wi' his left nief in the watch-pocket and knock him oot. Music in the hoose mak's cheerfu', happy hames, as Campbell the melodian man says, and noo the gramophone is up every stair in oor tenement, givin' sober men an excuse for gaun out to the public-hoose that they never had afore. The gramophone or phonograph, or whitever ye ca't, brings the maisterpieces o' music and a' the greatest singers of the age to man, and the humblest workin'-man, efter staundin't a nicht or twa, gets but the wan look o' the trumpet and mak's for the Mull o' Kintyre Vaults, where he'll hear Duffy singin':

'Oh Tillietudlem, nae matter whaur I be,
Tillietudlem Castle[9] 'll aye be dear to me.
'Twas there I met my Mary when first I went to see
Tillietudlem Castle and its bonny scenery.'

"Marconi telegrams withoot wires; Santos whit-dae-ye- ca'-him's flyin' machines; Edison phonographs; Welsback inconsistent gas light — a' foreign! a' foreign! The country's bein' fair ruined wi' them; I wish they had stuck by their slider machines[10] and their monkeys; we werena daein' that bad afore they took us in haund. The latest's a musicianer wi' a name like a cauld in the heid — Tschai- kowsky.[11] Oh I ken him! Noo and then on a Setterday nicht I gie a haund wi' the tickets at the Orchestral Con- certs, and I hear as muckle aboot Tschaikowsky as if he was the conductor o' the Govan Police Baun'. It used to be Beethoven and Mozart when I was younger, but nooadays they're coonted oot-o'-date, and there's concerts whaur there's naething else but whit they ca' programme music,

composed in his spare time by this Tschaikowsky. If ye
mention the name o' Beethoven, folk ye ken fine say, 'Tut!
tut!', dinna ask ye ony mair to their At Homes, and tell a'
the folk in their terrace that ye keep an orchestrion. Ye
might as weel ha'e the name o' keepin' the Sunday; it's a
shair sign that ye're awfu' faur behind. If ye talk aboot
Tschaikowsky wi' the richt kink in your voice ye're looked
on as a credit to Ethol Gairdens,[12] and if ye can go further
nor that and spell his name richt wi' three tries, ye'll ha'e to
look awfu' slippy and hide yersel', or ye'll be dragged into a
newspaper office to write aboot Tschaikowsky concerts.

"I'm no wantin' to be hard on Tschaikowsky; I have aye
a notion that his music's no near as bad as it sounds, but
gi'e me oor auld friend Wullie Frame. Whit folk likes aboot
the Tschaikowsky kin' o' concert is that he does the best he
can to help them. He's no' the man to see them worried
wunnerin' whit he's up to. A Tschaikowsky concert is a
great savin' o' time — a' the while ye're listenin' to't and
no' lookin' at your watch, ye're hearin' as guid a yarn as
ony that ever came oot in Horner's Penny Stories. When
the man wi' the drums is no' playin' but cuttin' his nails,
and lookin' sorry for ye, and the wee fiddler is sawin' awa',
the programme tells ye the eve was calm and clear, and the
moon was aboot the third quarter. When the trombone
begins ramming a yaird o' brass oot and in his throat, and
the Awfu' Clyde[13] almost bursts itsel', ye look at the programme again and see that the north cone has been hoisted
at Leith, and it's rough weather in the Channel. When the
strings ha'e't a' their ain wye, again the programme tells ye
that's the approach o' spring, and the wee kettle drums
come in to put ye in mind o' the annual cleanin', and the
beatin' of carpets oot in the back court. The 'cello gi'es a
'pom-pom' — that's the hero o' the story taking a walk
through the castle, and wishin' he had a pair o' cahoutchy
buits in case the lassie's faither hears him. There's no' a
bar o' the rale Tschaikowsky music that hasna as muckle
meanin' in't as a story by Annie S. Swan,[14] and, in case ye
should miss a chapter, it's in the programme. There's folk

that gleg in the ear wi' practice at thae concerts they can tell withoot lookin' at the programme when the Sleepin' Beauty snored; but for maist folk the programme's a Godsend they wad be useless wantin'.' "

43. *Erchie on Burns*[1]

"I'M GEY tired the day,' said Erchie to me on Saturday. "It was till twal' o'clock last nicht wi' the Haghill Wanderers' Burns Club, and it'll be the same again on Monday nicht wi' the Combined Maryhill District Peck o' Maut Club and Mother Haggis Lodge.[2] This is a great year wi' every son o' Scotland that has the stomach for two Burns suppers and the money to pay for them. I've aften thocht there was something providential in Burns ha'ein' his birthday on the 25th o' January: if it had been aboot the month o' July it wad ha'e clashed wi' the Gleska Fair, and if it had been three weeks sooner than it was, many a yin wad be bate whiles to think whether he was bringin' in the New Year or celebratin' the immortal memory o' the Bard in solemn silence. The proodest man in the country at this time o' the year is the man that minds the words o' 'Robin was a Rovin Lad'; they tak' him roon' in cabs frae ae Burns club to anither, singin' that as hard's he can in the hale o' them.

"The maist interestin' celebration I've heard o' this time was up Duffy's close last nicht. Duffy gangs every year to the Carlton Athletic[3] Burns Club supper, and his wife was aye castin' up to him it was gey droll that it was only the men got a chance o' honourin' the poet's memory, so this time Duffy gets a second-handed gramaphone and two Burns sangs to't — 'Kind, kind, and gentle was she' and 'A wee bird cam' to oor door', burst twa shillin's on a No. 7 haggis made in Koftinschafftachingen, Bavaria,[4] and left wife and family to work their will on them wi' pride and joy. Mrs Duffy entertained the hale tenement last nicht, and if the gramaphone hands oot there's gaun to be anither nicht wi' Burns on Monday. 'It jist shows ye,' Duffy says to

me, greetin' this mornin', and wi' an awfu' roopy throat
wi' singing the nicht afore; 'It jist shows ye whit a wee
kindness'll dae.'

"It's a guid thing the gramaphone was invented afore
the few that's left that ken Burns sangs dee. Anither generation efter this, when Scotch sangs is fair oot o' date and
naebody kens the airs o' them, they'll can get the gramaphone to oblige. Aboot the only sang they kent the richt
words o' at the Haghill Wanderers supper last nicht was
'He's a jolly guid fellow.' They sang it every noo and then.
It's a nice enough sang, but efter ye've heard it seventeen
times in the a'e nicht ye've a sair grudge agains the man
that made it. Whit's badly wanted is alterations inthe lines
to suit parteecular cases; everybody canna be a 'jolly good
fellow' exactly to the same extent, and there should be a
kin' o' graduated scale o' testimonial — 'He's a jolly guid
fellow' — 'He's a fairly jolly guid fellow' — He's a guid
enough guid fellow' — and 'He's a' richt when ye ken him,
which naebody can deny.' Burns had ha'e done a great
service to his country if he could have foreseen the need o'
something to tak' the place o' 'He's a jolly good fellow,'
and put thegither complimentary verses o' that character
for various occasions.

"But Rab, puir chiel! couldna think o' everything, as I
tell Duffy. He was jist yin o' oorsel's — a gey thrang man a'
his days, so that he had to mak' his sangs in his spare time.
It wisna a tred wi' him, and his photograph and the
photograph o' his wife and weans and his hoose, and his
study, and his favourite dug didna appear every other week
in 'Home Chat.' It was hardly worth while bein' a poet in
thae days, though there must ha'e been some money to be
made oot o't, too, for ye'll maybe ha'e noticed that Rab
was aye able to keep a di'mond ring. When his wark was
done at nicht and he had pit aff his plooin'-buits and on his
Sunday yins, he wad gang a' roon' the country-side writin'
verses on window-panes wi' his di'mond ring. I daursay
paper was dear aboot that time, but onywye Rab spoiled a
guid mony windows —Jist yin o' oorsels — a rale divert,

but gey-throughither. I daursay naebody wad ha'e kent there was onything wrang wi' him if he hadna said it himsel'. If he made a slip o' ony kin' he was aye the first to bluiter it oot, and these were the things, of coorse, his frien's aye kept mind o' langest.

"But nooadays things is different; every great poet — and ye'll notice whit a crood o' them there is — is jist as anxious aboot his reputation as he is aboot his sangs. He has aye his e'e on the Biography. The literary men o' the day are a' sober, earnest, God-fearing, and respectable, wi' money in the Savin's Bank. If you look at thon thick red book ca't 'Who's Who,' ye'll find that their favourite recreation's playin' dominoes wi' the wife. It serves them richt! Burns was the last o' the poets that took a dram and never denied it;[8] since his time the peppermint lozenge has been invented, and the clove has ta'en the place o' the shamrock as the national emblem o' Scotland. It's a mercy we're a' spared! And puir Rab's the frightful example for every person that's got a sermon to write on the frailties o' genius."

44. *Erchie on the Missive*[1]

"DUFFY'S CRYIN' his coals the day wi' an aufu' roopy voice," said Erchie to me on Saturday. "It's a shair sign he was doon at the Mull o' Kintyre Vaults late last nicht openin' his heid and lettin' in the cauld. I ken fine whit it wad be — the tyranny o' the factor's missive, for Duffy breaks his hert aboot the missives every February. I met him yesterday wi' his face by-ordinar black.[2] 'I'm no gaun to wash mysel' till I kill a hoose-factor,' says he. 'It's a fine ham'[3] says I; 'Jist gang on the way yer daein' and kill them wi' hert disease sclimbin' up and doon yer stair lookin' for the rent. There's nae need to spill blood.' 'Show me a hoose-factor,' says Duffy, 'and I'll brain him wi' a fifty-six!'[4] 'Man, ye couldna,' I says, 'there's no a fifty-six in your lorry.' I had him there! 'Still,' says I, 'if you're in the key for manslaughter, I'll no' be the yin to see ye bate; come into the post office and ask a wee lend o' their Directory, and we'll pick oot twa or three names and addresses.' 'Nane o' yer coddin'!' says Duffy; 'I'm tellin' ye I mean't; my face'll no' be washed afore I kill a factor.' 'Toots, man!' I says, 'there's no muckle savin' in that; ye were never very sair on the soap. If ye tholed your thirst till ye killed a factor it wad be mair o' a blessin' to your wife and weans.'

"'They say Rob Roy's deid,' says Duffy, 'but there's robbers gaun aboot Gleska faur waur nor Rob Roy. They canna see a puir workin' man gaun up a close wi' his hard-earned money in his pouch but they must slink efter him and slug him on the heid wi' a line tellin' him his rent's to be put up a pound at the May term. There was nane o' that aboot Rob Roy.' 'No,' says I. 'Rob wadna dirty his haunds wi' anything less than a drove o' coos, and he never touched ye unless ye were the length o' payin' Income-tax. The profession's greatly altered.' 'Ye should come doon to the Mull o' Kintyre Vaults the nicht,' says Duffy at that; 'We're gettin' up a Federation.' 'Whit for?' I asks. 'To— to— to federate and the like o' that,' says Duffy. 'See ye divna get catched at it,' I warns him. 'The chief plank in oor armour,' says Duffy, 'is that we're no' gaun to sign ony missives.' 'Indeed,' says I. 'Ye'll be jist gaun to mak' yer mark, the way ye aye did. If ye think that's gaun to vex the factors ye're awful' far up a close. They'll be ower thrang lettin' yer hoose ower yer heid to call for the missive. A factor, Duffy,' I says, 'is a busy man, and he dales with hooses in the bulk. You think the factor's laying wide awake at nicht sayin' to himsel', "There's a James K. Duffy, retail coal-dealer, aged fifty-five, and ten o' a family, daein' pretty weel at his tred, and engagin' an extra man to help him carry the coals on Setterday; he'll can staund thirty shillin's mair on his rent." But he's no, Duffy; he's no. There's a rale dacent auld widow woman oot maybe at Dowanhill, and she canna pay her coals unless she gets mair oot o' her hoose-property, and you're leevin' in her tenement, and she tells the factor she maun ha'e mair rent oot o't. To the factor

ye're no James K. Duffy at a', but jist two rooms and
kitchen, h. and c., three stairs up 4536 Dobbie's Loan,[6] and
the rent o' your hoose is jist as muckle as he can squeeze
oot o' ye.' 'Shame!' says Duffy. 'That's whit the auld
weedow in Dowanhill says aboot the price o' coal,' says I.

"The missive," said Erchie, pursuing a theme that I saw
had manifestly engaged a great deal of his thought; "The
missive, like the tenement hoose, the close, and the dunny,[7]
is an aff-set to the glorious preevelige o' being Scotch. It
wad be quite easy for the factor to hide on the stair-landing
at nicht when ye were gaun home and jump oot on ye wi' a
sheet o' paper, a fountain pen, and a pistol and mak' ye
sign on for anither twelvemonth, but he disna want to catch
the cauld daeing onything o' the kind, so he engages a
literary man, paid daily, weekly, or oorly as required and
the literary man writes a missive. It says, 'Hey, you there,
MacPherson, ye crawling wasp o' bleezes, look slippy and
say whether ye're gaun to tak' advantage o' your opportunities, and stay anither fifteen months in my bonny wee
hoose or no'. If ye divna like it, ye can lump it; God knows
there's hunders lookin' for hooses'll be gled to pay mair
rent nor you do. If the missive enclosed is no' signed in twa
meenutes four seconds efter receipt o' this, we'll consider
yer hoose to let, and send a jiner to put up a board in the
parlor window. — Yours truly, Gleg and Gleesome, house-
factors.' Then there's generally a postscript, 'From Whitsunday first the rent o' yer hoose'll be £16 10s. instead o'
£15, and ye should be gey gled, ye auld assassin, to get it at
onything like the money.' That's maybe no' the exact
words the literary man writes for this factor, but that's the
speerit o' them. When a man gets a letter like that afore
he's richt bye wishin' everybody a Happy New Year, it's no
wonder he feels nasty. Ye micht ha'e been a Tory afore that,
a member o' a kirk, and a fellow that wadna hairm a flee,
but that kin' o' epistle'll send ye oot into the street, hatin'
hoose-factors that bad ye canna pass yin o' their offices
without cryin' 'Boo!' Ye jine the Social Democratic Federation and the Unemployed Anarchists, and spend 'oors in

the washin'-hoose tryin' to mak' bomb-shells oot o' the
heids o' fusuvians[8] and threepence worth o' sulphur in a
condensed milk can.

"If Gleg and Gleesome's poet had ony sense o' respect
for his unfortunate fellow-craturs he wad write anither kind
o' letter a'thegither. He wad say, 'Dear Mr MacPherson,
— And hoo's a' wi' ye? We were aye thinkin' o' takin' an
efternoon and gi'en ye a ca' jist to crack aboot auld times.
Ye've been saxteen years a tenant o' oors, and aye payed
your rent afore twal' o'clock on the term day, and we're
prood to ha'e ye at 4562 New City Road. Is there naething
we can dae for ye at this time, such as white-washin' the
close and puttin' a new lock on the washin'-hoose? Yours
is an enviable condition, Mr MacPherson. Yer hoose is sae
muckle thocht o' that we have had fifteen applications for't
within the last week frae various neighbours o' yours, wha
are willin' to offer twa pounds mair rent in the year. But
knowin', as we dae, the value o' a guid tenant when we
have yin, we have refused to consider ony offers till we have
your customary assurance that ye intend signing the
missive' (enclosed with compliments) 'for anither year.
We had expected to be able to reduce your rent this year in
a substantial degree, but unfortunately the Income-tax still
remains very high since the war, and instead o' a reduction
we have reluctantly been compelled to announce an advance
o' thirty shillin's which, hooever, will be mair than recouped
to you by the reduction in the tramway fares gaun past
your street. Please remember us kindly to Mrs MacPherson
and, with kind regards, we are truly Gleg and Gleesome.'
A letter like that, noo, wad vex naebody.

"Every noo and then when I'm readin' the papers my
hert gi'es a stoon when I come on an advertisement that
asks, 'Why Pay Rent?' I look doon a wee bit to see that it's
no' onything about Mither Seagull's syrup or Bile Beans,
for it's gey suspicious, but no— it's richt-enough; it maks
oot that if ye write to somebody in London they'll show ye
a way ye can leeve in yer ain hoose rent-free. I'm aye gaun
to write, but havena done't yet. Ye canna believe a' ye hear

or see — even in newspapers. Advertisers are human and liable to error. But there's nae error aboot a missive. It means whit it says, as Duffy has found oot half-a-dizzen times he's tried to back oot o't when his wife took a notion to flit[9] a fortnight afore the term. And there's nae error aboot the rise o' rent; if the missive says it's gaun up, it's gaun up. It's gaun up the noo in Gleska on a' kinds o' excuses — because the skoosh caurs gang up your street, and there's a bawbee station at the close mooth; because the skoosh caurs dinna gang near your street, and it's nice and quate; because the public-hooses in the street are shut at ten and that improves the neighbourhood; because they're no' shut till eleven, and that's sae handy.

"The answer the factor has to a' the folk that say he has an awfu' neck on him to ask his missive signed in February is that half the folk in Gleska's lookin' for hooses already. There's a fair procession o' wives gaun up and doon our stair the noo gettin' mair sport oot o' looking into ither folks' hooses than you and me got frae the Exhibeetion the year before last. They aye gang in pairs, and they cairry the keys o' their ain hooses in their haunds to show that they're respectable. They aye look at hooses two rooms bigger nor ony they could pay for, because they're never ower auld to learn whit the gentry does. I wonder if ye ever noticed the fearfu' hatred a man that's gaun to flit taks to everybody that comes lookin' his hoose. I'm a beadle mysel', a flet fit, but a warm hert, and still and on, when I was gaun to leave a hoose, an' folks cam' lookin' at it, I wished the law wad let me meet them wi' a hatchet and chase them doon the stairs. The only folk I ever cared to ha'e comin' to see a hoose were the young anes that were gaun to be mairrit. The last hoose I was leavin' a lad cam' up wi' a red face and said he was lookin' for a hoose for his aunty that thocht o' flittin' in frae the country. It wad hae been a' richt if the hoose hadna suited and I micht never hae jaloused but it was just the sort o' place he thocht wad answer his aunty, and he said he wad tak' her up hersel' to see't. When he cam' up the next nicht wi' a lassie his ain age, that was as red in the face as himsel', I says, 'Weel, mister, is this yer aunty?' 'Ay!' says he, 'of course it is.' 'Man,' I says, 'ye're a bonny pair o' doos!' and gi'ed him the waiter's wink."

45. *Erchie in the Slums*[1]

I WALKED from church with Mr MacPherson yesterday, and found him somewhat out of patience with the Scottish climate. "Fine weather, Erchie," I said with feeling irony. "Man, isn't it?" said he; "I never pu' up the Venetian blinds to look whit kind o' mornin' it is, but I feel like to cry oot 'a baurlay! a baurlay![2] Fair rideeculous! Ye micht as weel be in the submarine miners a' the time." Erchie's idea of a submarine miner[3] obviously was the common one that he is a person who does his business in a diving-bell. "Oh! we'll have a change soon; it can't last for ever," I said, with that indomitable hope that springs eternal in the human breast. "Nae doot," said he, "if we're a' spared to see't. Jinnet's yonder spring cleanin' onywye. Man, yon's a wumman that's no' easy bate. The only sign o' Spring I ha'e seen sae far is her wi' a white-washin' brush in her haund and me wi' nae place to sit doon in my ain hoose. 'Ye needna bother, Jinnet,' I tell her, 'there's gaun to be nae mair springs nor summers; it's just gaun to be like this even on.' And wi' that she sends me roond to the fruit-erer's for tuppence worth o' mignonette seed for puttin' in the floo'erbox in the kitchen window. A cheery wee wumman I'm tellin' ye; I'm often that gled I married her."

'Hiv ye seen," said Erechie, "that a wheen o' the gentle-men that's gaun to abolish the single apairtment and gie everybody a but-an'-ben for tuppence a week and the taxes ha'e been takin' a turn roond the slums the ither nicht? It must ha'e been an awfu' trate to some o' them that never saw ony pairt o' Gleska afore except oot the windows o' a cab. They met just when the nocks were on the chap o' twelve at the front door o' the Municeepal Buildin's, every

man wi' a dark lantern, his auldest suit o' clothes on, and
his breeks turned up at the fit, Eau-de-Cologne on his
pocket-napkin, and his watch and purse left at hame. They
took the road for the Wee Doo Hill or wherever it wiz, in
cabs; it was a noble and invigoratin' sight to see, I'm shair.
When they reached the dwellin's o' the puir, they gi'ed
anither turn up to the fit o' their breeks, took a sniff o' their
scented hankies, and went quite game behind the bobby
up the stairs. 'No vestibule doors!' says they; 'point
number one. Nae hot watter in the baths!' they says; 'point
number two; this is dreadfu'!' And at that a man wakens
his wife to tell her no' to snore that lood; for there wiz
strangers in the hoose. 'Wha are they?' says she, turnin' to
gi'e a look at Cook's Tour.[4] 'It's mair nor I ken,' says he;
'they jist walked in. Wha the bleezes are ye?' he asks.
'We're bylies and the like o' that,' says some o' the gang,
'and we're here, puir man, to do ye a' the good we can.'
'That's fine,' says he, gaun to sleep again; 'Leave a shillin'
or twa on the dresser.'

"It was the first time the bylies had the chance o' seein'
their steadiest customers in their ain hooses. A bylie's is a
pretty thrang life. When he's no' on the bench givin' thirty
shillin's or fourteen days, he's looking for studs for his
dress clothes to gang to dinners in the Satinwud Salong;
and this was looked on as a rare opportunity o' seeing the
habit and repute[5] wi' his boots aff. It was expected that wi'
ony luck at a' they micht come on the wife-beater engaged
in his professional occupation, but the 'oor was too late for
that, and a' was hushed and calm, wi' naething but a black
eye here and there. As the bylies and the rest o' them went
frae hoose to hoose flashin' their bull's-eye lanterns on the
residencers, the guides gave speeches jist for a' the warld as
if it was the Zoo. 'Single apairtment of sixty-nine cubic
feet, scheduled for five adults and sixteen weans,' says the
guide. 'Here ye have the man the hoose belangs tae; 16s. a
week wages; observe his dogged aspeck and the no
pyjamas. On his left, gentlemen, the wife; notice partee-
cularly her intelligent and hard-workin' countenance. On

the other side we have the five lodgers, and if my assistant 'll ha'e the goodness to turn up that mattress ye'll see the sixteen weans in below it, as nate's ye like. The domestic utensils o' the degraded poor, gentlemen — the poker, the teapot without a stroop, the empty hauf-peck, the jeely-mug, the washin' boyne.[6] Art in the home, gentlemen — kindly direck your attention for a meenute to the grocer's calendar; mountain scene, wi' a whole squad o' deer; and pleasin' motto — 'My He'rt's in the Hielan's, my He'rt is Not Here.' 'Man, is't no' jist wonnerfu',' says yin o' the bylies; 'Ye see an appreciation o' the beautiful even here.'

"When the puir folk heard the bylies' feet skliffing on the stair comin' up, mair nor half o' them ran away and hid themselves, either because they hadna their faces washed, or because they thought it was the polis. Them that stood their grun' and were lectured on by the guides must ha'e been awfu' prood o' the experience. It's no' every day they could see a bylie aff the bench, quite cheery. But the introduction was a' on the a'e side; there was naebody to lecture aboot the bylies and the ither gentlemen. Somebody should ha'e said — 'Hey! you puir miserable dregs o' craturs that should be run into the Clyde if it wadna polute the watter, this is the Gleska bylies. They're a' richt; they'll no' bite ye. That's them. They havena thir gold chains on them the nicht, being feart for the damp spoiling them, and this is their golfin' clothes they're wearin' so that maybe ye think I'm a leear, but they're a' genuine. 'See that wet, see that dry, cut my throat if I tell a lie.' Them's the chaps that gi'e ye the blessin's o' ceevilisation — parks like the Green for handin' floo'ers, and macheenery for tellin' ye whit's the temperature and when it's gaun to be Set Fair; galleries cramfu' o' awfu' dear pictures; the Loch Katrine watter that ye mak yer tea wi' and wash wi' whiles; skoosh caurs that help to keep doon the size o' yer families by rinnin' ower them; libraries whaur ye dicht yer hands in the *Graphic*; and baths — and baths — oh! well, never mind about the baths, but they're there I'll gaurantee. Noo, touch yer keps to the bylies, and they'll see whit they'll can dae mair for ye. Their motto is doon wi' the single apartment, and every man his ain jawbox.'"

"Noo that the bylies have given the thing a start, veesits to the Gleska slums'll be a' the go. You and me, whenever we ha'e got hame frae oor wark and had oor tea, 'll mak' a rush for the haunts o' poverty and crime, and the music-halls'll ha'e to shut their doors for want o' custom. One half o' the folk in Gleska dinna ken whit wye the ither half lives; the folk on the ither side o' Charing Cross ha'e a notion that the puir oot on the east o' the Trongate are gey hard up when they ha'e to dae withoot cookies for their teas; that's a' they ken aboot it. Cook's gaun to organise slum excursions for the strangers to Scotland; they'll gang roon a' the Gorbals efter they've done wi' the Trossachs and Loch Lomond, and the degraded poor'll show them through the ticketed hooses, and sell their ain photographs. The fame of the Gleska slum'll be wider spread than the fame o' her shipbuildin' and the Commission on the Hoosing o' the Puir'll aye go on sittin'.'"

46. *Erchie's Sermon*[1]

ON SATURDAY nights, Erchie, in his sacred office as beadle of St Kentigern's, lights the furnaces that take the chill off the Sunday devotions. I found him stoking the kirk fires on Saturday, not very much like a beadle in appearance, and much less like a waiter.

"There's mair nor guid preachin' wanted to keep a kirk gaun," said he; "If I was puttin' in as muckle dross in my fires as the doctor whiles puts in his sermons when he's aff the fang, ye wad see a bonny difference on the plate. But it's nae odds — a beadle gets sma' credit, though it's him that keeps the kirk tosh and warm, and jist at that nice easy-osy temperature whaur even a gey cauldrife member o' the congregation can tak' his nap and no' let his lozenge slip doon his throat chitterin' wi' the cauld."

"This is no weather for big congregations, Erchie," I said.

"Man, ye're richt there!' said he. "Torrey[2] and the like o' thae gaun-aboot bodies is fair takin' the breid oot o' oor mooths. It shouldna be alloo'ed. I'll no' deny the chap's daein' guid; I hear he converted yin o' the Govan Polis Pipe Baun'. The puir sowl cam' wi' his pipes to the pipe-major and says, 'I'm gaun to gi'e up playin' the bag-pipes,' says he. 'Whit wye that?' says the baun'-maister; 'Are the neighbours complainin'?' 'No, it's no' that,' says the converted piper, and him near greetin', 'but nae man 'll gang into Heaven wi' drones ower his shouther.' 'Wha tellt ye?' askes the baun'-maister. 'It doesna maitter wha tellt me,' says the piper. 'I've been gaun to Torrey's meetings and I'm a new man.' 'Are ye, faith, Donald?' says the baun'-maister. 'Och! I think ye should hing on by yer pipes for a week or twa yet, and ye'll maybe get better.'

"The wye that Torrey and Gypsy Smith and the like o' them fancy preachers wi' the no dug-collars get on sae weel is that they're no preachin' a' the time to folks that ha'e their Sunday claes on and their clean collars that tashed at the laundry they hack them like onything roon' the neck. Torrey tak's ye in yer werkin' claes, wi' yer kep in yer jaicket pouch, and you jist as comfortable as if ye were sittin' in the Mull o' Kintyre Vaults. If a' the people in Scotland lost credit wi' their tailors for a twelvemonth it wad be the salvation o' the kirks; the like o' Duffy the coalman wad ha'e to gang to kirk[3] in his sleeved waistcoat, and his wife wi' a polka on, and the minister wad be speakin' to the rale Duffy and the rale Duffy's wife. The wye it is the noo is that Duffy on the Sunday mornin' cuts himsel' in fower places shavin', breaks a' the nails aff his fingers puttin' a stud in his dickie, and sits through the sermon in fair torment, wi' a tichtness aboot the knees and a pair o' 'lastic-sided buits two sizes ower sma' for him. Mrs Duffy's that thrang, at the same time, wonderin' if she washed her ears, and whaur the Macdougalls got the money frae to pey for sich grandeur, that the gospels' truths wadna get inta her he'rt if they were bawled at her through a speakin' trumpet. The finest sermon in the warld 'll no win through the black cord coat and waistcoat o' a plumber that on week-days kens the comfort o' sittin' in his shirt sleeves wi' a low red-and-white striped kahouchy collar on, contemplatin' a job that's chairged by the time. And it's a' yin onywye ye tak' it; if ye're no gettin' a sair heid stretchin' yer neck to keep yer collar frae sawin' yer lugs, ye're that prood o' yer new breeks, or that throng pullin' doon yer cuffs so that they'll be seen, ye never hear onything frae the openin' prayer to the Doxology.

"Scotland's curse is her Sunday claes. I've a flet fit and a warm he'rt, but I declare I hate to be comin' alang the street on Sunday and see sae mony black slop suits and last year's lum hats. I ken fine half the dacent folk that wears them think that's a' that's needed to mak' them A1 Christians, and if beadlin' wasna pairt o' my tred, I wad gang to the kirk mysel' wi' nickerbockers on and a straw basher.[4] There's my wife Jinnet — she's mair concerned aboot the wye her bonnet's sittin' on her heid on a Sunday than she is aboot her immortal soul a' the ither days o' the week. It's the only day she loses her temper, and when the bells start ringing and her no' ready, whiles she gets into such a tirravee[5] I'm feart she'll swallow her hair-pins. It wad be a bonny-like thing to read on a heid-stane — 'Sacred to the Memory o' Jinnet MacPherson, Died Dressing Hersel' for the Kirk. Erected by her lovin' Husband.' There's Hospital Sundays, and Lifeboat Sundays and Temperance Sundays; the wonder is to me nane o' the ministers ever think o' ha'ein' Parridge-and-Plain-Claes Sundays, when naebody wad be alloo'ed inside the kirk doors that had ony ither claes on than the kind he worked for his wife and weans wi'.

"But ye canna blame the folks, perhaps, for the ministers themsel's set the example, wi' their stracht waistcoats, and their dug-collars, and their Hallelulya hats. I daursay I could be puttin' up fine wi' the clergy if they wore claes like ony ither body. They wad ken a guid dale mair aboot the warld if they did. But it only needs the sicht o' a coat withoot lapelles and a dug-collar to put a damper on onything herty, frae a cock-fight to a cookie-shine.[6] Jinnet aye says they wear thae kin' o' collars wi' nae studs in them jist so that they'll no' ha'e to dae ony cursin'. Of course there's some ministers even a dug-collar'll no' strangle a' the humanity oot o'. There's oor ain Doctor; he wears his ministerial claes wi' a kin' o' flourish that wad mak' ye think he was a Gordon Highlander and sae free-and-easy wi' his flock that Duffy'll no' even stop kickin' his horse if he sees him comin'. Still, if ministers maun ha'e a uniform o' some sort, whit wye can they no' ha'e yin a wee bit mair cheery? A cocked hat for the Auld Zion and a feather bunnet for the UFs wad be a gran' thing, and baith o' them wi' kind o' tartan waistcoats, or a red stripe doon the sides o' their breeches. I aye say to oor ain yin, 'Doctor, if ye preached on Sunday wi' the red gowfin' jacket ye gang to St Andrews wi, ye wad fill the kirk,' but he doesna see't.

"Anither thing I'm no' in wi' at a' is the bells. It's gey droll that the like o' Torrey doesna need ony bells to bring croods to hear them. I'll alloo' it's a personal maitter, to a certain extent, wi' me, for jerkin' awa' at the rope o' a twa-ton bell three or four times on a Sunday's no' beadle's wark at a'; it's mair like navvying. But bells at the best's fair idiotic, and a kin' o' confession that folk ha'e an awfu' bad memory for whit o'clock the kirk gangs in at. There's nae bells needed for the Britannia[7] or the Zoo. I like fine to hear a nice wee bell bashin' awa' on the sclates o' a kirk in a Hie'lan' glen, where the folks ha'e nae watches, and maybe forgot to row up their nocks on the Seturday nicht wi' it bein' the pay; but the bells o' Gleska's waur nor the steam-hooters. If ye ha'e any ear for music they drive ye fair distracted. If the bells had a' the same sound, and gi'ed the bang at the same time, it michtna be sae bad, but wi' hunders o' them jawin' awa' in different keys, and every yin tryin' to hit at a different time frae a' the ithers, ye micht as well be in a rivittin' shop."

"But the poetic sentiment of the bells, Erchie," I protested; "there is something soothing in the Sabbath bells; why! poetry has been made about them. You read the work of the poets, Erchie, I hope?"

"Catch me!" said he; "It wad jist be encouragin' the deevels.

"If Torrey and the like's gaun to be bate on their ain grun', we'll ha'e to reform a' thae things, and forbye, abolish the choir. There's a choir o' braw singers in oor kirk that's rapidly reducin' the membership. In the guid auld days when we didna sing by the music, but jist oot o' oor ain heids, it was a great satisfaction for a man to pit in a big boom-boom in the bass, and I've seen mysel' (and I'm no' great shakes at it) gi'ein' a gey he'rty skirl at 'Coleshill' or 'Evans,' and feelin' I was a gey guid man efter a'. But noo the hale o' us ha'e to staun' like dummies, listenin' to five o' the choir — nearly a' bass — that hivna sleept in, and if ye try a wee chord a' the rest o' the congregation look at ye as if they wad eat ye for spilin' the thing. They've even invented a new hymn-book that's different frae a' the hymn-books that cam' oot afore, wi' the flyest kind o' falderals in the tenor to keep the man that winds up in a fine soh-fah-me frae jinin' in. That's the kirk nooadays; it preaches for us, prays for us, and sings for us. We divna need to do onything at a' for oorsel's except try and keep awake and pit the penny in the plate."

47. *Erchie Suffers a Sea Change*[1]

"I'M FEELIN' fine," said Erchie to me on Saturday night. He came up the street with a peculiar travesty of a sailor's walk, rolling as men do after a protracted exercise of their 'sea legs'. He laughed slyly, and made a comical attempt to imitate the stage jack-tar's manner of 'hitching up his slacks'. "Dae ye see that?" he asked. "Erchie MacPherson, A.B. the good ship Jinnet Grant, A1 at Lloyd's; no smokin' abaft the brig; all passengers on the efter deck pay cabin fare!" And he chuckled again.

"What's in the wind, Erchie?" I asked.

"Man! need ye ask?" said he. "Shairly ye never read the papers. There's been naething in them a' this week past but Lipton's yats.[2] Naebody needs to gang to the coast this summer; a' they need to dae's to bide at hame in bonny wee Gleska and spend their bawbees on newspapers. Deevil the hate else is in them but Sir Tummas and his yats. I get fair sun-burned readin' them; if I had a neif-fu' o' wulks[3] and my feet in a byne o' saut watter, I wad think I was at Rothesay a' the time. Naethin' in the papers but yats — 'The challenger in Gourock Bay'; '*Shamrock* dirty bate on a run to windward'; 'the Lipton fleet preparin' to start'; 'Sir Tummas mak's three speeches and says he'll bring back the cup or never smile again.' Naethin' in the papers but yats; I havena seen a guid wife-beatin' case since *Shamrock III* was lenched. Whit Erchie MacPherson disna ken noo aboot yattin' and ships and sails and port-the-helms and things is no' worth kennin'. The first half-croon I ha'e to spare I'm gaun to buy a cheese-cutter kep.

"It's terrible the dangers o' the deep! When I read aboot the gallant fellows strugglin' oot yonder aff the Gantocks[4] in a twa-knot breeze, and the puir sowls as dry's onything, and the accidents that happened them, I get fair sea-sick. They hadna their new main-sail a day till it was bent, and naething they could dae tae't wad straighten't oot again. Every noo and then they were breakin' oot their jib top-sail or daein' somethin' o' that sort; it must ha'e been awfu' chawin'. But Sir Tummas never lost he'rt. 'It's a' richt, boys,' says he; 'I'm wan o' ycrsel's, I'm jist the same as I used to be afore I made my money. If we bend a' the sails ever was sewed, or break the backs o' them, we'll bring back the cup.' A wunnerfu' man Sir Tummas! I ken him fine; him and oor Rubbert's aboot an age. I was waitin' at a dinner he got the ither day in Greenock, and I took the chance when haundin' him the ceegaurs to wish him luck. 'Thank ye, Erchie,' says he, 'I'm prood to see ye. Hoo's Jinnet?' 'Oh, she's no' complainin', Sir Tummas,' says I. 'She aye gets her tea in your shop;[5] the rale Ceylon — nane o' their foreign trash.' 'Ah! ye're weel aff to be the wye ye are,' says he. 'I never had better health than when I had my brattie on and was busy workin'. This sport's an awfu' harassin' thing; the eyes o' the warld's on me, and, forbye, I ha'e to keep mind o' the names o' the sails and ropes and things; ye ha'e nae idea whit a job it is. Never you tak' to the yattin', Erchie.' 'Nae fears o' that,' says I; 'My feet's ower flet, forbye, it taks a lot o' siller to keep it up.' 'It does that, Erchie,' says he, and he slips a shillin' and an aluminium rivet aff the *Shamrock* in my haund.

"A yat a year is Lipton's motto. He's fair hotchin' wi' yats; they're stickin' to his feet. When he's lyin' aff Gourock yonder the *Columba*[6] and the *Lord o' the Isles* canna get awa' frae the quay till they pick a dizzen or twa o' Lipton's yats aff their paiddle-wheels or propellers. Sir Tummas canna mind the names o' half o' them; he buys yats by the gross, the wye oor Jinnet buys her claes-pins, or the wye he used to buy the Irish eggs afore he was a company. If yats could win the America Cup it wad ha'e been here lang syne. 'Whit sort o' a cup will it be dae ye ken?' Jinnet asks me. 'It maun be awfu' fancy when there's sae much fracaw[7] aboot it. Dae ye think it'll be a wally[8] yin?' 'It's mair nor I can tell,' I said to her. 'It's maybe pewther, and hauds an awfu' lot. It's cost a bonny penny to Sir Tummas, onywye.' 'I think,' says Jinnet, 'he wad be better for to gi'e the money to the puir.' 'And whit wad the puir ha'e to hurrah at then, wumman?' I asks her. 'It's easy seen ye havena studied human nature. Lipton's keepin' the Americans in mind that there's a place ca'd Britain on the map o' Europe; they're that throng ower yonder makin' boots and nocks, and tinnin' salmon and corned beef, that they wad clean forget a' aboot us if it wasna for the *Shamrocks*. 'Lord! here's yon chap again,' they say when they see him sailing ower. 'Whaur in the warld does he come frae?' Then they scoor up yin o' their auld yats, or tack thegither a new yin, and hide the cup up the lum in case he gets a haud o't. The friendly rivalry o' nations — that's whit it leads to,' says I; 'at least, that's whit they ca' it in the papers.' 'Dod! dae ye tell me?' says Jinnet.

"Her and me gaed doon on Thursday to see the yats gang aff. It was a grand day; the only thing that vexed me was that I hadna a doo-lichter bunnet. Every man ye saw at Gourock Quay had bell-moothed troosers and an awfu' smell o' tar. The bay was jammed wi' Lipton's boats. The *Erin*[9] lay among them as big as a man-o'-war, and a brass baun' frae Greenock did the best it could at blawin' on the quay when the polis wasna lookin'. 'Whatna steam yat's that?' asked Jinnet. 'That's the *Erin*,' I telt her, 'Sir Tummas's floatin' palace home.' She got an awfu' start, puir body. 'Gae awa' wi' ye, Erchie!' she tells me, 'it has only ae lum, and the *Galatea*[10] has twa.' 'Believe't or no',' I assured her, 'that's the *Erin*; she has a silver keel, and the common sailors in her get their tea in their beds afore they rise in the mornin'.' 'She awfu' white,' says Jinnet. 'Of coorse!' says I; 'white's a' the go for yats noo.' 'Dod! it maun tak' a lot o' pipe-clye[11] to gang ower them a',' says Jinnet. Noo and then Sir Tummas he wad come on deck and gi'e a keek to see if naebody was lookin', for he wanted to slip awa' as quate as possible, and every time the Greenock baund saw him it played anither Irish tune as nice as onything. He was sair vexed to see croods and croods come poorin' aff the Gleska trains, and says 'Tut! tut! it's an awfu' thing a man canny dae onything withoot folk glowerin' at him; I wish I had gaun awa' through the nicht; I'll ha'e to mind and dae that next time.' A grand day! A' the wee boys plunked the schule, and a' the yats frae Rothesay and Hunter's Quay, as weel as frae Mudhook and Corinthia and them places that's no' in the maps, came puffin' up and got nearly run ower by the skoosh steamer, the *King Edward*. 'He maun be a prood man this day,' says Jinnet. 'He is that,' says I.

"When the quay was crooded that thick the folk were hingin' on by their tae nails, and Sir Tummas saw there was no chance o' their gaun awa', he threw aff a' disguise and ordered the yats to start. Cannons begood to bang, and every boat that had a steam whistle put a trained musician to the playin' o't till they nearly burst yer lugs. The twa *Shamrocks* were dragged past the quays that close that even the folk wi' the third-class tickets could get a fine

view o' Sir Tummas and his gallant men. He stood on the
deck o' *Shamrock III*, tryin' hard no' to greet at the sicht o'
his country's devotion. His kep was in his haund, and he
was lookin' as spruce as onything. 'Ye're no' a bad sort,'
says I to mysel'; ' I mind fine o' ye in Stockwell.'[12] It was an
occasion for a speech as the yat slipped past the quay and
anither special train from Gleska came in; Sir Tummas
raised his haund and I daursay he micht ha'e found
something new to say aboot the cup, but the Greenock
baund thocht it was a signal, and begood to play, 'Will ye
no' come back again?' while the sailors on the *Shamrock III*
started to gie their patent a'thegither-yin-twa-three yell.
Wan by wan the Lipton fleet poored oot o' the bay, and
though it wisna near the 'oor for't, the tide begood to turn.
As faur as the eye could see there was naethin' but Lipton's
yats. Flags wagged frae every hoose to let furnished, wi'
attendance in Gourock, every auld retired captain wi' a
pension in the place let aff a cannon and the coastgaird let
aff twa, no' ha'ein' to pay for the poother themsel's.

"At aboot Lamlash Sir Tummas, on the *Erin*, her wi' the
silver keel, got a' his fleet aboot him and bade his
challenger God-speed. It was a movin' spectacle. 'Boys!'
he says, and his voice jist clean choked wi' emotion. 'Boys!
the 'oor has come when ye ha'e to set oot across the
heavin' billow in quest o' the cup. Afore ye go I wad like to
mention whit I never tauld anither leevin' sowl afore —
that we ha'e a fine boat in oor new yat, that Mister Fyfe[13]
did the best he could, that I did the best I could, that
Wringe did the best he could, and that I'm confident we'll
bring back the cup. Whither we dae or no', my motto is to
please; mind and be good lads, and no' gi'e back-chat to
the Yankees. Mind the eyes o' the warld's on ye. They're
on mysel' too, but I'm used to't, and it disna put me aboot.
My last word to ye is — Bring Back the Cup!' Havin' said
that, he ordered every man a special tot o' rum, and then
broke doon, so that he had to be taken back to Gourock on
a tug steamer."

48. *Erchie in the Garden*[1]

ERCHIE HAD a flower in his coat yesterday evening, and looked quite rural, but had the self-consciousness of a man who thinks he is over-dressed. "Here's a floo'er to ye," he said, taking it out of his lapel and thrusting it on me. "Not at all, Mr MacPherson; I won't deprive you of it," I protested, but he insisted. "It's a fine thing a floo'er," he said, "and 'll no' dae ye ony hairm, but I never care to ha'e yin in my coat. It doesna suit the like o' me somewye. A red geranium in your buttonhole doesna gang awfu' weel wi' flet feet, and then, again, folk think ye've been awa' plunderin' a cemetery. There were two women at a close mooth I past up yonder in Springburn, and ane o' them said, 'See at the auld yin; I'll widger his first wife's deid, and he's coortin' again!'"

As I put the votive offering of my friend in my button-hole, he produced a bouquet, tightly wrapped in a hand-kerchief, from his coat-tail pocket, revealed its character, and hastily put it back again. "Ye see, I've plenty mair," said he. "An odd way to carry flowers," I said, astonished. "Do ye think I wad cairry them in my haund?" said he, "and it the Lord's Day? A bonny-like thing that for a beadle to dae. Forbye, it's no' the thing at a' for a dacent Scotchman that has his health to be seen cairryin' floo'ers aboot the street; it mak's him look like an Italian, or some ither o' they foreign trash that's no' hardy and releegious.

"I was oot at my dochter's yonder in Springburn, and my guidson's[2] great on gairdenin'. I don't ken awfu' much aboot floo'ers mysel', I only ken the names o' twa; yins a piano-rose, and the ither's no'. His gairden's lookin' fine the noo, and he's thrang at it till a' 'oors o' the nicht. Whiles I gang oot in the skoosh caur and sit on the summer sate and watch him weedin'. A man that weeds a gairden wad be nane the waur o' a hinge in his back, I'm thinkin'. It fair bates me to understand the wye weeds thrive sae weel whaur cabbage or syboes[3] 'll only grow wi' a grudge. Ye

may weed a plot o' grun' till it's as clean as the loof[1] o' your
haund, and if ye turn your back on't for a meenute to gang
for a drink o' watter, or wipe the sweat aff yer broo, ten
dandelions 'll come breengin' oot o' the grun' for every yin
ye poo'ed. They tell me that birds and bumbees and the
wind cairry the seeds o' the weed aboot wi' them, and
plant them onywhere they see a chance. It jist shows ye the
reediculousness o' Nature, that never tak's into its heid to
gi'e man a chance. When my guidson wants to grow cabbages, it's little help he'll get frae the birds and the
bumbees; he maun plank doon his bawbees for plants at
the bazaar, and sit up at nicht to chase awa' the cats aff
them. Whit Nature does wi' the aid o' a plain yellow and
black striped bumbee is mair nor my guidson can dae, and
him sixteen-stane wecht, a Rechabite, and a foreman
moulder. Half the things he puts in the grun' never come
up again, and the sowin' o' whit he ca's his annuals is like
the game o' neevy-neevy-nick-nack; ye canna tell which
haund the piano-roses is on, and which haund the no'
piano-roses is on. A'e day last April I saw him puttin' twa
wee sticks wi' 'R' on the yin, and 'P' on the ither, like wee
heid-stanes in the grun'. 'Whit's thae for?' I asks him. 'R's
for Radishes,' says he, and 'P' for Parsley.' I took anither
wee stick and wrote 'I' on it, and put it between the twa, so
that it read 'RIP', and I wisna faur wrang, for the seeds are
restin' in peace there ever since.

"The only floo'er that grows withoot much trouble in
my guidson's gairden is the rhubarb. It grows that hard he
has to clap a barrel on't in the end o' the winter to keep it
doon; if he didna dae that his rhubarb wad be sclimbin' the
fence, and spreadin' ower Springburn like a rash. The
quantities o't that he gi'es awa' at this time o' the year wad
mak' tarts for the British Airmy; naebody wants it, but they
ha'e to tak' it or he'll no' be pleased. There's a hale land o'
hooses near him that's a' shut up till the rhubarb season's
past; the folk that was in them are awa' to the coast to
escape frae Rubbert's rhubarb. They say at the start it's
fine red, sappy, sweet rhubarb, but efter a week o't they'll

no bide in the land. My guidson's cabbages and leeks and caulifloo'ers are no sae rife as a' that; there's nane o' them sclimbin' ower the dyke; he has to haul them oot the grun' by the hair o' their heids. He's growin' champion cabbage noo for the Springburn Floo'er Show and even the wee, sma' red-hot Springburn midge[5] has no terrors for him. It does me guid to sit in the summer-sate smokin' my pipe and watchin' him. Jinnet buys the cabbage for oor ain hoose at a bawbee the time, and I tell him they're jist as guid as his, and she rins no risk o' bein' eaten by the midges.

"There's a neibour o' my guidson's wha keeps hens. The hen is a fine, sonsy, usefu' beast for layin' eggs, and has excellent qualities, roast or boiled, but it disna mak' a nice stairheid neibour for a champion cabbage. My guidson's gettin' grey-hcided chasin' thae hens oot o' his gairden. He's an early riser, but they're up afore him, scrapin' aboot the cabbage and the peas, and excavatin' in the beds that's gaun to grow the floo'er that's no' the piano-rose but yon ither kind. There's ten thoosand wyes a hen can get into a gairden, but only the wan wye she can get oot, and it's gey ill for her to find it. I aften wondered what accoonted for the fine athletic legs o' the spring chickens I aften ha'e to serve to folk at dinners; it wisna till my guidson got a gairden I understood that they spent their days in runnin' roond gairdens, jinkin' a man wi' a hoe. Cats are jist as bad, my guidson tells me; there's millions o' cats in Springburn, and they a' come into his gairden when he's at his work, or in his bed sleepin' and play auld Hairry wi' the finest-raked beds in the place. A tax on hens and cats is what he says is badly wanted, and no' on the puir man's quarter loaf."

Erchie apparently found he had exhausted all he had to say on gardening, and, after a pause, turned to what might have been a more inspiring theme in the new invention of tabloid beer.[6] "Ye've read aboot it?" he said. "Man, it bates a'. The quart-pot and the schooner 'll be oot o' date in a twelvemonth, and every man that drinks beer 'll cairry his supply aboot wi' him in his waistcoat pooch. Ye'll ask a frien' to ha'e a schooner wi' ye, and tak' a No. 3 beer lozenge oot o' yer pooch, mak' wi' a tinny for the nearest pump-wall, and stir up the elements the same as ye were makin' sugarally. I'm vexed for Duffy; it'll spile him, for he'll cairry aboot beer lozenges in pokes and chow them like ju-jubes. It may be the cause o' Scotland's doonfa', too, for folk 'll maybe dae awa' wi' the peppermint and tak' the new tabloid to kirk. Afore the Fair's bye, ye'll see the Conversation Quart Drop,[7] a lozenge wi' a suitable motto on't such as 'Here's to ye!' or 'Ha'e anither wi' me this time'. The pubs may shut their doors, for the tred 'll be a' in the hands o' the Italian ice-cream shops. Whit was wanted maist, I think, was not a tabloid beer, but a new kind o' tabloid thirst; it wad be mair for the guid o' the country."

49. *Erchie on the Physical Standard*[1]

"THE FAIR'S nearly started," said Erchie on Saturday. "ye can feel't in the air. They're beginnin' to fry herrin's for their teas up oor close, and takin' in the new potatoes. I met Duffy an 'oor ago comin' alang the street haudin' himsel' up no' that bad, and tryin' to mind the words o' 'Dark Lochnagar.' 'The beer I've drunk this day!' says he. 'Man,' I says, 'ye wad be far better to bring't hame in a pail.' There's thoosands o' men like Duffy in Gleska this very day; they're that gled the Fair's comin' on they canna keep oot o' the public-hoose, and by the time the Fair's richt started they'll no' ken very muckle aboot it except that their money's near done. Last year Duffy comes to me at the end o' the Fair week and asked me for a wee len' o' my *Francis Orr's Almanack*.[2] 'Are ye wantin' to see when it's high tide, so that ye can go and droon yersel'?' I asks him. 'No, nor droon mysel',' says he, 'nae fears o' me; I want tae ken whit day o' the week it is, and whether this is the start o' the Fair or the end o't.' Man, is it no' jist peetifu' the wye men like Duffy spile their holidays wi' drink? A chap micht as weel mak' ready for his Sunday dinner by takin' a dram o' chloroform.

"Nae wonder the breed's fa'in' aff in Scotland. I see the Hoose o' Commons is awfu' sair vext at the condeetion o' the common people o' the country.[3] When an MP comes frae London to Scotland, and lands at Clachnacuddin Station, he can hardly get a men wi' strength enough to cairry his carpet bag. In the schools there's seventy-five per cent o' the weans needin' to wear specs; they hurt their e'en greetin' ower their hame lessons. They can tell ye the names o' a' the rivers in India gey near richt, but they canna tell whit 'oor it is on a clock withoot haudin' their heid to the side. The manhood o' the country's bein' sapped someway the Government canna understand; and there's hardly twa young chaps in twenty wi' good enough teeth to pass for the Army. They're fed that weel in the Army, ye ken, the teeth's the first consideration. The great big hame-made Scotsman that used to be bred on stiff porridge and Champion potatoes is nae langer to the fore, and sae faur as looks go, ye can hardly tell the difference between a Gleska man and an Italian if it wasna for the monkey. 'Something must be done, and that quickly,' says the Government, and then goes oot for lunch.

"The droll thing is that we were never daein' mair nor we're daein' the noo to keep up oor strength. They start in the school puttin' wee Wullie through his gymnastics, makin' him wag Indian clubs, and touch his taes wi' his fingers withoot burstin' the knees o' his knickerbockers; and he's no' richt oot o' the infant class when a potty gun's[4] clapt on his shouther, and he's made into a Boys' Brigade wi' a white belt and a pooch hingin' to't for haudin' his cigarettes. Look at the young man in his millions, sweatin' ower golf links lookin' for ba's, skooshin' oot to Fenwick Inn and the Black Bull at Mullguy on bicycles, walkin' by the 'oor withoot his waistcoat for yin o' Freedman's suits o' claes[5] or a £5 prize frae the Tivoli. The first thing the average Gleska young man puts in his kist when he's changin' his lodgin's is a pair o' twenty-pun' dumb-bells, a Sandow exerciser, and *The Whole Art o' Bein' Strong in Two Minutes' Practice a Week*. It's the same wi' the genteel young

weemen livin' at hame wi' their maws; they used to dae
naethin' but macrami doyleys for coupin' paw's decanter on,
or sit on deck chairs oot in the back green at Langside with
their feet up on the ash-pit lettin' on to themsel's it was the
country. Noo they're bikin' as hard as their brithers,
gowfin', playin' hockey, and daein' a' they can to get a fine
feegure.[6] Their maw keeps her feegure richt wi' jist dressin'
their polkas or blouses or whit is't ye ca' them?

"Me and you had to warstle into the state we're in on
stuff to eat that micht ha'e sent us early to oor graves.
Porridge, broth, soda scones, and a' that plain common
trash that tires the digestive organs, and has nae mair
science in't than a kippered herrin'. It's a mercy we're
spared; the risin' generation noo enjoys the blessin's o'
Force, Grape-nuts, Plasmon, Pianiolio, and Oleaginous.
Thae things may look like champed sandstane, bran-stuffin'
for dolls, or bath loofahs, but they're chokefu' o' science,
and there's hunders o' doctors' lines wi' every yin o' them.
Through the nicht, when ye're soond sleepin', the Pianiolio
Patent Provender is daen' its wark, buildin' up bone and
sinew for you, and makin' enough for the men that runs
the lumber and sawdust mills in America to buy yachts wi',
and live in Paris or London. Twa plates o' the Malted
Oleaginous are equal in nutritive quality to a butcher's
shop; a course o' Plasmon, persevered in for a fortnicht,
will tak' yer leg oot o' the grave, and mak' ye able to lift
prizes for wrestlin' at the Polis Sports.

"As for mysel', I'm daein brawly, thenk ye. I've maybe a
flet fit, but I've a warm hert, and I'm strong enough to be
daein' my bits o' turns. I can see signs that sooner or later
the people o' this country'll be made to rise at five every
mornin', walk ten miles afore breakfast, tak' cauld baths,
and pass examinations in the use o' bar-bells. There'll be
Government standards o' strength, weight, height, lung
poo'er, sicht, scent, and hearin', and them that canna
pass'll ha'e to gang abroad. But I'm fine, I'm no complainin' and neither's Jinnet. Daein' oor day's darg's aboot
as muckle exercise as we're needin'."

50. *Erchie on the War*[1]

There was a reference to the war[2] from the pulpit of St Kentigern's Church yesterday, and Erchie was somewhat annoyed that so much importance should be attached to a conflict of whose magnitude he has but a hazy idea.

"Fancy puttin' up a prayer aboot a bit war like thon!" he said to me afterwards. "The minister hadna much to dae to be bothered wi' them. It's jist yon o' thae foreign wars abroad in yin o' thae places ye gang to in a steamer. There's nae Black Watch nor Gordon Heilanders workin' at it; only a wheen o' folk that wear comic claes and eat ony kind o' trash. I wadna gie them ony encouragement."

"But war is always a dreadful thing, Erchie," I ventured to say; "and our own war[3] was abroad, too; that did not make it any the less dreadful."

"Maybe it was," said he, "but it was in a country whaur the places ha'e Christian names. I canna be bothered wi' thae fancy names they gi'e the places whaur this war's takin' place; it gi'es me a sair heid to read them in the papers. And I ken fine they're a' wrang spelled onywye. It's maybe a richt enough war, but there's nae money in't for Mrs Maclure in oor close, her that has a man in the Preserves. When he was ca'd oot to the front at the Transvaal, she was put on the War Fund, and did sae weel aff it that she started a green-grocery that's daein' fine. She got a wee lend o' a lot o' weans frae the neibours and got twa shillin's a week frae the Fund for each o' them, no mentionin' cairt-loads o' auld claes. The only body that I can see that's gaun to mak' money aff this war is Duffy; he's put a bawbee on the bag o' coals since he read somewhere that the Rooshians canna get fechtin' richt for the ice. 'That'll put up the demand for coal,' says Duffy, the same as if they were gaun to melt the ice wi' fires, and whips oot his lump o' chalk."

"Ah! Erchie," I said, "it means much more than a ha'-penny on the bag o' coals to Russia and Japan. War is war, foreign or at home."

"I daursay it is," he admitted. "They're no' gettin' awfu' guid weather for this yin onywye. Whit bates me aboot it," he went on, "is the wye the bonny wee Japs is daein' the trick. I'm acquent wi' the Japs; it's them that mak's the stuff for bleck'nin' grates, and ha'e the monopoly o' the draught-screen tred. They ha'e to be daein' something for a livin', puir sowls, them bein' sae far awa' frae onyplace. I seen them at the Exhibeetion[4] — gey peely-wally to look at, but as game as onything, and their prices for paper fans fair reediculous. It was them had yon wee trees hunners o' years auld and no' the size o' a savoy cabbage. A droll folk, but maybe God made them. We didna mak' a great fraca aboot the Japanese when they were at the Exhibeetion, and they had to keep their e'en open for fear some o' us smert Gleska folk dinna pinch ony o' their wee wally vawzes no' for haudin' onything. I mind o' the chaps fine; I was a waiter at the Grosvenor for a month at a time, and I could see them gaun aboot in their carpet slippers, their e'en up near their ears, and their claes ready-made. The Rooshians were there too; ye mind the wee toon they built in their spare time when they werena sherpnin' their hatchets. I learnt a lot aboot the Rooshians there; ye could see they were a thochtfu' people from the wye they contemplated ony parteecular job they were gaun to start. They had on top-boots nae maitter whit kind o' weather it was, slack breeks, and a language ye couldna mak' ony sense o'. We were awfu' friendly wi' the Rooshians at that time, even Duffy gave up the beer and took to drinkin' Rooshian tea. A great people, awfu' needin' shavin'. It was fine to watch them; it let ye see the curiosities o' nature. But they were the maist puttingaffinest folk ever I set e'en on. That's whit spiles them at this war; ye ha'e to be gey gleg when ye gang oot wi' a gun.

"It's a peety this war between the Japanese and the Roo-shians didna start when they were oot at the Groveries;[5] it wad ha'e been a fine pant and faur mair popular than the water-shoot. We could ha'e locked them up in the grounds when they got railly dangerous and watched them wi' spy-glasses from Park Circus. The papers wad be railly worth readin' for their war news then — 'Rooshian gondola torpedoed near the water-shoot,[6] and sinks in four feet o' water. Admiral Kaskowhusky wades ashore in the glare o' the search-licht frae Gilmorehill, and gets his feet a' wet.' 'Bungalow attacked by the Rooshians; great slaughter; no' a hale tumbler left in the place, and threatened intervention o' the Cranstonhill Polis.' 'Japs massing on Miss Cranston's tea-rooms;[7] great capture o' lemons, and exasperation o' the Rooshians, wha canna get their tea. Price o' the London bun goes up to threepence. Telegram frae the Rooshian Emperor — Hing on as lang's ye can till I spit on my hands and declare war; then God defend the right!' 'Six Japanese wi' five fans, twa draught-screens, and a battery o' paper lanterns, crossed the Kelvin on Setterday nicht and took up a strong poseetion in the laagar-beer bar. Rooshians reported in strong force in the neighbourhood o' the Art Gallery. Letter frae Sir John Shearer tellin' them they better mind whit they're aboot, and no' spile onything.' 'Fall o' the King's statue under the dome; blown up by dynamite by the Japanese. Great rejoicings.' 'Masterly move by the Japs; they retire on the Sunlight Soap Model cottage, and repel Rooshian attack wi' cakes o' soap. Rooshians protest that the use of soap is contrary to the Berlin Convention, bein' mair deadly than dum-dum bullets.'

"That wad be a richt sort o' war; ye could gang oot and see't goin' on every nicht efter ye got yer tea, and if things got dull they could ha'e Sousa's band[8] up at the flagstaff, forenent Park Circus, playin' 'The Mikado',[9] and 'San Toy'.

"This is the maist disappointin' war ever I read o'. Ye'll buy the paper at nicht, thinkin' it's gaun to be awfu' guid readin' because it says in the bill that three regiments o' Rooshian sappers went through the ice and were drooned, and ye find that though it's in the paper, the paper itsel' says it's maybe no' true. A bawr's a bawr, but that's no' fair horney.[10] Then, again, ye see that hunders o' Japanese ha'e been sunk in a transport ship; ye buy the paper as fast's ye can, and ye find their names is no' given. Whaur's the fun o' that? For a week or twa efter the war started the telegraph wires were kept red-hot wi' telegrams aboot the sinkin' o' Rooshian ships. The Japs sunk them daily or 'oorly as required; they wad jist daunder up where a Rooshian man-o'-war was lyin', and pit a torpedo on't as if it was a mustard plaister, and stand back smokin' their cigarettes and coolin' themsel's wi' their fans till the poother gaed aff. It generally happened that the Rooshian Admirals and their crews were awa' ashore in the punt to a dance, and when they came back their ships werena there, so there was naething for them but to tak' ludgings in the toon. 'Cowards!' says they, 'to hit us behind oor backs, and us no lookin'. Hoo wad they like it themsel's?' But the Japs jist went on fanning themsel's. Then the Rooshians made whit's ca'd a straggetic move, took some o' their ships oot o' dock and ran as nate's onything into their ain submarine mines. There was an awfu' bang. 'Tut! tut!' says Admiral Alexander (the chap that disna ken the wye to spell his ain name.) 'Tuts!' says he, startin' oot to sweem for shore withoot ha'ein' time to tak' his spurs aff. 'Tuts! wha left oot thae submarines this mornin'?' The Japs went on fannin' themsel's and agreed that if the war was cairried on this way they wad save a lot o' money. That's the droll thing aboot it: naithing ever happens to the Japs. They jist gang perusin' roond wi' a fan in wan hand and a torpedo in the ither. The Rooshian Emperor was awfu' annoyed at it. 'Hold on!' he wires to them. 'I'm jist gaun awa' to declare war as soon's I can find my bunnet.' 'We're findin' the holes in the Hoshkikoff and Ulbakx.' Admiral Alexander wires back whenever he got himsel' dried. 'They're a' above high-water mark, and we're fillin' them up wi' potty. The forces under my command are quite calm.' They micht weel be calm, puir craturs, for the maist o' them were in ablow the water, that awfu' deid nae potty could cure them.

"There havena been nae reports o' a' Rooshian disaster for three days; it's on accoont o' the snow fallin', yin o' the papers says. I suppose the Rooshians forgot to bring their galoshes to the front wi' them, and the Japanese divna want to wet their carpet slippers. This delay is Providential; it'll gi'e the American excursion steamers for the seat o' war time to be there for the next naval battle. Oh, aye! they're runnin' trips frae New York. Sixty days at the Seat o' War for Six Hundred Dollars. Every passenger guaranteed a front seat when the fightin' starts. Nicht engagements brilliantly illuminated by the electric searchlight. Band on board, and first-class cocktail bar.' I hear the German Emperor's thinkin' o' takin' a run oot on his yacht; if the weather's ower stormy he'll jist stay at hame and send the Rooshians a telegram."

51. *Erchie on After-Dinner Oratory*[1]

Erchie has had a busy season at his trade of waiting, for Glasgow this winter has been more convivial than usual. "I'm gled when it comes to Setterday," he said to me yesterday. "It's no easy job I'm tellin' ye; skliffin' aboot in a claw-hemmer coat tryin' to keep mind o' the French for potted-heid. Dinners is gettin' faur mair compleecated than when I begood waitin' in the auld Saracen Heid,[2] and they're gaun ower the score a'thegither wi' their fancy names for dishes. I'm no' sayin' onything against the French, but they should keep to their ain business, and that's the polishin'.

"When I started the tred, a waiter had some chance; ham was ham, and nane o' yer 'jambone', as they ca't noo; there wad be only four coorses; the folk got through them as smart as they could, and then made a breenge at the bottle.[3] But nooadays they keep chowin' awa' for two 'oors; their mind's made up they're no' gaun to their work on the morn's morn. For twenty years I ha'e seen the public men o' Gleska — Bylies and Professors, and Doctors and

Ministers, and the like o' that — gettin' fatter and fatter, a
new dress waistcoot no lastin' them mair than two winters,
though their wife's let it oot at the back and shifted the
buttons. That's the wye they ha'e to start the gowfin' — to
try and save their dress-suits. There was nae need for
gowfin' in my young days; folk jist took their meat like
Christians, and didna turn a dinner into an operatic show.

"I was at a dinner in the Fine Art Institute[4] the ither nicht,
and my hert was sair to wait on yon Deputy-Lieutenants,
them that wears the red-coats and gets their feet a' fankled
wi' their swords when they're gaun up or doon a stair. I
mind when thae Deputy-Lieutenants were as nate as onything, and could tak' their watches oot o' their waistcoast
pooches quite easily if they wanted to ken the time; noo
they ha'e to keep them in their trouser pouches, wi' whit's
ca'd a fob chain, and even then it's no' easy for them to
drag them oot, and they wad raither ask the like o' me whit
o'clock it is. A man's no' a Deputy-Lieutenant mair nor
three winters in Gleska when he has to start walkin' far
back on his heels in case he fa's on his nose. Fine, big,
sonsy chaps! — there's some talk o' startin' a tug-o-war
team amang them and challengin' the Govan Polis.

"The only thing that keeps some o' them frae bulgin'
oot that faur their sword-belts 'll no' meet on them is that
whiles they ha'e to mak' a speech. There's some that's used
to't, and wad raither be speakin' than no'. They like fine to
hear their voices bum-bumin' through the hall. That's the
kind that tak' twa helpin's o' soup to keep their strength up
for the toast they're gaun to propose. Ye can see when they
get on their feet that they're feelin' fine, and no' frichtened
for onything. When they sit doon efter they're done, and
looks roon to see whaur the champagne bottle's awa' to, I
like to be first at their shoother wi't, and tak' the chance o'
whisperin' in their ears (me bein' a lang while at the tred
and weel kent by the maist o' them) that it's the speech o'
the evenin'. I find that does nae hairm; there's aye
something slipt in my haund afore the nicht's bye.

"But it's them that ha'e speeches to mak' and divna like

the jab that keep thin the langest. An' shair's death I'm vexed whiles to watch the craturs afore their turn comes. Ye can see them breakin' a' their breid into muillins, smilin' in a kind o' ghastly wye to their next-haund nee-bour, and no' hearin' a word he's sayin' to them for their heid's a' in a whummle. They canna even eat, for whit they eat has nae taste, and curried sweetbreads micht be shavin's for a' the difference they can mak' oot. It wad be a mercy to them if the toasts cam' on afore the dinner; they wad get fat faur sooner.

"For weeks they ha'e been practisin' their speech; their wife kens it by he'rt, for they wakened her up at nicht to hearken them at it, and she said 'Oh, George! it's a beauti-ful speech, that's whit it is, and are ye gaun to buy me yon di'mond ring in Sorley's?' In his own pawrlour, when it's the servant lassie's nicht oot, and his wife's awa' callin' on somebody, George can gi'e that speech to the cat wi' such a grand delivery, he lets on to himsel' he's John B. Gough or Lord Provost Primrose, and winds up wi' openin' his sideboard for the least wee taste o' speerits as a reward o' merit. But when his turn comes on the toast list, he gets on his feet wi' his speech a' upside-doon in his heid, and an awfu' hole in the middle o't, and wishes he had stayed puir a' his days, and had nae need to suffer this, or had broken his leg on the way to the hall.

"I ha'e heard that mony efter-dinner speeches in my time as a waiter that if my feet failed me I could start a works for turnin' oot orations for all occasion. No' that I hiv only hankerin' to shine in that line mysel' — I ken whit it sometimes leads to. If ye yince get the reputation o' bein' a grand efter-dinner orator or awfu' guid at a bawr, ye're shair to be led astray in Gleska. Folk lie in wait for ye at the close mooth wi' a cab and kidnap ye, when ye're on yer wye hame to yer tea, and when you're thinkin' ye're daein' fine and keepin' the company lauchin' like onything, the folk that kidnapped ye's awa' back in anither cab to their shops and offices to work overtime to get the better o' ye in yer business. Na, na; if ye hiv a son that's showin' ony signs

o' comin' oot strong in the singin' or recitin' or speech-
makin' line — onything that canna be done in a shop or an
office — stop him as soon's ye can, for that's no' the wye to
fortune and a motor caur.[5] The men that's makin' the
money in Gleska's the men that were carefully kept clear o'
accomplishments and the public-hoose when they were
young. They're no' singers, they canna dance, they dinna
play Bridge, and they let the ither chaps dae the speakin'
and tell the funny bawrs. They themsel's jist stick into their
wark as dour as onything, and wear square-topped hats,
and ye think there's no' much in them till ye read in the
papers that they're deid worth half-a-million pounds, were
faithful adherents o' the Free Kirk, and did a lot o' guid to
the puir. I'm tellin' ye it's a rale divert!

"Och! but I could mak' speeches wi' my least wee bit
touch. I've heard the Imperial Forces proposed a thoosand
times in the last twenty years. It's generally proposed by a
man in the flannelette tred, wi' a wife that keeps his pocket-
money doon to haulf-a-croon a week, and wadna let him
oot to ony o' thae banquets if it wasna that his name'll be
in the papers and the Mackays roond the terrace'll see it
there — them that has a dochter mairried on a professor
and aye ca's her Mrs Professor Mackay. When he proposes
the Imperial Forces he begins wi' the battle of Waterloo
and the death o' Nelson, says the stuff's aye to the fore yet,
and the successors o' Britain's auld wooden walls can still
sweep the seas. A' the time the puir cratur's gled he hasna
the sweepin' o' the seas to dae himsel', for he couldna cross
frae Princes Pier to Cove on the Bonnie Doon[6] on a fine
day withoot feelin' no' weel. And he says the Airmy's a'
richt, fit to gang onywhere, and dae onything it's payed for.

"The man that responds for the Imperial Forces is
generally a dacent auld chap that never did onybody ony
hairm, and nearly jined the Volunteers when the movement started, but couldna get passed by the doctors, and
was gey gled o't. He says the bloodthirstiest things wi' a
fruit knife in his haund, the same as if he was jist gaun awa'
to the front to start slaughterin' as soon as the company

was done wi' 'Auld Lang Syne'. It's him and the news-papers that stir up bloody wars. Them that's at the dinner wi' him's no heedin' onything about the Rooshians or the Germans; they've eaten and drunken that much they wad stand ony Rooshian or German a drink, and tak' him hame in their cab if he hapened to drap into the banquet; but when that dacent auld chap wi' the fruit-knife grinds his teeth and says we have he'rts made oot o' oak and we're no' gaun to be bate by ony coalition o' the Poo'ers,[7] the meekest wee man in the company tak's anither soop oot his gless and hates the hale map o' Europe.

"My he'rt aye gangs oot to the puir sowl that has to propose the toast o' the evenin'. There's aye something fine and brilliant expected frae him, and he's that wrapt up in the attempt to be brilliant that he disna see the folk yawnin', and thinks that when they scrape their feet on the flair and say 'hear-hear-hear-hear-hear' they're eggin' him on, and a' the time they're wantin' to hear the chap that's to sing the comic sang. The finest toast o' the evenin' I ever heard was frae a Dundee man; he was to propose the toon and tred o' Dundee, and when he stood up he says, 'Ladies and gentlemen, I'm no' a speaker. Ladies and gentlemen, I'm— I'm— I'm a plumber. Ladies and gentlemen — ah — ah — ach, to bleezes!' and then sat doon. It was fine.

"Naebody ever said onything new at an efter-dinner speech — at least , no' in my time, and it's nae wonder, for they never change the text. Whit's the use o' aye wangin' awa' at the Royal Family, the Imperial Forces, the Magis-trates and Toon Cooncil, Art and Leeterature, and the like o' thae things that's been worn threadbeare. Whit's wanted's a change; gi'e 'Our Fitba' Clubs', 'The Temperance Move-ment', 'The Waiter', 'The Police Force', coupled wi' the name o' 'Captain Stevenson', and 'Photography' a chance.

"Perhaps it wad be better to abolish toasts a'thegither, and just tak' the dram the wye Duffy does, withoot makin' ony excuse for't. Toasts is a survival o' the auld days, when the country wasna sa wealthy as it is noo, and drink maybe wasna sae plentifu' at the social board. When a company

thocht a chap had plenty and was gettin' mair nor his
share, they put him on his feet to mak' a speech. By the
time he was feenished wi' his speech the bottle was done
and the folk said they had him on toast. That's the wye the
word toast cam' into use."

52. *Erchie at the Frivolity*[1]

"I'LL BATE ye canna guess where I was last nicht," said
Erchie to me some days ago.

"Let me see now," I answered; "Was it a wedding or a
temperance lecture, or a trip to Paisley? Or maybe it was
on a run with a motor-car?"

"No, nor a motor-car," said Erchie. "Catch me! I canna
stand yon things gaun skooshin' aboot like demented tar-
bilers, skriechin' 'Pip! pip!'[2] and runnin' doon folk that's no'
that awfu' auld they need to be killed that wye. No, it wasna
none o' yer motors; I was at the Frivolity Music-Hall."

"Oh, Erchie!" I exclaimed. "A beadle, too!"

"I don't see ony hairm in't," said Erchie. "Forbye, it
didna cost me onything. I got the ticket frae a gentleman I
waited on at a dinner the ither nicht; he was playin'
Bridge,[3] and it was a' the change he had left when he cam'
to gi'e me a tip. Theatres and music-halls is no' looked
doon on noo in Scotland the wye they used to be. I mind
when ye wad lose your place if ye were seen gaun into the
Britannia, and if ye were for a nicht in Davie Broon's[4] ye
had to disguise yoursel' wi' a false baird and the skip o'
your kep doon on your nose for fear ye met somebody
belanging to the same kirk as yoursel'! Nooadays the
genteelest and the best-leevin' folk gang to theatres and
music-halls if somebody gi'es them a ticket for naething.
Theatres and music-halls is gettin' as common as mulk
shops, and still the demand's greater than the supply, so
that every nicht noo the music-halls in Gleska ha'e to tak'
in their customers in two rakes, as Duffy says, the same as
they were coals.

"It's years since I was in a place o' that kind afore, but they're no' much changed. I noticed that the orchestra cam' in frae below the stage, the wye they used to dae, and ganted when they looked at the audience the same as to say, 'Here they are again, puir sowls, and them no' needin' to be here unless they liked; different frae us that mak's oor money by't.' The conductor pu'd doon the cuffs o' his shirt, breathed hard, rapped on the railin' that keeps the serio-comics frae fallin' into the big drum, and started the overture. It was the same overture — fine I kent it, though I canna gi'e ye the name, for the trombone won quite easy, and had couped the watter oot o' his instrument afore the rest were nearly done. The same chap at the flute, too! I'm shair ye ken him as weel's I dae; there maun be something melancholy aboot the flute to mak' every man that plays it look sae dejected doon his nose. It aye mak's me think that he swallowed yin o' the bits o' his instrument, and that it's no disjeested yet. Whiles I think we micht as weel dae withoot an orchestra, for naebody listens to't onywye and I daursay it wadna be there at a' if it wasna that the comedians need the drum to gi'e a bang when they kick yin anither, or fling each other oot at the side o' the stage. It's fine to see the fun the artists ha'e wi' the conductor, leanin' ower the fitlichts and coddin' him jist the same as he was yin o' themsel's. It'll need to be something extra on the puir chap's pay to stand their jokes — they're that auld and frail. If I was an orchestra mysel' I wad be the drummer. He has a lot o' instruments to look efter — the triangle and the cymbals, and the rickities and the bells, and a wheen mair; but he's aye in a nice corner whaur he canna see the stage, and that's whit mak's the drummers aye sae cheery. It's a great pant to see the drummer aye looking at a sheet o' music in front o' him, lettin' on ye need music to play the drum, when a' the time we ken fine that a' ye ha'e to dae is to gi'e a bang noo and then, and the head o' a drum's that big naebody could miss it.

"They had on a fine company at the Frivolity last nicht. It was ca'd a 'novel and stupendous aggregation o' talent,'

and it looked it frae the start. The programme opened wi'
the Sisters Sylvester,[5] comediennes. They sang a duet,
baith o' them at yince to save time, and it's me that wasna
sorry. It was a song where they said they were strollin'
doon a country lane, country lane, in the moonlicht, in the
moonlicht, but they didna look awfu' like it. They had on
yellow frocks, whit there was o' them, and awfu' tight
boots. Ye never saw sisters sae fond o' yin anither; the only
thing they couldna agree aboot was the key they were to
sing in, but that didna bother them. The yin couldna mak'
a step withoot the ither daein' the same, and they went oot
in each ither's airms kissin' their haunds to me like
onything, but me no' lettin' on. Jist when I thocht that was
the last o' them, and that the entertainment was noo gaun
to begin, they were back again wi' ither claes on, and did a
maist desperate song and dance. When they were
feenishin't twa fine booquets o' floo'ers were handed ower
the fitlichts, and the Sisters Sylvester looked as surprised
and pleased as onything, and kissed their haunds to me
and the rest o' the young chaps that micht ha'e sent them
the floo'ers, and then they handed them oot at the back o'
the stage, where the florist's boy was waitin' to tak' them
back to the shop. Oh! aye, there's a guid dale o' the hire
system in the booquet bisiness. Twa and six a turn if the
floo'ers is no' tashed, and the same booquet'll sometimes
dae five or six performance, the boy aye waitin' in a cab to
tak' it roon the different halls and theatres.

"Then came on the Star Comicue. Ye could see fine he
was comic by his false whiskers and his red nose — aye
look oot for them at a music-hall, and ye'll be shair they're
on the comicue. He sang a comic song wi' jokes in it. It was
aboot his mither-in-law — anither sure sign o' the comic;
got a licht for his cigarette frae the orchestra conductor —
anither sign o' the maist excruciatin' humour; and when he
was walkin' roond the stage atween the verses he tripped
ower tacks — a thing that I thocht awfu' funny the first
time I saw it aboot the time o' the Crimean War. I used to
think the last o' the star comicues wad be deid lang syne,

but there's mair than ever. It seems to me that whenever a man fails in the undertakin' business he turns to the music-hall stage and starts as a comic. When he comes on the stage the folk in the stalls smoke their strongest cigars to deiden the pain, or rush oot to the bar till the worst's bye. The only difference I saw between the star comicue and the twa knockaboots, Casey and Moyle, was that the knockaboots were twice as bad. They were Irish. Knockaboot artists on the music-hall stage are aye Irish. Yin o' them has aye a red whisker and a bald heid and checked claes; the ither has his claes padded for the funny bits, where he gets struck wi' a stick. It's when the knockaboots are on the stage the orchestra has its capacity strained to the utmost, and the big drum's whiles burst. The next turn I saw was some acrobats. It's ill-earned money they get, but at my time o' life I wad as soon look at a plewin-match. And the last run I saw before I came awa' was a chap loopin' the loop on a bicycle. It was the star turn — as they ca' it — o' the evening; and to look at the loop, there was aye the chance he micht be killed, so the folk crooded in frae the bar. But the thing was by in flash, nacthing happened, the chap wasna even hurt. A regular intak'."[6]

53. *Erchie on Golf*[1]

I WAS on my way to my customary game of golf[2] on Saturday when I met Erchie, who cast an understanding and, on the whole, sympathetic eye on my bag of sticks.

"Ye're weel aff," said he, "that has the time for't. It's a fine game, they tell me, and a' the doctors recommend it for want o' sleep, or palpitation, or dyspepsy or onything that's wrang wi' ye. I was jist readin' in the papers the ither nicht that if a wee, thin, peely-wally chap no' able to disjeest his meat gaes oot to the gowfing for a month or twa, he'll turn into a fair gladiator, that strong he'll no' ken his ain strength, and he'll be able to eat onything the same as if he was a connoshoor."

"It's a wonder you never took up golf yourself, Erchie," I said. "It would do you good."

"I daursay," said he; "but I'm ower throng at my work; besides, I'm savin' up for a yat. Yats is no' so common as gowf-bags. They're no' a craze. There's something aboot gowf, I think, that gangs to your heid like beer, and I can see even in the vestry on Sunday, when oor minister's pittin' on his goon, that his mind's wanderin' oot aboot Gailes or Troon,[3] where he aye gangs on a Monday. It's comin' tae't when the Toon Cooncils o' Gleska and Edinburgh neglect the interests o' the rate-payers for a hale day and gang doon to Ayrshire to chase a gutty ba'. It's nice, too; it shows there's nae ill-will between the places. But I'm vexed Edinburgh bate Gleska; surely the Gleska yins didna gi'e them enough to drink when they were at their lunch in George Square afore the game started.

"I see that yin o' the papers has been writin' to a wheen o' folks askin' them whit wye it is that gowf had such an attraction for clever men like them. Put like that, a paper was sure o' an answer frae onybody it wrote to, and some o' the clever men were so keen to explain the wye they felt aboot it that they made a breenge to the telegraph office and wired back the answer. It was plain from whit they said that gowf's the game for a' ages, a' complaints, and a' seasons. The only time ye canna play't is in the dark and even then ye can be lyin' in your bed keepin' your wife awake tellin' her hoo chawed Macphee was because ye bate him wi' three holes.

"Nae man's ower auld to learn gowfin'; at least if he's never likely to turn oot the champion at the age of 89, he can learn the wye to polish his clubs. I see auld chaps gaun to gowf that ye wad expect to be sittin' at hame readin' their Bibles, and the mair they gang gowfin' the mair they cling to this warld. It's awfu' aggravatin' to the friends that's waitin' for their money. The charm o' gowf, sae far as I could gaither frae the clever men that play't, and wrote their confessions on the way it effects genius, is that it's no' so relaxin' a game as dominoes, and still no' so violent an exercise as throwin' the hammer or playin' Rugby fitba'. It taks ye awa' frae yer business at the busiest time o' the day, awa' frae the worry and anxiety o' balancin' books and attendin' to customers in a stuffy atmosphere, oot into the glorious sunshine and face to face wi' the beauties o' nature and the problem o' gettin' your ba' oot o' the quarry near the ninth hole.

"There's no finer game for men that ha'e the doctor's advice to tak' plenty o' ootdoor exercise. Some o' them think the best way to mak' the maist o't is to drive in a cab to the links, ha'e twa caddies apiece — yin to cairry their bag, and anither for pittin' back the clods — ha'e a lie doon if the gress is dry, and smoke twa or three cigarettes between every hole. They come back to the warehouse in time to clear the tills, feelin' fine, at peace wi' all mankind, and awfu' glaury aboot the feet.

"It's a game ye can play by yoursel', too; it's no' like cricket, nor moshey,[4] that wye. At the start, I believe, maist men prefer to play't themsel's when there's naebody lookin'. They like to rise at six in the mornin' or maybe nine, mak' themsel's desperate wi' a cup o' no' richt warm tea, and walk wi' a brisk step to the gowf course. At that 'oor o' the mornin', and under thae circumstances, a' nature smiles. Whiles it rains, but the gowfer that has newly catched the disease never heeds rain. Far awa' frae the haunts o' men, as Duffy's sang[5] says, he reaches the place, looks roond to see the greenkeeper's no' in sight, for a greenkeeper mak's ye nervous; puts the bonny wee ba' in the tap o' as much sand as wad stock a grocer, spits on baith hands, swings his club, shuts baith his een to keep frae bein' blinded wi' the sand, and lets drive. He hits Bonnie Scotland an awfu' welt, then swears maist fearfu'. That's whit ye ca', I think, wan hole, and ninety-nine to play. He doesna mak' a hole every time, of course; noo and then he jist swipes the salubrious breeze.

"Ha'e ye noticed the sudden decline and fa' o' the daisy in Scotland? There'll soon be no' yin left, the result o' the deadly and unerrin' wallop o' the man new-started gowf,

who goes up and down the land, practisin' the swing for
the drive as explained in the different books. The modest
crimson-tipped floo'ers[6] perish in millions every time the
lonely sportsman gangs oot, but the ba's, except when the
tap's shaved clean off them, 's never ony the worse."

"Faith, you seem to have studied the ardent amateur at
pretty close range, and with some discernment, Erchie," I
said. "I suspect you have at some time or other in your brilliant and versatile career banged the elusive wee ba' yourself."

"Me!" cried Erchie. "Catch me. A flet fit and a warm
he'rt, but I never did a daisy ony hairm in a' my days,
except maybe when I tramped on't. But I ken something
aboot the gowfin' for a' that, for when the minister started
first he used to tak' me wi' him on the Mondays to cairry
his clubs. I never kent whit ministerial eloquence was afore
then. When he topped his ba' or garred the land o' the
mountain and the flood[7] dirl, there was whit the papers ca'
a weird silence that lasted five meenutes.

"And he kent less aboot gowf that I did, the minister, for
efter he had sclaffed a dizzen or twa o' divots a yaird square
aff the course, I tellt him it was considered the genteel
thing to replace the turf.

'Naething o' the kind,' says he as snuffy as onything; 'ye
only replace clods if ye lift them aff the puttin'greens.'"

"What did you say to that, Erchie?"

"I jist said 'Holy Frost!' and looked at the scenery.

"I had only the a'e season actin' caddie for the minister;
I found the experience was spilin' my respect for the
Church o' Scotland, and I couldna' stand yon awfu' tor-
rents o' silence efter he missed a four-inch putt so I tellt
him I had plenty o' better-payin' jobs at my ain tred, and
had to leave him. He took oot his wife then, to learn her the
game when naebody was lookin', and it was a movin' sicht
to see him and her comin' hame no' speakin' to yin
anither, for she bate him easy frae the start — a thing nae
man o' spirit cares to have happen to him.

"Oh, aye, that's anither advantage the game has ower
fitba', or harriers;[8] it's jist as weel suited for weemen as for

men. I'm gled Jinnet's no' ta'en up wi't, though, for it's sae distractin'. If she took the craze my tea wad never be ready; she wad be like Duffy's wife when she nearly went aff her heid ower ping-pong."

54. *Duffy's Fads*[1]

"DID YE hear the latest?" Erchie asked me on Saturday, when I met him going towards St Kentigern's Church to stoke the furnace for the morrow's service. "Did ye hear the latest? Duffy's wife's gane and left him!"

"I mind his first wife did the same thing," said I, "and I hope the separation will be as temporary on this occasion as it was then. But what did she leave him for?"

"Because the man's jist a fair Jenny," explained Erchie. "Fancy a coalman interferin' wi' the kind o' hats his wife wears, and challengin' her to put on boots that havena the richt kind o' heels to his notion!"

"These are the last things I should have expected Duffy to be much interested in."

"The cratur's whiles as daft's a maik watch,"[2] said Erchie. "A' fads, and changes his mind wi' every rake o' coal he gangs wi'. If he's no experimentin' wi' some o' his patent notions on his wife, he's experimentin' on himsel' and losin' money.

"This time last year he took a day aff and went oot to Carmunnock or the Mearns to gaither herbs for his blood. He said it was the finest thing gaun for a chap to tak' herb tea in the spring-time, and that it kept aff a' trouble.

"'You and your herbs,' says I to him. 'If it was thistles ye were efter I could understand it, for it's a great diet with cuddies, but to bother yer puir wife bilin' weeds for tea's a thing I ha'e nae patience wi'.

"'We divna ken whit the health is till we lose it,' says Duffy, and him wi' a bag of nettles and dockens,[3] and trash o' that kind in his haund. Everybody gets thin in the blood in the spring and needs herbs. Herbs is the life o' ye.'

"'The last time ye had the craze, Duffy,' I said to him, 'it was soor milk was the life o' ye , and the time afore that it was drinkin' a quart o' hot water afore breakfast in the mornin'.'

"'Oh, aye!' said he, 'but herbs is better than ony o' thae things. Herbs is Nature.'

"'Jist that,' said I. 'You gang on dietin' yersel' on herbs and I'll watch your horns sproutin'.'

"But that's Duffy a' ower; a new fad every time ye meet him, and I'm no surprised his wife's awa'. He wasna mairried to her a month when he started to be a vegetarian. When he said he was gaun to jine the vegetarians, his wife thocht it was some kind o' society like the Rechabites, whaur ye get 12s. 6d. a week if ye're ill and the committee doesna' see ye oot at a fitba' match, so she said she was gled to hear it. She wasna that gled when he begood to want turnips for his breakfast, and cry oot for dates, and oranges for his tea. Force, grape nuts, plasmon, pianola — he made her bring them in by the box, and raisins, aipples, figs, rice, till ye wad think Duffy's hoose was a co-operative store. He had maps stuck a' roond the kitchen, showin' ye the nourishment in different kinds o' meat, and the maps made oot that twa split peas were mair strengthenin' than a pun' o' pope's-eye steak, and that there was mair alumin-ium in an Irish egg[4] than wad mak' a yat for Lipton.

"'It's an awfu' trauchle this vegetarianin',' said Duffy's wife after twa or three days o't. "I wad sooner ye ett beef like a Christian.'

"'I'll never eat beef again, if I live to the age o' Methusalum,' said Duffy. 'I'm feelin' fine. I never felt as licht and cheery and strong in a' my life afore; if I had started sooner I wad ha'e been a richer and healthier man this day. Look at the money I'm savin' ye.'

"'Savin' me!' cries Mrs Duffy; 'it's costin' me far mair than if ye had kitchen[5] to every meal. I aye thocht that vegetarians ett naething but lentil soup.'

"But that wasna the kind o' vegetarian Duffy was; he said lentil soup was ower rich for his blood and fruit was the thing for the brain.

"When he tellt me that I lauched at him and advised him to buy his aipples by the barrel. 'It's no' yer brains ye need to nourish, Duffy,' says I, 'they're a' richt for a' the strain ye ha'e to put them to. Whit ye need's stuff to develop the voice, and there's naethin' like a flesh diet for that.'

"Efter three weeks o' vegetarianism puir Duffy lost that much wecht he couldna cairry a bag o' coal doon a dunny, and his voice got that wake he couldna hear himsel' speakin'. Wan day he cam' hame wi' twa pun' o' steak. 'Fry that!' says he to his wife, and she was that gled!

"'Are ye better?' says she. 'I was feart ye were gaun into a decline wi' yer vegetables. Nuts is no' a breakfast for ony man; they're maybe guid enough for Italians and foreign trash o' that kind,[6] but no' for a man that has a business.'

"It wasna lang efter that when Duffy took an awfu' bad turn, and started the teetotal. At first his wife thocht this was the best thing ever happened him, and she began to coont on saving money in the bank. But the coal tred's gey stoury, and Duffy had aye been used to slockenin' himsel' regular wi' a quart o' beer. He couldna dae withoot somethin' to be drinkin', even though he was teetotal, and he kept puir Leezie thrang makin' Broon Robin[7] and Boston Cream till she couldna find time to mak' the beds. He had to ha'e his half-a-dizzen bottles o' Broon Robin oot on the lorry wi' him, and instead o' gaun oot for an 'oor or twa at nicht to the Mull o' Kintyre Vaults the way he was accustomed to, he sat wi' his feet up on the kitchen hob, singin' 'Dark Lochnagar,' and findin' faut wi' everything.

"'Jimmy,' says his wife at last, 'ye were never a man that gaed ower faur wi' drink when ye were in the habit o' takin' it; dae ye no' think ye micht stop the Broon Robin and the Boston Cream and gi'e me time to wash the blankets. I'm tired bein' a kind o' Band o' Hope distillery for ye.'[8]

"'Ach, to bleezes! Leezie,' said Duffy; 'I'm tired o't mysel'; see's a sixpence and I'll awa' oot for a pint!'

"That was aye the way wi' Duffy's fads; they never lasted lang, but they aye cam' close on yin anither, and were an awfu' nuisance to his wife. If it wasna that he wad tak' nae sugar to his tea, it was that he wad tak' nae salt to his porridge, or had to ha'e a' the mulk biled. But when he began to mak' his wife wear boots wi' nae heels on them, and took to dae wi' the shape o' her bunnets, she went on strike. That's the way she's awa' frae him the noo. But I've nae doot she'll be back next week for she's a cheery wumman, and get's on wi' him fine when he's in his senses."

55. *Erchie on Tips*[1]

"WAITIN'S THE finest tred that's gaun," said Erchie, "if it wasna for the tippin'."

"Tipping is the last thing I should have expected a waiter to object to," I said.

"That's whit maist people think that has naething to dae but the tippin'," said my old friend.

"If ye were a waiter yersel' ye wad ken better. It's a fine tred for them that ha'e the feet for't, and can put their mind to't, and havena fingers that's a' thoombs, and can laugh at a guid baur, and understaun' Nature, the Rale Oreeginal. But ye need nerve; if ye havena nerve, and gang aboot the business blately[2] ye'll soon find oot that whit should be a bob tip'll only turn oot a tanner. Us waiters hate the tippin' system faur mair nor you dae but it's whit oor wifes and weans depend on. I kent a waiter yince that de'ed o' a broken hert because he never got ony credit for ony o' the finer human feelin's. His name was Macdougall. Him and I started to serve oor time thegither in the auld Saracen Heid Hotel. It was Macdougall invented the habit o' puttin' a hand up inside a customer's top-coat efter ye helped him on wi't and pu'in' doon the tail o' his jaicket. It took awfu' weel. At first Macdougall's customers got an awfu' start when he put his haun under the top-coat for they thocht he was gaun to ripe their pooches[3] but when they found the chap meant nae harm, and only wanted to keep the collar o' their jaickets frae crawlin' up aboot their ears, they were that pleased they aye gi'ed him an extra tip. It wasna for the tip Macdougall did it; it was jist his good nature, and, forbye, he was that prood o' inventin' the thing he took it awfu' sair to be gettin' tuppence, or maybe sixpence for't every time — or maybe mair if the customer was fat. He wad come to me near greetin' wi' a handfu' o' money, and say 'This is the rotten tred, Erchie; ye canna dae onything for the guid o' yer fellow-men but they think ye're on the mooch. Them and their tips! I wish I had never invented onything. It preyed on his mind that much his hert broke, and he de'ed, leavin' a weedow and four weans, and a guid pickle money in the bank. Since Macdougall's time the top-coat trick's practised by waiters a' ower the warld and maist o' them's in nae danger o' de'ein' o' broken herts either.

"There's sae mony wyes o' workin' a tip oot o' a customer nooadays that I think it wad be hard to invent ony new yin. When I begood the tred first tips were jist comin' in the fashion. A customer wad maybe gi'e ye a peppermint lozenger when he was leavin' the hotel, or when ye handed him his hat efter he had an extra guid dinner. If ye worked in a country hotel a regular customer wad maybe gi'e ye a ticket for last years' cattle show or a lift in his dugcairt if he cam' up wi' ye on the road. That was a' the length tippin' got for mony a day. Ye wadna get very fat on't if it was the tippin' ye were dependin' on; but then ye had a regular wage, and that's whit a waiter hasna nooadays. Maist o' the waiters get nae wage at a' noo, or maybe pay for their job, and that's the wye we canna afford to be blate. If Macdougall was to the fore yet, it wad break his hert half-a-dizzen times a day to see the wye the tred's degraded. Gang to an hotel and there's twa or three boots grabs yer bag and yer walkin' stick; anither chap runs awa' wi' yer hat; a hoistboy pushes ye into his machine, and tak's ye to the next flet in aboot twice the time it wad tak' ye to walk up the stair; waiters put on yer coat for ye, brush aff the stour that's no' there, light yer cigarette for ye, look the diary to see when yer train starts — they dae every mortal thing for a man that a man's quite weel able to dae for himsel', and it's a' for the tip. At least the customer aye thinks it is, and that's whit killed Macdougall.

"It's gey hard, that, on the like o' me that has maybe a flet fit but a warm he'rt. Mony a time I put mysel' aboot at a public dinner to get a chap a cigar frae the chairman's table instead of the Ne Plus Ultras, and I can see from the wye he looks at me he's wonderin' whit's the least o' a tip he can gi'e me when the dinner's bye, and thinkin' it wad ha'e been a savin' o' a sixpence if he had been content wi' the Ne Plus Ultras. London's the place, I'm tellt, where the tip's at its best. Gentlemen that ha'e been there tell me ye can hardly buy a stamp in London withoot gi'ein' the post-office chap tuppence to himsel' for the trouble ye put him to. And it's even worse, they say, abroad. The mornin' ye leave yer hotel abroad, the bell's sent roond the toon sayin' ye're gaun to start at nine for the station, and at nine o'clock the whole population stands on the steps o' the hotel wi' their keps aff the same as if ye were the King at Dublin. 'Tak' everything I ha'e, but leave me my gold watch,' says the puir tourist, and reaches the station wi' the skin a' peeled aff the backs o' his haunds wi' puttin' them oot and in his pooches. But the warst place for tips, I'm told, is a shootin' estate. If a gentleman wi' a shootin' up aboot Clachnacuddin asks ye to come and stay wi' him frae Friday to Monday, ye need to pawn everything but your gun and your dress suit afore ye start. The heid game-keeper expects his bunnet fu' o' sovereigns, and ony self-respectin' gillie that cairries hame the rabbit for ye wad snort at ye like onything if ye didna gi'e him the price o' a new suit o' claes.

"There's a fine chance in the tippin' system for a waiter to study human nature when he's no daein' onything else. I'm never very shair whether I like best the customer that gi'es ower much or the ither yin that gi'es ower little. Yince I took a young chap aside in an hotel I was waiter in, and I says to him, 'This half-sovereign ye gi'ed me wad be fine and welcome if I thocht ye were Carnegie,[4] but if ye're

gaun to start yer traivels roond the warld tippin' on this
scale, ye'll ha'e to work yer wye back as a stoker.' His face
got awfu' red; he was jist a laddie, and I kent fine wha's son
he was and that he was green. 'Whit dae ye mean?' says he;
'if it's no' plenty —' and he was puttin' his haund in his
pooch again. 'I mean,' says I, 'that half-a-croon's as much
o' a tip as ony self-respectin' waiter wad expect for a' that I
had to dae for ye.' The puir chap had nae idea o' whit he
should gi'e me, and was feart to hurt my feelin's wi'
onything less than gold. But that kind's no sae common as
the ither kind that think a sixpence 'll be plenty if they ca'
ye by yer first name, and ha'e a bit crack wi' ye aboot the
weather. I was yince on a job at Dunoon in the summer time
when some Americans cam' into the hotel for a plain tea.
They had a sma' bottle o' brandy wi' em, and feenished it
between them; and when they were gaun awa' the heid yin
says, 'There's an empty bottle; ye'll can get a penny on't.'
It was a' the tip they gi'ed me! There's ither folk'll gi'e ye a
sixpence in a nice wye that mak's ye respect them as much
as if it was twa shillin's, but ye needna put that in the
paper, for a lot o' people wad think they wad like to try't,
and they havena the knack o't."

56. *Erchie and the Stolen Hour*[1]

"WELL, ERCHIE," I said to the old man yesterday, "we
have seen the last night the public-houses will be open till
eleven."[2]

"We have that," said Erchie. "Efter this ye'll no' ken us,
we're gaun to be that sober, and guid, and weel-put-on.
We'll a' ha'e money in the Bank, and the peppermint
lozenge tred'll be a failure. We'll be an object-lesson to the
hale warld; they'll be rinnin' holiday trips frae the Continent and America to see the nation that gangs tae its bed
at ten o'clock; in ten or twenty years efter this ye'll see
them showing toddy-glasses and half-mutchkin bottles
and gill measures oot in Kelvingrove Museum, labelled:

'Ancient weapons found in the crannog³ at Buchanan Street Station?'"

"How's Duffy taking the change?" I asked, and Erchie held up his hands in mock surprise.

"Calm! He's keepin' wonnerfu' calm under the circumstances. He was chairman at a meetin' doon in the Mull of Kintyre Vaults last nicht, whaur the customers gave a purse o' sovereigns and a vote of sympathy to Macdougall, the manager. Duffy mak's oot that the result o' shuttin' the pubs at ten instead o' eleeven is that the workin' man's to be robbed o' an 'oor's liberty in the day, An 'oor in the day's aboot a hale day in the month; it's aboot a fortnicht in the year, and if a man leeves to the age o' 60 or 70, he's to be robbed o' mair than three years. Fine fun! 'We micht as weel be in oor graves,' says Duffy, and starts singin' 'Scotland the Brave!'"⁴

"It was a great nicht doon at the Mull of Kintyre, I'm tellt, and a' the regular customers turned oot wi' their Sunday claes on oot o' respect for Macdougall. There was talk o' hirin' a brass band, but Macdougall said that music o' ony kind wadna be ony help to him and his drawin's, sae they jist had a piper that played laments and things o' that sort in the wee room.

"Macdougall provided the soda-water free, and gi'ed a present o' a corkscrew wi' the name o' his Vaults on't to every customer. He was a cheery wee chap. When Duffy was handin' ower the purse o' sovereigns (I think there was twa in't and a pound in shillin's to mak' it look weel), he said this was the first nicht o' the new tyrannical law passed to mak' the workin'-man gang hame afore his money was done. It was anither blow at freedom. It was whit he would ca' a fair Staggerer. ('Question!' cries a chap half-sleepin' in the corner thinkin' Duffy was speakin' aboot him.) If the so-called Magistrates o' Gleska thocht gentlemen such as were gethered thegither this nicht to dae honour to their genial frien' Macdougall were gaun to be driven hame to their beds at ten o'clock, the so-called Magistrates were awfu' far up a close. Everybody that had ony experience o' a hame o' his ain kent weel enough that ten o'clock at nicht was jist the very 'oor when it was at its warst, especially on a Setterday nicht such as this, for it was the 'oor the wifes generally washed the kitchen floor efter she got the weans to their bed, and was aye in her warst temper.

"'No,' says Duffy, 'we're no' gaun to be driven hame at ten o'clock to please onybody. It wasna for that Bruce and Wallace fell. ('There was naething wrang wi' Bruce; shober as I am,' said the chap half sleepin' in the corner.) John Knox and the Covenanters and Rabbie Burns, the poet, werena driven hame at ten o'clock; not them! They jist pleased themsel's, and look at the wye they were respected! But if the so-called Magistrates o' Gleska think the gentlemen I see gethered roon me the nicht are gaun hame at ten, they're sair mistaken. (Great cheers.) It's like enough the so-called Magistrates 'll be sittin' in their clubs lang efter ten o'clock or eleeven either, drinkin' schooners o' champagne. My motto's live and let live, and I'm no gaun hame at ten ony nicht unless I'm awfu' tired.'

"Macdougall was nearly greetin' when the purse o' sovereigns was handed ower to him. The tear was standin' at his een and he had to wipe them wi' his brattie afore he could start. He said it was the saddest and the proodest 'oor o' his life. It was the saddest because him and his tred were bein' oppressed by a lot o' sneck-drawers in the iron bed and blanket industries that wanted sale for their stuff, and wad compel men to gang to their bed at ten o'clock. Thank heaven, he had never been in his bed afore twelve for a single nicht except on the Sunday since he left Clachna-cuddin, and he was as healthy as ony man in Gleska. And it was the proodest 'oor o' his life because he saw his frien's rallied roond him to show that they had confidence in the guid auld Mull o' Kintyre and in Dugald Macdougall.

"When it got to aboot ten meenutes to ten the company a' stood up and jined hands and sang 'Auld Lang Syne' as far as they could mind it. Ten meenutes later, Macdougall, who had to gang oot to attend the coonter efter the presentation, cam' to the room door and cries, 'Ten o'clock, gentlemen!' then burst into tears. Ye ken he had been used to cryin' 'Eleven o'clock, gentlemen!' since ever he left Clachnacuddin,[5] and nae wonder he took the change sae sair to he'rt.

"When a' the customers got oot in the street, they were that dazed wi' the novelty they didna ken whit to dae at first, and yin o' them actually proposed a walk in the West-End Park. There was naething for't but to gang hame, and hame they went. When Duffy's wife saw him comin' in at a quarter past ten on a Setturday nicht she cried, 'Oh, Jimmy! are ye no' weel?'

"'Whit dae ye think's wrang wi' me?' said he, quite snappy.

"'Ye're jist in time to gang a message,' said she; and afore puir Duffy kent whaur he was he was awa' wi' a basket to the greengrocer's for a half-a-stone o' potatoes the wife forgot.

"But Duffy tells me the Tred's keepin' wonnerfu' calm, too, and throng makin' up wee bottles, the same as it was near the New Year. The bottle manufacturin' tred's workin' nicht and day, and the price o' corks is gaun up. 'From scenes like these auld Scotia's grandeur springs,' Duffy says; 'Dae they think men's mice? We're no' gaun to be mice to please onybody.' Duffy says he's no' carin' for himsel'; he can aye get it in the hoose onytime he's needin't, but he's vexed for the publican. 'Whit's the puir chap to dae when his shop's shut at ten o'clock?' he asks. 'It's a gey lang nicht to put in by yersel' when ye're no' used to 't, and the nicht school's no' open till the winter time. As shair's death, Erchie,' he says to me, 'I'm vexed for the puir chaps hivin' to shut their bars at ten o'clock and gang awa' hame to their beds in broad daylicht. Hoo wad the Bylies like it themsel's?'

"It'll be as bad for the nicht polis, Duffy says. The streets 'll be that quate efter ten o'clock the bobby's'll get sae sleepy, they'll be standin' at the corners gantin' their heids aff and wearyin' for a fight. And the concerts, and soirees, and music-halls — whit's to come o' them? he asks. If they're no' shut afore ten the folk'll no' gang to them, for half the recreation o' gaun to the gallery's the chance o' breakin' yer neck breengin' doon the stairs to get to the corner afore the doors shut.

"The eyes o' the Empire's on Gleska. They talk aboot us abroad in foreign pairts whaur the nae Sundays is, and whaur the folk keep sober withoot tryin' hard, and they're gled they're no' us, but they're feared for us. 'If Gleska got into the prood poseetion o' bein' the Second City in the Empire when its public-hooses were open till eleeven, what'll it no' dae when they're shut at ten?' they're thinkin'. 'It gi'es the Gleska man, gaun to his bed at ten, two or three 'oors' start at risin' in the mornin' afore the rest o' the warld.'"

"But the Glasgow man may be no soberer than before, or earlier to bed than before, Erchie," I said; "He may take his whisky home in a bottle at ten."

"No fears o' him!" said Erchie. "That's whit the publicans expect he'll dae, and that's the wye there's such a preparation o' wee bottles, but the kind o' man that wad tak' a half-peck awa' wi' him at ten took it awa' wi' him at eleeven, and him and his mates aye feenished it afore they got the length o' his close. When they had it feenished yin o' them aye kent a Workin'-man's club three stairs up oot the Gallowgate, and if they had the price o' a quart left they went up there and had a fine time o't. But there's no' even the Workin'-man's Club noo; the polis ca't a shebeen, and fine the man that keeps it £50 the first time he's catched. So there's no chance noo for the workin'-man. It's an awfu' thing to think o' the puir chap, efter workin' frae six in the mornin', being put oot o' the Mull o' Kintyre Vaults at ten o'clock, and no' ha'ein' ony place to gang to except hame to his wife and weans.

"The time's comin' when the public-hooses'll ha'e to shut at three in the efter-noon the same as the banks and if Duffy and his frien's want to be jovial efter that 'oor they'll jist ha'e to gang to a tea-room and drink Russian tea or Broon Robin. It's the age o' the tea-room[6] and the lairge cup threepence. I mind twenty-five years ago whit they ca'd British Workman's Public Hooses were started in Gleska to try and keep men awa' frae the horrors o' drink. Ootside they looked like ordinary public-hooses and mony a puir cratur went into them wi' the delusion that they were ordinary public-hooses, but they never kept onything stronger than lemonade and Boston Cream and tea. The British workman never went into them unless he was the worse o' drink, and then it was his mistake. Nae ordinary man liked to be seen gaun into them in case folk wad think he was a chap that drank tea in the middle o' the day.

"Nooadays everybody drinks tea at a' 'oors and naebody's ashamed o't; the tea-room's takin' the place o' the tavern, and if Macdougall leeves lang enough he'll ha'e to furnish the Mull o' Kintyre Vaults wi' comic chairs and sell naething but tea."

57. *Erchie in the Park*[1]

"I WAS in the Park[2] the day," said Erchie on Friday evening; "It's lookin' fine, things is growin' yonder jist the same as if it was as easy's onything — trees, and bushes, and grass, and yon kind o' red floo'ers and roary dendrons, though they're no' ony roarier nor floo'ers I see in the women's bunnets. I'm fond o' the Park at this time o' the year, when I'm no' awfu' thrang at my tred. It's Nature; it's the Rale Oreeginal. It's fine to see the polismen beakin' in the sun, with their braw, sonsy, extra wide welt boots blackened that nice it fairly blin's the nurses to look at them.

"If I had my life to live ower again I wad be a polisman in the Park. There's nae hoose-breakin's in the Park, nor wife murders, nor shebeens, nor fights wi' moulders. A' a polisman has to dae there is to keep his feet close thegither when he's walking so that he'll no' tramp on the grass, and to birl his whistle[3] noo and then when he sees ony chaps bigger than himsel' stealin' floo'ers, so that the chap'll clear aff afore he gets near him. The rest o' the time he can lean on the railin' roon' the pond and watch the folk feeding the jucks[4] Abernethy biscuits, orange peel and quids o' tobacco. I'm gey gled I'm no' a juck; in the West End Park pond a juck has nae regular 'oors for his meals; people keep pappin' things into him even-on.

"I was vexed for the puir jucks in the Park this day. They're that fu' o' loaf and toffee, chewed pastry-pokes and broken bits o' delf that they're walkin' knock-kneed when they come ashore on the grass. It's nae bawr; I saw them mysel' some o' them that tight packed their tails curled up at the end."

"I thought you never went to the Park, Erchie?" said I.

"Me!" he cried. "I'm fair daft for the Park; I gang there twice or maybe thrice a year, and whiles aftener if the Govan Polis Pipe Band's performin'. I like to gang in the efternoon when the nurse-maids is oot wi' their pram-laters, misca'in' their mistresses to yin anither and lettin' the weans hing sleepin' ower the side o' the prams till they tak' watter-in-the-heid. But this was an extra day for weans in the Park —"

"The Children's Day!" I cried; "so it was; I quite forgot; I might have remembered your weakness, Erchie, for the bairns."

"I wadna ca't a weakness," he said reddening a little. "I had plenty o' trauchlin' bringin' up my ain. But, ach, they're fine fun, the wee yins. There were 123,000 o' them in the Gleska parks the day, and I tell you the jucks in the Kelvin-grove's gaun to be awfu' no-weel the morn's mornin'.

"I don't care," Erchie went on, "but I'm fond o' weans. Floo'ers is fine for them that understand them. There's Duffy; he was brocht up aboot a ferm in the country for a year or twa when he was a young chap, and he kens mignonette by the smell, but I hardly ken a'e floo'er frae anither except the dentilion, and the nettle, and the roary dendron.[5] When it comes to weans though, there's no' much I don't ken aboot them, and the Park never looks sae braw as when it's crooded wi' youngsters. Pair wee smouts, they're better there nor lying on a tarry pavement puttin' a lump of clye on the end o' a string doon a stank.

"I never saw the Common Good o' Gleska bein' better spent than it was the day. The Magistrates took twa thoosand pounds frae the Common Good to trate the weans — every mortal yin a poke o' buns, a poke o' sweeties, an oranger, and a big drink o' water frae a barrel, It'll tak' mair nor that to entertain the whit-d'ye-ca'-him — the Alake o' Abeokuta if he comes to Gleska as he's threatenin' to dae.

"When the Park polis saw 13,000 weans comin' into Kelvingrove they nearly grat, for there wasna a nurse amang the hale lot o' them, and whit the polis had been expectin' was a kindergarten. 'It's no' fair,' says they, 'to be lettin' sae mony weans oot wi' a lot o' schulemaisters; every yin o' them ocht to hae some sensible young nurse wi' him to keep him aff the jucks.'

"Thirteen thousand weans a' in a lump, man it was a fine sicht! Every boy wi' his face washed, his hair tidy, and a pure white kahoutchy collar; every lassie wi' scent on her hanky and a new string o' beads. As they merched into the Park the stirring strains o' the national anthem, 'Hiawatha',[6] rang from every lip. And the hale time they were there nane o' them did ony mischief; at least, they werena seen daen't, and the polis were that chawed they nearly swallowed their whistles wi' vexation.

"Less than five meenutes efter the Standard VI laddies got their pokes, they had et a' that was in them, an were swappin' the empty pokes wi' Standard IV boys that were willin' to gi'e a cookie and half an oranger for the fun o' fillin' the pokes wi' win', and bustin' it wi' a bang like a gun. It was rale nice, too, to see the big laddies offerin' to tak' care o' the wee yins' orangers for them till they were feenished wi' their sweeties, in case they micht lose them. I saw yin boy, no' awfu' strong-lookin', and he had such a nice wye wi' him that he sank seeven orangers, a dozen buns, and aboot a pun' o' sweeties the time the ithers were playin' fitba'. He said he had an awfu' sair heid and couldna' play, and the ithers fed him up the same as if he was a Sick Children's Hospital. When he et a' that, he went ower to the watter cairts and created an awfu' drouth.

"They werna supposed to gang near the pond, but a wheen o' them kent aboot the jucks, and had pooches fu' o' crusts, and corks, and tow, and stuff o' that sort that Corporation jucks thrive on, and they got awa' frae their schulemaisters and had a fine time. But it wasna fair feeding the puir, deluded birds wi' potty; hoo wad they like it themsel's?

"The Bylies went roond a' the Parks in a machine and made speeches at the weans. They wadna ha'e got the chance, for the sports were gaun on at the time, and the jucks were bein' fed, but when the machine wi' the Bylies drew up the weans thocht it was maybe jugglers, or mair orangers, and so they gaithered roond cheerin' like onything.

"'Children,' says the Bylies, baith speakin' at yince to save time and get the job owre, 'this has been a great day. For you. For us. For the teachers. For Scotland. For Gleska. For the crops. Ye ha'e nae idea hoo prood we are to see ye a' lookin' sae smert and nice, and bein' as weel-behaved as ye can. You are the future ratepayers o' this tremendous city; here ye are eatin' bun and quaffin' the crystal stream frae the Statute Labour water-cairts, and aye stick to't a' yer days and it'll dae ye nae hairm. It's a great preevilege for ye to get playin' in here withoot the polis bein' able to fin' fau't wi' ye for't, and we hope ye'll pye attention to the fine floo'ers that's planted here and there aboot the place, and maybe learn the foreign names o' em. It's the very thing for yer health to be here the day, and it'll help ye to grow up fine, big, strong ratepayers. We canna ha'e too mony o' them in Gleska. Whit ye got the day frae the Common Good ye'll nae doo't pye back a thoosand fold when ye're in business for yersel's.'

"'Hurrah!' cried the puir wee smouts, egged on by their teachers, and the Bylies were that pleased at this spontaneous and he'rty reception, they pu'd doon their shirt-cuffs, tightened their watch chains, cleared their throats, and started to speak again. 'Ah! children,' they said, jist like a Sunday Schule soiree, 'Ah! children, there are lessons to be learned frae the humblest floo'er in the Gleska Parks. There's the daisy; it's celebrated a' owre the world for its modesty, but it's up fine and early in the mornin' at business afore the ither floo'ers ha'e their een open. Let that be an example to you when ye begin the business o' life and ha'e bits o' shops o' yer ain; aye be up afore the ither shopkeepers, and aye ha'e yer een open.'

"When the Bylies got that length wi' their speech, I heard a wee red-heided boy near turn to his mate and sayin', 'Chairley, are ye gem to heave a clod?' Man! it just put me in mind o' mysel' when I was aboot the wee red-heided yin's age. 'Dinna heave ony clods, my fine, wee fellow,' I tellt him; it spiles the Park to lift clods, and ye divna ken but ye micht be a Bylie yersel' some day.'

"By five o'clock the water in the Statute Labour cairts was a' drunk; the jucks were refusin' ony mair corks, and the band was playin' 'God Save the King', sae the ex-Standard VI boys lit their cigarettes and went awa' hame."

58. *The Row on Erchie's Stair*[1]

I HAPPENED to mention casually to Erchie that Buffalo Bill's Wild West Show[2] was coming to Glasgow in the autumn. "That'll be fine," said Erchie, "but it'll be naething to the Wild West Show Carmichael's wife and Old Vengeance are ha'ein' this week on oor stair. The thing should be advertised to the papers; it's the comicalist kind o' variorum ever onybody listened to; there's half-a-dizzen performances in the day, and Old Vengeance is takin' oatmeal stout to keep up her strength, and a' the neebours ken by that it's gaun to last to the Gleska Fair."

"I'm glad you have the philosophy to appreciate a good-going stairhead row," I said, for I had heard of Mrs Carmichael before. "But who's Old Vengeance?"

"A raigular character,' said Erchie, chuckling. "She cam' to oor stair at the term; her name's Cam'ell, and she was aye flytin'[3] at the weans, and so they christened her Old Vengeance. She keeps ludgers. It wiz that started her on Carmichael's wife. Carmichael's wife was sweepin' the stair-heid on Wednesday when Old Vengeance on the flet above leaned ower the railin' and passed the time o' day as peaceable as onything. 'I've lost my lodger,' says she; 'he's awa' to a place in Bothwell.' 'It's me that's no' sorry to hear't,' says Carmichael's wife. 'I was sick tired o' that melodian o' his aye bum-bummin' awa' ower us at nicht so that my man couldna get his naitural sleep.'

"That set the heather on fire. The auld yin tied twa hard knots on the strings o' her brattie to keep hersel' frae burstin' wi' rage, and started there and then on puir Carmichael's wife. "If yer man got his dinner richt made for him,' says she, 'he wad sleep better, and if he didna spend that much o' his time round at the Mull o' Kintyre Vaults, he maybe wadna snore sae lood when he does sleep; as shair's death, its no' canny to hear him at nicht gurglin' awa' like a blocked jaw box; it gi'es the hale land[5] a bad name. When I cam' here first I thocht it was the drains was wrang, and I sent word to the Sanitary.'

"'Oh! ye needna be sae awfu' angry,' said Carmichael's wife. 'All I meant was that whiles the melodian wakened Rubbert.'

"'It wad need something to waken Rubbert,' said the auld yin. 'It wad vex onybody to see him crawlin' gantin' to his wark in the mornin' aye mair nor half-an-'oor late. Ye had nae business to rin doon me and my ludger nor his melodian either. He was a dacent chap, and took prizes wi' his melodian. It's mair nor ony o' yer dally dochters'll ever dae wi' their pianna. Them and their pianna. It wad suit them better if they darned the heels o' their stockin's.'

"'Awa, ye auld cat!' cried Carmichael's wife, fair exasperated; 'There was peace in the land till ye cam' to't wi' yer randy tongue and your drunken ludgers. They're no' awfu' parteecular aboot their ludgin's! I wonder at ye,

wumman! Awa' doon and clean the roost aff the washin'-
hoose biler; it's a fair disgrace the wye ye left it the last time
ye were washin' yer rags.'

"Old Vengeance got that mad at that she tied two mair
hard knots in her brattie and began to roar oot that lood ye
could hear her doon in the New City Road, 'Rags!' said
she; 'it was the rag tred that made the breid o' yer puir auld
faither, though ye mak' oot he was a tailor and clothier. If
the rag tred hadna furnished a room and kitchen for ye,
Carmichael wad never ha'e married ye. Let me tell ye that!
Ye think because I'm new come to the tenement I divna
ken a' aboot ye. Rags! There's no' a rag in my hoose, an'
it's like a new preen. Whit did the minister say the last time
he was ca'in' roond here? "Everything's a credit to ye, Mrs
Cam'ell," says he, "everything's that clean and nate, no'
like some o' yer neebours," and then he coughed. I kent fine
whit he coughed for, and maybe you'll ken tae, Carmichael.'

"That was the start o' the row. It was last Wednesday,
and it's gaun on yet. It's no' a' back chat on the stair
though; they carry't on like a war, and there's no' a man
stayin' up oor close'll ging oot efter his tea this week for
fear he'll lose a performance.

"On Thursday mornin' the auld yin was up fine and
early, and shook her door bass and her kitchen rug oot by
her kitchen window, so that a' the stoor went into the
Carmichael's kitchen window that was open at the time,
spiled Carmichael's parridge that were coolin'[6] on the
window sole, and fair took the breath awa' frae Carmichael's prize canary, so that it took a kink and nearly
de'ed. Mrs Carmichael cam' oot to the stairheid, and
made a few remarks up the stair. She's yin o' yon big, sonsy
red weemen that wears their bare airms, and never ha'e
onything wrang wi' them — that healthy it's no' naitural in
a wumman, Jinnet says; and if she could ha'e put her
hands on Old Vengeance the auld yin wad ha'e suffered.
But the auld yin jist waited inside till the harangue was bye,
and then she opened her front door a wee bit and says, 'Is
that you speakin', Carmichael? I'm no hearin' a word

you're sayin'. If ye were a wise wumman ye wadna be exposin' your ignorance skriechin' on a stair.'

"But Carmichael's wife had the better o' the auld yin afore dinner-time. A man cam' roond canvassin' for sewin' machines, and tried Carmichael's door first.

"'No, we're no' needin' a sewin' machine,' says Mrs Carmichael, as lood as she could so that the hale stair could hear her. 'I ha'e yin o' the very latest already. My man grudges me naething. There's an auld wife jist above us ye micht try; ye'll ken her door by the dirtiness o' the bell handle; she has nae machine the noo; the last yin she hed was ta'en frae her because she couldna pye the instalments.'

"The auld yin at that was oot on the stair in a meenute. It's my belief she stands behind the door a' day listenin' what Carmichael's wife's gaun to say next. At ony rate oot she breenges, and 'Thank ye very kindly, Carmichael,' says she, 'but ye needna bother sendin' ony o' yer relatives sellin' things to my door. I have enough to dae to support my ain frien's, though I'm proud to say there was never ony o' them in the rag trcd.'

"Carmichael's wife gaed into her hoose slashin' the door ahint her.

"Wee Wullie, Carmichael's boy, was oot in the back coort playin' moshy his lone, and his mither stuck her heid oot o' the kitchen window. 'William Alexander,' says she, 'come in oot o' that immediately or I'll sort ye. Ye canna tell the meenute a pail o' tawtie peelin's or ashes or onything micht be heaved ower frae auld Cam'ell's window. She's gettin' ower frail to gang the length o' the ash-pit.'

"She had her heid in jist in time to miss a dunt frae a scrubbin' brush the auld yin drapped by accident, and the auld yin stuck oot her heid. 'Yes, William Alexander,' she says, imitating Carmichael's voice. 'If ye see my cat, Thomas Peter Charles oot there, tak' it up to me and I'll gi'e ye a piece. Puir wee smout, mony a yin I gi'ed ye. If ye got your meat like a Christian ye wadna be aff the schule sae often no' weel.'

"Whan the boy went into his mither's hoose she gi'ed him a sixpence. 'Awa up wi' that to auld Cam'ell,' says she, 'and tell her that's to pye for the pieces she gi'ed ye. "My mama's compliments," says you, "and she'll thank ye no' to pushion[7] me wi' ony mair o' your ain makin' o' marmalade."' But the wee chap wadna gang.

"I was put aboot mysel' at the wean bein' dragged into the war, and I put my oar in for the first time. I gaed to Carmichael's wife and I said to her, 'Ye're no' cairryin' on this thing richt at a'; ye should ha'e a brass baund at the close-mouth, and pass round sandwiches among the spectators. A lot o' effort's lost through the folk no' richt kennin' the 'oors when the show starts; ye should get bills printed.'

"'Oh, Erchie,' said Carmichael's wife, greetin'. 'That wumman'll be the daith o' me. Whit am I to dae wi' her!'

"'Hire a hall,' says I, 'and engage the Terrible Turk and some mair o' thae wrestlers to dae wrestlin' between the times when you and her's restin'. There's money in the thing if it was richt managed. The sport's far ower guid to be confined to this close.'

"'I'll ha'e the polis to her,' said Carmichael's wife.

"Yin o' the Carmichael lassies has a lad that comes the length o' the close wi' her the nichts she's oot for her pianna lessons. Last nicht the twa o' them was standin' at the close-mouth, and Old Vengeance begood to trake oot and in on a' sorts o' excuses. At first she went sailin' by them wi' her heid in the air, grippin' her shawl tight aboot her so that it wadna touch them, the same as she was feared for something smittal. Then she went aye snortin'. 'It's a fine nicht the nicht,' says the chap at last bein' a sort o' comic. She turned on him like a teegur.

"'It's a bonny-like thing,' says she, 'that a body that pyes rent and taxes canna get oot in her ain close without trippin' ower dolls.[8] A chap like you wad be far better learnin' something at the nicht schule than hinging aboot here wi' a cratur that canna sew a seam nor wash her ain hankies. If ye kent as muckle aboot the Carmichaels as I dae, ye wadna come amang them. Piannas! If they wad pye whit they're owin' puir Lindsay, the grocer, it wad suit them better. I wish them and their pianna was burned; as shair's daith I canna get sayin' my prayers at nicht richt for the clatter of that pianna. Their grandfaither, that was in the rag tred —'

"The lassie and her lad skedaddled at that and left the auld yin victorious.

"I met her on the stair as she was comin' up lookin' as pleased as Punch. 'It's a nice nicht, Mr MacPherson,' says she as bland as onything. 'I think the weather's gaun to tak' up.'

"It's no the weather that should be ta'en up, I thocht, but I never said it. I'm no' anxious to tak' ony pairt in the Wild West show up oor stair."

59. *The Fair*[1]

"WELL, ERCHIE, the Fair[2] approaches," I said to him on Saturday.

"It does that," replied the old man, "ye can tell by the wye it's rainin'. I have a weather gless at hame yonder that's been pintin' to Fair for the last fortnicht. It's a fine cheery weather-gless that'll no' vex ye if it can help it, and if ye steeped it for a month in a byne o' watter it wad still keep on encouragin' ye."

"Where are you going this Fair?" I asked.

"If I get the length o' Yoker," said he, 'it'll be as faur as I'll venture. Gleska's guid enough for me. Noo that ye've made me into a book[3] wi' my photygraph as nate's ye like here and there in't, I can get fine fun gaun alang the streets lookin' in at the booksellers' windows to see mysel'. At first I was kind o' blate aboot the thing, and didna care to venture oot till it was dark and I aye hurried past the booksellers' windows as fast's I could in case the folk inside wad ken me frae the picture, but noo I'm fair brazen. I'm only vexed ye didna ca' me Archibald; it's genteeler nor Erchie, though I'm aye kent as Erchie in the tred. Gaun aboot lookin' at my ain picture's gaun to be the only trate I'm gaun to gi'e mysel' this Fair, unless, as I say, I tak' the notion o' a hurl on the skoosh caur as faur's Yoker.

"But Jinnet's gaun to Millport, her and my son Wullie. She was thrang packin' up jist when I cam' oot o' the hoose, and an organ-grinder oot in the back-court was playin' 'Hame, Sweet Hame' that nice it nearly made her greet. 'Oh, Erchie!' says she, 'it's a gey true sang; there's nae place like hame, and it's me that wad raither be comin' back than gaun awa'.' 'And whit for are ye gaun awa'?' I asked her. 'I canna tell ye,' said she, 'except it's for the pleesure o' comin' hame again.'

"And there she was, packin awa' as hard's onything, though she's no' gaun for near anither week, and a' she has to pack's the yellow tin trunk. Three or four hundred Gleska folk jist like oorsel's is packin' the same kind o' tin trunk at the same time. They're a' lookin' forrit to a fine time, that much uplifted the weans is neglected and no' gettin' their richt food. Yonder's Duffy; for the last fortnicht he's that fu' o' the Fair he canna walk at his horse's heid, but he's to sit on the trams o' his lorry singin' 'Dark Lochnagar,' and missin' mony a chance o' anither hundredwecht because his mind's wanderin' doon at the Skeoch Wud at Rothesay, so that he never notices folk twa storeys up wavin' at him. When Duffy comes back frae Rothesay and I say to him, 'Weel, Duffy, hoo did ye enjoy yer Fair?' he'll say, 'Immense, but by jove I've an awfu' sair heid.'"

"Well, Erchie," said I, "I don't know but your way of enjoying the Fair is as good as any."

"Of course it is," said he promptly. "There's nae midges in Gleska if it's a fine warm day, and if it's awfu' wet ye can staund in a close, and ye canna dae that in the country. There's mony a wye o' ha'ein' a fine time at the Fair withoot sailin' frae the Broomielaw. I kent a letter-cairrier ca'd Jock Wilson that used to spend a' his holidays in the Mitchell Library readin' books. He went in the mornin' when the place was opened, wi' a piece in his pocket, and sat readin' books till it was time for the place to shut at nicht. I used to say to him, 'Jock, ye should get the wife to bring ye a can o' soup in the middle o' the day, and keep up your strength.' But no; a' he wanted was the piece, and there he was for three weeks on end readin' a' the books, maistly aboot 'Half-'oors in the Country,' or 'Days at the Coast,' or 'A Summer in Skye,' or yachtin' or fishin' or sclimbin' hills. At least he told me so. And when the time was up, he wad come oot o' Miller Street fine and sun-burned, as happy's a lord, and enough money saved to buy a watch. He wad be daein' that yet, but he went and de'ed when he was just a young man, and I aye thocht it was for the want o' the can o' soup. It wad ha'e kept up his strength. His wife micht ha'e ta'en it to him for a' the bother.

"There's anither chap that I ken, a baker to tred, and when his bake-hoose shuts up on the Fair Setterday till the Wednesday, he jist washes his face and hands and gangs roond the other bake-hooses that's no' shut. Gi'e him the end o' a barm tub to sit on smokin' and watchin' the ither chaps puttin' in a batch, and he's as pleased as onything. He gangs the hale time o' his holidays frae the yin bake-hoose to the ither wi' his workin' claes on, except that his face is washed, and talks aboot barms, and bakin'-poothers, and pan breid, and the fancy breid tred, and the wye to kill clockers[5] and he starts his wark on Wednesday as fresh as onything.

"I used to ask him if he didna think it wad be a change to put on a collar and gang a sail on the *Edinburgh Castle*[6] as faur as Bowlin', but he aye said he couldna be bothered. I yince told him there were a wheen o' bake-hooses doon about Dunoon, and he cheered up, and said he wad like fine to see them. He was on his wye the next mornin' for the Broomielaw when he saw a bake-hoose he had never been in afore, and the temptation was that strong he went into't and spent the rest o' his time there.

"There's lots o' men in Gleska dae that at the Fair Holidays. Tylers gang to ither tylers' shops and keep back

the wark and save enough money for a rale spree afore they
begin work again. When the men in Dubs'[7] ha'e their
holidays they come doon to Buchanan Street Station and
strike matches to look at the insides o' the locomotives
there. I wadna say but they're maybe better to be daein'
that than shelterin' frae the shoo'er a' day in a public-
hoose doon at the Lairgs.

"The best Fair holiday I had mysel' was yince when oor
faimily was young. I packed Jinnet awa' to her guid-sister's
in Dalry, and took chairge mysel' o' a' the weans. The last
thing she said to me as she was leavin' the door was, 'See
and no' let onything happen the baby,' and I tell't her she
needna be feart, I was yince a baby mysel'. She wadna be
the length o' the street corner when the baby found the
door open and fell doon the stair. That was number wan
for the baby! I gi'ed it a big sweetie to stop it greetin', and
that sweetie stuck in its wee throat, and was chokin' it that
bad I had to thump its back. That was number two for the
baby. I had scarcely turned when it lifted a hot coal aff the
hearth-stane and started yellin'. Number three for the baby!

"Efter that I made up my mind to sit doon fornenst it
and watch it a' the rest o' the Fair Holidays in case it wad
keep up the sport and maybe sclimb up on the jawbox and
droon itsel'. But when I was watchin' the wee yin the ither
five went into the room, broke twa vawzes that were on the
chevalier and book-case, let oot the canary, and got their
haunds a' cut wi' the gless o' Gledstane's portrait they
knocked doon frae the wa'. The care o' the faimily was
becomin' ower great a strain on puir Erchie MacPherson, I
can tell ye. I sent for Jinnet's sister at the hinder end, and
sent a letter to Jinnet at Dalry, sayin', 'We are gettin' on
first class; nae bother; ye needna hurry back till the
Friday.' I kent fine frae my experience that a rest was whit
she was badly wantin'.

"I think the coast resorts on the Firth o' Clyde's no'
ha'ein' the vogue they used to ha'e, even wi' the Fair folk.
Do ye see the wye the folk's writin' to the *News* askin'
chape tickets for London? They see frae the writin's o' that

Cockney chap in the Setturday *News* that London's the only place ye can draw a dacent breath in, or get a dinner o' five coorses for eighteenpence, so the fever's on them. If it's no' London it's the Isle o' Man, whaur the cats wi' the nae tails is, or Blackpool. There's pictures o' Blackpool stuck ower a' the railway stations tellin' ye that it's beautiful and breezy, but it's seemin'ly no' breezy enough for the twa or three young weemen in the picture, for they ha'e a guid dale o' their claes aff them. If the Clyde's gaun to maintain its place wi' the holiday-maker, it'll ha'e to gang in for mair bands, mair minstrels, and a lot o' dancin' halls for the wet days. It's no use bein' beautiful if they're no' breezy forbye. But it mak's nae odds to Erchie; Gleska's guid enough for him."

60. *Erchie and the Free Church*[1]

"No," SAID Erchie, "I ken naethin' aboot whit's happened at the war this week back; the fight between the Free Kirks[2] is takin' me a' my spare time to keep an e'e on. I've nae doot the bonny wee Japs is daein' fine, and that they're still ha'ein' a sharp engagement wi' the Rooshians near Hanky-Pooh-Pooh, or crossin' the Poo Noo Paw under a heavy shell fire frae the enemy. It's like enough the Rooshians is still stoppin' British ships oot aboot the Red Sea yonder, and searchin' the sailors' bunks to see if they ha'e ony sweet tobacco, Florida water, or Song Folios planked, but we're ower much ta'en up wi' this Free Kirk affair to pye much attention.

"Jinnet asked me the ither day whit it was a' aboot. 'Are they gaun to shut up the Free Kirks a'thegither?' she says. 'If they are I'll be rale put aboot for puir Mr M'Cosh.' M'Cosh, ye ken, 's the minister o' the kirk that Duffy gangs to. He's an auld Free that turned U.F. It took me a' my time to assure Jinnet that Mr M'Cosh wadna need to gi'e up preachin' at yince and start canvassin' for sewin' machines and *The History o' the Clans*.

"'I'm gled to hear't,' says she, 'for he's a rale dacent auld man, and I wad be gey vexed if he lost his business. I'm shair I canna mak' oot whit a' this quarrel between Frees and UFs is aboot; there's that much aboot it in the papers, it mak's my heid dizzy to look at yin.'

"'Jinnet,' I tell her, 'if ye had Duffy the coalman here and a schooner o' beer in his hand, he could explain the poseetion to ye in ten minutes. If he couldna it wadna be for the want o' practice, for he's done naething since the Lords gi'ed their deceesion[3] except hing on to everybody he meets by the lapels o' their coats, tellin' them whit he said to M'Cosh when M'Cosh became UF, and whit M'Cosh said to him, and hoo he warned M'Cosh that he was jist makin' a cod o' the kirk jinin't on the UPs, that had nae richt releegion and hardly ever took ony coals frae him.'

"'Whit was wrang wi' the UPs?' said Jinnet. 'I'm shair I never could see ony difference between them and the Frees, except maybe that they were awfu' apt to be teetotal.'

"'Oh, but there was a difference,' I tellt her. 'I could never see whit it was mysel', but Duffy kens. He used to say the UPs was a' wrang in their fundamentals,'

"'Och! the puir sowls!' said Jinnet.

"'Aye, and Duffy, though he didna care to leave M'Cosh's kirk when it stopped bein' a Free and begood to be a UF because he had the contract for supplyin' the kirk wi' coals, was aye dubious if it was a safe thing to dae, and used to bide awa' frae the kirk, and sit at hame readin' the *Memoirs* o' M'Cheyne if he wasna feelin' weel.'

"'It's a mercy,' said Jinnet, 'the auld Established Kirk's no mixed up wi't; ye micht lose yer place at the beadlin'. But a' the same I canna understand it.'

"'Of course ye canna understand it,' says I to her. 'Neither, perhaps, does Duffy; but it's them that understands it least ha'e maist to say aboot it. If ye sit doon and darn a stockin' I'll tell ye a' aboot it.

"'First o' a',' says I to her, 'there were the Frees — the Rale old Oreeginal Frees, that cam' oot at the Disruption[4] bangin' the door behind them as dour as onything. They preached for a while in barns, and, by and by, they built kirks a' ower the country — fine, big, braw kirks, wi' rale bells on them, and nice wee manses, and folk left them money for mair kirks, and manses, and bells, and ministers, and they were gettin' on jist skooshin'. They had millions o' pounds in the bank, and the only thing that vexed them was that a' the ither kirks were a' wrang in the fundamentals, as Duffy says, and had a gey sma' chance o' gettin' to Heaven when the time cam'.

"'At the same time there were the UPs — mair fancy aboot the fundamentals, but that like Free's ye couldna tell the difference unless they had a quarrel. The only odds I saw between the UPs and the Frees was that whiles the Frees had blue hymn-books when the UPs had red yins, and Free Kirk elders aye wore clean white ties when it was their day at the plate. But there was only yin thing they were agreed on — neither o' them was fond o' the Established Kirk. The Established Kirk didna put itself awfu' much aboot ower that.

"'Everything was gettin' on fine till a'e mornin' the folk belangin' to the Free Kirk woke up and found they werena Frees ony langer, that when they werena lookin' the ministers o' baith bodies put their heids thegither and jined the Frees and the UPs and ca'd the result the UF. They were to sing oot o' the same hymn-book, put their bawbees in the same plate, sleep in the same pews, and save money.'

"'But a wheen o' the old Oreeginal Frees — the awfu' Free Frees that belang maistly to the Hielan's and keep the Fast Days, and hate the organ — maintained that they were the Rale Remnant, that the folk that went into the new UF werena Frees at a', and had nae business wi' Free Kirk buildin's or Free Kirk funds. They took possession o' the auld Free Kirks, took aff their boots and stockin's, and camped oot in the pews. They had free fechts wi' the UFs and the only thing that was wantin' to mak' the thing like an auld-fashioned clan war was that they hadna the bagpipes.

"'Twa dozen o' thae stench[5] auld Free congregations

held oot: folk thocht they wad jist wither awa' and disap-
pear in the coorse o' time, but they didna'. It's them that's
gaun aboot walkin' on their heels the day, with their hats
cocked to the side, for they're the Rale Remnants, and the
Lords say a' the kirks, manses, and money that belanged to
the auld Frees belangs to them, and no' to the UF at a'.'

"'Oh! the puir craturs!' said Jinnet. 'What'll they dae?'

"'Is't the UFs?' said I to her. 'Oh, they'll jist ha'e to trust
in Providence, and maybe keep a wheen o' hens.'

"'Noo that Duffy kens the money and the manse and
the kirk belangs to the Rale Remnant, and that it'll be
them, maybe, that'll ha'e the orderin' o' the coals efter
this, he's chawed that ever he ca'd himsel' a UF. He mak's
the excuse that he jined the UF because he wasna a scholar
and didna understand the thing richt, though he tried to
put M'Cosh against it. Since the deceesion cam' oot he's
even turned against puir Mr M'Cosh, and him and the
only ither Rale Remnant left in M'Cosh's kirk, an auld wife
that wears an ear trumpet, and canna stand the organ, are
gaun to put in anither minister in Mr M'Cosh's place.

"'It's as shair's ye're there, Duffy and the auld yin wi'
the ear trumpet's under the belief they're the only true
Christians left in this end o' the toon, and that they'll tak' a
place in Scottish history like the Scots Worthies or the
faithers o' the Disruption."

61. *Duffy's Day Off*[1]

DUFFY CAME to Erchie on Tuesday with a proposal that
they should take a steamer to the coast the following day to
see the Lochfyne Highland games.

"It'll be a fine tare," said Duffy; it's the kind o' thing ye
read aboot in the papers, wi' faur mair fun nor half-a-
dizzen fitba' matches."

"I wad gang in a meenute," said Erchie, "if I had a pair
o' kilts to put on; ye need the kilts for a Hielan' gaitherin',
and a 'Wee Macgreegor'[2] bunnet, and awfu' thick stockin's

and the slogan o' the clan, and a' that,'

"Whit are ye wantin' wi' a slogan?" said Duffy; "can we no tak' something in a bottle? Ye're the very man that should be there, and you a MacPherson. Here am I and the wife awa' on a veesit to a kizzen's in Heelensburgh, and me wi' a pound in my pocket. Are ye no' game? Jinnet'll let ye. A' ye ha'e to dae's to let on to her ye havena been feelin' awfu' weel for a week back — a kind o' dizziness in the heid ye didna like to say onything aboot. Says you to her, 'I think I'm jist rin doon; I'm needin' a wee change; I think I wad be the better o' a day at the coast wi' Mr Duffy.'"

"If I put it to her like that," said Erchie, "she wadna let me gang, for fine she kens a day wi' Duffy's nae cure for a dizzy heid. As luck'll ha'e it, I can gang to this gaitherin' withoot makin' up ony bawr aboot it, for Jinnet's awa' at her sister's the noo, and I'm no' on ony job to-morrow."

It was so that Erchie and his friend found their way to the Highland gathering. They were cast out upon the quay from a crowded steamer, and ten minutes afterwards reached a field where bagpipes were wailing ceaselessly, and gentlemen with very brilliant kilts were superintending proceedings of a singularly varied and occasionally bewildering character.

"My Jove!" said Duffy. "Is this a Hielan' gaitherin'? Whit are thae chaps doin' awa' in the corners o' the fields there blawin' their pipes the same as they were a wheen o' bumbees?"

"They're tunin' their pipes," said Erchie; "and if they can manage to get them tuned afore it's time to catch the boat they'll maybe play something fine. Bagpipes is a gey droll kind o' utensil; ye canna jist begin to play them the wye ye can a melodeon; they ha'e to be taken aside and argued wi', and half-throttled afore they'll dae onything wyse-like. They're awfu' dour things, bagpipes; but they never hairmed onybody that never hairmed them. See, yonder's a chap that's got his pipes fine and tame noo; he's gaun on the platform to play something."

The piper in question went on the platform and

proceeded remorselessly to play a pibroch. Two very fat
judges in kilts and a third in tartan knickerbockers sat on
chairs beside the platform and took notes on sheets of
paper as the pibroch unwound itself.

"Whit are thae chaps daein'?" asked Duffy.

"They're judgin'," said Erchie. "I've seen Hielan' games
afore. A' the prizes for bagpipe playin' gangs by points —
ten points for the natest kilt; ten points for the richt wye o'
cockin' yer bonnet; five points for no' gaun aff a'e tune on
to anither; five points for the best pair o' legs for the kilt;
ten points for yer name bein' Campbell and the judges
kennin' yer faither — that's the judges addin' up the points
and wishin' they kent the tune he's playin'."

The piper, having finished his pibroch, eluded the vigilance of the police, and got away behind the refreshment
tent. He was succeeded on the platform by a succession of
dancers, who did the Highland Fling, the sword dance,
and other terpsichorean deeds with great agility. They
were covered all over the fronts of their jackets and waistcoats with medals.

"That's a lot o' fine smert fellows," said Duffy. "They're
no' ill aff for medals. They must ha'e seen a lot o' wars."

"That's no' medals for wars," explained Erchie. "That's
championship medals. Every dancer ye see there's the
champion dancer. If he's no' the champion at Inverness or
Oban, he's the champion at Carmunnock, and he can win
a medal a week if it's a throng season for Hielan' games.
The wye the judges judge the dancin' is to coont the
number of medals each competitor has, bite the medals wi'
their teeth to see that they're no' pewter, and gi'e the first
prize to the man wi' the shortest kilt."

While the piping and dancing went on in one part of the
field, foot races proceeded in another; men put the ball,
threw the hammer, and tossed the caber, while committee
men, at regular and frequent intervals, hurriedly sought
their private tent, disappeared therein for five minutes, and
emerged wiping their mouths with the backs of their hands
and looking more active than ever.

The members of a pipe and drum band suddenly manifested themselves, running across the field to the committee tent, and something in the eager anticipation of their aspect aroused the interest of Duffy.

"Whit's wrang wi' thae chaps?" he asked. "They're in an awfu' hurry."

"Of course they are," explained Erchie; "they're awa' to ile their pipes. It's no' an easy job bein' a pipe band, I'm tellin' ye; ye need the nerve, and ye need to ha'e the richt sort o' feet for't. Wait you till ye see them comin' oot and playin efter their pipes is oiled."[3]

Duffy was struck with the intensest admiration when the pipe band came out and marched four deep round the field. He was particularly impressed by the player of the big drum. "My Jove!" said he, "that fellow put in a lot o' fancy work in his drummin'. I aye thocht onybody could play a drum."

"That's whaur ye made the mistake," said Erchic; "There's a science in't as weel as a gift. Ye see the wye the chap's got the big drum hooked on a belt roon' his neck; I've seen drummers that fou they couldna tak' the drum aff the hook whan they got hame at nicht, and jist had to gang to their beds wi' the drum on."

"My Jove!" said Duffy.

The steamer at the quay began to ring her bell for passengers returning to the city. "It's time we werena here," said Erchie, and they left the field. "I hope," said Erchie, "ye've enjoyed yer Hielan' gaitherin'. It's a rale divert!"

62. *Erchie's Views on Marriage*[1]

"THERE'S HARDLY a newspaper ye can tak' in yer haund the noo," said Erchie, "but whit's fu' o' letters frae folk that's either wantin' to be mairried or wishin' they werena. I read them ower to Jinnet efter oor tea at nicht, and mony a lauch we ha'e."

"Still it's a solemn problem, the matrimonial one," I

said to the old man, gravely. "Some marriages are full of tragedy, if we could only know it —"

"Ye needna tell me that!" he interjected. "I ken it mysel'; there's Duffy's second wife ta'en a notion o' improvin' hersel', and gaun every ither nicht to a cless for cookery and laundry-work. Duffy, the puir sowl, 's fair demented.

"'I never did ony hairm to her,' he says to me, and him nearly greetin'. 'It's gey hard,' he says, 'comin' hame frae yer wark tired and hungry, and ha'ein' to put on stairched cuffs on yer neck and eat Recipe 9 in Mrs Black's book for Lemon Snow. To bleezes wi' Lemon Snow! Whit ony man wants that's in the coal tred is his meat.'

"'Never you heed, Duffy,' I tells him, 'jist you tak' a biscuit and cheese and it'll soon blaw bye. Ye should buy her a bicycle or a chape American organ, and that wad maybe put her aff the notion.'

"Oh, I'm no denying there's tragedies, as ye ca' them, in mairrage — I yince broke a gasalier — but there's many a guid bawr tae.

"The great complaint some o' the women that writes to the papers have is that the man divna mairry fast enough, that they hang on till they're that auld and dune they canna lowze their ain boots, and ha'e to tak' twa rests on the stair afore they come up to their bed at nicht.

"'The thing that's wrang wi' the present-day so-ca'd Lord o' Creation,' writes 'Sensible Young Lady', 'is that they're ower much coothered up by their sisters and their mithers and their landladies that they grudge to tak' a wife they'll need to keep in claes and meat. Shairly we're no' that ill to keep. I wad be willin' to keep a genteel hoose and cleed mysel' and my man, if I had yin, on a selery o' fifteen shillin's a week. But the selfishness o' the brutes 'll no' let them gie us a chance.'

"'Vinolia Maud' writes: 'Whit's the use o' gaun through an expensive education and wastin' the best years o' yin's life learnin' German, Greek, Shorthaund, Astronomy and the richt swing at gowf if men gang awa' and hide themsel's up closes when they see ye comin', or mairry simpletons wi' crimpy hair that couldna tell ye the least wee bate aboot the Romans? Here am I,' she says, 'as cultured as onything, and a' in my ain time with my ain exertions, can wash a flair, mak' tasty dishes oot o' Vim, and embroider doylies, can read three languages if ye gi'e me time, talk aboot onything, and dress wi' faultless taste, and still at the age o' nineteen I'm gaun hame my lane at nicht frae my music-lessons. Is this,' she says, 'whit micht be expected frae the Second City o' the Empire?'

"Then the men tak' a haund at the writin', and a chap frae Gibson Street, signin' himsel' 'Common Sense,' says: 'It's a' very weel for the like o' 'Vinolia Maud' to say we'll no' drag her by the hair o' the heid to the conjugal altar, but the truth is we canna afford it on oor wee pays. Girls like 'Vinolia Maud' are used to the best o' everything — an egg to their tea, free-wheel bicycles,[2] and a' that; a chap couldna afford to keep yin on less than twa pounds a week. Whit would be left efter buyin' the like o' 'Vinolia Maud' a' her orders? It's no wonder,' he says, 'we don't mairry sae desperate reckless as oor forfaithers did; we see the young women o' the day are different frae whit they used to be. They're far ower smert, for wan thing, and ken as much as yersel', and they're that ambeetious they'll no' think o' mairryin' onything less than £180 a year, a hoose up a tiled close wi' a vestibule door and oriel windows.'

"'Vinolia Maud' talks aboot culture,' writes 'Indignant Hardware Assistant'; 'Culture's a' richt maybe in its ain place, but whit guid is it in twa rooms and kitchen at a rent o' twenty-four poun' ten? The question is — can 'Vinolia Maud' bake? Can she dae the washin' withoot takin' in a washerwoman? Can she turn her ain dresses? There was nae culture nonsense aboot the young women o' the good auld past. Sae lang's they had the kitchen range fine and polished and their weans fancier dressed nor the other weans on the stair, they worked like slaves and de'ed content at the age o' fifty.'"

"It's very sad, Erchie," I admitted. "These letters always seem to me to be written by chronic invalids who are

confined all their days to bed, and don't know the outside
life, but amuse themselves by writing to the papers about
one of its most interesting problems. Though 'Vinolia
Maud' can't get a husband, apparently, and 'Indignant
Hardware Assistant' is so fastidious about the kind of wife
he wants, the marriage market is just as busy as ever it used
to be, I fancy."

"I should think it is," said Erchie, "or it wad be a puir
look-out for the waitin' tred that I belang to. But it's no'
the difficulty o' gettin' mairried that's botherin' some o'
the folks; it's the impossibeelity o' bein' unmairried.

"It seems that in Society ye're awfu' apt to get wearied
o' yer ain wife. Ye rise in the mornin', and there she is wi'
her face sittin' fornenst ye at breakfast; ye come hame for
yer dinner, and there she is wi' the same blouse she had on
yesterday; ye try to read yer newspaper, and there she is
sittin' opposite ye in the same chair, knittin' the same sox,
wearin' her hair the same way, as she has been daein' since
ye mairried her five months ago, and it's awfu' exasperatin'.

"A chap ca'd Meredith[3] that writes novels, has been
asked whit he wad suggest to remedy this painfu' state o'
affairs, and he's for havin' mairriages last only twelve
years. When I tellt Jinnet that, she thocht maybe it was a
new law comin' oot, and she was fair astounded.

"'I hope ye'll no' leave me, Erchie,' said she, in the
nerves.

"'No, if ye behave yersel',' I tellt her, 'and promise no' to
tak' ony cookery lessons like Duffy's wife.'

"Yes, twelve-year-mairrages is Mr Meredith's cure for
domestic discord. Ye wad think that if a couple managed
to thole each other for twelve years they micht as weel hing
on the rest o' their lives. I canna understand whit mak's
him fix on twelve years ony mair than seeven, or fifteen.
But nae maitter whether he made it twa years or twelve
years, it wad be a bonny-like business — faur waur nor a
flittin' day."

"But I don't suppose Mr Meredith desires to compel
husbands and wives to separate at the end of twelve years;

he merely suggests what may be called a break in the matrimonial lease. If you, for instance, were, at the end of the twelve years, tired of Jinnet —"

"Catch me!" said Erchie.

"It's an absurd supposition, of course, I admit, but if you were, or she found your company no longer congenial, you could come to terms to leave each other and look out for new partners."

"It wad be an awfu' bother," said Erchie. "I hivna even my Sundays to mysel' for a tryst, me bein' a beadle."

"Oh! But the separation would not be compulsory. Mr Meredith doesn't contemplate that; if you're quite contented with each other, you remain as you are."

"Is that the wye o't?" said Erchie. "I thocht it had to be a swap, whether ye were willing or no', at the end o' the twelve years. And I was awfu' frichtened if I was free again I micht fa' into the haunds o' 'Vinolia Maud'."

"Do you know the real cause of a great many, perhaps the majority of these tragedies in married life, Erchie?" I asked.

"No," said he, "I'm nae scholar; maybe its the weather, or tight stays, or no' sleepin' wi' the window open at nicht, or the use o' saut, or —"

"It's poverty," I interposed, "grim, ghastly poverty. The rich are never given to domestic squabbles."

"Man!" he said, "I'm that gled I have a pound or twa by me; Jinnet and me'll no' quarrel when I'm gettin auld and doited."

"Listen to this," I said, and read an extract from a newspaper:—

"The discomforts of marriage — I don't speak of the more serious matters which appear in the law courts — are mostly confined to households with small means. A man and women must be incurably vicious if they jar on one another when they have a big house, motor-cars, a yacht, money wherewith to buy amusement, and a host of friends to share the fun. If in such circumstances the lady's husband annoys her seriously, she tells him a few home

truths, and motors down to Eastbourne for a week. The
man thereupon gives some neat little theatre dinners at the
Savoy, runs over to Paris, or goes to Newmarket. At the
end of the week husband and wife meet again casually on
the stairs of their London house, having forgotten the
whole incident. The propinquity of poverty is intolerable.
No man or woman with intelligence was ever born who
could live together from year's end to year's end without
quarrelling. Husband and wife may be the best of friends;
they may have found out all one another's faults and forgotten them, but sometimes if they are ordinarily human,
they must want to be alone. And whereas a single man or
woman with a small income can have a considerable
amount of solitude and amusement, a household at £500 a
year has little of either."

"Ma conscience!" said Erchie. "That explains the hale
thing! You and me'll ha'e to get a motor-cawr and a yat.
I'll rin awa' hame to Jinnet this meenute and say, 'Hey,
wife, I feel it comin' on me. I'll be breakin' bowls in an 'oor
or twa unless we ha'e a change. Awa' you doon to Millport
for a week and gaither cockles, and I'll put in the time wi'
Duffy till ye come back. We'll meet casually on 'oor ain
stairheid next week —'" Here Erchie took a fit of chuckling
that nearly choked him. "Do ye ken whit she wad say when
we met on the stair like that efter a week?" he went on.
"She wad say, 'Erchie MacPherson, ye're a bonny-lookin'
ticket wi' yer boots polishet wi' black leed, and the same
collar I left ye wi' , and such an awfu' smell o' cloves and
aromatic lozenges.' And I daursay she wad be richt, for I
wad sooner ha'e Jinnet a' the time and a quarrel noo and
then than ha'e her awa' for a week and live the life o' an
angel."

63. *Jinnet's First Play*[1]

ERCHIE IS an old playgoer, though he has long since ceased to take an active interest in the drama, which he maintains has fallen off sadly since the days of Mumford and Glenroy,[2] but his wife Jinnet's first experience of the theatre was had last Friday. It was at my instigation she went, for I was anxious to have the impressions of the drama from a mind as sophisticated as that of Mr W. T. Stead,[3] who thinks his first visit to a play of no little national importance.

"I have two seats at the Royalty,"[4] I told Erchie. "You can have them if you'll promise to take the Mistress with you."

He rubbed his chin and looked at me slyly. "Would ye no' raither say Duffy?" he asked, "and we micht ha'e a fine bawr. Jinnet's a' richt for a swaree, but I'm no' carin' to ha'e her mix hersel' up wi' thae theatricals at her time o' life. But wi' Duffy there wad be nae risk o' leadin' him astray or his gettin' stage-struck."

"No," I said, "it must be Mrs MacPherson or nobody."

He went straight home and bade Jinnet get ready for the theatre.

"The theatre!" she exclaimed, half afraid and half delighted. "I wonder if it wadna be thocht awfu' daft-like at my time o' life? Naebody wad need to ken onything aboot it—"

"Of course not," said Erchie. "It wad be an awfu' thing if it was fun' oot. They wad think ye were gaun to come oot as a ballet girl next. But naebody needs to ken. Ye could disguise yersel'. Put on my dress suit and a fause beard, and gang oot and in between the acts, trampin' on folks' corns, and ye'll pass for a gentleman."

"Oh! ye're jist bletherin'," said Jinnet. "I'm no' that feared to gang as a' that. I ken it's no' looked doon on the wye it used to be. Mony a time I've read that there's naething wrang with the morals o' the theatre, and that quite dacent people can gang to't."

"So they can," said Erchie, "if they get a pass, and don't pap orange peel doon on the heids o' the folk in the Orcestral Stalls. The theatre's a' richt. It's as good almaist as a sermon. The villain's a chap ye want to boo at, and if ye have ony he'rt at a' ye burst oot greetin' when the puir mitherless lassie is found oot to be the rale Lady Fitzgerald, and gangs aff to be mairried in the last act to the sound o' the chaps bashin' awa' at bits o' brass pipes, lettin' on they're kirk bells."

So they went to the Royalty.

"Whit's the name o' the play?" asked Jinnet, as they were entering.

"Letty,"[5] said Erchie.

"Letty," said she, surprised. "Are ye sure? I never heard tell o't. I thocht it wad be 'Rob Roy'[6] or 'East Lynne'.[7] Will there by ony singin' in't?"

"No, nor dancin'," said Erchie. "See's yer umbrella and slide in there; that's oor sates. Ye needna speak in a whisper," he went on, as Jinnet, in a state of palpitation, leaned towards him to express her astonishment at the grandeur of her surroundings. "Ye needna speak in a whisper, it's no' the church ye're in. Nobody'll touch ye. I wish I had thocht o't and I micht ha'e ta'en ye some chocolates."

"Chocolates wid choke me," said Jinnet, still whispering, and the curtain rose on her first play.

I fear I shall never get Jinnet's confidence regarding what she thought of 'Letty'. I know that I had only to mention the word theatre to her yesterday to see her face get very red as if I had referred to something very discreditable either to her or me. But Erchie has told me all about it.

"I'm gettin' an auld, din man," he said sighing. "I'm no' up to the latest ideas at a' and I'm feart I couldna be bothered wi' plays like 'Letty'."

"It's by a very clever man of great reputation," I ventured to inform my old friend.

"Like enough," said Erchie. "But it's ower rich for my blood, as the Englishman said aboot the oat-cakes. It's the story o' two men and wan lass."

"There's novelty for you!" I exclaimed.

"Stop you!" said Erche. "Yin o' the chaps is in a good way o' business — stockbrokin' or something like that, and the lass caws a typewriter for him in his works. He wants to mairry her. The ither man's jist yin o' thae chaps that gang aboot in plays, lookin' fine and generally in dress suit wi' nae tred nor ony ither means o' support sae faur as ye can discover, and he wants the lassie no' to bother aboot mairryin', but to come and tak' up hoose wi' him, and see Paris, and get nice frocks, and get her meat richt, for the puir cratur's no' strong, and gey thin. Noo ye'll no' hinder Jinnet from takin' the man that wanted to mairry the lassie for the villain, and the chap wi' the dress suit that had a wife already and living separate from her, for the hero.

"I'm no' astonished at her, for I was sooked in mysel' for nearly an act or two. The chap wi' the wife already, ye see, was a smert, even-doin' kind o' chap to speak to, that quate and nice, and fu' o' fun, and wi' fine ludgin's that wad maybe cost him a pound a week withoot board. I wad defy ony respectable woman, not engaged, to see the chap withoot takin' a notion o' him. He was the perfect gentleman. Ye could see't from the way he shed his hair.

"But the ither chap that wanted to mairry the lass, and was railly daft aboot her and wanted to tak' her to introduce her to his mither — he had nae mair manners than yin o' Duffy's coalmen on a Setturday nicht. When there was ony bawlin' or blawin' to dae; when there was onybody to get drunk and start fichtin' it was him. If there was onybody to look rideeculous, it was him. If the chap wi' the dress suit had a nice lang Englified speech to mak' he made it at the puir stockbroker, and he made it in such a noble and gentlemanly manner that the puirest man in the theatre wad be gled he wasna a stockbroker, and sorry he wasna livin' frae his wife. A' through the play it was the chap in the dress suit yer hert warmed to. The man that wanted to mairry the lassie was jist a nyaf, ye could see it frae the wye he aye kept his lum hat on the back o' his heid — the rale sign o' the snob — as ye see him in the theatre.

"It was jist as ill to find oot which o' the weemen in the piece was the clean potato. Letty hersel' — the lassie the men were aifter, and that had nae scruple aboot goin' at nicht to the dress suit chap's ludgin's, was a lassie naebody need to be ashamed to be seen talkin' to. It was her had a' the fine claes; it was her was gettin' the offers o' cairrages on this side and that; it was her got mairried at the hinder-end to a man wi' a fine business. Jinnet thocht Letty was the heroine, but by that time I was beginnin' to understand the wye plays is written nooadays, and I said to her, 'Haud on a wee, I'll bate ye she's no'.'

"And I was richt. It turned oot that the only wumman a respectable man wad care to mairry o' the hale ging-bang o' them was a wee sherp-nosed clerkess wi' specs, and the kind o' chape straw hat that's guid enough for wee men that'll no' go to grass weedower's lodgin's and drink champagne and smoke cigarettes —"

"That's the new school of realism, Erchie," I explained. "Virtue always wears spectacles and cheap hats, and has a sharp nose. Poor old boy, your dramatic education is a generation behind date."

"I can see that," sadly confessed Erchie. "Of course naebody wanted the wee clerkess. A' the fun she had was bein' good, and lendin' her money to Letty, and when Letty mairried the man wi' the guid business — he wasna a stockbroker; he was a phottygrapher — the wee clerkess humbly took a situation under her. That'll learn HER to be virtuous!

"There was a champagne supper in the piece. I suppose it was yin o' thae lightnin' suppers, for it was a' ower in five meenutes. It cam in maistly in bottles and it took twa glesses to mak' a stockbroker that fu' it needed three men and a German waiter to haud him back frae speelin' the wa'. It was a Society play —"

"It was bound to be that with Mr Pinero, Erchie. It is only in Society, I believe (on Mr Pinero's own contention) that you can get really interesting characters for modern drama."

"I'm gled to hear't." said Erchie. "He's welcome to them, for me. But he had twa or three dacent workin' chaps in the play. Yin o' them was a phottygrapher, and mairried Letty, though she made it plain a' alang she was vexed she couldna get mairryin' the fellow wi' the dress suit. Ye couldna help seein' he was a phottygrapher frae the start, for he wore a broon velvet jaicket, and his hair no' brushed, and business was aye bad wi' him. There was an insurance canvasser and a traiveller for furniture. I never in a' my life saw jist the same kind o' insurance agent, or traiveller, but they were rale comic when they werena tryin'.

"Letty changed her mind and didna run away wi' the dress suit, and didna mairry the stockbroker. The dress suit chap gaed into a decline, and had a hoast that wad vex ye. He came a'e day to Letty's phottygraphing werks efter she mairried and though he had this cough he was aye the gentleman, and such a superior lookin' chap to the phottygrapher Letty mairried that ye were vexed she didna run awa' wi' him. She was kin' o' vexed hersel'; at last she made it plain that she thocht mair o' the dress suit than o' her wee phottygrapher.

"And that's the play is it? Quite Pineroesque. Jinnet did not like it?"

"She did not," said Erchie, emphatically. "She thocht it rotten in every partcecular, and I agreed wi' her."

64. *Willie*[1]

THIS IS the history of Willie, Erchie's youngest son, and Jinnet's.

I would have liked to make it a story with a hero, one of those fine fellows who make you wish you had lived a better life when you read about them in print. Who have high, pale brows, and always get the first prize for English Composition in ex-VI Standard, or nobly take the blame on themselves when the other boy breaks the window. Who

Never Told a Lie. Never made any display, but marched bravely on to the last chapter with their hair always nicely brushed, modestly pretending the other fellow was much cleverer; always saying the beautiful, noble thing just at the right moment, and sharing their last penny with some poor devil who wouldn't have needed it if HE had taken pains and been a hero too.

I would have liked him to be handsome and tall, the way heroes are always constructed, with a fine, deep, manly voice, heard to perfection in the village choir, and afterwards when he shouted from the burning building, "Stand aside, men, I will save her myself!" or crying when the ship was going down in mid-Atlantic, "Women and children first. By heavens I'll shoot the man that puts his foot on that gunwale!" I would give anything to have a hero just like that who never caused his mother a single fear or tear, who never had any need to be ashamed of himself from the day he broke open his little tin savings bank to give the money to the organ-grinder's little lame daughter till the day his wife returned after eloping with the officer, and was met with the welcome words, "Darling, you have come back, I will try — I will try to be more worthy of you."

But I could not find, in real life, any model for such a hero, so I am forced to be content with Willie.

Even Willie's school teachers found nothing heroic about him. He cleaned his slate with the cuff of his sleeve, and sucked the blots from his copy-book with his tongue instead of drying them with botting-paper. He knew — for several days after he learned them — the heights of the chief mountains in South America, but he thought you could get to England only in a steamer. He had learned Algebra, and knew the multiplication table up to six-times, was at the start of French, and spelled "difficulty" with one "f". You can see from all this that he was just like you and me at the same age.

"Willie," said Erchie to him, when the boy was writing his first application for a situation that had been advertised. "Willie," said he, "ye're a fine, wee smert chap, and

yer mither and me's as prood as onything o' ye, but ye
shouldna spell 'difficulty' wi' wan 'f'. Ye needna grudge
the 'f's, there plenty mair whaur that yin cam' frae."

"Oh! it'll do fine," said Willie. "The man'll ken what I
mean. What's the use of two 'f's if one'll do."

"That's the way I aye spelt it in my time," broke in Jinnet. "Let the laddie feenish his letter, and get to his supper.
Even a man o' business needs his meat."

It was one night that marked an epoch in the history of
the MacPherson family. Willie, you see, was to be out of
school at last, and already, in his mother's eye, he was "a
man of business". He did not look very like one, sitting at
the kitchen table with a penny bottle of Perth Office Ink, a
sheet of ruled notepaper, and a piece of blotting paper torn
from a baker's passbook, stopping every now and then in
the act of composition to fondle a peerie he had in his
pocket. "I could keep books if they were not too difficult,"
he had written at his father's dictation.

"They micht ha'e spelt difficulty wi' wan 'f' in yer
mither's time," said Erchie to him emphatically. "She was
aye the sort o' wumman that made as little o' a difficulty as
she could. And maybe the man'll ken fine what you mean,
but at the start o' business it'll dae a young chap nae herm
to keep frien'ly wi' the dictionary. When yer fortune's made,
and ye ha'e to hurry up to get some fun oot o't afore ye
dee, ye may save time by droppin' a letter here and there,
but if I were you I wadna try't yet."

"Be shair and tell them ye're big for yer age, a guid riser
in the mornin', and ha'e fine health, and gang to Dr Mackay's
Sunday Schule," said Jinnet, leaning over the boy. "Tell
him ye're truthfu', and your faither's a beadle —"

Erchie chuckled. "It's no' a scullery-maid's place Willie's
wantin'," said he. "I hope he's truthfu', at least as truthfu'
as he's able to be, but it's no' an accomplishment to brag
o'; it's like haein' red hair, ye hae't or ye hivena't. And I
wad never mind sayin' onything aboot whit yer faither
does. The man that wants the 'Smert office boy — Apply
S23.438', disna want to ken onything aboot yer faither. He

wad sooner, maybe, ye hadna ony, for then he wad be shair naebody wad be comin' doon to his office to say it was time ye were gettin' a rise in yer pay."

"Tell him ye're fond o' work and got the third prize in Standard 3 for the Shorter Catechism[2]," advised Jinnet.

"Whit work?" said the boy, with apprehension, diving into his pocket to feel his peerie. "I never knew there would be any work. I thought an office boy sat on a stool and just went messages wi' blue envelopes."

"Jist that! Jist that!" said Erchie, soothingly. "Ye're daft for wark, as yer mither says, but ye're no' gaun to kill yersel' at it. I don't think, Jinnet, I wad say onything aboot bein' fond o' wark; the man wants a boy, and no' a nice wee clean angel. There's a chance that maybe he was yince a boy himsel' and minds whether he was fond o' wark or no. If there was a boy that was fond o' wark jist because it was wark, they wad put a hoardin' roond him, and start opposition to the Zoo. And as for his third prize for the Shorter Catechism, I think he shouldna mention 't. Hoo much do ye mind o' the Shorter Catechism, Wullie?"

"I mind — I mind the beginnin' o' the — o' the reasons annexed," said Willie, dubiously.

"Annexed to what?" asked his father, with an ill-concealed smile.

"To the — to the place we were at when I won the prize," said Willie, uneasily shifting in his chair, and wishing he could start business as a carter, where there was none of this preliminary bother.

"And whit was the reason annexed?" asked his father.

"The — the noun must agree with its nominative, as John, London, dog!" said Willie.

"Puir auld Scotland!" cried Erchie, and his wife held up her hands in horror.

"Ye should be ashamed o' yersel'," said Erchie, with a poor attempt at sternness. "Ye should mind every werd o' yer Catechism — like — like me. But it's like enough there'll no' be a Catechism in the office, and the man'll no ken whether ye ha'e the richt reason annexed or no'. The

Shorter Catechism's like porridge; ye tak' it when ye're wee because ye hiv to, and it mak's ye fine and strong; but when ye're grown up and ha'e a hoose o' yer ain, ye tak' ham and eggs instead. The man that's wantin' the smert office boy's no' trainin' missionaries, I'll wager. He wants a lad to be ready to answer the telephone the days he's awa' gowffin', and explain to the people that he's oot on awfu' important business. Nae man in his richt senses expects a Sunday School-book kind o' boy that kens everything for aboot seeven and sixpence a week. He wadna be comfortable in the same room wi' him. He wad be feared to gang oot at twelve o'clock wi' a customer in case the boy wad jalouse something, and be vexed for him."

"It's a gey short letter," said Jinnet when it was finished, and Willie read it out. "The man'll think Willie hasna very much to say."

"Och, it's lang enough," said Willie terrified lest he should have to write another. "If I put ony mair to't, I wad ha'e to turn the page. Can I get oot to play noo?"

"It's lang enough for ony kind o' letter," said Erchie, examining it critically. "Even a love-letter. Ye canna mak' them ower short, or ye'll maybe ha'e to mairry the lassie. The value o' a letter is no' whit ye put in it, but whit ye leave oot. It's the same wi' office-boys; it's no' whit they dae that a business man looks to, it's whit they divna dae. They're thrang trainin' philosophers in the Board Schools, and the demand's only for plain wee ordinary laddies that can cairry a basket withoot coupin' it, or turn up an address in the Directory."

"I hope ye'll aye be a guid boy, and tell the truth," said Jinnet.

"That's the main thing," agreed Erchie, "unless it's a lawyer's office. And even there, I think ye couldna dae better than copy yer mither."

"And aye be wyce, and no' throughither," went on the mother.

"Keep yer eye on me," said Erchie, putting his thumbs comically into his waistcoat's arm-holes.

"He micht dae waur; I'll say that for ye, ye auld haver," said Jinnet. "And aye be tidy and clean," she went on.

"And mind the back o' yer ears," said Erchie. "It's sore at first, but ye'll get used to't."

When Willie went out to post the letter that might be the key to his fortune, he left two rather sad parents in the kitchen in Grove Street (for all this, I should say, is an incident of the Erchie of a dozen years ago). Jinnet felt that this was the last of the flock going away from her in a sense, and her husband knew and sympathised with her feelings. "The puir wee smout," said he, beginning to fill his pipe. "He's startin' the rale school, and there's plenty o' palmies³ gaun in't."

"I aye think on that laddie o' the Carmichaels that was yin o' thae geniuses, and couldna dae onything but mak' poetry for the *Weekly Mail*, and lost his place, and —"

"Ye needna be frichtened for ony capers o' that sort aboot Willie," said his father. "There's naething o' the genius aboot him. He has faur ower muckle sense for't, and it's me that's gled o't, for it's an awfu' habble bein' a genius and ha'ein' to earn yer livin' at the same time."

"He's a fine wee chap, onywye," said his mother. "I'm gled he's no' se wild as ither boys."

"Maybe no'," said Erchie, and winked to himself.

Willie slid down the stair railing with the letter in his pocket, gave a wild whoop at the close-mouth that collected three or four other boys round him in two minutes and he began to brag.

"I'm startin' in an office," he said. "Twelve shillings a week the first year, and I'm to get cleanin' the boss's gowf sticks."

A great wave of envy swept over the others.

"I'm to start at yince," he went on, walking ahead of them, and wishing he had a cigarette. "The man said I wad get keepin' the foreign stamps aff the letters, and I'll gi'e ye some, Ferguson. It's a great big office wi' three hundred clerks and I'll ha'e a lot o' boys under me."

"Ye'll ha'e to wear a kahoutchy collar and speak polite,"

said one envious follower.

"Ye're a liar!" said Willie. "The man said he didna want ony toffs about his office. He's an awfu' nice gentleman; he said I wad maybe be foreman or cashier or something in a year or two if I took care o' the company I kept ootside. I'm thinkin' o' givin' up the Rosehall Street Swifts and learnin' short-haund. It's fine for writin' fast. Ye can write onything in shorthaund, and ye aye get on if ye ken't."

"I'm gaun to be a plumber," said the only boy who kept his head at the dazzling prospects for their friend. "My faither says a clerk's an awfu' poor job and no' good for yer health. A plumber has fine times, sowderin' things and workin' on roofs. I wouldna be an office-boy for a pound a week; they mak' ye wear a roond hat."

"A roond hat!" said Willie, remembering, with alarm, that round hats were an obnoxious feature of a great many office-boys he had thrown mud at in the interests of a simpler costume. "I didna exactly say I wad tak' the job," he added reluctantly as he dropped the letter in the letter-box.

And with what results I shall tell you later.

65. *Willie's First Job*[1]

THERE MAY have been hundreds of answers to the advertisement for the "Smart Office Boy — Apply S25,438," but you have probably guessed already that Erchie's son (and Jinnet's) was the lucky applicant, otherwise this story might never have got beyond one chapter. A letter in the following terms came next evening to "Mr William MacPherson":

> Middle Chambers,
> Hope Street, Glasgow.
> George Fraser Strang,
> Writer.[2]
> IN RE "Office Boy,"

Dear Sir, Please call on me at the above address at 2 p.m. prompt tomorrow.

Yours truly,

George Fraser Strang.

A profound depression seized on Willie when this portentous epistle was read aloud by his father, for the word "prompt" is hateful to any natural boy, and a career of kahoutchy collars and round hats was plainly suggested in the curt official character of the communication. There was no hint here at golf clubs to clean, or foreign stamps to be collected.

"It's a lawyer," said Erchie; "it micht be waur for a start. I yince kent a rale dacent lawyer, and naething was ever found oot aboot him. If ye're gaun to be a lawyer, Will, ye'll ha'e to start the nicht-schule again for coontin'; the accounts is the main thing in a lawyer's."

"I hope he'll no be mixed up wi' ony o' thae murder trials and breach o' promises," said Jinnet, somewhat disturbed at the prospect. "The papers is fu' o' them the noo. I wad be gey sorry if ony son o' mine was learnin' his tred in a polis office."

Erchie laughed at her. "Ye divna ken life, Jinnet," said he. "There's lawyers that never gang near a polis office or a polis coort unless some yin tak's it into his heid to examine their books."

Willie got an egg to his breakfast next morning to fortify him for his first encounter with the business world. He had to wash his face twice, put oil on his hair, and wear his Sunday clothes. It was a bitter hour! Many a time he had shouted ribald things after boys guilty of being seen in their Sunday clothes on a week day — unless, indeed, they were going to a funeral or a trip, when there was some allowance to be made for the temptation. Willie anticipated some trouble with the Rosehall Street Swifts for between one and two was the very hour they played their practice matches in Grove Street, and as he was having his clothes brushed for the fifth and last time by his mother he could hear the boys of the R.S.S. shouting.

"Mind and say 'Sir' to the gentleman," instructed Jinnet.

"And if he speaks awfu' fast and Englified, and ye canna mak' him oot easy, jist say 'Certainly!' noo and then," added Erchie.

"Be sure and tak' aff yer kep when ye gang inside," said Jinnet.

"But don't put it in your pouch," said Erchie. "That's low. There's nae fear o' onybody stealin't on ye, sae ye needna hide it that way. Jist haud it by the skip, and keep yer heid up, and look the chap in the e'e if he's no' skeely, and say, 'Certainly, sir,' noo and then when he gi'es ye a chance."

"Mind ye ha'e a hankie," said Jinnet, patting his pocket to assure herself, and pulling out a white corner.

"A hankie's a handy thing," said Erchie; "it can be used for mony a thing. It'll nearly haud yer first pay if ye can tie the richt kind o' knot."

"Is that a' I'm to mind?" said Willie at last, vexatiously.

"I think that's a'," said his mother, "except ye're to see and aye tell the truth. I'll be mindin' o' a lot o' things when ye're doon the stair, but the truth's the thing that's first and foremost."

"And after that the back o' the ears," said Erchie with an affectionate farewell joggle of the boy's shoulders.

Stopping on the stair a moment to push his white handkerchief into the bottom of his pocket, and pull up the collar of his jacket to cover the clean linen collar underneath so as to hide the evidences of week-day gentility from the Rosehall Street Swifts, Willie boldly ventured forth, whistling an air with a great display of unconcern. It was no use.

"By George! look at Willie, the toff! wi' his face washed and his Sunday claes," cried the captain of the Swifts, and the game stopped immediately, while the team gathered round the unfortunate victim.

"I'll hit ye a bat in the ear if ye say I'm a toff," said Willie. "Hoo wad ye like if yer ain aunty was deid? I'm gaun to a funeral."

This put another complexion on the situation; the R.S.S. could always sympathise with the necessity for dressing to attend a funeral, and so Willie escaped further comment. He found the office of George Fraser Strang up seven stairs in Middle Chambers. There was a hoist, but he thought you had to pay a ha'penny on the hoist like a car, or the Finnieston Ferry, so he climbed the stairs, rapped at the glass door of the lawyer's office, and entered at a shout of "Come in!"

It was George Fraser Strang's first office; he had become a lawyer on his own account exactly three days ago. A young man of about 24, clean shaven, and his fair hair cut very short on the top of his head to give an illusion of baldness, long experience, and brain-racking contemplation of intricate law cases. His chambers numbered two — the outer one furnished with empty Japanese tin deedcases, a desk, a stool, a letter-copying press, and a New York Life Insurance Office calendar; the inner one, to which he led the way, marked "Private" and containing a roll-top desk, with a spotless blotting-pad, a new inkstand, a book called *Bell's Principles*, and another called a *Table of Fees* on it: two chairs, one a revolving one, a bookcase filled with old Glasgow Directories, and Oliver and Boyd's Almanacks.

Willie, coming behind the lawyer, glanced hurriedly round to see if there was anything suggestive of sport or amusement in the place, and his heart sank when he failed to see even a bag of golf clubs.

The young man, having waved Willie into the other chair, took the revolving chair himself, and with a thrust of his foot, made it turn round rapidly several times, then turned to the boy with a faint show of pride in his new possession. "What do you think of that for a chair, eh? It goes round quite easy, without pushing with your hands or anything."

He was so much a boy himself, in spite of his pretence at baldness, that Willie was greatly reassured.

"It's a fine birler, sir" said Willie, promptly, eyeing the chair with a manifest desire to have a try at it.

Mr Strang put him into it, and sent him spinning like a top.

"It's your twist noo," said Willie, rising, and then Mr Strang realised that this was not business-like. "H'm!" he coughed, in a manner he had long studied under Lord Trayner without that judge being aware that he had a pupil. "H'm! That'll do for the chair. You're William MacPherson?"

"Certainly, sir," said Willie, remembering his father's advice. The hour had come when he must "speak polite"; he felt already the round hat entering his soul.

Mr Strang looked at him with some embarassment, for he could not think of anything more to ask him. Willie held up his head, and glared into the lawyer's eyes, which were, fortunately, without any flaw.

"Are you — are you — a Protestant?"[3] asked the lawyer.

"Certainly, sir," said Willie.

"Can you spell conveyance?" asked the lawyer; Willie did so, and came triumphantly through a test in interlocutor, bond, and disposition.

"Are you strong?" said Mr Strang finally, and Willie said, "Certainly, sir."

"It's like this, William," said the lawyer, leaning back in his chair and putting the tips of the fingers of both hands together. "It's like this: I'm a busy man; you have no idea the rush that is in this office. It's rush, rush, all the time; and the Sheriff-Principal said to me yesterday when I was having lunch with him, 'Mr Strang, you'll kill yourself if you don't get assistance.' He was right; I feel I'm doing too much. Two big proofs today; three wills; a bond and a disposition in security; consultation with seven clients, all wealthy men, and all determined on going to the Court of Session. It's too much for one man, now, isn't it?"

"Certainly, sir," said Willie.

"You're the very boy I want," said Mr Strang, delighted at such manly acquiescence. "You grasp my meaning. 'Delegatus non potest delegare,' as I said the other day to Lord Young[4] — to Lord Young, mind you. Just like that —

and though at first I could not entrust you with the — by the way, you know Latin?"

"Certainly, sir," said Willie, who had merely started Latin at the beginning of his last term at school.

"Good," said Strang. "You're the very man I'm looking for. You'll get on under me. Ask anybody and they'll tell you there's no office where you'll get more experience than in Mr George Fraser Strang's. Look at this —" He took Willie into the outer office, and, with a wave of the hand, indicated the japanned tin boxes. "Trusts!" he said, in a whisper. "Millions of pounds involved, my boy! You would wonder what these tin boxes were for, eh?"

"I though they were for gaun — I mean goin' to Rothesay wi'," said Willie.

"Not at all! Not at all! Trusts," said Mr Strang, eyeing them proudly. "I hold the situation — THE situation, mind you, in the hollow of my hand. Look at this calendar," he went on, pointing to the New York Life. "I'm agent of the company. You see my name printed there at the bottom — George Fraser Strang, writer, agent.' No humbug about it. I expect we'll clear hundreds — thousands — a year off this branch of the business alone."

Willie felt that this was like being in church, with no lozenges to chew.

"And now for your first lesson in law," said Mr Strang — "the desk, the stool, the ink — we use the best blue-black — the — the paper. Yes, here's the paper in this drawer — Process; feel that, hand-made, pott; Scroll, Deed. On the left, red tape, red thread — everything of the best. We spare no expense. Here, on a convenient stand behind you, you have the letter-press. See?"

It was an old-fashioned letter copying-press, with a handle that lifted off the screw, and was shaped like a dumb-bell. He gave two or three thrusts from the shoulder with it, as if it were really a dumb-bell. "Fine for the muscles," he said; "many a time I —" Then, noticing Willie's look, coughed in the Lord Trayner[5] manner and put it down. "That'll be enough for you to remember today. It's confoundedly busy," he said.

Five minutes later Willie was left alone in the front office, perched on a stool copying the draft of a Memorial to the Lord-Advocate[6] with injunctions to keep all visitors in the front office if they came in anyway crowded, admitting only one at a time to Mr Strang's room.

Willie had got three lines of the Memorial copied, his initials neatly cut with a pen-knife on the inner side of the desk-lid; a letter on the office notepaper written and addressed to "Tommy Ferguson, Esq., 179 Grove Street," several yards of red-tape secreted on his person for some purpose hereafter to be decided on, when Mr Strang rang his bell.

"Go out for six penny stamps and two ha'penny ones," he instructed his new assistant.

Willie's errands for the rest of the afternoon were for:

1. An ounce of cigarettes.
2. An evening paper.
3. Change for a pound.

Every time Willie left the object of his errand on the desk, and returned to the front room. Mr Strang rubbed his hands together, smiled with intense satisfaction, said to himself, "That's the style, George!" and then pulled himself up with a frown and a cough in the Trayner manner.

66. *The Young Man of Business*[1]

Willie came home from his first day in his first situation very full of a sense of his own importance, and no longer ashamed to show himself in his Sunday clothes to the sarcastic young gentlemen of the Rosehall Street Swifts Football Club. Indeed, he put himself to some trouble to meet some of them before he went upstairs to his tea.

"Shut up!" he said to the first who displayed anxiety to know how Aunty's funeral had got on; "I wasna at a funeral at a'; I was jist coddin' ye. I'm in an office."

"My George!" said the other boy. "Whit kind o' office?"

"A kind o' lawyer's," said Willie, doing a bar or two of a sand-dance on the pavement in a very undignified manner for any apprentice to so grave a profession as the Law.[2] "It's a fine job, wi' a hoist on the stair, and ye go up and doon withoot payin' onything."

"Whit do ye dae in a lawyer's office?" asked the other boy.

"Oh, lots!" said Willie. "Yet get ony amount o' fun. I have a room to mysel', and a desk wi' wee places inside it, fine for haudin' white mice or a rabbit. The man I'm wi' 's awfu' nice, a rale gentleman; he said I wasna to bother walkin' when I went ony message. I was aye to tak' a caur or a cab. We're awfu' busy in the place the noo; Mr Strang's makin' a hundred pound a minute, and he has a carriage and pair. I'm to get drivin' them some day next week."

"I ha'e an uncle that has a fine quick bicycle," said the other boy, enviously. "He's the second man in the depairtment in the Saracen."[3]

"I'm the heid o' the depairtment I'm in," said Willie. "A pound a week and my chance —"

"A pound a week!" cried the other, dubiously, and to carry conviction home, Willie proceeded to give him a share of the red-tape, the sealing-wax, the wafers, the pen-nibs, and the paper fasteners from Mr Strang's first stock of stationery material.

Jinnet had cookies for the tea of her new man of business.

"I declare!" she said when he came in, flushed and elated with the sense of manliness; "I declare I think ye're bigger than ye were a week ago, Willie. Ye must be fair stairvin', puir boy; ye never had a bite since dinner time. If I had kent ye were gaun to be sae lang I wad ha'e put a piece in yer pocket. Sit doon here in faither's chair and tak' yer tea."

She was afraid to ask if he had really got the situation; it would have been almost a relief to her to know that he had not, and that he was to be a boy a while longer. But her husband, with a more practical mind on the situation, put the question immediately.

"Well, Willie," said he; "whit did Mr Strang think o' ye?"

"I got the job," said Willie, "and I'm started."

"Are ye indeed?" said his father, whimsically. "Do ye hear that, wife? Willie's started. Everybody clear the road for wee Wille MacPherson! Stand aside or ye'll get hurt; he's gaun on the road to fame and fortune wi' such a breenge he canna stop himsel'. William MacPherson, Esq., writer, advice, wan shillin'; wills made while ye wait; sma' debt cases smertly attended to; licensin' coorts a speciality. And whit's the salary, Willie? I'm no' attachin' a great dale o' importance to't, for I jalouse I'll ha'e to help to keep the hoose mysel' for a year or two yet, but the salary's aye a point."

"I didna like to ask," said Willie.

"Of course no'," said Erchie, blandly. "Ye're yer mither's rale boy. It wad be a pity to put the gentleman aboot wi' thinkin' on the terible hole ye wad mak' every week in his bank account. And he wadna say onything himsel' aboot the pay?"

"No," said Willie.

"He wad likely forget," said Jinnet. "Ye'll see whit it is on Setturday. Is he a nice man, Mr Strang?"

Willie told all he knew about his employer, with none of the imaginary details which would have been so ready to come to his mind if he had one of the Rosehall Street Swifts for his audience.

Jinnet was impressed. She noted the most trivial particulars her son recorded regarding Mr George Fraser Strang, and was horribly depressed for a moment when she heard that Mr Strang was so busy the very Sheriffs said he would require assistance or he would die of overwork.

"Oh! I hope the work'll no' be ower hard for ye, Willie!" she cried.

"No fears o't," Willie assured her. "It's faur easier than daein' my lessons in the school."

Erchie rubbed his chin and reflected. "I'm thinkin'," he said, "there's nae fear o' Mr George Fraser Strang runnin' Willie aff his feet gaun wi' money to the bank. It's plain

he's no' long at the tred, but he seems to ha'e a lot o' qualifications for't to judge frae the stories he tellt ye."

"Do ye think he'll be mairried and ha'e boys o' his ain?"
asked Jinnet anxiously, a point on which her son was unable to enlighten her.

"It's no' likely," said Erchie; "but he'll be thinkin' aboot
it. Maist lawyers newly started at the business get engaged
in a month or two; they ha'e sae much time on their
haunds, and pen and ink's aye that handy on the desk afore
them they canna help writin' love letters and afore they ken
whaur they are the date's fixed. Ye didna post Mr Strang's
letters for him? No; it was the only job o' the day he didna
trust ye wi' for they werena addressed to men o' business.
And so ye think ye'll like the job, Willie?"

"I think I will," said Willie. "He didna say I wad need to
wear a roond hat."

"That's aye a savin'," said his father. "My auld hats is
the only thing yer mither canna mak' doon for ye."

"It's a start onywye," said Jinnet.

"H'm!" added Erchie, dubiously, "it's aye a start, but
it's no' exactly the same as if ye had fa'en feet foremost into
a gold-mine. Ye'll dae the best ye can wi' Mr Strang, but
that needna prevent ye keepin' yer e'en on the papers to
see if onybody's wantin' a smert young manager for a
railway company or onything like that. Three-fourths o'
the failures in life I see in Gleska (no' coontin' Toon
Cooncillors) are men that started work in the wrong job.
Look at mysel'; if I hadna been sent to clean knives in the
auld Saracen Heid Hotel when I was ten year old and
drifted into a dress suit afore I had my strength, I micht
ha'e been a tip-top lawyer."

"I wad far raither ha'e ye the wye ye are," said Jinnet. "I
couldna stand a lawyer in the hoose. Except a wee yin, no
awfu' far gone in the business," she added, quickly
remembering Willie's new situation.

"The start's everything," her husband went on; "It's no'
lucky for a young laddie to begin in a great big office,
whaur there's that mony men they need to ha'e a time-

keeper, and there's aye a subscription sheet gaun roond for a wreath for somebody's funeral. He micht as weel start stokin' in the Navy wi' the notion o' bein' an Admiral by and by. In a big office the bosses are that busy yachtin' and gowffin' and pushin' the business on the Continent that they never mind the name o' ony o' their clerks wi' less than £200 a year."

"Twa hunder a year!" cried Jinnet. "That's awfu'. Hoo much is that a week?"

"It's jist the same as a hunder a year," explained Erchie; "ye can manage wi't, but it's little enough; and there's folk no' half as smert wi' faur mair. But as I was sayin', the lad that starts in a job where he'll ha'e to steal the stamps or invent a patent afore the boss 'll ever hear his name is no' gaun to be a pairtner in the business in a hurry. It's better to start in the place whaur the boss kens yer name withoot turnin' up the books."

"It shairly wadna be ill for onybody to mind Willie's name," said Jinnet.

"He has wan advantage in bein' ca'd William, Willie or Will, that his maisters 'll aye be tempted to ca' him onything but Mr MacPherson. If ony man wants his boy to get on in ony business in Gleska, he shouldna ca' him Reginald or ony o' the fancy names; a maister's bound to feel faur warmer-he'rted to a chap he can ca' Willie than to a chap wi' a name in a penny story. Was it William or Willie Mr Strang ca'd ye?"

"It was whiles William and whiles Hie, boy!" said Willie, bolting bread and butter with incredible velocity that he might get the sooner out to the street, where the Rosehill Street Swifts were already to be heard whistling on him.

67. *Erchie's Son*[1]

I will not deceive you; Willie never became a laywer. He possibly might have been a dazzling light of the law today if it had not been for — among other things — a ninepenny rabbit. "A rabbit's a fine thing in its ain place," as his father said to him afterwards, "but they're no' heedin' aboot them in a lawyer's office; they wad faur sooner ha'e geese."

How the rabbit came between young MacPherson and a great professional career you may learn at once. It was on the second day of his employment with Mr George Fraser Strang he found it very dull. He had exhausted all the novelty of the desk and the stationery stock. He had tired of going up and down the hoist, and it was a terrible trial to have a pocketful of squibs (for it was approaching Hallowe'en) without being able to let one off now and then. When his mother asked him that night how he was getting on, and how he liked his work, he made no concealment of his real sentiments.

"I divna like it at a'," he told her. "I don't think it's good for my health; my heid's as sair as onything."

Jinnet was alarmed, in spite of the fact that his appetite at the tea-table might have assured her his illness was not necessarily fatal in character. "My puir wee Willie!" she cried; "was I no' feared the confinement wasna for ye? Whaur is't sair?" And she hovered over him as if he was to be plucked there and then from the very jaws of death.

Willie, hopeful that his strategy had succeeded, at the risk of bursting his collar, hurriedly gulped down sufficient bread and butter to make six sandwiches at an afternoon At Home, put a hand to his head, and loosely indicated the whole contents.

"It's an awfu' commandin' thing a sair heid," said his mother, putting a cooling hand on his brow. "Whit kind o' sairness is it?"

"It's— it's— it's whiles dizzy, and whiles jist like a red-hot knife gaun through't, and noo and then it gi'es a bang," explained the boy.

Jinnet stood wringing her hands. "Brain fever!" she said piteously to her husband. "I was shair frae the first the laddie hadna the strength for a lawyer. Oh! whit am I to do?"

"Gi'e him anither slice o' breid to start wi'," said Erchie, in a tone that made Willie blush. "Maybe it's jist a kind o' German brain fever,[2] jist a hairmless feverina, that can be staved aff if ye catch't in time. I used to hae't mysel' on the geography days when I was in the school. The thing for't, if it's no' to be shifted ony ither wye, is a dose o' caster ile. When did it start, Willie?"

"I had it a' day," said Willie, "but— but it's no' near sae bad as it was in the office."

"I could wager ye that!" said Erchie. "It's wonnerfu' whit the fresh air and a half-loaf 'll dae. I'll swear, if ye gang and ha'e a game o' fitba' wi' yer butties oot by, yer heid 'll be as hale as onything in twa meenutes. And whit for dae ye no' like the office?"

"I'm no' learnin' onything," said Willie. "It's jist sittin' on a stool and writin' things."

Erchie smoke his pipe and looked quizzingly at the hope of the household. "No' learnin' onything," said he in a little. "That's a peety! Did I no' think Mr Strang wad be learnin' ye Acts o' Parliament and cross-examination and a' that, the hale day. But he'll be that busy he'll no' ha'e time. No' learnin' onything! Man! that must be awfu' chawin' to ye, Wullie; you that was aye that keen to learn in the school. If the job disna suit ye, whit kind o' job dae ye think ye wad like?"

"If we jist had him in a wee shop," suggested Jinnet. "In a wee shop aboot the New City Road, whaur he could get hame for his dinner. He's no' strong."

"Jeck Macdougall's gaun to be a plumber," said Willie; "I wad raither be a plumber too."

"Ye wad be apt to get sair heids there, too," said his father. "Na, na, ye'll just ha'e to bide in Mr Strang's for a while, noo that ye're in it. And I hope and trust ye'll no' be bothered ony mair wi' thae awfu' sair heids. The only thing for them if they start again's the castor ile."

So Willie's strategy failed. There was nothing for it but to make Mr Strang's office as cheerful as he could, and casting round in his mind for some plan of lessening the loneliness of his daily toil, he remembered the possibilities of the desk for the accommodation of livestock, and after tea went forth to seek a boy who had a ninepenny rabbit that he might be induced to lend. For two lead pencils and an offer of unlimited free rides on the office hoist on Saturday, Willie next morning got a loan of the rabbit, and took it to the office, along with adequate fodder in the shape of dandelions and turnip tops. He installed the unfortunate animal in his desk.

Mr Strang went out and in, quite unsuspicious that his office was making a very promising start as a sort of menagerie, for the lid of the desk always went down at his approach, and his new boy was always discovered deeply engrossed in indexing the letter book. But in his hurry to shut up this ingenious hutch once, Willie left his store of dandelions outside.

"What's this?" asked Mr Strang, seeing them. "What are you doing with that stuff?"

"It was a boy gave me them," said Willie, prompt with the universal explanation of youth.

"Quite so, but what's it for? What are you doing with that stuff? You can't eat it," said Mr Strang.

"I'm— I'm fond o' floo'ers," said Willie; an apparently ingenuous explanation that greatly amused the young lawyer.

By the greatest ill-luck it was this very afternoon that a retired publican on the South Side, after ten year's consideration of the advisability of making his will, made up his mind. He was driven to this decision by the increasing number of dangers that seemed to beset his life. He had arrived at a period where he could not step off a car without falling on his nose, when it was difficult to get upstairs to his flat at night without accident; and when further escape from certain little blue creatures, which haunted him at intervals, was not much longer to be expected.

He came into Mr Strang's front office, enveloped in a genial odour of whisky, hot with lemon in it; shut the door very quickly and carefully to prevent any of his little blue friends from following him, and asked Willie if Mr Strang was in.

Willie, caught unexpectedly with the rabbit out of the desk, had thrust it suddenly into one of the empty japanned tin deed-boxes without closing the lid, and he had such a startled and confused appearance that the publican's befogged intelligence associated him somehow with the little blue imps on the other side of the door. He tried to brush him off his vision with his hand.

The boy did what he had been carefully drilled in; he first intimated to Mr Strang that a gentleman wanted to see him; upon which the young lawyer surrounded himself with books and red-tape-tied Records, and assumed the frowning and harassed appearance of a man who has been sitting up at night overtaking arrears of business. "Ask him to step in," he instructed Willie, and Willie went to the front and showed the client in.

The client stepped into Mr Strang's room, and hurriedly glanced round to see if any of his agile little cerulean friends were before him. He was reassured to find nobody there but a young gentleman so deeply engrossed in writing that he did not observe his entrance until he coughed.

"Ah, excuse me!" said Mr Strang, jumping up to receive his first client. "I was so busy — most important Memorial to draw up for the Lord Advocate; please take a chair."

"I'm Grant," said the visitor; "John Grant. I was wantin' my Will made oot, if that's in your line o' business" — and at every word he further impregnated the atmosphere of the room with the odour of good cheer.

The heart of George Fraser Strang beat with joy, but he lolled back in his revolving chair with a marvellous appearance of nonchalance. "Just so!" he said; "Just so! Wills are a special feature of our business, Mr Grant. Scarcely a day passes but that sort of thing engages my attention. I always give Wills immediate and careful personal supervision; life is so uncertain — in the midst of life, as the saying goes, we are, as it were, in death, and a Will always takes precedence to other business. Always, Mr Grant."

Mr Grant was proceeding to explain in detail what he wanted, and the lawyer's pen was poised over the ink-pot, when the ninepenny rabbit appeared on the scene, and brought dismay around. It had escaped from the deed-box, eluded the efforts of Willie to catch it, and ran lightly into the inner room, the door of which the client had left ajar.

The lawyer did not see it at first; he was too astounded at the horror on the face of his first client, who jumped to his feet with a yell of "Dalmighty! there's a new kind; I'm off oot o' this."

Mr Strang wheeled round on his chair to look for the cause of this outburst, and saw the rabbit on his hearth rug. He had so lately been a boy himself that he understood the whole thing in a flash. "Confound that boy!" he muttered, as his client bolted from the room.

"Come back, Mr Grant! Come back; it's a real rabbit!" he cried after him in a vain effort to begin business, but it was in vain — there came back to him only the sound of the client's frantic flight down the stair, and the aroma of whisky, hot with lemon in it.

That was why Willie's apprenticeship to the law suddenly terminated there and then. He came home with the rabbit under his jacket, and the circumstances permitted no deceit to his parents.

The process of looking for a situation had to begin again, with what results I may tell you by and by.

68. *Erchie on the Early-Rising Bill*[1]

IT WAS remarked by a good many people at our church
yesterday that the morning bell was nearly quarter-an-
hour later to start ringing, a thing which had not happened
twice in twenty years, for our beadle is a pattern of
exactitude, the rope in one hand and his watch in the other
five minutes before the latter indicates that NOW is the time
to call the town to prayer. We observed an unaccustomed
haste and nervousness about his appearance in the pulpit
when he placed the Books there, and it was further significant of mental perturbation that when he had shown the
minister into the pulpit he forgot to snib him in. Now, I
like to see Erchie snibbing-in the minister; it is a sacred rite
in itself; he does it with a flourish, as if it were the bolts and
bars of a dungeon, in which he thus confines the Champion
of Christendom to fight it out with the very Father of Sin.
Old Erchie's face stiffens as he pushes the pulpit door shut;
his mouth is pursed with firm determination as he bends to
turn the snib, and though the snib could be turned by the
push of a finger he is content with nothing less than an
emphatic and forceful gesture of the whole arm, which
gives the impression that he is saying to himself "THERE ye
are noo! Ye'll come oot o' that when I let ye!"

I confess I was so curious about his lack of promptness
and his perturbation yesterday that I waited behind the
rest of the congregation to walk home with him, and ask if
all was well with Jinnet.

"She's fine!" he assured me heartily. "She didna come
oot to the kirk the day because the kitchen nock went
wrang on us, so that she hadna time to dress hersel'."

"The kitchen clock seems to have upset yourself a bit today, Mr MacPherson," I said. "It's seldom we see you late
with the ringing of the bell."

He smiled a little grimly, and cocked his eye at me with
that sly look of his that always indicates a private joke,
which he is wondering whether I should be acquainted

with or not. "Did ye ever try to mend a nock?" he asked, irrelevantly, and I had to admit that I generally left it to the watchmaker.

"Ye're a wyse man there!" said Erchie. "I wish I had left my nock to the watchmaker too, and there wadna be sae mony wee brass wheels turnin' up on the waxcloth every time that Jinnet soops it. A nock's like your neighbour's character; ye can tak' it to bits wi' your least wee bit touch, but if ye try to put it thegither again, ye're shair to ha'e as mony bits o' the works over as 'll mak' anither nock, but nane o' the two nocks 'll be much use to ye. There's a lot o' human natur' aboot a nock — I don't mean ony o' thae wee, roond footry German tin nocks at 1s. 11¹/₂d. that the tylers use for birr-r-rin' them up on Monday mornin's, but a rale oreeginal wag-at-the-wa' nock made in Gleska, wi' a big sonsy face and a thrang, cheery-lookin' pendulum. I ha'e a wag-at-the-wa' nock o' my grandfaither's yonder that's almost human; it's that auld it has the hiccough afore it strikes the 'oor; it ticks in the Gaelic, for it cam' frae Mull; and whiles tak's asthma so that we hae to gi'e 't some ile and kittle it into humour again wi' a feather."

"It seems to have failed you today at any rate," I remarked. "What went wrong with it?"

"Did ye read in the papers aboot this new Daylicht Savin' Bill[2] a man ca'd Pearce[3] is introducin' into the Hoose o' Commons?" said Erchie, with a Scotsman's privilege of answering one question by asking another. "For years and years the German's ha'e been risin' an 'oor or two earlier than us in the mornin', every man o' them waukened wi' a 1s. 11¹/₂d. nock, that keeps on birr-r-rin' till ye put it in a byne o' watter. Startin' their day's business an 'oor or twa afore the British workin'-man has the wife heaved oot o' the bed to mak' a cup o' tea for him, the Germans[4] hae been gettin' a lot of tred that used to come oor way before we got a world-wide name for gowfing. If the tred o' the ither nations is to be kept from leavin' us a'thegither, it's argued noo that we'll hae to rise a wee bit earlier in the mornin' so as to be on the spot wi' oor samples before them graspin' foreigners."

"But the foreigner has only to forward his hour of rising, too, in order to leave us as we are," I suggested.

"Then there'll be naething for't but for us to sit up a' nicht, and at that, I'm certain, we could bate them easy," said Erchie. "But it's no' easy to mak' the sons o' the brave and the free rise before the milk comes, and the fire's richt on, so the men that's rinnin' the Daylicht Savin' Bill are makin' oot that it'll be an awfu' savin' in gas. You'll ha'e noticed that in the summer-time it's broad daylicht lang before the time that it's day-licht in the winter?"

"So I've heard; but it has never actually come under my observation," I replied; and Erchie chuckled for he has his own weakness in the matter of morning rising.

"Weel, this new Bill proposes to put furrit the clock an 'oor and twenty minutes in the summer, so that the folk like Duffy the coalman, that rises at six the noo, will be risin' at twenty minutes to five and never be ony the wiser."

"It will be very cruel to poor Duffy," I suggested.

"Naething o' the kind!" said Erchie, "for ye see he'll be gaun to his bed an 'oor and twenty minutes earlier than he gangs the noo, and as the Mull o' Kintyre Vaults and a' the ither pubs'll shut at twenty minutes to nine at nicht, he'll no' be missin' onything. Under the new plan we'll a' ha'e eighty minutes more daylight in the summer-time; it'll save the country gas, and lengthen your life when ye're no' lookin'. The Bill recommends that we've no' a' to put oor clocks furrit eighty minutes at a breenge, but to shift them furrit twenty minutes on the first four Sundays in April, putting them back again the same way in September for the winter."

"It seems delightfully simple," said I.

"It's no' that simple!" said Erchie. "It took me nearly an oor to mak' it plain to Jinnet. When she heard aboot it first she said it was an awfu' shame o' the Leeberal Government[5] puttin' up everything. 'They begood puttin' up the coals first,' she said, 'and then they put up the soap, and noo they're not content wi' puttin' up the butter mair than tuppence a pun', but they're wantin' to put up the puir wee smouts o' milk-laddies an 'oor and twenty minutes earlier than they used to be.'

"'Aye, but ye see, Jinnet,' I says to her; 'the milk-laddies 'll be in their beds an 'oor and twenty minutes earlier at nicht, so it's as braid as it's lang. If they're in their beds at ten the noo, they'll be there at twenty minutes to nine when the Bill passes.'

"'Twenty minutes to nine,' she says; 'that's jist the very time the puir wee things thinks the fun's beginnin'! And wha's to thresh them to their beds at that 'oor? — their faithers 'll no' be hame frae the public-hooses.'

"'Of coorse they will,' I tellt her. 'Do ye no' see that the faithers 'll ha'e to leave the public-hooses at twenty minutes to nine themselves?'

"'Ye needna tell me!' said Jinnet; it's hard enough to get them oot at ten!'

"'But it will be ten on the public-hoose clocks, though it's actually only twenty minutes to nine, and ye see the public-hooses 'll ha'e to shut an 'oor and twenty minutes earlier than they're daein' noo.'

"'I wadna say onything against that,' said Jinnet; 'It'll let a lot a' men hame on Setterday nicht wi' their wages before the shops shut, and it'll be a mercy for their wifes, puir things!'

"'Do ye no' see that the other shops 'll be shut an 'oor and twenty minutes earlier too, Jinnet?' I said, but she said she couldna see ony sense in that.

"It was jist as ill to explain to Duffy the coalman. When I tellt him a' the clocks were to be put furrit an 'oor and twenty minutes in the summer, he said, 'Thank the Lord for that, MacPherson; I aye thocht eight o'clock was faur ower late for a man to get his mornin'. When dae they start?'

"'Of course,' says I to him, 'the public-hooses 'll be shut correspondingly early at nicht, so that they'll ha'e to sling ye oot at twenty minutes to nine.'

"'I wad like to see them tryin' that! It's the very 'oor I'm gettin' into form,' says he, quite angry.

"'But they must!' I says, 'for a' the clocks 'll be eighty

minutes fast.'

"'Only in the mornin',' said Duffy, 'and that's fine, for it'll get the wife up.'

"'They'll be eighty minutes fast at nicht as weel as in the mornin', Duffy,' said I to him, nearly losing a' my patience. 'The Mull o' Kintyre Vaults 'll be shut at twenty minutes to nine, and ye'll ha'e as much as is guid for ye by that time.'

"'Hoo the mischief can I?' says he; 'It hardly gi'es me time to gae hame frae my wark, my hands washed, and my tea.'

"'But do ye no' see that intead o' stoppin' your work at five, the way ye're daein' the noo, ye'll stop at twenty minutes to four?'

"'Then that 'll be half a day wasted,' said Duffy, 'for it's nearly three afore I'm back from my dinner.'

"'Your dinner 'll be eighty minutes earlier,' I says.

"'That'll be half-past eleeven,' said Duffy; 'Man! I'm hardly done wi' my parritch then.'

"Who is to be responsible for the putting forward of the clock?" I asked my droll old friend.

"That's the point! said Erchie. "It wad ha'e to be a job for the nicht polis; at onyrate I'm no' gaun to be responsible for puttin' back my dacent auld grandfather's wag-at-the-wa' twenty minutes four times in September. I tried to put it back twenty minutes yesterday to show Jinnet hoo it could be done, and the big haund stuck, and burst a lot o' the works inside for spite. I have it a' richt noo except that it 'll no' go, and the wee wheels here and there aboot the floor are apt to hurt ye when ye're in your stockin' soles."

"Of course one needn't put the clock back actually in September," said I; "it will be sufficient to stop it for twenty minutes when required."

"Hoo are ye to tell when the twenty minutes are up?" asked Erchie.

"Well, you will presumably have another clock," I said, "and you will keep an eye on it while the first clock is stopped."

"And then I suppose I'll ha'e to stop the second clock and keep an eye on the first for ither twenty minutes. That'll be forty minutes day-licht wasted for a start. Na, na, Jinnet and me's made up oor minds we're gaun to put up wi' the time the way God made it."

69. *Erchie Reads the Papers*[1]

"WHIT'S IN the paper this week?" asked Jinnet, as she drew in her chair to the opposite side of the fire from that on which her husband sat, and proceeded to ply a frugal and skilful darning needle.

"It's jist fair runnin' ower wi' news," said her husband, looking pawkily over his glasses. "Here's a lang story aboot 'A Mother Saved from Certain Death in Lanarkshire'."

"Puir creature!" said Jinnet, sympathetically; "was it an accident?"

"No," said Erchie; "they were tryin'. It says that her name was Mrs Mary M'Graw, wife of a Coatbridge collier, and the mother of five robust and rosy little bairns. A year last November, efter a by-ordinar' hard day's wark in the washin'-hoose, she felt a shiverin' a' ower her, and her appetite clean disappeared. There was a curious tartan taste in her mooth in the mornin's, and awfu' buzzin's in her ears. She couldna sclim a stair withoot haudin' on by the railin'; crimson spots begood to dance in front o' her eyes; her feet swelled; she took palpitations every time she lifted onything; she lost flesh rapidly, and got that thin her claes had to be taken in three times in wan week. Fifteen doctors gave her up, and her man was lookin' aboot him for a nice young hoosekeeper wi' nae faimily, when by the mercy of Heaven she read in a paper aboot Murray's Mild Magenta Pills —"

"Ye auld rascal! it's jist an advertisement," said Jinnet.

"Tuts! so it is!" said Erchie, with a clever air of disappointment. "And I was expectin' a' the time she was near gaun to be run ower by something and snatched frae the

jaws of death by a young man wha modestly went awa'
refusing to give his name and address.

"Here's something else," said Erchie, turning to another
column. "'Important New Discovery About the Hair;
Baldness Will be Unknown in any Part of the World in
Another Twelvemonth.' It says that when the famous
American scientist Ralph K. Ford R.K.S.W.V. was
travellin' through the jungle o' Patagonia on his mission o'
love to the different tribes there he fun' a secret shrub wi'
berries on't which the natives used to oil themselves. Noo,
all the natives o' Patagonia are as hairy as onything, and,
bein' a bald man himsel', he tried some o' the secret shrub
berries, ca'd the Chichehuchas, on his heid, which was as
smooth as a curlin'-rink. In twa days he could shed his
hair; a week later he could dae withoot a hat at the hottest
time o' the ay, and had to tak' a steamer back to England
to get his hair cut. He brocht a cargo o' the Chichehuchas
wi' him, and he has cured hunders o' folk o' chronic baldness. John Jones, the well-known railway-porter at Leeds,
writes sayin' that efter three o' the 1s. 11½d. bottles —"

"Blethers!" said Jinnet. "That's jist anither advertisement."

"Tuts! so it is!" said Erchie. "And I thocht by the photography o' John Jones at the tap, it was gaun to be something comic. Here's anither thing— 'A College Education
in Three Months'. 'Many of our readers realise how much
they are handicapped by the want of a first-class University
education. Had they a knowledge of the history of Greece
and Rome, they would find their own value in the commercial world immensely increased, and their wages
doubled in the first six months. We cannot all afford a
University Education, but for the sum of threepence-
halfpenny a week, or one halfpenny per day, we can, by
means of the New History of the World —' "

"Never mind the History of the World," said Jinnet,
impatiently; "Is there no' onything aboot the Princess o'
Teck,[2] or the Princess o' Wales'[3] wee weans?"

Erchie sat back in his chair and laughed. "That's aye

your notion o' a newspaper, Jinnet," he exclaimed; "A' the
dear auld recipes for Shepherd's Pie, hoo to glaze in
starchin', and the way to make baby's bootees; a no' awfu'
cruel murder somewhere faur away in Germany, a Breach
o' Promise, where the lassie wins her case, and a' the rest
o' the paper aboot Royalty. Some of the Tories is frichtened to gi'e woman votes; if they only kent it, the workin'
women o' this country, if they had votes, wad be Tory to a
man, and determined Monarchists, jist to keep the papers
gaun wi' cheery news aboot waddin's and christenin's,
whaur the dresses are a' described and everything's o' the
best. Whit interest is the Princess o' Teck to the like o'
you? Ye never set eyes on the dacent body."

"Neither I did," said Jinnet, "but I'm shair she's a maist
respectable woman; her name's in the paper every noo and
then, and never in onyway to be ashamed o'. I've seen sae
much aboot her and the Saxe-Coburg family that they're
jist like auld friends. Ye needna laugh; mony a nicht when
ye're oot at your wark and I'm sittin' here my lane sewin'
or darnin' the time passes fine wi' thinkin' o' the cleverness
o' wee Prince Eddie,[4] and the number o' times a day the
King, puir man, has to sit doon to a meal or change his
uniforms. I was readin' the ither day that he tak's the
principal meal o' the day aboot twelve o'clock at nicht — it
must be an awfu' habble for the Queen, puir body!"

"Oh she's a' richt!" said Erchie; "she'll get assistance wi'
the dishes frae the lassies in the kitchen, if it's no' the nicht
their lads come."

Erchie turned to another page of his paper. "Mercy on
us! Here they're wi' their bombs again!" he exclaimed.
"They were fired at the Shah of Persia[5] when he was drivin'
to his palace and —"

"If it's awfu' bad, don't read anither word o't!" said
Jinnet, nervously. "If ye do I'll no' sleep a wink the nicht
wi' dreamin' aboot it. Oh! thae blagyards o' Fenians![6] A
King's life's no' worth livin' wi' them. I wad sooner be a
coalman like Duffy; any honest, sober workin'-man has a
better life o't; he can gang aboot the streets withoot a

regiment o' sodgers roon' him. Don't read a word o't the nicht, Erchie; I'll look at it mysel' to-morrow mornin'; I canna stand readin' aboot murders when the gas is lit."

"Jist that!" said her husband; "Then here's the very thing for ye a' aboot the Levée in St James's Palace Wednesday. I'm sorry to see, however, that the Royal Circle was the smallest for many a day, only the Prince of Wales and his brother-in-law, Prince Francis of Teck, being present to support the King. Sir Curzon Wyllie presented a bevy of India gentlemen, whose native costumes introduced a note of barbaric spendour into the— into the cowp de oil—"

"What's a cowp de oil?" asked Jinnet.

"It's French," said Erchie, meaningly. "When ye see onything in French in an English newspaper, ye'll be wise no' to ask what it means. Ye ken what the French are!"

"Oh! I'm shair I'm no' curious," said Jinnet, hurriedly; "I was jist wonderin'. Was there ony Princesses there?"

"'The placid countenance of Lord Li, the Chinese Minister,'" proceeded Erchie, still reading, "'was a conspicuous incident in the diplomatic body'. That's droll! I wonder whit he did wi't. He shouldna ha'e brocht it wi' him if it couldna behave itsel'."

"Was the Princess o' Teck no' there?" asked Jinnet.

"I'm lookin' for her as hard's I can," explained Erchie. "Ha'e patience, woman; ha'e patience! No; she wasna there, but I see further doon the paper that she was at Their Majesties' official Court on Thursday nicht. It says that 'the presentations were got through with that celerity which their Majesties have accustomed the Master of Ceremonies to observe, and a good many of the parties left the Palace well before midnight, withoot waitin' to enjoy the good things provded at the buffets. There were wonderful displays of patties, artificial cutlets, baked oysters in various forms, dainty morsels of game, and other things that do duty for solids at these times. The sweets in ample supply, and the white Muscat grapes and slices of pineapple, grown at Frogmore, were all a dream—'"

"Ye rascal!" exclaimed Jinnet; "It's anither advertisement."

"It's naething o' the kind," protested her husband. "Look for yersel'. Whit makes ye think it's an advertisement?"

"Ye said a' they fine things were a dream, and I jaloused it was just the start o' a new story to begin next week in *Home Chat*. Is there naething in't aboot dresses?"

"Plenty!" said Erchie. "The Queen wore black velvet; so did Countess Beauchamp and the Countess of Cawdor, black being of course very much in vogue this season—"

"I'm that gled!" said Jinnet. "I was jist switherin' last week whether to ha'e my new dress black or broon, and I picked black; if ye don't ha'e black, ye're shair to need it. Ye didna tell me whit ye thocht o' my new dress, Erchie?"

"It's top! I never saw onything that suited ye bettter. I like— I like—the—the crumpiness o' the frock; it's a' the go at pairties this winter. Weel, as I was readin' — 'The Duchess of Newcastle's brocade dress was richly worked with gold thread, and her ivory tambour lace train, edged with ermine, fell from the shoulders—'"

"What!" exclaimed Jinnet, incredulously.

"Fell frae the shouthers," said Erchie. "I'm no' a bit surprised at it. If ye jist seen them, sometimes! Mony a time, when I'm waitin' on them at a dinner pairty, I'm nearly askin' if they wudna like a wee lend o' my table-napkin. 'Among the diplomatic ladies were—'"

"Whit's diplomatic ladies?" asked Jinnet.

"Diplomatic's — weel, it means the same as being fly," explained Erchie. "Awfu' cunning, ye ken. 'Among the diplomatic ladies, Condessa de Villa Uretta (wife of the Spanish Ambassador), Marquise de la Begassiere (of the French Embassy), Madame Slavko Gruics (of the Serbian Legation), Madame Szokow (wife of the Bulgarian Agent), and Countess Gertrude Blucher von Wahlstadt (née Miss Stapleton Bletherton) were the handsomest.'"

"Are ye shair ye're no' among the advertisements again?" asked Jinnet, suspiciously. "Look at the bottom and see if it's no' a' aboot a competition for the biggest number o' cigarette pictures sent in before the tenth o' the month."

"No, it's richt enough," Erchie assured her; "that's the

diplomatic ladies; but it's likely it's no' their rale names, them bein' diplomatic. Ye see it doesna sae onything aboot their men bein' there wi' them."

"Was there no dancin'?" asked Jinnet.

"No' a step!" said Erchie. "But of course, it wasna a first-class soirée, concert and ball; it says here — 'It is expected that the second Court will be more splendid than the first, for the simple reason that, the first having been chiefly attended by official persons, there is more room for the nobility, aristocracy, and plutocracy at the second. The standard of dress and the display of jewels must therefore reach a higher level. Neither of these Courts, however, has any chance of equalling those which will be held in the summer, for then the entire Royal Family will gather on the day, and with them will be foreign Royalties, in brilliant uniforms and magnificent dresses ablaze with stars, Orders and splendid diamonds.'"

"Oh!" said Jinnet. "I wad faur sooner be the way I am, but I like to read aboot them; it's almost jist as good as gaun to a pantymime."

70. *Erchie's Great Wee Close*[1]

IN EVERY man there is some portion of all other men, so that Duffy the coalman now and then, not drunk but almost, discovers a Shakespeare in himself, who throws away tempting opportunities for short weight, and feels unutterable things (which he mistakes for more thirst), when he hears Syverina play a pensive penny whistle in the back court,[2] enrages the whole 'land' himself with nocturnal renderings of 'Dark Lochnagar', or has some maudlin sense of the width and splendour of life when he gets his quarterly dividend from the Store,[3] and goes to the pit to see 'The Father's Curse'. Every close[4] in Glasgow, similarly, is a microcosm, repeating in miniature the whole social phenomena of this life, with occasional glimpses of life in the nether world. "The greatest wee close in

Glesca," Erchie proudly calls his own; "I can study nature in't withoot puttin' aff my slippers, if I leave the door on the chain." He generously admits that there may be some justification for semi-detacheds and self-containeds: "For if ye hadna them there wouldna be mony jobs for us waiters." But he has argued with me before now that the intelligent appreciation of the opportunities afforded by residence in a Grove Street[5] close is as good as a liberal education. He lives on the street level — left hand — coco bass[6] (taken in at the gloaming), and his wife Jinnet has polished the letters of the name-plate into invisibility, but you know it is Erchie's door by the genial way the brass reflects your watch-chain; it is like his smile.

"We used to live in Broon Street," he remarked to me the other day, "but they gaed awa' and spoiled the place wi' fancy tiles, and cathedral gless on the doors, and changing the handy auld wooden baths for iron yins that wouldna haud mair than a bag or two o' coal, and it brocht the wrang kind o' tenants a'thegither. We kept on oor hoose there for a year, but it was nearly the death o' Jinnet — she couldna gang the length o' thc dairy withoot her bunnet on and was kept soopin' the close even-on, efter the processions gaun up to the 'days at home' on the second flet."

"Ye needna say that," protested Jinnet, dear old soul; "I'm shair I wasna compleenin' aboot ha'ein' to keep the close clean; I sometimes had naething else to dae; it was the callin'-cairds and the Indignant Gentlewomen[7] always collectin', and me no' bein' able to ha'e a wee servant-lassie, or enough o' plates for a day at home o' my ain."

"I had no idea the social conventions had penetrated to Brown Street tenements," said I.

"They were a' there," replied Erchie, "ragin' through the land like measles. Ye went to your bed a' richt at nicht, and in the mornin' ye had them bad. Ye were that dazed ye ca'd your dinner your lunch, and couldna tak' your tea withoot your collar on. When ony new tenant came to the land Jinnet had to put aff her ironin' for the day, and go and call on them afore they had the beds up, and sit for an 'oor wi' them talkin' aboot the trouble servants were, and the latest story in *Home Chat*. And they would be callin' back on her that smert, she had hardly time to be back in her ain hoose and the room fire on."

"I didna grudge the fire a bit, I'm sure," said Jinnet; "It was the way they used to bamboozle me talkin' aboot the awfu' nice neeighbours they had at Ibrox, and askin' me what I thocht o' the Italian Lakes. I'm sure I never was near-haund the Italian Lakes."

"We flitted just in time for Jinnet to escape bein' made a worker in the Women's Temperance League, and here we are quite cosy in the greatest wee close in Glesca, whaur the only use ye ha'e for a caird is to put it in the window so that Duffy'll ken he's to bring up anither bag. There's no' much style in this close, but there's lots o' the rale oreeginal human nature on every landin'."

"It's human nature I aye like best mysel'," said Jinnet. "I wisna brocht up to haud my teacup in my haund and play whit they ca' progressive whist in broad day-licht."

"It's the variety ye get here that's the great thing," said Erchie. "Next door there's Sergeant Macrae o' the nicht polis — as nice a chap when he has his uniform aff as ye could ask to see. Macrae's better for the close than hauf-a-dizzen newspapers: he kens things aboot the Bylies[8] that would stagger ye, and though he lives in the close like oorsel's — a pound a year cheaper than up the stairs — the folk upstairs look up to him. They gang oot and in on their tip-taes haudin' their breaths for fear they'll spoil his sleep in the forenoon."

"Mrs Macrae's a rale lady," said Jinnet. "Ye'll never hear her voice."

"On the first stair," proceeded Erchie, "there's Mrs Williamson — a sailor's wife. Her man's in the habit o' bein' awa' on his vessel somewhere roond aboot Calcutta, and every noo and then he comes hame wi' a wee tortoise or half-a-dizzen o' country ostrich eggs and his claes to wash. His name's no' like a sailor's at a' — it's Ebenezer;

and when it's awfu' cold winter weather his wife's aye lamentin' puir Ebenezer sclimbin' masts roond aboot Calcutta wi' naething on him but a Mizpah ring[9] she gied him and a thin suit o' dongarees. If it's a kind o' stormy nicht she gi'es her weans an extra jeely piece, and lets them stay up till a' hoors to keep her company; and if it's by-ordinar' stormy, she comes greetin' doon to Jinnet to get her to read a wee bit oot o' the Bible suitable for ships at sea."

"Revelation xxi, and 1st: 'And there was no more sea,'" quoted Jinnet piously. "She finds it rale consolin'. I had aye a saft he'rt for a sailor's wife."

"Ebenezer's wife mourns for him a' the time he's awa' on his vessel, and coonts the days till he comes hame, but he's no' a week at hame till she's wearyin' for him to gae back again afore a' his money's done."

"No' a bad sowl, either!" said Jinnet. "He has such a cheery laugh, and he's that nice to his weans!"

"When Ebenezer's at hame, it's like foreign travel for the rest o' us: there's a kind o' sea-breeze blawin' through the close, and a fine smell o' the rale Mrs Marshall Indian cheroots."

"Opposite Ebenezer's wife bides Johnny Syme, the poet —"

"Nae wife, puir body," said Jinnet, pitifully. "Does his ain bit turns; and such-like windows!"

"He used to be clerk for six weeks at a time aboot the Coonty Buildin's, but lately he's been daein' fine in the hoose wi' writin' Limericks. He mak's five pounds some-times wi' wan line, so he's lettin' his hair grow lang, and keepin' his bed till dinner-time, and eats naething but fish and vegetables — it's said to be awfu' nourishin' for poetry. He made a clever bit aboot Macrae that pleased him fine:

> There's a stalwart guardian of our street,
> Macrae, the champion of the beat,
>   Intelligent, strong
>   As he walks along,
> There's few with him can compete.

Compete — come Pete, ye see — Macrae's name's Peter. Every wee while Syme's name and address is in *Tit Bits*, and it gi'es the close a splendid reputation a' alang the street; he couldna be mair popular if he was a fitba' player. Macrae sees him hame wi' his ain haund on the nichts he's won anither Limerick."

"Jist a wee bit foolish, ye understand," murmured Jinnet, apologetically. "Maybe he hadna ony wise-like mither to guide him, but there's nae herm in puir Mr Syme; he wadna hairm a flee. It wad be faur better for him if he wasna a poet at a', and had some ither tred."

"On the tap flet," continued Erchie, seeing I was so obviously interested in the community of the great wee close, "there's Miss Carmichael —"

"An Indignant Gentlewoman," explained Jinnet. "I'm tellt she gets her rent aff them — and, indeed, puir body, it's a gey habble for her even withoot a rent to pay."

"Ye could see fine that she's yin o' the rale auld Indignant Gentlewomen," said Erchie, winking at me; "she domineers the hale close, and ca's me jist 'MacPherson'."

"Twa years in a boardin'-school, and has uncles high up in the law in Edinburgh," remarked Jinnet in an impressive whisper, as if she feared the distinguished Edinburgh relatives might overhear. "I must aye speak o' folks as I find them and Miss Carmichael's aye very ceevil-spoken to mysel' ... She hangs oot as nice a washin' as whit's in the land."

"But no' when there's onybody lookin'," added Erchie. "Ye never see Miss Carmichael daein' onything, though Jinnet tells me her stair-heid's like the snaw and her brasses beautiful. She's the Queen o' the great wee close, and keeps us a' in order aboot the key o' the washin'-hoose. Her lodgers —"

"Ye canna ca' them lodgers, Erchie," broke in Jinnet. "Ye don't ken. She ca's them aye her 'young frien's' hersel', and it's likely they'll be relatives, puir body."

Erchie laughed. "Ye auld humbug," said he, "ye ken they're jist twa dacent milliners payin' their way, but ye're

jist as prood in your notions as ony Miss Carmichael, and
ye're lettin' on ye're ignorant to save the body's feelin's. Ye
needna fash, she's no listenin'."

"Whether or no'," said Jinnet, "I ha'e a great respect for
Miss Carmichael."

"On the same stair-heid as Miss Carmichael there's the
Grants," said Erchie. "Five wee weans and nae work for
Grant for a month past. I'll wager there's no' a bit in the
hoose to eat."

"What? In the great wee close!" I exclaimed incredulously, and Erchie smiled.

"Man!" he said, "ye ken ower much; ye must ha'e lived
in a close yoursel'.[10] But whether there's meat in the hoose
or no', I wish to God I saw a job for Willie Grant!"

Oh! great wee close — grimy portals, drab stairways,
chalk-scrawled walls, and the eternal pipeclay fight with
the grime that degrades its neighbours. Oh! great wee close!
in whose back-courts sounds, each Saturday, the whistle of
Syverina, never unrewarded, sweetening the winter dusk
with old familiar melodies that for the time ennoble those
who in their kitchens hear — forget — remember. Oh!
great wee close! type of myriads (and so dear or so depres-
sing as they may have influenced our lives) that have heard
the names and voices of innumerable children now dis-
persed about the world, lovers' whispers, wedding music,
and the shuffle of the feet when coffins were carried down.
Oh! great wee close! lowly, but rendered venerable by the
trial and endurance of so many brave and unrecorded lives!

71. *Duffy on Drink*[1]

"What's your opeenion o' the Government's Licensin'
Bill?"[2] asked Erchie.

"It shouldna be alloo'ed," said Duffy; "guid drink's
hard enough to get already withoot a lot o' nyafs spilin' a'
the pleesure o' the workin'-man. They would tak' the
bottle oot o' your very mooth."

"Ay, but drink's an awfu' commandin' thing," remarked Erchie. "I sometimes think, mysel', we would be far better wantin't."

"I've felt that wye mysel', whiles, on a Sunday mornin', but whit could ye ha'e in place o't? There's nae ither thing near so handy to pass the time."

"Books," suggested Erchie.

"There's naething worse for spilin' the eyes; look at the lot o' folks ye see wi' specs on since Carnegie started a' them fancy libraries![3] A book's maybe no' bad in its ain place, and that's on a shelf or under the leg o' a cogly table, but when it comes your turn to staun' your hands, ye canna afford to pay for a roond o' *Pilgrim's Progresses*."

"And there's the Art Galleries," said Erchie. "I'm told the pictures in them's jist top!"

"But they're no' put up in flet bottles that'll fit the pouch," said the coalman, "and it's no' every workin'-man has the claes for perusin' roond a picture gallery. Pictures is solemn things the same as organ music; there's some that bad they mak' ye feel releegious."

"There's the soothin' charms o' music, too," persisted Erchie.

"It's easy seen there's no' a' gramaphone in your hoose!" said the coalman. "It's the talkin' machine and Harry Lauder[4] a' the time, wi' nae kilts on and his heid in a canister, that's drivin' the dacent workin'-man oot to the Mull o' Kintyre Vaults as soon's he's done wi' his tea. The warst o' music is that it spoils the conversation; ye micht as weel be passin' the time wi' your wife."

"Still-and-on," said Erchie, "there's a lot o' drink drunk in Gleska. I was readin' the ither day that in wan year Gleska spent twa-and-a-half million pounds on wines, spirits and ales."

"It's things like that mak's us workin'-men Socialists," said Duffy, gloomily. "When we're slavin' and toilin' awa', wi' nae chance o' gettin' ony o't except on Setterday, the upper classes is roound at their fancy bars and drinkin' the best o' everything. Two-and-a-half million! Man, I could-

na drink the half o't in twa years, even if I stop't my tred
and did naething else!"

"It's an awfu' money!" said Erchie, thoughtfully. "It
wad build a couple o' Dreadnought men-o'-war.[5] We're
no' sae bad as London either; there they perish nineteen
million pounds a year, and that's no' coontin' the price o'
the hansom cabs to tak' them hame. There's a hundred-
and-sixty-six-and-a-half million spent on drink in Britain
every twelvemonth."

"Fancy that!" said Duffy; "and my wife mak's a sang
aboot the wee drap I tak'! If she read the papers and had
figures like that afore her she wad see I was almaist what ye
micht ca' teetotal. And there's no' a tred that mak's ye
thirstier than cryin' coals. Whit's mair than that, it spoils
yer voice and mak's the publicans suspeecious. Last
Setturday, and it no' ten o'clock, I went into the Mull of
Kintyre Vaults and asked a schooner o' beer. Maclennan,
the barman, no' bein' very lang on the job, said, 'Ye'll no'
get onything here, my man; ye've jist as much as is guid for
ye.' 'Hoo do ye mak' that oot?' says I. 'I ken by your voice,'
says he; 'if ye had anither schooner o' beer ye would be a
dummy. Awa' like a guid chap and ha'e a sleep to yoursel'
and ye'll be a' richt in the mornin'.' I tried to argue the
thing wi' him as man to man, but he lost his temper and
gi'ed me the heave: he hadna ony come-and-go wi' him at
a' — a regular cuddy!

"It was five meenutes to ten o'clock; I kent by the wye
the folk was runnin', so I tried the Glue Pot at the ither
corner—"

"The Glue Pot?" said Erchie, interrogatively.

"Macrae's, ye ken; it's ca'd the Glue Pot because the
customers stick like glue to the counter yince they're up
against it. But the Glue Pot man was every bit as suspeecious as the Mull o' Kintyre Vaults; they're gettin' awfully
pernicketty. 'A schooner o' beer,' says I. 'No' wi' a voice
like that!' says he; 'Whit ye need's a bottle wi' glycerine
in't at the apothecary's.' 'Look here!' I says, 'as shair as
onything I havena seen a drap o' drink the day.' 'Did ye

no'?' says he; 'then ye're in the wrang shop; ye should try the Eye Infirmary,' and oot he flung me. I ran up the street and jist got into anither pub in time. 'A schooner o' beer,' I said, tryin' to speak like a tenor vocalist, and the man laid it doon in front' o' me. 'It's been a wat, mochy day,' he says, quite ceevil, and I like the look o' the chap, though I never gang much aboot his place. 'It's been that sort o' day that it spoiled a' my voice,' said I, meanin' to be quite nice to him, and show him what a lot o' idiots they were in the opposition pubs. 'Dae ye notice any sign o' drink aboot me?' 'No,' said he, lookin' at me; 'I wadna say there was much oot o' place wi' ye if he had yer face washed.' 'That's wi' my tred,' I explained. 'I'm a coalman. Ye'll hardly believe, but no' ten meenutes ago, roon' in the Mull o' Kintyre, and in the Glue Pot, they refused to serve me because they thocht I had plenty already.' 'Did they, faith!' said the barman, and he grabbed the schooner afore I could get haud o't. 'If they refused ye, then I'm no' takin' ony risks; there's yer tuppence back!' I was oot in the street again afore ye could say knife, and every other shop was shut!"

"There's a moral aboot that story somewhere," said Erchie.

"It's a moral that I was a gey dry man. I'm tellin' you," said Duffy, 'it learned me a lesson — never to put aff time when there's a schooner o' beer in front o' ye. And I had such a thirst! A beer thirst!"

"What's the parteecular specification o' a beer thirst ony mair than anither kind o' thirst?" asked Erchie.

"Ye can wager it's no' a thirst that'll bend the knee to Boston Cream or a bottle o' Kola," said the coalman. "The champion beer thirst ever I had in my life was wan time doon in Rothesay at the Gleska Fair. It's a droll thing, but there's naething mak's me thirstier than the sicht o' saut water; I think the thirst must gang in by the pores o' the skin. It was the year I married the second wife, and I was every noo and then a Templar;[6] so I wusna drinkin' onything but beer. I had been oot oarin' roond Rothesay Bay a' the evenin' with the wife and anither

woman; and the weather was so awfu' warm, and the
water looked that saut, I got thirstier than ever I was in my
life afore or since. If I hadna been teetotal at the time, I
would likely jist ha'e oared in to the quay as fast as I could
and made a breenge for the nearest bar, but I thocht to
mysel', 'this is a thirst that's so oot o' the ordinary, it's
worth studyin'.' It was a thirst that gaed doon to the very
soles o' my feet, and made my tongue and palate cheep
like a pair o' Sunday boots. I egged it on for a while wi'
thinkin' aboot beer in jugs, and cans, and barrels, and I
didna gang in wi' the boat for nearly anither half-'oor. I
sent the women awa' hame, and I hurried up to the
nearest bar, but jist at the door o't I said to mysel', 'No;
I'll thole five meenutes langer, for this is the thirst o' a
century. I'll walk the length o' the street to the next bar,
and THEN —!' But when I got to the front o' the next bar I
made up my mind other five meenutes mair would make
the beer taste five times better, and I turned at the door
and walked for a while on the Esplanade. I did the same
wi' other two public-hooses, till at last my thirst got
desperate, and I went into a corner shop. 'A quart o' beer,'
I gasped, quite dazed wi' thirst. 'This is a Temperance
Café,' says the man in chairge. I ran oot, and made for the
only other bar that I could see, and was jist the length o'
the door when the man shut it in my face. It was ten
o'clock. That was a lesson for me."

72. *Volunteering Memories*[1]

THE CITIZEN soldiers were returning from their last church
parade as Volunteers,[2] with a band whose brassy harmony
dispelled the solemn thoughts that come with the Sabbath's calm, and, watching them at a street corner, I saw
Erchie, standing a little more 'steeve' than usual, with an
umbrella at the trail. He made me an awkward parody of
the military salute, and jerked a thumb in the direction of
the passing companies.

"There's something awfu' cheery in a fine brass band," said he; "and a brass band never soonds sae nice as on a Sabbath day. I ken it's wrang; it's only pomp and vanity, and the man with the big drum micht as weel be at his tred in a biler-shop for a' the speeritual exaltation that he gets frae his bangin', but I'm a puir miserable sinner, and I like it fine."

"Are you going my way?" I asked, making west.

Erchie swithered, shamefacedly, a little, rubbed his chin and said he had been thinking to go east.

"After the band?" I suggested quizzingly, and he chuckled. "I was tryin' to let on to mysel' it wasna," he admitted, "but — pom-pirly-om-pom, pom, pom pom; man! I ken that tune; come on and we'll hear the feenish o't."

Erchie shuffled his feet to get into step with me, threw back his drooping shoulders and 'dressed by the right' suggestively.

"If the kirks used brass bands instead o' bells," said he, "there wadna be as mony folk sleepin' in on the Sunday mornin's. Look at the croods! Puir misguided craturs! They're sae uplifted they're forgettin' they ha'e on their Sunday claes. And this is the last o' the Volunteers! — it's an anxious time for the British hearth and hame."

"They've only changed their name," I said; "and we needn't sleep at night less soundly."

"Oh, I'm no' in the least bit feared," said he; "The only foreign invaders that put me about is yon chaps sellin' onions, and the ice-cream men that's sappin' the manhood o' the nation wi' their bawbee sliders. We're fed sae much on their foreign trash we'll soon be a' Italian oorsel's. Or French. It's a' a maitter o' diet, and even Duffy the coal-man, since his wife begood to gi'e him a supper o' sardines, is bloomin' into a kind o' parley-voo. If he had a waxed moustache and anither man's wife, he wad be a regular chef. Jinnet asked him the price o' his coals the ither day, and he says, says he, 'if ye tak' them a-la-cairt, mad-dam, they're 20s. a ton, but if ye tak' them cul-de-sack it's a shillin' extra for the bags.'"

"Were you ever a Volunteer yourself?" I asked.

"Nate!" said he. "I have the mark o' the kilts on the backs o' my knees yet, and if ye cried "Shun!' awfu' sudden, I wad burst a' the buttons aff my waistcoat. I was the regimental pet in two corps, and they only put me out o' them because they said I couldna' keep the step. That was a' nonsense; it was them that was always wrang in the step — the hale jing-bang o' them! The first corps I was in was the Sauchieha' Street — them that wore the tartan breeks and the shako wi' the pom-pom on the front o' it. Ye mind? It was the Enfield rifle[3] that we had — ye skooted water through't to clean't, and put a wee brass kep on the nipple, that gaed aff when ye shut your e'en and pu'd the trigger — if ye had ony luck at a'. I was five years in the tartan breeks, and then I jined the kilties — the auld Hunder-and-fifth. I thocht at first o' jinin' the Engineers, for though my feet were flet, I had a fine heid for the helmet, but I was newly mairried at the time, and Jinnet said she couldna bear the idea o' me awa' in steamboats. So my second corps was the Glasgow Highlanders. They were the boys!, A' bred on the heather, or roond aboot Garnethill.[4] Man you should see us trampin' aboot the Fleshers' Haugh[5] on a summer Setturday!

"When I marched oot wi' the Kilties I felt awfu' peely-wally, the maist o' the ither men had such tremendous legs! We had a drum-major that took the breadth o' the Gallowgate — and its no' that there was drink on him, but he was sae wide! We had a man, Mackendrick, wi' a leg like the gaitherin' o' the clans; when he merched in front ye couldna hear the drums. And there was anither chap we kept for tyin' on to the ends o' tugs-o'war: if weight was sodgerin' he would win the battle o' Waterloo wi' his least wee bit touch. Ye never saw onything like it!"

"A remarkably fine regiment, I am sure," I said.

"It was the Pride o' Scotland!" said Erchie with elation. "Harry Linn,[6] the comic comedian, had sangs aboot us. The only thing we wanted was the feather bunnet, and at one time it was thocht we micht raise the money for't at a

Grand Bazaar, but the War Office thocht it would maybe tak' the shine oot o' the Black Watch, and so it wouldna hear tell o't. We had the loodest pipers, and the maist determined bugle band in Scotland; gi'e them the least encouragement and they would blaw from here to Hamilton without a drap to drink.

"Yince a year, if the day was dry, and there wasna an important fitba' match, we merched a' over Gleska, and even the tramways couldna stop us. Gaun up Renfield Street a'e day, a tramway car in a hurry tried to break through the middle o' oor ranks. The Hieland blood o' the hale battalion biled; they chairged wi' a manly British cheer, put the fear o' daith in the guard and driver, and captured the punch and 650 penny tickets. It was afore the days o' the skoosh cars. When we marched oot in thae days, a' the West-End hooses and wally closes[7] had to put off their day-at-home, for they couldna' keep in their servant lassies — they were linin' Sauchieha' Street waving' their bits o' hankies, and nearly greetin' at the horrors o' war. But the Kilties werena carin', the Cornal rode in front, lookin' awfu' fierce, lettin' on he wasna weel acquent wi' the road, and the baund played up 'Good-bye, Sweetheart, Goodbye' from Charing Cross to Lauders.[8] Ye don't see onything o' the kind nooaways; the men's no' in't."

"But the Glasgow Highlanders are still a very fine battalion," I suggested.

"Maybe they are," said Erchie, changing step for the twentieth time since we started to walk together; "Maybe they are, but I doot they havena the proper Gaelic, and they're no' sae gallows[10] as they were in them days o' yore. The country's losin' a lot o' fun since they started education.

"My last appearance wi' the Kilties was the Review in 1881[11] when the Queen, puir body, peace be wi' her! couldna keep her eyes aff her Gleska darlin's. 'Them's men!' she said to the Duke o' Cambridge when we did the merch past in the glaur, wi' only the straps o' oor spats

handin' on oor boots and stockin's. I never in my life
before or since felt sae peely-wally. Ye mind the kind o'
day it was — it rained that hard it nearly washed awa'
Edinburgh Rock and Castle. My sporran wasna dry for
nearly two months efter't. I didna think much o' the First
Lanark — they had broon kid gloves, and broon kid gloves
is no' the go at a' since the war in Africa. Practically-
speakin', there was jist wan corps at that Review that the
glory o' the day depended on, and that was the Kilty lads
frae the Greenheid, Gleska. They did fine!"

"What was your rank in the regiment!" I asked.

"Oh, naething fancy," said he; 'jist a kind o' a private;
I'm no' the sort that had ony notion o' being an officer,
and getting' fankled wi' a sword atween my legs. Private
Erchibald MacPherson, Company 'K', no' much o' a shot,
but handy, because o' his tred, at a camp canteen."

The Home Guards, stepping smartly, had been gaining
on us; they turned the corner of a street and disappeared,
and simultaneously the band ceased playing. Erchie
stopped short, and with a "right-about turn!" wheeled
sharply on his heels. "I think I'm daft," said he, "to be
rinnin' efter a band on the Sabbath day the same's I was a
laddie. It was jist a kind o' notion. I kent the tune they were
playin' — pom-pirly-om, pom, pom, pom — and it put me
in mind o' big Mackendrick, and the chap we had for the
tugs-o'-war, and the croods on our merches oot alang
Sauchieha' Street, and the day in Edinburgh, and I clean
forgot that Jinnet was a granny. A sodger's life! Dod! I wad
be a sodger yet if they'd let me parade in my carpet-
slippers."

73. *Mrs Wetwhistle Provides a Text*[1]

STRANGELY ENOUGH, Erchie and I, in several years' intimate
acquaintance, never thought of discussing the Scotland ver-
sus England question till the other day, when that popular
theme was suggested in connection with the advent of Mrs

Wetwhistle in the 'great wee close'. There was never any doubt about my old friend's national sentiment; he was the first to call my attention to the fact that there is a difference in the pudding-plates of England and Scotland. "Oor deep dessert-plate," he said, "is aboot the last thing that's left to us o' the precious privileges oor forefaithers won at the battle o' Bannockburn. The English tak' their puddin' aff a thing that's only a tea-flet when a's said and done; on this side o' Carlisle we ha'e mair manly independence and use an extra-deep dish that hauds twice as much." Nor was my patriotic fervour ever doubted by him; he took it for granted without any parade on my part, and somehow I feel I should never have been honoured with so much of his confidence if I had been in the habit of going to Culloden once a year "to wag wee flags," as he one time put it, "and rin the chance o' gettin' yer death o' cauld in the kilts." "Flags is fine things," he said on another occasion; "There's naethin' handier for drapin' the wa's at a country dinner, but to be aye flap-flappin' them in the face o' folks that's no' daein ye ony herm is neither nice nor wyse. The best flag I ken's the yin my sailor son Willie ca's the Blue Peter; it means 'come on and see some ither place,' and it doesna' show the dirt."

But Mrs Wetwhistle's arrival in the 'great wee close', as I say, brought out his national sentiments in more detail. Willie Grant had got a situation in Kilbowie, and had flitted to be near his work; and his successor in the tenancy of the top-flat house was Mrs Wetwhistle.

"It's a droll name," said Erchie to me, "but it's genuine English, and it mak's me awfu' gled I'm yin o' the Hielan' clans. I went hame the ither efternoon and found a thing that's no' very common — three o' the neighbour women sittin' drinkin' tea wi' Jinnet. There was Mrs Williamson, the sailor's wife; the wife o' Macrae, the polisman; and Liza, her that keeps the dairy.

"'Wha's the sufferer this time?' I asked, lookin' roon' to see wha wasna there, and Mrs Williamson gi'ed a herty laugh.

"'Ye're aye there wi' your fun, Mr MacPherson,' said she, 'but it's no' scandal we're on this time, for Jinnet's the puirest hand at it; we're talkin' aboot the new tenant up the stair.'

"'Mrs Wetwhistle!' said Jinnet. 'Erchie, did you ever hear o' such a name? I canna bring mysel' to think it's no' a bye name jist picked oot o' a pantymime.'

"'It's richt enough,' said Liza. 'I ha'e her on my books for tuppence o' sweet and a penny o' cream for a fortnicht. She comes frae a place ca'd Woolwich,[3] and her son's an engineer.'

"'Still I canna believe there's ony Christian body wi' a name like Wetwhistle; I never heard o't in my life afore,' said Jinnet.

"'There's a lot o' things we never heard o' that's true enough,' said I. 'You put me in mind, Jinnet, o' the first time I took Duffy to the Zoo. He clapped the elephants on the legs, and whustled to the lions, and papped pea-nuts in among the monkeys; but when we cam' to the dromedary he got an awfu' start. "Great Scot!" he said, "whit dae ye ca' that?" "That's a dromedary," I tellt him; "they ca't a dromedary on account o' the hump." Duffy walked roon' aboot it hauf-a-dizzen times, examinin' it a' ower, and scratchin' his heid when it sneezed at him. "Ach! to bleezes!" he said at last, "there's nae such animal!" and he widna look at it only langer.'"

"I never saw Mrs Wetwhistle mysel' yet," said Erchie, "but I understand from the conversation o' the ladies she's a wee black-aviced women wi' a grand discoorse. She's a weedow, wi' a son in Dubs',[4] and she never was oot o' England in her life afore she came to Gleska, exceptin' maybe it was at the Isle o' Man. A lot o' things in Scotland's clean beyond her comprehension; the butchers dinna cut their meat the way she was accustomed to, and she says they ha'e the wrang names for a' the jints and things. When she ordered a loaf at the baker's, first, they asked her if she wanted a pan, and she tellt them that if pans were whit she was efter she wad ha'e gane to an ironmongers. They explained whit a pan-loaf was, and then they asked if she wanted it for cuttin'. 'I hope,' says she, 'it will not be necessary to blast it with dynamite. I am not acquainted with Scotch bread, but if it usually needs any other treatment than a knife, I'll have to bake at home.' Then they explained the mysteries of the cuttin' loaf, and she tellt them they should ca' it stale, for that was whit was always done in London. I can tell ye the bakers werena awfu' well pleased to ha'e their bread ca'd stale, and it no' mair that a day or twa auld.

"Mrs Wetwhistle's only a wee bit woman, no' nine stone, and haulf the time ye canna understand her, for she speaks that fast and misses oot her r's and h's; but she wants to shift the hale commercial system o' the district oot New City road. I gaither from the conversation o' the ladies that she's jist as sure they're a' next door to savage as they are certain that she's daft. She'll be writin' back to Woolwich lamentin' and tellin' her friends there we canna speak a word o' English, and on the ither hand Mrs Macrae's made up her mind that a' the women in England gang oot to buy potatoes wi' a Gladstane bag the way Mrs Wetwhistle does, and never saw a cookie. It's a droll thing, but we nearly a' form oor opeenion o' ither nations from swatches and no' from the piece. I kin' o' hate the Germans mysel' because I yince bocht a watch frae a gaun-aboot German as a rale Geneva, and it widna go. Ever since then I think o' Germany as a place the size o' Yoker, whaur a' the Germans that's no here learnin' a lot o' us the way to wait, are thrang makin' pewter watches and silverizin' them to pass them aff on Scotsmen.

"Naething aboot puir wee Gleska pleases the weedow frae Woolwich except the fancy bread; she admits she never in her life afore saw sae mony kinds. Mackay, the baker's boy, comes roond in the efternoons wi' a basket-load o' penny-things to sell at the doors, and she caught the influenza standin' on the landin' tryin' to mak' up her mind whit cakes, or buns, or cookies she wad ha'e for sixpence. She was aye seein' something new in his basket every efternoon. Last Wednesday — Jinnet tells me — Mrs Wetwhistle saw whit she thocht was a new and sonsy kind o' cookie on the tap o' the basket, and she said to the boy, 'That bun looks good value for a penny. I'll take some of them.' The boy lauched like to end himsel', and tellt her it wasna a bun at a', but the pad for puttin' in between his bunnet and the basket when he was carrying't on his heid!

"The oddities o' Mrs Wetwhistle gi'ed thae four women in my hoose a pleasant topic o' conversation for nearly two 'oors, and Mrs Wetwhistle was nane the worse o't, for she kent naething aboot it. A great deal o' the amusement o' life wad be lost if we hadna fau'ts to find wi' ane anither, and I'll wager the wee close 'll miss her when she leaves 't. They're learnin' to drop their h's already so as to gi'e her a chance to understand them, but I don't think she's likely to burr her r's and drop her t's to please them; that's the worst o' the English; there's nae come and go in them. Before I married I yince had an English landlady, and she thocht she could mak' parritch. I stood them as lang's I could and then ventured to tell her that whit we ca'd parritch was a little different in Scotland. 'Whit's wrang wi' them?' said she, quite snappy. 'They're ower thin,' I says, quite humble; 'in fact, they're sae thin that naething I send doon efter them 'll catch up on them.' But the body never heeded; she jist said that was the way they made them doon in Manchester."

74. *Duffy at a Music-Hall*[1]

"HOW'S DUFFY?" I asked, and Erchie gave the most favourable account of his friend, who had been off work for two weeks. "Influenza, ye ken; it catches the coalman jist as ready as the MP, and Duffy's no' the man he was a month ago. His voice is doon to a cheep, and he's missin' customers. But he's mendin', oh, aye, he's mendin'; he's at the stage whaur he finds the nicht air rale revivin' and ye'll no' guess whaur the pair o' us were last Monday."

"Give it up," I said.

"At a music-hall," said Erchie. "Ye needna be sae shocked; I'm no' makin' a hobby o't; it wad scarcely suit a beadle to be seen ower often in the stalls o' the Pavilion eggin' on comediennes and jinin' in the chorus o' 'The twi-twilight'. This is an enlichtened age; I can get a' the music-hall I want in the neebours' gramaphones, and naebody need be ony the wyser. I jist took Duffy to cheer him up; he was awa' doon in the dumps wi' his influenza, and he hadna been at a music-hall or onything classic o' the kind since afore the days o' Harry Linn.

"'Whaur will we get the wulks?'² he asked when I made the proposeetion.

"'What wulks?' says I.

"'For pappin' at the artistes when they come out for the encores; we had aye a supply o' wulks and things for sport o' the kind when I was a halflin gaun aboot the shows.'

"'Duffy,' I says to him, 'it's no' for a done auld coalman to be makin' an exhibeetion o' himsel' wi' games o' that auld-fashioned kind in the modern music-hall. It's a wonder to me ye havena mair refinement.'

"Weel, we went to the music-hall early hoose and it didna lift the load o' Duffy's melancholy; he was gloomier when he cam' oot than when we gaed in. I'm used to the music-hall mysel', me bein' there every ither year, and naething they can dae 'll vex me, but puir Duffy found the performance awfu' tryin'. The only thing he was much ta'en up wi' was the baun'; 'I ken that chap wi' the drum,' he says; 'he gets his coals frae me, and I aye thocht he was a tredsman; noo that I ken he's yin o' the theatricals I'll tak' an interest in him. Whit dae thae chaps playin' the fiddles dae through the day?'

"'They lie in their beds till twelve,' I says, 'and then get up and practice for the evenin'.'"

"'I think,' says Duffy, 'the yin that's waggin' the stick at them the noo slept-in the day, for he's missin' lumps, and no' lettin' on. I like the nerve o' him!'

"The first item on the programme was a lassie wi' the

bye-name o' 'Britain's Best' — the rale oreeginal Refined Comedienne. I never saw a mair determined singer; she cam' on twice, and would ha'e been on a third time if she had ony excuse at a'. First she sang 'The Valley o' Switzerland,' and then anither sang wi' nearly the same tune aboot the 'Island o' Anglesea,' and a' the time she was sae nice dressed and smiled that hard ye couldna be angry wi' her.

"'Is that Britain's Best?' says Duffy; 'I'm awfu' gled I can say I seen't. When does the fun start?'

"'Haud you on!' I says, 'and ye'll see life. No. 4 — The Yankee Wizard.'

"'I ken the kind,' says Duffy, quite delighted; 'mak's omelettes in a hat and tak's rabbits oot a quarter-loaf. They're no canny them chaps.'

"The Yankee Wizard cam' on, wi' a big brass baun' and a regiment o' men in livery to haud his kep and back him up. He suddenly pented a picture wi' his wan hand, and common pent, and then went oot and changed his claes. When he cam' back he was a monumental sculptor — ye could tell by his bunnet — and he started makin' monuments. He took saft clay aff a wee statue wi' his least wee bit touch, and brocht a clay-coloured woman oot frae behind a table when we werna lookin', and then cleaned his hands on a towel. Great cheers!

"'Keep your eye on him; noo he's gaun to dae a trick!' says Duffy, quite excited, but the Yankee Wizard jist went awa' aff the stage to put on another suit. A roar o' applause went up that nearly brocht doon the hoose, and Duffy looked at me wi' a peetifu' face.

"'Erchie,' he says, 'if this chap's gaun to tak' a' nicht makin' up his mind whit trick he's gaun to dae, there'll no be time for the ither performers on the programme. I wish to goodness I had my wulks!'

"The Yankee Wizard apparently had some frien's behind the scenes that cheered him up a bit and told him to go and try again, and he cam' back in a change o' claes and started shootin' wi' a wee laddie's bow and arrows at a piece o' paper. Dozens o' times he nearly hit the paper, and when he did hit it ye never saw a man sae pleased! Then for a diversion, he crawled under a rug and cam' oot again, as nate as onything, and ye could hear a preen drap.

"'It's the influenza,' said Duffy, in a kind o' hert-broken voice; 'it's brung me doon a lot, Erchie; tell me honestly am I at a show or at a flittin'?'

"'He's gaun to startle us immediately,' I said. 'Thae American conjurers aye work up the excitement gradual at first. Keep a grip o' your watch and don't look at his e'en or he'll ha'e ye up crawlin' aboot the stage lettin' on you're a steam-engine.'

"The Yankee Wizard then shoved twa or three pigeons oot o' the handle o' a big landin' net into the net, and dressed himsel' up to look like the King, and put on false whiskers to lead the brass band the way Sousa[3] wad dae. I've rarely seen a man mair willin' to obleege. He could ha'e kept on daein' thae wonderfu' things a' nicht, but time was pressin', and the management dragged doon the curtain for the next item before the puir Wizard could as much as produce a rabbit frae ony place.

"'Erchie,' says Duffy, 'tell me this; is there no' onything on the nicht at Vinegar Hill?'[4]

"He cheered up wonderfu' at the next thing on the programme — The Brothers Zim and Zack, Intellectual and Artistic Knockabouts. 'Michty!' he said, when he saw them, 'are thae chaps still gaun aboot yet? I mind o' them under other names in Davie Broon's, when I was learnin' my tred, the only difference I see on them is that the Zack yin's whiskers used to be blue instead o' red.'

"'Everything's mair refined in the music-hall line from what it used to be,' I tellt him.

"Zim was a tall thin man, weel-enough put on, wi' a fine big watch-chain and a bamboo walkin'-stick; Zack was a Ned, padded up to look like a beer-traiveller, wi' comic wide-check claes on, and a red nose. Zim stood in the middle o' the stage, and, lookin' up at the gallery noo and then to see that naebody was gettin' ready to throw onything at him, started to sing something comic. Ye could see fine it was comic from the way his feet gaed. 'He could mak' his fortune in the coal tred,' said Duffy, lookin' depressed. Then Zack chimed in, and Zim kicked him in the stomach, and slapped him ower the neck wi' the bamboo walkin'-stick — oh! he was the champion mirth-provoker! The orchestra played faster and faster to get it ower as soon as possible, and Zim was knockin' doon Zack and kickin' him fifty times to the meenute, but puir Duffy fell into a kind o' dover, and when I wakened him up the Intellectual and Artistic Knockabouts were makin' their escape, without a scratch.

"'Erchie,' he says, 'I doot the music-halls is gettin' too classic and refined for us; I wish they would put on a trained powney noo, and gie us some amusement.'

"But there was nae trained powney, and the hale way hame, Duffy was lamentin' that wulks were oot o' fashion."

75. *A Quiet Day Off* [1]

It was Erchie who prevailed on Duffy — still suffering a little from the influenza — to take a holiday on Victoria Day,[2] and they took their wives, Mrs Duffy with a collation of cold pies, poorly concealed by the meshes of a string bag, and Jinnet, a little sensitive about such a display, walking briskly in front with a pious pretence that no time was to be lost if the boat was to be got at the Broomielaw.[3] "I'm no' prood," was her explanation of her quizzing husband, "but there's something awful' common aboot pies, and you bein' a beadle I ha'e aye to think o' your reputation."

"You couldna expect the body to ha'e a luncheon basket wi' a chicken in't, and a bottle o' claret wine," said Erchie; "The coal tred's at its warst wi' the ludgers' fires bein' aff, and the tuppenny pie o' commerce, as the papers say, is the hurried hoosewife's friend. I wadna be ashamed o' the dacent woman even if she carried a string o' haddies."

"And neither should I," said the conscience-stricken

Jinnet; "It's silly pride; but I thocht ye maybe wadna like it; I'll gang back this minute and tak' a turn o' the bag mysel'," and as string bags are obviously things which men cannot carry with dignity, the ladies were left to carry the bag between them.

"Oh, whit a crood!" exclaimed Mrs Duffy, surveying the laden steamer with dubiety. "Are ye shair the boat'll no' be cogly?" And she hung irresolute, on the landward end of the gangway.

"She'll no' be a bit cogly, Liza, if ye haud your breath and stand nate in the middle," said her husband. "Are we a' richt, mate, for Ardgoilinglas?"

"Right you are!" the pursuer assured him; "Please step lively." And the steamer speedily filled up, and drew away from the wharf on her seaward voyage.

"A champion day!" said Duffy. "Liza, mind them pies. I'm awfu' gled I come; it's the life o' ye, a trip doon the water. The first time I was here was on the *Bonnie Doon*[4] — it was the year I started the Barr Street ree; we were aye gaun doon and seein' the engins[5] —"

"Yin o' the ancient customs o' the country, but it's oot o' date," said Erchie. "The best I can dae for ye's a picture post-caird at the sweety stall." And Duffy sighed, remembering more exalted days on the *Boonie Doon*.

"I never thocht there were sae mony steamboats," said Mrs Duffy, who had never been down the Clyde before. "Ye would wonder they would a' pay." And she fixed her gaze with admiration on the lofty hull of an Anchor liner.[6] "Whit a hicht that yin is abin the watter," she remarked; "The tide must be awfu' far oot the day!"

"It's no' by-ordinar," said Erchie; "it's jist up the length o' the paidles."

"I winna wonder but Ebenezer, the sailer wi' the wife in oor close, works on that big yin," said Jinnet. "It's in a boat like that he is, sailin' a' roond the warld and oot aboot Calcutta, and her, puir body, hardly ower the close except for her bits o' messages. It's quite romantic."

"Ye're right there," agreed Duffy; "Liza, mind the pies!"

The steamer made her way below the shipyards, through fields, over whose rag-weed gold the lark went whistling, past Bowling and Dumbarton, and soon the Firth received her in its wide-extended arms. The Voice of Glasgow rose above the churning of the paddles — "Mery, whaur's wee Alick?"— "Here's respects!" — "Michty, I've lost the tickets!" — "Is there no' anither caibin forrit?" "Wauken up, Jims, and see the scenery!" — "Fancy him wi' his knicker-bockers!" — "Gang doon to the engines, Jeanie, and ask for the fill o' that bottle o' hot watter; tell them it's for a baby." — "See's the bag, Sarah, I could eat a cuddy." — "Yon's the road to Rothesay." — "Mrs Jones, a lady frien' o' mine, has a summer hoose at Dunoon — ye never saw such rhuburb!" — "Whit are they ringin' the bell for?" — "Oh, my! luk at the man's straw basher in the watter! —"

"An A1 day!" said Duffy; "I feel like a brand-new man already."

"That's lucky for Liza," said Erchie, winking slyly at her. "She must ha'e been awfu' tired seein' the auld yin aye aboot the hoose."

"Will we soon be there?" asked Mrs Duffy, referring to her mountain park, Ardgoil.[7]

"We'll be there in an 'oor," she was assured by Erchie. "It's at Lochgoilhead heid."

"Does the boat stop there?"

"If it disna there'll be an awfu' dunt," said Erchie, who never scorns an old joke.

"Don't let yer e'en aff them pies, Liza," said the coalman, anxiously. "I wish I had my breakfast earlier. Whit dae the folk dae aboot here in the winter time? They're awful' faur awa' frae ony place."

"Oh, they ha'e their ain compensations, puir sowls," said Erchie. "They maybe ha'ena only skoosh caurs[8] to tak' them to their wark, but then they're likely no' in ony hurry, and can daunder alang, lookin' noo and then at the scenery. There's aye the hens to attend to, and ance a day a steamer ca's at the quay and lets a commercial traiveller aff; if twa come aff it's mentioned in the Dunoon papers, and ca'd a Revivin' Wave in Tred. Every ither day the residenters meet in each ither's hooses and look ower post-caird albums, and the weekly papers keeps them talkin' for a couple o' days frae Cove to Arrochar."

"They're aye sure o' fish, and milk, and eggs, and — and — cockles, onywye," suggested Mrs Duffy.

"They are," said Erchie, "as lang as the Gleska boat comes in. If there was nae bonny wee Gleska toon, half the folk roond here wad never see a herrin', or ken the taste o' butter; Gleska's the Pantry o' the West."

"If you lose them pies!" said Duffy to his wife, with menace.

"Noo for the mountain park!" was Duffy's exclamation when they had landed at Lochgoilhead quay.

"Were ye thinkin' to gang sclimbin' up Ardgoil?" asked Erche, innocently.

"I was," said his friend; "I'm feelin' fine; I could sclimb a land o' hooses. Whaur's the place?"

"Do ye see that hill wi' the no road on't and the preci-pices?" asked Erchie. "That's Ardgoil. Ye'll maybe get a ladder at the inn. Tak' the first turnin' to your right, turn up your trousers at the fit, and commend your soul to its Maker; then start spielin'. If you're gaun to tak' the mistress, and the bag o' pies, ye better get a rope as weel's the ladder, and leave the keys o' the hoose; we'll gi'e them to the factor."

"Don't dae onything rash!" prayed Jinnet, apprehen-sively. "It's a bonny hill, but I'm shair we canna see't ony better than whaur we are. Ye're no gaun to sclimb a place like that; are ye, Liza?"

"I'm no' daft," said Mrs Duffy; "I can see a' the rest o't I need in a picture post-caird.

"Whaur's them pies?" cried Duffy in accents of despair; and Liza almost fainted.

"I was sittin' beside the funnel, and I must ha'e left them there," she said; "Isn't it provokin? Is there ony use, do ye think, gaun back for them?"

"Nane in the world," said Erchie. "Ye wouldna ask, if ye kent them steamboat skippers and pursers; collectin' pies

is their hobby. But whit's the odds? I was plannin' a' the
way to stand ye your tea at Lochgoilheid; it's better fun
than sclimbin' mountains, and here we are."

"A champion day!" was Duffy's verdict, when they got
to the Broomielaw again in the evening. "There was
naething to complain o' if Liza hadna lost the pies."

76. *About Tips Generally*[1]

"I SEE they're thrang writin' awa' in the papers aboot tips
again," said Erchie; "It's a sure sign they're slack o'
murders. When there's no' enough murders nor scandals
in high life to keep them gaun, I think the editors tak' a
daunder doon aboot the quays to see if there's ony likely
chaps aff the Derry boat to write them letters sayin' the Tip
is a Tyranny, or that there's maybe no' a God."

"What's your own experience of the tipping system?" I
asked him.

"It's awfu' sair on the pouches," he replied; "I wad
sooner ha'e my pay in my haund at the end o' the week
than claut it up in coppers, and gang jinglin' hame every
nicht the same's I had been robbin' the kirk plate. When I
begood the tred o' waitin' there was nae such thing as tips;
if a customer was pleased wi' his dinner he jist ca'd ye
Erchie, and if he was extra well pleased he told ye a funny
bawr. A tip in thae days wad gi'e ye a red face. The first
time ever I saw a tip was when I was a halflin[2] in His
Lordship's Larder[3] doon in St Enoch Square; I found, a'e
day, a penny under a plate, and as shair's death I thocht it
was a clocker,[4] and made to kill't.

"'Whit does this mean?' I says to a German waiter in the
same hoose, and him bein' German he kent fine it was a tip
at the first glance. As for me, I was that new-fangled aboot
it I wanted to ha'e't enamelled and made into a kind o' a
brooch for the wife, but she wadna hear tell o't; she was
fair affronted. 'Little did I think,' she said, and her near
greetin' — 'Little did I think my husband would be

insulted this way; I micht as weel ha'e mairried a blin' man wi' a messan[5] dug and a tinny.'"

"The hobby grew, but it took me a gey lang time to get used to't. People papped pennies at ye if ye as much as helped them on wi' their coat, or handed them their umbrella. Ye couldna lift a dirty saucer but ye found a copper in below, for some of the customers werena sure but ye micht be angry wi' them if they put it in your loof as man to man. I'm shair I didna want their pennies, but I hadna the nerve to refuse. At first I put a' the tips in oor son Willy's wee tin bank wi' the bumbees skep on't, but the craze for tippin' grew that fast the bank was fu' in a fortnicht, and we had to burst it open and put him in the Savin's Bank. The warst o't was that the mair tips we got, as time gaed on, the less pay we lifted at the week's end, and nooadays ye canna tell whether a restaurant belangs to the man whose name's on the sign, or to the foreign chap that waits on ye and strongly recommends the Cliquot 1900. There's places whaur a shillin' tip would mak' the waiters grue wi horror, and there's ithers in London whaur it would be as much as your life was worth to try and put them aff wi' onything under a sovereign. A' the German gentry's sendin' their sons across to Britain to retrieve the family fortunes, as the papers say, and they dae't quite easy in the waitin' tred. Do ye mind Godenzi[6] — him that had the Sauchieha' Street Café? I'm tellt he made enough aff cups o' coffee and sliders[7] to buy a big estate and a rale chat-o in Switzerland, the place whaur the Milkmaid Brand is made. Godenzi was a wyse man — he kept the waitin' in the faimily.

"It's no' only in the waitin' tred that the tip's the go; I'm tellt ye're shair to ha'e a misfit wi' your coffin if ye divna dae the nice thing wi' the undertaker's man. If ye happen to be a gentleman, and get an invitation to a mansion wi' shootin's in the country, ye ha'e first to sell your shares in the railway companies and pawn the guidwife's di'monds. First there's the butler — bein' an Englishman he never clapt e'en in his life on less than a five-pound note, and if

ye tried him on wi' one-pound Scottish, he would think it
was a tract. The least ye can dae wi' a butler's to hand him
your Life Insurance Policy and a five-pound note to start,
if ye're on a week-end visit; if he has to hang up your hat
for a fortnight, ye'll be best to gi'e him a' the money ye ha'e
when ye leave, and ca' a meetin' o' your creditors. Then
there's the game-keeper — when ye gang shootin' wi'
anither man's gamekeeper, ye needna mind a gun as lang's
ye can keep him cheery every noo and then on the hill wi' a
sovereign. Ye needna lay't on a stane and turn your back to
gie him a chance to lift it; a' ye ha'e to dae's to throw't
onywhere, and it'll be shair to hit him on the open hand.
Ye've seen, yoursel', the lot o' pouches gamekeepers ha'e
in their claes; I'll bet ye they're no' a' for haudin' rabbits. A
lot o' the lairds in the Heilands would be richer men the
day if they let the tips to gamekeepers, instead of lettin'
their shootin's. When ye're leavin' the shootin' lodge, the
motor-caur 'll drive ye to the train and I'll wager the
chauffeur 'll be there in plenty o' time. He looks as if his
leather suit was an awfu' ticht fit, and it wad be hard for
him to get into his pockets, but ye needna be frichtened;
he'll get some place for your sleeve links and your watch
and chain if that's a' ye ha'e left. Anither way's to buy him
an annuity.

"I see often in the papers aboot new diseases like 'writer's
cramp,' the 'motor grin,' the 'skoosh-caur hop,' the
'telephone ear,' the 'rubber-neck,' and the 'gowf swing,'
but there's nane o' them near sae prevalent as the Tip Eye.
It's calculated that ninety per cent o' the male inhabitants
o' Great Britain ha'e the Tip Eye, and I've seen't mysel'.
Ye ask a railway porter if this is the train for Greenock; he
says 'richt ye are!' as quick as onything, and swings his e'e
doon to the place ye keep your pocket. He canna help it.
When the man comes roond to tak' the meter at Christmas
time, he has an e'e that's twice the ordinar' size wi' lookin'
among the gas-consumers for goodwill to men. The Tip
Eye's aye expectin' somethin'; it glowers that hard a' day
that it doesna shut at night, even when the man that has

it's sleepin'. The men that gi'es the tips are as likely to ha'e't as them that get them; mony a time when I'm daein' a bit turn for a man because I like the looks o' the chap, and think it's my Christian duty, I can see by the jink o' his e'e that he's calculatin' hoo much I expect, and hoo little he can offer me wi' decency. That's the curse o' the tip; it doesna mak' allowances for the better feelin's o' mankind."

77. *The Flying Machine*[1]

"WHAT CAPER'S this Johnny Syme efter, throwin' things oot at his window into the back coort and spilin' a' the washin's?" asked Mr Duffy.

"Is that a' ye ken?" replied Erchie. "Ha'e ye no' heard that Johnny's an inventor? Him bein' a poet, and the Limerick tred bein' awfu' slack the noo, he has a lot o' time on his haunds. A man that wasna a genius would get a fine character frae his minister and gang and look for work on the tramways; but that means risin' early in the mornin', so Johnny's gaun to mak' a fortune wi' a flyin' machine."[2]

"Puir cratur!" remarked Jinnet, sympathetically. "It's an awfu' peety aboot them poets; they canna help it, but it's aye some daft-like thing they turn their haunds to."

"There's a crood o' weans oot in the back coort hurrah-in' like onything, and every noo and then Johnny Syme leans oot at his kitchen window and draps a paste-board box with 'lastic bands and wheels on't," said Duffy. "They a' fa' wi' a dunt, and Johnny says 'damn!' It shouldna be alloo'ed in a respectable locality. Last nicht he nearly brained Macrae the sergeant's wife; she was bringin' in her washin', and he put his heid oot the window in a hurry and cowped a floo'er-pot. She got such a start she nearly swallowed a couple o' claes-pins, and a' he said was, 'My fau't, Mrs Macrae! A' my fau't, entirely.' What's the paste-board boxes for?"

"Models," said Erchie. "That's the way ye start the flyin'. It's a' in the principle o' the thing; if ye can mak' a paste-board airyplane that'll flee a couple o' yards wi' cahoutchy springs and a bit' coal inside o't, ye're on the road to what the papers ca' the Triumph o' the Skies. Johnny's in great hopes, he tells me; he's found the hale secret o' flight except the drappin' saft. If he keeps at it anither week, and the boys would gi'e him back his 'lastic bands, he would be flappin' roond the chimney-cans and liftin' prizes."

"Whit's he wantin' to flee for?" asked Duffy. "Wha's chasin' him?"

"That's whit I say!" interjected Jinnet, sagely. "There's such a lot o' pleesure jist in gaun aboot on the feet the Almichty gave ye."

"I'm no' gaun to start the fleein' mysel'," said Erchie, "but of late it's a' the go. It's said to be maist exhilaratin'; ye gang up wi' a breenge and come hame in the ambulance. In every pairt o' the warld there's geniuses like Johnny Syme inventin' airyplanes, workin' nicht and day to get a prize o' a hundred-thoosand pounds that somebody's offered.[3] Some o' them's poets, like Johnny — when they tell ye the way it feels to be skooshin' through the air at a height o' fully twenty feet, for fifteen seconds, their language puts ye in mind o' the Psalms o' David; it mak's ye ashamed to be crawlin' aboot on your feet. But maist o' them's only artists; when they get their airyplanes built and pented, they tak' their sate at the drivin'-wheel wi' a look o' quiet determination, and let the photographer tak' their pictures for the *Graphic*, then they say the wind's in the wrang direction, and that they'll start the fleein' maybe on Friday first, but they never da't. Catch their wifes allowin' them!"

"If it wasna for their wifes," said Jinnet, "men would mak' awfu' fools o' themsel's!"

"I thocht," said Duffy, "them balloons they used to ha'e were jist as comfortable for fleein' roond in as onybody wanted."

"The balloon's auld-fashioned and oot o' date," said Erchie. "It was handy enough in its way, but ye couldna steer it, and it cost a lot o' money and took up a lot o' room. Whit's wanted nooadays is the airyplane that ye can steer wi' your least wee bit touch, buy for aboot the price o' a pramlater, and keep in the lobby. When Johnny Syme mak's his, a' he'll ha'e to dae'll be to back it oot the kitchen window, shut his e'en in silent prayer a meenute, and then start soarin' across New City Road."

"I'm shair and I'll be thankfu' when it's in workin' order," said Jinnet; "It'll be an awfu' savin' in the cleanin' o' the close; he's such a man for cigaroots!"

"Johnny says a' the ither inventors is on the wrang lines a'thegither, tryin' to drag gas engines up in the air' wi' them. He says it'll tak' him a' his time to tak' himsel' and a flask on his machine withoot draggin a piece o' lumber like a gas-engine wi' him. Birds don't ha'e gas-engines — catch them! They're ower fly to be bothered wi' onything o' the kind, Johnny says, and he's studied a lot o' sparrows."

"Whit, does he flap?" asked Duffy.

"He's no' gaun to flap; he's jist gaun to kind o' skoosh or sklide," explained Erchie. "Ye see ye tak' the wind in an angle like a doo, or a gull, and the wind does a' the wark."

"I wish we could dae that wi' coal lorries," said Duffy; "It would be a terrible savin' in horses."

"Up till noo," proceeded Erchie, "Johnny's keepin' his plans deid secret; he says it's the only way to mak money at flyin' machines. A' the best inventors in the tred keep their plans secret and dae their biggest flees in the dark when there's nacbody lookin', and the newspapers is fu' o' the marvels they accomplish. Yince they show their hands the newspapers say there's naething in them. There's a couple o' men ca'd Wright[4] in America been workin' for years at an airyplane that was said to be so complete and bird-like in its motions it could dae onything a bird could dae except lay eggs. Even to read aboot the Wright machine for fleein' would mak' ye quite dizzy. Ye would think the Wrights spent a' their time skooshin' among the clouds, and only cam' doon at intervals to gang to their beds or see the foreign governments that wanted to buy their patent. If they had gone on daein' that they would ha'e been richt enough, but the idiots came ower to Paris the ither day wi' their airyplane in a Saratoga trunk, and they're gaun to gi'e a demonstration. Noo, demonstratin's the last thing an airyplane inventor should give in to; it jist gi'es the papers a chance to mak' a cod o' him. He should never gang further than ha'ein' his photograph ta'en, and sayin' that a twelve-month hence we'll a' be fleein'.'"

"Do ye think we will?" asked Duffy, anxiously. "I was jist gaun to order a new pair o' boots, and if I thocht I wouldna need them —"

"I would get the boots a' the same, if I was you," said Erchie; "ye could never carry hundredwechts o' coal upstairs on an airyplane, nor perch like a craw on the bar-rail o' the Mull o' Kintyre Vaults and tak' your usual. If flyin' machines were the vogue, where would the like o' you want to flee to? There's plenty o' fun in Gleska, and the skoosh caurs tak' ye to't as nate's ye like for a ha'penny."

"There'll be nae fleein' in this warld," said Jinnet with conviction, "and its aye an anxious thocht to me that maybe it'll be expected aff o' me in the next, for I'm that bothered wi' palpitation. I would far sooner daunder round the way I was accustomed."

"It's a' very weel, but ye canna tell," said Duffy, dubiously. "Look at the way they invented motor-caurs, and by-and-bye there'll no' be a horse left to put in the trams o' a lorry."

"Ye may tak' it frae me," said Erchie, "that flyin' machines are no' gaun' to tak' the place o' the birds o' the air or the tramways. The very hens that can only flee when ye shoo them are no' botherin' their heids aboot the competeetion. There's naething in't, and there'll never be onything in't but a job noo and then for the undertakers. The maist o' us can dae a' the fleein' we want, and that's in oor dreams."

78. *At the Franco-British Exhibition*[1]

ERCHIE HAD not long returned from London when Duffy called at his humble, but cosy, home. Erchie welcomed him with a little of the condescension to be expected of the travelled man.

"Ye ha'e been in London?" said Duffy for an opening.

Erchie smiled and nodded.

"An' did ye see the Exhibition?"[2]

"I did that," said Erchie. "Man, it's a great sight. When I was young and soople, I used to wish to gang to India. I've been there."

"I thocht ye said ye were at the Exhibition," said Duffy, a little mystified.

"It's the same thing," said Erchie, "an' a lot mair. It's India an' France an' Ceylon an' Ireland an' —"

"Whit aboot Scotland?" Duffy asked.

"I met a Scotch policeman," said Erchie; "He was very affable, an' asked me if we were a' weel North o' the Tweed. But I didna spend much time or money wi' him. There was too much to look at. I sat doon in the Court o' Honour, and there I was in India.[3] Round aboot me were the palaces o' the Rajahs glistenin' in the sun, wi' a sort o' filigree work in the windows where the gless should be, and a' kinds o' odd domes and minarets —"

"Are minarets savage?" Duffy broke in.

"Minarets are no' beasts, ye numskull; they're just a sort o' dome. An' in the middle o' the Court there was a big pond wi' swans shovin' boats in front o' them."

"Real swans?" said Mrs Erchie, incredulously.

"No' exactly real," Erchie replied cautiously, "but if ye didna notice the man on the bicycle ye might think they were real. An' a' roon' aboot were ladies in white frocks an' a lot o' ither colours, maist o' them talkin' foreign languages — I suppose it would be Hindoo, as the Court o' Honour is Indian — and fine set-up men in silk hats and frock coats. It may surpise ye, Duffy," he added, parenthetically, "but it's true that men in London wear silk hats and frock coats on the week-days as weel as on Sundays. An' then there was the cascade," he went on.

"What is the cascade?" Duffy queried.

"The cascade," said Erchie, "is a sort of fairy fountain,[4] only better. The water comes tumblin' doon a thing like a big salmon loup made o' gless, an' electric lights shine through it, an' gi'e it a' the colours o' the rainbow, an' a' that ha'e been invented since the rainbow. It wasna tumblin' doon very much when I was there," the truthful waiter added; "In fact the only thing I saw tumblin' was a glazier, that slipped on some putty, an' got a bath for naethin'. Somebody tellt him he must ha'e thocht he was in the Stadium — that's where they keep the ordinary swimming bath. An' so there I sat in the sun, an' fancied I was a Nabob in Bombay, with scores o' black servants to wait on me — an' a' for a shilling."

"Has the Exhibition got a switchback?" said Duffy, recalling the exciting times he had spent at the last Glasgow Exhibition.[5]

"Switchbacks," said Erchie, pityingly, "are clean oot o' date; it's the scenic railway that's the thing noo. Ye wad think it was a switchback when ye get into it; but somebody blaws a whistle, an' off ye go through tunnels an' up mountains as high as Ben Lomond, and doon passes like Killiecrankie; an' the tunnels are sae narrow ye are respectfully requested to keep your hands inside the car. Yours are that big, Duffy," he added mischievously, "ye wad need to keep them in your pocket. An' then, before ye ken what has happened, ye are back at the station."

"An' is that in the shillin', too?" said Duffy.

"Ye were aye great on bargains," said Erchie, severely. "No; it's no' in the shilling, but it's cheap at a sixpence. I had a shilling's worth on it mysel'. An' then I went to the Irish village, where they have a lot o' fine lassies they ca' colleens. I wasna so particular; I jist ca'ed them Red Riding Hood when I spoke to them. They have the hoose that President Roosevelt was born in there."

"I didna ken President Roosevelt was Irish." said Mrs Erchie; "It's no' an Irish name."

"Weel, maybe it was some other President," Erchie retorted. "I never was very great at history. But, onyway, it's a sma' hoose — no' unlike Burns' Cottage at Ayr. It's wonderfu' when ye come to think on it, hoo many big men ha'e been born in wee hooses."

"Harry Lauder's yin," said Duffy.

"They havena got his birthplace at the Exhibition yet," said Erchie, severely, "but if ye thocht o' gaun there, Duffy, they micht obleege ye. An' there's the flip-flap."[6]

"Whit ever's that?" Mrs Erchie asked in surprise.

"It's a contrivance that flips up on one side aboot as high as Tennant's Stalk, and flaps ye doon on the ither side. I didna sample that — at my time o' life—"

"Is that extra?" Duffy broke in.

"Aye, it's extra," said Erchie; "Hoo much wad ye like for your shilling. But I can see," he resumed, "that the Exhibition will be a fine thing for the waitin' tred. If I hadna been on holiday, I wad ha'e asked for a job mysel'. There's restaurants here, an' buffets there, an' tea-rooms yonder — ye need never be hungry there, I can tell ye."

"But they're no' in the shilling," said Duffy.

Erchie took no notice of the interruption. "It was really very thoughtful of Mr Kiralfy,[7] he said. "Efter he built a palace or twa, he said, 'The puir folk will be hungry here,' an' so he built anither restaurant. Then he built ither twa palaces, an' he said, 'They'll be gey thirsty here,' an' he built a nice cosy wee bar; an' as he went on buildin' palaces an' palaces, he said, 'They'll aye be gettin' hungrier, an' hungrier, an' thirstier, an' thirstier', an' so he kept on buildin' dining rooms an' bars. O, it's a great place, I'm tellin' ye. An' at nicht — ye should see it at nicht. The lichts on the palaces put the stars to shame; they shine on the white walls till they look like silver, and on the pond till it looks like burnished gold; and the ladies in their gay dresses flit aboot like butterflies, an' the bands play music that mak's ye want to dance or maybe jist to sit still an' dream. It's then ye are vexed to think ye ha'e to go back to Gleska."

"An' did ye see ony o' thae 'directory' costumes on the ladies?" Duffy asked, incautiously breaking in on the rhapsody.

Erchie's wife became suddenly interested. "Dear me," she said, "are they namin' costumes efter the Post Office Directory noo? They'll be namin' them efter the Dictionary next."

Erchie looked reproachfully at Duffy, and at length he said, "Ye must learn, Duffy, no' to ask such questions in the presence o' ladies; it's whit ye ca' embarrassin'."

"I havena heard ye say much aboot the exhibits," said his wife.

"Oh, there's plenty o' them," he said; "but I thocht I would leave them for anither visit."

79. *The Duffys Go on Holiday*[1]

DUFFY CAME down the close looking as if he had not shaved for weeks, and generally with an aspect melancholius.

"Anither fine day," said Erchie; "Haud on a bit and ye'll see this country wi' a climate. Ye have only to walk the length o' the Coocaddens to get a sunburn on ye the same's ye had been awa' a week at the yatin'. Whit's the maitter wi' ye. Ye're lookin' awfu' doon in the mooth; ha'e ye lost another customer?"

"It's no' that this time," said the coalman; "but we're gaun awa' a holiday."[2]

"A holiday!" said Erchie, with sympathy. "Man, I jaloused it was something serious. But maybe the case is no' just hopeless; if ye keep your wits aboot ye, ye'll maybe can lose the boat and just turn hame."

"Nae fears o' that!" said Duffy, sadly; "If ye kent my wife the way I ken her, ye would ken she'll be doon at the Broomielaw afore daylicht rappin' up the mate and captain oot o' their beds. Ye ha'e never ony chance to lose a boat unless ye happen to be a bachelor."

"How lang are ye to be awa'?"

"That's the aggravatin' thing aboot it; it's no' a nice wee shillin' trip to the heid o' Lochgoil and back at nicht wi' a bunch o' floo'ers in your kep; it's a week, nae less, at a place they ca' Kilcattan.[3] Fancy me awa' a week frae Gleska at a place they ca' Kilcattan!"

"Tut, tut!" said Erchie, "it's sad; I'm rale sorry for ye, Duffy. I'm shair ye had plenty o' trouble wi' your influenza, and the Co-operation startin' anither lorry. I ken whit holidays is, for I had them mysel' the year afore the Exhibection.[4] There's no' a worse infliction; they tak' ye doon terrible. They put ye aff your ordinar' meat, and spoil your sleep; ye ha'e such a lot o' thinkin' to dae wi' your heid aboot the steamboat tickets and keepin' mind o' the luggage that it mak's ye dizzy. I'm sorry for ye, Duffy, if there was onything I could dae —"

"It's a fair sickener!" said Duffy. "The thocht o't's puttin' me in the nerves the same's I was a woman, and a week ago, afore she took the notion, I was feelin' fine."

"A week's a lot," said Erchie; "It's jist enough to drive ye nearly despcrate, but it's no' a fortnicht; that's a consolation. Efter the Sunday's ower, and ye mak' a chum or twa, it'll soon pass bye. Ye micht even bring them to an end on the Wednesday by lettin' on to the wife ye lost the money."

"I didna lose it soon enough," said the coalman, "for she has a' the money, and she's no' gaun to lose't as lang's she keeps her senses. Whit did you do the time ye had the holidays?"

"I got a bottle o' stuff that keeps awa' the midges, and kept my bed when it was rainin'. Sometimes I gaed doon to the quay to see the boat comin' in frae Gleska, and a' the rest o' the time I had to talk wi' Jinnet aboot whit she could order for the dinner. I wouldna say but the wifes has the warst o't on a holiday; they get in the Gleska sausages, and they're kept in a fever a' the time plannin' the way to mak' eggs and kippered herrin' look like something new."

"Takin' holidays is a new complaint, the same's appendicitis; they didna ken the ravages o't a hundred years ago in Gleska. When a chap wanted a change o' air then he went doon the length o' Govan, ate grosets[5] and milk, and cam' hame along Sauchieha' Street wi' the coos at gloamin'.[6] He didna have to gaither up a' his silver plate and family jewellery and hide them under the coals in the parlour scuttle, nor get Macrae, the nicht polis, to try the handle o' the door every nicht and mornin' that he had mind. He kent when he was well aff, and was independent o' the weather, for in Gleska there's aye a handy close if its rainin', and in the country ye get wat to the skin standin' under hawthorn-bushes. I grant ye'll get cockles for naething at Kilcattan, and the best o' dulse; but it's likely, it bein' the Fair, there'll be nae sweet milk for love nor money, and a tuppenny pie on a Setturday nicht's a thing they never hear o'. A' the time Jinnet and me were awa' on the holiday we were thinkin' aboot oor ain wee hoose in Grove Street, and hoo handy it was, wi' the richt kind o' chairs beside the kitchen fire, and the jawbox that convenient, and the coals brocht in to ye, and the gas only two-an'-tuppence a thoosand, and nice folk we kent up the stairs, and a' sorts o' shops at the closemooth that aye kept the very things ye wanted, and —"

"Oh, ye needna be rubbin' it in," said Duffy, irritably, "It's bad enough to guess the way I'll be feelin' mysel' next Monday mornin'; it's bad enough to ha'e the horrors o' the packin'."

"Packin'!" exclaimed Erchie. "Puir sowl; ye're surely no' daein' onything sae rash as tak' to dae wi' the packin'?"

"Not me!" said Duffy. "I don't see onything to pack that ye couldna cairry in a hankie, but Liza's makin' ready for a fortnicht past the same's it was a flittin'. I canna even get my razor; it's doon at the bottom o' the basket wi' my sand-shoes."

"Sand-shoes," exclaimed Erchie, incredulously; "Ye're surely no' breakin' oot in sandshoes?"

"The wife insisted," said the coalman; "She says that ony ither kind at Kilcattan Bay would hardly be respectable. She read in an advertisement that they were a' the go, and gaun chape at a clearin' sale, so she bocht a pair for baith o' us. And that's no' the warst o't; there's mair nor that in the basket."

"Don't tell me there's a wee wudden spade and a barrow," said Erchie, holding up his hands in consternation. "If ye're in for sand-castle compeetitions, it's Millport ye should be at, and no' Kilcattan."

"I hate to tell ye," said Duffy, shame-facedly; "but don't say a word to onybody; she's bocht me a straw basher!"[7]

"Puir Duffy!" said his friend; "I kent there was something wrang, whenever I seen ye, but little did I think o' this calamity. Sand-shoes and a straw basher! I'm feart ye're in for an awfu' holiday!"

80. *The Age of Sport*[1]

"THEY TAK' up an awfu' room in the paper nooadays wi' things that naebody wants to read," said Jinnet, putting down the newspaper and taking off her specs. "Everywhere ye look it's naething but cricket, gowfin', soomin', rowin', shootin', yachtin', sodgers' camps, and Canadian boolers; ye wad think we had naething in the world to dae but play at games."

"What would ye like?" asked Erchie, blandly — "recipes for rasp jam and new crochet patterns?"

"No," said his wife; "but there used to be nice wee bits aboot workin'-men oot at Motherwell bein' left a hundred-thousand pounds frae an uncle in Australia; or aboot horses that ran aff in the Gallowgate; I canna find onything to read noo except the drapers' sales. I think the country's gaun clean daft for sport — look at yon awfu' cairry-on at the — at the Stadium!"[2]

"Whit did they dae there?" asked Duffy, who was visiting.

"It's a place in London," Jinnet explained; "They made a lot o' puir Italians and Americans and foreigners o' a' kinds breenge roond and roond it for three 'oors till they got dizzy and had to be cairried awa' on the ambulance."[3]

"Serves them richt!" was Duffy's comment; "What guid's an Italian onywye? If ye seen the things they eat!"

Erchie lit his pipe, flicked the end of the match at the cat, which lay on the kitchen hearth-rug, and smiled at his wife and the coalman.

"Ye mustna misca' the Italians, Duffy," he said; "they're daein' their best, and if ye say a cheep aboot the Americans it'll hurt their feelin's, and they'll no' play. Thae Olympic Games in London were faur mair important than Jinnet thinks; it's on oor common interest in whit the papers ca' the realm o' sport that the peace o' the world depends; if ye leeve lang enough ye'll see that instead o' competin' in the buildin' o' big men-o'-war ships, the Great Powers 'll put a' their money into trainin' likely chaps for hammer-throwin' and the hundred yards sprint. The wonderfu' effect o' athletics on the finer feelin's o' humanity has jist been discovered; if ye pay a shillin' to see a mixed lot o' champions o' the world daein' the hop-step-and-jump or heavin' javelins , ye're filled at yince wi' the deepest affection for a' yer fellowmen, foreign as well as Christian. When I read the other day aboot yon puir chap Dorando careerin' roond the Stadium in the airms o' his devoted countrymen, I felt that fond o' the Italian nation I was nearly gaun alang the street to Quadracini's Ice-cream Emporium to jine him in a slider."

"Was that him they gi'ed the cup to?" asked Jinnet.

"It was. If he had happened to be an American they wad ha'e gi'en him the jyle for fa'in' and spoilin' the track; the wonderfu' effect o' athletic competeetion on the finer feelin's o' humanity's confined to the nice, quate, wee nations we're no' feared for."

"It's a fine thing, sport, though Jinnet doesna unders-taund it," proceeded Erchie, "and Great Britain's glory is that she can tak' on a' the nations o' the warld at their ain games and mak' a good thing oot o' the gate-money."

"I couldna tak' on the nations mysel' at onything," said Duffy, "unless it was cryin' coals and coupin' bags in a bunker, for I havena played ony games since I played moshey[4] at Nelson's Monument[5] — I hadna the time. "

"Ye should mak' the time," said Erchie, firmly; "It's your duty as a British ratepayer to keep up the manhood o' the nation. Ye can get in to see ony fitba' match for sixpence. There's far aulder men than you, Duffy, trampin' the golf links every ither day and sittin' up to a' 'oors cleanin' their clubs in case the lamentable need should ever arise for them to turn oot and preserve the land from foreign invasion. Dae ye think when ye see them hurryin' frae the offices to their trains wi' a bag o' sticks that they're gaun for the fun o' the thing? Not them! They're daein' it for their health and the glory o' Great Britain.

"They're weel aff," said Duffy; "I ha'e to pick up my health gaun alang the streets wi' a lorry."

Erchie surveyed him critically. "Ye're no' the man ye were Duffy," he said candidly. "Ye're gettin' fat; your step's no' sae licht on a stair as it used to be; I see ye come hame earlier at nichts frae the Mull o' Kintyre Vaults — there's nae surer sign o' physeecal decline. Whit ye want's exerceese."

"Did ye ever try cairryin' bags?" asked Duffy, significantly.

"Cairryin' bags is a' richt, but it's your tred, and it doesna coont," said Erchie. "That's no' exerceese; exerceese is daein' something ye're no' paid for daein'. When a gamekeeper's trampin' the hills efter deer and grouse it's wark, and he's no' awfu' keen on't, but when the gentleman that keeps him tramps the hills the same wye its sport, and exerceese, and he's willin' to spend a lot o' money for the chance o' daein't. If there was ony money gaun for chasin' a wee ba' roond parks and puttin' it every noo and then in a hole in the grun' nae gentleman would dirty his hands wi' a golf club, the job wad be left to the caddies."

"Ye wadna shairly ha'e puir Mr Duffy trampin' efter deer or gaun aboot wi' gowf-bags?" said Jinnet; "The man has plenty o' trampin' and cairryin' bags in his business."

"Right!" said Duffy. "If I was gaun in for recreation, gi'e me draughts."

"Draughts is nae use for a man like you," said Erchie;

"it's — it's sedentary; whit a chap wi' your figure needs is scientific physical trainin'; ye can read aboot it in *Home Chat*.⁶ Get oot o' your bed an 'oor afore ye rise and open the window wide. There's naething bates the fresh air if it's no' blawin' frae Tennant's chimney.⁷ Draw ten deep breaths, and then begin to swing a pair o' licht dumb-bells till ye feel a gentle perspiration. Then tak' a cauld bath —"

"Ach! ye're coddin'!" said the coalman, enlightened by the last suggestion; "I'm shair ye never try ony o' them fancy tips yoursel'."

"Me!" said Erchie. "Catch me! I'm no' needin'; I'm faur ower much interested in my wark to be bothered devisin' ways o' passin' the time. The best recreation I can think o's waitin'; I wad dae't for naething if I hadna a wife to keep."

81. *The Presentation Portrait*¹

A JEWISH-LOOKING gentleman with a neat leather case in his hand and a huge Masonic emblem for a scarf-pin, rang Erchie's bell with all the brisk assurance of a letter carrier, and took off his hat politely to Jinnet when she opened the door.

"Mrs MacPherson?" he asked suavely, inserting one foot inside the doorway so that she could not make the emphatic retort with which his preliminary advances were often met.

"It'll be my man ye're wantin'," said Jinnet, nervously. "He's no' in."

"Ah!" said the visitor, "that's a pity; our firm wrote last Monday to say I would call today. Most important. The Home Art Supply Association. We wrote saying he had won a place in the ballot, and asking him to select a portrait. Possibly the letter is at the post office; they are so busy at the post office at this season of the year, letters lie over for days. Never mind; you may be able to choose a picture yourself; it will save time." And despite the timid obstruction of Jinnet, he brushed past her, calmly entered her kitchen, and proceeded to open his leather case with business-like alacrity.

"The Home Art Supply Association, Mrs MacPherson," he said glibly during this proceeding, "has just started a Glasgow branch. It was all explained in the letter. We have introduced a new style of Art portrait which is all the rage; done in pastel, very chaste; fit for the King's palace as well as for the working-man's parlour. I will show you —"

He produced a neatly-framed crayon portrait of a well-known actress and held it at an angle over the jaw-box[2] so that the light should fall upon the picture most effectively.

"This," he said, "is just an example. It was ordered for a lady in the West End, and I am now on my way to deliver it."

"Would ye no' come back and see himself?" asked Jinnet, much embarrassed by this sudden intrusion of Art and West-End beauty upon her preparations for her husband's tea.

"I might," said the visitor, reflectively; "but it will be difficult; we are so busy. The New System is so popular we are kept on the rush night and day. I am surprised about the letter not reaching you. You see we wish to introduce our portraits into this district, and instead of advertsing in the ordinary way, we select by ballot a few of the most prominent householders in the neighbourhood, to whom we give a presentation portrait free, believing that their visitors will be so pleased with it they will come to us to buy some for themselves. The portraits are valued at five pounds, but we charge you positively nothing."

"It's rale kind o' ye," said Jinnet. "We havena mony veesitors, except Mrs Duffy next door and ane or twa ither neighbours, and I'm afraid ye wouldna mak' much aff the pictures they would buy. I'll no' deceive ye; they're jist puir people like oorsel's."

The visitor magniloquently waved his hands. "That is of no importance, Mrs MacPherson," he said. "You have been fortunate enough to draw a lucky number in the ballot, and the free portrait is yours. If you kindly give me a photograph of yourself or your husband, or anybody you wish treated in the chaste pastel method, I shall put it in hand at once and deliver the portrait next week." He glanced round the wall and pounced upon a framed cabinet photograph hung on the side of the window. "Ah!" he said, admiringly; "That's a fine head! Noble! It would made a beautiful portrait. I suppose this is Mr — Mr MacPherson?"

"Naething o' the kind!" said Jinnet; "It's Macrae, the nicht polis. My man mak's a joke o' hangin't at the window to keep awa' burglars. My man's no' like that at a'; he hasna ony whiskers; I'll show you him!"

The Hebraic-looking visitor left with Erchie's portrait, with a guarantee of its safe return, accompanied by the free pastel portrait taken from it, in the course of the next few days, and Jinnet eagerly broke the news of her husband's good fortune to him when he came home for tea.

Erchie listened gravely, with his lips tightly pursed. "Man!" he said, "it's a wonderfu' age for gi'en awa' things for naething. If it's no' samples o' cocoa and washin' poother, it's bam-zuk for sprained wrists, or polishin' paste. If ye want a wee bottle o' brandy or a book wi' pictures in't, a' ye ha'e to dae is to cut a coupon oot the papers and send it wi' yer name and address. Whit was he like, this chap that ca'd?"

"A rale smert, weel-put-on man, that spoke awfu' polite and had a parrot nose," said Jinnit, graphically.

"Jist that!" said her husband, stirring his tea; "Carnegie![3] If it wisna Carnegie, it was some ither millionaire; the country's packed wi' them, and they're fair distracted tryin' to get rid o' their money."

"Mercy!" exclaimed Jinnet; "I never thocht it was Carnegie."

"Ye're no' half 'cute," said Erchie; "Ye should ha'e asked him to a cup o' tea and gi'ed him an egg wi't; them millionaires, when they're distributin' leebraries and organs and pictures, aye expect a wee attention. It wad ha'e pleased him. He micht ha'e come roond again wi' a pianolo. Of course ye didna gi'e him onything?"

"Naething but your photygraph," said Jinnet, "and he promised to tak' care o't."

"My photygraph!" exclaimed Erchie, who now heard of this part of the interview for the first time. "Ye're an innocent, auld cratur! I only hope I'm in when he comes back wi't."

By good luck, Erchie was in when the hook-nosed philanthropist returned a few days later. He drove up in a cab well-filled with picture frames, and carried in his hand a photographic enlargement of Erchie's portrait.

"Ye're no' a bit like the picture o' ye I've seen in the papers, Mr Carnegie," said Erchie blandly to him. "Hoo are they a' at Skibo?"[4] But this was a sort of humour that passed uncomprehended over the head of the visitor, who proceeded to point out the excellence of the picture he had brought.

"And it's no' to cost me onything?" said Erchie, beaming on him through his spectacles.

"Certainly not," said the visitor. "We give ten thousand of these portraits — valued at five pounds each — away free."

"Tut! tut! it's fair extravagance," said Erchie; "a twa-pound ane would ha'e done me fine. Still, it's a nice picture; coudna be better!" He lifted it up, placed it on the mantel-piece, and stood back to regard it critically. "Champion!" he said. "Me to a hair! I canna understand the way ye dae't."

"Of course it's not quite finished yet," explained the philanthropist. "It wants a little colour put in. Let me see, what colour are your eyes?" and he whipped out a note-book to record this important detail.

"They're no' green," said Erchie, innocently. "In fact, they're no' ony colour that's worth botherin' aboot; the picture's fine the way it is."

"Oh, dear, no!" protested the visitor, with the fastidious-ness of real art; "I'll take it back and have the colour put in. Besides, you'll want it framed. The portrait is yours, absolutely free, but you may just as well let us have the framing of it. We are the biggest picture-framers in the country, and understand exactly the sort of frame to go properly with our presentation portraits. I have some neat frames with me which run from thirty shillings upwards —"

"Frames!" cried Erchie. "Man! I ha'e the very frame already to fit that picture; I got it in a restaurant I used to wait in. Rale oak!"

The philanthropist, using language quite lacking dignity or reserve, was edged to the door, and departed in his cab the loser by the value of a cheap enlargement, and Erchie returned to hang up his new possession in the parlour.

"It was lucky we didna need to bother Mr Carnegie for a frame," he said, as he and his wife admiringly regarded the portrait hung in a frame which bore the attractive legend:

BOTTLED ON THE PREMISES

82. *Harry and the King*[1]

"I HEAR," said Duffy, "that the King went the ither nicht to see Harry Lauder.[2] He's awfu' far behind; I heard Lauder a couple o' years ago in the pantymime."

"It's the ither way aboot," said Erchie. "Harry's been to see the King.[3] He couldna help himsel', even if he wanted no' to gang; he went by Royal Command."

"Whit's that?" asked Duffy.

"It's a sixpenny telegram sayin': 'Come here wi' the first train, and bring yer ain piano, Edward Rex.' When a man gets a message like that, he has to drop whitever job he's at, and ca' roond a' the newspapers tellin' them the train he's gaun wi' so that the reporters and photygraphers 'll be able to dae the occasion justice. The King was newly back frae his holidays on the Continent, and puttin' in a day or two extra wi' Lord Savile[4] in the country. Ye ken what the country is yersel' — nae relaxation; naething but wuds and parks, and he got awfu' tired o't.

"'Would ye like a book?' Lord Savile asked His Majesty.

"'I've read a' the books there is,' said the King, lookin' at his watch and gantin'. 'Is it no' near bed-time?'

"'Would Your Majesty no' like to hear a band?' asks Lord Savile, and the King said he was tired o' bands; he had heard that many on the Continent. 'I would raither a gramaphone,' said he.

"'Right-oh!' said Lord Savile, and hires a gramaphone and twenty records.

"It was a guid enough gramaphone; there was 'Put Me Among the Girls', 'Waltz Me Around Again, Willie', a piccolo solo, a banjo, and a bell effect, 'True Till Death' and 'The Cock o' the North' on the bagpipes, but naething wad please His Majsty till near the end, when he said, 'That's a champion yin! We'll ha'e the Italian again.'

"'It's no' an Italian,' said Lord Savile; 'it's Harry Lauder singin' Scotch.'

"'I've heard the name,' said His Majesty. 'Let me think, noo, dae I ken him?'

"'He's a' the go,' said his Lordship, windin' up the gramaphone again for anither start. 'Mak's his twa or three hundred pounds a week and drives his motor-caur.'

"'Heavens!' said His Majesty, "that's mair than we pay Winston Churchill. Whit can he dae wi' a' that money and him Scotch?'

"'He buys lands o' hooses,' said Lord Savile. 'Every week a tenement — that's Harry Lauder's motto, and he's a fly wee chap.'

"'Does he look jist the way he sounds on the gramaphone?' asked the King.

"'Jist the very same,' said Savile; 'only funnier, for ye see his legs.'

"'I wad like fine to see the chap,' said the King; 'Dae ye think he'll ha'e a dress suit?'

"'Shair,' said Lord Savile. 'He needs it when he's singin' 'Rocked in the Cradle o' the Deep'.'

"'Then I'll command him for the morn's nicht,' said His Majesty.

"'He's busy the noo at the Tivoli in London,' said Lord

Savile; 'The place is packed wi' people every nicht.'

"'Is it?' said the King. 'They wad be faur better at hame for yince wi' their wifes, and there and then he sent off the telegram.

"When Harry got the telegram, he was jist startin' for the Bank wi' a bag, and whustlin'.

"'Tuts!' he says to the chap that was helpin' him wi' the bag; 'this fame 'll be the death o' me.'

"'Is't anither marriage proposal?' asked his friend.

"'No, not this time,' said Harry Lauder, lettin' on he was readin' the telegram. 'It's frae the King. He says, "When are ye comin' to see me, Harry?" I think I'll start wi' the 2.10 train.'

"'It'll be in a' the newspapers,' said his friend.

"'So it will!' said Harry, lookin' awfu' chawed. 'That's the warst o't! But I ken the way to dae the deevils — I'll gang in disguise.' He went into the hoose, and disguised himsel' in a kilt o' the Leslie tartan, stuck a cairngorm brooch the size o' a soup-plate on his shouther, put on a Glengarry bunnet wi' a rampant lion as big as a door-knocker on the side o't, and a sporran that hung doon below his knees.

"'Ye're awfu' like Harry Lauder yet,' said his friend.

"'Am I?' said Harry. 'It's maist deplorable; but we'll tak' the back roads for it to the station, and naebody 'll be ony the wiser.'

"They went up the Strand and Fleet Street on their way to the station, and every time that Harry saw a man that micht penetrate his disguise he ran into a newspaper office until the man was past. By the time he got to the station, there was a crood o' 10 000 people efter him, and the tramway caurs were stopped. When he got into the railway cairrage they cried, 'Speech! speech!' and Harry jist put his heid oot the window, waved his Glengarry bunnet, and said, 'Ta-ta the noo, chaps; I'll put in a word for the hale o' ye."

"The King was lookin' oot the room window o' Lord Savile's hoose, watchin' the rain, when he saw a man in Leslie tartan kilts come in by the front gate. 'Savile,' he cries, 'Look here! Here's yin o' thae chaps from Braemar that flings the hammer or plays the pipes; go oot and tell him he's no' to start here.'

"'It's Harry Lauder,' said Lord Savile. 'Stop you, Your Majesty, and ye'll see a pant! Come on in, Harry; mind your feet on the lobby lamp. Soda or jist plain water? Say when.'

"'Harry did a step o' the Hoolichan, and then begood to sing 'Afton Water'.

"'Hold on! hold on! hold on!' cried His Majesty; 'This is no' gaun to be a Sunday School soiree, I hope. I was led to understand you were a comic.'

"'So I am, Your Majesty,' said Harry. 'A fair topper; but I didna bring my comic music wi' me. I thocht ye maybe wouldna think it cless.'

"'Then ye thocht wrang!' said the King. 'Whit ither sangs ha'e ye wi' ye besides 'Afton Water'?'

"Harry mentioned a dizen o' sangs like 'Mary Morrison', 'The Bonnie Banks o' Loch Lomond', 'Fareweel to Lochaber', and 'O' A' the Airts'.

"'Ye micht as well ha'e brung doon a wee red hymnbook and a harmonium,' said His Majesty. 'Ye'll mind that I'm on my holiday. Whit's yon song wi' the foreign chorus on the gramaphone, Savile?'

"'Stop your ticklin',' your Majesty,' said Lord Savile.

"'Then I command, 'Stop your ticklin',' said the King, settlin' doon in the easy-chair, and makin' ready to laugh.

"So the bold Harry starts 'Stop your ticklin' Jock', followed it up wi' 'Tobermory' and worked aff 'The Saftest o' the Family', 'I love a lassie', 'O'Callaghan', 'The Weddin' o' Sandy M'Nab' and 'When I get back again to Bonnie Scotland', before it was time for supper.

"'Ye're a great man!' said His Majesty. 'I don't ken whit way ye dae't.'

"'It's jist a gift.' said Harry, turnin' his Glengarry bunnet roond and roond in his hands, till he twisted the toorie aff.

"'Weel, I'm shair me and Savile's awfu' obleeged to ye,' said His Majesty. 'It's been a fine entertainment. Is there onything I could dae for ye? If there is, ye'll write me, and let me ken. Ye'll see my address in the Directory.'

"When Harry went awa' to the station to get the train back to London, His Majesty said to Lord Savile, 'That's a nice wee chap! No' a bit stuck up. But I thocht ye said he would be shair to ha'e a dress suit?'

"When Harry got to London he was met by a' the newspapers. 'Whit did ye think o' the King?' they asked him.

"'Oh, him!' said Harry. 'He's a perfect clinker. Right enough!'"

83. *Erchie on Heroes*[1]

"WE'RE IN for great time," said Erchie; "Carnegie's put by a quarter-a-million pounds to encourage the breeedin' o' British heroes, and a' the papers 'll be fu' o' gallant deeds.[2] Duffy, are you a hero?"

"Not me!" said the coalman, frankly. "I micht ha'e been, but I never got the chance. I ken a hero though — Wull Macintyre, that drives my lorry;[3] he saved a life in the Port Dundas Canal a week ago and got himsel' a' wet."

"Did he, faith?" said Erchie, with interest. "Then he should put in for Carnegie's pension. Tell him to get the application and fill it up."

"It's nae use," said Duffy. "Ye're no' a genuine hero unless ye're 70 years o' age, ha'e less than £31 a year, and havena been in the polis office."

"Tuts! man; ye're a' mixed up," said Erchie; "That's the Auld-Age Pensions."[4]

"I'll be a leear, then!" exclaimed the coalman. "I'm shair I went to the Post Office mysel' last Thursday, and tellt them I kent a hero that saved a life. 'That has naething to dae wi' us,' said the lassie at the coonter, lookin' through her specs at me; 'If it was money he saved I could recommend oor Savin's Bank.' 'Isn't it here ye apply for the pensions?' says I. 'Ye should ha'e said that first,' said she; 'Is he over 70?' 'No, nor over 40,' says I. 'Does he mak' £31 a year?' says she. 'He mak's his pound a week,' says I.

'Has he been in ony trouble?' says she. 'Often enough,' says I; 'but it's naething against his moral character; he's in the Camperdown Street Polis Office at this very minute.' 'Come back, if ye're spared, in anither forty years,' says she, snappin' aff her eye-glasses, 'and maybe he'll be eligible then.' So ye see, Erchie, Carnegie's money's no' for ony young or middle-aged heroes; ye must be on your last legs afore ye get it."

Erchie looked at the coalman with patient resignation. "Ye're sair mixed up," said he; "Carnegie has naething to dae wi' the Auld-Age Pensions. That's the warst o' never readin' the newpapers except in your bed on Sunday mornin'. They're two different things a'thegither; the Government gi'es the pension for Auld Age and Carnegie looks efter the heroes."

"They didna say onything aboot that to me at the Post Office," remarked Duffy, dubiously; "and it cost me three-pence in stamps, for I didna like to bother them aboot Wull Macintyre's case withoot buyin' something for the guid o' the hoose."

"Weel, I'm tellin' ye noo the richt way o't," said Erchie. "We're a' takin' oor share in paying the Auld Age Pensions, but Carnegie's payin' the heroes oot o' his ain pocket.[5] Ony man that's a hero efter this can depend on losin' naething by 't except maybe a leg, or his life, and then he'll ha'e the consolation o' kennin' that the money'll gang to his weedow."

"A' the heroes I ken are men's wives," remarked Jinnet. "There's puir Mrs Cameron up the stair — seven weans, and a man workin' only three days a week. She puts them a' oot clean and nice put-on, and ye never hear her voice complainin'. I can hear her sewin'-machine gaun birr-r-r at twelve o'clock at nicht. That's a hero if ever there was ane!"

"That's no' heroism," said Erchie; "it's jist auld-fashioned Scotch. It used to be quite common. Besides, it's done when naebody's lookin'; to qualify for Mr Carnegie's pension, ye need to ha'e a crood roond watchin' ye."

"Sandy Boyd the slater's a hero, then," said Duffy; "Mair than a hunder folk was watchin' him sclimbin' alang the tap o' a land in Grove Street yesterday, and him as fu's the eye o' a pick. It wad mak' yer hair stand on end."

"That's no' bein' a hero, either," said Erchie; "that's bein' an idiot. Besides, Sandy Boyd was daein' something he was paid for daein'. To be heroic, is to dae something desperate ye're no' paid for."

"I'm shair Mrs Cameron's heroic enough," said Jinnet. "She gangs to Maryhill on Setturdays to clean doon the stair for a puir auld body that canna dae't for hersel', and its a' because the puir auld body comes frae her native place, Kilbarchan."

"Tuts!" said Erchie, "wha' ever heard o' a she-hero exceptin' Grace Darling and Florence Nightingale? The heroic's a' in the hands o' the male sect; its like sailing ships, sodgerin', warking in the Fire Brigade, or throwin' the hammer; ye canna dae't in a frock."[6]

"Ye wad wonder whit we could dae if we tried," retorted Jinnet.

"Them flyin'-machine men'll come in for a' the money," suggested Duffy. "Ye'll no' deny it tak's a hero to skoosh ower the taps o' hooses on a machine that looks like a run-awa' washin'?"

"The flyin'-machine men'll no' ha'e a look in at a'," said Erchie. "Ye don't get ony o' Carnegie's pensions for hero-ism if bein' a hero's your tred. The men on the flyin'-machines are riskin' their lifes every day. So's doctors, and policemen, nurses, engine-drivers, colliers, quay-lumpers, sweeps, coalmen, and whiles waiters, but a life o' deleeb-erate heroism doesna mak' a hero; ye can only be a hero by daein' something awfu' sudden. A' the medals and a' the rewards for heroism are for the man that's been a hero for ten minutes; there's nae recogneetion for the deleeberate hero that keeps it up six days a week and a' the year roond, except at the Fair, when he gangs to Dunoon, gaes oot in a boat, and nearly droons himsel' to gi'e a job to some fancy hero that can soom wi' his claes on."

"Macintyre pu'd a chap oot the Canal in three meenutes and was that prood o' himsel' he was aff his wark for a week," said Duffy.

"Exactly! Quite richt too! The glory that comes frae bein' a hero o' that kind doesna last very lang, and Macintyre was as weel to mak' the maist o't as lang's it lasted. They'll cry 'hurrah!' efter ye for a week, and then they'll deny ye're a hero efter a' because ye're in debt wi' your grocer."

"Mrs Cameron's no' a penny in debt to onybody," said Jinnet. "And ye'll hear her singin' like a lintie in the mornin' so that naebody'll think she's bothered wi' her man. I yince was bold enough to say to her he was a wee bit foolish, and she nearly snapped my nose aff. 'If ye kent whit he cam' through!' says she; and I don't believe the crature cam' through onything by-ordinar'; it was the only excuse that she could mak' for him. She's the only kind o' hero I ha'e ony regaird for, but perhaps it's because I'm no' comin' much in contact wi' ony o' the ither sort."

"Neither am I," admitted her husband; 'But whiles I think I would like to be a genuine hero mysel', no' for the sake o' Carnegie's money, but for the pure sensation. I'm eften a hero in my ain mind. The gallant deeds I've done walkin' to my work or dozin' in the kitchen chair beside the fire. I've swum oot to wrecks and cairried hunders o' folk ashore; I've gane doon coal-pits naebody else wad venture in, and saved the hale nicht shift; if ye'd seen me rescuin' women from a fire, or leadin' a chairge o' cavalry against the Germans, it's a sicht ye wad never forget in a' yer deys. But I'm like you, Duffy; I never got the chance to be a hero, and maybe it's just as weel. I doot I'm ower auld to earn Carnegie's pension, and it's ane o' the consolations o' auld age that heroism o' that kind's no' expected aff ye."

"It's rale nice o' Mr Carnegie," said Jinnet, 'and I wish he kent aboot Mrs Cameron."

"It's nice enough o' him," agreed her husband, "but it'll no' mak' heroism ony mair heroic; Geordie Geddes'll no be able to dive into the Clyde[7] noo withoot makin' shair that somebody's lookin' that 'll maybe tell Carnegie. Chaps'll mak' it a profession, the same as writin' Limericks; they'll dae naething else but look aboot them for a chance to be heroes and get an independence, and the man that saves a life jist for the fun o' the thing'll never get ony credit."

84. *Mrs Duffy Disappears*[1]

DUFFY CAME tearing down Braid Street on Saturday night without his cap, looking like a man demented, and banged into Erchie at the corner.

"Hold on! hold on! hold on!" said Erchie; "Whit's the awfu' hurry wi' ye? It's no' near ten o'clock."

"I'm a lost man!" said Duffy, piteously; "The wife's gone awa' an' left me!"

"Has she, faith! My puir wee Duffy! If you had held on by her frock and no' gone loiterin' behind lookin' at the sweety-shop windows, this wouldna ha'e happened. The puir woman'll be fair crazy thinkin' she's lost ye, and I'll bate ye she's up at Camperdown Street Polis Office report-in' to the Sergeant. Gi'e me yer hand, and I'll tak' ye hame."

"Don't be comic wi' me, Erchie; it's no' a comic maitter, this," said the distracted coalman; "It's a case o' Suffra-gitis."[2]

"Is it you or her that has it?" asked Erchie, anxiously. "I aye tellt ye that ye should wear a camphor locket and breathe only through the nose when ye're takin' coals to thae tenements wi' the wally closes. Maybe it'll no' be an awfu' bad case. But there's a terrible lot o' trouble gaun aboot the noo; it's the open weather. See the doctor; he'll gi'e ye something in a bottle, and ye shouldna be oot in the nicht air withoot a bunnet on."

Duffy almost blubbered. "It's no' me that has it at a'," he said; "it's her, an' she has it bad. I never suspected onything till Macrae, the nicht polisman, chapped at the door ten meenutes ago an tellt me she wasna comin' back. Ye didna see the ambulance, did ye?" And the coalman

was about to pursue his impetuous flight again, when
Erchie caught him by the collar of his coat.

"There's nae ambulance needed for a case o' Suffragitis,"
said Erchie; "they tak' them a' in the prison van."

"My puir Leezie!" moaned Duffy. "There's four weans
to wash yonder, and naething in for my supper! If I had
kent it wad come to this, I wad ha'e been a better man to
her. Do ye think there's ony chance o' her gettin' better?"

"Whiles they dae get better," said Erchie, sympathetically, "but it's a trouble that ca's for great attention. Where
dae ye think she got it?"

"I canna tell ye," answered Duffy. "I never heard there
was such a disease till Macrae cam' in and tellt me. I was to
be hame at twa o'clock for my dinner, but I met a lot o'
chaps, and didna get hame till half-an-'oor ago, and she
wasna there, and the weans were in Mrs Macrae's. 'I'm sorry
to tell ye that your wife's awa',' said Macrae to me; 'Ye've
spiled her constitution wi' yer cairry-on, and she's taken
Suffragitis.' He says they'll maybe need to operate. Whaur
she got it I canna tell ye; there's naebody else in the land[3] has
it, and there I am, left wi' four weans, and no' a bit o' supper."

"As faur as the supper goes," said Erchie, "that's naething desperate; come awa' up to my hoose and Jinnet'll
gi'e ye something to ease the awfu' feelin' o' desolation."
And Duffy, a little comforted, went with him.

"If there had been ony warnin'!" said Duffy, as they
walked together. "But there was nane; it just cam' on wi' a
bang. She was a' richt in the mornin'; took her breakfast,
and looked tip-top. 'Be sure and be here at twa o'clock,'
she says, 'and I'll ha'e something special for the dinner.'
And Macrae says my no' comin' hame for my dinner was
on her mind. But ye wad think they wouldna cairry her
awa' withoot my sanction."

"The victims o' Suffragitis," said Erchie, "don't need to
be carried awa' in the early stages; they gang themsel's,
and ye canna stop them. I'm surprised that ye never saw't
comin' on. Was she no' droll in ony way!"

"She was sensible to the very last," said the bereaved

husband. "A' I saw oot o' the usual in her was the craze she had for readin' the papers and talkin' aboot the 'richts o' women.' I don't ken onything aboot the richts o' women, me bein' jist a coalman. It tak's me a' my time to look efter my ain richts, no' to mention the ree."[4]

"That's wan o' the symptoms," said Erchie. "If I heard Jinnet talkin' aboot the richts o' women, I would hide her boots, and buy her a present — an umbrella or a pair o' gloves, or something. The great thing is to catch the trouble in time. A man that has a wife showin' signs o' Suffragitis should never gang ower the door at nicht except to tak' her to a soiree; he should pay her every attention, the same as if he was coortin', cairry her parcels, gi'e her the best chair, tak' notice o' her new hat, praise her makin' o' scones, and say he never saw a bonnier dancer. He should tell her a' aboot his business, ask her advice, and let on he's gaun to tak' it. He should never be late for a meal, nor lose his temper, nor ha'e the look o' drink, nor put his dirty boots on her new-polished fender. He should —"

"Oh, bleezes!" said Duffy. "Gi'e us a chance!"

"I'm sorry for ye, Duffy," said Erchie, "but Macrae's richt — ye brocht it on yersel'. Is there onything missin' oot o' the hoose besides the wife?"

"Missing?" repeated Duffy, vaguely; "Naething that I ken o'; whit would be missin'?"

"No' the chains o' the kitchen nock, for instance?"

"Whit would she dae wi' the chains o' a nock?" asked Duffy with surprise.

"They're the first thing that a Suffragette mak's for," explained Erchie, "unless her husband keeps a watch-dog. Ye woudna believe the cravin' they ha'e for chains. The chain is whit oor minister would ca' the symbol o' female freedom. Gi'e her a railin' to fasten hersel' to wi' a nice thick chain and a padlock, and she'll reason wi' ye till the blacksmith comes to chip her aff wi' a cauld chisel. If your puir wife had Suffragitis in its maist aggravated form, ye're apt to come on her at ony moment padlocked to a fence to prove that she is free."

"My puir Leezie!" groaned Duffy. "There never was onything o' the kind afore either in her faimily or in mine. I had nae idea Suffragitis was like that; thocht it was something inward."

"It's the scourge o' modern times," said Erchie, "and if you were in the habit o' readin' onything else in the newspapers besides the triumphs o' the Celts, ye would ken that it's ragin' in London, where they can hardly keep them gaun in chains. The victims are padlocking themselves a' over the place. Whenever a Suffragette sees a nice thick railin' and a wheen o' men standin' close by, she fastens hersel' to't and swallows the padlock key. It would be a guid bawr to walk awa' and leave her there till the fit was bye, but the polis seem to be frichtened for the infection; they lift baith the railin' and the victim, tak' them awa' in the prison van, and ha'e them fumigated."

"Oh, Leezie! Leezie!" moaned Duffy. "Fancy her bein' fumigated!"

"Here's a man that's lost his wife," was Erchie's introduction of the coalman as they entered Jinnet's kitchen.

"Dear me! did ye lose Leezie?" asked Jinnet, gravely; 'That's an awfu' awkward thing to happen on a Setturday. But there's plenty mair to be got where she cam' frae."

"I'm no' wantin' onybody else but Leezie, and she's awa' wi' Suffragitis."

"Oh, thae Italians!" said Jinnet, holding up her hands, and Duffy's wife, unable to stand it any longer came out from behind the press door, where she was concealed.

"Did ye think I was lost?" said she, as he stared at her incredulously.

"Macrae said ye were aff with the Suffragitis," he stammered.

"It was jist a bawr we made up to frichten ye; I cam' here and sent Erchie oot to look for ye. I see it gi'ed ye an' awfu' fricht."

"And ye havena Suffragitis at a'?"

"Not me! there's naething wrang wi' me!"

85. *Erchie and Carrie*[1]

THE LADY came down the street, with her eyes on the signboards; she looked rather in a hurry, and the head of a quite business-like hatchet was protruding from her muff.

Erchie stepped off the pavement to give her room, and was much impressed by the hatchet.

"It's a wonderfu' thing the fashions," he said to himself. "Jist the ither day, as ye micht say, it was wee hairy dugs they were cairryin', and noo it seems to be the beginnin' o' a tool-chest. She's either a Suffragette gaun to a meetin', or she's startin' to hack her way into High Society. A business-like body! I'll bate her name's Sarah."

The lady stopped in front of him, sniffed suspiciously, and surveyed him with a searching eye.

"Say!" she remarked with an American intonation, "do you drink?"

"I have nae great grudge against a drink in its ain place," he replied, "but I never touch it, thank ye, through the day. If ye tak' my advice, ma'am, ye would be faur better wi' a nice hot cup o' tea."

"I'm looking for a saloon," said the lady, apparently heedless of this disinterested advice; "Are there any round about here?"

"Saloons," repeated Erchie thoughtfully. "Lots! There's Quadragaheni's Ice-cream Saloon[2] — the Rale Oreeginal — five doors doon, on the richt hand; there's Cam'ell's Hairdressin' Saloon at the fit of the street, and a shootin' saloon along the Garscube Road —"

"What I am looking for," said the lady, "are the hell-shops," and she fondled the handle of the little hatchet.

"Beg pardon!" said Erchie, with some astonishment. "I see ye're foreign. That's no' whit we ca' them in Gleska; we ca' them kirks. They're a' shut up except on Sunday, but I can recommend St Kentigern's; it's the best-heated and the cleanest kirk in Gleska, and I should ken for I'm the beadle. But ye wouldna need — ye wouldna need the hatchet to break your way in; it's hardly ever done here."

"Are you sure you haven't been drinking?" asked the lady, dubiously. "I understand that all you Scotsmen start drinking early in the morning."

"I daursay," agreed Erchie. "It's the best way; if ye tak' it in the mornin' ye get the guid o't a' day. But I'm a kind o' oddity; I havena the heid for't at ony time. Man! that's a nate wee hatchet!"

"Right here I want to know where I can find refreshment saloons," said the lady, impatiently.

"Oh, them!" said Erchie; "noo I understand. Ye're a lang way aff them; they're on the steamers. Tak' a skoosh caur[3] doon to the fit o' Jamaica Street; then the first turn to the richt, past a piper that's tryin' to play the 'Cock o' the North'; roond the end o' a red shippin'-box, and there ye are! Mind your feet on the gangway. It's a penny cheaper in the steerage end than it is in the first-class caibin, but they tell me the stuff's the same."

"You don't know who I am?" remarked the lady, with apparent disappointment.

"Ye have the advantage o' me, ma'm," said Erchie.

"I'm Mrs Carrie Nation,"[4] explained the lady. "I'm starting out right here to reform your saturated city."

"Carrie Nation!" said our friend, astonished. "And I was batin' mysel' a pound your name was Sarah! Noo I have ye. You're the Champion Bar-smasher o' the West. I'm prood to see you. Ye'll be finished noo in America? Whit are the puir publicans there turnin' their haunds to noo that ye've shut up a' their shops?"

"Ah!" said Mrs Carrie, sadly, "they're as bad as ever. What's a broken barrel or two, or the work of one weak, timid little woman?"

"True!" said Erchie, "true! But I thocht ye were sure to ha'e feenished them aff at hame in America afore ye cam' over here. Let me tell ye this — a hatchet's no' much use in Bonnie Scotland; what ye would need's a lot o' dynamite. We're an awfu' hard folk to shift."

"It rests with the women to remove this cursed evil," said Mrs Nation.

"It does that!" agreed Erchie. "If they would jist put sawdust on the kitchen floor, a brass rail alang the dresser to lean on, lay doon a gless case fu' o' pork pies, and a row o' fancy bottles, their men would stay at hame."

"Why *will* men go to to these infernal haunts of Satan?"

"That's the way I put it! Nae moral elevation, nae intellectual up-lift, nae money to be made in them. It's deplorable! I says to my frien' Duffy, 'Whit's the good o' gaun aboot the public-hooses?' and Duffy says, 'Nae good in the world, Erchie; but they're the only place where I can find my friends.' Ye'll excuse Duffy, Mrs Nation — he's jist a coalman. My! that's as smert a wee hatchet as I ever seen!"

"I am the sunshine carrier," said Mrs Nation. "I have brought hope to a myriad miserable homes. In the Middle West I am known as Birdie. You Scotsmen must strike a blow for freedom, and my axe is the symbol of the revolution."

"They say ye canna mak' a nation sober by Act o' Parliament," said Erchie, "but maybe ye'll can dae't wi' a hatchet, though my wife Jinnet has a faur better argument than a hatchet, and that's a hame-made haggis for supper."

"The Scots are the drunkenest people in Britain," said Mrs Carrie Nation.

"That's where ye're wrang, ma'am," answered Erchie; "We drink faur less in a year than the English or the Irish, a fact that's awfu' aggravatin' to Mr Duffy. He thinks it's no' fair horny. We drink less than oor neighbours, but they're mair discreet wi't; they can cairry't better. Ye see we're younger at it, we havena had the experience o' ither countries. Maybe we'll get better; it's jist a kind o' infantine disease like the hives or whoopin'-cough."

"It is the sin of the century," said the lady with the hatchet.

"Worse than that," said Erchie; "it costs a lot o' money, and it's unbecomin'. If ye're in a hurry to smash a bar or

twa afore your tea, I would recommend the Mull o' Kintyre
Vaults to start wi'; except for a gramophone whiles, they
havena ony entertainment. Maybe it wad be better if ye
sent them word that ye were comin', and they wad put up
a bill in the window:

To-night

at

8 p.m.

CARRIE NATION

Sardines and Cake

"Where are the public houses?" asked Mrs Nation,
preparing to go.

"A' roon' aboot," said Erchie; "ye canna miss them if ye
follow the croods. It's a pity ye havena a chain and a
padlock and ye could fasten yoursel' to the brass rail. Start
wi' the pork-pie In Memoriam case, and then mak' a
breenge for the wee gless barrels o' Extra Special, twopence ha'penny. Don't bandy words wi' the barman —
he'll be a large, big, red-haired, healthy man, wi' his mind
made up and it's nae use arguin' wi' him; hit him on the
heid wi' the hatchet, and that'll coont wan in the game to
you. I'll awa' hame and tell the wife I saw ye; her and you's
in the same grand movement to keep the men at hame,
only she believes in attractin' them there and you're for
drivin' them wi' your hatchet. It's a nice wee hatchet, but
in Gleska I think it wad need to be a gun."

86. *Duffy's Horse*[1]

DUFFY THE coalman came down from his stable in Dobbie's
Loan with a woebegone aspect, and, encountering Erchie,
explained that his dejection was due to the prospect of
losing another horse.

'I've done everything I could," said he, "but the mear's[2]
booked for a better land. That's the third I've lost in six
months. Cost me six pound ten and a couple o' mangers
she bit to pieces. Ye're weel aff, MacPherson, that has nae-

thing to dae wi' horses; there's nae dependence on them. Worse than women!"

"Did ye ever try corn?" asked Erchie. "They tell me it's a sure cure for onything wrang wi' coalmen's horses."

"It's a' richt if they have teeth for corn," said Duffy, "but this yin hasna ony. She's no' exactly a filly, and she spiled the twa or three teeth she had when I got her, wi' chewin' up her manger."

"It's time she was on the road to Rotterdam,"[3] said Erchie. "Aye, Rotterdam via Grangemouth, ye ken; I understood a Continental trip was the final stage for coalmen's horses. It's a kind o' Cook's Tour[4] for the puir craturs; a horse maun be gey far through if the Continental chefs canna mak' ony use o't. Hurry you up and send the mear away. It's no' a time for us to hesitate when there's ony chance o' anither wipe at Germany."[5]

But the coalman's melancholy was not thus to be dispelled. Walking down the street with his old friend, he discoursed upon the trouble he had always had with horses. They were costly to buy, and only to be fed at ransom prices. You had to groom them once a week at least, and all the vets in Glasgow, put together, couldn't keep pace with their invention of new and complicated ailments. "There's mair things wrang wi' that mear o' mine than ye would think four legs could stand under," he said, bitterly. "Every ither day, a new disease wi' a fancy foreign name for't. Macdougall the vet says he could run a College on her. He's takin' an awfu' interest in her case. 'Duffy,' he says; 'she's no' a mear at a'; she's a museum.'"

"What you want," said Erchie, "is a motor lorry. The day o' the horse is done, and ye should put on a leather jecket and a pair o' leggin's, an' move wi' the times. Look at the savin' a motor would be in mangers! A motor lorry wouldn't ca' for ony curry-combin' or ony o' Macdougall's fancy bottles."

"Jist that! but ye canna get a first-cless motor lorry for six pound ten, and that's the price o' a first-cless horse," the coalman pointed out. "And it costs far mair to feed a

motor lorry than a mear. There's such a thing as ile, Erchie
— petrol ile. If a motor lorry went wi' win' it would be
capital, but it doesna."

"Then there's naething for ye but a camel," said Erchie.

"A camel! I never heard o' a camel in a coal-cairt. The
thing would be ridiculous."

"A camel in a coal-cairt would be tip-top," said Erchie.
"Look at the advertisement! 'James Duffy, the only camel-
delivery coalman in the Tred! Coals by camel frae the pit-
bing to the bunker! Your coals will not cost you more though
brocht to the close-mooth by the Ship o' the Desert.'"

"Ship o' the Desert?" said Duffy; "I thocht ye were
talkin' aboot camels."

"So I am; the camel is ca'd the Ship o' the Desert, as ye
micht ha'e kent if ye had feenished your education. It covers
the trackless sands in great big spangs. The beauty o' the
camel is that it can go for days withoot meat or drink —"

"Eh!" exclaimed the coalman, roused to interest.

"— for days without meat or drink. It takes in a big
supply o' water at the oasis afore it starts wi' the caravan,
and doesna get the least dry till it reaches the ncxt oasis,
maybe thoosands of miles awa'."

"Michty!" said Duffy. "Whit aboot the puir drivers?"

"An oasis is no' a public hoose," explained Erchie, realising that his friend had made a perfectly natural mistake.
"In ony case ye may be sure the drivers'll ha'e refreshments wi' them; a bunch o' dates, maybe, and a skinfu' o'
wine."

"Drunken deevils!" said Duffy. "But maybe ye couldna
blame them, it bein' the desert. It'll be a sandy job drivin'
camels."

"Then, as for meat, the camel's easy put bye, for it lives
on its ain hump."

"Man! ye're an awfu' leear, Erchie!" said the incredulous coalman.

"It's a fact; ony book'll tell ye! Nature has provided the
camel wi' the hump, to keep it goin'. If it wasna for their
humps there would be nae camels. Pursuin' his way wi'

incredible celerity frae oasis to oasis, the camel needs nae feed but whit it carries on its back."

"I've seen a camel," said Duffy. "A camel's no' constructed in a way that would aloo o't turnin' roon its heid and biting its ain back."

Erchie laughed. "I didna say it had to bite its ain back," he explained. "It doesna need to bite onything; the hump kin o' dissolves inside, the hungrier the camel gets, and the beast gets a' the nourishment, and keeps on crossin' the desert in great big spangs."

"Criftens!" exclaimed the coalman; "it's like perpetual motion. If ye had a big enough stick ye could keep on raisin' new humps as lang's the camel had its twa legs to stand on."

"Twa legs," said Erchie. "A camel has four legs."

"Only twa," protested Duffy. "I've seen a camel — a great big coorse beast wi' twa legs it goes shauchlin' alang on."

"Tuts, man! ye're thinkin' o' ostriches," said Erchie. "That's a different kind o' quadruped a'thegither. It's the ostrich buryin' its heid in the desert sand that's confused ye."

"I could swear the camel I saw had only twa legs," said Duffy; "What'll ye bet on't?"

"I'll bet ye onything ye like," said Erchie, "and seein' we're near the Zoo, we'll jist gang in and see yin."

They went into Mr Bostock's[6] establishment in the New City Road. "Hae ye onything in the way o' camels?" Erchie asked an attendant in a uniform.

"Camels, sir; yes, sir — to the left. It's about your last chance to see the genuine camel in Glasgow," said the attendant. "The whole collection of wild beasts is to be sold off on Tuesday."

"We're jist in time," said Duffy, looking round the Zoo.

"You weren't thinkin', sir, of buyin' a camel?" asked the attendant, with an eye to trade; the visitors, for all he knew, might be in the showman business.

"My frien' here had a kind o' notion o' a camel if he got the exact kind to suit," said Erchie quietly, as Duffy walked up to where the camels raised their haughty brows and sneered at things in general.

"He couldn't get better in Great Britain," said the attendant, leading the way to the starboard side of a Ship of the Desert and slapping it affectionately on the hump. "Docile to a degree, gentlemen; a child could play with it. Never saw a pleasanter-dispositioned camel."

"Is he no' a bit chafed aboot the sides?" asked Erchie, and Duffy counted four unmistakable legs, and scratched his head.

"Chafed, sir?" said the attendant; "No, sir; not more than camels ordinarily is; he's a perfectly good camel. Money couldn't buy better. The children's pet we call him; lor'! many a little innocent child's been on that 'ump!"

"I thocht the Gleska Toon Cooncil was gaun to buy the hale Zoo for themsel's," remarked Erchie, paying no attention to the the coalman.

"It was proposed," said the attendant; "but they was afraid to go in for a Zoo on account of the opposition."

"Oh! I'm shair the ratepayers wouldna oppose the notion," said Erchie, innocently; "A Zoo's a kind o' education, like a picture gallery."

"It wasn't that sort of opposition I meant," explained the attendant; "They didn't want to support any counter-attractions of the same character, as you might say, to their own show."

"I could swear the yin I saw last time had jist two legs," said Duffy. "Is this the only kind o' camel ye ha'e? Ha'e ye no' ony two-legged camels?'

"The two-legged camels must be the Cam'ells that's comin'," said the attendant with a twinkle in his eye, "but they haven't come this length yet." And he turned his attention to other business.

87. *Erchie the Cheer-up Chap*[1]

"I'M AYE sorry when the days is lang," said Jinnet, pensively, as she pulled down the kitchen blind and lit the gas.

"Whit for?" asked Erchie.

"Because," said his wife, "it's almost like the start o' winter; the days'll soon be creepin' in again. Mind ye, Erchie, this winter I'll be needin' a new umbrella, and —"

Her husband burst into ribald laughter. "Oh, Jinnet!" said he; "ye're an awfu' woman. We're no' at the height o' summer yet, and here ye are lamentin' because it'll soon be bye. Ye put me in mind o' Duffy, the coalman — afore he was teetotal — and his beer. If ye put him in front o' a schooner he was aye sweirt[2] to start and drink it, 'because,' says he, 'if ye drink it, it's done.'"

"Ye canna chairge me wi' drinkin' beer," said Jinnet, irrelevantly; "I never could stand the taste o't."

"I never said ye could," protested Erchie. "What put that in your heid?"

"Ye said I put ye in mind o' Duffy afore he was teetotal —"

"Oh! to the mischief wi't!" said Erchie. "That's the worst o' arguin' wi' women; they tak' ye up a' wrang. Not another word! Ye'll get your umbrella when the time comes; ye'll get it the morn's mornin' if ye want it, but if I was you I would put it aff and buy a parasol; it's mair like the month o' June."

"I think I see mysel' wi' a parasol!" said Jinnet, picking up a stocking she was darning. "I wouldn't ha'e't a day when the weather would be shair to break. I've been looking for't to break every day for the last six weeks."

"That's six weeks lost then," said her husband; "Oh, ye o' little faith! I think, mysel', that things is jist tip-top. Cheer up, Jinnet! Look at the price o' eggs — they're doon to nine-pence, Irish, and ye hardly need a fire except to cook the dinner wi', or dae a bit o' ironin'. I'm feelin' fine! I'm fair exuberant! I'm strong! I'm well! I'm happy! I'm a great success and the world's magnificent!" And he slapped himself upon the chest, and pushed his specs up on his forehead, and blinked at his wife with roguish gaiety.

"Oh, Erchie!" she exclaimed; "ye're that joco![3] Ye should be humble, humble! Ye divna ken when onything might happen; ye might lose your job, or break a leg to-morrow. I canna sleep at nicht whiles, thinkin' wha would darn your socks if I was ta'en awa'."

"Look here!" said her husband, firmly, "what you want's a course o' the new magnetic treatment o' the mind; it would set ye singin' like a lintie in a day or twa."

"I never heard o't," said she, as she busied herself on the heel of her stocking.

"Of course ye didna," cried her husband; "ye never read onything but the news aboot the Royal Faimily and the fancy mairrages, whaur the bride gaes awa' in a navy-blue silk director dress, wi' a Merry Widow hat and a bunch o' lily o' the valley. Look at me! I'm studyin' Mental Science; its in a' the books — the *Don't Fret Series*, the *Cheery-up Primers*, the Christian Science Tracts."[4]

"I don't believe in Christian Science; it's a' a parcel o' nonsense."

"It's naething o' the kind; it's a branch o' Mental Science; it's as right as rain, and ye needna ha'e the toothache or a sair he'rt if ye ha'e the will-power no' to ha'e't. Listen to this — 'Has your life been one long winter, have the dark days of sickness settled down upon you? Have your plans miscarried? Have you erred? Take heart again. Have faith; for there is a good time coming right here on earth, that will not be dark for ever. 'Twill not be all disappointment, you will yet look into eyes that are true, you will yet hear lips that love; soon you will walk in the sunlight and say, "Behold, my Spring is here!" Have faith!' And Erchie, pushing back his specs again, looked up from the penny weekly paper in which this precious and inspiring counsel was provided.

"The man that wrote that hadna a sair back when he was at it," said Jinnet cynically.

"A sair back!" repeated Erchie; "There's nae such thing. It's a' a sheer delusion. Your back's no' sair when ye're sleepin'; that shows ye the pain is only in your mind. Ye may think ye ha'e a sair back, and go through a gross o' porous plasters, but it's a hallucination. Whit ye ha'e got to dae is to pull yoursel' thegither, and say to yoursel', 'I THINK my back is sair, but it's naething o' the kind; it's only kitly,' and then laugh. Keep on sayin' to yoursel', 'I'm fine! I could sclim' Ben Lomond or Dumbarton Castle!'"

"Indeed, and I would dae naething o' the kind," said Jinnet; "it tak's me a' my time to sclimb the stairs wi' a basket frae the mangle. If ye had my back whiles, ye would see it was nae hallucination."

"But I havena your back" said her husband; "and what wya ha'e I no'? Because I'll no' alloo' mysel'. I could ha'e the symptoms o' a whole Infirmary if I put my mind to that, the way I had when I started readin' *Buchan's Domestic Medicine*, but I'm no' that daft; I'm one o' the Cheer-up Chaps. Listen to this I'm gaun to read ye — 'Say that your stomach is all right; not only once, but any number of times, and mean it; your stomach will appreciate the compliment by making a special effort to be all right. Speak of every organ in the body in the same way, and they will do their very best to be as good as you say they are. Say that you have the best eyes in the world, the best lungs in the world, the best digestive system in the world. Say it to yourself, and mean it; say it to others when you are asked as to your health. If people think you are only talking, never mind; continue to praise your body, and it will positively prove worthy of more and more praise; continue to stand by all the organs in your system, and they will continue to stand by you.'"

"Indeed and I wouldna spoil my stomach wi' such flattery," said Jinnet. "If it'll no' dae the best it can withoot lavishin' a lot o' compliments on't it'll jist ha'e to dae the ither thing."

"The secret o' health, happiness and success," said Erchie, "is deep breathing, buttermilk instead o' beer, your bedroom window open, the *Path to Power Journal*, a penny a week, and a mind weel disciplined. Mak' up your mind for't, and ye can dae onything — be onything — stand onything. If ye don't believe me, listen to this." — and again he quoted from his paper — "'When you realise your birthright you will not be disturbed by anything that may happen; you will be so filled with thoughts of health, of harmony, gladness and peace that accidents and misfortunes cannot touch you. You will live in an atmosphere of love and joyousness. You are one with the spirit of joy; and are destined to a life of peace and gladness.'" He rose in his enthusiasm, reading aloud as he paced the floor, and Jinnet, fascinated, put her darning down, and said, "Oh, Erchie! ye would mak' a bonny minister!"

"The thing's as easy's onything," he proceeded, turning over a page. "'In the first place steady your mind and calm your feelings. Then pause for a moment and say the words, "I AM", calmly and forcibly, at the same time forming a mental picture of yourself as a Centre of Force and Power in a Great Ocean of Mind. "I AM WELL!" says you; "I AM JECK-EASY! I have no pain, no care, no worry. Everything is going fine. I'll NOT be anxious. I'll NOT be ill. This is NOT toothache; it is a plate of early strawberries. Is this a gumboil? No; it is a new gold watch I got the present o', and I am glad.'" That's the motto — Just be Glad! Oh, Jinnet, think what you and me has lost thae forty years thinkin' things was jist as bad's we thought they were!" And Erchie resumed his chair on which his wife had thrown her stocking.

He jumped up with a violent exclamation.

"Keep calm!" said Jinnet, solemnly. "There's naething wrang; ye're shairly some hallucination."

"Hallucination!" cried her husband, with a grimace; "it's twa inch o' darnin' needle."

"It's naething o' the kind," protested Jinnet; "there's nae such thing as a darnin' needle! Ye wouldna feel't at a' if ye were soond sleepin', and that shows you it's only jagged ye in the mind. If I was gaun to be a Cheer-up Chap, I would be a Cheer-up Chap and no' gang rampin' aboot the floor like a dancin' dervish!'

88. *Erchie and the Theatre Nursery*[1]

"TUTS!" SAID Erchie, putting down his newspaper with
some appearance of vexation, "you and me was born forty
years afore the right time, Jinnet; we're ower auld for half
the fun that's gaun on."

"If it's them flyin' machines ye're at again," said his wife
emphatically, "I'm no carin'; I would never put a fit in yin
o' them, for they're no canny; they micht cogle ye oot at
ony meenute, or gang that high up ye could never get doon
again."

"I wasna speakin' aboot flyin'-machines," explained
Erchie; "but aboot anither epoch-makin' invention you
and me 'll never be able to mak' ony use o' noo — the
Metropole Night Nurseries.[2] To get the full advantage o' a
Theatre or a Music-Hall noo, ye need to ha'e a baby, and
we've been kind o' oot o' babies in this hoose ever since
Willie went to sea."

"Dear me!" said Jinnet, quite interested; "babies seems
to be a' the go nooadays; Mrs Cameron was tellin' me the
Government's gaun to give £10 a heid o' Income-tax for
every child,[3] and her and Big Cameron's calculatin' that if
they're spared they'll be makin' enough to put the twa
auldest yins through the College by the time they're ready
for't. I'm shair it'll be a great help to mony a puir family. A
body needna be ill-aff noodays if she has a wheen o' weans
and a granddfaither maybe ready for the auld age pensions.[4]

Erchie beamed upon his wife admiringly. "Ye ha'e a
great grasp, Jinnet," said he, "o' the general situation. Ye
ought to be in the Liberal Caibinet wi' that cheery wee
chap Lloyd George. Whit dae ye think o' the Metropole
Theatre doon in the Stockwell? Listen to this." — and he
put on his glasses again, and read from his paper —

"'Mothers need no longer miss the Play; Fathers need
no longer miss the companionship of their Wives to
share their night of pleasure, so often experienced on
account of Baby! Henceforth the comfort of the Bairns

will be considered equally with that of their parents by the opening of Night Nurseries for their reception, in premises adjoining the Theatre, with access therefrom.'"

"Keep us!" cried Jinnet; "they're shairly gaun ower the score when they mak' ye bring a baby wi' ye to the Theatre. Whit'll ye dae if ye havena ony?"

"Oh, ye'll jist ha'e to get a lend o' yin frae a neighbour; it'll no' be ill to dae that in Gleska. Perhaps the Corporation 'll start a Baby-lendin' Bureau for hirin' oot puir wee smouts by the 'oor or evenin' as required."[5]

"They would be faur better in their wee beds," said Jinnet. "I'm shair the last time we were seein' 'Rob Roy'[6] I couldna hear a word o' Helen Macgreegor wi' babies greetin' in the gallery."

"It's to prevent the like o' that the Night Nurseries is bein' started," explained Erchie. "Ye mind when Willie was a baby, you and me couldna even get to see the pantymime."

"We werena wantin', I'm shair. Willie was a guid enough pantymime himsel'."

"Under the new system," said Erchie, "we could ha'e gane wi' Willy fine; put him in the Left Luggage Office wi' a half o' a ticket gummed on his back, and the other half in oor pouch to produce when we wanted to lift him again when the play was done."

"Mercy! I couldna leave my wean like that for the sake o' any play!" protested Jinnet.

"The weans 'll be a' richt," said Erchie; "this is whit they dae wi' them." — and he read again from the advertisement—

"'Spacious Rooms. Perfect Sanitation. Cosy Cots. Experienced Nursing Service. Toys for the Juveniles. Cakes, Milk Foods, and other Infantile Necessaries will be supplied at Moderate Cost, but Mothers will be quite at liberty to bring their own supplies, and, doing so, will not be expected to purchase on the Premises. If so desired, a young Sister, or Brother, may accompany and remain with Baby, thus ensuring his or her complete contentment.'"

"It bates a'!" exclaimed Jinnet; "I would be feared there would be such a habble when the theatre came oot that the weans would be a' mixed up, and they would give me the wrang yin."

"There's nae danger o' that; ye would hae the Left Luggage Ticket for that:

"'The Manager reserves the right to refuse to deliver up any Child to any Person whose claim, or Identity, he may have any reasonable cause to doubt until such is fully established. Also, Children must be Healthy, Clean and Tidy, and the Manager further reserves the right to refuse acceptance of any Child where such conditions are not complied with.'

"So it's a' richt, ye see, Jinnet; naething's left to chance. The parents are at liberty to come oot between the acts and see the babies, and it says here that 'Other Patrons may Inspect the Nurseries on Payment of three pence, the proceeds of which will be divided equally between the Nursery Expenses Account and the Actors' Orphanage Fund.'"

"There'll be a great run on them threepenny tickets," said Jinnet, "for babies, if they're nice, clean, happy babies, is faur greater fun than ony play. But oh! Erchie, I hope and trust there'll be nae accidents. Ye mind when Duffy's first wife brocht her wee lassie Patricia to the Wild West Show, and lost her among the Red Indians. Mrs Duffy was near demented; she was shair they would eat her child, and she jist newly into the Infant Standard!"

"There'll be nae fears o' Patricia at the Metropole Night Nurseries," said Erchie, "for there'll be nae Red Indians in them; and the only risk there'll be is that they'll maybe spile their stomachs wi' the Infantile Necessaries, and then their ain mither 'll be to blame for buyin' them. For a thing like that the Management is no' responsible:

"'Whilst every precaution will be exercised for the safety and welfare of the little Charges — the Manager realising that thus he will be ensuring the confidence of the future 'Met.' Patrons — their temporary housing will only be undertaken subject to the understanding (and such understanding shall be an essential of the agreement to accept their care) that neither the Metropole Theatre Limited nor any of its servants shall be held responsible to the parents, or any other person, for any Accident, Illness, or untoward Incident which may befall any child arising from any cause whatsoever.'

"Ye see it's a' richt," continued Erchie; "I aye like to see the word 'whatsoever' in a notice like that; it looks fine and fancy, and doesna dae onyboy ony hairm."

"What's an Untoward Incident?" asked Jinnet.

"Between oorsel's it's — it's anither name for colic," said Erchie; "They'll hae to put a limit on the cakes supplied to each baby."

"Ah, weel," said Jinnet; "the Night Nurseries 'll be awfu' handy for faithers and mithers that need them; it's a pity they havena got them in the kirks. If the kirks kept babies in the vestries, they micht be better filled on Sundays."

"Fitba' matches, too," suggested Erchie; "It's sad to think o' the thoosands o' well-deservin' faithers and mithers in Gleska that canna get to see a fitba' match on a Setturday because they canna get takin' a pram wi' them. If the Night Nurseries catches on at the Theatres, ye'll see the Celtic wi' a day yin at Parkheid. And they'll need yin, too, in the Hoose o' Commons, when the women ha'e the vote and are alloo'ed to sit in Parliament. Then ye'll read in the papers that the leader of the Opposition stopped her speech on the Budget for ten meenutes to gang oot and attend to Baby and that the weans of Westminster are makin' a demand for votes!"

89. *Duffy's Pianos*[1]

"TALKIN' ABOOT pianos —" began Duffy.

"We never said wan word aboot them," said Erchie, a little surprised at this abrupt departure from a discussion on horses.

"No, but I've put a wheen o' horse and a lot o' pianos through my haun's in my time, and the yin leads up to the other, as ye micht say. Ye can come to the last word aboot horse, but ye canna exhaust the subject o' pianos. I've been studyin' pianos for the last twenty years, and I could write a pamphlet on them if ye gi'ed me time."

"I wouldna write onything o' the kind if I was you," said Erchie. "I would mak' a lectur' o't, and ha'e lantern slides. 'Professor James Duffy on The Piano and How to Cure It'; 'Pianos I Have Handled,' 'Breakin' in the Young Bechstein,' 'Grand Pianos o' the Past' — man that last yin would be a fine lecture; you've had some droll experiences wi' yon grand auld piano ye used to ha'e in Braid Street; I mind the kitlin's."[2]

"There wasna much wrang wi' yon yin," said the coalman; "Ye could aye depend on gettin' a line o' some sort oot o't, but it took up an awfu' room. I never could see the sense o' spreadin' pianos a' over the floor when ye jist get the same noise frae them if ye back them flet against the wa'. But the grand was a' richt compared wi' a black piano I bocht in an auction sale. It looked a fair clinker — every note complete, wi' twa candlesticks, and only yin o' the castors aff, and when the wife had touched it up wi' a bottle o' embrocation, ye could see your face in't."

"That's the main thing in a piano," said Erchie, sagely. "Had it ony inside works?"

"Works!" said Duffy; "It was fu' o' works! Genuine iron-strung. It took me and four ither chaps to lift it up the stair. If it had only been the works! But ye see it was a piano that had been in a restaurant whaur they had smokin' concerts, and it got abused. Whenever the lid was lifted at the smokin' concerts, chaps begood to pap in corks and cookies and things, and the inside o' that piano, when we had up the tuner to't, was a perfect revelation. The tuner said it must ha'e been in use a while as a cinder-sifter, and there was mair lemonade wires tangled up in't than there was o' the wires that mak' the music. 'If I was you,' says the tuner, 'I wad put it awa' and buy a mangle; there's faur mair come-and-go aboot a dacent mangle.' I sent it to anither sale-room, and it lay for three years there; naebody would mak' an offer. Then the unctioneer sent me an account for stablin' it, and I tellt him just to keep the piano. It turned oot that the piano was that weel kent for years in the unctioneerin' tred they ca'd it the Lorryman's Pet. It was never aff the lorry."

"That wasna the first yin ye had," said Erchie; "I mind o' a yellow yin that looked like an auld-fashioned side-board."

"The Broadwood,"[3] said Duffy; "that was the yin that Sally learned on. It cost aboot a hundred pounds when it was new, but of course I got it second-handed. Ye could play onything on't and it never cost a penny for a tuner; it kept tuned itsel'. We should never hae pairted wi' the Broadwood, but ye see my wife said it looked that like common furniture folk never kent it was a piano at a', and your parlour got nae credit wi't. 'If we're gaun to ha'e a piano at a',' said she 'let us ha'e a piano that'll look the thing, and no' disguise itsel' like a chiffonier.'[4] Except for that, there was naething wrang wi' the yellow Broadwood; at least there was naething wrang wi't that ye couldna put richt yersel' wi' a tack or twa. A fine Setturday-nicht piano — nane o' your awfu' lood yins that annoy the land. But the wife would have it awa', and we got a Genuine Rose-wood Cottage. It was an upricht; at anyrate, it was upricht enough if ye put a book or something below the aff hind leg. The worst o' the Genuine Rosewood Cottage was that a note was missin' every noo and then, and that vexed Sally; she said at last she would sooner ha'e a mandolin or a dulcimer. The tuner was that often at it that he took a hoose in the next-door close, and was almaist whit ye micht ca' yin o' the faimily. He made a study o' the Genuine Rosewood, but he confessed at last it bate him. 'There's twa ways o' hatin' music,' he says; 'wan way is to like the melodeon, and the ither is to ha'e a piano like that.'

"Then," proceeded Duffy, "I saw a weedow lady that was gaun abroad was advertisin' a Walnut Tricord Cottage Upricht Grand that was a perfect marvel at the money. Ten pounds ten, and cost sixty-seven guineas jist a week or twa afore that. I went to see her oot in a private hoose at Shawlands,[5] and she wasna in, but a chap that said he was her only son explained the instrument and guaranteed the highest satisfaction. 'If it wasna a tip-top piano,' says he, 'we wouldna lower oorsel's to sell it; look at the solid hand-done carvin' on the panels! It's a piano (he says) that micht adorn the palace, and still-and-on be nae disgrace to a workin' man. There's pianos (he says) I would be ashamed to see comin' up my stair, but this is a piano that the Prince o' Wales himsel' micht tak' pride in.' I mesured it wi' a piece o' string, and found it was four inches ower lang to go roond the turn o' oor lobby. "That's a' richt,' says the chap, 'ye're in luck, for I happen to ha'e anither yin next door jist the very length, the same price, and if onything a bit better.' He took me to the back, and as shair as death, MacPherson, the room was fu' o' pianos. 'Your mither was shairly in the musical profession,' says I; 'she's awfu' weel supplied wi' pianos.'

"'To let ye ken,' says the chap in a whisper, 'she's no' my mither at a', but the wife's, and she's ta'en a craze for buyin' fine pianos; that's the way we're shiftin' her abroad. Buy this yin, and ye'll never ask to buy anither.' I paid the money for't, and took it hame. I'd ha'e been faur better if I'd bocht a big drum; the wud was new; it was warped in a week, and I see by the papers the weedow's still carryin' on business at Shawlands."

90. *Erchie Explains the Polar Situation*[1]

"THERE'S AN awfu' rush for the North Pole; what is't for?[2] Is't the skatin'?" asked Duffy.

"Skatin's the last thing a man would think o' trying' at the Pole," said Erchie; "It's no' for recreation folk go there; it's to mak' a livin'. Fifty years ago, when I was a laddie gaun wi' the mornin' rolls for Paterson the baker, the Arctic regions was considered awfu' dangerous; noo the only danger is ye'll maybe bung your heid in the dark against a flag-pole, or trip on a theodilite."

The coalman looked at his friend with some suspicion; "Ye're coddin'," said he.

"I'm daein' naething o' the kind; gaun to the Pole's a craze, like roller-rinkin'; it's a regular Royal Route; it would pay MacBrayne to run a steamer."[3]

"I would nae mair think o' gaun to the Pole than flyin'; I canna see what sport they get in't."

"Look at the ice and the fine fresh air ye get," said Erchie; "and the bawrs ye can hae wi' the Eskimos. If ye stun them first wi' a tune on the gramaphone, they'll swap ye £20 worth o' ivory tusks for a string o' beads, a couple o' tinnies, or a handfu' o' jujubes."

"They must be awfu' Neds!"

"Oh, aye, but they're fine for Polar explorin'. They reach the Pole as soon as onybody, but they never get ony o' the credit, for the puir sowls hae such comic names that naebody can mind them. It's only white men coonts. A chap like Peary or Dr Cook 'll take an Eskimo, a darkey, or a dug to the Pole wi' him, but he aye shoos back a man a mile or two frae the goal in case he'll no' get a' the glory to himsel' when he gets hame.[4] It would be rale confusin' for the women in New York if they had to mak' a selection who they would kiss."

"Kiss?" said Duffy.

"Yes. Did ye no see that when Dr Cook went ashore at New York it took an 'oor and a half for the women that were waitin' on the quay to kiss him. I'll wager the puir sowl was wishin' then he had brung back his Eskimos."

"What way do ye gang to the Pole?" asked Duffy.

"Ye start oot in the mornin' wi' an early boat, takin' wi' ye a gramaphone, a cinematograph, a hunderweicht o' jujubes, a bundle o' flags, and a box o' tacks —"

"What's the tacks for?"

"To scatter on the ice as ye gang alang, so that ony ither body comin' up behind 'll get their feet a' jagged. Every noo and then ye stop and mak' an observation."

"I would think," said Duffy, "it would be the chap that got his feet jagged wi' the tacks that made the observations."

"Ye reach the Pole, if ye've ony luck, afore it's dark; pick up a' the flags and things that ony ither explorers that micht had been there afore ye left, and put up some flags o' your ain. Then ye tak' your ain photograph in a dizzen different positions, and load your gun."

"What dae ye need wi' a gun?"

"In case there's onybody else aboot the place. Ye hae nae idea, Duffy, hoo narrow it is at the Pole; if there were twa men there at the same time yin o' them micht shoogle the ither aff, so ye tak' nae risks, but shoot at the first heid ye see that's no' an Eskimo. Then ye make a breenge for the nearest telegraph office scatterin' a' the tacks that's left, and send a wire to President Taft[5] tellin' him the Pole's his for the liftin'."

"Was it Peary or Cook got to the Pole first?" asked Duffy.

"I canna say, but Cook was first at the post office. He ran that hard he dropped his Penny Diary wi' a' his notes, a lot o' valuable instruments and a couple o' quite good Eskimos. But he had his telegram handed in afore the office closed, and the next day the whole civilised world kent that Dr Cook had found the Pole."

"Peary says he didna."

"Peary can say what he likes, but Cook was before him on the wire. When Peary reached the telegraph office a' oot o'breath, he was awfu' chawed to find that Cook had been there the nicht before.

"'What was he like, the chap that handed in the telegram?' he asked the lassie.

"'A black-avised man, awfu' needin' shavin', and he had a lump o' the rale oreeginal North Pole ice wi' him in a pocket-hanky,' says the lassie in Battle Harbour P.O., Labrador, puttin' on her muff to get oot to the roller rinkin'.

"'I kent it!' says Peary, near greetin'; 'it shows ye the man's a leear. Hoo could he be at the Pole and me no' see him?' And then Peary spends a pound on telegrams to a' the Crowned Heids tellin' them no' to believe that Cook was ever a dozen miles frae an hotel.

"When Cook and Peary had sent aff their telegrams, they started for New York. Cook got first to the place where the newspaper reporters were waitin'.

"'Ye fun' the Pole?' says they wi' their pencils ready.

"'I did; nate!' he says.

"'Hoo did ye get there?' they asked him.

"'Walked,' says he; 'if ye don't believe me, see my feet!'

"'What direction is the Pole?' says they.

"'North,' said Dr Cook.

"'Right enough!' said the reporters; 'was there onybody that seen ye there?'

"'Zermkzoo and Ookszleek, twa Eskimos; if ye don't believe me ask them yoursel' the first time that ye see them.'

"'Did ye tak' ony soundin's?' says the reporters, and the Doctor gi'ed yon genial laugh. 'I didna tak' soundin's or onything else,' says he; 'for there's naething at the Pole to tak' except it's your death o' cauld.'

"'Noo, hoo did ye ken ye were at the Pole?' says the reporters.

"'Fine!' says Dr Cook, 'because it's twelve o'clock in the day in front o' your face there, and twelve o'clock at nicht behind your back. I looked at my watch.'

"'Ye didna come across Mr Peary?' asks the reporters.

"'Peary,' says Dr Cook; 'wha's Peary? I never heard o' the chap. There was nae Peary yonder, that I saw; if ye don't believe me I can prove it on the cinematograph.'

"But if Cook didna ken onything aboot Peary, Peary kent a' aboot Cook. When he was makin' his way frae Battle Harbour, he spent a' his spare time on the road writin' a life o' Cook. He showed Dr Cook's grandfather was an escaped convict; that his father was an un- discharged bankrupt, and that Cook himsel' was a body- snatcher. 'What did Cook do?' he says. 'Stole a bunch o' my Eskimos that I was feedin' on the fat o' the land for years; plundered the places where I had planted pemmican —'"

"What's pemmican?" asked Duffy.

"It's a kind o' potted heid,"[7] said Erchie; "it's the favourite food o' the explorers. Pemmican and jujubes. 'This ruffian Cook was never near the Pole,' continues Mr Peary; 'and I can prove it. He's no gentleman. He had never ony intention o' goin' to the Pole; he hadna the richt sort o' boots for't, to begin wi', and he doesna know a word o' the Polar language. He was never oot o' sicht o' land. I've examined over a hunder Eskimos that's been keepin' their eye on the Pole since 1862, and they swore they never saw Cook there wance. The man should be put in jyle.'"

"They're jist spoilin' the Pole wi' a' their argyfyin'," commented Duffy. "But a' the same, it must be a gey ill place to get to."

"It's no' nearly sae ill to get to the Pole as to prove, when ye get back, that ye were ever there," answered Erchie.

91. *Erchie's Politics*[1]

"THERE'S something faur wrang wi' my eyes," said Jinnet, putting down the newspaper, and cleaning her spectacles with a corner of her apron. "I'll need to get a new pair o' specs, or something. I've looked, and I've better looked a' ower that paper for onything to read, and I canna see a thing but speeches aboot the price o' the loaf in Germany. I'm shair I'm no heedin' whit's the price of the loaf in Germany. I was never there. They must be awfu' hard up the noo for news to fill the papers."

Erchie finished his shaving, having used the Election Address[2] of one of the local candidates to clean his razor, and turned to his wife with a pawky smile.

"There's naething wrang wi' your eyes," he assured her; "and the price o' loaf in Germany's maist parteecular; everything depends on't."

"Is it different from ony ither kind o' loaf?" asked Jinnet.

"It's no like oor loaf at a'," said Erchie; "the German kind is made o' Indian corn and gunpoother, and it's black. The Germans eat it even-on, and that's whit mak's them so ferocious. They keep on eatin' it because they canna be shair whit the price'll be for ten minutes; the cost and the weight of the German loaf changes that fast ye would think ye were seein' it in yin o' thae cinematographs. It weighs two pounds at twelve o'clock, and at half-past three in the afternoon, when the evenin' papers comes oot, it's up to four pounds. It's fourpence the loaf if ye buys for your breakfast, sixpence ha'penny if ye want it for your tea, and elevenpence in a' the months that have an 'r' in them."

"Isn't that silly!" exclaimed Jinnet; "I'm gled I'm no a German. It would be an awfu' sin if Lloyd George brocht in a loaf like that to this country to bamboozle us. But of course we could a' dae oor ain bakin'."

"Then you're a Free Fooder?" said her husband.

"I am," she answered, "and thank the Lord we have aye

had whit would pay for't. I'm no owin' a penny to Mackay the baker."

"But look at it this way," continued Erchie, lighting his pipe; "Ye ken whit the Dukes are — livin' in their castles and carryin' on like onything? They want twa shillin's a quarter extra tax on corn because it's a raw product."

"Well let them!" said Jinnet, firmly; "Corn's a thing that never comes inside the hoose. It's the Dukes themsel's that keep the horses."

"I admit that's an argument," said her husband, with the air of a candidate who has to confess that his heckler has cornered him. "But on the ither hand the price o' the half-loaf would go up a ha'penny if foreign corn was taxed. Whit did George Adam Smith,[3] the great Free Trade man say to Mr Gladstone in 1863? He said — well, ye can see for yoursel' in the papers whit he said, and he was a man that studied the subject."

"Was he a Free Trader?" asked Jinnet.

"He was. He invented it. He was a Tariff Reformer, too, and the things he wrote aboot tariffs were like the ace o' clubs, nae maitter whit end of them ye look at it, they're aye the same; at least that's whit I gaither from readin' the Letters to the Editors."

"I wouldna be in favour o' a ha'penny on the loaf at a'," said Jinnet. "It's dear enough at threepence ha'penny, and they don't even gi'e ye a farden Abernethy wi't, the way they used to dae before they started politics."

"Then you're a Protectionist?" said Erchie,

"Indeed I am! If we didna protect oorsel's, what would dae't for us?" said Jinnet.

"It doesna maitter whether there's a ha'penny on the loaf or no if ye havena the money to buy a loaf at ony price, and that's the argyment on the other side," continued Erchie. "If you calculate that the Germans can build three Dreadnoughts[4] a month; that a suit o' claes costs six pound ten in America; and, that £5,604,324 worth o' boot protectors came into this country from abroad in 1893, ye can see for yoursel' that somebody must pay for the extra cost o' country eggs."

"Eggs is dear enough this winter," said Jinnet, sharply; "and wha's to pey the extra?"

"That's the point," said her husband. "I've gone into the thing carefully, and I see quite plain that the exporter, the importer, the shop-keeper, and the hen-farmer are gaun to quarrel among themsel's to get payin' 't. The only body that's jeck-easy about the hale thing is the hen. And that leads us up to anither point — do we pay for imports wi' exports, or do we jist send the money? There's no' the slightest doot that when we imported £2,646,408 worth o' Geneva watches into British ports in 1908, the Geneva watchmakers must have got something in exchange. What did they get? They got Bills o' Exchange. They cashed them pretty smart at the Post Office for gold. That bein' so, they got gold for their watches, and £2,646,408 of good British gold that micht hae paid the wages o' 6,432 British workmen for seventy-nine weeks at £2.10s. a week no' coontin' the Gleska Fair, went to pamper the foreigner."

"It shouldna be allood!" said Jinnet, emphatically. "I'm against puttin' money oot o' the country."

"Exactly!" said Erchie. "You're a Retaliator. But if ye look at it this way, gold's no use —"

"It's gey handy, whiles." said Jinnet; "I wish I seen mair o' 't."

"— It's no use; it's jist a medium o' exchange. Ye canna eat it, nor mak' a topcoat oot o't, nor use it in the kitchen grate. The gold the chaps in Geneva got for their watches was the equivalent o' labour. You tak' a man on a desert island, where there's nae minin' royalties, and say that in three years he imports 654,000 tons o' beet sugar and exports 1,642,000 tons o' whale bone —"

"Tuts! I'm aye startin' to read aboot that chap on the desert island," interrupted Jinnet; "but there's naething worth while readin' aboot ever happens to him. And ye needna try to bamboozle me wi' a' thae figures, for I canna understand them."

"Right!" said Erchie. "Neither can I. But they sound fine and big, and that's politics. When a man starts to be a politician he buys a Ready Reckoner, an almanack for the year afore last, and a book aboot astronomy. He multiplies the day o' the month by 79 and divides by the distance to Jupiter, and havin' got his information that way sends it in a letter to the papers heided 'Exports v. Imports: Which?'

"I'm aye feared for thae Germans," said Jinnet, a little irrelevantly. "Dae ye think they're gaun to fight us?⁵

"Them!" said Erchie, contemptuously. "They'll no' fight us as lang's we tip them dacently. I ken hunders o' German waiters here in Gleska, and ye coudna chase them hame — nice enough chaps, tae. They mak' faur mair money aff takin' orders in the restaurants here than they would mak' by fightin' us. Forbye, they havena the time to fight, the Germans; they're so busy buildin' men-o-war."

"Whit for?" asked Jinnet:

"For fun," said Erchie. "And the mair they build the better for us, for that mak's us build men-o'-war tae, and brings work to the Clyde. The warst thing that could happen to the Clydebank rivetter would be a Universal Peace."

"But we ha'e to pay for the new boats a' the same," Jinnet pointed out, and her husband twinkled.

"H'm!" said he; "ye're awfu' ready wi' your argyments; if ye don't tak' care ye'll be a politeecian yoursel' before the election's over. Leave you a' the politics to men;⁶ we understand them better."

"I'm no' so shair," said Jinnet. "Are you a Liberal or a Tory?"

"As shair as daith," he replied, "I canna tell. I'm baith o' them time aboot, and I canna mak' up my mind as lang's I read the papers."

92. *A Menagerie Marriage*[1]

ERCHIE CAME home two hours late for his supper.

"Whit in a' the world's come ower ye?" said his wife, with a significant glance at the clock.

"I was at a mairrage," replied her husband, taking off his coat. "Bostock's Jungle.[2] A.1. They played 'The Voice that Breathed O'er Eden' on the drum and cornet, and the bride, hypnotisin' the lions, wi' yin e'e', and keepin' her ither on the bridegroom in case he would change his mind, swore to love, honour and obey. It went aff wi' a bang. I've never seen a cheerier weddin'."

"Tuts!" said Jinnet; "ye're haiverin', will ye ha'e an egg?"

"I'll ha'e twa eggs, and I'm no' haiverin'. I've been at a mairrage in the jungle. The determined and happy couple went into the lions' cage. The bride wore a white silk dress and a bunch o' lily o' the valley, and the bridegroom, in a dark blue corded mornin' coat, took his posection next the gate. 'Whit new game is this?' says the lions to themsel's, gantin', and the minister hurried through wi' the thing in case they would mak' a breenge. At a distant part of the arena the monkeys sat disconsolate on their hunkers, wonderin' whit way they were neglected. 'Where's them peanuts?' they says to themsel's. 'Are we, or are we not, entitled to some public recognition?' But the fickle public hadna a single peanut or a gingersnap for the monkeys; that's the worst of a mairrage matinee — it distracts attention from the regular hands."

"I suppose ye're talkin' aboot that lassie that mairried the lion-tamer," suggested Jinnet. "He must be awfu' busy when he had to tak' her into a cage to mairry her. Was the lions no' awfu' angry?"

"It wasna a lion-tamer at a'," said Erchie; "it was jist a common workin' chap. 'Noo's the chance for ye to mak' a reputation for yoursel',' they tellt him; 'Be mairried in a lions' cage, and ha'e your name in a' the papers.'

"'Could I no' be mairried among the love-birds, or sittin' on an elephant?' he says.

"'There's naething for't but the lions' cage,' says Mr Bostock, firmly; 'Whit we want to prove is the sagacity o' the animal.'

"'But the lions micht mak' a dash at us,' said the chap.

"'Whit's the odds?' says Mr Bostock; 'Ye're gettin' mairried onyway! Everything'll be tip-top — a rale minister wi' Geneva bands on, a brides-cake, a cab, and a poke o' confetti. Whit mair could ye ask for?'"

"I'm gled," said Jinnet; "there were nae operatics o' that kind at my weddin'. I would rather no' be mairried at a' than mairried in a cage, like a canary. Whit's the sense o't?"

"It's an American idea," said Erchie. "A kirk's the last place on earth onybody would think o' mairryin' in in America; the ceremony must tak' place in a balloon, or doon a coal-pit or in a warehoose window. The thing's so common there that they ha'e a special breed o' minister that spend most o' their time in balloons, coal-pits or warehoose windows. We have been a little late in taking up the idea in Scotland, but if ye're spared ye'll see mairrages on the stage before the transformation scene in the pantomime; on the roller rinks; in billiard-rooms; and at half-time at the fitba-matches. The common mairrage in a kirk, or up a stair wi' a wheen o' laddies cryin' 'Hard up!' at the fit o' the close 'll be oot o' date in nae time; ony pushin' young man that's thinkin' o' enterin' the sacred bonds o' matrimony 'll no' be blessed unless he can hae a brass band, and five or six thoosand folk lookin' on."

"Did the lions growl?" asked Jinnet.

"They did not!" said Erchie, taking off his boots. "They didna want to ha'e anything to dae wi' the thing at a', and the trainer had to egg them on. I was vexed for them lions, they would be faur happier scourin' the desert plains o' Africa than sittin' like a lot o' neds at a mairrage pairty wi' naething to eat. They never got the least chance, for three or four tamers with a pistol in every hand stood between them and the blushin' pair, and—"

"Were they railly blushin'?" interrupted Jinnet.

"They were," said Erchie. "At least the bride was; the bridegroom he had his back to the lions, and every noo and then he gi'ed a glance over his shoother to see if onybody was gaun to heave a coconut. The minister kept near the gate, handy for backin' out if there was any need for't; and he had the pair mairried before the lions could mak' up their mind whether they would start wi' the bride or bridegroom."

"'Ha'e ye that ring aboot ye?' says the minister to the bridegroom.

"'It's in my hip p-p-pocket!' says the puir chap trimlin' in his shoes.

"'Oot wi't slippy then, and put it on her finger,' says the minister; 'The big yellow yin's lickin' his lips.'

"The bridegroom slipped on the ring, and then dashed for the door, and ye never saw lions mair chawed."

"Did he no' kiss his wife?" asked Jinnet.

"He hadna time. Forbye, he wouldna like to dae't wi' such a lot o' strangers lookin' on."

"I canna understand whit in the world ye went to such a performance for, and you a beadle," said Jinnet. "I'm sure ye've seen plenty o' weddin's."

"Hundreds," agreed her husband. "But this was a bye-ordinar' weddin'. There was aye a chance that the lions micht be hungry, and I've never seen a lion swallow a bridegroom. Duffy was wi' me, and he was awfu' disappointed; 'I wouldna care though the lions let the newly-mairried couple aff, for it's bad enough to be mairried,' he says, 'but the least the silly brutes could ha'e done was to chase the minister. Whit did we pay oor shullin' for? I doot, MacPherson, the management's gaun awa' and fed thae lions up afore the weddin' started. Either that or they should ha'e a fatter minister.'"

"Was he a rale minister?" asked Jinnet, with surprise.

"Of course he was a rale minister; he made a speech to the audience frae the inside o' the cage, and tell't them that he wouldna ha'e been there that nicht at a' if it wasna that

he was sure a mairrage in a lions' cage was a moral and
spiritual exhibeetion. Some o' the people laughed at that,
and later on he expresed his surprise that they didna realise
the solemnity of the occasion. It was solemn enough for
the puir lions — no' a bite of onything a' the time."

"Was he no' nervous?"

"He must ha'e been, for he forgot to mak' a collection;
and he didna dwell on the moral lesson."

"Whit was the moral lesson o' the mairrage in a
menagerie?" asked Jinnet.

"I would ha'e to see the Rev. Mr Morris and ask him,"
said her husband; " I couldna find out mysel'. But I can
tell ye I was vexed for them puir lions!"

93. *Erchie and the Earthquake*[1]

ERCHIE, WHO had fallen asleep by the kitchen fire in an
effort to discover, by the utmost concentration of his
intellect upon a newspaper leading article, whether it was
the Unionists, the Liberals, the Nationalists, the Irish
Americans, or the Socialists who were winning the
Election, awoke suddenly with a startled movement which
upset the winter-dykes on which Jinnet had been toasting
some of his own professional linen.

The tin tea-caddie on the mantelpiece had toppled over
on its side, and was trickling a sample of the Finest Tea the
World Produces, at 1s. 7d. per pound straight from the
Plantation, on to the hearth-stone; the Bonnie Lass of
Ballochmyle (Wilson the Grocer's Calendar, 1910) was
strangely swinging from side to side on the tack
suspending her over a pair of cast-iron sheep which Jinnet
faithfully black-leaded every time she did the grate. Two
highly-polished Britannia-metal dish-covers that had
never been used for their legitimate purpose, and were
merely ornamental, like the cast-iron sheep, were shaking
and tinkling against the wall they hung upon above the
coal-bunker, and every plate on the dresser rattled.

"I'll bate ye whit ye like that's McCallum the sailor hame from another voyage," said Erchie, looking up at the ceiling; "I wonder what he brought this time; it sounded awfu' like a chevalier-and-bookcase."

Surprised to get no answer from his wife, he turned about in his chair, and was even more surprised to see her bent below the set-in bed.[2]

"My! what a start I got!" she exclaimed, when she had emerged. "I was shair that Williamson's cat had got in this afternoon when I was washin' doon the stair, and shut himsel' up in the wee tin trunk I had at Rothesay. But there's nae cat there, and I'm a' in a palpitation!"

"Did it soond like a cat?" asked Erchie.

"It wasna exactly a soond, but jist a queer sensation. First I felt the soles o' my feet a' prinklin'; then the caddie coupit, and the delf begood to rattle on the dresser. I could swear the hale o' the land was shakin'."

"It's whit I tellt ye; it's McCallum hame from sea," said her husband, confidently. "Wait a wee and ye'll hear yin o' his kahootchy top-boots gaun bungin' into the back coort through his kitchen window. Ye canna blame the chap. Awa' from his wife and weans for nine months even on, and nae sport!"

"It's no' McCallum, whatever it was," said Jinnet, picking up the winter-dykes. "She tellt me yesterday he was awa' where the nutmegs comes frae, somewhere aboot Calcutta, and wouldna be hame till February."

"Then it's Willy Grant comin' up the stair, and the wrang man's in for the Curmunnock Burghs.[3] Gang to the door and see if he hasna tummelt on your bass."

Jinnet went to the door and returned to report that nobody was on the stair. "It wasna like a man comin' hame at a', for there wasna ony noise wi't," she said to Erchie; "It was mair like something happenin' at a distance; it was — "

She was interrupted by a second tremor of the house; the tea-caddie toppled over again, the Bonnie Lass of Ballochmyle fell off her tack, and the crockery clattered even more extraordinarily than before.

"We'll hae to look into this wi' a candle," said her husband, when he had recovered from his astonishment. "I'm afraid the gasalier's awa' wi't in the paurlour. Naething less than the fa' o' yon twa hunderweicht o' chains and weichts and brass bunches o' grapes, and curly-wurlies, and cut-glass globes, no' to mention a gallon o' water I put into't last week, would account for ony dacent hoose behavin' like this, and me, as ye micht say, quite teetotal. And I thocht it was McCallum! McCallum couldna mak' a stramash like that, even if his wife, puir body, kept a mangle."

They lit a candle, and went apprehensively into the room.

The gasalier was still suspended from the ceiling, as magnificently ponderous as Erchie had suggested; but a what-not, the pride of Jinnet's heart since her son had made it mainly out of empty cotton-reels, had fallen forward, and its contents were scattered — fortunately little damaged — on the floor.

"Oh Erchie! Erchie!" she exclaimed; "I was shair frae the start it was Williamson's cat."

"If Williamson's cat was the size o' a dromedary, and was dancin' the Hoolachan afore your very e'en, it couldna shake the hoose like yon!" said her husband, with impatience, looking, with the candle, underneath the table. "It looked to me mair like as if they had started to tak' doon the Hoose o' Lords."[4]

"Do ye think it micht be that?" asked Jinnet, seriously, thinking of explosions.

"Weel, no," he admitted; "it hadna the proper dunt for that."

"Maybe it's a judgment, for them middlin' wi' the Hoose o' Lords," said Jinnet, setting up her what-not. "If I was gaun to tak' doon onything o' that kind, I would start wi' the Hoose o' Commons. Naething'll convince me it's no' that cat o' Williamson's!"

"A cat couldna stop a nock, and there's the nock stopped," said her husband, when they returned to the kitchen;

but this, at least, was not to be attributed to any mysterious agency. Jinnet pointed out that the weights of the wag-at-the-wa' had naturally run down.

"If it's no' a cat, and ye have yet to prove it's no' a cat," said Jinnet; "it's electricity! Look at a' thae 'lectric lights in the butcher's windows; and their motor-caurs, and their skoosh-caurs scourin' up and doon a' day; and their telephones and telegrams and cinematygraphs — they're usin' up the substance o' the air, so that even a tack'll no' haud up a calendar. I was readin' in the papers just this very day that the way its awfu' wet in London is because they're cuttin' doon a lot o' trees in Canada."

Erchie laughed. "Hoo could cuttin' doon trees in Canada bring on the rain in London, ye wee fuiter?" he asked.

"It's a thing they ca' the Gulf Stream," she explained; "and I'm no' a fuiter! There's hot air, and there's cauld air; and every time ye cut a tree in Canada there's a blash o' moisture comes on the Gulf Stream — Mercy on us, whit's that?"

The door-bell had rung violently; Erchie went to the door himself, and gave admission to Duffy the coalman in a state of intense excitement.

"Did ye feel it?" he inquired, when he reached the kitchen.

"The only thing I feel is a smell o' the Mull o' Kintyre Vaults," said Erchie. "I hope you and your friends doon there are daein' the best they can to keep the country gaun till this election's settled."

"Did ye no' feel the earthquake?" asked Duffy, heedless of this irony. "Man, the hale o' Gleska's shooglin' like a calf's-feet shape."

Erchie looked at the stopped clock with some surprise; it indicated only a little after nine. "I had nae idea it was efter ten, Duffy," he remarked. "Oor clock's stopped. Was it jist an ordinar' ten-past-ten o'clock shoogle, or something extra-special for the Elections?"

The coalman sat down in a chair and recounted a thrilling tale; which carried conviction with it. Tea-caddies, calendars, and tin dish-covers had been falling all over the city, and a man he knew had had a pint of ale upset. Mrs Duffy had taken the weans with her, and had left her house to take refuge in her sister's out at Maryhill, with some idea that she could depend on the protection of the British Army.

"Oh, Erchie!" wailed Jinnet. "I tellt ye it was a judgment. They didna need to touch the Hoose o' Lords; they could jist let on they were gaun to tak' it doon."

"And they say, doon at the Mull o' Kintyre Vaults, that we havena passed the worst o't yet," proceeded Duffy with gloomy pleasure. "There's aye three shocks; the third'll come afore twelve the nicht, if it comes at a', and then ye'll see a pant!"

"Oh, mercy be aboot us!" cried Jinnet, wringing her hands, "and me wi' a great big ironin' the morn!"

"Wha tell't ye that aboot the three shocks?" inquired her husband.

"A gentleman that's an expert aboot earthquakes," answered Duffy. "He was yince a stoker on a boat that went to Demerara, and he's sellin' alarm clocks. Splendid sonsy, wee, round, tin, white-faced yins, wi' an awfu' birl; he was askin' haulf-a-croon for them till the earthquake happened, and noo he's takin' eighteenpence to get them aff his hands afore the toon collapses. I tell ye there's a wheen o' wiselike clocks changed hands the nicht doon yonder at the Mull o' Kintyre Vaults."

"And whit are ye a' wantin' wi' alarm-clocks if the earthquake's gaun to swallow Gleska in anither oor or twa?" asked Erchie. "Are ye frichtened that ye'll sleep in and miss it?"

"And we havena even the richt time!" moaned Jinnet, hauling up the clock-chains.

"Do ye railly think there's ony danger, Erchie? We micht sleep for the nicht in Mrs Williamson's."

Erchie laughed. "I would sooner risk the earthquake than her cat," he answered. "There's no' enough o' fushion in a Scottish earthquake to upset a barrow."

"Onyway," said Duffy, making his departure, having duly warned them; "I'm gaun to live a better life if I get ower the nicht wi't."

Twenty minutes later Jinnet was in bed, convinced that that was the safest place to be in case of an earthquake.

"Erchie," she said to her husband, who had resumed his paper; "push back that tea-pot on the hob a wee; if Gleska's gaun to be swallowed up, I would be vexed to lose my good new teapot. And me plannin' for a great big ironin' in the mornin'!"

Five minutes later she was fast asleep.

94. *Erchie and the Census*[1]

DUFFY THE coalman came round to MacPherson's house on Saturday night with his Census schedule[2] carefully wrapped in a newspaper as if it were an exquisite rare etching or a Commission of the Peace.

"Do ye understand anything aboot this?" he asked, unfolding it. "There's a chap comin' roond to lift it again on Monday mornin', and it'll tak' me all that time to read it."

"I've jist filled up my ain this efternoon," said Erchie. "A solemn occasion, Duffy! We're ten years aulder than we were when we did it last, and I sair misdoot we're no' much better men. Have ye read the instructions carefully?"

"I have not! It cam' to us yesterday, but I didna want to examine it much till I washed my hands for Sunday, and noo that I'm washed I canna find my specs. I wish ye would gie me a hand. I'm tellt that if ye mak' the least bit slip-up in fillin' it up it's a five pound fine. Nae wonder sae mony folk's gaun awa' to Canada!"

Erchie's wife produced the ink-pot and a pen; he took off his coat, drew up his chair to the kitchen table, spread Duffy's schedule out before him, and glanced over his glasses quizzingly at the coalman.

"I see they've put ye doon here already as the heid of the family," he remarked. "Whit does Mrs Duffy say to that?"

"That's richt enough," said Duffy; "I'm the heid o' the hoose: I pay the rent o't."

"But it's her that saves it; if it wasna for her I doot ye wouldna hae a hoose to be the heid o', and would be haein' your name put doon to-morrow nicht for a lodger in a Model. Whether we pay the rent or no', Duffy, I'm afraid it's the last chance we'll hae in a Census paper to put oorsel's doon for heids o' faimilies; the Suffragettes is gaun to parade the streets on Sunday to show that they hae no heids o' any kind."

"Number o' rooms," proceeded Erchie, "including kitchen, wi' one or more windows occupied by the person or persons entered on the schedule?"

"I never occupy a window frae wan end o' the week till the other," said Duffy. "If there's ony windows that ye could ca' occupied in oor hoose, it's by the wife, and it's the parlour yin; she's generally hingin' oot[3] o't watchin' funerals."

"Hoo mony rooms hae ye wi' windows in them no' coontin' sculleries, pantries, or bathrooms?"

"Twa rooms and kitchen, a fine big lobby,[4] and a share o' a washin' hoose."

"Washin' hooses don't coont," explained Erchie, "nor lobbies either. There's nae windows in a lobby."

"There's a window in oors," insisted Duffy, "a wee yin wi' a broken pane above the ootside door."

"But ye canna live in a lobby, man," said Erchie; "It's only rooms ye can live in that they're wantin'."

"Can ye no'? When my wife starts spring cleanin' in a week or twa the lobby'll be the only pairt o' the hoose I'll can turn mysel' roond in. I think I would chance the lobby, Erchie; twa rooms and kitchen for a faimily o' nine looks awfu' shilpit. Forby, there's three fine presses."[5]

"Three rooms," said Erchie, emphatically. "No' a room more, or they'll fine ye! Noo for the names and ages — James Duffy, heid o' faimily; aged 69 —"

"Haud on!" cried Duffy. "Nane o' that! I'm naething like 69; I'm nearer 59."

MacPherson put down his pen. "Tak' my tip, Duffy," he said, "and don't be an idiot tryin' to pass yoursel' aff for 59. Ye'll be wantin' an auld age pension in a year or twa, and then ye would look awfu' silly if your ain Census paper made ye oot a leear. Whit's your actual age?"

"It's 65," said Duffy, hastily. "The very day I was born in Wishaw they started the Caledonian Railway."

"Nae Gaelic?" proceeded Erchie. "Mairried, of course; Personal occupation — coalman, own account; born in Lanarkshire, Wishaw.[6] Ony infirmities?"

"I racked my back a week ago liftin' my horse on its feet in the stable," said the coalman.

"That's no' an infirmity under the Act; it's a lesson to ye to put props under that kind o' horse whenever he's oot o' the trams. I think that's a' for you, Duffy, but of course ye must tak' care and be alive at midnicht to-morow nicht or else ye'll be in for the fine. And ye must be shair and pass Sunday nicht in yer ain hoose; if ye step over the door between the time ye get your tea to-morrow nicht and Monday morning, Lord Pentland'll[7] be awfu' angry. Noo for the mistress; whit's her full maiden name?"

"Bella Carmichael," answered Duffy, breathing heavily, and perspiring with the intellectual stress of the occasion. "Whit the deevil's the use o' botherin' aboot the like o' that? She's weel enough kent as Mrs Duffy."

"Jist that! but it's a point Lord Pentland's awfu' parteecular aboot," said Erchie. "Ye canna tell whit he may be wantin' her maiden name for, and onywye it would look gey droll if your wife hadna a maiden name. Age?"

"Fifty-three, but she mak's oot hersel' it's only fifty."

"Mairried, of course. Hoo mony years has she been mairried?"

"Fifteen."

"Puir cratur! Hoo mony children born alive and still livin'?"

"Six livin' and wan in Edinburgh," said Duffy after a moment's reflection.

"Is that Jamie, the paper mill yin?" asked MacPherson. "He's livin' too, isn't he?"

"Ye could hardly say he was," said Duffy, seriously, "him being in Edinburgh. By all accoonts, there's no much life in Edinburgh."

"All the same he'll be lingerin' on, we'll put the family doon at seven. Personal occupation — your wife hasna ony Personal occupation."

"The busiest wee woman in Gleska!" interjected Jinnet, who had occupied herself with her knitting hitherto. "It's no' fair to let Lord Pentland think that mairried wives does naething. I saw Mrs Duffy wi' a great big washin' yesterday."

"Lord Pentland doesna want to ken aboot the wash-in's," said her husband. "Washin's no' an occupation; it's jist a way o' passin' by the time. Where was the mistress born, Duffy?"

"Cambuslang, but I couldna say whit county."

"We'll leave Lord Pentland to fill the county in for himsel'," said MacPherson. "In ony case it's on the Gleska tramway system. Infirmities? — I better tell the truth aboot that and put her doon as 'totally blind'. There's nae ither way o' accoontin' for her mairryin' you."

Having filled in all the details regarding the Duffy family, Erchie winked at his wife and proceeded to invent a variety of interrogations which Lord Pentland and the Registrar-General had omitted from the schedule.

"Ony cats, dogs, canaries, or other domestic pets?" he asked solemnly.

"Michty!" exclaimed the coalman. "I didna think they would cairry the thing as far as that. We hae a cat — a — a kind o' Tom, like."

"Cat — Thomasina," said Erchie, with a graphic pretence at writing down this interesting item. "Whit spechie?"

"Torty-shell."

"Torty-shell, richt!, Hoo mony pianos, gramaphones, motor-caurs, or other musical instruments?"

"The only musical instrument we hae in the hoose is Maggie's mandolin, and she doesna play on't," said Duffy.

"A mandolin's no' a musical instrument within the strict meanin' o' the Act, we'll hae to put it doon under Infirmities," said Erchie scribbling away with a dry pen. "Ony live stock in the shape o' horses, cattle, goats, or sheep?"

"Jist the wan horse," said Duffy, "but whit's the sense o' them takin' ony accoont o' horses?"

"It'll be for the Airmy," explained MacPherson. "Lord Pentland'll want to ken hoo mony horses are available for military purposes if we were gaun to start a war."

"Unless he's startin' gey soon he needna lippen ower much on my horse; it's no' a chicken."

"Are ye shair it'll be livin' at twelve o'clock the morn's nicht?"

"It has a fair chance," said Duffy with some hesitation, and MacPherson apparently credited him in the Census schedule with a horse. "Next," he proceeded; "whit money hae ye in the bank?" But this was carrying the joke too far in Jinnet's opinion, and she interposed.

95. *The MacPhersons at the "Ex."*[1]

ERCHIE TOOK his wife on Saturday to the Exhibition[2] where they spent ten solid hours of the most determined gaiety, and each consumed as many cups of tea. It was only by having it with a cup of tea that they could enjoy the luxury of a seat, and though Jinnet could stand a whole day over a washing-tub without expressing weariness, the tread-mill of gaiety revealed a hitherto unsuspected weakness in her legs. Wherever they saw a restaurant they looked for its least imposing entrance, and worshipped again at the shrine of St Bohea.[3] They tried it by the cup and by the pot. "The doctors say that tea's no' a food at a'," said

Erchie late in the afternoon. "That's where they're wrang; its that extraordinar' satisfyin'. I feel I could dae withoot ony mair o't a' the days o' my life."

But to his wife it was like a continuous series of banquets. Sustained and fortified by these libations, she compassed the whole show, exhausted its every feature to her own satisfaction — a feat beyond the average season ticket-holder, even though he attend each day till next October.

The philosophy of Exhibitions was imparted to her early in the day by Erchie. "It's no' the fun ye get yoursel' that's to be looked for at oor time o' life," he told her; "But ye can get a lot o' sport frae watchin' ither people screichin' themsel's hoarse on the Scenic."

"Mind I'm no' gaun on it!" she warned him as she watched the crowded cars pop in and out between the painted hills, and heard the hysterical screams of their passengers as they plunged down the precipitous places.

"I'm no' askin' ye," he retorted. "To dae the Scenic properly, ye need to be under five-and-twenty, and hae a lad to haud your hand. A sport that would suit ye better is the whirly-whirly washin'-bynes."

"Whit are they like?" she inquired with interest, and he took her to the Whirlpool.

"In a' creation' whit are they daein' in the bynes?" she exclaimed, amazed at the sight of giddily gyrating tubs with their load of frenzied occupants.

"Jist whit ye see," he answered. "They're birlin' roond and roond, first yin way, and then the ither. It's a game they got the idea for frae the sweetie-works. 'It must be fine to be a pan-drop!'[4] said the inventive sowl, and skooshed awa hame at yince and took oot a patent."

"Puir craturs," said Jinnet, under a natural misapprehension. "Look at that yin wi' her hair a' doon! And it's likely they'll no' get much in the week for daein't."

He laughed. "Instead o' bein' payed for daein' it, they pay to get daein' it. They couldna be hired to dae it for ony money. I have nae idea the way ye feel when ye come aff a thing like that, but I'm shair it would mak' my heid bizz like a seidlitz poother."[5]

"Whaur's the place they ca' the Joy Hoose?" Jinnet asked, when her interest in the Whirlpool was exhausted.

"Up here on the left; I'm shair ye can hear them laughin'."

They went up and watched a stream of convulsively amused devotees of Joy go staggering along the balcony whereby the ingenious inventor of the House of Mystery made it plain to the hesitating looker-on that fun of the most excruciating kind was to be had within.

"Whit in a' the world dae they see inside?" asked Jinnet.

"I havena the least idea," said her husband, "but I'm certain shair ye couldna get a sonsy, big, wise-like woman like that yin haudin' on to the rail to laugh like that unless it was something extra comic. I believe they must tak' aff your boots and stockin's and kittle[6] your feet to start wi'. Then, in anither room, they'll hae a chap tellin' funny bawrs. Further on again they'll hae waiters trippin' on a mat and smashin' trays o' delf — in my experience as a waiter there's naething on earth mair laughable than that."

"Mercy on us! See at them comin' skytin' oot o' yon place!" exclaimed his wife. "Dae ye think there's been an accident?"

"That's the concludin' moral; when ye reach the height o' Joy ye get the heave, and land wi' some loss o' dignity on the solid, solemn firmament. I'm tellt the star comic o' the Joy House stands at the top o' that slide and gies every customer a push-aff wi' a wooden leg in the sma' o' the back."

"A wooden leg!" said Jinnet, incredulously.

"That's his speciality," said her husband solemnly. "Engaged for the season at great expense. The last wild pang o' Joy's a pin leg in the sma' o' the back."

Jinnet protested that though so much apparent joy was ridiculously cheap at sixpence, she would not venture to indulge in it, a sentiment with which her husband quite agreed, so they passed along and examined the Mountain Slide and the Joy Wheel.

"A proof," said Erchie, "that ony kind o' hasty motion's joyous so lang's it's no' walkin' to your work. Ye would think that slidin' doon a funnel on a bass, or sittin' on a wheel for a second or twa afore it whirled ye aff would be sports that an athletic nation would tire o', but here they're keepin' it up frae mornin' till nicht. I watched them the ither day when I was here wi' Duffy for mair than a couple o' hours, hopin' to see a Bylie or a Gilmorehill Professor on the slide or on the wheel, but nane o' them turned up. They seem to have awfu' nerrow views aboot an Historical Exhibition."

"I havena seen onything historical aboot it," said Jinnet.

"Then we'll try the An Clachan," said Erchie briskly. "It's a risk, I'll admit, for though I'm a MacPherson, I havena a word o' the language, and I'll maybe no' understaund a word o' whit they're daein'. Here ye are, roond here: ye can tell it's the An Clachan by the smell o' peats and the chap wi' the kilts and medals."

Jinnet was delighted with the Clachan. "It's jist the same as it was rale," she said; "I've seen the like o't afore in Islay. Whit are they lads gaun to dae on the pletform?"

"They're gaun to dance a reel," said Erchie, without hesitation. "They're aye daein' that in the genuine An Clachans. Whenever the weather's dry the native Hielandman puts on his medals and goes on a pletform on the An Clachan green and does a step o' the Hoolichan. They're daein' it at this very meenute, the day bein' fine, a' ower the Hielands, and here it's brung to your very door. It's a triumph o' science, like Loch Katrine water.[7] There ye hae their wee bit hooses; there's the smiddy, and I'll bate ye whit ye like the blacksmith's no' in, for there's the Inns quite handy to him."

"I don't see ony Inns," said Jinnet.

"It's the Inns richt enough, I assure ye; though they ca't the Tigg Osta,[8] them no' haein' ony English. I see they sell tea in't; ye havena had ony tea for nearly twenty meenutes;

we'll gang in and try a cup in Gaelic. Watch ye don't tramp on a hen."

"They're rale wise-like lassies that's waitin'," said Jinnet as they took their seats at a table. "Boots and stockin's and a' their orders."

"Of course they are! the genuine Clachnacudden. Did ye think ye would find them postin' blankets? Man, I wish I kent the language! — Whit's the kind o' signs ye mak' for twa cups o' tea and some soda scones."

But the attendants, fortunately, were bilingual; signs were quite uncalled-for, and the pair emerged, refreshed anew, to pursue their studies of the Celt at Home.

"Whit I like aboot an An Clachan," said Erchie, "is that it's fine and self-contained. The inns is handy to the smiddy, and the kirk's next door to the inns; everything's contrived for comfort and conveniency. I don't see mony people croodin' to the kirk, either, they're a' at the picture post-caird coonter; faith, naething seems to have been overlooked. And I declare to ye here's a wee private still as nate as ninepence workin' awa' beside that burn."

"Oh, Erchie!" said Jinnet, "are they no' feared? If the polis was to catch them!"

Erchie chuckled. "Nae fears o' that!" he assured her. "The polis is Hieland themsel's, and if ye asked them if that was a still they would likely tell ye it was a soda-water works."

From An Clachan to the African Village was to Jinnet like a transit by magic carpet from Paradise to a pagan orgy. She clung close to her husband's arm as they passed the dusky sons of Shepherd's Bush and Saughton Park; regarded the dancing women with pity and dismay, and felt every domestic instinct outraged by their heathen kitchen.

"Whit are thae men yowlin' and bangin' the wee barrells for?" she asked.

"They're no' yowlin!" said Erchie; "They're croonin' the plaintive sangs o' the dear auld Mother Land but they're kind o' croupy wi' the Scottish climate. And they're no' bangin' barrells; them's the genuine native drums; they're ca'd tom-toms."

But the native babies pleased her most. "It must tak' an awfu' black-leadin' to mak' them look like that. The wee smouts! I wonder whit'll they feed them on!"

"Monkey nuts," said Erchie, "and noo and then a banana. If ye're tired o' the shows by noo we'll hae anither cup o' tea and pass on to the rale Historical!"

But of the Historical Section, all she could recall when they got home was a case of old Church tokens. And she was grieved at old familiar features they had somehow missed. "If I havena come awa' and clean forgot to hae my name embroidered on a hankey!"

96. *Togo*[1]

"I SAW Togo[2] drivin' oot to the Exhibeetion yesterday," said Duffy. "He's a fine big strong chap; I would back yon chap to shift coals if ye put him to't. He was smokin' a substantial cigar wi' wan hand and recognisin' the folk in the street wi' the other."

"Had he on a pot hat?" asked Erchie, suspecting some mistake.

"Yon's a heid that never had a pot hat on it, Mac-Pherson; he was wearin' a yachtin' bonnet."

"Then ye're wrang again!" said Erchie. "Yon was Lord Provost M'Innes Shaw in the Loch Katrine uniform. When the Gleska Magistrates go to a Water Trip[3] they aye put on a deep-sea kep, and the Lord Provost wore his yesterday oot o' respect for the Japanese Admirality."

"I was tellt it was Togo richt enough," said Duffy. "And the crood was cheerin'."

"Togo was the wee blate chap sittin' in the shade o' Mr Shaw, wi' a jerry hat on, broodin' on the mystery o' the East and lookin' awfu' like a man that micht hae a steady job in the Prudential. I'm tellt he asked the Lord Provost through an interpreter if the weather was aye like this in

Gleska. 'There's whiles a drap o' rain,' said Mr M'Innes Shaw, 'but this is a time of the year that's special; we ca' it the Fair Week, and it's aye that hot that a' the folk in Gleska gang doon to the coast to dook⁴ themsel's, Your Admirality.'

'"It minds me of Nagasaki,' said Count Togo, takin' a hankey from his sleeve and moppin' the back o' his neck wi't. 'I could dae fine wi' a drink o' Lemon Kali and a piece o' ice in't.'

'"Ye'll get that!' said His Lordship; 'Jist you hold on till we're at the Garden Club!' Togo edged up in his seat to get mair into the shade o' Mr Shaw and wished he had brung his fan."

"They're makin' an awfu' palaver aboot the Japanese nooadays," said Duffy. "They werena in't at a' when I was young; the only place ye saw ony sign o' them was on a tea-kist or a willow-pattern plate."

"That wasna the Japs! it was the Chinese, but there's railly no' much difference, for the Chinese and Japs is kind o' Hie'lan' kizzens. Japan's an island aff the coast o' China, the same as Arran's aff the Lairgs."

"They focht the Chinese,"⁵ Duffy reminded him; "There wasna much o' the kizzen aboot that."

"I said Hie'lan' kizzens. Ye couldna expect them no' to fight at some time or other. Ye see the Japanese were wakenin' up, but the China yins werena wakenin' up at a', and it's awfu' aggravatin' to hear another body snorin' and you at your work. At first the Japanese thocht o' landin' a cargo o' yon wee roond tin wan-and-elevenpenny alarm clocks on the China coast, but there's 750 million Chinamen, and there wasna enough o' clocks to go roond, so there was naething for't but to send an Airmy. I tell you the China yins got a deevil o' a start! They werena richt ready for a war. They hadna even wise-like claes for't, to begin wi' — naething but felt slippers and a kind o' cretonne ulster, and they hadna done onything in the gunpoother way since they invented it. The hardy wee Japs went in at the wan end o' China and cam' out of the ither the same's it was a through-gaun close.⁶ My Jove!"

"Was Togo leadin' them?" inquired Duffy.

"No, he was on a different shift; if I mind richt, they were led roond China by a chap Band's Eye. They did a feaful lot o' damage to the China yins, and then went hame."

"Togo is close on bein' the Nelson o' the East; if he had an eye awantin' and an empty sleeve, he would be the very ticket! The Rooshian[7] fleet went sailin' roond by the Dogger Bank, and anchored aff Japan at a place they ca'd Yahoo.[8]

"'What's this?' says Togo when he seen them. 'Do they imagine that we're handin' a Coronation? See's my spy-glass.'

"'It's Rodjestvenski[9] richt enough!' says he. 'Fancy the neck o' him!' And he cleared his ships for action. He wiped aff the Rooshian fleet afore his tea, and then went doon the stair to the caibin o' his boat and had a sleep to himsel'. When he came up he was feelin' fine and fresh, and, puttin' his spy-gless to his e'e again, he sweeps the hale horizon. 'My Jove! chaps,' says he, 'there's been an awfu' stramash here! This sort o' thing 'll spoil boat-hirin' in Yahoo for July and August.'

"The Mickado[10] — that's the heid yin o' the Japs; that goes aboot below a paper umbrella — made Togo a Count, and the British Government made oot that the Japanese were a civilised nation at last, and made an alliance wi' them as fast's they could. They're a hardy race, the Japanese. They used to feed on naething but rice and cherry blossoms up till a dozen years ago, when they started takin' tinned meat from Chicago. Immediately their manly instincts was roused; they put aff their Paisley plaids and started wearing breeks. The future o' the human race is wi' the folk that ha'e a pocket at the hip for haudin' money."

"If yon was Togo, then, he wasna my idea!" said Duffy in tones of doubt and disppointment. "Yon chap might be a UF Elder. He didna look half as fierce as Provost M'Innes Shaw."

"He micht look like a Christian elder, Duffy, but he couldna richt be wan since he's no' a Christian," answered

Erchie. "The Japanese believes in naething but ancestors; they're hunders o' years behind the time aboot releegion. I'll bate ye that some day they'll be sorry for't! The only thing that's to be said for their releegion is that it's chape; there's nae Sustentation Fund nor Foreign Mission in't, and a' they want when they're worshippin' is a wee wooden temple and a box o' fuzee lichts. Sunday and Setterday's the same to them: the rice and cherry-blossom's in their blood yet, and they're only heathens."

"Ye would think," said Duffy, "that him bein' an Admiral, he would put on his uniform gaun to the Exhibeetion."

"Nae ordinar' uniform would stand the strain o' a' yon Coronation banquets he's bein' haein' up in London; he would hae a uniform to start wi' richt enough when he landed."

"I would hae liked to hae seen him in't," said Duffy.

"Ye wouldna be awfu' ta'en up wi't if ye had, for a Japanese Admiral in his uniform is just like an English yin, and that's no' half as fancy as the Fire Brigade. The days when a Japanese Admiral would go into action wi' a satin quilt and a parasol is a' by wi't, and the ambeetion o' the poorest Japanee noo is to hae a pair o' trousers turned up at the foot, and a there-and-back[11] collar five inch deep."

"What were they daein' afore they woke up and started fightin'?" asked Duffy.

"The puir deluded sowls were quite content makin' draught-screens, wee ivory elephants, ash-trays, and things to put in lucky bags. Their needs were few; their tastes were simple — a handful o' rice or cherry-blossoms, four bamboo poles and some sheets o' caird-board for a hoose; a vase wi' a single orange-lily in't, and a bass to sleep on. Noo they hae splendid factories, and turn oot a jute art square at 3s. 11½d. that's the terror o' Dundee.[12] They cam' ower to Dubs and Fairfield to learn some engineerin', and went hame wi' the genuine Gleska accent and a heid fu' o' plans for battleships. The China yins are still doverin', as ye micht say, but the Japanese are up afore it's daylicht in the mornin' pushin' tred, and I'll warrant Togo never felt sae much at hame in ony place in England as he did in Gleska."

97. *Strikes*[1]

"DID YE hear a noise on the stair last night?" asked Jinnet. "I was just gaun over, when it wakened me wi' an awfu' start. I thought at first it was the Grants bringin' hame their new piano, but naebody in their sober senses would bring hame a new piano in the dark, for naebody in the land would see't."

"I never heard an article," said Erchie, tapping his breakfast egg, "but I'll guarantee it wasna Grant's piano onyway. When the Grants get their piano it'll be on a Setturday efternoon, accompanied by a grand procession. It was mair like to be Jack Macallister, the tramwayman. It spiles your step on the stair to be hangin' a' day aboot the depot peacefully persuadin' your fellow-workmen to come oot and jine the strike."[2]

"It's me that's sorry for his puir wife! Nine o' a faimily and never oot o' the habble at the best o' times; she has plenty to dae withoot Macallister himsel' thrown on her hands. Whit in a' the world will he be daein' when he's no' at work?"

"Peacefully persuadin'; have I no just tellt ye? Macallister's a man that mak's a pet o' his ain parteecular tramway-caur; it's his only hobby and it would break his hert to see ony other chap tak' chairge o't."

"Whit's peacefully persuadin'?" Jinnet asked.

"The popular way in the tramways is to twist the neck o' a trolley-pole, or hit the chap ye want to reason wi' behind the ear wi' a drivin'-handle. I met Macallister yesterday gaun doon the street wi' a pocketfu' o' stones, and he was nearly greetin'. 'The champion caur in the Duke Street depot,[3] Mac', says he, 'and I had her trained that fine she would spark like a human bein' if a dug was in the road or she saw a woman frae Carmunnock standin' on the pavement ready to mak' a breenge in front o' her. I could drive her wi' baith hands aff the crank and my een shut — she was that dependable; and noo she's in the chairge o' a ticket-inspector! If there was onything my caur couldn't thole it was a ticket-inspector; she hated the very sicht o' the uniform, and whenever yin o' them put his foot on the step she would try to jump the trolley.'"

"Whit in a' the warld 'll Gleska dae if there's nae tramway caurs? asked Jinnet.

"Maist unfortunate! Couldna hae happened at a waur time, jist when horses is nearly oot o' date and airyplanes[4] is only startin'. Duffy the coalman tellt me he was gaun to Maryhill this mornin' wi' a couple o' horse and cairt on the chance o' liftin' a wheen o' businessmen no' fit to walk to their businesses efter a substantial breakfast. 'There's money in't!' says he, 'if the tramwaymen stand firm for a month or twa, for the Gleska folk hae lost the use o' their legs since the skoosh-caur started ha'penny tickets.' It's richt enough whit Duffy says; my hert was sair, in the mornin' yesterday, to see sae mony dacent, weel-put-on, weel-daein' business gentlemen toilin' in frae Hillhead on their ain feet. You could see they werena used to't; they peched maist dreadful and the sweat was drappin' aff them. I'm tellt that hunders o' them frae the south-side suburbs lost their way and landed oot near Paisley; it's sae mony years since ever they came into the toon or oot o't except wi' their e'en glued on a newspaper, that they didna ken the road. A couple o' year after this it wouldna maitter; if the tramway-caurs stopped then, a man in a hurry for the office would only need to birl a whistle on the roof o' the washin'-hoose and tak' his pick o' half-a-dozen airyplanes that would come skytin' doon to lift him."

"But maybe the airyplane men would strike, too," suggested Jinnet shrewdly.

"Richt ye are! There's naething mair likely. It's yin o' the drawbacks to an age o' science that the mair conveniences ye invent for yoursel' the mair ye miss badly when ye get the heave back on your ain resources."

"It's mercy the strike is ended," said Jinnet, some days later in the week, comforted by the resumption of the normal tramway traffic going past her window. "I felt that eerie wi' the want o' the noise o' the caurs; at nicht it fair put me aff my sleep. I've nae patience wi' their strikes; whit way can folk no' be agreeable? Everything would be fine if everybody was agreeable."

"Ye were cut oot for a Capeetalist; that's the rale Capeetalist p'int o' view," said her husband slyly. "It's the p'int o' view that's held by thoosands o' tip-top gentlemen busy shootin' grouse and scourin' roond the country in their motor-caurs. But it looks as if the habit o' bein' agreeable was gaun oot o' date, for half the country's oot on strike, and if I was you I would buy a bag o' potatoes and lay in a stock o' eggs."

"What in a' the world for?"

"The trains 'll no' be runnin' efter Setturday; a' the railway men are gaun to strike."

"It doesna' matter to me; I'm no gaun onywhere on a railway," said Jinnet.

"Maybe no', but an awfu' lot that needs a railway comes to you. Stervation stares us in the face! There'll be naebody to bring the beer frae the breweries, beef frae the markets, wheat and flour frae the docks, and coals frae the mine. Naething to drink but water! Naething to eat but hens, for they're gaitherin' the hens thegither roond the country and gaun to shoo them into Gleska[5] on their ain legs and save the need for trains or cartage. Tak' you my advice for't, Jinnet and buy potatoes. Look at London last week; I tell you the folk there got a start! They were packin' up their bits o' things and gaun to mak' tracks for the coast and country so's to be near the raw material, and only changed their minds when the cairters tied their trousers below the knee again and brocht oot their cairts once more in front o' the motor traffic. And that was only the cairters, mind ye! Up till then the cairter was always thocht to be a harmless kind o' chap, that sat on a lorry-tram and damned maist dreadful wi' nae ill-will to onybody. When he stopped work on a sudden he was found to be mair important than the Hoose o' Lords. If the Hoose o' Lords struck work for a month it wouldna hae the least effect on the price o' beef or stop the motor-omnibuses, but the cairter had only to drop his whip for a day or twa and London was in consternation. Whit'll it be when we havena ony railways?"

"I'll jist hae to set to and bake scones," said Jinnet, philosophically. "But whit in a' the world's the maitter wi' the country, gaun on strike wholesale like this?"

"The doctors say it's owin' to the heat," said Erchie, "but I think mysel' it's partly the heat and partly the rideeculous price o' stimulatin' beverages. Since ever Lloyd George put up the price of the workin'-man's refreshment[6] there has been what they ca' in the papers a smoulderin' discontent among us. Noo he's gaun to take aff us fourpence a week to pay for oor insurance. If that becomes law he'll maybe tak' other fourpence aff us for an annual health-restoring fortnight in the country; twopence for the upkeep o' a Dolly washer[7] in every home in the interest o' national cleanliness and a penny a week for the Popular Educator to keep us up-to-date wi' the Germans.

"I only hope the waiters 'll no' strike anyway' said Jinnet, with a natural solicitude for her husband's profession.

"We'll be the last to think o't." said Erchie. "We're no' in a poseetion to come oot on strike for oor customers could bide at hame and fa' back on their wives to dae their waitin'. Its their naitural occupation."

"Aye, but whit if a' the women were to strike?" asked Jinnet. "That would be a strike wi' a vengeance!"

"The peaceful persuasion would be a' on the ither side then; awa' and buy potatoes."

98. *Cinematographs*[1]

"ERCHIE," SAID Jinnet, knitting with a concentrated and determined air which showed that something far away from wires[2] and three-ply fingering was in her mind, "Could a man's heid swell up the height o' a four-storey land o' hooses?"

Her husband turned from the kitchen looking-glass with his face half-lathered, and regarded her with surprise.

"Don't you try to be comic, Jinnet," he advised. "It's no' in your line. An auld married woman has nae mair use for the sense o' humour than she has for a fancy box o' chocolates."

"I'm no' trying' to be comic," she protested with a little indignation. "I'm only askin' ye if ony mortal man's heid could swell up the height o' a hoose?"

"No," said Erchie, curtly, proceeding with the preliminaries of shaving. "A phenomena like that couldna happen to an ordinar' mortal man. It might happen wi' a provost. What are ye askin' for?"

"Oh, jist for curiosity!" and the wires clicked more furiously than ever.

Her husband stropped his razor on the full calf cover of a solitary volume of Gibbon's *Decline and Fall* he had bought for that purpose years ago from a barrow in Stockwell,[3] and expressed a hope that these remarks were not personal to himself.

"Did ye ever hear o' a man called Lieutenant Rose?" was the next startling inquiry addressed to him.

"Look here, Jinnet," he replied impatiently, "if this is a guessin' competition, I'm no' playin'. And if it's yin o' them catches where ye cry 'Kelly!' ye're no' gaun to catch me. I never heard o' ony Lieutenant Rose. And there never was ony Lieutenant Rose."

"Oh, but there was!" she replied with great assurance. "A fine young strappin' chap in the Navy. I'm awfu' surprised we didna read aboot him in the papers at the time. The Captain o' the man-o'-war cried him ben to his cabin, and says, 'Lieutenant Rose, when the Royal pairty come aboard tomorrow they'll be in serious danger o' bein' blawn up wi' a bomb. I hae a letter here that tells me the anarchists[4] are plottin' and I'm awfu' put aboot.'

"'Let me ashore in disguise for the efternoon,' says Lieutenant Rose; 'I ken a wheen o' thae gentry, and I could maybe find oot their plan.'

"So the Captain o' the man-o'-war sent the Lieutenant ashore disguised wi' a straw basher[5] and his breeks turned up at the feet, and he went to an Italian restaurant and ordered a snack. When he was waitin' for't, the hale jing-bang[6] o' the anarchists passed through the room he was sittin' in and into a room but-and-ben.[7] Ye could see at yince they were anarchists; they had the very hats.

"Lieutenant Rose lifted a bass aff the floor o' the room he was sittin' in a' by himsel' and waitin' for his snack, and there was a trap-door doon into a cellar. He went doon the trap and in below the other room where the anarchists were plottin', and he heard every word they said. They were gaun to hae a motor-boat a wee bit aff frae the man-o'-war, and a man wi' a divin'-suit. The diver was to tak' a bomb wi' him and put it in below the very middle o' the man-o'-war. When they had him hauled aboard the motor-boat again the anarchists would set the bomb aff wi' electricity, and the man-o'-war and the Royal pairty would be blawn to bits."

"Is this a *Home Chat* story or a dream ye had?" her husband interjected.

"Oh, it happened richt enough," his wife assured him. "It must hae happened just the ither day, and no' a word aboot it in the papers.

"Lieutenant Rose got another motor-boat, and a divin'-suit o' his ain, and when the anarchists were thrang pumpin' win' doon to the chap that was layin' the bomb below the man-o'-war, the Lieutenant put on his divin' suit and went doon a wee bit further aff. The anarchist was walkin' roond the bottom o' the water in the weeds to find a place to put his bomb, when Lieutenant Rose crawled up ahint and cut his wind-pipe —"

"Horrible, Jinnet! horrible!" exclaimed her husband. "I aye warned ye no' to eat afore ye go to your bed; there's naething worse for nicht-mares."

"I mean the pipe that his friends pumped doon the air to him wi'. And then Lieutenant Rose did something to the bomb to keep it frae explodin', and was hauled up on the anarchists' boat, them thinkin' a' the time it was their frien'. I tell ye they got a start when they screwed the helmit aff and found Lieutenant Rose wi' a revolver orderin' them to haud up their hands! They were a' ta'en awa' to jyle, and Lieutenant Rose, back on the man-o'-war again, was introduced to the Royal pairty, and got a title on the spot."

"Where did ye hear such haivers?" asked her husband.

"I never heard the tale frae onybody," answered Jinnet; "I saw the hale affair wi' my ain e'en in the Cinematygraft. That's where I went wi' Duffy's wife on Setturday, and I didna like to tell ye. Yon bates a'! I saw boats fishin' cod near Iceland; and the way that corks are made; and a man wi' leggin's and a helmit catchin' lions in the bush. If I hadna seen the man wi' a heid that swelled and swelled till it reached the top o' a tenement, I would have said such a thing was hardly possible."

Erchie laughed. "Ye never were acquainted wi' a Provost, Jinnet, nor even a first year's Bylie. What ye saw at the Cinematygraft was only pictures."

"They were movin', Erchie; and they were actual photygraphs; ye canna deny't if ever ye saw a cinematygraft. The photygraph was taken aff the genuine Royal pairty and a genuine Lieutenant Rose, and when he cut the — the air-pipe, ye could see the bubbles risin' in the watter. There was anither yin wi' a horse that belanged to a married woman, Mrs Grundy, wi' a man that was awfu' foolish and went awa' noo and then gallivantin'. Mrs Grundy had only to tell her horse to go and bring her husband hame and it would trot awa' as nate as onything and follow him to a public-hoose or a picnic pairty and chase him hame. The way that horse could run! Ye saw it a mile awa', and afore ye could wink it was almost doon on the tap o' ye."

"Only movin' pictures, Jinnet, movin' pictures! It's a' arranged."

"Hoo could they manage to arrange Lieutenant Rose, and the deep-sea divers, and the Royal pairty, and hoo could they arrange the lend o' an actual man-o'-war? For it was an actual man-o'-war to start wi'; and the very smoke was comin' frae its funnels."

"Science," said Erchie, finishing his shaving. "The deevils can dae onything! The man-o'-war was maybe genuine, but Lieutenant Rose and the Royal pairty would be actor-bodies dressed in uniforms."

"But I tell ye, Erchie, I saw the diver wrastlin' wi' the anarchist in the bottom o' the sea and the very partans[8] walkin' roond aboot them."

"Rale partans?" said Erchie, incredulously.

"So rale that I could almost feel them nippin' me," said Jinnet with conviction.

"I don't understand aboot the partans; it's no so easy to act a partan as a Royal pairty," confessed her husband; "But I'm certain sure the thing never happened, or ye would hae seen it in the papers."

"Would ye say the cod-fishin' was genuine?" asked his wife.

"Oh, like enough; there's nae cod aboot that; cod-fishin' and cork-cuttin' could be photygraphed at ony time."

"And Mrs Grundy's horse?"

"Oh, jist a trained horse."

"Could ye train a horse," asked Jinnet, "to go gallopin' doon a crooked street and breenge richt through a motor-caur, comin' oot at the ither side as brisk as onything, and jump frae the pavement through a three-storey window?"

"Science!" said Erchie. "Jist science. You weemen don't understand, and you shouldna bother yer heids aboot it."

"I'm certain shair, at onyrate, that what I saw was genuine," said Jinnet. "I can see how it a' micht happen, but I'm bate to understand the man wi' the heid that swelled."

"That's easy," answered Erchie; "They had jist to photygraph a provost."

99. *Duffy's Coals*[1]

ERCHIE DROPPED into Duffy's house on Saturday afternoon, and found the coalman washing himself in the kitchen jawbox but otherwise quite cheerful.

"Ye're late," said Erchie, looking at his watch. "A' the banks is shut hours ago, and ye'll no' can get your money lodged afore ten o'clock on Monday mornin'. If I was you, I would start a burglar- and fire-proof safe. It's temptin' Providence to hae a' that money lyin' in the shuttle o' a kist."[2]

"What money?" asked Duffy, drying himself.

"Fine ye ken what money! Ye're gettin' bald wi' haudin' up the lid o' the kist to coont it. If this coal strike was to last another month, we would see ye up at Skibo playin' gowf wi' Mr Carnegie. If ye tak' my tip, Duffy, put your money into quarries; the whin-stane quarry is the great investment o' the future. There's fortunes to be made in quarries; the India Rubber Boom[3] is naethin' to't."

"I havena the least idea what ye're talkin' aboot," said Duffy.

"I wish to Providence I had been brocht up to the coal tred," said Erchie. "Wi' a wee bit quarry, a half-a-dozen stone-knappers, and a couple o' cairts, I could retire before the Gleska Fair. What's the price o' the hunderweight the day?"

"Two-and-six — no, two-and-nine." said Duffy, hastily. "It'll be three shillin's on Monday."

Erchie held up his hands in admiration. "It's an astronomer ye should be, Duffy," he exclaimed. "What a heid for big figures! That gigantic mind o' yours is quite at hame in the higher mathematics, and ye turn half-croons

and three shillings roond in your mooth withoot a bit o'
harm to yoursel', like a woman bitin' hair-pins."[4]

The coalman stared at his visitor dubiously, conscious
of some irony, but unable to discern exactly where it lay.

"Erchie's only takin' a rise oot ye," explained Mrs Duffy
with great good humour, largely due to the fact that her
husband had at last been induced to see the absolute
necessity for a new sewing machine and a piano. "He's
grudgin' the price o' coals."

"Not me!" exclaimed Erchie. "If coals were whit they
used to be and burned awa' to ash the time ye would be
lookin' at them, I micht grudge the price; but no' the price
o' coal as improved by modern science in the last three or
four weeks. Jinnet and me sat up the maist o' last nicht wi'
a fire in a slow decline that's been lingerin' on since
Wednesday. It's the first o' a couple o' bags we got frae you
on Monday, Duffy. I can gie ye them back as guid as when
I got them — no' a chip the waur."

"Ye're the first customer that I've heard makin' ony
complaint o' my coal," said Duffy, now on familiar
ground. "Everybody else is astonished at the quality."

"I'm astonished mysel'!" said Erchie. "When we tried
them first, I thocht somebody had opened a new coal seam
in a cemetery; every noo and then we cam' on a heid-stane.
Genuine Peterheid granite.[5] If ye send up another bag on
Monday I'll be able to build mysel' a mausoleum. I
couldna understand it at first, but at last I minded o'
readin' somewhere a while ago aboot the Fuel o' the
Future, and then I saw it was it I had at two-and-three a
bag. Lasts a lifetime! A' ye have to dae is to turn it twice a
day and open the window. There's no' a better thing for
makin' ice-cream. Highly recommended for rale ice skatin'
rinks; they're usin' it oot at Crossmyloof.[6] Whaur is it ye
get it?"

"Whaur would I get it except in coal-pits?" replied
Duffy. "The best coal —"

"Na, na! Duffy, ye needna tell me yon comes from coal-
pits," said Erchie. "If it's no' from abandoned cemeteries,

it's frae the South Pole. Thon Swedish chap that got there first[7] must be coinin' money."

"The best coal in the market!" insisted Duffy. "And I'm payin' weel mysel' for it."

"I hear," said Erchie, "that the Gleska Fire Brigade's layin' in great bings o't. It's the very thing they've been lookin' for for years."

"What for?"

"For puttin' oot fires," said Erchie.

"A' the same," said Duffy, "if ye're wantin' ony mair coals, ye should lose no time in orderin' them; there's no' saying what the price'll be this day week, for the supply's runnin' short."

"No' as lang's there's a quarry open in the country, or chuckies[8] lyin' on the shore for the gaitherin' at Rothesay or Kilcreggan. But a' the same, your price is rideeculous high, Duffy; ye'll soon be wrappin' every lump in a piece o' tissue paper wi' a motto on the ootside like New Year short-breid, and sellin' it at threepence. A young chap coortin'll be in a swither whether to gie his lass a bag o' coal or a bracelet."

"I can assure ye I'm no makin' much aff them!" protested Duffy. "Ye should see what they cost me at the bing!"[9]

"That's the miraculous thing aboot the new fuel; naebody's makin' onything aff it, I hear. It's bein' distributed at two-and-six to three shillin's the bag jist for the sake o' the advertisement. The coalowner's losin' money on every ton; if he wasna a philanthropist he would sell it for pavin'-setts to the Corporation. The retail traders — that's you, Duffy — wi' coal-rees chock-a-block since the New Year, when the genuine old fashioned coal was fifteen shillin's a ton, are breakin' their herts at havin' to throw it awa' in bags at fifty to sixty shillin's."

"A' the same, Erchie, I wish the strike was over," said Mrs Duffy. "Everybody's abusin' my man, the same's he could help it!"

"Oh, I'm no' complainin'," said Duffy, cheerfully. "I can stand it a week or two longer."

"I daursay ye could stand it for anither twelve-month if the slate-quarriers didna go on strike," said Erchie. "But I'm no' for ony mair o' your patent fuel till the weather's warm. Efter a', a fire o' ony kind's a luxury; if I'm cauld I can put on a couple o' extra waistcoats, and start an argument aboot the minimum wage;[10] there's naething brings oot a genial glow so fast."

"There's aye briquettes,"[11] suggested Mrs Duffy, not disinterestedly, since her husband did some business in them also.

"The briquette," said Erchie, "is purely ornamental. It fills up a grate as well as onything, but like everything ornamental in a hoose, it means extra work."

"I don't see that," said Mrs Duffy.

"We have a 6 by 4 yin yonder for a fortnicht back, and it's a perfect he'rtbreak, Jinnet says; she has to black-lead it every time she does the grate. If coal's bottled-up sunshine, as I saw a man writin' the ither day, the briquette's fossilised Gleska fog, and it's no' quite ripe yet."

"Does Jinnet no' try gas?" asked Mrs Duffy, this time more disinterestedly.

"She micht as weel try Vesuvians," Duffy interposed, with professional repugnance to the latest enterprise of the City's Gas Department.

"Duffy's richt," said Erchie. "I have no ill-will to gas for illumination purposes,[12] and it's a fine thing on a stair, but the very sicht o't in a grate aye gies me influenza. The Corporation's crackin' it up like onything and lendin' oot gas stoves for naething noo, I see, but I never saw a gas stove yet in the Municipal Buildin's. They're auld-fashioned enough there to be content wi' a rousin' open fire. Jinnet got the gas put in the oven a year ago, and ever since she's a victim to palpitation."

"Dear me!" said Mrs Duffy; "Is't the fumes?"

"No," said Erchie. "Fricht. Every time she lichts it, it gangs aff wi' an awfu' bang, and it spiles the hale week for her to think o' the explosion that she'll hae to face afore she can mak' ready Sunday's dinner. Where a gas fire's fine is in a picture or in a scene in a pantymime.[13] If workin'-men cam' hame on winter nichts to gas-fires in their kitchens, the public-hooses wouldna haud them later on. A gas-fire fits fine in a dentist's waitin-room or a factor's office, where a man's mind's taken up wi' other things, but it's no adapted for a Christian household where there's boots to dry."

"Was he tellin' ye himsel' we're gettin' a piano?" asked Mrs Duffy, changing the conversation.

"Of course ye are!" said Erchie, heartily. "He never tell't me, but I kent ye would be gettin' something. Good luck to ye! I'll see ye yet in your motor-car. Ye'll see me when ye're skooshin' by[14] — I'll be walkin'. Ye'll ken me by my feet."

"And we're gaun to Lamlash on the Easter holiday aren't we, Jamie?"

"So ye say yersel'," said Duffy, gloomily.

"I hope the trains is on again by that time," remarked Erchie.

"Are they aff?" asked Mrs Duffy, anxiously.

"They are!" said Erchie. "Maist deplorably! The coal tred may impose on the general domestic public wi' it's patent fuel, but it canna deceive a locomotive."

100. *The Conquest of the Air* [1]

JINNET WAS going out upon her Saturday evening shopping. "Tak your umbrella wi' ye, and keep weel in on the pavement," Erchie advised her.

"It's neither wet nor windy: at least it's no' sae bad's a' that," replied his wife. "Ye're surely getting' awfu' anxious aboot me; I'm no' that auld!"

"It's no the wind or the rain I'm thinkin' on," said he; "It's them derisible machines from Germany[2] skooshin' aboot in the air at nicht that's botherin' me; ye dinna ken the minute that they'll drop a soda-water bottle on ye."

"Surely they're no' sae bad as that?" said Jinnet, incredulously.

"Bad!" said he; "they're a fair scunner! It shouldna be put up wi' — breenging over the British Isles in droves and puttin' the fear o' daith on folk that never did them ony hairm. Nae wonder we have to light the gas that early; it couldna be otherwise, and the sky congested every nicht wi' German trips! A bonny-like thing when a puir wee laddie canna get fleein' his draigon[3] for them! That's whit Duffy told me; his boy went oot to the West-End Park the other day and cam' hame greetin' because he couldna get his kite to gang; 'There'll no' be room in a while for us to draw oor breaths,' says Duffy; 'It's time we were awa' to Canada.'"

"There's a lot aboot them in the papers," said Jinnet, "but I've never seen them. Are they big?"

"They have them a' sizes'," explained her husband, twinkling; "Wee chats the size o' a washin'-boyne up to monsters bigger than a land o' hooses. But, wee or big, they're as fast as lightnin': the wan meenute they're seen in Portsmouth and the next aboot the Orkney Islands. Every thrivin' man in Germany noo has his private air-machine; whenever it comes to gloamin'[4] he puts a piece and a bottle o' laager beer in his pocket, fills his machine wi' gas at the kitchen bracket, and comes fleein' over the German Ocean[5] jist for a bit o' a pant before he goes to bed.

"Airship moonlight trips to the South o' England is the craze just now aboot Berlin; it's supposed to be a tip-top cure for sleeplessness. If ye picked up ony German paper and could read it, ye would see't full o' advertisements o' moonlight cruises to the British Isles, 'the Land o' the Settin' Sun.' 'Now is the time to see them to the Best Advantage!' says the Berlin airship advertisers.[6] 'See the White Chalk Cliffs before the gas goes oot! The Greatest Bird's-Eye View in Europe! Monster Attractions! Magnificently Illuminated Upper Decks! Band of the Emperor's Imperial Guard in the Fore Saloon! England and Back Again in Three Hours! Tickets, 5s. 6d. Infants in Arms, half-price! Meat Teas, 1s. 6d! Suppers, 3s. Opera-glasses, 9d.'"

"Infants!" said Jinnet, indignantly. "It's a cryin' shame bringin' weans awa' at nicht in the cauld when they should be in their beds and no' gallivantin' through the heavens. I wonder whit mothers is comin' to! But whit could ye expect o' Germans! I hope to goodness they have proper railin's round the airships so that the puir wee smouts'll no' fa' oot."

"I'm no sae sure aboot that," said Erchie; "There's some gey funny young German waiters[7] in Gleska that must ha'e fallen over the side o' something. They may have a railin' richt enough aboot their airships, but you tak' my advice and keep up your umbrella!"

"Do ye think they'll be here the nicht?" said Jinnet, anxiously. "Surely no' on a Setturday nicht; they couldn't get hame again afore the Sabbath."

"The Sabbath's naething to them!" said her husband, solemnly; "They're puir deluded Continentals. I wouldna' be a bit surprised if they were makin' specialities o' week-end trips, 30s. inclusive wi' electric baths. There's wan thing certain — they've spoiled the countryside for courtin' in; a lad and his lass'll no' can venture oot the length o' Carmunnock or Canniesburn Toll withoot the risk o' a fleein'-machine wi' a pairty on board comin' swoopin' doon and makin' a cod o' them in German wi' their search-lights. I'm awfu' gled my coortin' days is bye wi't! There was nane o' that in oor time, Jinnet."

"Whit in a' the world's the meanin' o't?" said Jinnet.

"Science!" replied her husband, putting on his waistcoat. "It's the age of progress, and you tak' my advice and keep weel in on the pavement; if it's no' an infant in arms that'll drop on ye it micht be a German waiter; whenever they see the lichts o' a toon that's likely to have an hotel they give the heave to a chap called Fritz, and he lands wi' a dunt, haudin' on to his dinner-naipkin. Ten minutes after that he's handin' roond sardines and daein' his best to let on he was born in Coupar Angus."

"It's droll I never heard a word aboot them," said Jinnet.

"If you would read the papers!" said her husband.

"Ye're far ower much ta'en up wi' the motions o' the Royal Faimily. The thing has been goin' on for weeks! The first o' the German air machines was seen by the Chief Constable o' a place in the North o' England comin' home from a Thursday prayer-meetin'. He took in a couple of holes in his belt and birled his whistle on them to stop till he brought out his diary and made a pencil note. But they didna stop – not them! The band played on, and fifteen minutes later the lights were seen distinctly in the neighbourhood o' Hull by a solicitor in a large way o' business. Exactly a minute and a half after that they were seen at Ipswich as sworn to before a JP and a man in the horticultural trade wi' a church connection."

"We were far better the way we were," said Jinnet, "and nane o' their cairry-on wi' their fancy flyin'! It's a wonder to me the government doesna interfere. Ye never can tell whit they'll drop! I yince let a methylated lamp fa' oot a cairrage in the train frae Greenock when I was nursin' Jimmy."

"The British Government daurna interfere," said Erchie. "They're far ower deeply implicated in the flyin' tred themsel's."

"I always thought their home was on the deep,"[8] said Jinnet, who knows a song or two.

"So it is," said Erchie, "but that needna hinder them from takin' lodgin's and the conquest o' the air's the latest battle-song o' Britain. Did ye no' notice the flight o' the aerial squadron frae Farnborough to Montrose?"[9]

"Mrs Macrae has an auntie in Montrose; she's mairried on[10] a linen-draper and he's daein' awfu' weel; they have a grand piana."

"Never mind aboot that the noo," said Erchie; "The aerial squadron from Farnborough for Montrose begood to get ready to start at the Auld New Year, and landed safe and sound on Thursday last. They call it the Royal Flyin' Corps,[11] and I tell you it's a clinker! It's no' so fast as the German derisibles, but man, it fairly cuts the air! It started off at the rate o' seventy miles an 'oor, and kept it up for fifteen seconds; then the Royal Corps cam' doon and landed on a flesher's park to light its cigarette because the wind was blowin'.

"Exactly at half-past two by Reuter's telegram,[12] it got in the air again, pursuin' it's way wi' grim and darin' energy to the North, and stopped for lunch at Chorlton-on-the Hill, a place wi' a bottle licence.

"'Is this, can onybody tell us, Chorlton-on-the Hill?' says Commander Becke and they tellt him he was near enough, that the place was roond the corner wi' a Black Bull signboard. The Royal Flyin' Corps dragged roond their airyplanes and had a snack, and started off again in a drizzle o' rain to Scotland marked on the chart distinctly wi' a cross.

"They put up that night at a place in the South o' England; they could see the lichts o' France across the English Channel, and they grat thegither feelin' awfu' far frae hame.

"On the Thursday week the Royal Flyin' Corps (all ither kind's no' right Royal, just a kind o' imitation) got the length o' Doncaster, and their airyplanes a' wet."

"'Is this Scotland?' says Lieutenant Waldron.

"'No,' says the chap in chairge o' the railway buffet; 'first to the left, then third to the right, and ye're there when ye drop doon deid; that's Edinburgh'.

"Wi' dauntless resolution the Royal Flyin' Corps resumed its weary journey to the North; and a fortnicht later, wind and weather favourin', havin' travelled at the terrific speed o' a cushion-tyred perambulator, landed at the very door o' the Provost o' Montrose.

"'Are you the Royal Flyin' Corps frae Farnborough?' says the Provost, puttin' off his brattie.[13]

"'We are!' says Commander Becke, lookin' roond aboot him for the demonstration.

"'We've often read aboot ye since ye started,' says the Provost; 'I mind o't fine though I was jist a laddie,' and he takes them roond to the Council Hall and gies them a gless o' wine and an Abernethy biscuit!"

"Man, ye're jist an auld haiver!" said Jinnet, but as she went out of the close a little later she cast an apprehensive glance at the heavens lest the Germans should throw out a bottle, and put up her umbrella.

101. *Jinnet's Visitor*[1]

Before Jinnet could quite grasp the situation, her first alarming thought being that the gentleman was from the Sanitary,[2] he had passed her with his strange machine into the lobby.

"There's nae disinfectin' needed here," she told him tremulously. "It must be some mistake; there hasna been an illness in this hoose since Wullie was a baby."

"Just a little demonstration," he said to her. "Won't take ten minutes. Can I have a little flour, or meal — a couple of handfuls, say?" He was such a stylish gentleman, Englified, and with a handkerchief stuck up his sleeve, that she couldn't think of asking what he wanted flour for, so she simply went and got a bowl from the kitchen. When she came back he was in the parlour, busily screwing on a metal hose-pipe to the strange machine, and with his coat off.

"Now we shan't be long!" he said to her gaily. "The leading merit of the Dinky[3] is simplicity. You only have to see that the dust-container's screwed up tightly; lower the footboard, so; select and fix the nozzle suitable for carpets, mouldings, or upholstery, as the case may be; grasp the handle, so; work back and forward slowly, and direct the nozzle to the part required ... Excuse me, madam," and he took the bowl of flour from her.

"Has it onything to dae wi' the drains?" she asked him, anxiously: she had some slight experience of smoke-test machines.[4]

"Not at all," he said briskly. "Just dust, which is quite as deleterious to the health as drains. No doubt you think this room is thoroughly clean?" and he looked at her with the compassionate eye of a well-informed English gentleman who knows better.

"If it's no' clean," she said indignantly, "it's no' for want o' elbow-grease. Far wiser-like if ye would see aboot the ashbins at the back there — no' a lid on them; a bonny close they leave us in the mornin'! … Lord be aboot us! what is that ye're daein'?"

He had strewn the bowl of flour upon the carpet, and was rubbing it thoroughly into the fabric with his feet.

"I will now demonstrate how effectively the Dinky removes the finest dust. There are scores of imitations in the market costing twice as much, which do not have one half the suction power of the genuine Dinky. A child can work it — see!" and working the bellows of the vacuum cleaner he ran the nozzle of the hose across the carpet, leaving it as thoroughly clean as it was before.

Jinnet stood bewildered, now convinced the man was a lunatic; they both were so engrossed in the performance that they never heard the opening of the outside door nor a footstep in the lobby; and Jinnet's husband was looking in on them before they realised his presence.

"What's this?" he asked astonished.

"Oh, Erchie!" cried his wife, relieved to see him; "I'm glad ye're here! This gentleman is — is — is tryin' an experiment."

"I thought at first it was the Fire Brigade," said Erchie, looking at the metal hose-pipe. "But then I saw the gentleman hadna on a helmet or a hatchet. Bless me, Jinnet, ye're surely no gaun in for a vacuum cleaner?"

"A vacuum cleaner!" she exclaimed. "Is that what ye ca' a vacuum cleaner. I didna understand; I thought the gentleman was frae the Sanitary."

"Cheapest in the market — £1.10s.," said the canvasser. "You have no idea of the saving —"

"Saving!" cried Jinnet. "Bonny on the savin'! I couldna keep the thing in flour!"

The canvasser unscrewed the lid of the dust receptacle, took out a little bag, and exhibited a small amount of dust in the bottom with an air of triumph.

"Fairly eats it up, you see!" he remarked as if the Dinky was a horse.

"We could dae that for oursel's," said Jinnet, "but we like it baked first; there's naething in your poke but my guid flour."

"On the instalment system of easy payments, the Dinky — " he began, but Erchie cut him short with the intimation that under no conceivable system could a Dinky be thrust upon that household.

"It's three and forty years," said he, "since I got a vacuum cleaner, and I have it yet; it's jist as good as ever, and it hasna got the wheeze. It's a faur better yin than yours, and I like the smell it leaves — it's something like saft soap and water."

"Three and forty years!" said the canvasser, dismantling his machine. "Let me tell you, sir, that the vacuum cleaner was invented only — "

"'Toots!" said Erchie, cheerfully; "I'm talkin o' the wife. Cleanin' and dustin's no' a task wi' her; it's her principal recreation. It would break her he'rt to think it could be done wi' a pair o' bellows flyped."

"It's a great highjinckie age!" said Erchie, taking off his coat to have his tea when the canvasser was gone. "If yon machine had a few improvements on't: could wash a blanket, darn a sock, sew on a button, cook a meal o' meat, and nurse a wean, a body wouldna need a wife. But it's comin! I'll bate ye that chap Edison's[5] thrang thinkin' o' a combination o' the phonygraph, the kinematygraph, the sewing machine, the vacuum cleaner, the Thermos flask, and the incubator that'll relieve women o' their domestic bonds, and gie them leisure to gang roond the country lettin' aff their bits o' bombs."

"Ye needna talk!" said Jinnet, with conviction; "Ye couldna dae withoot the women! Him and his dust! There's no' a morsel o' stour in the four wa's o' this hoose!"

"Nae mair than what's in the top flet, No. 29," said her husband, alluding to the next-door close. "When I went oot the day, a half-a-dozen nice bit lassies and an aulder yin in specs, every yin wi' a brattie in a parcel, were troopin' up to 29 the same's it was a waddin'."

"What on earth are they daein yonder?" asked Jinnet. "Every day in the week they're there a different gang, except the wee yin wi' the specs; she's spachial."

"Domestic science!"[6] said her husband, solemnly. "It's a' the rage in Gleska. The like o' you was just heaved oot o' school when ye got the length o' Long Diveesion, to nurse your mother's weans, and mak the beds and dae the best ye could at makin' porridge, but things is different noo. No. 29's a trainin' ground for Gleska's comin' house-wifes. I tell you, the stour's goin' to get a fright, even withoot the Dinky vacuum!"

"Hoots, ye're haiverin' again!" said Jinnet; "What science is there aboot keepin' a hoose? It's jist a trauchle!"

Erchie helped himself to sugar. "That's your notion," said he; "but ye're far behind the times. The School Board has twa-room-and-kitchen hooses, h. and c., here and there through a' the tenements, and every wise-like lassie has to go and learn in them the way to wash a floor, and clean a grate, and mak' a bed, and cook a shillin' dinner. Every day they're up in 29, and scrubbin' at it till I'm tell't the boards is worn as thin's a tramway ticket, and the grate's as shiny as a shillin'. They've polished at the handle o' the door so much it's worn away so bad it jags ye."

"Perfect nonsense! It would be far mair like the thing if they cam' and helped puir Widow Grant doon stairs to clean her hoose on Setturday."

"Aye, but that wouldna be Domestic Science," said Erchie.

102. *Black Friday*[1]

It would be idle to deny that an almost universal gloom prevails in Glasgow in anticipation of the new Act[2] which, on and after Friday first, will shut all public-houses from ten o'clock at night till ten o'clock next morning. The innovation is looked upon as a dastardly blow at a fine old national custom, and as certain to have the most serious effects upon the social, economic, and physical conditions of the people. To have two hours per day lopped off our period of refreshment means about 600 hours per annum; which is to say that this iniquitous Act robs us in the aggregate of 25 days of what time we have in a year for stimulus and conviviality. It will be impossible to make up for the loss of those two morning hours by dispensing with dinner and tea, or by the exercise of more agility in getting washed and out again at night; there was something in those magic morning hours[3] now stolen from us that is best indicated in the words of Mr Duffy: "If ye tak' a dram at a', tak' it in the mornin', and ye get the guid o't a' day." No wonder Scotland this week is solemnised. You see apprehension and revolt in every face. Everywhere are mutterings of rebellion. Home Rule and the Suffragettes,[4] and all the clamant national topics of the hour are quite forgotten in the sense of intimate and personal injustice.

I have interviewed Mr James Duffy, the well-known coal vendor, on the crisis, as a citizen whose views were likely to be representative of those held by the rugged sons of toil for whom peculiarly the ten o'clock opening law will be a hardship.

"It's just a fair sickener!" he said with unmistakable disgust. "Ten o'clock's far ower late for ony man's breakfast. Nae wonder folk's flockin' to Canada! Everything here's against the workin'-man."

"The theory may be that it will save you money, Mr Duffy," I suggested.

"There's no' a greater mistake," he replied, "than tryin' to save money at the expense o' your health. If a man has a hard day's work to dae he needs to start weel and keep up his strength. Eight o'clock was richt enough; seven, or even six, would hae been better, but eight did fine; it kind o' broke the back o' the day; it kep' ye cheery watchin' the clock from six till eight, and after eight a schooner and a wee hauf-gill[5] made your work nae bother to ye."

"How will the new opening hour affect your own practice?" I inquired.

"I don't see hoo it'll work at a'," he answered gloomily. "I've thocht o' turnin' oot at eight instead o' six, and gettin' the better o' them that way, but there's the risk that I'll be hungry afore I get my mornin',[6] and spoil my thirst wi' tea. Anyway ye look at it, the thing's a persecution. It's a' the harder on a man o' my tred that has to dae a lot o' roarin' in the morning'; ye canna cry coals dacently on milk and jujube lozenges."

Behind the rather flippant confidences of Mr Mac-Pherson, whom I next interviewed, I thought I discerned a genuine antagonism to the new measure.

"Ye mean the Daylight Saving Bill?"[7] he said. It doesna' affect me personally, for I'm no' an early riser, but it's hard on the like o' Duffy, and it's a blow at Scottish history. Everybody kens that the secret o' Scotland's greatness is the 'morning'. A' the finer qualities o' the race come oot at eight o'clock. It comes from the national food bein' oatmeal porridge."

"How?" I asked, surprised.

"In the olden days," said Erchie, "when the tinned salmon and the closed fish[8] werena thocht o', a Scotsman's breakfast never was anything else than porridge. It's a fine upstandin' meal, and we won the Battle o' Bannockburn on't; but when there was naething else except on Sunday, the very thocht o't cast a gloom on the mornin' hours o' the workin' man, and he honestly couldna face it without a tonic.[9] The immediate result I see o' the ten o'clock openin' is that Mrs Duffy'll have to use the mornin' money on fancy breakfasts wi' ham and eggs."

"That might be a gain all round," I suggested.

"I'm afraid ye're no' better than an Englishman!" said Erchie, shaking his head. "Where's your patriotic spirit? Hae ye no feelin's for the thoosands o' chaps like Duffy gaun hame to a breakfast, even o' ham and eggs, past the

Mull o' Kintyre Vaults, and its shutters on? It'll look like every day a funeral."

"Will it not make us a more sober people?" I inquired.

"It will not," said Erchie. "That's the way that the wine, spirit, and beer trade's against it. They wouldna open till twelve if they thocht it would make Scotland soberer, but thcy ken fine Duffy and his friends'll spend as much as ever on refreshments; at least, that's whit they say, so I suppose they like, themsel's, the early risin', jist for health's sake. My own idea is that it's playin' into the hands o' them Italians.[10] There's an eight-o'-clock-in-the-morning feeling in a town like Glasgow — maist depressin'. Nothing gives relief to't but standin' at a coonter."

"A dairy might serve the purpose," I suggested.

"Milk!" cried Erchie in horror. "Full o' germs! Ye'll recommend Broon Robin next! Ye're surely no' teetotal. Na, na! the ice-cream shops'll get the tred, and ye'll see the riveters[11] next Friday standin' oot in raws forenent[12] the ice-cream shops at breakfast time, for their turn at the slider coonter.[13] Scotland's done! There's nae inducement left for us to get up in the mornin' or bide late up at nicht."

There has, plainly, been no more staggering blow to Scotland's custom and sentiment since the days of Forbes Mackenzie.[14] Closing at ten instead of eleven was, by comparison, a step of no importance; that only called for a little more expedition in the orders. But the abolition of the traditional 'morning' is involved in the newest Act; for a time, at least, it will have bewildering effect on the working-classes who discovered long before the doctors did that alcohol was a food, stimulating and sustaining, for the morning use of men, though not at all to be recommended to their women. So Glasgow this week is gloomy, though it is lucky that the new conditions start in early summer rather than the mirk morns[15] of November.

103. *Down-Hearted Duffy*[1]

"You'll see!" said Duffy. "Just you watch! In twa or three weeks there'll no' be a single steamboat sailin' — "

"Of course there'll aye be the *Fairy Queen* on the canal,"[2] said Erchie, cheerfully. "As lang as she keeps runnin', Britannia rules the waves."

"I'm layin' in a lot o' onions and oranges," proceeded the coalman gloomily.

"Ye have no idea the way onions and oranges'll go up when the blockadin'[3] starts, for there'll no' be ony ships get through, and the price o' foreign eggs'll be something fancy. They'll be worth their weight in —"

"In coal," said Erchie quickly. "Man, Duffy, I doot ye're a pessimist!"

"What's a pessimist?" asked the coalman.

"A pessimist's a kind o' man ye want to gie a bat on the lug to. So far as I can see, all men in the coal tred are pessimists. I think that when they gang hame at nicht and get their teas they stick their heids for the rest o' the nicht in yin o' their ain coal-bags, and say, 'Michty! doesn't things look black!' Ye have nae mair idea o' war than my leg, Duffy. Neither have I, but I aye ken bluff when I see it, and every time I see the Germans bluffin' whit they're gaun to dae, I aye cheer up, for I ken it's no' that way that war is won. I would be far mair anxious aboot the Germans if they kept their mooths shut."

Still Duffy shook his head; he had had a counterfeit half-crown passed on him by some miscreant customer unknown that afternoon, and this personal disaster augmented — if it did not even wholly account for — his sombre view of the international situation.

"Hoo lang will the war last?" he asked in one of those flashes of intelligent curiosity which come at times to so many of us.

"Man, I daurna tell ye that, Duffy," said Erchie solemnly. "I'm on my oath. But I'll venture this length if ye don't repeat it — it'll finish sooner than some folk think, and it'll last langer than others imagine. But for goodness sake, don't let on I told ye! I had it special frae a man that has a brother in London that cuts Lord Kitchener's hair when it's needin' cuttin'.' "

"Ye can depend on me!" said Duffy, exceedingly grateful for this reassuring confidence. "I'll no' say a wheesht to onybody. I was railly gettin' anxious, for Macrae the polisman swears it'll last three years."

"When it comes to European wars," said Erchie, "ye canna depend on the polis for the very latest information. They're a' richt for tellin' ye when the watter's to be cut aff, or showin' ye your close at nicht if the tenement looks kind o' shifted; but for the deeper secrets o' State, it's rarely ye can trust them; they'll mislead ye if they can. My ain private opeenion is that the polis is making' a fair hash o' things at present — a'thegither mismanaging their ain depairtment. The Germans come over here week-ends and murder weans, and ye never hear a word o' the polis doin' onything."

"If I could only mind wha I got that half-croon frae, things wouldna look sae bad," said Duffy in a little. "I doot, Erchie, I'm a comer-and-goer."

"What's that in English?" asked his friend. "Since they began puttin' wee French dictionaries in the packets o' cigarettes, ordinary human conversation's kind o' spoiled for folk like mysel' that havena ony foreign education."

"A comer-and-goer's no French," said Duffy. "I mean that I come and go aboot the war; some days I'm whistlin' at my wark, and ithers I canna cry my coals wi' ony kind o' melodiousness, I'm that doon-hearted."

"I see!" said Erchie. "My mistake! Ye're no a genuine pessimist after a', ye're jist an auld wife."

"Ay, but jist you consider this — we havena won a naval battle for nearly twa weeks; whit's the Navy daein?"

Erchie MacPherson sighed. "Man, Duffy," he said, "ye put me awfu' in mind o' an aunty my wife had oot at Stra'ven. She had a hundred and eighty hens when the

Boer War started and every time ye went oot to see her she would boil ye eggs. Every time De Wet or Cronje was mentioned in the papers, and it was aye for something dashing that didna agree wi' us at a', she sold a dozen hens in an awfu' panic, sure this country was done for, and that sooner or later she would have to leave it and tak' a wee bit hoose in Gleska. 'Whaur's the Navy wi' its hunder-ton guns?' she would ask in desperation; 'Here am I wi' a' they hens!' — the puir auld body had never seen a man-o'-war in her life; she never was even the length o' Gourock. At every British reverse she sold some mair o' her hens and got very little for them, for she grat that much they were plashin' wet, and looked as if they werena ony weicht at a'. And when the Boers were smashed, and my wife and me went oot to celebrate Cronje's capture, she hadna a hen in her possession nor an egg to boil us for oor tea. 'Oh, dear me,' says she, 'wasn't I the silly woman no' to trust in God and keep my hens?'"

"What I aye like to see in the papers," said Duffy, "is a regular battle. This week or twa I'm a wee bit disappinted. I hate to see them hangin' on."

"It's a mercy you're no' in the poultry line like Jinnet's aunty; ye can greet if ye like on a bag o' coals and no' lose onything on the transaction; quite the contrary. Admiral Jellicoe,[4] wi' the best will in the world, canna indulge ye to a battle every nicht to yer tea; buy haddies if ye want to keep yer strength up."

"I'm a' richt if I don't read whit the Germans say; they're most annoyin', Erchie," said Duffy.

"Ay, that's their nature; they canna help it. And a' they German wireless stories are meant particularly for folk like you and my Aunty Bella. They want to cause a flurry among auld wifes' hens. You attend to the coal tred, Duffy, and be as honest as ye can wi' the scales, and leave Lord Kitchener[5] and French[6] and Jellicoe to dae their business."

"Ah!" said Duffy, "but a man must read the papers; I'm readin' them even-on."[7]

"I have naething to say against the papers in moderation," said his friend. "They're fine for linin' presses — naething better. But ye have to read them wi' discretion. I'm a busy man mysel' just now, for I'm daen' the wark o' twa or three waiter chaps called Fritz or Hans so the most I can read o' the papers is the heidlines. And I'm no like you, at all, when I see naething startlin' in the heidlines I say, 'Thank God! — another battle won!' For, Duffy, every day wi' naething doin' is a battle lost for the Germans."

104. *Erchie on the Egg*[1]

"EGGS ARE doon. They're a great deal lower this week," said Jinnet, returning with her grocery order.

"No' the yin I got yesteday: it was as high as Tennant's Stalk," replied her husband.

"Oh, Erchie!" cried his wife, remorsefully, "and ye never said a word! It was the last o' my ain preservin'."

"Tuts! Whit herm's a high egg in the time o' war? There's countries where they eat them fair blue-moulded. It's just a fad the new-laid egg. Nae sensible body wants new-made cheese or a fresh saut-herrin'. The Gentry like their venison and grouse hung up till it's dangerous to go past the larder door wi' a naked licht."

Jinnet shook her head. "I don't understand their tastes: it's silly! Anyway I'm glad the egg's doon; ye'll can get a couple the morn's mornin'. They're one-and-eight the dozen, fresh frae Arran."

"The Arran egg," said Erchie, "is an egg I'm very fond o'. If ye get the genuine inland Arran egg there's nae humbug aboot it; ye can almost taste the heather. I'm no sure aboot the seaside egg, though; it aye tastes like a cross between a Dorking and a cockle. I suppose it's the diet o' dulse and sand hoppers gies them the doon-the-watter flavour."

"I aye think an egg's an egg, and that's the whole o't," said his wife. "If they're fairly fresh I'm no' much heedin' aboot their genealogy."

"Ye have a coarse uneducated palate."

"That's the kind that pays a puir-body best; sae many people educate their palates till they canna eat onything that's easy got. Half the money that's spent on meat and drink is spent just on a flavour."

Her husband looked at her with mock alarm. "Jinnet," he said, "ye're gettin' awfu' close on bein' a philosopher, and I wouldna like that to break oot in ony wife o' mine; it's the first step to bein' an atheist or an emaciated[2] female. Tak' you my word for't, that there's eggs and eggs, and whenever ye can afford it, give your custom to the hens o' the motherland, the hens o' bonny Scotland, where the heather and the bluebells grow. The alien egg is aye suspicious, even if it's frae a neutral country like Ireland, though I'll no' deny the Irish egg is a good enough put-by for fryin' when there's nane frae Arran. I'm never sure o' the Continental egg, though, till the heid's chipped aff; it micht be just a spy. The further awa' ye go for eggs, the less ye can depend on them. Yon guaranteed Egyptian yin I got last Sunday was a case in point; ye could see quite plain it cam' frae the tomb o' the Pharaohs, and if there's onything I hate to make a breakfast o' its ancient relics."

"I don't understand eggs nooadays," said his wife, taking off her bonnet. "They used to be sixpence a dozen in my time, and plenty o' them. ... If I had just a wee hoose in the country —" she sighed. That was an old ambition with very little prospect of ever being realised.

"My dear Jinnet," said her man, "if ye had ten wee hooses in the country and a thousand weel-daein' hens thrang layin' nicht and day for ye, I'll guarantee ye would never eat an egg. Ye would send the hale jing-bang to the market and buy sausages. The folk in the country that brings up eggs by haund or by machinery never eat an egg except when they come to stay wi' a friend in Gleska, and then they canna help it; they get yin o' the yins they brocht for a present in a box wi' them — a dirty trick to play on onybody.

"Forby," continued her husband, filling his pipe, "egg production nooadays is a science, like playin' the fiddle; there's naething to be made at it by rule-o-thumb. The auld-fashioned hen of Caledonia was a simple, honest, hard-workin' creature that had na conceit o' itself', and just went on layin' day after day, if ye gave it onything oot o' a bowl yer werena needin' yoursel'. It lived at the back, in ony auld box that was handy, and when the nicht was cauld would come in the hoose and jine the faimily pairty; wrought hard a' its days in scrapin' at the neebours' gairdens, and dee'd the naitural death o' a hen at last when full o' years and nae langer able to contribute to the Sustentation Fund."[3]

"Don't joke aboot the Sustentation Fund, Erchie," said Jinnet with pious reproof.

"In these days there was just the yin kind o' egg — genuine and unadultered, no different from the modern egg o' commerce till ye broke it open. Ye never needed to haud it up to the gas to see its age; it was aye in the prime o' youth. The hardy and frugal sons o' Scotland were reared on such-like eggs at their breakfast, dinner and tea. And an extra yin on Sundays, and keepin' a wheen o' hens was a lady's occupation, like playin' the pianola.

"Some silly idiot took it in his heid that the hen could be educted and refined, and that a little extra money spent on its board and lodging would rouse its gratitude to that extent it would double its egg production. They began puttin' up fancy semi-detached hooses for the hens, wi' a southern exposure, the watter laid on, and bauks[4] it was a trate for a hen to sit on. They put in fixed grates to keep them warm in winter, spent money on buying meat for them and the hen-hoose was cleaned oot as regular as the parlour. It was before the vacuum cleaner; they'll have the vacuum cleaners in them noo, and the O-Cedar mop to gie the bauks a polish."

"Ach! ye're just haiverin'," said Jinnet.

"Naething o' the kind! The thing developed. Whenever the hen got into its heid it was a bird o' consequence, it had to get a title — Buff Orpington, Minorca, or the like (it was just a common 'hen' before) — and had to get a course o' champed shells in its daily menu, and a' its orders. If ye let a draught blaw on it, it took the jee. A' the same there's nae doot it laid mair eggs; and this encouraged the poultry-fermers to keep on coddlin' it. I'm tellin' ye they fair spoiled the hen! Just pampered it! Ye'll no' get a hen to lay an egg for ye noo unless ye put a bass at the door for it to wipe its feet on, and a hot-watter bottle in beside it when its clockin'."

"It must be fine to be a hen," said Jinnet.

"Not at all! Just hold you on!" said Erchie, warningly. "It was all a plant to cheat the puir things oot o' mair eggs than the Almichty meant them to provide. At first the hens thocht they were on velvet — eatin' the best o' meat withoot the trouble to scratch for't and even spared the trouble o' sittin' on their ain eggs, a thing the hens in the auld days just detested, for it's no joke sitting on a dozen o' eggs at a time and them maybe no' your ain at all, but some silly juck's."[5]

"They got fine and fat — that fat that at last they couldna put their minds into their business, and stopped layin' a'thegether. 'What they need,' says a poultry vet that had his eye on them, 'is exercise. The hen is like the human Bailie, unless it works for its livin' it runs to creesh, and ye micht as weel have a wally yin or a weathercock, for a' the eggs ye'll get!'

"The very next day after this discovery there wasna a hen in Scotland, except the no-weel yins, that wasna workin' for its livin'! In the best-regulated egg factories noo, the hens are never let over the door at all, but kept at business even-on. They still get the pick o' meat, but they have to scratch for't in the litter, or it's hung frae the roof and they have to jump for't. Muscle like gladiators! Ye can see't in knots on them when auld age comes to them and they're slipped on a plate in front o' ye as roasted chicken. It's called the intensive system o' poultry-fermin' because it's awfu' hard lines on the hen. If it doesna lay sae mony eggs a week for the twopence that's put oot on it for meat, there's a blue mark put aginst it in a ledger, and if it's gaun to keep on bein' a dour yin at the layin', up its number goes, and the bauk's cleaned oot for a better yin."

"Poor things!" said Jinnet, feelingly.

"That's science for ye!" said her husband. "Eggs is dearer than ever they were, and the hens, for a' their luxuries, are no' a bit the happier. They were daein' fine the way they were, and noo they're payin' dear for hygiene, sanitation, clean feet, and tooth-brush drill. I never see a hen noo but I'm someway vexed for't, as if it were a human body. There it's tied doon to layin' eggs for other folk wi' a' its micht, when it's natural inclination is to live the simple life and no' be an egg-machine."

"Still," said Jinnet, "I would like fine a wee bit hoose in the country, wi' a dozen hens."

105. *Erchie on Prohibition*[1]

"Whats a' this aboot shuttin' the pubs to sodgers?" Duffy asked. "What harm would the sodgers dae in a pub ony mair nor onybody else? I think at a time like this the sodgers should get a' encouragement, to cheer them on."

Erchie looked at the coalman with humorous resignation. "Man, Duffy!" he replied, "ye're aye a week behind wi' your news the way ye are in takin' tuppence aff the bag when the coals come doon. It's no' against the sodgers that they're gaun to shut the pubs; they're maybe gaun to shut them a'thegither."[2]

Duffy was staggered, but incredulous. "Nane o' your coddin', Erchie! Hoo could they refuse to serve ye if ye hae the money and nae signs o' drink aboot ye? They widna daur! They would lose their licence!"

"Duffy," said his friend, "your education's painfully neglected; ye should have stayed another quarter in the night school. Ye've heard o' an Act o' Parliament? Wi' an Act o' Parliament they can dae onything. They could stop ye eatin' eggs or gettin' your hair cut. It used to tak' years to pass an Act o' Parliament, and even then a smert-like chap could march through the middle o't the same's it was a triumphal arch. But noo an Act o' Parliament taks less than twenty seconds; they dae't wi' a rubber stamp. If they took a notion to stop the sale o' coals the first ye would hear o't would be a telegram frae the Hoose o' Commons, sayin' that coals were contraband, and ony man found wi' a bunker in his hoose on and after Monday first would be put in jyle."

"Somebody should write to the papers and expose them!" said Duffy, warmly; "It shouldna be allo'ed! I'll never vote for onybody again! What sense is there in shuttin' pubs?"

"Oh, they're no' shut yet," said Erchie; "But a lot o' folk's got an awfu' start. I got a wee bit shake mysel'."

The coalman gloomily stared at vacancy. "My George! It's gettin' worse and worse!" he said despairingly at last. "First it was Zeppelins, and then it was submarines, and noo it's pubs blockaded! It's perfectly redeeculous! What herm's a dacent pub if ye don't abuse it?"

"Ye don't understand," said Erchie. "It's military tactics; it's to get recruits. If ye want a people to win a war, ye must mak' them desperate. Look at the Russians and the French! The Russians, for ordinar', like to put past the time wi' a foreign drink called vodka because it jist tastes like that, and the French mak' a habit o' drinkin' absinthe, if there's ony left over when they're polishin' a chest o' drawers or a sideboard. When the war broke oot half the French kept on busy polishin' and the Russians moved that slow from the vodka shops to the fightin' line they ca'd them the steam-road-rollers.

"'If things go on like this', said the Czar to the President o' the French Republic, 'the war'll last a lifetime. We'll need to tak' steps to mak' them move a little slippier.'

"An Act was passed prohibitin' the sale o' vodka and absinthe till the war was settled, and the Russians and the French flocked to the Army determined to end the war at

the earliest possible moment. Ye couldna stop them goin'
noo that there was naething to keep them at hame."

"And what did the Germans dae?" asked Duffy.

"The Germans did the same in a different way. 'If ye
want good beer,' says they to their sodgers, 'there's plenty
in Belgium, and France is full o' champagne cellars.' That
made them breenge across the border, and they'll stay in
Belgium and France as lang's there's a barrel or a bottle
left.

"If they shut the pubs in Scotland, Duffy, it's because
your king and country needs ye quicker than ye come.
Stayin' at hame and shirkin' must be made to lose its main
attraction. When it's generally understood that the only
place in Europe where ye can get a tot o' rum is in the
trenches, every high-spirited young man'll 'list."

"It'll be gey hard on us that's no' that young," said
Duffy. "Could they no' just mak' the Act apply to chaps
that's under forty?"

"Na; na! if it comes at a' it'll come a' roond. The King
himsel's teetotal[3] noo; no' a drop o' onything in the hoose
for him but butter-milk, or maybe a bottle or two o'
raspberry cordial. 'What'll ye hae, your Majesty?' says his
butler, bringin' in the tray at nicht. 'I suppose there's
naething for't but butter-milk as usual,' says the King.
'Right-o!' says the butler, and slaps him doon a jugful. It's
a lesson to us a', Duffy. If ye want to get royal noo ye can
get the whole concomitants o' a spree at the kitchen
jawbox."

"But still I canna picture the pubs a' shut in Gleska,"
says Duffy. "Everybody'll mak' a rush for Paisley."

"Tuts! if they're shut in Gleska they'll be shut in Paisley
too. But I'm like you — I canna figure to mysel' a total
prohibeetion Scotland. Whaur would millionaires like you
in the coal tred spend their money. A small limejuice and
soda's a nice enough beverage in moderation, but ye canna
spend a nicht wi't, and if there's nae pubs, a lot o' chaps,
when their day's work's done, 'll no' hae any place to go to
but straight hame. They'll be driven to't!

"And then," continued Erchie, "consider the effect on a' the associated industries! The peppermint and aromatic-lozenge tred'll suffer dreadfully. The cultivation o' the clove'll stop, and the cork-screw manufacturies may just as weel shut their doors. It'll tell on the fishin' tred, for naebody'll go fishin'; ye canna keep the midges aff wi' eau-de-cologne or barley-water."

"I simply WILL NOT stand it!" protested Duffy. "I need a moderate refreshment noo and then to keep my strength up. You carry fifty hunderwechts o' coal —"

"Fifty bags ye mean," corrected Erchie.

"— Up them tenement stairs and ye'll find it canna be done on butter-milk!"

"Oh, ye'll get used to that," said Erchie cheerfully. "Drinkin's just a habit, like wearin' boots or sittin' in your shirt sleeves to your tea. There's days and days I never think o't, and if I was in a lichthoose I would clean forget that such a thing as drink existed. ... My Jove! what would happen to Campbeltown?[4] I would be vex't for Campbel-town!"

"Ye micht be vexed for yoursel'," suggested Duffy. "There wouldna be the same demand for waiters."

"Oh, just the same!" said Erchie. "They canna stop folk eatin', except in Germany, where ye need to get a ticket before ye can cut a loaf. The only difference wi' us waiters would be that we would get hame sooner frae their public banquets; there wouldna be ony aifter-dinner oratory."

"Ach! the thing's a' nonsense!" said Duffy. "If ye met a chap ye kent at nicht, what could ye stand him?"

"Oh, ye would jist slip him an oranger or a tin o' Nestle's milk, and say 'Here's to ye!' The springs o' human kindness needna be a'thegither dry because o' prohibeetion. At the worst ye would aye be at liberty to tak' a crony into Craig's or Cranston's,[5] and fill him up wi' Russian tea, a drink that's fairly ragin' noo across the Blue Carpathian Mountains."

"Tea's a' richt in its ain place," admitted Duffy, "but ye couldna be aye nip, nip, nippin' awa' at tea. It's maybe fine

for folk that hae the time to spend on't, but it's no' for
workin' men. If this calamity is railly gaun to happen us,
I'll hae to lay in something in a press till the war blaws bye."

106. *Duffy Will Buy Bonds*[1]

THERE IS every indication that Mr Duffy has been doing
well in the coal trade lately. For the first time in his
business career he has a horse that can lie down in its stall
and get up again without the least assistance — a coal-
black, long-tailed, feather-footed, haughty-looking horse
with an astonishingly masculine 'nicher,' which, coming
from between the trams of a coal-lorry, provokes much
interest every time it is heard, and almost saves Duffy the
trouble of crying "Coal!"

It was whinnying in the most inviting way to a passing
taxi-cab on Saturday when Erchie came along the street
and congratulated Duffy on his new steed.

"Man," he said, "that's a great, big, fine, lump o' a
horse ye hae, Duffy! He's like his meat. Is he a genuine
Clydesdale ?"

"If ye kent aboot horse, ye would see quite plain he
wasna a Clydesdale," answered Duffy; "He's a Belgian
refugee. I bocht him frae Meikle the undertaker. A wee bit
saft, like a' them funeral stallions, but, man, he's got the
style!"

"What's he nich-nich-nicherin' for?" asked Erchie.

"If ye'll no' let it ony further, I'll tell ye," whispered the
coalman. "He's blin' in wan e'e, and he canna see wi' the
other, and he jist gangs by the sound o' wheels. That horse
would nicher to a tramway caur!"

The last raik of the day had been delivered, and Erchie
went to the stable with the black Belgian and its owner.
Duffy gave it corn!

"That's because it's Seturday," he explained.

"Nae wonder he nichers!" said Erchie. "Pampered like
that! The coal tred must be daein' weel the noo, Duffy."

"Oh, I'm no' daein' that awfu' bad!" the coalman admitted. "But, man, ye canna keep money; the wife's never aff my face noo to buy her a pianna."

"A pianna!" exclaimed his friend. "Whit on earth does she want wi' a pianna? I'm shair a' your lassies is merried and aff your hands! I would think your wife had plenty to dae to keep the grate in order. Don't you encourage her, Duffy; if she got yin she would maybe try to play't — "

"Oh, I'm no' givin' in to her," said Duffy; "but I'll go as faur as a vacuum washer." He turned to his friend with an amazing outburst of confidence. "Man, Erchie," he said, "I'm makin' money! Ye have nae idea o' the fine sensation it is. I have mair than a hunder pound this very meenute in behind the meter — "

Erchie sighed. "A hunder pound!" he said. "Nae wonder ye have a horse that nichers; it's just pride! But I wouldna keep a' that money in behind the meter; the man that comes to tak' the meter micht tak' mair. Ye should invest it, Duffy."

"I thocht o' that tae," said Duffy. "A buildin' society —"

Erchie waved the suggestion aside impatiently.

"A'thegither oot o' date! Ye micht as weel put it in the Sustentation Fund or doon a stank.[2] Before ye kent where ye were ye would be landed wi' a hoose and naebody to pent and paper't for ye. Whit you should dae wi' your hunder pound, Duffy, is to put it in a Bond."[3]

"I thocht aboot that tae," said Duffy, brushing down the Belgian. "Everybody's sayin' ye should put money in a Bond, but I went doon and looked at yin below a railway arch, and I wouldna trust a penny in't. As dark as a ree,[4] and an awfu' smell o' drink."

Erchie laughed. "Man," he said, "ye're a comic, Duffy! It's no' in a bonded store ye're advised to put your money noo, though I daresay mony a penny ye put there indirectly through the Mull o' Kintyre Vaults; the thing I mean's a War Bond. Gie your money to the country and get 4$\frac{1}{2}$ per cent."

"But would it be safe?" asked Duffy, cautiously.

"Onything would be safer than havin' it in beside a City o' Gleska meter. A Bond's safer than a bank, and ye ken whit banks is; every weel-daein' man in Gleska puts his money into banks, and it's there as guid as ever when he's deid. But a bank'll only gie ye twa per cent; the Government'll gie four-and-a-half, backed up wi' the security o' the British Empire, and there's naething mair secure than that unless it's the jyle at Peterheid. You buy Bonds, Duffy! Never you heed the wife and her pianna; a vacuum washer's far mair like the thing. Onybody can work it and it doesna need a tuner. And mind you this — that every sovereign ye lend the Government's a sodger to fight the Germans. There's no sense keepin' sodgers in beside the meter, or locked up in a Cottage Upright Grand that aye needs polishin'."

"It's a lot o' money, mind ye, a hunder pound!" said the coalman. "It's nearly twa pounds a week for a year; a man could live first-rate on that."

"Tak' my advice, and put it in a War Loan Bond! It'll gie ye the status o' a landed gentleman. 'There's Mr Duffy,' the folk'll say, and touch their keps to ye; 'He keeps the country goin'!' If I had a hunder pound to spare the noo ye wouldna see my feet for stour,[5] running to the G.P.O. or the bank to get the best investment that this country's every seen."

"I'll dae't!" said Duffy, putting on his coat. "Will they use it for buyin' shells?"

"That's jist whit they want it for," said Erchie. "And if ye buy a Bond ye're daein' your wee bit to bash the Germans. It's likely there'll be a badge for the genuine War Investors. Ye'll get a button to stick in your coat lapel to show ye're no' a shirker."

"I'll awa' this very meenute and buy a vacuum washer!" said Duffy.

107. *An Ideal Profession*[1]

JOHNNY DUFFY, the coalman's son, having reached the age of seventeen, and being now, in his father's estimation, thoroughly educated, is not going back to school again.

"Whit are ye gaun to make o' him?" Erchie asked the father on Saturday.

"That's the bit!" said Duffy. "I havena ony notion — not the least! He used to hae a fancy to be a tramway guard, but that was afore they had the petticoats;[2] he would nae mair think o' bein' a guard noo than o' bein' a milliner. His mother was thinkin' o' puttin' him in a bank."

"In a bank!" exclaimed Erchie. "There's naebody puts onything in banks noo since the War Loan started. It would just be throwin' the chap awa'."

"Ay, but banks is aye looked up to; it's no' the same as sellin' coals. A clerk in a bank can keep his mind aff anything till he gets his breakfast, and his work's a' done at three in the efternoon and twelve on Saturday. And there's money made in banks; folk just come and put it in."

"Duffy," said his friend, solemnly, "don't you be so misguided as put Johnny in a bank. It's no' done nooadays at a'; it's oot o' date. This time next year, if ye're spared, ye'll see naebody workin' in banks but the directors, and a wheen o' smert wee lassies new passed wi' their Intermediate. Has Johnny no' got his health?"

"There's naething wrang wi' his health since Dr Jordan sorted him efter the measles," said Duffy. He might have been talking about a clock.

"Very well," said Erchie, "if he has the health, and a' his wits aboot him, ye couldna dae better than put him into the Wine, Spirit, and Beer Trade; it's gaun to be the popular profession o' the future. Get him started richt aff. There's bound to be a rush for't. It's gaun to be a far better tred for a smert young chap than slavin' awa' in a bank seven or eight hours a day. Put Johnny in a pub, and he'll no' need to start his work till twelve o'clock. He'll get aff from half-past two till six, and be done for the day at nine, in time for the second hoose at the music-halls. On Seturday he'll only need to work frae four till nine. Five to five-and-a-half hours a day! Man, it would just be sport for the fellow! He wouldna hae mair time to himsel' if he was a stock-broker!"[3]

"Five hours!"[3] said Duffy, who rarely reads the papers. "Maclachlan o' the Mull o' Kintyre Vaults is toilin' awa' in his place from efter nine in the mornin' till efter ten at night; it's no' sport keepin' a pub."

"That's true aboot Maclachlan noo, but it'll no' be true o' him efter Monday week; he'll have time, if he likes, to attend the College and come oot a minister. Man, that would be a capital chance for Johnny! Ye see, Duffy, under the new Act, Gleska and the Clyde is an infected area; naebody'll dare sell a drap o' drink except at the hours I've mentioned."

"My Jove! I wish this war was ended," fervently said the coalman.

"If you and me survive these hardships for a year or twa," said Erchie, "we'll see an awfu' difference in Gleska and the Clyde doon as far as a line drawn between Camp-beltown and the Heads o' Ayr. The 'mornin'' is abolished at wan fell swoop. Efter his dinner a man may just as weel go back to his work, for the pubs 'll no' be open till six o'clock, and at nine at nicht there'll be naethin for't for even the maist determined and independent man but just to gang awa' hame."

"And they talk aboot the land o' the brave and the free!" said Duffy, bitterly.

"That's richt!" said Erchie, cheerfully.

"It's a blow at British liberty. But, of course, ye'll can get tea and coffee and Kola and Broon Robin, and onything of that sort at ony reasonable hour o' the day; the pubs can keep open for the sale o' them if they like."

"I can tell you there'll be a bonny run on half-peck bottles!" said Duffy, and his friend gave a chuckle.

"Na! na!" said he; "they thocht of that tae. It's only on

twa hours and a half a day ye'll can tak' away a bottle or have yin sent to the hoose for ye, and maybe no' at a' on Seturday. The bottle-blowin' tred is in a state o' panic, and every cork-cutter in the country's listin' in the Airmy. That's no' the worst o't," proceeded Erchie. "Ye'll no' get staunin' your hand."

Duffy's aspect brightened; momentarily he regarded the new regulations as being not entirely unreasonable.

"Treatin' is abolished. Every man'll have to buy his ain drink, and ye couldna order a drink at the bar for me unless ye gave me my dinner wi't, or at least a twopenny pie; I'm no richt sure yet whether a twopenny pie's to be regairded as a meal or no'."

"Who on earth can keep mind o' a' that?" asked Duffy. "It was far simpler the way it was."

"That's just it! It was far ower simple. The idea noo is to bamboozle ye and mak' gettin' a drink as hard a job as gettin' the VC. It's gaun to be a grand thing for the watchmakers; everybody'll hae to keep a wristlet watch, and a printed caird wi' the hours for drinkin' on it. Ye couldna keep mind o' them ony other way. And look at the flyness o' them — 4 p.m. till 9 on Seturday'. By the time 4 o'clock comes round on Seturday, a poor chap must go hame for his dinner. His wife'll get his pay and have it a' squandered in grocers' shops before he has his face washed. If he's no' wide awake, he'll be hurlin' a perambulator or at a picture-palace wi' her before the pubs is open, and that's no way to start a jolly Seturday nicht."

"I never richt understood afore what they meant by this 'policy o' frightfulness'," said Duffy.

"And forbye," said Erchie;' "there's gaun to be a change in the strength o' whisky. The publican can sell it 35 under proof instead of 25, the strength he sells it at noo. Perhaps he'll sell it cheaper, but it's likely no'. The weaker it is, the better it is for the health, the government says, and ye daurna contradict them!"

"A' nonsense!" said Duffy. "Water's adulteration. I wouldna put Johnny in a tred like that."

"Ay, but consider the gentlemanly leisure Johnny would have!" said Erchie. "As good as a schoolmaster. And, besides, he would be a kind o' a Civil Servant, bein' strictly under Government control. I wouldna say but by-and-bye there'll be a uniform for barmen, and superannuation pensions."

108. *Margarine for Wartime*[1]

ERCHIE MACPHERSON came home on Saturday afternoon with a pound of margarine. He had bought it away in another part of the town, where he wasn't known, by instruction of his wife. "If we must hae margarine," she said, "we needna let a' the neighbours ken. Ye can let on it's just for cookin'.""

It looked all right when Erchie put in on the table — firm and clean, nutritious and faintly golden; it had actually a vague attractive odour of the fields, as if of clover; to the taste it was absolutely indistinguishable from ordinary good butter. Jinnet was astonished.

"That's no what I thocht margarine was like at a'," said she. "I thocht it would just look like a daud o' creesh and taste like monkey-nuts."

"It's the rale Muir o' Stra'ven Margarine," said Erchie. "It's made that like the genuine article that the coos in the Stra'ven district's up in arms against blackleg compiteetion. Ye should hear them mooin' roond the munition factory!"

"The munition factory!" said Jinnet.

"Ay! The Muir o' Stra'ven Margarine's a' made in a munition factory under Government control. Lloyd George[2] has nearly as much high explosive shell noo as he needs to feenish the war, and maist o' the munition factories is makin' margarine three days a week. A' female labour! It's a trate to see yon smert and sonsy Stra'ven lassies in their clean print wrappers churnin' awa' at margarine made o' the very purest ingredients. There's nae monkey-nuts in the Stra'ven stuff — the pick o' Scottish hazel-nuts left over frae Hallowe'en and a reasonable proportion o' sweet milk, and whiles when there's naebody lookin' they fling in a bit o' genuine butter for the sake o' Auld Lang Syne. It's inspected every five meenuts by a chap in brass buttons wi' a microscope in case o' hairs. Just you taste the taste!"

He spread some of it on his toast, and ate with apparent relish.

Jinnet spread it on her bread as thin as possible, and nibbled dubiously. "It's just exactly the same as butter," she remarked, "but it's someway different, and I ken I'll never like it. Oh, Erchie! Little did we think we would ever be reduced to margarine, and us wi' no ill-will to onybody. But I kent for years there was something brewin' for us; we were needin' a chastisement. Look at the way we were cairryin' on! The lust o' the flesh and the pride o' the eye! We werna' half humble. Naething in our minds but pleesure, the raiment we should wear and the worship o' the belly; gallivantin' here and there: chamberin'[3] and wantonness; tiled closes, pianos, mandolins, and fancy cookery classes. When ye bocht me yon new boa a year last January I felt there was something wrang!"

"Is it moths?" asked her husband anxiously.

"No, no! Nae fear o' that; it's aye in camphor. But it was the display o' the thing. Erchie; you were that built up on my ha'en' it. And I was that conceity wi't on Sabbaths."

"Dae ye actually think," said Erchie, "that your boa brocht on the war!"

"I don't ken, but I'm shair it helped. It was the cope-stone of mony indulgences in things corruptible. Ye canna' deny, Erchie, that we were a wicked and extravagant generation."

Her husband twinkled. "So we were," said he, "I'm no' denyin'. Naething would dae me but the tramway-caur frae my work instead o' walkin' the way I used to dae. Every noo and then a shillin' tie. My bottle o' porter every Setturday, whether I was needin't it or no'. The History o' the Clans in forty pairts wi' a' the different tartans. A yin-and-penny-ha'penny bottle o' embrocation every time my back was the least bit sair. The money I've spent on raffles in the past ten years would come to a pound or twa, I'm shair, if it was coonted up, and there's only that model in the room o' the steamer *Bonnie Doon* to show for't. It's nae wonder I havena onything to put in the War Loan, the way I was cairryin' on!"

"Indeed," said Jinnet, bridling, "ye needna blame yoursel'; ye worked hard enough for your wee bit comforts. But when I think o' that boa —"

"If ye mention that boa again I'll tak' the heid aff ye!" cried Erchie. "There was naething I ever bocht in my life I got better value in — unless it was a waddin'-ring."

"Ye're an auld haver!"[4] said his wife, smiling, with a little flush of colour. "Dear me, that's awfu' like good saut butter! I believe I could get used to 't if it hadna the taste o' nuts; no strong, but I can feel it. And, onyway, there's naething cleaner than a nut."

"But it must be rale Scotch hazel," said Erchie, firmly. "Nane o' your foreign trash! That's the motto o' the Muir o' Stra'ven Margarine Manufactory."

"We micht weel come doon to margarine," said Jinnet, sighing, "considerin' the wastery in Scotland this past twenty years. I'm black affronted when I think on't. There was me with my brand new bonnet every second year — no' even content wi' alterin' the auld yin. The last yin I got cost 10s. 6d. I used to buy the print and get a wrapper made o't for twa shillin's by Katie Broon, and naething would please me at the hinder end but a costume frae a shop at thirty shillin's, and it wouldna last me mair nor a year or twa. Oh, Erchie, we were needin' a chastisin'. ... When I think o' my boa, and Mrs Duffy's Alick deid among the Germans!. ... The pride o' the eye and the lust o' the flesh! We were faur astray."

"So I see in the papers," said her husband; "Mr M'Kenna's[5] rale disappointed wi' us. When I think o' the money I spent on tobacco — sevenpence every week!"

"That's naething!" said his wife, impatiently. "A bonny hoose it would be wi' a man that didna smoke! It's my ain extravagance that vexes me. I couldna keep money. I'm shair I could hae done fine without the sewin'-machine, and think o' a' the money it cost us every year for a week at Ro'say! We werena needin' incandescent mantles for the gas, and the wee hoose that we had in Raeberry Street was fine; I'm sorry I ever egged ye on to leave it. Whit would my mither — peace be wi' her! — think o' me gaun twice to a picture-hoose, and sendin' oot your washin' to a la'ndry! A penny a collar! It's ruination! But I canna help it Erchie; in your tred linen needs a gloss, and, though it's me that's willin', I'll assure ye, I'm no langer fit for 't."

"If ye try to iron a shirt or collar o' mine again," said her man, "I'll leave ye."

"And here we're at the margarine!" said Jinnet, sadly. "There was never in this hoose afore but honest butter. But I'll no repine: there's mony a puir body waur aff, though I ha'e my boa, and Alick Duffy's deid. I think I'll gang roond and gie Mrs Duffy a tastin' just to show her margarine's no' sae very different frae butter efter a'. Whit did ye pay for't, Erchie'!"

"One-and-nine a pound," said her husband, chuckling. "are you sure ye feel the taste o' nuts?"

"One-and-nine!" cried Jinnet. "Man, that's the price o' butter!"

"And that's just butter that ye're eatin' — plain Danish butter; I bocht it doon the stair in Campbell's. For a' we eat o' butter we can afford it. It's no whit you and me can save in pennies that's gaun to win the war: we couldna' save enough in margarine to run the war a week!"

109. *Duffy in the Dark*[1]

AT EIGHT o'clock on Saturday night, through the darkness and the snow-soup of Garscube Road, Duffy drove his empty lorry home. The night might be filthy, but he had had a good day — a real good day. There had been a delightful public uncertainty as to the selling price of coals. It varied according to circumstances. In Raeberry Street, from desperate women who saw an Arctic Sunday in prospect and had already burned up their clothes-pins for the tea, he had got as much as two-and-three the reputed bag. For carrying bags to the upper flats of tenements he had charged a War Bonus of threepence, and in at least five grateful houses he had got a small refreshment extra.

Duffy was feeling fine.

He was whistling the war-song of the trade: 'Keep the Home-fires Burning', and seeing himself in fancy half an hour from now with his face washed and dry clothes on, sitting before his excellent wife's idea of a Saturday supper. He hoped it would be sausages.

At the corner of Hopehill Road a young man jumped on him out of the dark and said, "For the love of Peter, have ye ony coals!"

"No' as much as you would heave at a cat!" said Duffy. "I'm done for the day."

The young man groaned. "Oh, Jerusalem," he exclaimed. "I've been a' over the toon for a ton at ony price, and I'm bate!"

"Whit would ye ca' ony price?" asked Duffy.

Great thoughts, great instincts, come to men.
Like feelings unaware

as the poet says,[2] and his commercial instincts as a coalman had instantly swamped his vision, as a human being, of an early sausage supper.

"Ony mortal thing!" impulsively said the stranger. "I'm wantin' them for the kirk in Dobbie's Loan. My faither's the beadle, and he's let himsel' run oot, and the place'll be like charity the morrow."

"Whit kirk is't?" asked Duffy.

"It's the yin at the ither end," said the stranger. "Ye'll easy find it."

"I think I mind o' yince seein't," said the coalman. "It's a good bit aff my bate. Forbye, it's late on a Setterday nicht and forbye, my horse and me's clean wabbit. Ye'll mind ye coals is coals them days: it's a favour to get them. They'll cost ye £2. 5s., and that's wi' a half-croon aff, for kirks is a kind o' charity."

"Right-o!" said the young man. "It's stiff, but we'll pay it. Ye'll no' be lang!"

"I'll be there in half an 'oor," said Duffy.

He was quite mistaken.

It was only when he got into Dobbie's Loan a half hour later with the load of coals that he realised fully the drastic character of the Lighting Regulations[3] and the inconspicuousness of churches. By the merest chance he came on one at the corner of Charlotte Street, but not a living soul was to be found in charge of the edifice, which looked as if it had been shut since the Coronation.

"Wasn't I the eediot?" thought Duffy. "It was 'the ither end' he said, and the ither end o' Dobbie's Loan's awa doon somewhere near the Necropolis."

That was somewhat to exaggerate the length of Dobbie's Loan, but in truth it is a ridiculous thoroughfare, in parts the dreariest in Glasgow, and twenty minutes later found Duffy at its extremity in Parliamentary Road with the church of his search still undiscovered. The only helpful information he could get in a public house (with a little nourishment) was that though Dobbie's Loan itself was rather short of churches there was a good selection in the neighbourhood, including the Catholic Apostolic.

"That sounds like a place they would be needin' coal," said Duffy. "The silly Ned micht ha'e gi'en me the richt direction. I'll ha'e a chaser."

"Nine o'clock," said the barman firmly, and began to

clear up his counter.

When Duffy rejoined his horse the night seemed blacker than ever. The snow was falling thickly. Only the faintest light came from the public lamps; the tramway cars went past as black as hearses. Tenements were like cliffs without a chink of light in them, and the shops that were open still appeared to be using candles.

"Oh frost!" said Duffy to himself.

Twenty minutes later Duffy cried 'Woah' to his horse, jumped off the lorry's front, and peered about for somebody to speak to. A man came round a corner, feeling his way with caution.

"Do ye ken ony Catholic church?" asked Duffy.

"There's yin in Glebe Street," was the reply; "but man, ye're far ower early for't!"

"Whaur's Glebe Street frae here?" asked Duffy.

"I could tell ye if I had a licht," said the man; "but the way things is I have nae idea. I'm lost mysel'. Sae far as I can mak' oot we're near the Blin' Asylum. Whit are ye wantin' a church at this time for? Is it Easter Sunday or onything o' that sort?"

"I'm gaun to't wi' a rake o' coals," said Duffy. "Do ye no see I have a lorry?"

"My Jove!" said the man, "is that a lorry ye're standin' in front o'? I thocht it was a pend close."

"Ye micht weel think that!" said Duffy. "I have nae mair idea o' whaur I am than my horse has. It's the first time I ever took a job on for this end o' the toon, and I'll bate ye it'll be the last. I would gang hame the way I am if I only could fin' oot Dobbie's Loan."

"Dobbie's Loan!" said the other. "Ye're richt enough for Dobbie's Loan; it's scattered a' roond here; ye canna miss it. If ye see a tramway caur go efter't. And if ye don't see onything at a' its Sichthill Cemetery."

"Gee-up!" said Duffy to his horse. "This is a bonny warnin' to me to have naething to dae wi' papists. If I had kent I would have asked for £2.10s."

The idea of following the tramway lines appealed to

him. At least they would prevent him from straying out of Glasgow altogether. By now there was nobody on the streets; the cars that went past at intervals one way or another had hardly anybody in them, so far as he could see into their dimly lit interiors. The shops were shut. Great blocks, pitch black, were on either side of him.

"And yet they say ye canna get stuff to mak' briquettes," said Duffy.

At the end of another mile or two he came on a standing tramway car, and the driver in front of it lighting matches.

"Can ye tell me where I am?" the driver asked him, with an Irish accent. His conductor was a lady who was in tears, and she was lighting matches also.

"God knows!" said Duffy. "Where were ye bound for?"

"Sure and I was makin' for Barrachnie," said the driver. "I came from the Paisley Road way and it's my first time on the rowte. I always disbelieved there could be any place wid the name Barrachnie in Glasgow, and now I'm sure av it. I've drove this kyar since eight o'clock on both sides av the river; I've been in the Roukin Glen and the Celtic football ground and the barracks at Maryhill, and divill the ticket the girl has got in her bunch 'll fit the passengers. I should be back where I started an hour ago, but the only place I knew since I started was the Cattle Market and I've passed it half a dozen times."

They stood helplessly in the darkness till a policeman came up and shone his lamp on them.

"What's a Barrachnie car doin' here?" he asked with some astonishment.

"Do ye ken a Catholic church that's needin' coals?" asked Duffy.

"No," said the constable, "nor a UF neither."

"Where the divvel are we?" asked the driver.

"You're within a kick of Bishopbriggs: you're on the High Possil Road," said the constable.

"Oh frost!" said Duffy.

110. *A Bawbee on the Bobbin*[1]

"THAT'S an awfu' thing that's happened in Paisley," said Erchie, putting down his paper and removing his glasses.

"What in the world is't?" cried Janet, trembling already in anticipation of some dreadfully tragic news.

"A Mr MacGallochary," said her husband, "yin o' the largest shareholders in J. & P. Coats'[2] business, went into the works on Friday mornin' and attacked the manager."

"Isn't that awfu'!" said Janet. "What did he attack him wi'?" Her sense of the tragic always depends very largely on the nature of the weapon.

Her husband pretended to consult the paper again. "Positively monstrous!" he remarked. "Bashed him ower the heid wi' a poke o' sovereigns!"[3]

"I thought ye couldna get sovereigns the noo: there's surely no' enough o' them aboot to hurt onybody."

"I havena seen yin mysel' since the year o' the Exhibition," said Erchie; "but there must be plenty gaun aboot for onybody that's in a dacent way o' business."

"What did he attack him for?" inquired Janet.

"For makin' an awfu' mistake in his calculations. MacGallochary said he was just efter gettin' his dividends from the business, and he noticed at yince there was something wrang, they were that rideeculous for the time o' war, and his anger got the better o' him."

"It was gey hard on the puir manager," said Janet. "Ony man can mak' a mistake in coontin'; there's whiles I'm no very sure o' mysel' wi' the price o' everything different to what it used to be."

"MacGallochary didna look at it that way, though, him bein' a kind o' Christian and parteecular to a faut."

"I hope we're a' Christians, Erchie," said the wife gravely.

"Oh ay, of course we are, but MacGallochary must hae belanged to a brench high up in the Christian body that canna stand the least wee deviation frae the Ten Commandments. It doesna say his age, but I think he must hae

been an auld, auld man that doesna realise there should be
some come and go in Christianity. ... What dae ye pay for
your pirns o' threid?"

"Threepence a piece," said Janet. "It's mair than a year
since they put them up a ha'penny. It's an awfu' money for
threid! I suppose it's the war."

"That's just it! That's what vexed MacGallochary. Ye
see it's like this — when the war broke oot the Coatses say
'The cost o' raw material and labour's bound to gang up
like onything, and we'll hae naething left for dividends at
the present price of the cotton bobbin. We must dae
something.' The manager made a calculation wi' a pencil
on the back o' a bit o' paper he had brung his piece to the
works in and said the way things was the pirn would hae to
be raised to threepence. Somebody asked if a farden[4] extra
on the bobbin wouldna dae, considerin' that threid would
be mair in demand in the world than at any other time in
its history. But he says 'No, gentlemen, the farden advance
is oot o' the question. Naebody ever has a farden except on
the Greenock tramways. It's no' a coin in circulation. We
couldna be handin' back the customer a packet o' preens
or an Abernaithy biscuit for change for every pirn she
bought. No, gentlemen, it must be a threepenny bobbin to
do justice to the shareholders.'"

"There's nae doot," said Janet, "that the farden's oot o'
date since they stopped the missionary boxes in the
Sunday schools."

"Weel, ye see, when MacGallochary found that Coats
made a profit o' £3,387,395 last year, or threequarters o' a
million mair than in the year afore the war began, he saw
the manager's calculation was lamentably wrang, and that
he was far ower smert in puttin' the bawbee on the bobbin
when there wasna ony need for't. When the manager came
to his senses efter the poke o' sovereigns struck him on the
neck, MacGallochary tellt him he wasna gaun to tak' a
bonus o' a bawbee extra on the pirns, for sewin' sodgers'
shirts, and that the three-quarters o' a million must be
handed back to the Government, and the price o' the

bobbin reduced to what it was afore the war."

"I don't care," said Janet, "but there must have been something nice aboot Mr MacGallochary to think o' such a thing."

"When the manager heard this extraordinary proposal he swooned awa' for the second time, and it wasna' till they sent oot for a little brandy he cam' tae again."

"He must ha'e been awfu' badly hurt," said Janet, sympathetically, "Just fancy you a poke o' sovereigns on the neck!"

"And the best o't is that they werena sovereigns efter a'," said Erchie, consulting his newspaper. "It said sovereigns right enough on the ootside o' the poke, but the polis found it was filled wi' naething but auld communion tokens.[5] He was a clever man that thought o' that!"

"What did they dae wi' Mr MacGallochary?" inquired Janet.

"They took him to Gartnavel,"[6] said her husband, solemnly. "They kens that nae shareholder in his senses would be such an awfu' idiot and act like that. On the way to Gartnavel in a taxi he kept stickin' his heid oot at the window every noo and then cryin' "Paisley pirns! Paisley pirns! Gie the women and the Army back their maik.'[7] Awfu' vulgar! Fancy him sayin', 'maik'."

"And are they gaun to bring doon the price o' pirns noo that they hae found oot they were mistaken?" asked Janet innocently.

Her husband look at her with pity. "My, Jinnet," he said, "ye're almost fit for Gartnavel yoursel' to hae ony such idea! Do ye no' ken that the nation's slogan is 'Business as usual — and a wee bit better.' They found MacGallochary was aff his heid for months back, and that he never was a shareholder in Coats' or onywhere else. He was only lettin' on — like mysel'."

111. *Nationalised Eggs*[1]

DUFFY, THE work of the week accomplished, walked home with the essentials of a satisfactory Saturday tea for himself — a half-a-pound of ham he had bought at the corner, and two fresh eggs. On Saturday afternoons he always caters for himself; a wife has quite inadequate ideas of a coalman's needs.

"I'll bate ye what ye like it's a present for the mistress," said Erchie, with a finger on the parcel.

"Then ye're wrang!" retorted Duffy. "I gi'ed her a present last New Year. It's my supper. Do ye ken what country eggs is, Erchie? Four shillin's a dozen! For eggs, mind ye! — just common country eggs, no' ostriches. Four shillin's! I've seen the day 4s. would cairry ye roond every licensed hoose in the Coocaddens district and leave enough for your fine on the Monday mornin'. What's the maitter wi' the hens?"

"It's no the hens," said Erchie. "The loyal and patriotic hen is willin' to dae her bit. It's the faut o' a Coalition Government.[2] The London *Times* and the *Daily Mail* at the very start o' the war pointed oot that the egg situation was desperate and that only firm and immediate action by a Poultry Board would save the situation. The government paid nae heed. It had nae relations in the egg trade for wan thing, and there was nae ootstandin' statesman wi' that devotion to his country and intimate knowledge o' the hen to mark him oot for Egg Minister. What's the result? The country eggs at 4d. to $4\frac{1}{2}$d.! — a price that puts it oot o' the question for workin' men and mak's it the monopoly o' shipowners and teetotallers."

"Somebody's makin' a fine thing o't anyway," said Duffy, gloomily. "I'm shair the country's fair hotchin' wi' hens."

"On the contrary," said Erchie, "there's no' near enough o' them, and them we hae are fair mismanaged. Just you think! — there's 20,000,000 acres o' Scotland under deer, and half as much set aside for growin' grouse. Hoo much o' the land dae ye think is devoted to poultry? Man, ye could hardly play a fitba' match on't! It's silly! There's naething tae be got frae deer besides the eatin' o't except the horns, and maybe a bass for your parlour, and grouse doesna lay eggs! — at least I never saw them. But you tak' a hen! — a hen's producin' something a' the time, providin' the people's breakfasts and the coalman's tea, and whiles a surplus over for elections. Even when it's deid at the end o' a lang and busy life, it's chicken croquets, a thing ye get in restaurants. Economically, for the State, a hen's worth twenty deer and a gross o' grouse, but it gets nae support frae the Game Laws and the Government.

"If the country realised the value o' the hen, it would clear the deer and grouse frae the land they occupy, and put on a good-layin' strain o' Leghorns and Minorcas. The sportin' gentry would soon adapt themselves to stalkin' Wyandotes in the shootin' season and a' the rest o' the year the hens would be busy layin'. Nae waste! On the 18th o' August ye would read then in the papers that the Duke o' Sutherland (3 guns) shootin' over the Castle Moor bagged 30 brace o' Black Minorcas and 15 Dorkins. A' the rest o' the time the hills and moors would be full o' quite fresh eggs!

"But nobody thocht o' backin' up the natural enterprise o' the hen by givin' it this expansion. Run on large intelligent lines, hen-farmin' might have been the country's salvation. We would be independent o' the foreign egg and the egg wi' the Irish accent, and the price would never be over a shillin' a dozen. It's too late to start hen forests noo that the war is on, but a sensible Government would have done the next best thing a year ago, and put the nation's egg production on a scientific basis. The business is a' in the hands o' auld wifes wi' nae capital. A farmer's wife oot about Mearns employs thirty or forty hens; a minister's wife in the parish o' Balfron keeps a hundred gaun; thoosands o' country women wi' nae appliances but a bauk and a couple o' stucca[3] eggs tak' up the tred wi' a dozen or twa auld-fashiond hens that never had any education or

technical trainin', and it's on the like o' them the supply o'
a reasonable breakfast for the British workin' man
depends! The thing's silly!"

"Four shillin's a dozen!" said Duffy.

"If the Government had done what the newspapers
wanted, they would hae pooled a' the poultry-stock in the
country'; shooed a' the hens into a big kind o' national
muneetion factory, and speeded them up under expert
management. Mind ye, there's a lot o' labour troubles wi'
hens workin' in small concerns. They're aye gaun aff to
moult or cleck, or onything that'll tak' them aff their work;
put them a' into half-a-dozen big national Egg Factories
wi' the right kind o' supervision, and a' that nonsense
would be ended. Half the puir auld wifes that's super-
intendin' hens the noo hae nae idea aboot science; they
fling oot the heel o' a loaf and some potato peelin's, and
waste half the day lookin' through the hay or under
hedges for the product. Meanwhile the country's waitin'
for the National Idea — and that's the All-Round Penny
Egg."

"I wish I seen it," said Duffy. "Four shillin's the dozen!"

"Ye'll no see it till the government wakes up," said
Erchie. "Not till the egg production o' the country's put in
the hands o' Mr Winston Churchill[4] or Mr. Bottomley.[5]
They're cut oot for the job. They have the very cackle
for't."

112. *A Slump in Zepps*[1]

"IT'S ME that's vexed for the poor!" said Janet. "I don't ken
hoo they manage at a' in the country-places where there's
naething extra comin' in frae bonuses and muneetions.
Everything's gaun up."

"No' exactly everything," said her husband, looking
over his spectacles "Zepps[2] is comin' doon. There's a
slump in Zepps. We're baggin' them by the pair like kipper
herrin'. Onybody in this country that's needin' a second-

hand Zepp for gaun home wi' at the New Year, can buy yin then for the price o' a pramlater, or I'm sair mistaken. If I could stable yin in the lobby I'd have it. The airyplane chaps is gettin' fair fed up wi' them, and the country's flooded wi' aluminium souvenirs. There's nae reputation to be made noo bringin' doon a Zepp. The first man that did it got the VC, and ony amount o' money; noo they only gi'e ye a coconut."

"There must be some contrivance for puttin' them on fire," suggested Janet.

"I'll tell ye what it is if ye'll no let bug," said Erchie, mysteriously. "To let ye understand, they're lined ootside wi' flannelette. A' the airyplane chap has got to dae is to light a cigarette afore he rises, and drop it on the Zepp when he's fair above it. Every time a coconut!"

"Oh, dear me!" sighed Janet. "Ye would wonder folks would risk their life in them."

"There's nae risk!" explained her husband. "It's a deid certainty! When a German's sent aff in a Zeppelin noo his widow at yince goes into mournin'. A' his friends go doon to the airship shed to see the last o' him, and slip him a couple o' floral wreaths, and then go back to read the will. The heid o' the German Zeppelin service noo is no' Count Zeppelin at a'; he's away back to the toy tred and makin' a fortune oot o' penny squeakers. The whole Zepp business noo is superintended by a firm o' funeral undertakers in Berlin; they're the Wylie & Locheid[3] o' Germany, and aye had the reputation o' turnin' oot a classy job in ony line o' obsequies."

"If I was a German —'

"God forbid!" cried her husband, shocked. "Please moderate your language, Jinnet!"

"If I was a German, I wouldna put a foot in their Zeppelins."

"Ye would ha'e nae choice in the maitter," said Erchie. "The Kaiser picks the crews. They're made up o' expensive auld Army and Navy chaps he's tired o', or found oot daein' something. He gies them an iron cross apiece and puts up a prayer. The cruel thing is the cross is far far ower wee for puttin' up in cemeteries. It's just makin' a cod o' the deceased. When the Zeppelin starts for England, His Majesty drives hame in the first o' the mournin' coaches and says to his wife, 'We're daein' fine! There's another thirty pensions saved!'

"What does a Zeppelin look like?" inquired Janet. "I never saw yin."

"It's the shape o' a Trades Hoose cigar, if ye understand, and the size o' a pencil when ye see't first; then there's a bang, and a bleeze o' light, and the next time ye see it, it's spread ower a field like the start o' a new Corporation gas-works."

"Puir things! There's no much sport in that," said Janet.

"Oh, there's an element o' sport wi't tae! The *Milguy Chronicle* is offerin' £3,000 to the first o' a Zeppelin crew that can land on his feet withoot stottin'."

"What good does it dae them tryin' to come here at a'?"

"I can tell ye that!" said Erchie, promptly. "It's 'frightfulness.'[4] They want to put up the price o' potatoes and milk that high we'll no' can buy them. There's nae other reason for their droppin' bombs ower the rural districts. It frightens the coos and make an awfu' hash o' the potato pits. Nae wonder the fermer greets into the tinny when he's measurin' oot the milk, and laments that he has to charge sae much for his potatoes."

"But the Germans is aye talkin' aboot hittin' fortified places; what's a fortified place?"

"It's a place," said her husband, "where there's two or more JPs, a Young Women's Guild, two good kirks, and an esplanade. If there's a Casualty Sick Poorhouse in the place, it comes under the cless o' 'heavily fortified'."

"I don't care what ye say, I wish I saw the last o' their Zeppelins," said Janet. "I can hardly mak' oot the dairy doon the street, it's that dark. Did I no' mistake the door and gang into Maclintock's public hoose last Seturday? Fancy that! And me wi' my jug in my haun'! What would they think?"[5]

"Oh, they would just think ye maybe had lodgers. What did ye dae wi' the beer?"

"Fine ye ken I never got it!" said Janet indignantly; "I came oot whenever I saw the barrels, and who did I bang into when I was comin' oot, but Duffy!"

"I hope ye explained to Duffy!" said her husband anxiously.

"He didn't gie me the chance; he jist said 'I'll no' mention it Mrs MacPherson,' and in he went!"

Erchie chuckled. "That shows ye," said he, "that the darkenin' o' Gleska's no' withoot its compensations. It gave ye an opportunity to see what Maclintock's is like inside, and to learn the naitural kindliness and courtesy o' the coalman."

"It gave me an awfu' start!" said Janet. "It's just yin tribulation after another; I sometimes think its the end o' the world."

"Nae fear o' that!" replied her husband. "If I thocht it was the end o' the world, I would tak' the first boat for Carrick Castle."

113. *The New Pub* [1]

DUFFY THE coalman came up to Erchie on Saturday with a face like a fiddle. "They're fair puttin' the lid on't now," said he. "Did ye hear the latest?"

"Don't tell me the Scottish Command has gone awa' and commandeered your horse!" exclaimed his friend. "If they've done that I'll vote for President Wilson and Peace, for it shows this country's situation is desperate."

"It's no' that," said Duffy hastily. "It's the pubs; they're shutting them a'thegither!"

"They've done it on Saturday nichts for years and years ever since the time o' Forbes McKenzie," said Erchie. "But they'll be open again at twelve o'clock on Monday. If yer wife's taken ill, or onything like that, mind I havena a drop o' beer in the hoose!"

Duffy snorted indignantly. "Ye ken fine what I mean! They're shuttin' them efter the first o' January and maybe they'll never be open again, for a' the refreshments that's in them's to be sent to France to carry on the push."

It took Erchie several minutes to recover his solemnity. "Ye're a' mixed up, Duffy!" he explained with the tears of laughter in his eyes. "It's na the pubs they're shuttin' up after the New Year's Day; it's a wheen o' railway stations[2] that naebody ever went into except when it was rainin'."

"Oh, jeepers!" exclaimed the coalman, much relieved. "I was tellt it was pubs! There's far ower mony railway stations onyway at this time o' year; they jist tempt folk to trevel, instead o' stayin' at hame and keepin' on good fires."

"Ye needna be the least feared aboot the pubs," said Erchie, "They'll no be shut for a lang while yet, but before the war's feenished you and me'll be teetotal. There's no' gaun to be Prohibition, for ye can dae ony mortal thing ye like wi' the free-born British citizen except prohibit him from takin' a drink when he wants it. Ya can tak' awa' his business and his bairns, and even tak' his life, but ye daurna tak' his beer. The Government kens that fine, so it's no gaun to mak' ony frontal attack on the public-hooses; it's gaun to flank them on the lines o' what Duggie Haig[3] would ca' the higher strategy. When there's naething left in the public-hoose to drink but Boston Cream and Broon Robin it'll shut itsel'."

"When are they gaun to start?" asked Duffy anxiously looking at his watch.

"Oh ye canna lay in onything noo till Monday afternoon," said Erchie. "They've started already. Ony whisky they're makin' noo wi' ony puff in it is a' gaun ower to France in iron barrels for presentation to the Germans; what's left for sale here's half Loch Katrine, good enough for funerals but no' for first fit purposes at Ne'erday. And look at the price o't! There's thousands o' dacent workin' men in Gleska this week switherin' whether they'll buy a wristlet watch for the wife or bring hame a bottle o' five-

year-old. There's no' half the opportunity for gettin'
cheery there was twa years ago, the 'oors for sale in hotels
and pubs is reduced exactly that much. But the clincher is
to come wi' State control!"[4]

"What's that?" asked Duffy, anxiously. "Put me oot o'
pain."

"When a' the wee pubs is shut up and bankrupt because
they canna get whisky or sell't any langer at a profit, and
it's the price o' champagne wine, the Government'll tak'
over a' that's left and put 'GR' over the doors o' pubs, the
same's they were letterboxes. They've started already at
Annan and Carlisle. When the Mull o' Kintyre Vaults is
run by a chap that had to pass a Civil Service examination
and is workin' for a pension, the place'll be that different
ye'll no' ken it. It'll be a kind o' place ye wouldna like to
gang into unless ye had your face washed and your Sunday
claes. The barmen'll be in uniforms wi' red stripes doon
their breeks, and ye'll have to sign an order form for the
least wee thing ye want to drink that's no teetotal.
Duplicates o' the form'll be sent to your wife and your
minister, if any; if not, to the police. The new-fashioned
pub under State Control'll be a large commodious place
the size o' a skatin' rink, furnished to the last degree wi'
high art and a string band in behind some bushes playin'
'Draw the sword, Scotland!' or 'Why left I my hame?' It'll
be great on snacks; ye'll hardly can get a ginger cordial
unless ye tak' a threepenny shepherd's pie alang wi't, and if
ye tak' tea they'll gie ye a bonus. Nae standin' up'll be
allooed; ye'll hae to sit at a wee table wi' a crochet
centrepiece and a jar o'chrysanthemums in the middle.
Facilities'll be given for readin' the papers and writin'
home. Every wee while in the winter they'll have lectures."

"A chap might as weel be in the Royal Infirmary," said
Duffy, with disgust at such a prospect.

"The great aim o' the State Pub'll be to get the women
to come. Efter the first six months nae married man'll be
served unless he brings his wife wi' him. One free cup o'
Bovril will be given to every woman that tak's her knittin'

wi' her. If she tak's the cookery clesses on the Seturday nights, she gets a coupon every Seturday, and 150 coupons'll be value for a 15s. 6d. war savings certificate at ony post office. The alcoholic strength o' spirits'll be gradually reduced till ye could put oot a fire wi't, and the State-brewed beer'll be officially guaranteed to quench the thirst. Of course, there'll be a great reduction in the 'oors o' openin'. The State Pub'll open at six in the evenin' and shut at nine, and everything'll be done to prevent panic when the rush to get oot begins. Efter it has been established for eighteen months the like o' you and me, Duffy, 'll stay at hame at nichts and carouse on Boston Cream. Then they'll shut up the public hooses on the ground that naebody wants them."

114. *Marriage a la Mode*[1]

THE CLOSE was strewn with confetti and rice when Erchie got home for tea. In the house on the right-hand side of the second landing somebody was playing a melodeon. A perfume of oranges and Florida Water pervaded all the stairs. "There's surely a waddin' in Johnny Simpson's," he remarked to his wife as he put his umbrella upside down in the kitchen jawbox.

"It's his dochter Julia," said Janet, "— the typist yin. What a carry-on! Ye wouldna think there was a war!"

"Do ye tell me Julia's merried!" cried Erchie with surprise. "The lassie's daft; she was makin' her thirty shillings a week. Wha is she merried on!"

"He's a kind o' Sergeant in the Fusiliers," said Janet. "His name's Macrae. Ten minutes after they were married he went awa' back to the Front wi' a bit o' the bridescake in his pack and her address written doon on the batters o' a Bible he got frae her Auntie Marget. Such a carry-on! Him awa' to the trenches, and them wi' a waddin' party that's shakin' the very land! And they're only engaged since Seturday!"

"Nane the waur o' that," said her husband. "I aye believed in short engagements."

"Weel, I don't," retorted Janet. "They should be happy as long's they can."

"It's the age o' short engagements," said her husband, putting on his slippers. "Yon daft-like way we had o' daunderin' in the gloamin' for months roond the Three Tree Well and alang the Canal is oot o' date entirely. Look at the money it cost for gloves and conversation lozenges alone!"

"Ye canna cast up that I chased ye!" exclaimed his wife warmly. "Ye had to ask me six times."

"Ye're right," said her husband, twinkling; "it was exactly six times. I got 'no' every time and then my luck changed. But nooadays a' that kind o' palaverin's over; the bright young sodger home for seven days' leave is no' richt oot o' the station wi' his goatskin coat on, than some smert young lassie tracks him by his footprints to his lodgin's or his mother's, and has him gassed afore he can mak' a grab for his respirator. If he's an officer they're roond at ten o'clock next morning at the photographer's gettin' their picures taken for the *Bulletin*, and the lassie's wearin' a di'mond and ruby ring for four-and-twenty hours afore she finds oot whether its him or his brother Alexander. Ye get awfu' mixed up wi' them in their uniforms; they look a' alike."

"I never saw such merrages!" said Jinnet. "What a carry on! They go awa' and get married the same's it was fit-on for a costume; it would put me in the nerves!"

Her husband laughed. "Ye belang to a past age, Jinnet; but if you were five-and-twenty and makin' a muneetion wage ye would nick a sodger as quick's the best o' them. There's naething that's alarmin' nooadays aboot a merrage to ony chap that's come through the war. In the old days he would have to go roond her relatives for inspection, and haud her hand at soirees, and study for months the kind o' claes to wear that would please her, and maybe have to join the YMCA if her faither was parteecular. There's nane o' that noo. There's no' ony time for't, wi' him to be back in

France on Sunday. The whole world's speeded up, and ye pick a partner for life the same's it was for a polka. Merrage has been made attractive. What used to put   fellows aff the notion was the need for rentin' a hoose and furnishin't on the instalment system; goin' awa' on a   honeymoon wi' a perfect stranger; jinin' the church, and handin' ower your wages every Seturday afternoon."

"Ye never rued it, ye auld rascal!" his wife rejoined. "Men have nae sense wi' money."

"The very thocht o' the jeely-pans and cruet-stands he was sure to get frae the lassie's cousins was enough to frichten a young chap. That's a' bye wi'! The sodger lover doesna need to bother about a hoose in Gleska as lang as he has his villa in France. He's married in the claes he stands in, a gift o' the Royal Family — the very latest fashion. The engagement ring's an aluminium yin made oot o' the nose o' a German whizz-bang, and the bridegroom's present to the bride is a couple o' German helmets and a rare collection o' the different rifle cartridges as used by the Allies. The relatives canna pass onything aff on him in the way o' presents except a pair o' socks and a box o' a hundred fags, and he's up and awa' for the train afore the minister gets richt started wi' 'The Health o' the Happy Couple.' At eight o'clock next mornin' the sodger's wife's on her way to business as usual and lookin' at a' the newspaper bills on the road to see if her gettin' married to a corporal had made ony difference on the war."

"What a carry on!" repeated Janet. "Whit'll happen when a' they married men come back? There'll no' be hooses² for them, and lots o' them couldna keep a wife."

"That's the only thing that bothers me," confessed her husband, more seriously. "And I'm no' denying that there's risks that lots o' them in their hurry's makin' a raffle o' a serious business."

"Just that!" said Janet. "But merrage is a raffle onyway ye tak' it. Julia Simpson's sergeant looks a wise-like lad; she maybe couldna pick a better if she took a year to't, the way I did mysel'."

115. *Bad News*[1]

I FOUND my old friend Erchie very depressed on Saturday night. "What's wrong?" I asked him. "Is it the weather, or the aftermath of the festive season, the new alcohol dilution order, or the fall of Braila?"[2]

"It's far worse than that," he responded gloomily; "It's the news aboot Wanton Wee Willie.[3] His health has broke doon; he's oot o' the Airmy, and awa' wi' his wife to a hydro. I doot he'll never get over it this time; his constitution is bound to be dreadfully undermined for the want o' proper nourishment. There's no' as much fat left in Germany as would grease a saw."

"Perhaps it's not true that the Crown Prince has retired," I suggested hopefully. "You mustn't be a pessimist."

"I doot it's true," said Erchie, sadly. "It's in the papers in twa places. Nerves a' shattered. It's a gloomy start wi' the New Year for the Allies: as lang as Willie was kind o' daein' his bit they could depend on him. Next to the British Navy, Willie was the guarantee o' our security. He was the Allies' Best Battle-winner; the French sodgers thocht that much o' him they had his picture printed on their pocket naipkins. A favourite a' roond! I doot his faither was gettin jealous o' Willie's popularity among the French and British; did Haig no' send him a case o' ten-year-auld and a cake o' shortbread on Christmas?"

"We'll just have to win our own battles in future, then," I suggested.

"That's a' richt," said Erchie, "but the best way to win battles is to have a chap like Willie in command on the other side. Muneetions is no' everything; 'tanks'[4] is no' everything; ye need somebody on the other side ye can depend on to mak' a cod o' himsel' every time, and Wee Willie's presence on any pairt o' the battle front aye kept oor chaps cheery. He was the honorary Regimental Pet o' a lot o' the French battalions ever since the Indian Contingent ate up their goats.

"'Wha's in front o' us the day!' General Joffre[5] would ask, comin' up the trenches.

"'Six diveesions o' the Prussian Guards, three Grand Dukes, an awfu' smell o gas, and Wee Willie,' the Sergeant would say, like to burst himsel' wi' laughin'.

"'Mong jew!' General Joffre would cry, at that, wavin' his kep at the artillery, 'Stop firin'! Ye'll maybe hit him! I'm no much heedin' aboot the Prussian Guards and the Grand Dukes, but you're no' goin' to spile oor Willie.'

"What made Willie beloved o' a' the troops he fought against was the way he put his mind into an attack. The Grand Dukes was frichtened for him. Whenever Willie sat up for two nichts wi' a wet towel on his heid, and came roond to the tent in the mornin' wi' a fine new scheme for smashin' in the French line, the Grand Dukes made up a parcel o' a' their clocks, watches, and other nicknacks collected since the start o' the campaign, and posted them to their wives wi' a tender letter o' farewell; they kent it was domino! Him bein' the Croon Prince, of course they daurna heave him oot o' the tent and tell him to go and tak' a sleep to himsel'. But a Grand Duke — except that he's fatter — is jist like onybody else; he doesna want to risk his life keepin' up a pretence that Willie's a kind o' new and improved Napoleon, and him only a Ned.

"There was nae herm in Willie; if he had been put into the drapery tred he would have done fine at dressin' windows. His faither spiled him. Every Christmas Eve since he was oot o' petticoats, they put swords an' helmets and uniforms in his stockin' and encouraged him in the notion that he was a warrior. Oh, michty! No' wi' a chin like yon! But he suited us.

"I tell you, Willie's dismissal frae the German Airmy, if it's true, is a great blow to the Allied cause! Something should be done! What's the use o' havin' diplomatists when they canna keep a chap like Willie where he's most use? It's the worst news we had since the fall o' Warsaw. So lang as the Kaiser kept Willie in a responsible job, jist because he was his son, a' the bluff o' the Germans that they're up to date wouldna deceive a polisman. Mony a time I cheered mysel' wi' the reflection the Germans is maybe super-human, but they're wantin' in common sense or Willie would be in the drapery line and his faither would be trevellin' for beer.

"I'm vexed for Willie! There he's away to a hydro in his plain clothes wi' a bowler hat on, and nae chap ever suited a bowler hat and plain clothes worse than Willie; if he cam' to your door ye would think he was comin' to tak' the gas-meter or sell ye a sewin' machine. Imagine a hydro efter Verdun!"

"All the same I question if our interesting young friend is permanently out of action," I said; "They may give him a trial yet on the German fleet; a Hohenzollern must naturally be of amphibious genius."

"I wish they would!" said Erchie. "There's awful little sport or recreation comes in the way o' Admiral Beatty."[6]

116. *Erchie on Allotments*[1]

"DID YE pick your wee allotment[2] yet?" asked Erchie of Duffy, and the coalman looked at him dubiously, suspecting it was a catch.

"Where dae ye pick them?" said he. He was at least determined to conceal his ignorance of what an allotment was. A vague impression floated through the woolly parts of his intelligence that it might have something to do with those extraordinary but probably deceptive loans of unlimited money the banks were offering to all and sundry who wanted to carry on the war.

"Where dae ye pick them?" repeated Erchie. "Ony-where ye like that's suitable and near a tramway line. There's a thousand picked already roond about Mount Florida, Bellahouston, Alexandra Park, Whiteinch, and Plantation. If ye don't hurry up, ye'll not get as much as would fill a floo'rpot. A' ye have to dae is to write to Sir John Lindsay, The Town Clerk, tellin' him ye're gaun in

for growin' cabbages, and he'll send a polis sergeant oot wi
ye to measure aff a bit o' land that's no encumbered wi' a
tenement or used for fitba'. It's the chance o' your life,
Duffy! There's bound to be fine-growin' ground aboot the
depot where ye get your coals at Port Dundas. A' ye need
to start wi' is a seedsman's catalogue and a wab o' wire-
nettin' to keep oot the deer and rabbit. I'll buy my potatoes
aff ye."

"Ye're no gaun in for yin yersel'?" said Duffy, who had
now a more or less hazy undertanding that amateur
agriculture was Erchie's topic.

"I thocht o't," said Erchie, "but Jinnet and me concluded it would be nae advantage wi' us no ha'ein' a family
to dae the delvin' and the weedin'. You're in a different
poseetion a'thegither, wi' a fine strong family roond ye: a'
ye would need to dae would be to put up a bit o' a summer
hoose and sit in 't watchin them workin'."

"It takes me a' my time to sell coal," said Duffy, with
conviction.

"Ye'll be sorry for't if ye don't tak' the chance when it
comes!" declared Erchie. "Look at the price o' potatoes!
Before the summer's on ye'll only can get a half a pound o'
them in the week at the grocer's if ye buy a cheet[3] o' tea
wi't. And cabbage'll be the price o' pineapples; a wealthy
man that gets yin 'll gie a dinner pairty. Tak' my advice,
Duffy, and you go back to the land if it's only to clean the
canisters aff it and plant rhubarb. You would be independent! There's naething easier; try a stone o' seed potatoes,
borrow a potato chip machine to slice them, bury them no'
too deep, and watch till ye see the shaws, then grab them
up like lightnin' afore they have time to change their
minds. Ye would ha'e potatoes to your dinner when the
best in the land was reduced to rice and savoury balls."

"What's savoury balls?" asked Duffy.

"God knows, but it's no' potatoes, though we ha'e to let
on ye can hardy tell the difference. If I was you, Duffy, I
would go in for a wee allotment, and the sooner the better,
for there's gaun to be a great demand. I saw a Bylie

yesterday lookin' awfu' keen at a plot in George's Square. Ye'll see barbed wire and rabbit nettin' roon the plots in George's Square before the spring, or I'm mistaken."

"I don't see ony signs o' their new allotments," said Duffy.

"Do ye no?" said Erchie, ironically. "Ye'll maybe hear aboot them when your wife gangs oot in the mornin' some day to the washin' green and trips on a cart o' manure or tramps on a bed o' syboes. Everybody's no indifferent, like you, to the Board o' Agriculture's orders. If ye took a walk roon the ootskirts o' Glasgow ye would see the vacant land beginnin' already to blossom like the rose. There's a rush in graips⁴ that would astonish ye! Ye can hardly buy a waterin' can, and the dandelion's gaun to be that rare next summer it'll be worn at weddings instead o' the camellia. Look at the way the deer's cam a' doon frae the Hielan's, that close on Gleska that the police hae to shoot them."

"Wha tellt ye that?" asked the incredulous coalman.

"Man, it's in the papers! At the first hint that Gleska was gaun to be an agricultural community under powers conferred by the Government, the deer has deserted the mountains and the crofter's corn and I'm tellt that Possilpark is fair infested wi' them. If the polis didna keep them down, they would be a' ower the town at nicht like Redskin hooligans."

"I don't believe wan word of it!" cried Duffy.

"Do ye no?" said Erchie. "Have ye no' see the poulterers' shops? The best o' venison at eightpence and a shillin' a pound — a perfect glut in the market! Man, at eightpence and a shillin' a pound it wouldna pay for kilts for the gamekeepers! They're first-rate deer; there's naething wrang wi' them, and they couldna be sold at the price o' potted heid if ye had to sclim the hills for them. The way they're sold that cheap is that they're got at the door. The folk in Strathbungo canna get their sleep at night wi' listenin' to them baain'."

"I don't care!" said Duffy firmly; "Gleska's no' a place to grow potatoes in. There's far ower many rats. If land's gaun to be put under cultivation, it should be in the country."

Erchie looked at him with pity. "Man, Duffy," he remarked, "it's easily seen you haven't studied the situation. The country's the last place that ever does anything to spoil the rural peace o' the rabbit, irritate the pheasant, mar the beautiful solitude o' the parish, or adopt any reckless measure, even at the Government's request, that would put a penny on the Rates. Do ye see ony o' the rural County Councils, or the wee Toon Councils botherin' themsel's to start and encourage allotments. Not them! A' the enthusiasm for garden allotments is roon the bigger toons where they're least needed and like to dae the least good. Maist o' the local authorities in the country have personal reasons to let things go on as they are, and they've got used to livin' in a kind o' graveyard. They'll no more think o' exercisin' intelligently and disinterestedly the powers conferred on them by the Board o' Agriculture than they would o' stalkin' deer in Possilpark. Just watch them and ye'll see! I have no great hope o' getting chape potatoes oot o' them! You start a garden, Duffy!"

117. *The Last of the Bridescakes*[1]

"If ye gang doon the street to Maclachlan, the baker's shop," said Erchie, coming in, "ye'll see the Last o' the Bridescakes in the window. It's a topper. Near as big as the Stewart Fountain in the West-End Park.[2] Three storeys, and a couple o' angels on the garret flat blawin' trumpets. There's a crood roond the window stretchin' oot as far as the tramway lines; naething like it in the street since the pawnshop fire!"

"I seen it," said his wife. "It's Sanderson, the slater's dochter; she's merryin' a mason."

"He'll be a monumental sculptor," suggested Erchie. "Ye can see the monumental touch in it; there's bits o't awfu' like some o' the Necropolis buildin's. I never saw a bridescake that better filled the eye, and I've passed a lot through my hands."

He sat down to his tea, and first cast a depreciatory eye on the sugar-bowl, which was almost empty.

"Is that a' the sugar ye ha'e?" he asked.

"It is," said Janet, "and it's a' I'll get till Seturday.[3] They'll no gi'e me it."

Erchie sighed. "It's what I was expectin'," said he; "They must ha'e used up the maist o' the sugar in Gleska to cover Miss Sanderson's mausoleum. I'm no grudgin' it to her. It'll no be cut, that bridescake. Years efter this ye'll see't in the Kelvingrove Museum in a case wi' camphor balls and a ticket sayin' it's the only survivin' specimen o' Early British Architecture. Naebody'll tak' it for a thing that ye could eat."

"What's the crood for!" asked Janet.

"Am I no' tellin' ye? It's the Last o' the Bridescakes. The Food Controller got a piece o' bridescake sent to him last week and put it in below his pillow to see what he would dream. He was hungry through the night, and he sat up and ate a' the marzipan. A' his dreams were nichtmares, and the first thing he did in the mornin' was to pass an Act o' Parliament puttin' sugar-coated bridescakes oot o' bounds. Efter the 1st o' March ye daurna hae a cake wi' icin' on't, or the polis'll be on your track. It's an awfu' blow to the tred o' the Italian modellers and marble cutters unless they use stucca. Worse than that, it's a blow at the sacred institution o' Christian marriage. Everybody kens that yin o' the main attractions to a lassie merryin' was the joy o' seein' her bridescake in MacLachlan's window. The Post Office people's furious! It'll put the livin' expense o' the letter carriers up 25 per cent; they used to could keep their families gaun wi' bits o' bridescake cut up and posted in boxes wi' the labels kind o' torn."

"I think they were jist extravagance!" declared Janet. "Jist a show aff! The silver floo'ers were maybe kind o' nice on a parlour mantelpiece wi' a gless on them, but there's mony a hoose where they made ye kind o' melancholy —"

"Souvenirs o' a great mistake," said Erchie; "I've seen them."

"It's time they were daein' something o' the sort, to gi'e us sugar for oor tea," said Janet.

"Just you stop till the 1st o' March," said her husband, "and ye'll get that much sugar ye can start the fire wi't again. Lord Devonport[4] is thinkin' o' everything, and it shows ye he's in earnest, for he's in the fancy cake line himsel'. The stoppage o' monumental bridecakes in Gleska alone'll save the country a couple o' hunderweight o' sugar every week. That in itsel' would mak' the sugar situation easy. Then there's chocolates; they're stoppin' the sale o' a' chocolates over four shillin's a pound."

"Four shillin's a pound!" cried Janet. "There's no chocolates at four shillin's a pound!"

"Oh yes!" said her husband, "Lots! If you were carryin' a flag in the pantomime, or I had ships, ye wouldna look at ony chaper chocolates. It's the cocoa that's in them. And then there's the box! When you were young the fashion was motto lozenges and conversations. They're entirely oot o' date! The great mass o' people in this country noo eat chocolate at threepence an ounce and over; it's them that's makin' the sugar scarce, and the Food Controller's no' gaun to have ony mair o't."

"I don't believe in it!" said Janet oracularly. "They micht as well put a stop to valentines to help the paper tred."

"I daresay you're richt," admitted her husband, "but Lord Devonport's only feelin' his way. Him bein' English, he hasna the least idea what folk live on. He recommends the people to take no mair than 2½ lb o' butcher meat a heid in the week —"

"I couldna dae't!" cried Janet; "It would mak' me ill! And where could Duffy, wi' a family o' eight, get a' that meat? Wi' coals at their best he never had the money for't."

"But the Food Controller never lived in Scotland, Jinnet, and he doesna understand that maist o' us in Scotland 'll never feel the pinch o' war till they put us on

an oatmeal ration and commandeer oor girdles.⁵ We've
aye lived nearer the bone than ony other folk in Europe,
and Devonport's scheme o' rations'll look to a lot o' us like
a continual Trades Hoose banquet. The only thing to
bother aboot is the sugar."

118. *How Erchie Spent the Fair*¹

THE GLOW of health was on Erchie's face when I saw him
yesterday; he had a sparkling eye and a springy gait that
seemed to betoken the utmost physical wellbeing.

"Been having your holidays?" I asked him.

"Exactly!" he responded, chuckling. "Finest Fair I've
spent in fifty years. It's done me and Jinnet a' the good in
the world. What a blessin' we had such bonny weather!"

"Where did you go?" I asked.

"Oh, just circular tours," said Erchie. "I was aff frae the
Monday to Seturday. We couldna mak' up our minds at
first where to gang to, so I bought a Murray's Diary², and
went over a' the names in't frae Aberdeen to Winchburgh,
but couldna find ony place ye could exactly ca' attractive.
'It's a droll thing,' says I to Jinnet, 'that the only place
that's no' mentioned in the Diary is Gleska.' 'It's bound to
be there!' says she. 'It's naething o' the kind,' I told her;
'It's missed oot althegither. There's ony amount o' places
like Lugton and Fintry and Markinch mentioned, but
naething at a' aboot Gleska.'

"She wouldna believe me till she put on her specs and
looked the Diary for hersel'.

"'What dae ye want to look up Gleska for?' she asked
when she couldna find it.

"'Because I think it's here we should spend oor holidays,' I tellt her, and she gave a great sigh o' relief. 'I'm
glad to hear ye say't,' says she; 'I havena slept a wink these
twa nichts thinkin' o' a box to pack and a' the habble.'

"But you said circular tours," I remarked to Erchie.

"Weel, they were circular. Oot the close and back again;

landed at your very door. Dalrymple's[3] personally
conducted tours. Ye must have noticed there was a lot o'
threepenny bits in your change this few days back — they
were mine and Jinnet's, saved up for a twelvemonth to be
spent on the most luxuriant and cheapest trevellin' in the
world. I never thocht there was sae much to see in Gleska.
We took Duffy the coalman and his wife wi' us, and Duffy
said it was a fair eye-opener to him. 'If I just had a sair heid
and a hanky-fu' o' dulse,'[4] says he, 'it would be the best
Fair I ever had in a' my puff.' Do you believe me? — Duffy
had never seen St. Jocelyn's crypt[5] in the Cathedral nor the
back o' the Necropolis though he's lived in Garscube Road
a' his days! 'Carrick Castle's no' in it wi' this!' says he
when we came to the Kelvingrove Art Galleries and seen
the ruins in front o't."

"Your trips seem to have been more instructive than
amusing," I suggested.

"Oh, there was ony amount o' sport, too," said Erchie.
"Every other mornin' we went doon to the Broomielaw
and watched the folk losin' the *Lord o' the Isles*."[6]

"It's just ridiculous," continued my old friend, "the way
Gleska folk neglect the advantages o' Gleska for a holiday.
They think it's only a place for workin' in. They go awa' to
Gourock, Dunoon, and Rothesay to hear pierrot bands
and see picture palaces that's no' half sae good as they
could get just roond the corner; daunder up and doon
esplanades that's no' near as crooded wi' folk as Argyle
Street or the New City Road."

"Rural sights —" I suggested.

"Ye'll no' get rural sights ony better than ye'll get in
Gleska. We went oot and watched the folk workin' their
allotments; hoein' potatoes and showin' their gallowses jist
the same's it was the wilds o' Inverness-shire. The only
thing ye missed was midges.

"The great thing aboot Gleska for holidays is that ye can
aye buy something for your tea and needna be feared ye'll
get wet if the rain comes on. It's the only place where your
lodgin's cost ye naething, and ye run nae risk o' missin' the

last boat or the last train hame. There's nae luggage to pack. When Jinnet and me used to gang doon the watter at the Fair we were in a perfect turmoil a' the time. The trains would be crooded and ye lost your hamper: there's naething o' that in Gleska. We used to let on in Arran there was something fine and fancy aboot washin' your face in a burn, and a' the same it's no' half as handy as a jaw-box."

"It is quite clear," I said, "that the perfect Guide to Glasgow as a Holiday Resort has still to be written."

"Then don't write it!" said Erchie with mock alarm. "It would spoil the fun o' the Fair in Gleska if everybody found it oot. The more folk that gang and scramble for trains to the coast and country, the better for us that bide at hame. It gi'es the air a chance to become salubrious. The country was a' richt for a holiday so lang's it could depend on plenty o' breid, and eggs, and ham, and fish frae Gleska, but the war's put an end to that; ye risk landin' somewhere where there's naething to eat but rhubarb. The country's a' richt for coortin' in when you're young, but it's spoiled even for that by the Daylight Savin' Bill,[7] and when ye're auld like me and Jinnet it's no' great catch at the best; better to stay at hame and hear the milkboy's cheery whistle."

119. *Erchie's Work in Wartime*[1]

"WHAT'S best on the bill of fare today, Erchie?" I asked as I picked up the table napkin.

The old waiter blinked his eyes with a sly expression, glanced at the card, and replied in non-committal tones. "There's Paysau soup — that's lentils; herrin', sauce moutarde — the sauce moutarde's in season and it's champion; then there's devilled eggs —"

"Put it in the singular, Erchie," I said. "The devilish thing about that dish is that there's only one egg to it, and it looks so lonely on a plate!"

"Has nae appearance! I admit it! Ony gentleman in

good health would feel the same aboot a solitary egg. Fancy a doo's cleckin' o' eggs[2] for the main stand-bye to a Bylie's lunch!"

"And about the cheese, Erchie? Is the cheese still a fragrant memory o' the past?"

He sighed. "I havena seen," said he, "what ye would ca' a rale man's cheese for a year and a half. Guidness kens what's happened to the Stiltons; they must be makin' them into muneetions. At the best we can only get American cheddar, and ye ken what the Americans are — fine fighters[3] and good enough for aipples, but wi' nae richt skill o' cheeses. It's a terrible time, sir! Do ye think we'll ever get back the Gorgonzola?"

He hovered about me while I romped through a light table d'hôte menu that hasn't varied in any particular from day to day for months, and he brought in the culminating two square inches of roly poly with a comical flourish.

"There!" said he. "Don't blame me! I said roly-poly plain enough, but they must have misunderstood me, and thocht I mentioned dominoes."

"What about a coffee and cognac?" I inquired with malice prepense.

"Coffee," he repeated. "Right, sir!" and turned away. He came back without the cognac, which was just what I expected of his good sense. But I 'registered' surprise, as the cinema artists say, and asked for the liqueur.

"At twa shillin's the gless!" he whispered. "It's mair than your hale luncheon used to cost ye. Tak' my advice and instead o' liqueur hae a biscuit to augment the insufficient solids. I noticed ye didna eat your breid; nae wonder! A shave o't looks like a wee lassie's peever,[4] and it tastes like flannel. Terrible times, sir! Terrible times!"

"You seem to thrive in them, all the same." I remarked, regarding his rosy gills, his bird clear eye, and his undiminished figure.

"If I dae," said he "it's no what I can scran here. It's parridge — jist parridge! Naething better if ye have the wife to mak' it. It's the only thing in Scotland that tastes the way it used to."

"What about the band?" I asked. "It seems to me they ought to have continued it. With mixed light operatic selections we might be beguiled into the illusion that we were really lunching."

"Quite right!" said Erchie, as he moved away. "It's noo we need the music to droon the bad language o' the customers."

120. *Government Milk*[1]

"I NOTICE," said Janet, "that the Government is gaun to tak' control o' the milk supply; that'll be an awfu' blow to puir Mrs MacGlinchy, the dairy, and her wi' six o' a faimily!"

"I'm vexed for the MacGlinchys, but the day o' the wee dairy's done," said Erchie. "If they want to cairry on the business they'll hae to concentrate on the soda-scone[2] department. Before the winter's on, the mornin's milk'll be delivered to ye at the door by the letter carrier."

"Ye don't tell me!" exclaimed his wife, a little incredulous.

"Right enough! It's a moral certainty that the distribution'll be put in the hands o' the Post Office. They can dae't fine; they have the time, forbye the uniform."

"Then I'll miss the wee boys whistlin' on the stairs," said Janet, sentimentally. "Some folk didna like the clatter o' the cans[3] and the milk-boys whistlin', but I aye thought them cheery. Whit harm was the MacGlinchys daein' that the Government should tak' away their tred?"

Erchie shook his head. "I doot ye'll no' can grasp it, Jinnet," he said, "but it's part o' the great national scheme o' Industrial Reorganisation. Under private ownership the British coo has been a pampered and unprofitable animal, slackin' aff its milk supply at the very time when milk was scarcest. Under government control it'll have to fall into line wi' the riveters and hurry up. Then, again, the hale system o' milk collectin' of the country was ancient and oot o' date. When the Government tak's it over, all the output o' Renfrew, Ayr, and Lanark 'll be collected in a big dam near Dalry and run in to the main distributin' centre oot aboot Dalmarnock. Dairy farmin' will be revolution-ised; instead o' risin' at the blythe hour o' 3 a.m. gantin'[4] their heids aff for the want o' sleep, the dairymaids 'll come daunderin' oot to the Governmental byres efter breakfast, press the button that starts the electric milkin', and have naething mair to dae but sort the product into the various classes o'

Warm Milk,
Skim Milk, and
Milk.

"The dazed coo'll be fed on scientific principles; her output'll be weighed every day, and whenever she drops below the gallon or twa as the case may be — it's domino for the coo! The Government'll no' stand ony hanky-panky, mind I'm tellin' ye!"

"Well, I'll say this," said Janet; "I couldna get ony better milk than I get frae Mrs MacGlinchy. And a civil, earnest, honest woman! I never had ony complaint against her."

"Ye'll hae plenty against the Post Office," said her husband. "And ony time ye're a half-cup short in the measure for your four pence worth o' milk, ye'll hae to write to the Postmaster-General. All he'll dae will be to send ye a wee blue printed form saying 'Your letter has been received; the complaint is bein' inquired into. Any further communications on this subject should be marked XC40295, M. Department!'

"I never heard such nonsense," exclaimed his wife. "We were daein' fine wi' Mrs MacGlinchy!"

121. *Coal Rations*[1]

DUFFY, WITH a heave of the shoulder, emptied the bag of coals into Mrs MacPherson's bunker, and dryly remarked, "Ye're gettin' a bargain; if it was next month, they would cost ye a bonny penny."

"They're costin' plenty the way it is," said Mrs MacPherson. "And full o' sclate stanes!"

"If there's any stanes in that lot," retorted the coalman, "lay them aside and I'll gie ye a pound a ton for them; it's the price they charge for them at the quarry."

"Ye're in a poseetion to ken the quarry price o' coal best," interposed Erchie. "When do ye start the rationin'?"[2]

"Whenever I get word," said Duffy, wiping his brow. "I'm fair in the dark yet, like yoursel's. But I'm tellin' ye this'll be a cauld winter; as far as I can see, the ration o' coals for a hoose o' this size'll be a stane a week."

"I got twenty stanes oot o' the last bag ye left," said Janet. "Ye can gang doon to the ashpit an' coont them for yersel'."

"A bakie o' coal'll no' gang far in them close-and-open ranges,"[3] pursued the coalman, unheeding her suggestion whether it was ironical or in earnest. "But it's wan mercy ye havena a big family. A dozen o' weans hingin' roond a kitchen fire takes up an awfu' lot o' heat; it's the big families I'm vexed for. The ration for hooses o' this cless should be accordin' to the number o' folk in them, but I needna speak to the Government; it has nae sense. A' the same, ye'll be better aff than the English; the ration's to be 20 per cent mair here."

"We'll need it a'!" said Erchie. "There's awfu' little warmth left in the national beverage.[4] But listen, Duffy; Jinnet'll use a bag o' coal betwixt Monday and Wednesday: what'll be to cook the dinner for Sunday?"

"She'll can burn her claes-pins like mony another woman," suggested Duffy unfeelingly. "A' I ken is she canna get ony extra allowance frae me. It wouldna be allo'ed."

"I'll jist hae to borrow a bakie full frae the neebours, then," said Janet, resignedly.

"Ye daurna!" said Duffy. "There's to be nae treatin' under the Act."

"Then I doot," said Erchie, solemnly, "that I'll hae to dae withoot my hot baths and wear two or three waistcoats."

"Hot baths is a luxury under the Statute," explained the coalman with authoritative tones. "So's mair than wan waistcoat if I'm no' mistaken. I could lay ye in anither bag or twa on Monday if ye cared; I clean forgot ye had the bath."[5]

"Nae fear o' me!" said Janet. "Ye'll not mak' a coal-bing or a quarry o' my bath! What we'll dae is this — I'll get the Corporation to put in a gas ring,[6] and save the coal."

"A gas ring!" exclaimed Duffy with contempt. "God bless my sowl, Mrs MacPherson, dae ye ken whit gas is made of. Naethin' but coal tar and analine dyes: I wouldna have it in the hoose for cookin'. Ye couldna boil a wilk wi't. You stick by the coals and I'll see what we can dae for ye."

122. *Celebrating Peace*[1]

DUFFY, THE coalman, on Saturday afternoon, had gone to the stable to feed his horse, and fell asleep on a bale of hay, as may happen to any man in the coal trade in these melancholy times when Saturday assumes no real holiday hue till 4 p.m. He was wakened by a passing char-a-banc that shook the street, and had on board of it a bagpiper who was giving a sketchy performance of 'The Barren Rocks of Aden.'

"That's something like the thing! That's what I ca' cheery!" said Duffy to himself, combed the hay partially out of his whiskers and hurried to the pend-close mouth.

The char-a-banc was disappearing in the distance and had a flag.

"Whatna trip's that?" inquired Duffy of a woman passing with two loaves and a bundle of firewood.

"It's this Peace,"[2] she informed him without a scrap of enthusiasm, "The Germans is signed. Man, ye're a' hay!"

"Hokey!" said Duffy, "that puts the lid on it! And there's no' a flag in the hoose! It's a thing that should be celebrated."

Intent upon celebrating with the requisite patriotic spirit, he consulted his watch anxiously, and was astounded to find it close upon seven o'clock. With incredible velocity he locked up his stable and made for the Mull of Kintyre Vaults, reaching the door just as the owner was shutting it with that inhuman emphasis and gladness which all publicans manifest in the most unsocial operation of their working day.

"Haud on!" panted Duffy. "Great news! The Huns has heaved in the towel!"

"Whit towel?" asked the barkeeper suspiciously with his foot firmly against the inside of the door, which was only a few inches ajar.

"They've signed the Peace and handed the Kaiser[3] ower to a squad o' the Princess Louisa's Own Argyll and Sutherlands," said the coalman wiping his brow, and trying to clear some ticklish hayseeds out of his eyebrows. "They're bringing him up to Maryhill in a barrow. Gi'e us half a chance, Peter! It's not seven o'clock yet, let alone eight or nine!"

"Are ye shair they're bringing him to Maryhill?" asked the barkeeper with crafty irony.

"He'll be passin' in ten meenutes," said Duffy.

"That's a pant I should be in!" said the barman with apparent eagerness. "Haud you on a meenute till I get on my jecket," and pushing the door to, he turned the lock leaving the coalman outside.

Duffy waited five minutes, coughing up hay dust, then realised that the Glasgow Wine Spirit and Beer Trade was shamefully unwilling to rise to the occasion.

He went homeward reluctantly, looking everywhere about him for signs of those Great Rejoicings in Glasgow, which would certainly figure prominently in the papers on Monday morning.

There were none. The char-a-banc and the piper appeared to have had an absolute monopoly of any rejoicing that might be going.

Crowds were tearing their way into the already full tramcars; perhaps they were hurrying home to get on their Sunday clothes and illuminate their windows. Big Jock Mackay, the night policeman, was chasing boys out of a close; they might have been trying to start a celebrative bonfire. But, on the other hand, the populace seemed depressingly sober compared with what Duffy recalled of Mafeking night and Armistice day. Without exception they looked like men and women having one common solemnising thought — such as that hooker-doon caps were likely to be dearer yet on account of the dispute in the Gorbals hat and cap trade.

"They hiv nae sense," said Duffy to himself. "Jist clods! Micht as weel never hae been ony war. It's my belief there'll no' be a single fight this night in the hale Northern Diveesion."

It was then he saw his old friend Erchie on the other side of the street, and hurried across to him, waving his cap and giving a tentative 'hurrah!'

"Ye should slip up a back street where naebody kens ye, get hame as quick's ye can and hae a good strong cup o' tea," said Erchie, looking at him with disapproval under a quite erroneous impression. "Man, Duffy, I'm rale surprised at ye! Fair makin' a Ned o' yersel! Put on your bunnet like a wise man and I'll see ye hame. The hay's comin' oot o' your very lugs; it's the stuffed animal department o' the Kelvingrove Museum ye should be in."

"There's naething wrong wi' me," retorted the coalman indignantly. "You're aye finding' faut! Hae ye no heard the news?"

"Whit news?" asked Erchie, "Is the bag o' coals gaun up."

"The Germans has signed the Peace!" cried Duffy.

"It's three or four 'oors since I heard o' that," said Erchie, calmly. "Allooin' they have, it's nae excuse for you makin' a cod o' yoursel' and affrontin' me in broad day-light in New City Road. It'll no' bring doon the price o' ham."

He took the coalman by the coat sleeve, brushing some of the hay off him, and accompanied him towards the street to which his own and Duffy's residence give distinction.

"Ye don't see onybody wavin' keps and cryin' 'hurrah' except yoursel'," said Erchie. "That shows ye're under some kind o' a delusion. There's an awfu' lot o' hay in your composection."

"Look at the fun we had at the Armistice," retorted the coalman. "I hadna oot my lorry for a couple o' days except for carryin' joy-parties."

"That's right, but the Armistice was different; there was something aboot that to understand and cheer for. It meant for at least a dozen folk in oor ain tenement that their ain particular Jocks were oot o' danger at last and that was aye worth a flag or twa. But the Germans signing a scrap o' paper's a thing that makes nae appeal to the imagination. Ye wuldna even wave your kep if ye saw them daein't wi' your ain e'en at Versailles. A' that was in the ceremony this efternoon was that twa fat middle-aged German business gentleman that never saw ony o' the fightin' dipped their pens in a penny bottle o' blue-black ink and wrote their names doon wi' the usual flourish, then went oot on the balcony wi' the others and had their photographs tooken.

"There's nae occasion for hingin' up flags and gaun on the batter over that. For years we have been told that onything signed by the Hun wasna worth the paper it was written on, and there's nae guarantee that their scrap o' paper this time's ony different from the others just because twa auld chaps that signed it had their minds made up for them by the Allies."

"Still the Peace is signed," said Duffy firmly, "and that's aye something."

"Oh, it's something, right enough. It lets Lloyd George and President Wilson[4] hame to their wives and families.

They're fed up wi' Paris. But do ye ken whit I'm gaun to tell ye, Duffy? I'm nae gaun to hing oot ony flags or jine ye on a skyte even o' the very mildest till boots is doon again to 12s. 6d. and the price o' a topcoat's something less than three weeks' wages.

"I'm no gaun to cheer till the last British sodger's landed on this side o' the English Channel and back at his tred; till the Territorials is gaun to camp at Stobs or Gailes at the Fair wi' red coats on and a toppin' brass band for their gymkana; till butter and beef's demobilised —"

"And beer," suggested Duffy.

"Till the Gleska tramcar system is equal to its reputation; till the factors are chasin' folk up to rent their hooses; till a trip doon the watter wi' high tea included is again within the means o' a waiter; till oranges are a ha'penny, bananas a penny, eggs a shillin' a dozen, and the kipper herring again in the home o' the British workin' man."

"Ye'll maybe wait a lang while," suggested Duffy.

"I'm beginnin' to doot it," admitted Erchie. "Come up and see the wife."

Jinnet opened the door to them.

"Peace is signed," said her husband, on the threshold.

"That's nice," she said, simply. "Come awa' in the pair o' ye and I'll bile ye a couple o' eggs for your teas. Oh, Mr Duffy, ye must be celebratin'; ye're full o' hay."

123. *The Coal Famine*[1]

ERCHIE WENT round on Friday night to Duffy's ree to order coals. He wanted a couple of hundredweights at the earliest possible hour on Saturday morning.

"What kind would ye like?" asked the coalman, who seemed to be in a sardonic mood.

"The kind for heatin'," replied Erchie, blandly. "Oot o' coal pits, ye understand. The stuff we've been gettin' frae ye for some time back must hae come frae a quarry. Nae wonder they canna get buildin' material for a' the new hooses needed in this country, when the coal tred's cornered the hale o't and sellin't at 1s. 11½d. the bag."

"Would nuts dae ye?" inquired Duffy, putting on his muffler preparatory to shutting up and going home.

"Fine!" said Erchie; "so long's they're no' peanuts. Any mortal kind that'll boil a kettle!"

"A' the coals o' ony kind that I hae at my command the noo, I can gie ye wi' ye, if ye have a hankie," said Duffy. "And there'll be nae coals the morn's mornin'; your wife'll just hae to burn her claes-pins."

"Ye're gettin' awfu' snotty!" said Erchie, warmly.

"I've got mair impudence the day frae my customers than ony human bein' could put up wi'," said the coalman. "Ye would think I was made o' coals, or could conjure them oot o' a hat. I canna get coals for mysel', but I'll tell ye what I'll dae — I'll gie ye a bakie full if ye come roond to the hoose for them, and it'll hae to carry ye ower the Sunday."

"What we're needin'," said Erchie, walking homewards with his friend, "is Lord Leverhulme[2] in the coal tred. Look at soap! Ye can get soap onywhere if ye're willin' to pay for't. There's never ony shortage. And noo his lordship's takin' in hand wi' the fish tred; ye'll find no shortage o' herrin' this year at the Gleska Fair; he's sittin' up at night and plannin'."

"Is he in the fish line noo?" asked Duffy, incredulous.

"Up tae the neck!" said Erchie. "His lordship was aghast at the scarcity o' finnan haddies and the price o' real Rock Turbot in the fish and chip shops. What Britain wants, he says to himsel', is more brain production to pay aff the National Debt that's noo six hundred billions. Fish makes phosphorus, and phosphorus is the chief ingredient in brains; the need o' the nation is for fish.

"What does his lordship dae! He buys up a bunch o' islands in the Hebrides[3]; carts in the native crofter populace to Stornoway; runs them through a sapple o' Sunlight Soap, cuts their nails; learns them the English language; gies them an eight-'oors day, and starts them fishin' on scientific principles. Stornoway becomes the Port Sunlight o' the North; every man has a nice wee red-tiled cottage, and a picture palace at his door, and the cod-fish is fair worried oot o' its life.

"There's nae fun in catchin' fish by the ton unless ye can sell them, and the next step for Lord Leverhulme is to buy up a' the fish shops he can lay hands on in London, Edinburgh, Gleska, and Greenock. For the last three weeks his lordship, disguised in a Harris tweed ulster and a hooker-doon[4], has been buyin' fish shops right and left."

"What way do ye buy a fish shop?" inquired Duffy.

"Quite easy," said Erchie, "There's naething in a fish-shop at maist times except slabs. The hale o' the stock's sold oot each day, and ye start each mornin' wi' a hose-pipe and a bundle o' cards marked 'Fresh Loch Fyne'. There's nane o' your fancy glass-fronted cases — naething but marble slabs, a guttin' knife, a Cash Register on ball bearin's, and a sign-board. The rest's good-will."

"What's good-will?" inquired the coalman.

"The only tangible good-will I ever saw," said Erchie, reflectively, "belanged to a druggist. He had a fruit-shop next door to him; the public aye slid on the orange-peel on the pavement and sprained an ankle, and he had a great tred in lint and embrocations. On the other side o' him he had a public-hoose that didna open till half-past twelve, and he had a toppin' line in pick-me-ups.

"Mark you my words, Duffy, twa or three years efter this the Sunlight Fish Shop'll be Gleska's great feature next to her tea-rooms.

"What spoils the fish trade noo, is mainly the want o' art and imagination. Ye go into a shop and ask for a pair o' kippers or a couple o' pounds o' ling; they're clapped in front o' ye, wrapped up in a sheet o' newspaper and the bell o' the Cash Register goes 'ping'!

"The fishmonger has nae human touch aboot him; he is just a large damp man that wants to get his stuff oot o' his sight and his hands dried as fast as possible. Ye never catch him whisperin', 'That's a herrin' I don't sell every day, a genuine Tarbert. Look at the lustre! Feel the resiliency! That's a pre-war herrin', there's very few left but for an old customer —' Not him!

"The Leverhulme Fish Shops'll make fishmongin' a High Art, like the sellin' o' motor-cars or four-shillin'y chocolates. Next year ye'll no see Gleska fish shops exposin' big fat cod and mammoth salmon in their windows, and ladlin' fillets into the market basket wi' the naked hand. The silvery denizens o' the deep'll be put up in nate wee cardboard boxes o' half-a-pound, wi' a coloured picture on the ootside o' the Hebridean fisherman pursuin' his avocation oot in the stormy Minch, or a view o' Stornoway Castle in a sunset.

"A box o' Sunlight Haddies tied up wi' red silk ribbon'll be the popular gift o' the young man o' the period to the girl he wants to marry, and ready-cooked sprats'll be the favourite thing for passin' round the stalls between the acts at the pantomime, or 'Chu Chin Chow'.

"In the past, the supper o' fish and chips has been regairded wi' disdain by a' but the workin'-classes; Lord Leverhulme's gaun to mak' it a' the go wi' the aristocracy. Ye'll see his big palatial fish-supper saloons start in Sauchiehall Street and extend to ev'ry part o' Gleska. 'Hot on the plate!' is to be his motto, and he has got a new way o' cookin' the potato chip that maks it as crisp as toffee. I'm tellin' you the butchers'll get a start!

"And everything centred on Stornoway! Fast steamers and express trains. The Hebridean herrin'll hardly realise it's catched till it's flappin' its tail in the Sunlight shops. I wish to goodness his Lordship should noo tak' up the coal-tred."

124. *A Turned Suit*[1]

DUFFY THE coalman at any time looked awkward and unhappy in his Sunday clothes, but to-day they appeared to fit him worse than usual, and he was as dejected and restless as a pup with a tin tied to its tail. There was nothing wrong with the texture or hue of his garments, which were of his favourite pepper and salt character, yet they seemed odd to Erchie.

"Ye're an awfu' swell the day, Duffy," he remarked. "I never saw ye in a tastier suit o' claes. They would cost ye a bonny penny."

Duffy shrugged up a shoulder to get his coat collar back on his neck again and made a fumbling, ineffectual attempt to fasten up a waistcoat button with his left hand.

"It's no' a new suit at a'," he explained, irritably. "It's my auld yin turned. The wife said she'd dae't as easy as onything, and she's made a fair hash o' the job!"

"I don't see onything wrang wi't," broke in Jinnet, putting on her glasses to make a more critical survey. "Jist like new!"

"A tip-top job!" said Erchie. "Ye couldna get better in Gunn and Collies. Wi' a suit like that and a silver-mounted umbrella ye could trevel the Continent. Whit way dae ye no button your waistcoat and gie your dickie a chance?"

"That's the cursed thing!" said the coalman, perspiring with vexation. "I canna button wan particle unless there's somebody helps me. The wife buttoned up my coat and waistcoat richt enough afore I left the hoose, but I had to tak' them aff when I was roond at the stable feedin' the horse, and noo I canna get them richt again for love nor money."

He was again, making feeble fumbling efforts to master his button holes.

Erchie gazed at the clothes intently, his lips pursed and his eyes puzzled.

"There's something oot of the ordinar' aboot that coat and waistcoat o' yours," he said. "But whit it exactly is I canna tell. It's no the cut o' them — the cut's a' richt for a coalman. The pockets is in the richt place; the sleeves is the proper length — at least yin o' them is; there's the richt amount o' slack a' roond. But there's something!"

Jinnet, with quite a professional touch, plucked at the shoulders of the coat and pulled down the lapels, to her husband's admiration.

"A' ye need to be a regular foreman cutter, Jinnet," he said, "is a moothfu' o' pins, a lump o' chalk, an inch-tape, and a few aromatic losengers."

Duffy sighed, resignedly submitting himself to this expert survey.

"I canna see a hait² wrang wi' the claes!" declared Jinnet. "They're a credit to your wife, Mr Duffy. It's mair than I could dae — turn a man's claes, and I'm no easy daunted. Were they made to your measure to begin wi'? Whaur did ye get them?"

"I bocht them aff a sodger, split new," said the coalman. "They were gi'en to him by the Government when he left the Army, but he was a piper to tred, and had to wear the kilts, so he had nae need for them, he telt me. There was naething wrang wi' them then; I could button them quite easy."

"It's an awfu' affliction ha'ein' a suit o' claes ye canna venture out o' the hoose wi' unless ye bring your wife," remarked Erchie sympathetically. "I never seen a waistcoat afore that ye needed a button-hook for unless it was a Bylie's. If I was you wi' a magic suit o' that kind, I would never go ower the door withoot a waterproof."

"Tach! the pair o' ye's just haiverin'," said Jinnet, rapidly buttoning up the recalcitrant waistcoat. "Ye're fingers is a' thumbs, Mr Duffy."

The coalman surveyed himself with incredulity and scratched his head.

"I canna for my life see hoo ye dae't!" he exclaimed. "It fair bates me to get in them buttons even if I grease them. They're either ower big or ower wee, or they're no' canny. Jist let me get anither chance."

He ripped open his waistcoat and made a serious effort to re-button himself. Not one button could he restore to its proper orifice, whichever hand he used, or even with both of them together.

"Ye would think it was a pair o' spats ye were wrestlin' wi'," said Erchie; "Let me try my hand."

But he, too, found Duffy's buttons unaccountably stubborn; he couldn't fasten one. He gave it up in despair.

"If I was you, Duffy," he said solemnly, "I would gi'e that suit to a guid-brother or send it to a jumble sale. There's something far far wrong wi't! It's something no canny in the buttons; ye micht as weel try to fasten up your claes wi' biled gooseberries. If it hadna been your wife that turned that suit, I would say it was a drunk tyler or wan o' them Spiritualists. They're up to onything! It's a clear case for Conan Doyle.[3] Ye havena heard ony rappin' aboot the watch-pocket, have ye?"

"I wish to goodness Bella had left the suit alane!" said Duffy, almost weeping. "It was fine the way it was, except for a beer-stain. This'll be a lesson to me!"

Jinnet again, quite easily did the buttoning

"You gang hame, Mr Duffy," she said, "and ha'e your tea, and tak' a bit sleep to yoursel', and ye'll find your waistcoat 'll button a' richt next Sunday. They've jist ta'en a kind o' tirravee. I've seen something o' the same kind wi' Erchie, efter comin' hame frae' a funeral."

"Efter the cheeriest funeral I was ever at, I never saw buttons like them!" protested her husband. There's something wrang! I can see't in the very look o' your coat and waistcoat, Duffy. It's a classy-lookin' suit, enough, but there's something oot o' the ordinar' in it. Ye havena, by ony chance, put it on back-side foremost?"

"I'm no' that daft," said Duffy. "If it was back side foremost, hoo could I get showin' my watch-chain?"

Erchie had another look, and held up his hands in amazement. "I see whit's wrang noo!" he cried; "Bella's put on the buttons on the wrang side!"

"They're on the right enough side," said Duffy; "they're

opposite the button-holes. Whatever's wrang, that's no' the trouble!"

"But wise-like buttons is aye on the right and yours is on the left," said Erchie; "The thing's ridiculous! I couldna understand whit way ye were workin' awa' at them wi' your caurry haund. Am I no richt Jinnet?"

"Onybody wi' ony gumption kens," said Jinnet, "that if ye turn a man's claes, the button holes is bound to be on a different side from whit the tailor put them. They're wrang to start wi', and when a woman turns a man's claes, she's glad to put them richt, even though she canna help it. Buttons on the right-hand side o' onything's jist silly; it's a man's fad, and nae woman would put up wi't. I couldna, for my life, mak' oot whit you twa men were bogglin' over. Tak you my word for't Mr Duffy, ye have a clever wife and she has your coat and waistcoat buttons on the side God meant them for!"

125. *Erchie on Divorce*[1]

"FANCY YOU," said Duffy. "Mary Pickford[2] mairried again! It's no' a month since she divorced her man; she canna be richt oot o' mournin's for him!"

"A woman doesna gang into mournin's when she loses her man that way," said Erchie. "She buys hersel' a new sealskin coat and a Pekinese terrier, and mak's for the nearest hydropathic. If there was ony mournin' over Mary's sad bereavement, it should have been her man that wore them, for she was makin' a wage o' £4,000 a week, and a wife like that's no' to be picked up in a tearoom or a laundry."

Duffy sighed. "Jerusalem!" he exclaimed; "ye would think ony hoose would be happy wi' a' that money comin' into't! Whit did she gi'e up Mr Moore[3] for?"

"It was Moore gied Mary up. As far as I can mak' oot, the chap got fed up hingin' on at the film factory every Saturday nicht wi' a barrow to hurl hame her pay. He got nae credit in the public eye; he was jist 'Mary Pickford's man', and got to abominate the very sicht o' her picture on the hoardin's. He dropped the barrow, shaved himsel', changed his name, and hid in the Rocky Mountains, refusin' to come hame, so Mary jist divorced him.

"As soon as the news got aboot that she was quit o' him, there was a gold rush to California from every pairt o' the United States. Thoosands o' smert young Americans that were jist dune winnin' the war and had seen Mary on the films and kent aboot her earnin's, cam pourin' into Los Angeles in Pullman trains to mairry her, but Douglas Fairbanks,[4] a fellow in the same line o' business as hersel', was on the spot and nicked her first. He chased her alang the roof o' a land o' hooses, sclims efter her doon a rhone-pipe, galloped on horseback twenty miles through a forest, shootin' aff his revolver a' the time, and made up on her jist as she was divin' into a coal pit shaft.

"'Tig!' he says. 'You're het! Come on and get spliced afore the crush starts.'

"'Richt-oh!' says Mary, pechin'. 'Haud on till I get my hair up.'"

"By a' accoonts," said Duffy, "Douglas Fairbanks was jist divorced the ither day himsel'."

"That's richt," admitted Erchie. "Matrimony's a wan reel picture wi' the cinema star; it's only wi' the like o' you and me its a lang sensational serial runnin' on frae day to day and week to week and feenishin' wi' a close-up view of Darby and Joan in the Poorshoose, frail in health but faithful until death. A cinema star gets tired sooner than onybody else o' the humdrum business o' comin' hame at nicht and takin' his tea with the same face forenenst him. It spoils his art. If the star's no' sick o' his wife, she's sick o' him. Ye would think that onybody could put up wi' Cherlie Chaplin,[5] he's such a comic, but his wife's divorcin' him. It's likely she'll no can staund his shauchly feet."

"Whit a crew!" said Duffy. "Thank God I'm in the coal tred!"

"The only difference between you and Cherlie Chaplin or ony ither cinema star is that ye're no' a public pet. If William Duffy, the Coalman Comedian, had his picture in a' the papers, and thoosands o' people were croodin' to see him jugglin' wi' briquettes or daein' a refined song-and-dance turn on a lorry, there's nae sayin' whit he would be up to."

"I don't think there's ony excuse for ony wife gaun awa' and leavin' her man," said Duffy with conviction.

"Man, but ye're awfu' nerrow!" retorted Erchie. "Ye're still in the dark ages! Whit could be mair proper and releegious than Mary Pickford's merriage? Ye could see for yoursel' in the papers that the minister that married her read Ephesians 5: 22-32[6] frae a Bible Mr Fairbanks, the handsomest man in America, got frae his mither on her death-bed. It shows ye the cinema tred is quite respectable.

"Ye have only to read the papers," continued Erchie, "to see that Divorce is noo recognised by a' the best Authorities as a kind o' Sacrament. The time's comin' fast when the rulin' elders o' the kirks'll go roond the congregations twice a year deliverin' tokens for the Coort o' Session, and I'll bate ye that in maist o' the hooses they'll get a dram."

"Criftens! ye're no' in earnest?" exclaimed Duffy, shocked.

"Of course I am!" Erchie assured him solemnly. "This rideeculous habit o' hingin' on to the wan husband or the wan wife a' your days is jist breakin' doon. It was a' richt enough in the days when ye had to gang hame if ye wanted a meal o' meat or wanted a waistcoat linin' mended, but noo that there's ony amount o' eatin'-hooses and the Valet Services, a man needna be behauden to ony wife in parteecular. On the other hand, noo that she can get a Divorce as easy as a dug licence nae wise-like woman needs to mak a hobby of her hubby.

"There was a time when gettin' a Divorce was a luxury only for weel-aff people that were payed by the month or had a lot of property. It's now within the means o' the riveter or the railway porter, and it's catched on like wildfire. Mony a man that used to swither whether he would strangle his wife or jine the Airmy under anither name is noo in the happy position o' bein' able to get quat o' her by rookin' her o' the money he gaithered for the rent and goin' to a lawyer wi't.

"Look at the papers on Seturday nicht or Monday mornin' — a list o' Divorces as lang's the programme for the Grand National. If ye live lang enough ye'll see folk advertisin' their Divorces the same's they were Silver Weddin's or In Memoriams:

At Edinburgh on Saturday. Before Lord Sands, Jon Diveen M'Grory and Margaret Skelford Black — by mutual consent. 'Unpleasant and unhappy in their lives now they are divided.'

"That's the kind o' thing ye'll see whenever the housin' situation is relieved."

"What has the hoosin' situation got to dae wi't?" demanded Duffy.

"Everything!" retorted Erchie. "It's only the shortage o' hooses that prevents the wave o' divorce frae sweepin' the country. Noo that the war's over and the world's determined on peace, everybody's sick o' his wife, and every wife finds it hard to thole her man."

"I don't believe wan word o't!" exclaimed the coalman. "My wife and me gets on fine. Three months efter I married her, I couldna see for my life hoo I could put up wi' her anither twelvemonth, and for twenty years noo I couldna see whit way I could dae withoot her."

Erchie shook his head. "That's a' richt for you," he replied, "but whit aboot Mrs Duffy? And whit aboot my ain wife Jinnet? Do ye no' think, Duffy, they must whiles be awfu' fed up wi' us? There's neither o' us ony great catch and never was. Ye canna deny but we're gettin' gey chafed and shabby — the only part o' the household furniture that canna be spring-cleaned. We are oot o' date completely, and don't go richt at a' wi' the new linoleum.

It's my belief that oor wifes must often wish they could send us to a jumble sale. Keep your eye on Mrs Duffy; if ye find she's takin' a suspicious interest in the divorce cases, awa' richt oot and buy her an umbrella."

126. *Our Mystery Millionaire*[1]

THE FACT, as reported in the newspapers, that a Glasgow man had bought five million pounds worth of stock in an American company so staggered Duffy the coalman last week that he rushed off at once to consult his old friend Erchie on the subject.

"Fancy you! Five millions!" he exclaimed. "A' that money gaun oot the country, and us needn't! Whaur's the polis?"

"Whit are ye yappin aboot?" inquired Erchie.

"That chap, Sir Harry M'Gowan,"[2] explained the coalman, "gaithers up five million pounds nate, and goes awa' to America and buys a motor-caur business wi't. It's a fair do! He's feared he's gaun to be taxed for his war profits, and he's awa' wi' the lot in a kit-bag before they can get on his track. Wha is he?"

"He's the Mystery Millionaire," responded Erchie, without hesitation. "Ye'll hae to wait for six months afore ye see him on the films. When the story came oot, the newspapers were offerin' a guinea apiece roond a' the best villas in Pollokshields for photographs o' Sir Harry, after tryin' a' the photographer's shops, and they couldna get yin. He has never been took. He's either the most modest man in Gleska, or he's no' pleased wi' his face for it seems he never stood in front o' a camera.

"I never heard o' the chap afore," said Duffy. "Is he in the Toon Cooncil?"

"No fears!" said Erchie. "Ye don't get that kind o' man in the Toon Cooncil; he can buy his cigars for himsel'. The Toon Cooncil's a' richt for men that has plenty o' time on their hands, but when ye're onywhere near the millionaire class ye would as soon tak' up wi' the Boys' Brigade. To tell you the truth, Duffy, I never heard o' Sir Harry mysel', and I thocht I had seen everybody in Gleska worth mentionin'. If his life story appeared onywhere in print afore this it could only be in The Gospel Trumpet, and I don't read it regular."

"The Southern Polis-office'll ken something aboot him!" suggested Duffy.

"They don't," said Erchie. "I asked a Sergeant in the Maxwell Road and he said that so far as he kent there was absolutely naething that could be brung hame to him. Sir Harry, he reports, was a quate sober chap that went to his work in the mornin' regular wi' the University car,[3] and came hame punctual at six o'clock for his tea, never steppin' out over the door efter that at nicht except whiles for a game o' bools or a visit to a cinema."

"He must have a whupper o' a bag!" suggested the coal-man. "Hoo could he cairt hame a' that money?"

"He never had a bag at a'!" replied Erchie. "Just a wee attachy case they surmised he had his piece in. They followed him nicht after nicht for weeks after he got the KBE, thinkin' they would nail him, and they photographed his fingerprints aff the bell-handle o' his door, but there was naethin daein'. He had an alibi every time.

"It's only since this American deal o' his that his career has been revealed. Thirty five years ago he was a boy that kept the petty cash in the Nobel Explosive office[4] in West George Street. He was a tip-top boy ye could aye trust on a message to the station wi' a bag o' golf clubs, and never smoked cigarettes. He was born in Gleska withoot onybody takin' ony particular notice and passed through Allan Glen's School[5] as fast as ever he could for fear they would finish his education. Efter that he had what wan o' the daily papers ca's 'a meteotric career'. But it wasna till the country was in the throes o' war that he got a richt chance to prove the stuff he was made o'. He pushed Nobel's products wi' such success that a' the Allied nations were fair clamourin' for them, and auld Hindenburg, the comic German General and story writer, had to engage a poet to write a special Hymn o' Hate addresed to Harry M'Gowan at St. Andrew's Drive, Pollokshields.

"I see from a mornin' paper," continued Erchie, "that it has been remarked by his friends, amongst whom he is a great personal favourite, that 'Sir Harry's commercial career has not only been rapid, but of the genuine type that can only be associated with pre-eminent business qualities.' I couldna put it better mysel'.

"It is also mentioned in the same quarter, that, 'apart from his business, he has led what might almost be termed the life of a recluse, although it could be more correctly put that he is one of those silent forces that effect great revolutions, without produing great public commotion.'

"As far as I can gather," continued Erchie, "that's richt. A recluse is a man that strictly looks after his ain business, tak's hame a lot o' work frae the office to feenish at nicht in his ain hoose, and has nae hobbies except the pianola or stamp collectin'. A silent force is a man that canna be prevailed on to contribute onything vocal to the harmony o' a smokin' concert; he gets a' the fun he needs frae watchin' other folk makin' Neds o' themsel's singin' 'Out on the Deep' wi' in-growin' tenor voices, or recitin' 'Jim the Fireman' in a suit o' evenin' cla'es."

"But Sir Harry's a keen gowfer at the Troon Club, I see frae the papers," mentioned Duffy, "and an auld member o' the Queen's Park Futba' Club, and goes to a' the games."

"That's a' a plant," patiently explained Erchie. "A strong silent force is a member o' ony number o' clubs, but he never goes near any o' them; he hasna the leisure for't. He jines them jist to mak' folk think he's wastin' his time like themsel's, and the mair clubs he belangs to the less they keep an eye on him, so he's weel on his way to win the millionaire stakes before they jalouse he's puttin' in his Seturday efternoons wi' his correspondence.

"The polis sergeant in the Maxwell Road assures me he has never seen Sir Harry in a pair o' plus-fours nor a striped jersey, so he canna be desperate keen on either gowf or futba'. He maybe had his name doon on the books o' the Troon Club and the QP, but he had his money in Explosives, Dunlop Rubber, and British Dyestuff Corporation. There's ony amount of millionaires like him in Gleska noo; ye would never suspect them. They're the only folk that doesna want their exploits put in the papers. But my opeenion, Duffy, is that millionairism should be among the notifiable diseases, the same as chicken-pox; it's spreadin' like onything."

"If I was shair it's bad in Pollokshields," said Duffy, " I would give up the coal tred and drive a Belvidere ambulance."[6]

127. *Erchie Sorts the Clock*[1]

"I'M TIRED lookin' at that clock and it no gaun for the last three month," said Erchie. "Could ye no bring it doon to the watchmaker and get it sorted!"

"A clock like that!" exclaimed Jinnet; "Ye micht as weel ask me to carry doon the kitchen grate to get the gas put in't! Are ye wantin' to get rid o' me?"

The time-piece on the parlour mantel-shelf was, unquestionably, not to be lifted like a teapot by any lady; it was a vast Corinthian black marble temple that would weigh about half-a-hundredweight.

"But could ye no' get Durward to come up and see whit's wrang wi't?" pursued her husband. "It's maybe only needin' oilin'."

"It's mair than twa months since I asked Durward to come and see't," said Jinnet, "but he says he canna; he has as mony clocks and watches in his shop to mend as 'll keep him thrang till the New Year."

"Then he'll no get the chance o' mendin' this yin," said Erchie with impatience. "I'll dae't mysel'!" He got to his feet with an air of firm determination, the light of conquest in his eye, and his pocket-knife in his hand.

"For goodness sake, Erchie, don't you meddle wi' the

clock!" pleaded Jinnet. "Ye'll spile it a'thegither! I'm shair you don't understand clocks!"

He paid no heed to the protest, but lifted the Corinthian temple into the kitchen, where he placed it on the table, and then took off his collar. The dusk was falling.

"Licht the gas," he ordered; "— or no, don't licht the gas. I'll can see better whit's the maitter wi' the clock if ye gie me a candle."

"I wish ye wouldna touch it, Erchie!" implored his wife. "Ye mind the last time ye worked awa' at the kitchen clock till ye made a mess o't. There's a bit o't still in the dresser drawer there."

"That was a different kind o' clock a'thegither; it was the weights bamboozled me. This is a clock wi' a mainspring; onybody could sort it. Get you me the candle, a wee drap castor oil and a feather."

"Where on earth could I get you a feather?" piteously inquired Jinnet, lighting the candle. "There's no a hen in this hoose."

"Then the next best thing's a hairpin," said Erchie, in the most confident businesslike manner. He was beginning thoroughly to enjoy himself.

He prised open the brass back of the timepiece with his knife, bent down, and looked into the interior of the temple. "We'll ha'e to shift this pendulum to start wi'," he decided, putting in his hand. The pendulum was unhooked with a little difficulty, but escaped from his fingers and fell jangling noisily against the chiming spring with which it got entangled.

"There ye are!" exclaimed Janet. "Ye've broke the bell already! A body would think ye were shellin' mussels wi' your knife. Would ye no' just put it aside for the nicht, and I'll see Mr Durward the first thing in the mornin'. Clock-mendin's a tred, Erchie; ye need the skill for't. I'm no gaun doon to ony watchmaker wi' a' the works in a pail."

"I wish ye would calm yersel'!" remarked her husband with dignity. "I'll ha'e your clock gaun in twenty minutes; there's hardly onything wrang wi't."

He took from her hands the short piece of lighted candle and held it inside the temple, the better to see the mysterious and intricate contents. His eye, as if fascinated, swept over the brassy mechanism in search of a main-spring. With a pair of scissors he captured and extracted the pendulum.

"There!" he cried triumphantly. "I tellt ye this was different a'thegither frae a kitchen clock. I'll need a wee screwdriver — that yin ye hae in the sewin' machine."

She brought him the screwdriver. Humming blithely to himself — for the novelty of this delightful entertainment was entirely to his mind — he took out the screws which kept the movement of the clock in situation, and, as the glass on the dial was open, his next touch on the back of the mechanism sent it toppling over the front in a mass on the table, whence it rolled to the floor with an appalling clatter.

Jinnet held up her hands in horror. "I tellt ye!" she exclaimed. "Ye were daft to meddle wi't! Your own guid presentation clock that ye got at oor marriage! It'll never gang again, and it's a lifetime's ill-luck to let it drop like that."

Her husband picked up the movement, considerably abashed at the mishap but cheered up instantly to find it seemed to be none the worse.

"Tuts!", he said. "It's no' a hait the waur for ye to mak' a song aboot. Ye would think I was a wean. Ye think I can dae naething. Durward would take a week sortin' this clock and charge ye seven shillings. I'll feenish it the nicht. Look at that — it's tickin' awa' already! Clock mendin' wi chaps like Durward's a' a humbug, it's my belief they just drop half the clocks they get to mend frae the bench on the floor to start them."

"If ye tak' my advice, Erchie," pleaded his wife again, "ye'll put they works the way they are in a newspaper, and I'll tak' them doon to Durward in the mornin'."

"I wish to peace ye would go awa' and tak' up your knittin'!" said her husband peevishly. "You women don't understand the least wee thing aboot mechanics, it's a' Greek to ye. If I could get the mainspring I would fix it up wi' a drop o' oil."

He made Jinnet hold up the candle while he scrutinised the mechanism from the sides, prodding at the wheels tentatively with the hairpin. The complication of them astonished him. Compared with the kitchen clock, of whose anatomy he had distinct recollection, this clock appeared fantastically intricate. And nowhere could he see any sign of mainsprings.

"Of a' the clocks that ever I handled this yin bates them a' for swank!" he declared, as if he had dealt with thousands. "It's fair jammed up wi' wee brass wheels. Ye couldna' get your knife in! And there's nae mainspring that I can see."

"What mak's it gang then?" inquired Jinnet, her mechanical curiosity for the moment wakened.

"I'll soon tell ye that," replied her husband, taking off his coat, picking up the screwdriver again, and briskly proceeding to extract screws with reckless impetuosity.

"Is your watch richt?" pathetically inquired Jinnet.

"What are ye askin' for?" he inqured without a pause in the fascinating task of loosening screws.

"Because we'll hae to depend on't for the time for the rest o' oor days," said Jinnet seriously. "I can see this clock's a waster. Ye're awfu' heidstrang, Erchie! It's my belief ye would try and mend a pianola if we had yin!"

The last of the accessible screws was extracted, he lifted the brass plate they had passed through; the majority of the mysterious little brass wheels collapsed, and he held in his hands a hopeless mass of disintegrated machinery from which screws fell pattering like hail on the kitchen waxcloth.

Jinnet was dipping a hairpin in a phial of castor oil.

"Are ye ready for the oil?" she asked, not quite realising the tragedy of the moment.

"What oil?" inquired Erchie irritably.

"For the mainspring," replied Jinnet meekly, but with deep ironic meaning.

"Mainspring!" cried her husband. "There's nae springs o' ony kind in this clock. Ye can see for yoursel'. Nae wonder it wouldna go! They left oot the mainspring a'thegither an' filled it up wi' wee brass wheels for fair swank. Haud oot your brattie."

Jinnet obediently held out her apron and he poured into it all the internal fragments of a once satisfactory presentation marble clock which still dripped screw nails on the waxcloth.

"Ye would hae been faur quicker to hae ta'en a hatchet and gien it a good clourin'," she sobbed. "There's naething for't noo but the ashpit. I wonder when ye'll get sense!"

Erchie put on his coat and collar and made for the door.

"We've made a fair hash o' that clock between us!" he remarked coolly. "This wouldna hae happened if you had a wise-like feather. But, I couldna bide the look o' that marble clock since ever I got it, it aye put me in mind o' the Necropolis. I'm gaun awa' oot to buy ye a fine wee tin yin wi' an alarm."

128. *The Soda-Fountain Future*[1]

DUFFY NEVER heard of the Soda Fountain till last Saturday night. That glad new American institution had crept into Glagow without his observing it, and it was a startling revelation to him to find that in many parts of the city there are frightful evening orgies over Walnut Sundaes and Manhattan High-Balls sucked through two straws to the strains of a jazz band.

He had been talking gloomily to Erchie about the prospects of Prohibition.[2]

"If they shut the pubs," he said, "whaur's a chap to go when the kitchen's full o' his wife's washin' drying'!"

"There'll aye be the Parks," suggested his friend, "and the Kelvingrove Museum. In the winter there'll be lectures. You'll see the time'll pass fine."

"And do ye mean to say we'll no' get onything to drink at a'?" pursued the coalman, still somewhat vague as to the devastating influence of Pussyfoot.

"Oh, that'll be a' richt," Erchie assured him genially. "A' ower the toon they're openin' Soda Fountains. The naitural human fondness for a tumbler'll get every consideration."

"Whit's a Soda Fountain?" inquired Duffy.

"It's a branch o' the Fire Brigade depairtment," Erchie informed him. "It's principal stock-in-tred is genuine Loch Katrine watter, but they don't use a hose. Ye go in wi' a ragin' conflagration o' thirst, and come oot wi' hoarfrost on your whiskers. Awa' you hame, Duffy, and put on a collar and I'll tak' ye to a Soda Fountain."

Half an hour later, Duffy was walking downstairs to a Soda Fountain, stepping softly, with his cap in his hand, for the band below, at the moment, was playing almost classic music, and, so far, his entrance had been through scenes of grandeur.

"Are ye sure we're a' richt here, Erchie?" he whispered anxiously. "It looks awfu' cless."

"As lang's you don't start singin' 'Dark Lochnagar' or interfere wi' the orchestra ye're as richt's rain." Erchie assured him. "Put on your bunnet! It's no' St Jocelyn's crypt ye're in; ye're oot for fun. Whit'll you hae?"

They had seated themselves at a little round table in a hall filled with little round tables, practically every one of them occupied by young folk, male and female, who blissfully supped ices or sucked at an infinite variety of flavoured soda water through straws.

Duffy perspired at the very sight of this extraordinary spectacle.

"Whit in the name o' Peter are they chewin' at them sticks for?" he inquired, as his friend consulted a long list of quaintly-christened beverages.

"Them's no sticks," Erchie informed him. "They're straws to sook through. Everything to drink here's new aff the ice and if ye didna use a straw to't it would jar the teeth oot o' your heid. ... Ye'll hae a Mint Julip."

"I will not!" said Duffy firmly. "Whatever it is, I don't like the name o't."

But under pressure he consented to experiment with a Mint Julip, a green concoction in a bell-mouthed wine-glass, whose restricted size and unusual shape prejudiced him from the outset. Fortunately no straws were necessary with a Mint Julip. Erchie watched him narrowly as he sipped.

A spasm went over his visage; his eyes rolled; his mouth puckered.

"Somebody's drapped a' peppermint lozenger in this," he stuttered. "I was dubious o' the colour o't; green's no lucky. I would raither ha'e Broon Robin."

"Ye'll jist hae to tak whit ye hae," retorted his host. "There's nae local veto here. That green taste's mint. It maks a' the difference on Loch Katrine watter. To enjoy a Soda Fountain ye must concentrate your attention on the band, and then ye think ye're drinkin' champagne wine. Listen! They're playin 'Till We Meet Again'; does it no' put ye in mind o' a fine Fair Seturday afore the War?"

"It doesna' put me in mind o' onything the way a dacent drink would dae," declared the coalman. "And this green drink just puts me in mind o' the Sunday School. Could we no' get something at yon bar wi' the fancy bottles in't."

The bar, which was the most prominent feature of the Soda Fountain, had certainly a delusive air of unlimited and variegated wassail with an arrangement of entrancing taps, which, to the casual eye, recalled the beer-pulls of the Mull of Kintyre Vaults. Two ministering angels busily kept filling up glasses with water charged to the highest degree with carbonic acid gas, having first put a teaspoonful into them of some flavouring syrup; or they dexterously slapped down on saucers an exact shilling's worth of sundae — sundae being ice-cream just a little more sophisticated than Duffy had known it in the days of his youth.

Loudly the band played 'Indianola'; but it hardly drowned the animated cackle of the assembly, or the protests of an infant-in-arms whose fond parent was initiating it into the delights of a sundae supped from a teaspoon.

"There's naething in that bar ye would fancy, Duffy," Erchie said. "Ye're too late o' startin' the Soda-Fountain habit, and that's bad luck for you, for the age o' the Hole-in-the Wa' wi' the sawdust floor and the tuppeny schooner's by."

"Ye're no' in earnest, Erchie!" said the coalman, genuinely alarmed.

"Of course I'm in earnest!" retorted Erchie, as they departed from the scene of revelry. "This time next year the Mull o' Kintyre Vaults'll hae a soda fountain and a fish and chips depairtment, and Big MacGlashan, instead o' ladlin' oot halfs and schooners o' beer in his shirt sleeves on a Saturday nicht'll be gaun roond his saloon in a claw-hammer coat recommendin' some new ice-cream o' his ain invention. It's me that's vexed for the Italians! The competeetion o' MacGlashan's gaun to ruin them."

"Ye couldna dae in this climate w16hoot pubs," protested Duffy. "Look at the weather!"

"Ye can dae without onything except graveyairds!" retorted Erchie. "Ye're daein' noo without a half in the mornin' afore your breakfast, and a few years ago that would spoil the day for ye. But I doot ye're ower auld for the Soda Fountain; for that ye need to start in your teens, wi' an inside like a Thermos Flask. There'll be naething for it, for the like o' you and me, Duffy, but to go hame at nicht and stay there, fillin' in the time wi' the wife wi' a cup o' cocoa."

"I couldna' dae my work on cocoa!" said Duffy, emphatically.

"Tuts, man!" said Erchie, in a more reassuring mood. "By the time that comes ye'll no' be needin' to work. Ye'll hae made your fortune aff the coals."

129. *Reminiscences*[1]

"WHIT IN the name o' fortune are ye writin' there?" asked Erchie, with a look of mock alarm at the discovery of his wife in the throes of composition, with a twopenny bottle of ink and a threepenny jotter.

"I'm just puttin' doon, as lang's I mind it, a recipe I got frae Mrs Duffy for a jumper for her dochter," replied Jinnet.

"Ye gied me an awfu' start!" said Erchie. "I thocht ye were beginnin' a book o' your Reminiscences — and me with my trunk no' packed for Canada. I warn ye that if ye ever dae onything o' the kind ye'll hae to gie me a month's full notice so's I can clear oot o' the country."

"Haivers!" exclaimed his wife. "Naething ever happend to me that was worth puttin' in a book."

"I'm no' so sure o' that!" retorted her husband, darkly. "Efter this, I'll never see ye wi' a pen in your hand but I'll think ye're clockin' on something. Look at Mrs Asquith!"[2]

"Indeed and I wish I could write a book like Mrs Asquith — look at the money she's gettin' for't!" said Jinnet. "The papers doesna gie half enough o' bits oot it; I laughed like onything at yon aboot her gallivantin' wi' the lads afore she married Henry."

Erchie looked dreadfully shocked. "I'm surprised at you, Jinnet!" he remarked solemnly. "I wonder whit kind o' woman I married! Surely you didna cairry on flirtin' and philanderin' the way Margot Tennant did. Ye hadna the education for't."

Jinnet laughed. "Hoots awa' wi' ye!" she cried. "There's nae education needed to be naitural and young. And do you think the lads a' passed me by before I met in wi' you? Well they didna! There was half-a-dizzen I could hae married."

"Ye don't mean to tell me they tried to kiss ye?" exclaimed her husband with a look heroically fierce. "Wha were they?"

"Na, na!" said Jinnet blithely. "I'll no tell ye that — except that the last o' the batch was a ne'er-dae-weel ca'd

Erchie MacPherson. The only fau't I hae wi' Margot is that she clypes the names o' the honest lads that liked her. That's no fair horney."[3]

"She's was a besom!" protested Erchie.

"She was naething o' the kind!" insisted Jinnet. "She was jist a licht-he'rted hullockit[4] lass that liked a ploy and could laugh at a boy, and was as brave as a wee bantam."

"But look at the lot o' gentry she has made to look redeeculous!" said Erchie. "And them no' deid!"

"A' the better for them! There's still time for them to get ower bein' rideeculous, noo that Margot's shown they had that failin'. Let me tell you, Erchie MacPherson, every man's redeeculous to a clever woman — except perhaps the man she means to mairry. I laughed like onything at the way she took the measure o' a' they namely men and showed they had jist the ordinar' human frailties. The bigger the man in the eyes o' the world the mair he's inclined to posturin', and its fine, for ance in a while, to see them scuddin' like hares in front o' a smert wee whitterick o' a wife that's feart for naebody."

"A randy!" said Erchie with emphasis. "Naething in her book but clatters!"

"Naething o' the kind! A rompin' lass; she's jist that yet, though she micht be a granny. I would like her fine for a neibour on the stair; she would get plenty o' cheery clash[5] in this close to put in another book."

"Thank goodness, there's nae material for a book o' that kind to be found in Braid Street," said Erchie with pious fervour. "Fancy her ridin' a horse into a hoose in London and pullin' down the lustre chandelier!"

"There's whiles I would like to pull doon a lustre chandelier mysel' if we had yin," said Jinnet. "But I never had Margot's chances," she added regretfully.

Erchie, somewhat shaken in his usual mood of irony, was now regarding his wife with genuine surprise.

"Ye're a most amazin' woman!" he exclaimed. "At your time o' life I thocht ye micht hae sense. Would you be seen smokin' a cigar?"

"I ance smoked a pipe — when I had the toothache," replied Jinnet brazenly. "And I felt I was awfu' gallant. That's the way Mrs Asquith would feel aboot her cigar; ye can see it wisna a habit. And that's true aboot half the escapades she was up to; they astonished hersel', and mak' her laugh at herself noo when she minds o' them."

"It's a' wi' hersel' she's ta'en up in her writin' as far's I can see," said Erchie. "There's naething aboot serious affairs in life — and — and politics. There's nae moral uplift."

"There's nae pretence at it," admitted Jinnet. "If there's ony upliftin' to be done in the Asquith family, Henry'll[6] see to't; that's his business. Wha could she be better ta'en up wi' than wi' hersel' in writin' her book? There's naebody she kens better. If she wasna' a plucky yin, she wouldna' say sae much aboot hersel' that ither folk keep secret. If her man was to write his life he would come oot like yin o' the Apostles, as glossy as a figure in a wax-work."

"It's no' a book for the youth o' the country; it'll mak' them think the highest society in the land is awfu' frivolous and peery-heided,"[7] pleaded Erchie. "That's whit the papers say."

Jinnet chuckled, as she put aside her jotter.

"Noo ye're jist making fun o' me, Erchie!" she retorted. "The newspapers wouldna' daur say that, for they're a' competin' wha'll give maist aboot the frivolity and peery-heidedness o' Society. Do ye think ye could get a lend o' the book frae the minister? He's sure to hae't frae the library. I would like fine to read it if it's big print."

130. *Glad News*[1]

ERCHIE CAME home in the evening, radiant, whistling an old air of the Seventies as he hung up his coat in the lobby, and grinned at his wife with a sly congratulatory air as he took off his boots.

"Ye're awfu' cheery the night" said Janet. "Did they raise your pay on ye?"

"I don't want my pay raised," he informed her. "Another shillin' or twa and I would be into the Income-tax. That would be the last straw!"

"Indeed and I wish we had the Income tax," said Janet. "If ye're on the Income tax ye get an allowance o' £225 for yoursel' and your wife."

"Who the mischief gi'ed ye that information?" inquired her husband, with surprise.

"Duffy's wife. She says her man's in for't and she's getting a new room grate on the strength o't. She's expectin' a lot o' money, too, for the weans."

Erchie chuckled. "Faith, that would mak' it a land fit for heroes to live in![2] If Duffy and his wife think the Income-tax is as lavish as that, they're goin' to get an awfu' start when the thing's explained to them. You tell Mrs Duffy no' to go in for a room grate in the meantime, but to get a good gas ring for the kitchen and stop coals. As far as I can hear from the chaps that's sufferin' it, the Income-tax is the worst o' human afflictions. It puts ye aff your sleep."

"But whit are ye whistlin' for?" pursued Janet.

"Great news!" said Erchie. "I ran a' the way hame to tell ye. THERE'S TWOPENCE AFF THE BOBBIN O' THREAD! Whit de ye think o' that?"

"It'll be bastin' thread," suggested Janet dubiously.

"No, it's no' bastin' thread; it's twopence aff the best bobbin o' thread ye ever put your teeth to. There's a chance noo I'll can get that button on my waistcoat I've been speakin' aboot for the last twelvemonth."

"Ye auld haiver! It only come aff yesterday, and it would be on afore this if ye had put on anither waistcoat in the mornin'. Wha's takin' the twopence aff?"

"Coats,[3] of course! Wha else could dae't? I havena heard the parteeculars, but it's rumoured there was a mass indignation meetin' o' the Coats shareholders in the St. Andrew's Halls, where they demanded that the English pirn[4] should be eightpence instead o' tenpence, so as to bring doon the cost o' livin' in the tylerin' tred. They said they were fair affronted wi' their dividends. It gied them a bad name."

"Whit's the difference between an English pirn and a Gleska yin?" asked Janet.

"The English pirn, bobbin or reel," blithely intimated her husband, who had learned of it only an hour ago, "contains 400 yards. The Scotch pirn, bein' mainly used for kilts, is only 300 yards, wi' a choice o' a 200 yard pirn that contains only 200 yards suitable for chaps in lodgings that does their ain repairs. The English bobbin is reduced from 10d. to 8d., the Scotch 300-yard pirn from 8^1/$_2$d. to 6^1/$_2$d. and the 200-yard chat to 4^1/$_2$d. There's goin' to be a torchlight procession among the young students at Gilmorehill; the 4^1/$_2$d. pirn means a lot to them."

"It's the first time ever I heard there was ony difference between an English and a Scotch pirn," said Janet. "I never kent hoo many yards o' thread was on a pirn; I must look."

She pulled out the drawer of her sewing machine and produced a new bobbin.

"Ye're richt enough," she agreed. "It's 300 yards. That's a big lump! It'll be as far as frae here to Maitland Street."

Erchie, took the bobbin into his hand and regarded it critically.

"Did ye ever measure a pirn to see if ye were gettin' the richt length?" he inquired.

"Not me!" replied Janet. "I couldna be bothered."

"Nae wonder we're poor!" exclaimed Erchie. "I'll bate ye English wifes measure their pirns! I wouldna tak' a 300-yard pirn withoot measurin' it for mysel' ony mair than I would buy a dozen o' eggs withoot countin' them. Get me your inch tape."

"Oh, Erchie!" exclaimed his wife apprehensively; "Ye're shairly no' gaun to waste a pirn o' thread measurin't wi' a tape. It'll be a' richt. Mr Coats wouldna lower himsel' to gie short measure. I never in a' my life heard o' onybody measurin' thread."

"Get you me the tape!" imperatively said her husband. "We'll hae to go into this. I'm dubious aboot the twopence aff the bobbin."

The tape being produced with tearful protestations, he began to unwind the thread and measure successive lengths of it with all the cheerful flourish of a ribbon counter.

"One yard, twa yards, three yards — you get a pencil and put doon the yards as I measure them. If ye don't I'll never can mind them efter the first fifty."

"I think ye're daft!" cried Janet. "Mind the way ye spoiled the clock. Ye would be far better to let things alane."

"They're no gaun to diddle me oot o' a single yard if I can help it!" declared her husband firmly. "Whaur did the Coats get their yachts?"[5]

Already the thread unwound was beginning to curl about his feet; he kicked impatiently. Thread caught on his buttons; the bobbin slipped from his fingers, and when he picked it up from the floor he was already knee-deep in a spider-web of cotton.

"Fifty yards, fifty-wan, fifty-two, fifty — did I say fifty-seven — "

"I'm gaun oot o' the hoose!" wailed Janet. "I would be better wi' a man that took drink. That thread'll never be ony use to me noo, the way it's fankled."

Indeed, it was very unlikely to be of any use to anybody, for her husband was now wrapped round with it as if he was making himself a cocoon.

"Oh, to the mischief!" he exclaimed at last; "Are ye shair it says 300 yards? If I'm no' mistaken, I've measured miles. The Coatses is just palmin' aff the stuff on us! There's as much thread here as would reach to Mars; this must hae been a bobbin specially made for astronomers."

By the time the thread was all off the bobbin, he was wrapped in it up to the eyebrows, and his spectacles were lost somwhere in the mass.

"My good bobbin!" wailed Janet. "I tellt ye to leave it

alane. Cost me 8½d! I couldn't get enough oot o't noo to put on your waistcoat button."

"I'm no botherin' aboot my waistcoat button!" warmly declared Erchie. "A' this cairry-on for the sake o' a waistcoat button! I wish ye had left me alane and no nag-nagged on at me to measure thread when I'm wantin' my tea. Hoo am I to get oot o' this fankle o' thread? Paisley was aye a place I fair abominated. See if ye can find my specs."

"Men's a' the same; they're a' silly!" declared Janet, as she started snipping him into freedom again with a pair of scissors.

131. *The Footballer's Life*[1]

"DID YOU notice this week," asked Duffy, "that a fitba' player by the name o' Tom Hamilton[2] at Kilmarnock, has been bocht by the Preston North End for £4,500?"

"I didna notice." replied Erchie. "That's a terrible lot o' money for a human bein'! I've seen the day ye could get tip-top fitba' players in the prime of life for five pounds apiece, delivered at the door for ye. I've seen half-backs, and goalkeepers that had twenty years' experience, ye could get for a schooner o' beer."

"They're surely gettin' scarce," suggested Duffy. "Criftens! £4,500 would buy a champion entire horse like the Baron o' Buchlyvie.[3] Ye could buy a tenement land wi' that money! Whit'll they dae wi' him?"

"The first thing they'll dae 'll be to insure his life, tak' his measure for an evenin' dress suit o' clothes, and show him aff at a conversazione and soiree at Preston North End. That's the usual procedure. It's done like an induction dinner to a new minister. The wifes and dochters o' the Preston North End Club'll present him wi' a new silk jersey and a revolvin' bookcase. I'll bate ye Hamilton's sittin' up at nicht trainin' for his speech."

"I wish I had gone in for fitba', instead o' the coal tred," said Duffy. "I had nae idea there was that much money in it. I hope Hamilton has the gumption to put it in the Bank and no' play the goat wi't, backin' horses."

Erchie laughed. "Ye're under a delusion, Duffy," he remarked. "Tom Hamilton doesna' handle a' that money; it maistly gangs to the Kilmarnock club that sold him. A' he gets frae the Preston North End is his wages and expenses. Bein' a champion fitba' player's no great catch; he's the last relic o' slavery left in modern times. He has nae sooner settled doon in a nice wee hoose wi' a bit o' gairden, and the ground a' delved, than somebody comes and buys him and cairts him awa' to anither pairt o' the country where he doesna ken a livin' soul and has to learn the language.

"He canna ca' his life his ain; at the top o' his fame it's jist fair martyrdom. You and me, Duffy, can live whaur we like, and dae whit we like; eat and drink onything that we can pay for or get on credit, but a fitba' player micht as weel be a canary except for the glory o' seein' his picture in the papers.

"The life o' the famous fitba' team in the season is beyond description, cruel. They havena even their Seturdays to themselves. The chap that trains them watches them like a hawk, and if he seen yin o' them eatin' a pie, or oot o' his bed efter nine o'clock at nicht, he would gie him an awfu' doin'. If their legs gets saft he goes ower them wi' a nutmeg-grater; at the slightest sign o' puffiness under the eyes he scrapes them wi' a curry comb and rubs them wi' embrocation.

"Ye canna alloo ony man ye've paid £4,500 for to spoil his health attendin' mairages or keepin' the New Year; the only dissipation that's permitted is to go to Hydros."

"Do ye tell me they tak' them to Hydros?" asked Duffy.

"They do," said Erchie.

"Well it's a bloomin' shame! I've heard aboot them Hydros. A' teetotal!!"

"That's the very reason they tak the fitba' players to them every noo and then to feenish their trainin'.

"Just fancy you big strong chaps like Tom Hamilton

taken under escort to a Hydro for a weekend or a couple o' days afore a match.

"'Whit would ye like for your dinner?' asks the trainer — aye a brutal character wi' nae human feelin's.

"'Could we no' have hare-soup, steak and kidney pie and a dumplin'?' says the goalkeeper, speakin' polite.

"'Yous can not,' says the trainer; 'yous'll have a small underdone beefsteak and a couple o' water biscuits.'

"'Whit aboot a spot o' beer?' says the Best Half-Back in Britain. 'Ony kind o' reasonable wee refreshment.'

"'A' the reasonable refreshment I hae wi' me in my bag is for mysel' and the committee,' says the trainer. 'Wha says lemonade, and wha says dry ginger? It's no' a Gleska Corporation Water trip ye're on, it's a trainin' session. Efter ye're done gorgin' yersel's, yous'll come oot wi' me and dae a nice wee five miles across country. I seen some o' ye yesterday eatin' chocolates and ye'll hae to work it oot o' the system.'

"When the team comes back, a' glaur, efter scourin' roond the countryside, they're taken into the Hydro baths and washed and massaged till they're as glossy as ony-thing. The trainer gi'es them a lecture on the muscles, and then they put on their Sunday clothes and go into the room where the ither Hydro guests is having a meal o' meat.

"The League champions toy at a side table for a while wi' Glaxo, chemical food and rusks, and the ither folk in the room says, 'Is that the Celtic? Oh, what a treat!' and a fine old gentleman in the sweetie tred moves up to the trainer and asks permission to hand the team a tract on Foreign Missions or Rome and the Irish Situation.

"Efter that the team would like fine to jine the dancin', but they don't ken the Hesitation Waltz, and the toppin'est girls in the Hydro go aff jazzin' wi' a lot o' young neds in the stockbrokin' business that couldna stop a hot shot for goal even if they had a bill hoardin' behind them.

"The auld Roman gladiator ye used to read aboot in the Sevenpenny was on velvet compared wi' the fitba' players o' today. The crowd on the field heaved bags o' money or their jewels at him every time he got a wallop hame on the chap frae anither pairt o' the country, and every Seturday nicht he went hame wi' a bagful o' souvenirs o' that sort. When he got up in years and a wee bit groggy, he was bocht a bit o' a ferm and retired, respected and free o' care for a' the rest o' his life.

"But the fitba' player, passed aboot frae wan club to anither for the best ten years o' his life, and naething to show for't but cuttin's aboot him frae the *Evenin' News*, retires wi' naething but a worn-oot reputation, and a promise o' a' the influence that's needed to get him a public-hoose.

"Boxers and fitba' players, Duffy — they're the people's pride jist as lang's there's the puff left in them; efter that they're no' half as much in demand as coalmen."

132. *Celebrating the Eclipse*[1]

ERCHIE STEPPED out of the close on Friday morning with a feeling that somehow official Summertime had missed a cog, and looked at his watch to make certain he had not mistaken the hour. It was exactly 9.45. But somehow the morning had not a breakfast-hour look. There was sunshine, it was true, but a curious wan sunshine, more like a Fintry moonlight. The shadows were unnatural (as his instinct though not his consciousness at once detected); the air was too cold. At the corner where the Mull of Kintyre Vaults ought properly to have the dismal deserted pre-noon aspect, there was already a crowd.

"The General Strike's started, or else there's a change in the licensin' regulations," he said to himself. And then he observed that the crowd were looking at the sun through bits of glass with as much fascination as if it were a keyhole or a film of Charlie Chaplin.

At that instant Duffy's coal cart came round the corner, the horse as usual, dejected, apparently wholly unaware of the cheering fact that the coal pits were out of business;

Duffy with a collar and a jacket on — both indicative of some unusual occasion.

"Whoa!" he said, and the docile animal stopped with a jerk as if actuated by electricity, with two feet suspended in the air.

"Whit's up that ye're in your evenin' dress for?" asked Erchie. "Are ye gaun a trip?"

"Nae trip aboot it!" replied the coalman. "The wife made oot I would need to put on a jecket to celebrate the eclipse. I don't see onything patent aboot it to celebrate. Do ye no' think there's some mistake aboot the date? It should be on by this time accordin' to the almanacks. I'll bate ye they forgot the clocks was shifted!"

Erchie chuckled. "Man ye're a character Duffy!" he exclaimed. "Ye don't see the eclipse and you're standin' richt in the middle o't. I have a canary yonder wi' far mair observation; it stopped whistlin' as soon's the demonsteration started, and the cat went oot like lichtnin' on the washin'-hoose slates and began yowlin'."

"I canna see onything different in't," said Duffy, shutting an eye and blinking with the other at the crescent orb of day. "Forby, whaur's the moon? They bragged ye would see the moon in front o't. There's a catch in't somewhere, Erchie. They're takin' a rise oot o' us."

"To see an eclipse proper," explained Erchie, "ye need a gless."

"Hoo the bleezes can ye get a gless wi' the pubs no' open till half-past twelve?" inquired Duffy indignantly. "If there's an eclipse to celebrate they should celebrate it richt and gie us a chance o' some refreshment. Tomorrow there's to be thoosands o' chaps in Gleska frae England to see the fitba' International,[2] and the restaurant bars is to be opened for them in the middle o' the day; but there's nae consideration for the Gleska man that pays the rates and taxes and wants to celebrate a Scotch eclipse."

"It's no' that kind o' gless I mean at a'," patiently explained Erchie. "Ye would lose yer eyesicht if ye looked at the sun through the bottom o' a tumbler; the glare o't's maist tremendous. Whit ye need's a bit gless smoked; there's a wee boy'll lend ye his; he must be tired noo lookin' for his eyes is waterin!"

"I'll dae naethin' o' the kind," said the boy when appealed to by the coalman. "Awa' and get an eclipse o' your ain."

Duffy unhesitatingly grabbed him by the back of the neck, purloined the astronomical essential from him and turned his penetrating gaze upon the heavens.

"I see the moon a' richt," he said to Erchie. "It's a new yin but there's nae sun," and he searched at large across the heavens for the missing luminary.

"That's the sun ye're lookin' at, ye idiot!" said Erchie. "The moon's in front o't."

"Nane o' your coddin'! There's nae moon there; I'm no' that silly."

"It's the moon ye're lookin' at!"

"Ye said a meeenute ago it was the sun."

"Ay, but the black bit that ye see's the moon."

"Well, it's no' lichted, onyway," declared the coalman.

"Lichted!" retorted Erchie contemptuously, "Do you think they would licht the moon in the middle o' the day?"

"They should ha'e the eclipse at nicht then," said Duffy. "It's awfu' badly managed. If ye seen the baith o' them lichted ye could believe it."

"Do ye no' believe there's an eclipse at a'?" inquired the astounded Erchie.

"I'm no' denying' it," replied the coalman, cautiously, "for I saw aboot it in the papers, but that's no' my idea o' an eclipse."

"Maybe no'," said Erchie; "but it's God's."

"I'm wantin' my eclipse! Duffy the coalman stole it!" wailed the weeping owner of the glass; but Duffy again was rapt in the higher astronomy.

"Gi'e the laddie his gless," commanded Erchie. "Ye'll see as much eclipse as ye need, reflected in the Mull o' Kintyre window."

Duffy restored the glass and pursued his studies in the

way suggested. "It's a perfect education!" he declared at last. "I wish the wife could see't. She's aye in the hoose and never sees onything. Would ye watch my horse till I go roond to Braid Street for her."

"It'll be a' past before she could get her furs on," said Erchie. "But ye can tell her a' aboot it."

"The next eclipse o' the sun like this I'll ha'e her oot in time. I'm vexed she missed this yin, fir it's an education."

"If ye can get her oot at the next eclipse like this it'll be fine," said Erchie. "It's shair to be visible frae Sighthill. It's to be in 1960 or thereaboot."

"Criftens!" exclaimed Duffy with genuine surprise, "I thocht they were gaun to hae them regular, efter this, like the Summer Time."

"That was talked about, but it canna be managed. It tak's an awfu' lot of plannin', like a Gleska Exhibition. The last eclipse o' this sort was sixty years ago, efter the Crimean War. But there's to be a topper — a total yin — in 1999. Be shair and ha'e a bit o' smoked glass ready for't."

133. *Firewood* [1]

"DID YE no' get some sticks?" inquired Janet, when her husband returned on Saturday. "I tellt ye I must hae sticks if there was to be ony dinner for ye. There hasna been a morsel o' coal in this hoose for a fortnicht, and dear knows whit I'm gaun to dae ower Sunday!"

"I couldna get as much stick as would gie ye a skelf in the finger," he said hopelessly. "I think the Royal and Ancient Foresters[2] is jined the miners and struck work. I saw a procession o' them wi' a brass band gaun oot the Maryhill road."

"Whit am I to dae?" lamented Janet. "I couldna even mak' ye a cup o' tea."

"Whit did I get ye gas in the range for?" inquired her husband.

"Ye ken fine," she retorted, "that I daurna licht the gas

in the range when I'm my lane; I'm frichtened for't. It starts wi' a bang that shakes the hoose, and lang efter I've screwed it oot, it gi'es a terrible explosion. Oh Erchie! I was dependin' on ye gettin' some sticks to mak' your dinner."

"Ye don't need sticks nor coal either, to mak' a dinner. I've seen a chap in the music-halls mak' a first-rate omelette in a tile hat, that wasna ony the worse o't."

"But ye ken fine there's no' a tile hat in this hoose," said Janet, quite seriously, as if that were really all that was wanted to secure an excellent omelette. "Ye sent it awa' yoursel' a week ago to bring it up to date."

Erchie calmly opened up his parcel. "I'll licht the gas ring for ye," he said. "But what you're badly needin' is philosophy."

"It's not!" she retorted; "It's fuel."

"If you had philosophy," pursued her husband, "you would mind that food came into the world afore fuel. I have here a pound o' the best boiled beef ham."

"I wish we lived near a wud," sighed Janet, but half-resigned to the situation.

"Far better livin' near a grocer's shop in the New City Road district!" said her husband. "There's an awfu' lot o' humbug aboot cookin'. Naebody needs fires in weather like this as lang's they can get boiled ham. Life, Jinnet, is full o' merciful compensations; we're no actually dependin' on the coal tred as lang as there's pies in the bakers and boiled ham in M'Sorley's shop. When ye come to think o' it — coal's a sheer extravagance."

"But it's handy for washin's," pleaded his wife, "and I was gaun to hae a washin' on Monday."

"Haven't ye a vacuum washer?" asked Erchie. "As far as I've read aboot the vacuum washer, ye have only to give it a start, and then ye can go awa' and leave it."

Janet held up her hands despairingly.

"Oh, dear! you men!" she exclaimed, "Ye havena the least idea! ... Whit in a' the world am I to dae for sticks?"

"I've never in a' my life seen such a craze for sticks!"

exclaimed her husband impatiently. "You're lettin' it get the better o' ye, Jinnet. It's worse than drink or cigarettes. The first thing ye think aboot in the mornin's a fire, and it's the last thing at nicht wi' ye. I'm gaun aboot my work a' day and I never think aboot a fire. Even when coals was plentiful, I could pass a score o' coal-rees withoot the least temptation to go in an hae a half-a-hunder-wecht. But I'm begining' to be frichtened you're yin o' the secret fire-eaters that's tipplin' awa at the bunker a' day when yer man's at his business. And I don't like the way ye're aye clamourin' for sticks. Whit did ye dae wi' the clothes-pins!"

"If I hadna burned the clothes-pins last Seturday, ye couldn't hae got to the kirk on Sunday," retorted Janet, indignantly. "There was naethin' else to mak' a fire to iron your shirt and collar wi'."

Erchie was only for a moment rebuffed. "There ye are!" he said, "I tellt ye! Ony excuse for a lowe[3] in the chimney! As if I couldna be daein' fine at a time like this wi' a muffler. Ye'll be ruining your constitution. A confirmed fire-eater! Cairry on the way ye're daein', and the furniture'll gang next. Ye'll be ha'in' a fine spree wi' the what-not and the chiffonier, and takin' in other neibour women like yoursel' to finish off a' the doors and skirtin'-boards."

"I never can tell when ye're in earnest, Erchie," said his wife. "It's no' very nice o' ye to be makin' fun o' me, and me wi' no' a morsel o' coal."

The doorbell rang. Erchie went to open it, and let in Duffy, who marched into the kitchen carrying some heavy object wrapped in newspapers.

"Here's Duffy," said Erchie; "wi' a couple o' quarter loafs."

"It's naething sae common. It's a good lump o' coal. The wife tellt me ye were in desperation for a fire, and feart to use the gas. Nae wonder! I never believed in gas for onything but lightin'. Tak's the flavour oot o' everything in cookin'."

He unwrapped a substantial block of fuel with an air of triumphant benevolence.

"There's the stuff for ye, Genuine Barrachnie! Pre-war, and full strength. I'll bate ye there's no' a bonnier lump o' coal in Kelvinside. I came on half-a-hunder-wecht this efternoon in the stable loft where I put it at the last big coal strike to keep it frae bein' commandeered."

"Oh, Mr Duffy, what a trate!" exclaimed Janet, with delight. "It's rale considerate o' ye. I couldna be better pleased if ye brocht me a seal-skin jacket. But I hope ye're no' deprivin' yoursel'."

"Not me!" the coalman assured her. "But ye mustna let bug to onybody. A lot o' my customers in Braid Steet jaloused I had coal in the parcel, and there's twa score o' them at your close-mouth this meenute, followin' me with zinc pails and baskets."

"Puir things!" said Janet, sympathetically, "It's hard times."

"By jings! If I had coal, I could mak' money o't," said Duffy, wistfully.

"It would be a blessed thing if we could dae withoot coal a'thegither," suggested Erchie. "There's sae many people that abuse it."

"Whit would ye use instead?" asked Duffy, feelingly. "Peats! Ye couldna richt boil a potato wi' peat; it's only a smell."

"Coals is a curse," continued Erchie solemnly. "If people only kent when to tak' and when to leave it alane, there wouldna be much herm in't. But it's the ruin o' mony a hoose. There should be the Local Veto for coal, the same as drink. I hope the Pussyfoots'll start that next. If I had a' the money that's been spent in my hoose on coal I would be a rich man the day."

"Haivers!" interjected Duffy, with warmth. "Ye couldna dae withoot coal. The trouble is there's far ower little o't."

"That's what ye say aboot drink also, but I'm tellin' ye ye're wrang. I've jist proved to Jinnet here that so far as cookin' goes coals is an extravagance — as lang's ye can get bully beef, boiled ham, and tuppenny pies at threepence ha'penny. Forby, there's nuts, tinned herrin', and bananas."

"Then ye'll no' be needin' my lump o' coal," said Duffy moving towards it.

"Na, na," said Erchie, shifting it hurriedly to the bunker. "Jist leave it alane; I'm gaun to get it silver mounted for a trophy o' the Great Peace."

134. *Duffy's Flitting*[1]

DUFFY'S FLITTING was getting on all right on Friday till Archibald the tailor came, quite uninvited, to his assistance.

He had done two raiks with his own coal-lorry and the aid of his wife and her brother Peter. All the stuff put out first on the pavement, carefully selected by Mrs Duffy as best fitted to bear the prolonged scrutiny of the neighbours, was now in the new house, three streets away, and there remained but beds to take down the stairs, the chiffonier to negotiate round the bends, three clothesbaskets full of crockery and pots, some valuable works of art, the what-not, the kitchen clothes poles, lobby linoleum, the bird cage and a couple of grates.

"We're gettin' on top!" said Duffy. "I'll be feenished afore my dinner."

"Ye're a fair champion'!" said his wife with honest admiration. "And there's no' an iota broke, I never had a luckier flittin'."

It was exactly 12.25 p.m., and Archibald came round the corner.

The eye of Archibald, the reformed actor, lit up. A flitting to him was a joyous thing, like a trip to Rothesay or a Hogmanay. He had never had one of his own, but had helped at scores of them.

"I'll gie ye a hand," he volunteered agreeably, taking off his coat and throwing it on the lorry. "For shiftin' a cottage grand or a massive cabriole sofa, put your money on Baldy ev-e-ry time! There's no' a more willin' performer in the far-flung flittin' line. Could ye get me a brattie, Bella!"

"Are ye shair ye're a' richt?" inquired Mrs Duffy, dubiously. "I'm no' wantin' onythin' bashed."

The tailor drew himself up with a dignity not seriously impaired by the fact that his dickie scarcely filled the opening of an old evening-dress waistcoat, and cast on the lady a reproachful eye.

"Mrs Duffy," he said "— or in the words o' the vernacular, Bella, — I'm as right as the far-famed trivet, the same bein' an appurtenance made in the Sun Foundry and warranted OK. In all great congeries of thought, the British patriot, first at heaven's command, in these parlous times canna even greet the orb o' day wi' a modicum o' cheer till the efternoon. Is there, by any chance, what, when I played wi' John Clyde in his 1889 season, we called without divagation a bo'le o' beer?"

"Oh, you tylers!" exclaimed Mrs Duffy. "Ye'll get no beer here till the flittin's by."

Archibald sighed. "Most noble and worthy!" he said, bowing; "Kismet! We maun just thole! If there is no beer at least let me have the brattie. I'm wearin' a customer's trousers for what ye might call the nonce."

Mrs Duffy had no sooner disappeared upstairs in search of an apron for Archibald, than he turned to her husband, and the brother Peter.

"Gentlemen all," he said engagingly.

"Nothing under the cope and canopy[2] is more con-ducive to a flittin' than a little homologation of thought. Methinks I see now the Mull O' Kintyre Vaults open. If there is one thing more than another I can shift furniture on, it is a glass of the nut-brown. It ameliorates. In the words of the Vulgate,[3] Duffy, are ye on?"

Duffy scratched his chin. Flitting was certainly warm work, and he had had no breakfast.

"A' richt!" he agreed. "But jist the wan pint, mind ye! Peter's teetotal. Hing on by the horse, Peter, till we come

back. Tell the wife I'm awa' to Mactaggart's for the lend o'
a bed-key."

"The bed-key," said Archibald, putting on his coat, "is
the palladium o' British liberty. Lead on, MacDuffy!"

At ten minutes past one o'clock Mrs Duffy came round
to the Mull of Kintyre Vaults, manifestly angry, with a
bird-cage in her hand.

"Listen! Is this a flittin' or a funeral?" she inquired
acidly. " I wonder ye're no' ashamed o' yirsel's! Me moilin'
and toilin' wi' a linoleum and yous-yins drinkin'!"

"Just a small scintilla o' the nut-brown, Bella, and a
chaser — nothin' more, so help me, Peter!" explained
Archibald. "First the day! Can I relieve ye, madam, of the
songster?"

Mrs Duffy refused to surrender the bird-cage. "I
wouldna trust ye wi' a stuffed gold fish," she declared
indignantly. "Ye jist came here to spile a flittin'. We were
daein' fine withoot ye."

"Fair do, Bella!" pleaded her husband. "Baldy and me's
as richt as rain. Ye must aye mak' some allooance for a
flittin'."

"I'll mak' nae allooance for a big sumph that's cairried
awa' by a bletherin' auld play actor tyler," retorted Mrs
Duffy. "Come awa' oot o' this and feenish my flittin'. A
bonny example, the pair o' ye, for my brither Peter; he's
awa' to a public hoose o' his ain, and the horse is
stravaigin' the City Road wi' naething in the lorry but a
what-not and a jeely pan. Whit'll the neighbours think?"

Twenty minutes later Peter and the horse were collected; Archibald took off his coat again, and regardless of
the protestations of Mrs Duffy, helped to remove the
grates. Duffy and Peter and he bore them down the stairs,
his share of the burden being the dampers only, which he
absent-mindedly carted up again.

"Whit on earth are ye playin' at?" asked Mrs Duffy,
exasperated. "It's a wonder ye dinna bring up the horse."

"My mistake, indubitably, Bella," confessed Archibald
handsomely. "A lapsus lingus, which in the original Hebrew

means a bloomin' error. Now for the portrait gallery! My, that's a clinkin' picture o' Mr Duffy; we'll need to mind the gless o' that yin."

He was already in posession of this gem of the art collection.

"Keep your hands off that and cairry doon a bass if ye cairry onything!" cried the anxious housewife. "But I would raither ye went awa' to your tylerin'. We're no needin' ony help."

There was an ominous crash of wood on the landing, where her husband and Peter wrestled with the chiffonier; she rushed out, leaving Archibald, who got up on a stepladder and took down the gasalier by the simple process of taking off its weights first. Luckily the gas had been turned off at the meter.

With three of the ancestral portraits draped round his shoulders by their cords, the gasalier in one hand and a coil of clothes-rope in the other, he got down on the landing, where Mrs Duffy was already weeping over a sadly-damaged chiffonier.

"Mercy on me! Whaur did ye get that gasalier?" she cried, distracted, as she turned from watching nervously the further progress of the chiffonier downstairs. "A body's no' safe to turn her back on ye a meenute!"

"Never saw a nobler gasalier!" said Archibald, blithely. "Massive in the extreme, and still chaste to a degree. For cleanin' a gasalier the best authorities mention beer. It might be best to clean it now; I could run across and get a quart in MacKirdy's Home of Geniality."

"It's no' oor gasalier; it belangs to the hoose!" gasped Mrs Duffy. "Ye're far ower smert at shiftin' things."

"My mistake, Bella, indubitably," said Archibald, without any symptom of contrition. "Methought, most noble and worthy, ye had overlooked it."

"Overlooked your aunty!" exclaimed the lady, plucked it from him rudely, and broke two globes against the railing of the stair.

"Amn't I the puir harassed woman!" she wailed. "Wi' a

lot o' silly men! Whit are ye daein' wi' my clothes rope? I was keepin't up here to tie the beds."

She grabbed the cord from him; a loose coil of it had got about his feet, and he staggered. There was a clatter of the art collection, and the glass of Mr Duffy's portrait as an Ancient Forester was splintered hopelessly.

"That's a feenisher!" she cried. "Awa' hame like a wise man, Baldy, and leave this flittin'; ye're jist in the road."

Archibald, however, esteemed the duties of human friendship and aid too highly to abandon the flitting at that stage. He was now in the vein of a score of old-time flittings, when the world was carefree and unperplexed. The spirit of youth restored, he whistled like a mavis up and down the stair, his every step attended with disaster.

It was he who let the handle of a basket slip to the manifest damage of its crockery contents that sounded too alarming to be investigated at the moment, and in carrying down the kitchen clothes-poles he put one of them through a staircase window.

"Ye have surely an awfu' spite at gless!" cried Mrs Duffy, wringing her hands. "It's a mercy I havena a bookcase."

"At bookcases," said Archibald, "I am par excellence. Many a yin I shifted in the old Royal Princess'[4] days wi' my coajutor, John Clyde."[5]

"It's shiftin' scenery ye should be yet!" said Mrs Duffy.

"Right! most noble and worthy," agreed Archibald. "I have shifted the Clachan o' Aberfoyle[6] in fifteen minutes — the cloud-capped towers and palaces[7] — and now, base scullion, am engaged in turnin' suits o' clothes. Crockery and the like is for women, and boys to handle; I wish ye had a bookcase or a grandpa clock."

"Thank God, there's naething noo but saft stuff," said Mrs Duffy piously. "Gie Peter a hand wi' that feather bed."

"Flittin's is no what they used to be," said Archibald. "I miss the geniality."

135. *After the Fight*[1]

ERCHIE, THE beadle, perfunctorily rang the bell of St Kentigern's yesterday forenoon, as if for once his mind was not in his occupation, finished its pealing at least three minutes earlier than usual, and then, in the vestry, heaved the minister into his gown in the shortest time on record. He had no sooner snibbed him into the pulpit than he shuffled hurriedly out to join two elders who were counting the copper contents of the plate with a worldly jingling that penetrated even to the congregation and was painfully out of harmony with the opening prayer.

"Did ye see a paper?" he anxiously inquired and Mac-Coll, the elder, reaching into his coat-tail pocket, handed him the latest *Life and Work*.[2]

"Ach, to the mischief!" said Erchie, impatiently, "It's no' that I mean; it's a paper for readin'."

"It's no' a day for papers for readin'," replied MacColl, solemnly.

"I ken that fine," said Erchie; "But wha won?"

"Mind I have nae interest in't mysel, but I did hear last night afore I went to my bed that ten minutes efter it started Carpenteer[3] was a corp in the fourth round," said the elder in a whisper.

"And that's a' the time it took to feenish the thing!" exclaimed Erchie. "Fancy you, the whole mortal universe hingin' in suspense for the last six weeks on a fight that's settled in the time ye would smoke a pipe! I thocht the battle would rage for a month, wi' a' the sang they made aboot it."

"The twa ruffians that was involved in the shameful proceedin's would make a lot o' money, onyway," commented MacColl. "It's that that vexes me! Everybody's wantin' everybody else to put aff his coat and work for the national prosperity, but they'll pay ony money to see chaps takin' aff their coats for nae mair useful purpose than to bash each other. The job could be far better done wi' machinery."

"Nae doot they would make a lot o' money," admitted Erchie, "but as far as I can see they were throwin' awa the chance o' makin' far mair if they just had a little gumption. Prize-fightin's badly mismanaged in a commercial way. Instead o' drawin' wan day's gate money they could be liftin' weeks o't if they opened the trainin' quarters o' the combatants and ran charabangs and trains."

"It's no' the fight that I would want to see; it would be Carpenteer and Dempsey[4] grindin' their teeth as described in the newspapers, and makin' speeches aboot the exact way they were gaun to knock each ither's block aff. I was backin' Dempsey mysel', for he has a toppin' set o' teeth accordin' to his photographs, and he confessed frae the first he was confident o' winnin'."

"But so was Carpenteer," pointed out the elder; "and he kept on grindin' his teeth till I'm sure they must be worn doon to the gums. Grindin' your teeth in the French language means a lot o' wear and tear that Dempsey escaped, bein' an American and maistly speakin' through his nose. But I'm no' sayin', mind ye, that I wouldna like fine to see the fight if I happened to be in America — that's if there was nae bloodshed."

"Bloodshed!" exclaimed Erchie, contemptuously. "There's nae bloodshed in a prize fight nooadays, unless the pugilist bites his tongue by accident when he's dictatin' his daily message to the world's Press tellin' them he's feelin' fine and fit. Ye daurna draw claret[5] in America, it bein' a dry country.[6] I would far sooner see the prepar- ations than the fight itsel'; better value for the money!

"A' the excitement's in the trainin'. Day efter day, for weeks afore a match, Carpenteer spends the mornin' brushin' his hair wi' Anzora cream to give it the proper polish. They talk aboot the Frenchman's deadly left, but believe you me, there's far mair in the way he sheds[7] his hair and keeps it glossy. That's whit mak's him the most popular pugilist pet o' the century wi' the female sect, and sells his photographs. Dempsey was badly handicapped wi' his hair — it's far ower tousy and nae sensitive woman would put his photo on the top o' the piano, he looks that brutal. If I was Dempsey's trainer, the first thing I would dae would be to mak' him spend a couple o' 'oors a day wi' a pail o' gum-arabic and a set o' stiff army hair-brushes. It would mak' a' the difference.

"Efter twa 'oors strenuous exercise at his hair and a smert bout wi' the tooth-brush, Carpenteer in his trainin' under Descamps takes a sleep to himsel' and then gets up and shaves twice. From eleven to twelve he reads the best French poetry, wi' an occasional glance at selections frae the letters from his wife and his fair admirers. Then a snack o' something, an omelet or a bunch o' grapes, and he's ready for the serious business o' the day.

"Half a dozen interviews wi' the novelists that's engaged by the newspapers to explain the mystery o' his fatal gift, and then an 'oor or twa wi' the photygraphers. That's a killin' part o' the trainin'; a' the time Carpenteer has to look like the film hero in the Western drama 'Tried and True, or The Manly Curate,' and it takes a lot o' doin', for the heat in America's that great, the Anzora cream runs into your eyes."

"I saw last nicht from the papers that Carpenteer said his morale was spendid, and that he had a perfect con-tentedness o' the mind that filled him wi' every hope o' victory. He mentioned, too, that shakin' hands last year wi' the Prince o' Wales and Sir Philip Sassoon[8] was wonder-fully helpful to him." remarked MacColl.

"The thing that tells wi' him mair than shakin' hands wi' onybody is the hypnotic power o' Mr Descamps, his trainer," said Erchie. "Descamps puts the 'fluence on him afore the fightin' starts; he's in a kind o' trance when he enters the ring, and thinks that every wallop on the heid's a presentation bouquet o' flooers. It gives him a great advantage unless he's up against a man wi' tin ears and a solid brain pan.

"Dempsey's just a coorse hairy man that I'll wager ye never read Milton's poetry through, and canna conceal the fact that his face is quite unfit for puttin' on chocolate boxes. He hasna the Frenchman's classical education, and was sadly handicapped by the fact that he never shook hands wi' the Prince o' Wales in his life, an' couldna be put in a trance unless wi' a whack from a steam-hammer. If he asked him aboot his morale, ye would need to gie him a diagram o' what ye meant. But brutal in the extreme! That's the way he won — nae poetry in his composeetion.

"Still I would pay a shillin' or twa mysel' to see Dempsey in his trainin' quarters. The hack that he had above his eye that needed a pad on't up till the 'oor o' battle was, likely enough, a bit o' camouflage for his heid's a' made o' pewter, accordin' to the Frenchman's backers. Day efter day, when he wisna gettin' the muscles o' his back photygraphed as an offset to the refined and handsome dial o' Carpenteer, he would put in a while at stunnin' the strongest boxin' men they could gather together in America to face him.

"A rare speaker, too — ye could hear him dictatin' his reports for the newspapers at a distance o' half a mile. Of course they had to be translated for the European papers, but they read fine."

"Fifteen and sixpence and a couple o' trooser buttons," said MacColl, concluding the counting of the offertory. "This fight's fair spoilin' oor gate the day! I'll wager half the members o' the kirk are stayin' at hame to read the Sunday papers."

"They micht hae kent that Carpenteer would lose! I had nae hope for him wance I saw he went and got his hair cut," said the beadle.

And Erchie and the elders filed silently into the congregation, while it rose to the opening strains of 'Peace, Perfect Peace'.

136. Saturnalia[1]

THERE WAS a great demand for coal on Saturday. Out New City Road way every second housewife wanted a couple of bags so urgently that Duffy was sold out by a little after noon.

"Coals is gettin' too chape!" said Duffy. "If they cost a sixpence mair they would be mair appreciated."

He felt genuinely aggrieved. For, usually, on Saturdays, his lorry load was not exhausted till about 3 o'clock, an ideal hour, which enabled him to partake of some liquid nourishment before going home. If he went home now at the ridiculous hour of 12.30, the consequence would likely be a Saturday wholly ruined. He would have to wash himself and take his dinner, so spoiling the natural human Saturday appetite for beer. Nothing more likely, too, than that his wife would want to come out with him to a picture-house or on one of those dreary perambulations down Cowcaddens to see the shops. She might even want some extra money!

"If this is the comin' revival o' tred they're talkin' aboot," said the coalman, "I wish they had picked anither day for't than the Saturday."

He had stabled his horse, and was dolefully walking homewards, carrying the can that had boiled his breakfast tea, when turning the corner of the street, he found himself on the fringe of the students' carnival, the nature of which was beyond his comprehension.

"Criftens!" he explained. "Galoshans![2] It's either that or Hengler's."[3]

A nice old lady with spectacles and a rabbit-skin collar-ette slipped twopence into his can and remarked in warmly sympathetic tones, "For a good cause," and passed on.

Duffy stood and stared after her, amazed, incredulous, suspicious.

"Cocaine," he reflected. "Or jist dotty." He didn't know what to do about the twopence.

Before he could make up his mind whether to put them

in his pocket or run after the lady, he felt his sleeve tugged, and turned round to find two laughing girls confronting him. "Isn't he a scream!" one of them exclaimed in an ecstasy of enjoyment, and behold another twopence was in the can!

Duffy flushed, as could be seen through the bare patches on his face.

"Hey you!" he exclaimed. "Do ye think I'm a blin' man? I'm sure ye see I havena a dug wi' me!"

"It's perfectly killin'!" giggled one of the girls; "Duffy to the life!" and already quite a crowd was gathered round the coalman. A shower of coppers rattled into his can.

"Speech! Speech! How's the coal trade, Duffy?" somebody shouted.

He was utterly bewildered. He didn't know one of these poeple, who seemed to know him well, and have some mania for throwing away good money. Could there, by any chance, have been a sudden change in the licensed hours for Saturday? A closed pub immediately in front of him firmly negatived any such inspiring idea. These people, then, were either escaped lunatics or taking a rise out of him.

"Awa' hame and tak a strong cup o' tea to yersel's," he advised them, filling his pocket from the contents of the can. "And ye can whistle for yer money; it'll dae for the plate the morn."

He was swept away with his can in the tumult, between a pierrot and a policeman with white spats and an incredibly red nose. The policeman evoked much laughter from the public on the pavement, but Duffy was plainly regarded as the star performer. Everyone knew his name and occupation (the latter not difficult to guess from his appearance), and his can once more was getting heavy with contributory coin.

"I wish to goodness I had brung a pail," he said regretfully, every time he put the contents of his receptacle into his pockets. ... "Whit was I eatin' last nicht afore I went to my bed? Afore I wake up I hope they'll make it sovereigns."

"A great make-up, old chap!" said the policeman to him. "Perfect masterpiece! But you ought to have brought your horse and lorry. ... Ygorra! Ygorra! Ygorra!"[4]

"I know you; you're Charlie Dunn!" said a bold young lady from Queen Margaret College[5] with a red gown, and a trencher, putting her arm through Duffy's.

"No," replied the coalman. "I'm the manager o' the Penny Savin's Bank. Whaur did ye get the comic bunnet? If you waken first don't mak' a noise; I never had a greater pant o' a dream since I dreamt I was Napoleon Bonaparte, an' I want to enjoy every minute o't."

"Are you a student or a real coalman?" asked the lady dubiously, suddenly removing her arm.

"Of course I'm a student," replied Duffy mockingly. "My name's Skerry.[6] I wish that brass band would clay up; it would waken a Necropolis monument ... Do you think ye can flee? That's yin o' my dreams too. Yer claes is a' richt; ye have on a red flannel nichtgown; it's no' exactly the thing for Charin' Cross, but naebody's noticin'."

Sauchiehall Street was a riot of bizarre costumes, bands, strange vehicles, grotesque encounters, supplicatory collecting-boxes, shouts, shrieks, and laughter. A host of irresponsible and fantastic characters seemed to have taken possession of the city for the time being, its customary traffic was ludicrously impeded; a wild spirit of Disrule prevailed. Duffy with his can drifted like a leaf in a current of whose constitution he was ignorant; he was finding his accumulating coinage something of a burden.

"Old Bean," said the red-nosed policeman, by whom, instinctively, he had stuck, "what football match are you going to after we've lunched with the Lord High Provost?"

"I'm no' gaun to ony lunch nor ony fitba' match," replied Duffy, firmly. "I ken fine this is something I ate last nicht, for if we wis daein' this wide-awake in the streets o' Gleska they would gie us the jyle for't. I'm gaun to wake up in twa meenutes, and hear the clock chappin' six."

"I say, old fruit! are you by any chance a genuine coalman?" inquired the policeman anxiously.

"A' the time — when I'm no' sleepin'," Duffy informed him, again emptying his can.

"Then, by George, you'll have to hand over all the coin you've collected," said the policeman. "This is a students' stunt, and it's for the Unemployed."

"I kent I was only dreamin'" said Duffy sorrowfully, emptying his pockets into the policeman's helmet. "It's only in a dream that Gleska mak's a cod o' itself. But man — I enjoyed it fine!"

137. *Keep to the Left!*[1]

DUFFY SAW it first on the front of a tramway-car which was approaching him as he got half-way across the street. Mr Dalrymple's peremptory order to the citizens to 'Keep to the Left' was in such emphatic large blue type that it immediately impressed him. He stopped suddenly, confused between an urgent desire to get as quickly as possibly into the Mull of Kintyre Vaults, whose door was just opening for the afternoon, and the problem what, exactly, the tramway manager's order meant.

Keep to the left of what?

And why?

The car was up on him before those two questions were solved by his slow-moving mind, and he would have been run over, but for the ferocious abruptness with which the driver put on his brakes.

"Somebody should be in chairge o' ye'," shouted the driver. "Take my tip, and never you step oot o' yer peramblator, or ye'll get hurt."

Next Duffy saw the great new slogan swinging from a wire above the pavement. "Keep to the Left!" it shouted in even bigger type than on the tramway-cars.

He stopped and looked all round to discover what particular left his attention was demanded for, quite prepared to be agreeable and acquiesce in anything reasonable.

The only possible left he could discern as practicable for him at the moment involved his going round an impressively stout lady who was looking intently into a jeweller's shop. So he passed between her and the window, brushing against her as he did so.

She gave a little scream, hauled in the slack of her vanity-bag, opened it quickly to see if her purse was still in it, and stared at Duffy with much suspicion.

"Sorry!" said Duffy. "My mistake."

"Imphm! Just that," she remarked with icy coldness.

He passed on, pondering on the mystery of this new message to the people, which he now perceived was on all the cars, and hung at intervals along the vista of the street.

A man with sandwich boards hung round his neck, boldly inscribed with the Dalrympian slogan, came towards him on the right-hand side of the pavement.

Now, Duffy understood! "Keep To The Left" was obviously the title of a film.

He stopped the sandwichman. "Where can ye see it?" he inquired politely.

"See what?" retorted the sandwichman.

"That picture o' yours, 'Keep To The Left'; it seems to be a' the rage."

"Awa and bile yer can!" said the sandwichman.

"Criftens!" thought Duffy, "Everybody's aff their heid the day. It must be the Rangers and the He'rt o' Midlothian."[2]

He was now being swept on in a stream of pedestrians who faithfully kept to the right-hand side of the pavement as their ancestors had done, simply because it was the side next the shop windows, and the pubs and the closes they might at any moment feel like entering.

There was only one man on the outer side of the pavement, and he was, apparently, under a misapprehension as to where he was, for he was led by a dog on a string, and tapped with a stick on the flagstones as he walked.

"If that blinny doesna look oot he'll fa' aff the kerb in the gutter and hurt himsel'," thought Duffy, who has a kindly heart.

He had turned round to look after this touching spectacle and failed to perceive the approach of a painter who emerged from a pend close[3] carrying a twelve-foot ladder ingeniously balanced on his shoulders in such a way as permitted him to keep his hands in his pockets. His head was through the rungs, and a nice equilibrium was maintained by means of a pail of whitewash stuck between two other rungs in front of him.

The man turned round as the rear end of the ladder cleared the close-mouth, the fore part of it caught Duffy on the shins, the pail fell off, and the whitewash splashed over Duffy's boots.

"Whaur the bleezes are ye gaun?" angrily demanded the victim of this mishap. "Can ye no' watch yer bloomin' lether?"

"Watch yer aunty!" said the painter indignantly; "It's you that's aff-side. Ye should keep to the left."

"Hoo the mischief do ye ken whether I should keep to the left or no' when ye don't ken whaur I'm gaun?" demanded Duffy.

"It doesna matter! If ye keep to the right ye go wrang; I'm on the right side o' the pavement."

"Then ye must be wrang!" said Duffy.

"Awa' an' bile your can!" concluded the painter. It is the one unanswerable retort in Glasgow.

"It's time I was awa' hame," thought Duffy. "This is yin o' they days I'm bound to get into trouble unless the wife's wi' me," and at that moment he was overtaken by his old friend Erchie, going in the same direction.

"Ye're aff-side!" said Erchie, elbowing him over to the left. "What's the use o' Mr Dalrymple takin' in hand wi' your education when ye'll no' tak' a tellin'?"

"What's a' this aboot keepin' to the left?" asked Duffy. "Are they expectin' a procession?"

"No," said Erchie; "Mr Dalrymple's cairryin' on the noble work o' trainin' Gleska to keep oot o' the road o' his tramway cars. Ye have nae idea the trouble he has wi' folk crossin' the street. They'll cross the street in spite o' him, come bangin' against his cars, and scrapin' a' the paint aff them; he's fair demented! Lots o' folk used to spit, too — a habit that's fair ruination to the tramway rails; noo that he's put a stop to spittin' in ony shape or form, he's determined they'll no keep on gettin' fankled up wi' the wheels o' the finest tramway system in the universe. If we keep to the left, we can see when a car's comin' and keep oot o' the road o't."

"Half the pubs o' Gleska's on the right-hand side," Duffy pointed out. "Hoo could ye get near them if ye kept gaun left?"

"They're gaun to be shifted," said Erchie, cheerfully; "Efter the May term[4] a' the pubs are to be on the left-hand side o' the pavement for convenience."

"Hoo could they dae that?" asked Duffy, considerably bewildered. "The left-hand side micht be the ootside o' the pavement — it depends on the way ye're gaun — and ye canna build pubs there."

"Can ye no!" retorted Erchie. "Jist you wait and ye'll see! Dalrymple can dae onything. He'll have a' the pubs on yin side o' the street and a' the soda fountains and ice-cream bars on the other. Naebody ever fa's oot o' an ice-cream shop in front o' a tramway car."

"Come on in to M'Gashan's shop and hae a wee refreshment," suggested Duffy, feeling depressed at the very prospect of new obstacles to geniality in Glasgow.

"We canna," said Erchie. "Ye see yoursel' already it's on the wrang side. But I'll tell ye whit we'll dae; I ken a soda fountain on the left side, roond the corner; we'll go and hae a raspberry vinegar."

138. *Glasgow in 1942*[1]

"THE ONLY consolation I ha'e in gettin' auld," said Erchie, "is that wherever I am in twenty years it'll no' be in Gleska."

"Ye'll may be in a far waur place," suggested Duffy, drily.

"I couldna be. Conan Doyle[2] has nae intelligence o' trams and motor-cars on the Ither Side; ye jist skliff aboot

on your feet or whiles tak' a flee to yoursel'. There's nae
vehicular traffic. Mr Dalrymple'll get an awfu' start when
they hand him a trumpet and gie him a job in the
orchestra. There'll be naething in his ain line for him to
dae."

"What'll we get to dae oorsels?" inquired the coalman,
entering into the spirit of these speculations.

"I'm a' richt!" said Erchie blythly. "There's bound to be
some jobs suitable for a chap accustomed to handing
round a tray. You bein' in the fuel tred of course ye'll be in
the ither department. ... Did ye ever in your life see such a
habble?"

They stood at the upper end of Jamaica Street, held up
by a maelstrom of traffic that made any attempt to cross
look suicidal. North and South, as far as the eye could see
was an unbroken line of inanimate tramcars. On the
narrow margins on either side, automobiles, waggons,
lorries followed each other closely.

"When I mind first o' Gleska," said Erchie, "there was
some kind o' pleesure in gaun aboot in't; ye didna take
your life in your hand if ye stepped aff the pavement. The
folk that came in frae the country then — ye would see
them daunderin' up the middle o' Jamaica Street the
same's it was the Crow Road oot to Fintry. As late as the
early 80s I've seen the point polisman oot in the middle o'
the crossin' there talkin' Gaelic for half an oor at a time wi'
a wheen o' his kizzens new aff a trip frae Campbeltown.
Just every noo and then he would birl his whistle and let a
hearse or a beer lorry past. Some o' the polismen had their
books wi' them and carried on their studies for the college.
They were fed up with the loneliness o' their job at Jamaica
Street, and the craze wi' some o' them was to get a nice
wee manse in some brisk place like Invergordon.

"It's gettin worse and worse every year; a man's no safe
to tak' drink noo on a Setterday if he's gaun to venture
nearer the centre o' the toon than Possilpark or the
Halfway Hoose. He'll get nailed as sure as fate unless he
tak's a tramway car.

"That's maybe Mr Dalrymple's notion — to abolish walkin' althegither. But the problem will aye be hoo to cross the street.

"Aboot 1942, if I'm no' mistaken, everybody in Gleska 'll have his jeckets made wi' a ring in the middle o' the back."

"What for?" asked Duffy.

"To cross the streets wi'. They'll sling him across on overhead wires, and the ring's 'll be needed to hook him on wi' 'The Dalrymple Patent Safety-First Slinger. Ball bearin's. No jerk at the start and no jar on landin'.' There'll be cross-traffic underground escalators too; ye'll go doon a hole at Simpson's corner; slide under the main drain-pipes and come up at Chrystal Bell's Soda Fountain."

"This is a fair beezer!" said Duffy, surveying the congested thoroughfare. "Maybe we should go doon to the Boomielaw and work oor way roond by Finnieston."

"Whit ye're seein' there, Duffy," said Erchie, gravely, "is the Triumph o' Civilization, and the Age o' Progress. It's maybe a bit awkward for the like o' you and me no' to get the safe and rational use o' the Gleska highway, but consider the swellin' revenue o' the Tramway Department and the praise that Gleska gets in the foreign newspapers for tramways that mair than pay their way!

"Do you know that 10,000 tramway cars and other vehicles no' coontin' bassinettes pass this corner every day? There's gaun to be mair, too. They're gaun to chip aff the corners o' the crossin' here, and mak' a kind o' circus."[4]

"It'll take the place o' Hengler's," suggested Duffy seriously. "We'll can see Doodles again."

"It's no' that kind o' circus exactly," explained Erchie. "You and me 'll be the Doodles. It'll look fine on the map, the circus, but it'll no mak' the least wee difference on the problem o' congested traffic in Argyle Street, Jamaica Street, and Union Street; there'll no' be ony mair room for jazzing between the cars."

"I see," said Duffy, "they're gaun to ha'e a 'No-Accident Week' in Gleska soon; it should bring a lot o' folk in frae the Mearns[5] that's frichtened to venture in at ordinar' times. Whit'll be the safety tips, I wonder?"

"I hear a rumour that, over the city generally, pedestrians is only to get movin' aboot on the convoy system — twelve at a time, in the chairge o' a policeman carryin' a red flag. For the No-Accident Week every car 'll ha'e a cow-catcher on the front and a steamboat bell. Naebody allo'ed to walk in the main thoroughfares except athletes; women and children that'll no tak' the trams 'll be conveyed in tanks kindly lent for the occasion by the War Office. Motor car and locomotive boiler traffic confined to the West-End Park. First Aid Hospital at the corner of Gordon Street and Hope street and a bulletin board in George Square givin' the casualties from hour to hour.

"Any bloomin' thing, Duffy, that'll mak you and me believe that life and limb's as safe in the streets o' Gleska as in Balmoral Castle. Of course they're no', and never will be in oor time.

"The streets in the middle o' Gleska were laid oot for a population no' the size o' Greenock. The great mistake was that they werena made o' kahouchy."[6] As lang as Menzies' buses and the horse had the cairryin' traffic there was nae great inconvenience to the foot passenger; he could stop in the middle o' the street and tie his laces, and there wasna ony need for an ambulance.

"But any kahouchy quality the streets had vanished when the tram-rail and the motor came in vogue. Nae human ingenuity noo can widen them to accommodate safely what's expected o' them. In the past ten years the population's risen a quarter o' a million; the traffic's speeded up at least four times what it used to be when the horse was bloomin'; and twenty years from noo, when everybody has a motor-car, ye'll see some fun! The Tramway Department in 1942 'll need to hae break-doon gangs continually on the move, wi' derricks to deal wi' the street fatalities."

"But maybe there'll be nae tramway cars," suggested the coalman hopefully.

139. *No Accident Week*[1]

ERCHIE WAS astonished this morning to meet Duffy, the coalman, walking towards his stable with what looked like a red burgee in his hand.

"I knew the coal tred was daein' no' that bad," he remarked, "but I never thought it was payin' that weel that ye could start the yachtin'. Ye have the wrang kind o' bunnet for it, Duffy; ye should have wan o' they deep-sea keps wi' brass braid on't. Whaur's the regatta the day?"

"Ye're awfu' comic," retorted the coalman. "At least ye think ye are."

"I'm no' bein' comic at all," said Erchie. "I'm ower anxious for ye gaun awa' yachtin' at this time o' the year. Ye'll get your death o' cold, or maybe ye'll droon yersel'. Whitever ye dae, hang on by the spinnaker. Wha gie'd ye the flag?"

"Big Macrae, the polisman. It's for No Accident Week. He said I was to wear it on my horse, cart, lorry, or other vehicle."

"As sure as daith," said Erchie, " I thocht it was the Royal Mudhook Yacht Club flag, or maybe the Corinthians! I clean forgot aboot the Accident Week, an' me wi' a safety button for it in my pocket! It was handed to me yesterday comin' frae the kirk."

He took the button out of his pocket as he spoke, and passed it through the hole in the lapel of his coat.

"There!" he said; "I'm a' richt noo; it's as good as a life insurance. All the same, I'm gaun oot for the week wi' the wife to Eaglesham[2] till this No Accident ploy blaws by. It'll no' be safe, I'm tellin' ye, in the streets o' Gleska! They're bad enough at ony time, and haein' six or seven days of a kind o' Cairter's Trip gaun through them a' the time is no gaun to help them ony. Whit did they gi'e you a flag for, Duffy. Are ye on the committee?'

"I tellt ye," said Duffy, "I got it frae Big Macrae to put on my horse and lorry."

"Whit fur?' asked Erchie.

"So that I'll no' rin doon onybody," replied the coal-man.

Erchie laughed. "Rin doon onybody! There's no' a safer coalman's horse and lorry gaun through the streets o' Gleska. They micht as weel gi'e flags to Wylie & Lochheid or a book-barrow. I doot Macrae was pullin' your leg. Take my advice, and keep you oot o' the commotion althegither. Them No Accident Weeks is no' for a horse like yours that couldna raise enough wind to mak' a flag fly unless ye helped it with a pair of bellowses. Stick by the back streets a' this week, or, better still, come out wi' the wife and me to Eaglesham. It's gaun to be a rale No Accident Week in Eaglesham, unless, maybe, a hen run over by an ice-cream barrow."

"Macrae said Mr Dalrymple would be awfu' angry wi' me if I didn't put on the flag," said Duffy, somewhat shaken in his first intention.

"Never you mind Mr Dalrymple! He's the cheeriest chap in Gleska — always thinkin' o' some new dydo to speed up his tramway-cars and mak' the walkin' popula-tion skliff along a wee bit quicker. It'll be wan o' the busiest, brightest weeks in the year — every other man, woman and child wi' a Mind The Step button, and everything on wheels, except the hearses, with the red burgee. There were Safety First sermons in the kirks yesterday, with special intercession for pedestrians weel up in years. There's a whole lot o' them no' deid or disabled yet. A special service for members o' the Scottish Auto-mobile Club, the Motor Trade, professional chauffeurs and owner-drivers was arranged to be in the Cathedral, but was put off at the last meenute.

"There's gaun to be cinema shows at the Tramway Office, decorated cars, and the Tramway Pipe Band. The polis 'll wear white gloves and every constable 'll carry a flag wi' the motto 'Keep to the Left' in the Gaelic lan-guage.[3] The ambulance is to get a holiday, and the Infirmaries to be put on half-time."

"We were needin' something to brighten us up," said Duffy. "There has been naethin daein' in Gleska since the 1911 Exhibeetion. Will there be fireworks?"

"I havena heard o' ony fireworks yet," replied Erchie, "but I wouldna wonder if Mr Dalrymple's keepin' them up his sleeve for a grand surprise. There'll be illuminated cars. The Orpheus Choir[4] is engaged for the week to sing 'God Save the King' every half 'oor at the corner o' Jamaica Street, and a couple o' hardy auld chaps that's been walkin' conscientiously on the left-hand side of the pavement for the last six months are to be exhibited at Kelvingrove and gi'e lectures every afternoon on the way it feels. It's understood they're gaun to get the Freedom o' the City.

"Cheap excursions 'll be run from a' the country districts within 20 mile radius o' the city and a bumper week's expected for the tramway cars."

"There's bound to be accidents," said Duffy. "Ye canna help them, whiles."

"The idea is that there's gaun to be nane. The magic wee button's gaun to impart a cautious sense o' Safety First on everybody that wears it. That's the reason I'm gaun to Eaglesham."

140. *The Grand Old Man Comes Down*[1]

WITH REMARKABLE expedition, and unaccustomed cheerfulness, as if for once they were thoroughly enjoying their job, a gang of workmen had hoisted Gladstone[2] from his pedestal. Suspended by the neck in a most sinister manner, the grand old statesman swung at the end of the winch-chains, oscillating slowly. A fine, crisp, clear day, with the touch of Spring in it.

"Criftens!" exclaimed Duffy. "Whit are they daein' here?"

"Fifteen feet o' a drap," replied Erchie, solemnly. "Ate a good breakfast o' bacon and eggs, and asked for a cigarette. Ellis[3] was assisted by William Johnson, a young shoemaker from Northampton, and before hurryin' back to England visited the Cathedral, havin' a keen interest in Gothic architecture and stained gless."

"Awa' and tak a runnin' jump at yersel!" said Duffy impatiently. "Nane o' your cod, Erchie; whit are they ca'in' the Grand Auld Man aff his feet for?"

"They have every richt to dae't," said Erchie; "He's five-and-twenty years deid."

"It's a statue that was daein' nae herm to onybody," remarked the coalman with feeling. "It's a hanged shame shiftin' it! I suppose it's Mr Dalrymple; he'll be gaun to bring his cars roond here. He has nae respect for onything."

"It's no' Mr Dalrymple this time, Duffy," said Erchie, chuckling. "It's the general consensus o' public opeenion that the time's come when public statuary and triumphal arches should be annually revised, and scrapped when necessary. In an electric age, wi' wireless and a' that, ye canna be bothered wi' them when they're the least oot o' date. To you and me, Gladstone was the greatest man o' his time; but by the growin' generation all that's kent aboot him is that he wrote 'The Land o' the Leal'[4] and invented a portmanteau."

"If it wasna' for him Ireland would never ha'e had Home Rule!" said Duffy with loyal admiration.

"Whisht!" warned Erchie, "say naething aboot that. He meant it for the best."

"There's far aulder monuments than Gladstone's here," said Duffy; "They should start wi' the auldest; it's only the other day they put up the Gladstone; I mind o't fine; there was a great furore and brass bands."

"Just you wait and ye'll see the others shifted, too. Gladstone came first because, standin' aye there lookin' in at the front door o' the Municipal Buildin's he fair got on the nerves o' the Labour members. It spiled their Corona cigars for them. That's the way sae mony o' them went to London,[5] where a bronze Presbyterian conscience is no' aye glowerin' at ye. A' the time auld Willie has been standin' there he's seen a lot o' life."

"But what are they flittin' him for?" asked Duffy, who never keeps abreast of local movements by reading newspapers.

"I've told ye already," replied Erchie patiently. "Statues nooadays are like comic songs; they go awfu' quick oot o' fashion. Naebody looks at them efter they're mair than a twelvemonth in position. The only yin in George Square that attracts attention noo is Mr Oswald[6] wi' the lum hat, for it has never occurred to onybody to put a lid on the hat to keep the boys frae pappin' stones in't.

"It's like this, Duffy — ye've seen yersel' wi' a grocer's calendar in the kitchen showin' The Genius of Scotland Findin' Burns at the Plough'. For the first three months your eye was never aff it; a' the rest o' the year ye would never look at it unless the wife put it on the table in front o' ye on a plate. It's the same wi' statues — there's auld General Peel[7] at the other side o' the Square; naebody looks at him unless it's a polisman to see that there's naething chalked on the pedestal.

"Under the new movement for brightenin' up Gleska the authorities is gaun to put a' the statues on wheels and hurl them to different sites in the city twice a year. The priceless gift o' Art is to be brung hame to the toilers o' Brigton Cross and Maryhill. I wouldna say but ye'll have Watty Scott's monument sometime next winter clapped at the end o' Raeberry Street. Walk you roond it, Duffy, if ye're coming hame at nicht; mak' nae attempt to sclim' it."

"Ye're aye tryin' to pull my leg," said Duffy, impatiently. "I wish you would talk sense."

"I'm talkin' naething else. The perambulatin' statue is going to solve a lot o' civic problems: it's surprisin' they never went in for it wholesale sooner, seein' they had some experience wi' King William[8] at the Cross. They're goin' to shift him again. There's no' an equestrian statue in Europe that's done mair gallopin'. It's the only way to keep up wi' the urgent needs o' the greatest Corporation tramway system in modern times.

"Whit can be done wi' King William can be done wi'

every monument in sicht as occasion requires; the only site for a memorial regarded as perpetual should be the Necropolis.

"Put them a' on wheels from the start, and hurl them where they're maist required from year to year. I wouldna destroy them althegither as lang's the memory o' the departed's green, but as soon as it's only folk frae the country on a trip that looks at them, I would send them to the stone-knappers and introduce a brand-new lot."

141. *The Doctors' Strike*[1]

JINNET PUT down her newspaper on her lap, and, looking over her spectacles, threw one of those quite unexpected queries at her husband Erchie, when he came home late in the evening.

"Did ye mind yon bottle o' fruit salines I asked ye to get me?"

It rather staggered him; he had quite forgotten all about the fruit saline. In these circumstances, the tactical way of averting unpleasant recriminations was obviously to raise some other controversial issue.

"There's naething worse for ye than fruit salines," he remarked with emphasis. "Ruins the constitution! They start a crave, like drink, and afore ye ken where ye are, ye're nip-nippin' awa at them. The secret drinkin' o' fruit salines is the ruination o' thousands o' homes. Whit on earth do ye want them for?"

"Ye'll find that oot soon enough," she retorted. "Did ye' no see aboot the doctors' strike?[2] It's fair ragin'. They're leavin' their work in droves. If you or me was taken ill we would be in a bonny habble withoot some medicine in the hoose. Every panel doctor in the country's liftin' his graith."[3]

"But that'll no shut the chemists' shops," said her husband; "Ye can aye get a bottle. That's where the doctors is at a disadvantage; they're no' in the strong position o' the bakers or the colliers."

"Ay, but just you wait and ye'll see the chemists 'll come oot too. They a' hang thegither."

This naive assumption of his wife's provided Erchie with what he had been looking for — a really plausible excuse for his failure to bring her fruit saline.

"By Jove!" he said, "ye're right! I doot the druggists is oot already; they were a' shut when I came by." — a statement strictly true though false in its implication. "Have ye nae medicine o' ony kind in the hoose."

"Not an article!" said Jinnet.

"Tut! tut! That's maist annoyin'! If a miners' strike was threatenin' ye would hae your bunker full o' coals. I'm awfu' surprised at ye, Jinnet! I'm a busy man; I canna think o' everything. When you learned the doctors were goin' to strike, ye should have taken steps to lay in something — a bottle or twa o' mixture and some peels. Here we are noo at the mercy o' Providence."

"I saw in the papers a week ago the doctors were goin' to strike, but I didna tak' it awfu' seriously," said Jinnet, contritely, and apparently blind to the strategy that transferred the blame to her. "I never in my life before heard o' doctors strikin' and they're no' in ony trade union."

Her husband gave a sardonic laugh. "Are they no'?" said he. "They're in the auldest and the strongest union in the country. They pay pretty sweet to get into it; it involves a lot o' money. They have funds that'll afford them strike pay for a couple o' years if need be. God pity the man that canna keep his health till this thing's settled."

"Isn't that just deplorable!" exclaimed Jinnet. "Whit's the world comin' to? I thought naebody ever went on strike except puir chaps wi' cloth bunnets. Are the strikers makin' ony trouble doon the toon?"

"Naething serious yet," replied Erchie, airily; "Just the usual processions. Eight or nine hundred o' them gaithered in front o' the Municipal Buildin's, every man wi' a tile-hat and a wee black bag, and wanted a deputation into the Lord Provost. He wouldna see them. There was a bit of a commotion, and somebody flung a mustard poultice at a

Bylie, but efter a while the strikers formed four-deep and merched doon Buchanan Street and along Argyle Street to the Green, where they made the usual speeches. They had twa or three tasty banners, a pipe-band and an awfu' smell o' iodoform; but I must say they were very orderly. I think they must have got a lot o' money in their collection cans; there's a good deal o' popular sympathy wi' the doctors."

"Whit are they strikin' for?" asked Jinnet. "I canna' mak' it oot. It's something aboot 8s. 6d. for five years; is that a' they get for their panel work?"

"Off and on," said her husband, now thoroughly enjoying himself. "It's no' enough to keep a doctor in carbolic soap. It's a' very weel for the auld chaps in the tred that get fancy prices for appendix jobs and neurasthenia, but the young panel doctor new oot o' his time must have an awfu' struggle to mak' ends meet. He's up against the most cruel competition from the multiple chemists shop and the grocer. Ye can get noo, in the shops, patent medicines that'll cure onything, and there's every inducement to buy them, for when you're cured ye get your picture in the papers.

"Forbye," continued Erchie, warming to his theme, "folk play the dirtiest tricks on the doctor; a chap'll get a prescription for a hack on his heel and pass it round the whole tenement so that it does for palpitation, gastric catarrh, blotches, scarlet fever, spine o' the back, and general paralysis, and not a penny does the puir doctor make oot o' the bunch o' them; the only man that benefits is the undertaker.

"And that's no' the only competition the doctor's up against; there's a lot o' bloomin' blacklegs breengin' in wi' patent tips for curin' yoursel' o' onything by the simple power o' the will. Christian Science struck a heavy blow at the tred, and noo there's a chap called Coue[4] that started everybody sayin', 'I'm better and better every day,' an' they keep on sayin' it withoot a doctor bein' called in till the relatives send for one to give the death certificate."

"I hope to goodness they'll no' stay oot twa years," said

Jinnet. "It's an awfu' prospect! It's no' that I ever had ony
need for doctors, but it's aye a kind o' comfort jist to ken
they're handy if ye need them."

"If the worst comes to the worst, we can aye mak' a shift
wi' Mrs Duffy; she's an awfu' skilly woman," said Erchie
consolingly. "Wi' her Aunt Kate's Domestic Medicine,
she's fit to tackle ony complaint that ever baffled science,
short o' what the doctors call 'rigor mortis', and that's a
corker o' a trouble, terrible lingerin'."

"Mrs Duffy!" exclaimed Jinnet, with disdain. "I wouldna be behauden to her for a cloth on a cut finger."

She smiled slyly, put down her paper, went to the
dresser drawer, and produced a tin of fruit-salts not yet
opened.

"I kent fine ye would forget it, Erchie," she remarked.
"Ye're that througither and puttin'-aff. I jist went doon to
the grocer mysel' an 'oor ago and got it."

"And what's a' the row aboot?" asked her husband
indignantly. "Botherin' me wi' your doctors' strike! Ye
have nae consideration. Whit way do ye drag me into it?"

"Jist to hear ye bletherin', Erchie; ye have the grandest
imagination. Tell me again aboot the procession."

He looked at her with admiration. "By jings!" he
exclaimed, "ye're gettin' awfu' fly. There's nae pullin' o'
your leg at a' noo."

142. *The Coal Crisis – Duffy Explains*[1]

"It was high time the folk o' this country got a lesson in
the value o' coal; they treated it like dirt," said Duffy.

"There's no other word for the last bag I got from
yoursel'," remarked Erchie, agreeably. "But, mind, I'm
no' blamin' onybody! Accidents will happen! All my wife,
Jinnet, said when she looked in the bunker this mornin'
was 'Somebody's smashed a guid marble clock near
Duffy's ree! I wonder what happened to the works?'"

"Ye couldna get better coal in the city o' Gleska at the

money!" protested Duffy warmly. "I picked it special for ye."

"I'll no deny it was good enough coal o' the kind," said Erchie. "A capital coal for Sundays, when the breakfast's never in a hurry. The last word in smokeless fuel! The black smoke problem solved at last! But it's too rare and too dear at 3s. 6d. a bag for puttin' in grates. It should be kept for rockeries and crazy pavements. If it's a fair question, do ye get it direct frae the quarry, or did it come frae the demolition o' St. Enoch's Kirk?"[2]

"Away you!" retorted the coalman, impatiently. "Ye haven't the least idea the way I'm badgered wi' people like you that think I mak' the coal mysel'. I sell it just the way I get it."

"That's the mistake you make," said Erchie, solemnly. "Ye're losin' money on it that way. Ye should take it to the lapidaries and get it cut into Scotch pebble brooches ... Ye havena, by any chance, a bag o' pre-war full-strength coal aboot ye? I could come roond in the dark wi' a basket and slip it awa' in instalments."

"As shair as daith," said Duffy. "I have naething but whit ye see! If I had a single bag o' the auld inflammable stuff, I doot I would keep it for myself. It's no' to be got! I never kent I had so many frien's in the world as turned up in the last week to ask aboot the health o' my wife and family. Men that has motor-caurs noo call me 'Mr Duffy' and hands me a cigar. A cousin o' the wife's that we hadna heard o' for fourteen years comes in yesterday frae aboot Milguy[3] to call on us wi' a print of butter[4] and a dozen o' eggs. She had them in a bag that would hold a hunderweight. Of course I had to gie her a trate, and coal was what she was efter, so I took oot the bag and nearly filled it. She'll get an awfu' start when she coups it; it was a' half-bricks at the bottom; I'm no' gaun to perjure my soul and break the law for onybody in Milguy!"

"Ye're quite right there," said Erchie; "Ye have your regular customers to consider! I'm no' that awfu' put-aboot mysel' for the want o' coal; I could dae withoot it at this time o' year so long as the gas-ring's gaun and there's cooked ham at the grocer's. What surprises me is to see them sellin' ice-cream bricks off barrows at a time like this when the best folk in Pollokshaws and Kelvinside is desperate for ready-made hot boiled eggs."

"The only folk that puts on side wi' me is the chaps that has a ton o' coal in their cellars," said Duffy. "It shouldn't be allowed! And they lift their weekly ration jist like onybody else."

"A ton doesna go far if ye have a conservatory. If this coal Prohibition movement lasts, ye'll see all the coals in Gleska put in a central depot run by the Magistrates. A couple o' pounds a week, includin' coke, for every household. Ladies' wear next winter'll be maistly a string bag or a perambulator, and ye'll see them standin' in queues at the City Hall. Already, a well-filled bunker in the home is better than a book-case. ... Ye'll no have ony dross ye could spare?"

"No' as much as would fill your pipe," said Duffy, hopelessly. "The rale old genuine dross, if I had it, would sell at the price o' the best loaf sugar."

"I dare say that!" said Erchie. "It must be an awfu' job just now in the coal ree and lorry trade to decide what the price is; there's nae agreement among ye on the question; do ye jist mak' a guess at hoo much is in the customer's pocket?"

"There ye go!" said Duffy, bitterly. "I'm fair sick o' hearin' aboot prices! There's no human gratitude. What ye don't understand is that there's different qualities o' coal, and different prices for it at the bing. There's coal ye couldna boil a kettle wi' at the best o' times — "

"I know," said Erchie. "It's greatly in demand for heatin' churches. Ye have to light it the week before."

" — and there's coal that's only safe for use in the hands o' the fire brigade, and the salvage corps, and costs a lot more money at the pit."

"Don't vex me!" pleaded Erchie. "All I'm wantin's just a plain medium coal at a medium price for democratic purposes. Ye must be makin' your fortune, Duffy."

"Fortune," exclaimed the coalman, "I'm sick o' the whole business and wish I could start a wee green-grocery. I'm only keepin' on this business for the sake o' my horse. What would he do if I was shuttin' up the ree?"

Notes

1 Introductory to an Odd Character

1 A church officer occupied in a variety of tasks, most of them useful. St Kentigern's is of course entirely appropriate, being an alternative name for Mungo, the patron saint of Glasgow. Beadling is Erchie's "day-job"; he also acts as a waiter and thus satisfactorily serves both God and Mammon.

2 Since 1843, when Thomas Chalmers led more than a third of the ministers and congregations of the Established Church of Scotland "along the High Street" to set up the Free Church of Scotland. The issue which led to the Disruption or sundering of the kirk was Parliament's right to intervene in its affairs. It is not totally clear which cause is espoused by St Kentigern's—we learn that it is a "genteel congregation", which may indicate the established kirk, and in "Degenerate Days" Erchie speaks disparagingly of the beadles in United Free Kirks who lack the "rale releegious glide". On the other hand St Kentigern's seems to be well-attended and the old rhyme may be relevant here:
    "The auld Kirk, the cauld Kirk,
    The Kirk that has the steeple,
    The Free Kirk, the wee Kirk,
    The Kirk wi' a' the people!"

3 A flat foot but a warm heart.

4 Cold, chilly.

5 Suppose or suspect.

6 Onomatopoeic name for a turkey.

7 Whisky.

8 A curling match played in the open air on a frozen pond or loch.

9 Dress shirt front.

10 A reference to the Russo-Japanese War of 1904-5, which ended in a humiliating defeat for Russia. Erchie's apparently neutral stance was not shared by H.M. Government, which had ended a period of "splendid isolation" by forming an alliance with the Japanese Empire in 1902.

11 In a tenement property, the communal wash-house was an essential and collective responsibility, and a possible source of unneighbourly strife.

12 Not a scholastic usage. A Term was one of the four days of the year (Candlemas, Whitsunday, Lamas and Martinmas) on which payments such as rents fell due.

13 A pie dish. The word is derived from the French *assiette*, a plate, and

is probably one of the relics of the Auld Alliance between Scotland and France.

14 Fold his own socks. Evidence of his good intentions and Erchie as an early example of a "New Man".

15 Scuffing the feet carelessly.

16 Looking glass on stand.

2 Erchie's Flitting

1 Here used intransitively, in the sense of leaving one house to move into another. A flitting can also mean the act of moving household belongings, in this case on Duffy's coal cart.

2 Vases. More fragile items would be safer in the flitting if carried to the new abode by hand. The picture of William Ewart Gladstone (1809-98) the great Liberal leader and Prime Minister is an obvious clue to Erchie's political sympathies—in this respect he differs from Para Handy, who is unwilling to vouchsafe more than that he has voted for the "right man" (*Para Handy at the Poll* no. 84 in the Birlinn edition of the Complete Para Handy Stories.)

3 Because of the impression it would make on the new neighbours if the flitting needed two "rakes" or loads on the cart.

4 A superior kind of grate or fire-basket was one which had "wally" or porcelain sides and not simply cast iron throughout.

5 A valance or pelmet was needed on the mantelpiece to set off the grate nicely.

6 Extraordinary. A dram given to those helping with a removal is expected to be an extraordinarily large measure (probably a "glass" or "double double".)

7 An ornamental cabinet with shelves or drawers.

8 The residents of the same landing shared a rota for brushing, then washing out the landing and stair or, if on the ground floor, the closemouth or common entry. Finally the close would be pipe clayed to give a good appearance. A frequent cause of dispute with complex arrangements for determining "whose turn of the close" it was.

3 Degenerate Days

1 An extremely thin person, as in the children's rhyme:
   "Skinymalinky longlegs, big banana feet
   Went tae the pictures, fell through the seat!"

2 In the Gallowgate of Glasgow, built in 1754 by Robert Tennent, of "good hewen stone", taken from the ruins of the Bishops' Castle. Boswell and Johnson stayed in the Saracen's Head in 1773. Erchie explains that he began his career as a waiter there forty-five years previously, when the Gallowgate was more prosperous.

3 A half-grown fellow. In this case a country bumpkin from Strathaven in Lanarkshire.

4 Vesuvian lights—a brand of safety match.

5 A coalman was dependent on a strong pair of lungs for calling his wares, so that he could be audible in the farthest recesses of tenement buildings.

6 Erchie is reminiscing about the good old days when waiters could be

so weighed down with purloined bottles or food after serving at dinners that they had a list rather like a Clyde steamer. Blythswood Square (designed by John Brash in 1823-29) had at that time been a fashionable residential area. It was originally called Garden Square after its developer Hamilton William Garden and, with its four regular ashlar terraces facing on to the central gardens, formed a fine centre piece to the patrician "Blythswood New Town". Much later, it was to be a haunt of many professions, including the oldest of all.

7   Playing hide-and-seek. Kee-hoi so-called because of the cries uttered by the participants in the game.

8   The Baillies, senior Councillors or Aldermen, of the Corporation, whom one once would have expected to have had well-rounded waistcoats, were now but poorly fed according to the dictates of culinary fashion.

9   To loose the neckties of the recumbent causalties of the groaning board. A well established Scottish custom: Henry Mackenzie (1745-1831), the author of *The Man of Feeling* tells how he collapsed under the table after a convivial evening and was alarmed to discover hands tugging at his neck; however this proved to be merely a helpful servant who identified himself as "the lad that louses the cravats."

10 Infusing tea: an essential skill for the hostess.

11 With a yawn. The Baillie in question is not enamoured of the combination of light suppers and musical accompaniment.

12 Erchie regards smoking concerts, where the organisers simply hired a room and the refreshments were mainly liquid, as an inferior social occasion for a waiter.

4   The Burial of Big Macphee

1   The Second Reform Act of 1867 had extended the vote to artisans, or working men, including lodgers, in large towns and cities. The Third Reform Act of 1884 gave the vote to all male householders and lodgers, so that about eighty per cent of the male adults in the country were now enfranchised.

2   As Chancellor of the Exchequer in Balfour's Unionist Ministry of 1902-5, Joseph Chamberlain espoused the cause of tariff reform in a time of economic depression. This introduction of Protectionism meant that imports of cheap foreign food, including grain, were taxed on entry. Whether economically correct or not this measure proved politically inept, enabling the Liberal Free Traders to take up the cause of the "poor man's bread" and led to Big Macphee and thousands like him voting the Unionists out of office at three successive General Elections.

3   High tea was a substantial meal, incorporating a "knife and fork" dish of perhaps fish and chips, in addition to bread and butter, teabreads and cakes. The whole served with the best china and cutlery.

4   Fuss about trifles.

5   The Britannia Music Hall in the Trongate played host to most of the leading figures of the Victorian variety stage. It was later bought by the kenspeckle Glasgow eccentric A. E. Pickard and renamed the Panopticon.

6 Hired mourners paid to accompany the funeral cortege.
7 Mourning bands worn by relatives or close friends.
8 An oaf or slow-witted person.
9 A member of one of the many orders of Friendly Societies which
   played such an important part in Victorian and Edwardian life.

5 The Prodigal Son

1 The courtyard at the back of a tenement block. A scene of a great deal
   of bustle and activity; as well as its designed use as a drying green for
   the tenement's occupiers, it might at various times serve as a trysting
   place for "winching" couples, as a playground or even as an audito-
   rium for "backcoort singers".
2 A street in north central Glasgow linking Cowcaddens with Great
   Western Road.
3 David Stow (1793-1864), educational reformer, had created in
   Dundas Vale in 1827 the first "Normal Seminary" or teacher-training
   institution in Britain. This was followed in 1846 by a Free Church
   Normal School, also used for the purposes of teacher-training,
   situated in the Cowcaddens, and attended by Willie MacPherson.
4 Mint sweets also known as "Imperials", famed for their long-lasting
   qualities.
5 Mean or stingy.
6 On a binge or drinking session.
7 Troubled, disturbed. This evocative description recalls other passages
   from Munro's writings, e.g.:
   "In such an hour and season we forget the cost of mercantile supremacy, and see in that wide fissure through the close-packed town a
   golden pathway to romance, or the highway home to our native hills
   and isles." (*The Clyde, River and Firth* p. 75)
8 To bring under control. The figure of speech is derived from haims or
   hems, the two pieces of wood forming the collar of a draught horse.

6 Mrs Duffy deserts her man

1 A topical reference to one of the celebrated divorce scandals of the
   day. Such references serve to remind us that divorce was, at this
   period, a very uncommon phenomenon with only 801 decrees
   absolute being recorded in Britain in 1910. The comparative figure for
   1997 is 161,815.
2 A steep street or brae in central Glasgow leading northwards to Rotten
   Row from George Street. Now in the area occupied by the buildings
   of Strathclyde University.
3 A dish made from the head (or shin—potted hough) of a cow or pig,
   boiled, shredded and served cold in a jelly made from the stock.
4 An Irish Catholic, who would be infuriated by Duffy's singing of
   Boyne Water, a battle hymn of the Orange persuasion and Protestant
   Ascendancy. Like many other, this song celebrated the victory of King
   William of Orange ("King Billy") over the forces of James VII at the
   Battle of the Boyne in 1690. Those familiar with the socio-religious
   map of Glasgow and the West of Scotland will nevertheless be puzzled
   by Duffy's behaviour on this occasion and his avowed support for Glas-

gow Celtic Football Club (see notes to No. 13 *Erchie goes to a Bazaar*).

5 The inhabitants of the flat above the Duffy domicile would be so disturbed by the racket from downstairs that they would knock on the floor (i.e. Duffy's ceiling) with a poker, to tell them to be quiet.

6 A type of cloak with large cap-like sleeves. Dolmans had been in and out of fashion during the nineteenth century but had fallen out of popularity around 1892.

7 From the French *ménage* or household. A mcnodge or menoj was a kind of savings club to which each member contributes a fixed sum weekly for an agreed period of time. An easily administered arrangement, hence the popular accusation that a poor organiser "couldnae run a menodge".

8 Insignificant impudent rascals. The nyafs living above Duffy are bringing down the ceiling plaster by their "rapping doon".

9 Duffy is incapable of even washing up for himself. A poorie is the milk or cream jug which he should have cleaned and taken to be filled at the travelling milk cart.

10 Rubber.

11 So affected is the hapless Duffy by fending for himself, that in his distraught condition he fills the bags with the correct weight of coal, instead of, as is the invariable practice of coal men, giving short measure.

12 Edward VII's Coronation in 1902 had had to be postponed because of an operation for appendicitis. Because of the trend-setting influence of Royalty this operation actually became fashionable for a while. Whether Duffy's G.P. has made a similar diagnosis or not is not made clear.

13 Part of the children's pursuit game of tig, meaning "You have been tagged!" An affectionate touch, signalling the end of hostilities between Duffy and his wife.

14 Similar to the above; meaning "Are you 'in the Den' with me".

7 Carnegie's Wee Lassie

1 Andrew Carnegie (1835-1918), son of a Dunfermline handloom weaver, had emigrated to the United States and, in the course of becoming a multi-millionaire, was instrumental in making that country the leader in steel production, based on Pittsburg.

2 On his return visits to Scotland Carnegie stayed at Skibo Castle in Sutherland.

3 The Bessemer Process for producing cheap steel from iron ore had revolutionised the Pennsylvanian based industry.

> "It was not until the advent of Bessemer that the Americans found how lavishly nature had endowed them ... That solid mountain of iron, the greatest ore-bed known to man, the richest in metallic content, the most easily mined, the most readily transported—and at the same time practically free from phosphorus—that, in fine, is the story of the Lake Superior fields. Such a miraculous conjunction of forces a nation has seldom had laid at its feet. The result has been to give industrial leadership to the United States."
> (Burton Hendrick : *Life of Andrew Carnegie*)

4 The historic first flight of a powered aircraft by the Wright Brothers at

Kitty Hawk in North Carolina would not take place until December 1903 and at this time a "fleein' machine" would be a hot air balloon or one the new-fangled dirigibles such as those being developed by Zeppelin in Germany.

5 Many towns benefitted from Carnegie's generosity, a particular feature being his support for libraries (over 600 being endowed throughout the world) as an expression of his improving, philanthropic intentions. As for the kirk organs, Carnegie seems to have had little difficulty in reconciling material success with religious zeal— "The gospel of wealth but echoes Christ's words". All told he was to give away £70 million, in keeping with his doctrine that "The man who dies rich ... dies disgraced."

6 "Go ahead and search my pockets."

7 Buy sweets.

8 Weasel.

8 A Son of the City

1 A reference to the annual movement of Glaswegians to Clyde Coast resorts like Rothesay and Dunoon at the Glasgow Fair holidays, in the second fortnight of July. Boarding the steamers at Bridge Wharf, the trippers had their bedding and other household goods as well as clothing packed in tin trunks, which were piled on deck.

2 Merry passengers, on disembarking, would celebrate with a "clog-wallop" or clog dance on the pier.

3 The electric powered tramcar. Tramcars were generally known as "cars" or "caurs" in Glasgow—"skoosh" refers to the speed of the vehicle (as compared to their horse-drawn predecessors), as well as, onomatopoeically, to the distinctive sound produced by the release of the brakes. Tramways had been introduced to the streets of Glasgow in 1870, a service which was taken over by the Corporation in 1894. Electrification was completed in 1902, to general satisfaction.
"The experience of the Tramway Department has been that the working expenses for electric haulage are 2.35 pence per mile less, and the average return 2.57 pence greater than for horse haulage. Beyond question, the Corporation have deserved well of the citizens by their management of the cars."

4 Keating's Powder was a proprietary treatment used for delousing.

5 The rookeries was a popular term for any densely populated slum building.

6 A room and kitchen or two-roomed house would be regarded as an immense improvement in living conditions by most slum-dwellers; "wally jawboxes" or sinks with running water would be an unimaginable luxury.

7 A term for no place in particular, but obviously in the Gàidhealtachd, since there is an obvious reference to the Gaelic greeting "Ciamar a tha thu?" (How are you?).

8 *Clansman* was a much used name in the shipping fleet of David MacBrayne, with no fewer than four vessels having carried the name under their flag. The vessel Erchie refers to was the second of the line, build in 1870 at Clydebank at the yard of J & G Thomson (later John

Brown's). She was employed on the company's year-round Glasgow to Stornoway service. *Clansman II* was sold out of MacBrayne's service in 1910, when another steamer, the less romantically named *Ethel*, was re-christened *Clansman*, to preserve what was a familiar and popular name in the West Coast shipping trade.

9 Deid Slow is rather like Kamerhashinjoo in being no place in particular—somewhere beyond the Glasgow boundary, where ships proceeding up-river were signalled to proceed with engines at Dead Slow. An unsophisticated place—"in the sticks".

10 Spring onions.

11 When the weather was at its worst. A weather station was maintained on the summit of Ben Nevis (4406 feet) between 1883 and 1904.

12 See notes to No. 5 *The Prodigal Son*.

13 i.e. to the Britannia Music Hall. See notes to No. 4 *"The Burial of Big Macphee"*.

14 Strolling along the Cowcaddens. The Cowcaddens was once a densely populated district of central Glasgow, lying to the north of Sauchiehall Street. It is now largely given over to motorway flyovers and multi-storey car parks.

9   Erchie on the King's Cruise

1 In August 1902, shortly after his delayed Coronation (see No. 6 *Mrs Duffy deserts her man* Note 12), King Edward and Queen Alexandra sailed from Cowes up the West Coast, calling at Weymouth, Pembroke Dock, the Isle of Man (see note 3 below) and on into Scottish waters, visiting Arran, Skye and Lewis, and visiting Andrew Carnegie at Skibo Castle (see No. 7 *Carnegie's Wee Lassie*) before sailing round to Invergordon. Thereafter the Royal party proceeded by land to Balmoral for the usual Autumn visit.

2 The Royal Yacht, the third to bear this name, was a screw steamer of 4,700 tons, built in 1899 at Pembroke Dock, and served until replaced by the present Royal Yacht *Britannia*. She was broken up, after war service as an accommodation vessel, at Faslane on the Gareloch in December 1954.

3 Here Erchie accidentally or facetiously (and who would know with Erchie) has transposed the surnames of two famous writers of the day—Marie Corelli and Hall Caine. Marie Corelli, was the pseudonym of Mary Mackay (1856-1924) whose romantic melodramas, such as *The Sorrows of Satan* and *The Mighty Atom* were immensely popular among a wide range of admirers, including Gladstone. Her theories about matters ranging from morality to radioactive vibrations soon dated, however, and her reputation was to decline sadly in later years. In fact Hall Caine (1853-1931) was the "great novelist", resident in the Isle of Man, mentioned by Erchie. Caine gave many of his stories a Manx setting and acquired a sensational reputation leading to the banning of his books by several circulating libraries.

4 Very great struggle.

5 Plunged away suddenly.

6 Campbeltown was noted for the distillation of its distinctively full-flavoured malt whisky. The town undoubtedly bore an industrial front

(coal mining and fish curing were carried on in the neighbourhood)
which contrasted with other towns on the West Coast.
7 Raking or gathering in the money. A bawbee was originally a coin
   worth six pence Scots—later a halfpenny sterling.
8 This was an epithet bestowed on the town of Oban by the Victorians,
   because of its importance as a centre of road and steamer, and later
   rail, communications.
       "Oban is a place of passage and not of rest. Tourists go to Oban
   simply for the purpose of getting to somewhere else." (F. H.
   Groome: *Ordnance Gazetteer of Scotland*)

10 How Jinnet saw the King

1 The "him and her" are of course King Edward VII and Queen
   Alexandra. The King and Queen visited Glasgow on Thursday, May
   14th 1903, and the Glasgow magazine *The Baillie* noted this was the
   first recorded visit of a reigning King to Glasgow. Edward's mother,
   Queen Victoria, had of course visited the city on a number of
   occasions. The King and Queen carried out, as Erchie's comments
   will suggest, a busy programme of engagements; chief amongst which
   was laying the foundation stone for the new buildings, in George
   Street, of the Glasgow and West of Scotland Technical College, later
   the Royal College of Science and Technology and still later
   Strathclyde University.
2 Gairbraid Street is in the Maryhill district of Glasgow.
3 The "Sunny Jim" in question is probably the character invented by
   Edwardian advertising agents to publicise the strength-giving cereal
   "Force". Sadly, any thoughts that Munro is introducing the cook of
   the *Vital Spark* into the Erchie tales will have to be resisted on
   grounds of chronology, Sunny Jim not making his first voyage on the
   Vital Spark until February 1908. Erchie himself appears in the Para
   canon (in *The Disappointment of Erchie's Niece* No. 24 in the Birlinn
   edition of the Complete Para Handy Stories) and Para's shipmate,
   with his brio and irrepressible nature might well have served as a
   model for any kind of life "Force".
4 The association of the Co-operative and Labour movements was
   reflected in the working classes' habits and attitudes. Thus Jinnet, as a
   member of the "co-op" or the "store", would be expected to have left-
   wing and anti-establishment views.
5 *Reynolds News* was published between 1850 and 1967 and was a
   popular Sunday paper supporting the Labour and Co-operative
   movements.
6 A gloomy expression. A tontine was a club in which all the participants contributed a sum all of which went to the last survivor, thus the
   surviving member of a tontine would be well used to mourning the
   deaths of his fellow members. The usage "a ... face on him" is
   typically Glasgow and has survived to the present day.
7 A non-alcoholic beverage.
8 The Edinburgh and Glasgow Railway Company had opened the route
   between the two cities in 1842. One major problem had been the
   Cowlairs incline (1 in 45) leading to the Glasgow terminus at Queen

Street. This was beyond the capacity of the locomotives of the period and a winding engine was installed to haul trains up the hill. The provision continued until 1908 and from then until the end of the steam era banking engines were provided to assist trains leaving Glasgow.

9 As the King moved out of the station into George Square he would have seen the many statues of politicians, national heroes and writers arrayed there. Erchie avers that he mistook them for monuments, as it were in a cemetery.

10 In Victorian days the citizens of Glasgow insisted on this honorific for their city. "James Hamilton Muir" (Neil Munro identified, in one of his pieces reprinted in *The Brave Days*, the writers behind the pseudonym as Muirhead Bone, the etcher; his brother the journalist James Bone and Archibald Hamilton Charteris, a lawyer) writing in 1901, expressed some doubts:
> "Considering the situation of the town there are few traces anywhere of decoration or ornament adequate to its opportunities. Frankly, Glasgow seems a thriving city, but as little as Manchester or Liverpool does it look the 'Second city of the Empire'"(*Glasgow in 1901*).

11 The junction of Argyle, Jamaica and Hope Street was formerly known as the Hielan'man's Cross or "Umbrella"—A reference to the Central Station bridge which covered that part of Argyle Street. It was given this name because of the fondness exiled Highlanders had for meeting "Celtic compatriots" here.

12 The principal throughfares of Glasgow were well made with hard-wearing granite setts or paving stones, unlike many of the streets of the capital. Another cause for local pride.

13 Glasgow has a considerable artistic tradition which perhaps can be considered as beginning with the early nineteenth century topographical painter John Knox. The late nineteenth and early twentieth century saw a flowering of talent which put the city at the forefront of British art—particularly the group of painters, many influenced by the French impressionists, who became known as the "Glasgow Boys", artists such as Hornel, Melville, Lavery, Henry, Guthrie and Walton. The presence of works by these living Glasgow artists, and their Continental contemporaries in Kelvingrove is testimony both to the Glasgow taste for *avant garde* art and to the enthusiasm with which the civic collection was built up.

14 A tall black silk hat, with a supposed resemblance to liquorice, worn at one time by the Glasgow constabulary or "polis".

15 The King and Queen had been visiting the Duke of Buccleuch at his magnificent residence of Dalkeith Palace, just outside Edinburgh.

16 Kinderspiels (from the German "child's play") were groups for young children supposedly run on the best educational principles of the day.

17 The student was no doubt dressing up as a black-faced minstrel. Gilmorehill was the site of Sir George Gilbert Scott's Glasgow University buildings. The university had moved west from the Old College in the High Street in 1866. Students from the "Yooni" were known for their energetic pursuit of extra-curricular activities,

including the Charities Day pranks, when undergraduates would dress up in exotic costumes and spread out all over the city with collecting tins. (See also No. 136 *Saturnalia*)

11 Erchie Returns

1 An expressive exclamation meaning something like "Isn't it just like Erchie!" or "Good old Erchie!".

2 Edinburgh tenement blocks featured drying poles arrayed outside their windows, looking rather like hay rakes to the sceptical Erchie. Erchie here is indulging in the time-honoured ritual of "misca'in'" or poking fun at Scotland's capital city. Edinburgh-Glasgow rivalry really begins to emerge with the mercantile and industrial rise of the western city in the nineteenth century, a century which saw Glasgow overtake Edinburgh in population.

3 Literally dredgers scraping up the mud from the river. It was dredging and river deepening operations of course which in the nineteenth century had made the Clyde navigable to Glasgow for ocean-going ships and made her thriving shipbuilding industry and ports possible.

4 Another example of Erchie's assertion of the innate superiority of Glasgow. While the independent Leith tramway system had been electrified in 1905 the capital city itself persisted in cable cars until the first electrified route was opened in June 1922 between Pilrig, Churchhill and Liberton.

5 Milliken Park is a rural suburb of the small industrial town of Johnstone in Renfrewshire.

12 Duffy's First Family

1 Patriotic fare indeed; porridge and soor (sour) dook or buttermilk was plain wholesome food from readily available local produce, if rather unappetising for the "wean" or "wee smout".

2 Unclear. Most probably this is a reference to the left wing of the Conservative Party, known as Tory Democrats, who favoured a policy of social reform and were therefore likely to appeal to a working class entrepreneur like Duffy.

3 "From scenes like these Auld Scotia's grandeur springs". There is a school of thought which attributed the former greatness of the nation to a mixture of porridge and regular dosing with Gregory's mixture; a foul-tasting purgative blend of rhubarb, magnesia & ginger, invented by James Gregory (1753-1821), Professor of Medicine at Edinburgh University.

4 A general term for unpleasant illness in children, including inflammation of the bowels and skin eruptions—almost any ailment, but certainly not including "gymnastics".

5 One of a number of practitioners specialising in phrenology, or the study of cranial features and their relationship with character and illness. Munro seems to have, with justice, regarded them as quacks and often makes sport of them. The scene from Para Handy where Para tells how Dougie had his bumps read by a mesmeriser at Tarbert Fair comes to mind (*Queer Cargoes* No. 12 in the Birlinn edition of the Complete Para Handy Stories)

6 Bowl-money was money thrown to children at a wedding, especially by the bride or groom on leaving for the ceremony. The coins would be scattered or "bowled" along for the children to scramble after. Probably a survival of a propitiatory or sacrificial practice.

13 Erchie goes to a Bazaar

1 Glasgow at the time this story was published was very much to the fore in European contemporary art and design. The work of Charles Rennnie Mackintosh and his contemporaries was recognised internationally and commented on locally, as we will see in story 22 *Erchie in an Art Tea Room* which takes our hero into the art nouveau delights of Miss Cranston's Willow Tea Rooms.

2 A bassinette is a form of perambulator and Jinnet is assumed to be past child-bearing age.

3 Glasgow Celtic were founded in 1888 by a Marist Brother and attracted a loyal following from the East End of the city largely from the many people of Irish Catholic descent. Traditionally the rivals of Glasgow Rangers, they played in green and white; these obviously are the colours favoured by Duffy.

4 A tall silk hat or top hat, so named because of its resemblance to a "lum" or chimney.

5 St Andrew's Hall, built by James Sellars in 1873 in Berkeley Street in the West End, was the city's principal concert hall, with an international reputation. Originally commissioned by a private association of well-to-do citizens, the halls were the centre of Glasgow's musical life for generations, until burned down in the disastrous fire of 1962. The west facade of the Mitchell Library is all that remains and "there is no more masterly or powerful classical facade in the city" (*Central Glasgow—an Illustrated Architectural Guide.*)

6 The Grosvenor Restaurant formed part of the impressive Grosvenor Building in Gordon Street and for many years was frequented by the Glasgow *glitterati*; hence the comment from Erchie about "the richt kind o' claes, wi' a crease doon the front o' their breeks." Like the St Andrew's Halls, the Grosvenor has vanished from the Glasgow scene; a great loss, with its resplendent centrepiece the German baroque banqueting hall extending over both the second and third floors.

7 Erchie argued or contended persistently that the winning of the pony was all a mistake.

8 Jinnet was worried that the pony would scrape the linoleum floor with its iron "buits" or horseshoes. One of Erchie's tallest tales.

9 Dandelions.

14 Holidays

1 The Glasgow Foundry Boys Religious Society founded in 1865 was an organisation devoted to the religious, moral and physical improvement of the lot of city children. Originally concerned with, as the title suggests, boys working in the foundry trades, later the society's activities widened to other employment areas and to work with girls. They had religious classes on Sundays and educational classes, drill exercises, banking and other provident facilities, musical and social

meetings during the week. An interesting Munro connection is that in 1869 the 8th Duke of Argyll became Honorary President of the Society and took a great interest in the movement and encouraged the Society to bring the boys to the grounds of Inveraray Castle for their week's camp at the Glasgow Fair. Doubtless young Neil would have been very aware of the excitement caused by the annual arrival of the "Foondry Boys" in his quiet Highland town.

2   A dish of oatmeal or rolled oats boiled in salted water and forming part of the staple diet of Scots for centuries. Still, in Erchie's time, treated as a plural noun ("taking them every mornin'").

3   The musician assaulted with an egg was presumably playing the ophicleide, a brass instrument, related to the bugle, playing in the bass register.

4   An area in the East End of Glasgow, near the Gallowgate, used by travelling circuses and the "shows" or fairs.

5   A glee party was a singing group, usually male, which favoured close harmony singing.

6   Another East End location, close to the Saracen's Head Inn.

7   A paddle-steamer, built in 1876, by T. B. Seath and Co. of Rutherglen, named after the song by Robert Burns, and appropriately enough saw service on the Glasgow-Ayr route. Due to her frequent mechanical problems, she acquired the nickname of "Bonnie Breakdoon" or "Bloody Breakdoon".

8   Gooseberries. Wee Hughie has presumably plucked them, unripe, from a kitchen garden. Erchie is ironically contrasting a rural, coastal idyll at the Fair which contrasts with city life during the rest of the year.

9   A game of marbles (also called bools or jiggies), which involves rolling marbles into hollows scooped in the soft ground.

15   The Student Lodger

1   The Calvinist doctrine of predestination, lampooned by Burns in "Holy Willie's Prayer"

> "What was I, or my generation,
> That I should get such exaltation?
> I, wha deserv'd most just damnation,
> For broken laws
> Sax thousand years ere my creation,
> Thro' Adam's cause."

2   In a densely populated tenement like Erchie's any activity or noise out of the ordinary could attract the comments or disapproval of the neighbours.

3   The Carter's Trip was a high spirited annual event when the cart drivers of the city, and there were many in an age when horse-drawn transport predominated, went off to the country for a day's merry-making.

4   A Gaudiamus, so called from the student song *Gaudiamus igitur, Iuvenes dum sumus* (Let us rejoice, for we are students), was a "smoker" or drinking party for students.

5   Divinity students were generally acknowledged to be the wildest of all undergraduates; hence Erchie's alarm.

6 Mr Tod, showing off his learning, is quoting from the ballad poem by
   Walter Scott *Jock o' Hazledean*
   > "Why weep ye by the tide, ladye?
   > Why weep ye by the tide?
   > I'll wed ye to my youngest son
   > And ye sall be his bride;
   > And ye shall be his bride, ladye,
   > Sae comely to be seen:
   > But aye she loot the tears down fa'
   > For Jock o' Hazledean."

7 Gibson Street is situated close to the University on Gilmorehill; the
   references to the Rectorial Election and Conservative Committee-
   rooms are reminders that university politics and national politics were
   closely intertwined with major political figures standing for election as
   Lord Rector of the University and graduates having two votes at
   General Elections until 1948 by virtue of the University seats. This
   story would seem to have been sparked off by the November 1903
   Rectorial election which saw the victory of the Conservative M.P. for
   Dover and Chief Secretary to the Lord Lieutenant of Ireland (in effect
   Secretary of State for Ireland) Rt. Hon George Wyndham (1863-1913).

8 Soda syphon.

9 Gash means pale. This is a reference to an old tale from
   Dumbartonshire, illustrating the convivial habits of the eighteenth
   century gentry. Garscadden lies on the north bank of the Clyde near
   Yoker.
   > "Some of the Kilpatrick lairds had met together and ... as the
   > evening wore on, the whisky bottle was passed round and round
   > until even the hardest drinker began to weaken. It was in the small
   > hours that one said to his host, "Garscadden looks unco gash,"
   > pointing to the pale face of the Laird of Garscadden. "De'il mend
   > him!" was the reply, "He's been wi' his Maker these last two hoors.
   > I saw him slip awa' but I didan' like to disturb good company by
   > saying aught aboot it." (I. M. M. MacPhail: *Short History of
   > Dumbartonshire*)

10 He took me on in argument.

11 Mixed up or muddled—hasn't sorted himself out yet.

16 Jinnet's Tea Party

1 Duffy is swollen up and bloated with a surfeit of milk from the dairy
   where his lady-love works.

2 By the early years of the century, the U.S.A., and to a certain extent
   Germany, had gained economic leadership from Great Britain;
   American production of coal, iron and steel as well as most foodstuffs
   outstripped Britain's and Joseph Chamberlain's proposals for
   protectionist tariff reforms were the result. Duffy's reference is to the
   Americans' ability to dump cheap coal on the British market, because
   of the traditional British policy of Free Trade, something which
   Chamberlain proposed to end.

3 Duffy comments that Jinnet is very smart, quick on the uptake and
   has noted that he is "chief" or especially friendly with Leezie.

4 "Dough-feet", as Erchie describes the policeman, is sulking, or in the
   huff, because he has correctly surmised that Leezie has bestowed her
   favours eleswhere.
5 Wash out or rinse. The impression given when "syning" is used is one
   of perfunctory or hasty washing—as here when it is only the tea-things
   which have been deployed by the lady of the house. Greasy dinner-
   dishes or pots would require "scoorin'".

17 The Natives of Clachnacudden
1 Erchie, as a Lowland Scot (despite his Highland surname), is
   describing the Gaels' conversing in their own language as "tearin' the
   tartan."
2 A door-mat, especially one made of coconut fibre.
3 Even allowing for Erchie's reporting, this is a misquotation from the
   "Canadian Boat Song", a popular, yearning song of exile. The stanza
   ought to read:
       "From the lone shieling of the misty island
       Mountains divide us, and the waste of seas-
       Yet still the blood is strong, the heart is Highland,
       And we in dreams behold the Hebrides."
   The authorship of these lines, which first appeared in Blackwood's
   Magazine in September 1829, is disputed; the Oxford Book of
   Scottish Verse states authoritatively—"Anonymous", while other
   authorities attribute it to David Macbeth Moir ("Delta").
4 Harry Linn was a Scots music-hall entertainer of the generation before
   Harry Lauder specialising in the portrayal of the comic stage Highlander. Jack House in his *Music Hall Memories* (1986) describes him as
   "a tall, thin man with a somewhat lugubrious expression". His most
   characteristic piece was the comic song "The Fattest Man in the
   Forty-Twa". This story seems to be about the Glaswegian's stereo-
   typical portrayal of the Gael, yet Munro, as a Highlander himself,
   suffuses the knock-about stuff with his customary affectionate
   humour. Like the Clachnacudden folk themselves—and of course
   Clachnacudden (though boasting a Highland League Football Team)
   is a generalised construct rather than a specific locality—he is given to
   humour "that kind o' codded themselves".
5 Bamber's superior hairdressing establishment was at the corner of
   Hope Streeet and Gordon Street (very close to the Grosvenor
   Restaurant).

18 Mary Ann
1 A maid of all work. In this, Erchie's ironic commentary on the middle
   class household and the "servant problem" reference is made to
   various categories of maids and others in service; a "general" is a
   maidservant with general duties, and one likely to be found in smaller
   establishments. The extent of domestic service in early twentieth
   century society should not be underestimated—many comparatively
   modest households would employ a "general"—thus contributing to
   the employment of 25,947 persons in domestic service in Glasgow in
   1901—or 7.25% of the total labour force of the city.

2 A favourable reference.

3 A South African town, scene of fighting during the Boer War (1899–1902). In the early period of Boer success and several heavy British defeats, Kimberley, the wealthy centre of the diamond industry, was besieged by smaller Boer forces and not relieved until the first half of 1900, together with Ladysmith and Mafeking. Thus was Queen Victoria's defiance vindicated—"we are not interested in the possibilities of defeat: they do not exist."

4 An area in the West End of Glasgow noted for its large impressive terraced houses, establishments which would certainly require servants.

5 Glasgow had experienced as much of municipal enterprise as any town in the Kingdom with tramways, electricity, gas, telephones, bath-houses, water-supply, slum clearance, etc. being provided by the city council. Erchie, in his role as social satirist advocates taking domestic service into the public sector.

6 Perambulator, or pram.

19 Duffy's Wedding

1 The new Mrs Duffy, with undoubted social ambitions, considers that her husband's normal way of advertising his wares is beneath his (or more probably) her dignity.

2 A surtout coat, similar to a frock coat. From the French "sur tout"—"over all", and therefore a translation of "overcoat".

3 Probably the dance hall of that name in Dumbarton Road, Partick. Dance halls at this time served refreshments.

4 Literally wooden ("timmer" is timber) in the tune—i.e. tone deaf.

20 On Corporal Punishment

1 An area in the East End of Glasgow between the Gallowgate and Glasgow Green.

2 One of the city's leading enterprises was the locomotive works of Henry Dübs.

3 A tautology. "Wee;" means small and "smouts" is a generally affectionate appellation given to small children or other creatures.

4 The palm of the hand.

5 A leather strap used in Scottish schools; punishment was administered by striking the offender's palms. "The belt" as it was also known, had two, three or four tongues or "fingers", came in different weights and was probably manufactured by Messrs. Dick of Lochgelly in Fife, who enjoyed a virtual monopoly. Indeed a "Lochgelly" was another eponymous term for this terror of the classroom.

6 Alick is finding his "coonts" or arithmetic difficult and is dreading the inevitable punishment on his return to school, if he doesn't get them right. The arithmetic wee Alick is wrestling with might be "mental arithmetic" or "speed and accuracy", but in this case is the dreaded "problem arithmetic"—as we learn from Erchie's comic recital of the cistern problem—a real "staggerer".

21 The Follies of Fashion

1 The fashion of a fore and aft crease in men's trousers became popular
   only in the 1890s and the acceptance of the new style by the Prince of
   Wales (later Edward VII) resulted in its widespread adoption.

2 Fussy or obsessed by detail.

3 Neat, smart.

4 Also "galluses"—trouser braces. The spelling used here more
   accurately conveys the idea of hanging or suspending the trousers.

5 Iron suits—or suits of armour.

6 One of the small passenger steamers operating to various piers on the
   Clyde between Victoria Bridge and, as here, Whiteinch, on the north
   bank of the river.

7 Left-handed. Also corry-handed or corry-fisted; from the Gaelic *cearr*
   wrong or awkward, thus imparting to left-handedness a similar
   pejorative quality to the Latin *sinister*.

8 This would be the book in which the weekly payments to the "penny a
   week man" of the Prudential Assurance Company, a noted life
   insurance agency, would be recorded. Erchie jokingly reacts to
   Jinnet's fears that he was drowned by suggesting that she would hurry
   home to check what she would collect from the insurance.

9 Jinnet states her intention of not being dependent on anyone.

22 Erchie in an Art Tea-Room

1 The year is 1904. Erchie and Duffy are patronising the newly opened
   Willow Tea Room in Sauchiehall Street—an appropriately named tea
   room since Sauchiehall is from *sauch* (willow tree) and *haugh*
   (meadow). Glasgow's tea rooms were famous and numerous, and
   were seen as emblems of the Temperance Movement, and increasingly as temples to good design. The Willow Tea Room was the work
   of Charles Rennie Mackintosh (1868-1928) and formed a fitting
   climax to his association with Kate Cranston (see below). It was
   restored in the 1980s by Geofrey Wimpenny.
       "It is not the accent of the people, nor the
       painted houses, nor yet the absence of Highland
       policemen that makes the Glasgow man in London
       feel that he is in a foreign town and far from home. It is a simpler
       matter. It is the lack of tea shops ... Glasgow, in truth, is a very
       Tokyo for tea rooms." J. H. Muir *Glasgow in 1901.*

2 Kate Cranston, noted businesswoman and temperance advocate had
   set new standards in tea room service and design, since opening her
   Argyle Street premises in 1892, followed by others in Buchanan Street
   and Ingram Street. By employing the best architects and designers like
   Mackintosh and George Walton and imparting her own special
   combination of verve and shrewdness, her establishments gained such
   a reputation for excellence that they became synonymous with beauty
   and taste. So it might be said of something well designed; "It's quite
   Kate Cranstonish!"
       "Miss Cranston has started large restaurants, all very elaborately
       simple on the new high art lines. The result is gorgeous! And a wee
       bit vulgar!" (Letter from Sir Edwin Lutyens, 1897).

3 Three pound notes and a ten shilling note (£3.50). The affluent Mr Duffy assumes that the impressive decor implies a hefty bill. In fact, Miss Cranston's policy was to keep prices reasonably low so as to compare favourably, if not actually compete, with public houses such as the "Mull o' Kintyre Vaults".

"(The expatriate Scot) returns with pleasure to his town, where he may lunch on lighter fare than steak and porter for the sum of fivepence amid surroundings that remind him of a pleasant home." (J. H. Muir *Glasgow in 1901*).

4 The shafts of a coal cart.

5 The Room de Luxe was the jewel of the Willow Tea Rooms. The colours ("o' a goon Jinnet used to hae") were silver grey and pink and in fact Erchie gives a fairly good account of the decor, if more than slightly tinged with irony—"ye could easy guess they were chairs" being a reference to Mackintosh's specially designed seating.

6 Not "purple leeks" as they are called by Erchie, but the classic *art nouveau* rose of the Glasgow style. The "gasalier" was not precisely that, (illumination was by electricity) but a magnificent chandelier with a flower-like arrangement.

7 Glass balls or marbles as big as your fist. Glass and mirrored glass was very much a feature of the Willow Tea Room.

8 Erchie's joke is a play on "bead"—"to tak a bead" is to take a good drink or quantity of spirits. There are still photographs showing waitresses wearing the red beads just as Erchie describes them.

9 The Zoo referred to is Wombwell's Menagerie (see No. 92 *A Menagerie Marriage*).

10 The batters are the front and back covers of a book.

11 Pairs of matching ornamental china dogs were very popular on tasteful Edwardian mantelpieces.

12 Different coloured glass balls, representing items on the menu of the restaurant (or "solid meat department"), were sent down a tube to the kitchen. "Moshy" is a game of marbles. As to Mackintosh's idea of "Miss Cranston's" as a "total work of art", Duffy appears irredeemably Philistine, but Erchie's true opinions are not revealed.

23 The Hidden Treasure

1 Mrs Duffy is referring to the contemporary craze for pianolas or player pianos.

2 A sign of a superior neighbourhood. Note that the upwardly-mobile Mrs Duffy does not use the term "wally-close".

3 Nonsense, tricks.

24 The Valenteen

1 The Trades House (1791), designed by Robert Adam for the Trades Guild. A sign of the "increasing respectability of the Trades Rank" and erected in Stockwell Street in what is now termed the "Merchant City". Erchie's dinner would be held in the magnificent pilastered Great Hall.

2 A diminutive of Euphemia.

3 A form of embroidery carried out on a cloth stretched over a hoop—

the name comes from the frame's resemblance to a drum or
tambour.

4 Diamond tiaras

25 Among the Pictures

1 Late or sports edition of the evening newspapers—note that Munro
resists the temptation to "plug" the *Evening News.*

2 Erchie and Duffy are paying a visit to the annual exhibition of the
Glasgow Institute of the Fine Arts at their Sauchiehall Street gallery,
now vanished beneath the mass of the Sauchiehall Centre. The
Institute Galleries were designed by the young J. J. Burnett and
opened in 1880.

3 After the International Exhibition of 1888 it was felt that provision
should be made for an exhibition of arts, crafts and sciences in the
working class area of the East End and in December 1890 the East
End Exhibition was opened in the old Reformatory buildings in Duke
Street by the Scottish Secretary, Lord Lothian. The exhibition ran for
four months and attracted a total attendance of 747,873. The surplus
of £3000 went towards the achievement of the long-held ambition to
build a People's Palace in the East End. The People's Palace on
Glasgow Green eventually opened in January 1898.

4 Henri-Eugène-Augustin Le Sidaner (1862-1939) was a distinguished
French artist, honoured by the French Government by being made an
Officer of the Legion of Honour. Sidaner exhibited two paintings at
the Spring 1904 Exhibition of the Glasgow Institute of Fine Arts, of
which "La Terrasse" seems the more likely than "Le Bouquet" to fit
Munro's description of a "foggy impression by Sidaner". Munro's
comment reminds us that one of his roles on the *Evening News* had
been as art critic and his comment on Sidaner's style accords with the
remark in Bénézit's *Dictionnaire critique et documentaire des Peintres,
Sculpteurs, Desinateurs et Graveurs*, that Sidaner was particularly
praised for his twilight effects ("on a particullièrement vanté ses effets
de crespuscule").

5 Calandering is a finishing process in the textile trades and involves the
smoothing and pressing of the cloth.

6 Duffy's "culture-shock" leads him to suppose that he is at the kind of
entertainment where "pass-outs", i.e. tickets which entitle the holder
to leave and later gain readmittance, are issued to patrons seeking
alcoholic refreshment—the "something" which they might have "at
the tea bar".

7 The 1904 Exhibition included a watercolour of this title (price £45)
by Margaret Macdonald Mackintosh (1864-1933), the wife of Charles
Rennie Mackintosh, and one of the most distinguished of the Glasgow
"weemen painters". "The Sleeper" was later exhibited in London
(1911) and Chicago (1922) but when, in 1987, the Hunterian
Museum in Glasgow organised an exhibition on Margaret Macdonald
Mackintosh this work was listed as untraced. Margaret Mackintosh's
somewhat attenuated *art nouveau* style and use of muted colours could
certainly lead Erchie into his later comment that she "wasna ower
lavish wi' her pent".

8 Duffy wonders how lady painters (assuming them to be of the house-painting variety) can get up and down ladders, whilst wearing skirts.

26 The Probationary Ghost

1 Garnethill (originally Summerhill) is an area of fine red sandstone tenements on a steep-sided hill to the north of Sauchiehall Street. This was the second hill on which the Blythswood New Town grew up and it was called Garnethill after Professor Thomas Garnet (1766-1806), whose name is associated with the Observatory which stood there in the first half of the nineteenth century.

2 Wandering or roaming about.

3 Buccleuch Street in Garnethill subsequently gained some further celebrity from No. 145 "The Tenement House", owned by the National Trust for Scotland and, coincidentally, a splendid evocation of tenement life in Erchie's day.

4 See note 2 to No. 16 *Jinnet's Tea Party.*

5 Stairs to climb.

27 Jinnet's Christmas shopping

1 Even in the early years of the new century, Jinnet is drawing on the collective memory of the disastrous collapse of the City of Glasgow Bank in 1878.

> "Most of [the shareholders] were local people. The first call on them was for five times the amount of the investment. The majority found themselves ruined ... Depression swept over the wintry city, factories closed, buildings stood half-completed." (J. M. Reid *Glasgow*).

2 In receipt of poor relief—"on the parish".

3 A wooden pail

4 Busy, here in the sense of full up or crowded.

5 In front of or before.

28 A Bet on Burns

1 "The chap" is quite right to challenge Duffy's ideas about the authorship of *Dark Lochnagar* and Erchie is right too in attributing it to Byron. However Byron used another form of spelling, as may be seen from these lines from the final stanza:

> "England! thy beauties are tame and domestic.
> To one who has roved o'er the mountains afar;
> Oh for the crags that are wild and majestic!
> The steep frowning glories of dark Loch na Garr."

Just to add to the confusion the poem is titled *Lachin Y Gair.* It may be noted that Burns did not in fact write any of the songs on Duffy's list.

2 Another gaffe from Duffy, Burns met Mary Campbell in Ayrshire, where she was in service.

29 The Prodigal's Return

1 A sailor's kit bag.

2 China was a principal theatre of war for the Russo-Japanese conflict of 1904-5, in which the Japanese inflicted a decisive defeat on the forces

of the Tsar. Britain, although allied with Japan since 1902, was bound
to remain neutral in the event of a war with Russia.

3 Turning a handle. Probably in the case of the Captain a ship's
   telegraph, and in Jinnet's mind's eye her son is ca'in a handle rather
   like the driver's control on a tram car.

4 A beating or hammering.

5 A sore heart. This was the story chosen by Munro to end the collected
   edition of Erchie stories published in 1904, and, as the story title
   suggests, provided a charming and touching finale.

30 Erchie

1 This, the first-ever Erchie story, appeared in the *Glasgow Evening
   News* of 10th February 1902. It is also the first of the uncollected
   stories and it is absolutely fascinating for the connoisseur of Erchie to
   see how Munro experiments with the character and the material.
   Munro is obviously intent on finding inspiration in topical events and
   we can already detect the acerbic edge to Erchie's views on the news
   of the moment. This early, the material is perhaps more loosely
   arranged — some of the later stories are more like complete rounded-
   off essays than newspaper columns.

2 The first paragraph here, ("On Sundays he is the beadle of our church
   ...") was transposed to the beginning of the first story in the 1904
   anthology — *Introductory to an Odd Character*.

3 This is the first of many references to the Temperance Movement. In
   the second half of the nineteenth century Temperance had become an
   issue that concerned political parties as well as social reformers.
   Regulation of the drink trade became an important plank of both
   Liberal and Labour platforms — the initial breakthrough had come
   with the Forbes Mackenzie Act of 1853, which had introduced
   Sunday closing and 11pm weekday closure.

4 The policemen's "sugar-awlly hat" is so-called because, being black
   and shiny, it resembles liquorice.

5 Scott Gibson was an up-and-coming politician, whose power-base was
   the Springburn ward.

6 An early example of Erchie's fondness for the malapropism — he
   means hydra-headed or many-headed.

7 The "ree" referred to is Duffy's coal-ree or coal bing.

8 Captain Byde was the Chief Constable who had evidently been
   offered a golden handshake. He and the Corporation of Glasgow had
   agreed to part company over some matter involving drink.

9 The Lord Provost is Samuel Chisholm, who was later this same year
   forced to resign over his policy of what might be called "creeping
   municipalisation".

10 Glasgow's many slums are a regular target for Erchie's dissertations,
    but on a subject that might indeed be seen as no laughing matter. (In
    1901 more than 1 in 10 houses in Glasgow had only one room and
    half of all houses had 2 rooms or less.) Erchie clearly accepts the
    difference between the "deserving" and the "undeserving" poor.
    Described as a "New Slumming Crusade", the initiative described by
    Erchie is one of a long series of middle-class good works.

11 The playing of the mandolin and the game of ping-pong or table tennis were examples of crazes — i.e. more frivolous demands on middle-class ladies' and girls' time. A feature in the *Evening News* notes the disappearance of the older sort of parlour games, such as "Spin the Platter" and laments:

> Today the old order is changed, for I learn from a juvenile friend that things aren't as they used to be out in "Kelvinsighed". The programme for the last Saturday afternoon function this young hopeful attended, according to the "invite", included "ping-pong, an obstacle race through the house, and a scratch lunch".

12 Keating's Powder was a product used in delousing.

13 The Garden City was a concept outlined in 1898 by the Englishman Ebenezer Howard, in which the expansion of cities would be absorbed by cottage-type homes with separate front doors and gardens. This was seen as a response to the problems of the slums.

14 "Deid Slow" is Erchie's term for any place down-river from Glasgow, based on the sign for river traffic to that effect.

15 "The Wee Doo Hill" or Little Dovehill is a short street off the Gallowgate. The inference is that there are familiar features of life (like "pawns and shebeens") in the slums that would need to be exported to the garden suburbs.

31 Erchie is Ambitious

1 This previously uncollected story appeared in the *Glasgow Evening News* of 24th February 1902.

2 The war is the second Boer War that did indeed end in 1902, but not until the Peace of Vereeniging on 31st May. Erchie's conceit is that soon-to-be discharged soldiers are suitable material for appointment to the vacant post of Chief Constable of Glasgow — "Captain Byde's place" at the enormous salary of £1000 a year. Even a corporal can offer "discipleen" to the post, having been sentenced to C.B. (confined to barracks) "a hundred times".

3 Khaki had been the colour of the army's new combat uniform since 1900.

4 "A signkenone" — Erchie means a *sine qua non*.

5 By "Lord Chisholm" Erchie means the Liberal Party's Lord Provost Chisholm.

6 The schooner is a measure of beer served in the characteristic shaped glass still to be seen in some Glasgow public houses. The variable opening hours of public house was to be a topic often returned to by Erchie, who himself favours the mythical Mull of Kintyre Vaults.

7 The usual epithet reserved for the electric tramcars (introduced in 1902) is "the skoosh caurs", after their capacity for attaining high speeds. "Sparky-caurs" seems equally evocative, however.

8 Geordie Geddes was the celebrated boatman of the Royal Humane Society whose boathouse on the Clyde near the Glasgow Green was the centre for rescuing the victims of boating and other water accidents. He is on the "doon" side of Argyle Street and accordingly can now only drink up to ten o'clock at the riverside locals.

9 The supervisers in the Toon Cooncil might "lift their graith" or books

or personal documents in preparation for leaving their posts. The
description of local government bureaucracy has a familiar ring even
today.
10 The building of new houses "seeven minutes walk frae a caur
terminus" may refer to places like Townhead. These were the
precursors of the vast municipal housing programmes of the remain-
der of the twentieth century.

32 Erchie on Windfalls

1 This previously uncollected story appeared in the *Glasgow Evening
News* on 24th March 1902. It ranges across a number of themes and
talking points of the day.
2 The story begins with a rare glimpse of Erchie at his beadling in St
Kentigern's Church.
3 Gutta percha is rubber. Erchie's rationale for not wishing to be a
millionaire — even in the days when a million pounds meant something — is much to be admired.
4 The "teegurs" or tigers were to be found in E. H. Bostock's Scottish
Zoo and Variety Circus (a neat conflation of three marketing points)
in the New City Road.
5 The Tobacco War was a price-cutting war and another example of the
intense rivalry, in trade and other matters, between Britain and the
USA.
6 To "speak through his nose" is to Erchie a mark of an American
accent.
7 Munro next speirs Erchie about the celebrations being prepared in
Glasgow for the Coronation of Edward VII. These are evidently to be
of modest proportions and Lord Provost Chisholm, as a notable
teetotaller, is to be blamed for the conversaziones replacing any lavish
municipal banquets at which Erchie would no doubt find employment
in his other capacity as a waiter. Samuel Chisholm would be expected
to drink the King's health in kola — he was known to blame all the ills
of society on the drink trade. Similarly, Erchie expresses his disgust at
the absence of processions and sees the presence of schoolchildren in
the parks as a poor substitute.
8 Clog-walloping, the glide and La-va are all variations of dancing.
Glasgow has always been "dancing daft".
9 The Moolders' Hall was a social centre for moulders or iron-workers.
10 The "gress" or salad sandwiches are a symbol of the feeble replace-
ments being offered for a full-blown banquet.
11 The *Fusilier* was a steamer built in 1888 by McArthur & Co. of Paisley
to serve on David MacBrayne's West Highland services. With her
clipper bow she was regarded as the epitome of elegance.

33 Erchie on the Cars

1 This previously uncollected story appeared in the *Glasgow Evening
News* on 5th March 1902.
2 The "skoosh caurs" or electric-powered tramcars were to become one
of Erchie's abiding obsessions. This is the earliest burst of his
invective which reached its apotheosis in story no. 138 in this edition

— *Glasgow in 1942,* in which he looks into a future ruined by the "skoosh caur".

3   The "room-and-kitchen" variety was a double-decked car with seating accommodation at the top of the staircase (the kitchen) as well as in the main upper compartment (the room). The tartan buses were their horse-drawn predecessors.

4   Gleg means quick or speedy.

5   The tramcars in Edinburgh were of the type drawn by cable, and were slow-moving compared to Glasgow's "skoosh caurs".

6   Erchie's opening salvo in the Glasgow-Edinburgh rivalry draws attention to the individual nature of the capital's architecture — his jibe is directed at the towering lands of the Old Town with their "bowsprit" windows. See also story No. 11 in this edition for a jocular description of the citizens of Edinburgh with "their washin's on hay-rakes stuck oot at their windows ..."

7   A bass is a doormat.

8   "The man that ca's the haundle in front" is of course the tramcar driver, and when the car reached the terminus he would move to the other end, for the return journey.

9   Erchie is having fun at the expense of the Corporation in suggesting that one of the bailies is wearing a brattie or apron to serve in a new Co-operative municipal-run store. By 1902 the extent of Glasgow's municipalisation was greater than it was anywhere else in the UK. One journalist made a long list of those services affected, from which this is an extract.

> (A citizen) may live in a municipal house; he may walk along the municipal street, or ride on the municipal tramcar and watch the municipal dust cart collect the refuse which is to be used to fertilise the municipal farm ...

10 Erchie's description of the network of responsibilities and rivalries within the walls of the Municipal Buildings has many points of resemblance with bureaucratic structures even today a hundred years later.

34   Erchie on the Volunteers

1   This previously uncollected story appeared in the *Glasgow Evening News* on 19th March 1902.

2   The "auld 105th" was one of the regiments of the Argyll and Sutherland Highlanders known as the Glasgow Highlanders. A fictional member of this regiment in later years was J. J. Bell's character 'Wee Macgreegor'.

3   The "dreel" was the military drill.

4   The Royal Exchange was in the square of the same name, connecting Buchanan Street and Queen Street. It subsequently became Stirling's Library and is now the Gallery of Modern Art (GOMA).

5   Edward VII was known for his dress sense and he set many trends avidly copied by his lieges, not on by Erchie, however, who confesses himself too "kittly" or ticklish for frequent suit-fittings.

6   Sandringham in Norfolk was Edward's favourite out-of-town residence.

7 A *ménage* or "menoge" was a savings club to which each member
   contributed a fixed sum weekly for a stated period. Erchie is talking
   about the transatlantic sales methods recently adopted by door-to-
   door salesmen representing *Encyclopedia Britannica*, which despite its
   origins in Scotland (the first edition was issued in 1771 in Edinburgh
   by the 'Society of Gentlemen in Scotland') was by this time an
   American company.
8 Jacobus Hercules de La Rey (1847-1914) was a Boer General who,
   with the better-known Botha and De Wedt, was to come to Britain
   later the same year to arrange the detailed peace terms, following the
   Treaty of Vereeniging.

35 Erchie on Things in General

1 This previously uncollected story appeared in the *Glasgow Evening
   News* of 23rd June 1902.
2 Another story (no. 26 in this edition) offers Buccleuch Street in
   Garnethill as one of Erchie's many addresses.
3 More than one pandemic of influenza had visited the UK before 1902,
   the last having been in 1890. Most remembered was to be the
   dreadful visitation of 1918, which is said to have taken more lives than
   the First World War. A small ad. In the *Glasgow Evening News* of the
   period states:
      Thompson's Influenza specific "acts like magic", reduces the fever,
      and dispels the disease. Post free, 1s 9d and 3s 9d, from
      Thompson's, 17 Gordon Street, Glasgow.
4 The Prudential Insurance Society was one of the most remembered
   agencies for family insurance. Its 'shillin' a week man' is mentioned in
   many plays and stories of the time.
5 The "black squad frae Fairfield Yaird" in Govan was the elite
   rivetters' squad with their noisy rivet hammers.
6 Electricity had begun to be used for public and some private lighting
   purposes from the 1880s onwards.
7 Blaming inclement summer weather on vulcanite explosions, telegraphs without wires and so on seems only a short step away from
   atom bombs and global warming. "Auld Horney" is the Devil or Auld
   Nick, to give him another of his favourite Scottish names.
8 Horatio Herbert Kitchener (1865-1916), as commander-in-chief
   during the Boer War, was instrumental in moderating the terms of the
   peace settlement.
9 Barbed wire had been invented in 1873 by Joseph F. Glidden for use
   by farmers and later ranchers in the American West in fencing the
   open range. It was then introduced to the South African War for a
   quite different purpose.

36 Erchie at the Water Trip

1 This previously uncollected story appeared in the *Glasgow Evening
   News* of 7th July 1902.
2 The forenoon service was the morning service — it is interesting to
   note that the "Looker-On" or Munro himself is a worshipper at what
   is obviously a large and prosperous city-centre church.

3 Light summer clothing in chiffon.

4 This is truly intriguing. Erchie has evidently become, merely a few months after his first appearance, a celebrity created by the press.

5 Water Trips, or annual civic inspections of the buildings and plant associated with the water supply, became a by-word for occasioning "junketing" and over-indulgence by the councillors and their guests. This reputation was upheld even to a much later date. The Highland Tour is a reference to the Loch Katrine Water Supply Scheme in the Trossachs, opened by Queen Victoria in 1859.

6 Erchie "cannot possibly comment" to a journalist on the junketings — with his tongue firmly in his cheek he mentions lime juice, herb beer and Broon Robin, a noted health drink of the time. According to Erchie, such is the fear of being exposed by zealots like Scott Gibson, that Pommery or champagne is to be replaced by herb beer and the innkeeper at Aberfoyle feels constrained to demand payment in advance, because of the collapse of trade brought about by the 'unco' guid'.

7 The Christian Endeavourers were another of the groups like the Band of Hope, designed to encourage health-giving and temperate ways among the young.

8 To "burke" here means to avoid or thwart someone's endeavours, to hush up. After William Burke (1792-1829), Irish murderer and resurrectionist, along with his accomplice, William Hare (1790-1860).

37 Erchie on the Coronation

1 This previously uncollected story appeared in the *Glasgow Evening News* of 11th August 1902.

2 The Coronation of Edward VII had taken place two days earlier.

3 See the preceding stories for more on the Lord Provost and Bailie Scott Gibson and their opposition to alcohol and other forms of junketing. Munro is quoting Sir Toby Belch in Shakespeare's *Twelfth Night* Act II scene 3: "Dost thou think, because thou art virtuous, there shall be no more cakes and ale?"

4 The "light lunch," about which Erchie is so scathing, is evidently being held in the City Chambers in George Square.

5 "Chateau Loch Katrine" is of course water from the Corporation Water Scheme mentioned in the previous story.

6 The Royal Bungalow Restaurant had been regarded as the best of the tea rooms at the previous year's International Exhibition. A surviving photograph shows it at night reflected in the River Kelvin and indeed bearing some resemblance to the Municipal Buildings.

7 Theodore Napier (1845-1920) was a noted Jacobite enthusiast, known for his eye-catching Highland dress. Evidently he cut a fine figure in the kilt, hence Jinnet's admiration — although as well as that, in story no. 10 in this edition, there is also a hint that Jinnet may be inclined towards nationalism or even republicanism. The tartan-clad Napier was born in Ballarat, Australia — a fact that immediately conjures up a certain affinity to one Mel Gibson and the *Braveheart* phenomenon.

8 *Reynolds News* was a popular socialist-minded Sunday newspaper,

584 ERCHIE, MY DROLL FRIEND

published between 1850 and 1967. An indication that Duffy was present at Parkhead, the home of Glasgow Celtic in London Road, on this occasion. It is not clear however whether he is a Celtic supporter. (See also story no. 6 in this edition.) The reference to the Irish flag has to be seen in the context of Ireland before the creation of the Free State — but it does seem to anticipate an alleged cause of antagonism in later years — namely the flying of the Irish tricolour at Parkhead.

9 A slop was a kind of loose-fitting jacket or tunic.

38 Erchie on the Preachers

1 This previously uncollected story appeared in the *Glasgow Evening News* of 15th September 1902.
2 A halflin callant was an adolescent youth.
3 A tare or tear was boisterous behaviour or a carry-on. Still found today in 'a rerr terr'.
4 A baur was a joke or story — a term forever associated with Para Handy.
5 In pursuit of novelty or pulling-power for his minister's presbyterian services Erchie now suggests something of the Episcopalian form of service ("back to the congregation"), or even as far as the "Babylonian Wumman" — the Roman Catholic Church itself.
6 Next he suggests the extreme Protestantism espoused by preachers like Mr Primmer, evidently a Pastor Glass of his day. His choice of what would now be described as a sectarian song, "Boyne Water", resembles that of Duffy, who also favoured that ditty — story no. 6 in this edition.
7 "Doverin' ower" means nodding off.
8 Not fair play.
9 "Kale through the reek". Erchie is being ironic and using a phrase that means to be given a severe scolding.
10 Erchie is reminiscing about Hengler's Cirque or Circus as it was when situated in Wellington Street after having been brought to Glasgow by Charles Hengler in November 1885. In 1904 it was to move to the Hippodrome building in Sauchiehall Street.
11 Dwight L. Moody and Ira D. Sankey were the celebrated American revivalists who had had a great impact on Scotland in the previous century, and had toured the country as recently as 1892.

39 Erchie on the Modern Young Man

1 This previously uncollected story appeared in the *Glasgow Evening News* of 29th September 1902.
2 "The lad that dunts the dominoes". This appears to be a nickname for an accordionist — the dominoes presumably are the black keys.
3 A besom or broom.
4 A keelivine pencil was a lead pencil.
5 This magnificent paddle steamer was built in 1891 for the Glasgow and Inveraray Steamboat Coy. By D. & W. Henderson at their Meadowside yard. She was designed for the daily Glasgow to Inveraray service.
6 All male householders and male lodgers had been enfranchised by the

Third Reform Act of 1884. Eighty per cent of the male adults of the male adults in the country could now vote.

7   The Empire Theatre (the notorious "graveyard" for English comics) was situated in Sauchiehall Street, and the Britannia in the Trongate.

40   Erchie on Hooliganism

1   This previously uncollected story appeared in the *Glasgow Evening News* of 20th October 1902.

2   Keir Hardie (1856-1915) was one of the principal founder-members of the Labour Party. He was born in Holytown in Lanarkshire and worked in a local pit from his early years. Hardie was the first ever Labour parliamentary candidate. Defeated at Mid-Lanark, he then secured the seat at West Ham South. Chairman of the Independent Labour Party from its inception (1893-1900) and again in 1913-14, he lost his seat during the Boer War, mainly because of his avowed pacifism.

3   A cuddy is a horse or donkey.

4   Andrew Carnegie, Scots-born multi-millionaire and philanthropist, was known for his generosity in funding higher education.

5   The Common Good Fund, in Glasgow as in many other burghs of Scotland, was often used to subsidise various kinds of civic junketings.

6   Sir James Marwick (1826-1908) had been the town clerk of Glasgow 1873-93 and, uniquely, had held the same post in Edinburgh 1860-73. He was the author of *The River Clyde and the Clyde Burghs*.

7   Duncan's auld horse-crawlers were the horse-drawn trams which had been completely replaced by the new "skoosh" or electric cars earlier in 1902.

41   Erchie on the Election

1   This previously uncollected story appeared in the *Glasgow Evening News* of 3rd November 1902.

2   Belvidere Fever Hospital was on London Road in the East End of the city.

3   The Art Galleries and Museum were opened in 1901.

4   Yet another reference to Scott Gibson, the representative of the Springburn ward and apparently a *bête-noire* of Erchie because of his constant activity and interference. One of Erchie's most satirical salvoes.

5   A cleg is a savagely-biting gadfly or horse fly.

6   "Rekerky style" — Erchie appears to mean *recherche*.

7   Mugdock Reservoir is on the outskirts of the suburb of Milngavie.

8   An indication that, notwithstanding the gradual introduction of electric lighting, street lamps were still gas-lit.

9   "Rax me" means to reach over.

10   Soap-sapple or soap lather.

42   Erchie's Resolutions

1   This previously uncollected story appeared in the *Glasgow Evening News* of 12th January 1904.

2   I began at twelve o'clock.

3 Erchie intends to fold his own socks.
4 Preens are pins.
5 A marvellous example of Erchie's alertness in response to what's in
   the news. In this case the former owner of a Glasgow ice cream
   parlour is conflated with Gulielmo Marconi, inventor of wireless
   communication or radio. In 1901 the first wireless (or "telegraphin'
   withoot ony wires") signal had been sent from Poldhu in Cornwall to
   St John's, Newfoundland. In 1904 Erchie is still reeling from
   inventions such as the telegraph and the electric tramcar and is
   alarmed at the prospect of even more technology giving him a dunt or
   blow on the ear.
6 Erchie's awareness of the fact that ships could receive messages in
   mid-ocean has curious echoes of the still-to-come arrest of the
   murderer Dr Crippen on a transatlantic liner in the year 1910.
7 The world's first commercial turbine passenger steamer was the *King
   Edward*, built by William Denny & Bros. of Dumbarton in 1901. She
   was a screw steamer and sailed on a service between Greenock,
   Dunoon, Rothesay and Campbeltown.
8 Fitzsimmons and Corbett were leading British heavyweight professional boxers. Bob Fitzsimmons (1862-97) was New Zealand-born
   and is remembered for his boast: "The bigger they are, the further
   they have to fall".
9 Interesting. Tillietudlem Castle is the name invented by Walter Scott
   for Craignethan Castle, which stands on the Nethan close to the
   Clyde in the upper ward of Lanarkshire. This was in Scott's novel *Old
   Mortality* published in 1816. The novel — about the Covenanters of
   the seventeenth century — was so well known at one time that the
   Caledonian Railway company built a railway station called
   Tillietudlem used by literary tourists visiting the castle. The prov-
   enance of Duffy's song is unknown, but here is part of Scott's
   description of the fictional Tillietudlem:
        … the fortalice, thus commanding both bridge and pass, had been,
        in times of war, a post of considerable importance, the possession
        of which was necessary to secure the communication of the upper
        and wilder districts of the country with those beneath, where the
        valley expands, and is more capable of communication.
10 A slider is a Glaswegian's name for an ice-cream wafer — another
   reference to the large group of Italian immigrants, who were to be so
   influential in Scotland's leisure industries. The monkeys were the traditional accompaniment to the organ grinders of the same nationality.
11 Difficult to imagine Peter Ilich Tschaikowsky (1840-93) being
   considered *avant garde*. The *News* critic, writing in 1904, recollected
   "the vogue of Tchaikowsky" beginning in the 1880s and continuing
   until his own day, when the "Pathetic Symphony" was voted most
   popular among Glasgow audiences. Munro himself seems to have had
   catholic tastes in music.
12 "Ethol Gairdens" is a rendering of the posher sort of Glasgow accent.
   Athole Gardens are indeed in the West End, just off Great Western
   Road.
13 The "Awfu' Clyde" is Erchie's version of the name of the musical

instrument the ophicleide, an obsolete keyed wind instrument of bass pitch.

14 Annie S. Swan (1859-1943) was an immensely popular writer born in Edinburgh who was said to have produced over 150 books in addition to numerous stories in magazines such as *The People's Friend,* to which Erchie may be referring.

43 Erchie on Burns

1 This previously uncollected story appeared in the *Glasgow Evening News* of 26th January 1903. For more of Erchie's observations on Scotland's Bard see story no. 28 above in this collection (but actually written some years after this story).

2 Fanciful names for institutions celebrating the cult of the Burns Supper. There was a Haggis Club and another was known as the Mother Club, but not so far as we know a Mother Haggis Club.

3 This should read Calton Athletic, surely.

4 Another reference to the current intense commercial competition between Germany and Britain, and what those like Duffy saw as a Teutonic invasion of our traditional markets.

5 *Home Chat* was a popular weekly.

6 "… the last of the poets that took a dram and never denied it." As in the above-mentioned story, Erchie reveals considerable insight into the character of and affection for Burns.

44 Erchie on the Missive

1 This previously uncollected story appeared in the *Glasgow Evening News* on 9th February 1903.

2 Extraordinarily or unusually black or dirty, even for him. Rather like Dougie on the *Vital Spark.*

3 A brain

4 The unwontedly pugnacious Duffy is proposing to assault a house-factor with one of his half hundredweight (56 lb) weights.

5 Rob Roy Macgregor (1671-1734), the famous Highland freebooter pales in comparison with house-factors, according to Duffy. Rob Roy was, of course, familiar to generations of Glaswegians, through the medium of Walter Scott's 1818 novel and a well-known theatrical adaptation that ran for years on the Glasgow stage.

6 Dobbie's Loan was one of Glasgow's many overcrowded tenemented streets, running from the Garscube Road to North Hanover Street. A century later there is scarcely a single dwelling house to be found on a thoroughfare more noted for warehouses and retail outlets.

7 The dunny is the basement or cellar — occasionally a euphemism for toilet.

8 'Vesuvian Lights' were a brand of safety matches.

9 Duffy's wife took it into her head — as they say in Glasgow — to flit or move house.

45 Erchie in the Slums

1 This previously uncollected story appeared in the *Glasgow Evening News* on 23rd March 1903.

2 Erchie is so scunnered with the weather, uncommonly wet even for Scotland, that he cries out for a truce — "a baurley" — as in children's fighting or play.

3 Munro would be familiar with submarine miners — there was a Royal Engineer detachment based at Fort Matilda, Greenock, just a mile from his Gourock home. The Clyde Division, Submarine Miners, R.E. (V) were responsible for the minefield which formed part of the Clyde's defences and stretched between Greenock and the Rosneath peninsula. The minefield was removed in 1904.

4 Thomas Cook (1808-1892) was the English inventor of the "conducted tour" and founder of Thomas Cook & Son, the celebrated travel agency. Previously acting as a Baptist missionary, Cook organised a special train between Leicester and Loughborough for a Temperance meeting in 1828 — this was the first-ever publicly advertised excursion train. During the Paris Exposition of 1855, he organised tours from Leicester to Calais. In the following year Cook led his first Grand Tour of Europe. The business expanded and for a while in the 1880s Cook's were organising military transport and postal services for England and Egypt.

5 "... habit and repute" — slang for a criminal.

6 The washin' boyne (usually pronounced 'bine') was a washtub.

46 Erchie's Sermon

1 This previously uncollected story appeared in the *Glasgow Evening News* 6th April 1903.

2 Dr Reuben Torrey (1856-1928), an American evangelist (or "gaun-aboot") in the tradition of Moodey and Sankey.

3 Something of a mystery this, at least to those who are alert to certain nuances of West of Scotland society. Duffy, evidently a Presbyterian church-goer, is at the same time a supporter of Glasgow Celtic. Later still in story no. 60, we learn that Duffy is of the United Free inclination, but he seems to have 'shopped around' a bit. Erchie's job naturally makes him stick to the "auld kirk".

4 A straw hat is really a leisure accessory and quite unsuited to church-going.

5 A tantrum or temper.

6 A cock fight is clear enough but the meaning of a "cookie-shine" seems to be lost.

7 The Britannia Music Hall was situated in the Trongate. Most of the great music hall artists of the Victorian era played there, and later renamed the Panopticon, it saw appearances by such as Stan Laurel, Jack Buchanan and Cary Grant. (The Panopticon has actually survived to the present day, walled up on the upper floor of a building in the Trongate. The founding of a Panopticon Trust has recently been announced in 2002, with the aim of restoring the hall.)

47 Erchie Suffers a Sea Change

1 This previously uncollected story appeared in the *Glasgow Evening News* on 1st June 1903.

2 Thomas Johnstone Lipton (1850-1931), born in humble circum-

stances in Glasgow, established a chain of stores through an original and dynamic approach to food retailing and made his first million by the age of 30. Noted for his philanthropy he also spent a fortune on repeated but unsuccessful attempts to win back the *America's* Cup from the USA with a series of yachts called — in tribute to his Irish ancestry — *Shamrock*. Knighted in 1898, he had been made a baronet in 1902 by Edward VII — another keen yachtsman.

3   A fist-full of whelks.

4   The Gantocks are rocks off the Cowal shore in the Firth of Clyde near Dunoon.

5   Jinnet is not alone in buying her tea at Lipton's. We learn in a Para Handy story ('Among the Yachts', no. 41 in the Birlinn edition) that Dougie, the mate of the *Vital Spark*, also patronises Lipton's.

6   The *Columba* and the *Lord of the Isles* were two of the most famous Clyde steamers.

7   Fracas.

8   Jinnet wonders if the *America's* Cup is a china one.

9   Lipton's splendid steam yacht, built at Scotts of Greenock in 1896 as the *Aegusa* for an Italian owner, she was purchased by Lipton and renamed *Erin*.

10   Jinnet confuses the *Erin* with the *Galatea*, a yacht owned by Lieutenant Wm Henn and built in 1885 — most unusually — of steel, by John Reid & Co. of Port Glasgow, as a previous challenger for the *America's* Cup.

11   Pipe-clay is used by house-proud women like Jinnet to decorate the stairs in the MacPhersons' close.

12   The first Lipton's store was in Stockwell Street.

13   *Shamrock*'s builders were W. Fife & Sons of Fairlie.

48   Erchie in the Garden

1   This previously uncollected story appeared in the *Glasgow Evening News* on 29th June 1903.

2   The gardening enthusiast is Erchie's guidson or son-in-law.

3   Syboes is a Scots word for spring onions.

4   The palm of your hand.

5   The red-hot Springburn midge is a species not mentioned in the definitive account of *cullicoides impunctatus* given in the Para Handy story *Mudges* (no. 66 in the Birlinn edition).

6   Tabloid beer is about concentrated ales rather than anything in the red-topped press.

7   Erchie is referring to that well-loved sweetmeat, the Conversation Lozenge or Loveheart.

49   Erchie on the Physical Standard

1   This previously uncollected story appeared in the *Glasgow Evening News* on 13th July 1903.

2   Francis Orr's Almanack, another in the tradition of Old Moore. Almanacks or almanacs contain a calendar of the days, weeks, and months of the year; a record of various astronomical phenomena, often with weather predictions and seasonal suggestions for farmers;

and miscellaneous other data. Erchie does not appear to be numbered among the credulous.

3 A concern for public health was in the news at the time this story appeared and revealed that in many respects Glaswegians failed to measure up to the specified physical standards. Public health records from the beginning of the twentieth century show that, for example, the average height of adults had hardly improved at all in the whole of the nineteenth century. Even as late as 1935 Glasgow clerical workers were on average one inch smaller than their equivalents in London.

4 A potty gun is a child's toy that fires small potties or marbles.

5 Freedman was a fashionable tailor.

6 The emancipation of women was proceeding apace in 1903, but was as yet largely confined to the middle classes — at least according to Erchie.

7 Doing a day's work is about as much exercise as Erchie and Jinnet find they need.

50 Erchie on the War

1 This previously uncollected story appeared in the *Glasgow Evening News* on 22nd February 1904.

2 In the Russo-Japanese War of 1904-5, Russia was decisively defeated by the emergent power of Japan. Britain had been allied to Japan since 1902, but this was only a limited change in the UK's policy of isolation — she was bound to remain neutral in the event of such a war.

3 By "our own war" Erchie means the recently concluded Boer War.

4 Erchie as usual has his own uniquely Glaswegian take on world politics. In this case what he knows about the Japanese nation — and indeed the Russian — is in the context of the Glasgow Exhibition of 1901, where both nations had popular pavilions. In a passage perhaps not quite to modern taste, Erchie goes on to sketch a fantasy about what would have happened if the war had begun at the time of the Exhibition, with gunboats on the Kelvin and so on.

5 "The Groveries" was a popular, if unofficial, name for the 1888 and 1901 Exhibitions at Kelvingrove. See also the Jimmy Swan stories (nos 31 and 36 in the Birlinn edition).

6 The water-chute into the River Kelvin was one of the most popular attractions at the 1901 Exhibition.

7 Kate Cranston (1850-1934) was of course the *doyenne* of Glasgow tea rooms, as well as a noted patron of the Glasgow School of Art and its associated designers, such as Charles Rennie Mackintosh (1868-1928) and George Walton (1867-1933).

8 John Philip Sousa (1854-1932), the American composer whose name is synonymous with march tunes and other military music. Known as "The March King", he was born, appropriately enough, in Washington D.C., the son of a Portuguese father and German mother. Sousa mastered several instruments at an early age and at the age of 14 enlisted in the Marine Corps as a bandsman. In 1892 he formed his own band and toured the US and Europe. As well as 136 military marches he wrote 11 operettas and many other pieces.

9 *The Mikado*, by W. S. Gilbert (1836-1911) and Sir Arthur Sullivan

(1843-1900) had had its first performance in 1885. It was, of course, ostensibly set in Japan.
10 That's not fair play.

51 Erchie on After Dinner Oratory
1 This previously uncollected story appeared in the *Glasgow Evening News* on 7th March 1904.
2 The Saracen Head in the Gallowgate in the East End was and is one of the city's most well-loved hostelries. It was originally built in 1754 by Robert Tennent, of 'good hewen stone' taken from the ruins of the Bishops' Castle.
3 The Scots' preference for drink before sustenance was given as a reason for the poor physical condition of the people throughout the nineteenth century. Erchie, as social trend-detector, has noted a move towards a more cosmopolitan approach to cuisine.
4 In the Sauchiehall Street Gallery of the Glasgow Institute of the Fine Arts, designed by J. J. Burnett and opened in 1880.
5 The motor-car had been fairly late in appearing on Scottish roads, following its development in Germany in the 1880s by Daimler and Benz. The "Red Flag" Act, limiting speed to 4 mph, had not been repealed until 1896. At the time of this story the car was beginning to replace the horse-drawn coach and was the emblem of prosperity. Early British makes included the Austin 3-wheeler of 1895, the British version of the Daimler of 1896, and the Lanchester of 1896.
6 The *Bonnie Doon* was a paddle steamer built in 1876 by T. B. Seath & Co., of Rutherglen, named after the song "Ye banks and Braes o' Bonnie Doon" by Robert Burns. Appropriately enough, she operated on the Glasgow-Ayr run. A certain degree of mechanical unreliability led to her being dubbed 'Bonnie Breakdoon'.
7 "... we're no' gaun to be bate by ony coalition o' the poo'rs". Under the Conservative premiership of Lord Salisbury (1830-1903), Britain had generally sought to avoid European entanglements. Salisbury (and Erchie it seems) believed in "splendid isolation", although he also ought to be remembered for describing Britain as an integral "part of the community of Europe".

52 Erchie at the Frivolity
1 This previously uncollected story appeared in the *Glasgow Evening News* on 4th April 1904.
2 "Skooshin' aboot like demented tar-bilers, skriechin' 'Pip! Pip!'". Erchie doesn't care for the motor-car any more than he cares for the electric tramcar. For another Scots writer's description of one of the early cars, here is an excerpt from *Wind in the Willows*, written by Kenneth Grahame (1859-1932) in 1908:
    ... far behind them they heard a faint warning hum, like the drone of a distant bee. Glancing back, they saw a small cloud of dust, with a dark centre of energy, advancing on them at incredible speed, while from out of the dust a faint "Poop-poop!" wailed like an uneasy animal in pain. Hardly regarding it, they turned to resume their conversation, when in an instant (as it seemed) the

peaceful scene was changed, and with a blast of wind and a whirl of sound that made them jump for the nearest ditch, it was on them! The "Poop-poop" rang with a brazen shout in their ears, they had a moment's glimpse of an interior of glittering plate-glass and rich morocco, and the magnificent motor-car, immense, breath-snatching, passionate, with its pilot tense and hugging his wheel, possessed all earth and air for the fraction of a second, flung an enveloping cloud of dust that blinded and enwrapped them utterly, and then dwindled to a speck in the far distance, changing back into a droning bee once more.

3 Bridge is a card game of English origin, but with strong Russian influences. The world-wide craze in Erchie's day was for a variety of the game called auction bridge, developed around 1900. An American, Cornelius Vanderbilt later developed the modern form of contract bridge in 1926 while on a long shipboard cruise.

4 Erchie is reminiscing about music halls as they had been some thirty years previously. The Britannia (still active in 1904) was in the Trongate, while Davie Broon's Royal Music Hall flourished in Dunlop Street from 1853 until 1887. However, no trace can be discovered of the Frivolity, the subject of this story — perhaps an amalgam of the Tivoli and the Gaiety?

5 The Sisters Sylvester appear to have been in the tradition of other sisters' acts beloved of the exacting Glasgow audiences, such as Billie and Renée Houston and — nearer our own day — Fran and Anna.

6 It's a proper fraud or deception.

53 Erchie on Golf

1 This previously uncollected story appeared in the *Glasgow Evening News* on 18th April 1904.

2 Munro's diary records his first game of golf in 1892 at Alexandra Park.

3 Erchie's minister's golf clubs of choice are Western Gailes (founded in 1897) and Royal Troon, founded in 1878. Ministers have always had an association with the game of golf — the invention of the gutty ba', which replaced the "feathery", is credited to a St Andrews clergyman, the Reverend Robert Adams Paterson (died 1904.)

4 Moshey is a game of marbles played with target marbles in each of three hollows scooped in the ground.

5 Duffy's "sang" is normally *Dark Lochnagar* — but this quotation does not come from Byron's classic poem.

6 This is a quotation from Burns's *To a Mountain Daisy On turning One down with the Plough, in April 1786*:
   Wee, modest crimson-tipped flow'r,
   Thou's met me in an evil hour;
   For I maun crush amang the stoure
      Thy slender stem:
   To spare thee now is past my pow'r,
      Thou bonnie gem.

7 This, the well-read Erchie's third literary quotation in one story, comes from Walter Scott's long narrative poem *The Lay of the Last Minstrel* (1805):

> O Caledonia stern and wild,
> Meet nurse for a poetic child!
> Land of brown heath and shaggy wood,
> Land of the mountain and the flood ...

8   Harriers were cross-country runners.

54 Duffy's Fads

1   This previously uncollected story appeared in the *Glasgow Evening News* on 2nd May 1904.
2   "As daft's a maik watch" — i.e. completely silly. A maik was a half-penny — a half-penny watch was obviously a thing of no value.
3   The docken is the weed-like Broad Dock (*Rumex obtusifolius*).
4   Duffy seems to draw the line at the kind of vegetarianism that excludes eggs from the diet, still more at out-and-out veganism.
5   Anything served in addition to plain food such as bread or potatoes.
6   Erchie's antipathy to Italians is a trifle tiresome at times.
7   A proprietary brand of non-alcoholic drink.
8   A Band of Hope distillery is something of an oxymoron.

55 Erchie on Tips

1   This previously uncollected story appeared in the *Glasgow Evening News* on 16th May 1904.
2   Blately — i.e. shyly
3   "... ripe their pooches" or pick their pockets.
4   Andrew Carnegie (1835-1918), the well-known Scots-born multi millionaire.

56 Erchie and the Stolen Hour

1   This previously uncollected story appeared in the *Glasgow Evening News* on 30th May 1904.
2   Changes in the opening hours were a recurrent feature of Glasgow life, and indeed of Erchie stories.
3   A crannog was (probably) a prehistoric lake dwelling, found mainly in Scotland but also in Ireland and Wales. Two main theories exist about their function — their builders may have retreated to them in times of danger, or they may have served as fishing platforms. Remains of crannogs have been found mostly in freshwater lochs, although one example was discovered in the nineteenth century at Dumbuck on the Clyde. The remains of a canoe taken from this site are exhibited at the Hunterian Museum in Glasgow University.
4   Duffy sings *Scotland the Brave*, which appears to be an earlier song unconnected with that composed by the late Cliff Hanley.
5   This story gives us more information about the Mull of Kintyre Vaults than heretofore. Here we learn that the landlord comes from Clachnacuddin (in Erchie-speak anywhere in the Highlands) and this, coupled with the tavern's name, suggests one of the public houses frequented by expatriate Highlanders, possibly in Partick or around Argyle Street. The suggestion that Duffy and his fellow drinkers go for a walk in the West End Park — or Kelvingrove Park — appears to confirm this.

6   The age of the tea-room this undoubtedly was — a story included in the 1904 anthology (no. 22 in this edition) has Erchie and Duffy visiting one of the many tea rooms which had sprung up like "purple leeks" — a reference to the distinctive style of C. R. Mackintosh. Glasgow's tea rooms were famous for good design, as well as emblems or temples of the Temperance Movement.

57   Erchie in the Park

1   This previously uncollected story appeared in the *Glasgow Evening News* on 13th June 1904.

2   The Park in question turns out to be the West End Park, or Kelvingrove Park as it is known today. Glasgow was justifiably proud of its many parks on both sides of the Clyde.

3   The policeman is not turning his whistle round but blowing it.

4   Ducks.

5   The "roary dendron" is better known as the rhododendron and has nothing to do with Sunny Jim's famous set of nature notes about the whale in the Para Handy story No. 29 in the Birlinn edition:

> This is no' yin o' thae common whales that chases herrin' and goes pechin' up and doon Kilbrannan Sound; it's the kind that's catched wi' the harpoons and lives on naething but roary borealises and icebergs.

6   *The Song of Hiawatha* first appeared in 1855. It seems hardly likely that the Glasgow schoolchildren were reciting the narrative poem in unrhymed trochaic tetrameter by Henry Wadsworth Longfellow (1807–82). On the other hand, the *Oxford Companion to English Literature* states that its "incantatory metre and novel subject matter made it immensely popular, and attracted many parodies ... "

58   The Row on Erchie's Stair

1   This previously uncollected story appeared in the *Glasgow Evening News* on 27th June 1904.

2   William F. "Buffalo Bill" Cody brought his "Wild West", as he preferred it to be described, to Glasgow in 1904. The show had been touring since 1883. It featured sharp-shooting and acts including an attack on the Deadwood Stage, the Pony Express, and a "grand, realistic battle scene depicting the capture, torture and death of a scout by savages".

3   Scolding or chiding.

4   Apron.

5   A term for a tenement building, more often associated with Edinburgh.

6   Among older people like Erchie, porridge was a word that took the plural.

7   "Pushion" is poison in Scots.

8   An unkind way of describing a young woman — a herry.

59   The Fair

1   This previously uncollected story appeared in the *Glasgow Evening News* on 11th July 1904.

2   The Glasgow Fair is normally celebrated in the middle fortnight of July.

3   Erchie was indeed made "into a book" in 1904, in the anthology
    Erchie, My Droll Friend.
4   Not the tramcars but the shafts of a wagon.
5   Clockers are cockroaches or beetles.
6   The paddle steamer *Edinburgh Castle* was built in 1879 by Duncan &
    Co. of Port Glasgow. In 1888, as an experiment, she was fired by coal
    briquettes in an effort to cut down on smoke emissions. Throughout
    her 33 years of service she sailed on the Glasgow to Lochgoilhead run.
7   Düb's engineering firm — the Queen's Park Locomotive Works —
    was one of Glasgow many companies active in the field of railway
    engineering.

60   Erchie and the Free Church

1   This previously uncollected story appeared in the *Glasgow Evening
    News* on 8th August 1904.
2   In the second half of the nineteenth century there had been two
    principal Presbyterian churches apart from the Church of Scotland
    itself, with its formal connection with the state. These were the Free
    Church of Scotland (since the Disruption of 1843), and the United
    Presbyterian Church (the U.P.), formed out of earlier secessions from
    the Church of Scotland. Then, in 1900, they agreed to a Union and a
    United Free (U.F.) Church was formed, leaving outside a small but
    determined minority in the Free Church, whose members came to
    known as the "Wee Frees".
3   Following the 1900 Union, there was a dispute over church buildings
    and funds between the "Wee Frees" and the United Free Church.
    This led to a legal case and associated violent scenes that caused a
    gunboat to be sent to Lewis, where feelings were running particularly
    high. The Free Church Case was finally settled in 1904 in the House
    Of Lords in favour of the "Wee Frees". Further legislation in 1921
    and 1925 eased relationships between the Church of Scotland and the
    U.F. Church and in 1929 they combined to form the new Church of
    Scotland. That, more or less, is the situation at time of going to press.
4   The Disruption of 1843 was crucial to all of the foregoing. In Scottish
    presbyterianism's complex history of disputes and secessions one
    event stands out — the departure of one third of the established
    Church of Scotland to form the Free Church of Scotland. A struggle
    had raged over the relationship between church and state. The
    increasingly powerful evangelical wing felt that judgements made by
    the House of Lords and the Court of Session undermined the Kirk's
    claim to spiritual independence and sought this in a new Church. The
    defining moment came on 18th May 1843 at the General Assembly,
    when the dissidents tabled a protest and walked out.
5   Staunch.

61   Duffy's Day Off

1   This previously uncollected story appeared in the *Glasgow Evening
    News* of 22nd August 1904.
2   The popular character "Wee Macgreegor" had been created by J. J.
    Bell (1871-1934) in the rival *Glasgow Evening Times* and published in

book form in 1902. Wee Macgreegor — Macgregor Robinson — was an archetypal Glasgow tenement-dwelling boy whose adventures were chronicled by Bell through to the First World War period. The cover illustration by John Hassall depicted Wee Macgreegor wearing a huge and floppy bonnet of the "Tam o' Shanter" style — oddly enough one of the stories insists that Wee Macgreegor's favoured headgear was the much neater Glengarry.

3　The "oiling" of pipes — or of pipers — is a frequent source of humour. The thirstiness of pipers is legendary — for further evidence see the Para Handy story *Para Handy's Piper* (no. 14 in the Birlinn edition)

62　Erchie's Views on Marriage

1　This previously uncollected story appeared in the *Glasgow Evening News* of 10th October 1904.

2　From the mid-1890s the bicycle had become a symbol of the "new woman" with its possibilities for unsupervised independence and "rational dress". Arthur Conan Doyle's Sherlock Holmes story "The Solitary Cyclist", published in January 1904, but set in the 1890s, featured just such an independent woman, Miss Violet Smith, who was making her own way in the world and was an enthusiastic cyclist.

3　George Meredith (1828-1909) was one of the most distinguished English literary figures of the Victorian era. His novels include *The Ordeal of Richard Feveral* and *The Egoist*. Taking on the role of the grand old man of English letters, in his later years he published many statements of opinion on matters of public interest, such as marriage. Meredith's own experience of marriage was not uniformly happy. He described his first marriage as "a blunder" and his wife deserted him in 1858.

63　Jinnet's First Play

1　This previously uncollected story appeared in the *Glasgow Evening News* of 24th October 1904.

2　Mumford and Glenroy were among the many operators of "geggies" or booth theatres providing popular entertainment in Glasgow in the second half of the nineteenth century. Mumford's Geggy was sited in the Saltmarket while Glenroy and the other "penny geggy" proprietors pitched wherever a vacant space could be found.

3　William Thomas Stead (1849-1912) prominent English journalist and social reformer. His campaign on child prostitution in the *Pall Mall Gazette* was a defining moment in the rise of the "new journalism."

4　The Royalty Theatre in Sauchiehall Street (demolished in 1962) would, in 1909, be the venue for Munro's own play about Erchie — *MacPherson* — staged by Scottish Playgoers Ltd. Munro was a director of this attempt to bring high quality repertory theatre to Glasgow.

5　*Letty* by Arthur Wing Pinero (1855-1934) was one of this acclaimed dramatist's "problem plays" and was first produced in 1903.

6　*Rob Roy* by Isaac Pocock, a dramatisation of the novel by Walter Scott, had an enormous popularity throughout the nineteenth century as the "Scottish National Drama."

7 *East Lynne*, the dramatisation of the sensational novel by Mrs Henry
Wood (1814-1887), was one of the staples of the turn of the century
theatre.

64 Willie

1 This previously uncollected story appeared in the *Glasgow Evening
News* on 7th November 1904.
2 The Shorter Catechism was drawn up by the Westminster Assembly
of divines in 1643 and among other products of this meeting was
adopted by the Church of Scotland. The Shorter Catechism, with its
memorable first question: "What is the chief end of man?" and its
answer: "Man's chief end is to glorify God, and to enjoy him forever",
continued in use for religious instruction in Scotland into the mid-
twentieth century.
3 Strokes of a leather tawse on the palms of the hand. For Erchie's
views on corporal punishment see story no. 20 in this edition.

65 Willie's First Job

1 This previously uncollected story appeared in the *Glasgow Evening
News* on 14th November 1904.
2 A writer is the old Scots term for a solicitor
3 Protestantism was as essential a qualification for many posts in early-
twentieth century Glasgow as a School Certificate. An anti-Catholic
or anti-Irish sentiment was widespread and many jobs were not open
to Catholics.
4 George Young, Lord Young, (1819-1907) sat on the Court of Session
from 1874 to 1905
5 John Traynor, Lord Traynor, (1834-1929) sat on the Court of Session
from 1885 to 904.
6 The Lord Advocate is the chief law officer of the Crown in Scotland
and responsible for public prosecutions.

66 The Young Man of Business

1 This previously uncollected story appeared in the *Glasgow Evening
News* of 21st November 1904.
2 Munro wrote that he himself had, as a youth in Inveraray, been
"insinuated, without any regard for my own desires, into a country
lawyer's office." Munro's first employer, William Douglas (1824-
1903), was however a somewhat better established lawyer or writer
than George Fraser Strang — being Clerk to Commissioners of
Supply of Argyll and Clerk to the Lieutenancy of Argyll and, after
Munro left his employment, Sheriff Clerk.
3 Walter Macfarlane & Company's Saracen Foundry in Possil was the
leading centre for the manufacture of ornamental ironwork. The
Saracen Foundry produced a vast range of architectural castings
including iron bandstands, railings and gates.

67 Erchie's Son

1 This previously uncollected story appeared in the *Glasgow Evening
News* of 28th November 1904.

2   While the medical dictionaries do not enlighten us as to German brain
    fever, the parallel with German measles — the popular term for
    rubella — a mild viral disease similar to measles suggests itself.

68   Erchie on the Early-Rising Bill

1   This previously uncollected story appeared in the *Glasgow Evening
    News* of 17th February 1908.
2   Daylight Saving or Summer-Time schemes did not in fact come into
    operation until 1916, when the exigencies of war resulted in the
    "tamperin' wi' the time o' day the way God made it" (to quote Para
    Handy in *Summertime on the Vital Spark*, no. 69 in the Birlinn edition.)
3   Robert Pearce, later Sir Robert Pearce (1840-1922), Liberal MP for
    Leek from 1906-1918, introduced a Daylight Saving Bill into
    Parliament in 1908, along the lines proposed by William Willett
    (1857-1915) a London builder.
4   Another reflection in these stories of the growing rivalry between
    Britain and Germany. On the same page of the *Glasgow Evening News*
    as this story was a report of German press anxiety about British naval
    expansion and a report of the construction of fortifications at the
    mouth of the River Ems.
5   The Liberal Government, under Sir Henry Campbell-Bannerman
    (1836-1908), had taken power in December 1905 and had won a
    large majority for their reforming programme at the General Election
    of January 1906. Campbell-Bannerman died in April 1908 and was
    succeeded by H. H. Asquith (1852-1928).

69   Erchie Reads the Papers

1   This previously uncollected story appeared in the *Glasgow Evening
    News* of 2nd March 1908.
2   Alice, the daughter of H.R.H. Prince Leopold, the 8th child of Queen
    Victoria, married Prince Alexander of Teck in 1904. Prince Alexander
    was created Duke of Athlone in 1917 when the House of Saxe-
    Coburg & Gotha re-created itself as the House of Windsor.
3   Victoria Mary Augusta Louise Olga Pauline Claudine Agnes of Teck
    married George Frederick Ernest Albert the second son of King
    Edward VII, later King George V in 1893.
4   The comprehensively named Edward Albert Christian George
    Andrew Patrick David, born 1894, succeeded to the throne as Edward
    VIII in 1936 and abdicated the same year.
5   In 1908 Persia was ruled by the Shahs of the Qajar dynasty
6   The Fenians were a secret Irish nationalist organisation formed in the
    1850s and developed strong links with Irish emigrant groups in the
    United States. Their involvement in the affairs of Persia is as yet
    undocumented — but the word Fenian had descended, as Janet
    demonstrates, to a generalised term for any extreme political activist.
    The original derivation of the word was from the *feinne* — the warrior
    companions of Ossian in Celtic legend.
7   Lieutenant Colonel Sir William Hutt Curzon Wyllie (1848-1909)
    after a career in the Indian Army and as a political agent in India was
    political ADC to the Secretary of State for India in London from

1901-1909. He was assassinated by an Indian student in London on
1st July 1909.

70 Erchie's Great Wee Close
1 This previously uncollected story appeared in the *Glasgow Evening
   News* of 16th March 1908.
2 The common area, incorporating drying green, washing house and
   cellars behind a land of tenement houses. Syverina is something of a
   mystery and we can only suggest that Munro intends to apostrophise
   the spirit of the streets — a syver is a common Scottish term for a
   street drain.
3 The Co-operative Society.
4 The entrance to a block of tenement flats.
5 Grove Street — a now-vanished street in the Cowcaddens District of
   Glasgow, close to New City Road (see below.)
6 A doormat made of coconut fibre.
7 The collector might have been representing the Royal Society for the
   Relief of Indigent Gentlewomen of Scotland, founded in 1847, or a
   similar locally based body.
8 Bailies — senior members of the City Council who served *ex officio* as
   Justices of the Peace.
9 In Genesis 31 Jacob raises a heap of stones called Mizpah (literally a
   watchtower) which conveyed the meaning: "The Lord watch between
   me and thee, when we are absent one from another" (Genesis 31 v. 49).
   Rings and other jewels with the word "Mizpah" were popular gifts.
10 Erchie was of course correct. Although by 1908 Munro was living
   prosperously and in some style at a villa overlooking the Clyde at
   Gourock he had as a young man lodged in various tenements and in
   his early married life had lived in closes in the New City Road area of
   Glasgow and would have experienced at first hand the joys and
   hardships of "a great wee close".

71 Duffy on Drink
1 This previously uncollected story appeared in the *Glasgow Evening
   News* of 30th March 1908.
2 Temperance was one of the great issues of the late nineteenth and
   early twentieth centuries, and nowhere more so than in Scotland, where
   control of the drink trade was a major plank in the programme of the
   Scottish Labour Party, founded in 1888. The Scottish Prohibition Party
   was founded in Dundee in 1901 and would claim one remarkable
   victory in 1922 when Edwin Scrymgeour (1866-1947) became Britain's
   first and only Prohibitionist MP by unseating Winston Churchill.
3 Dunfermline-born Andrew Carnegie (1835-1919) acting on his motto
   that "the man who dies rich dies disgraced" devoted much of his
   wealth, gained in the American railroad and steel industry, to providing
   public libraries both in the United States and the United Kingdom.
4 Harry Lauder (1870-1950) the Scots entertainer had by 1908 started
   on his annual tours of the United States and the Commonwealth.
   Lauder became the first music-hall star to be knighted when he was
   honoured for his war charity work in 1919.

5   HMS *Dreadnought*, launched in 1906, the first of the "all-big-gun"
    battleships was a symbol of the German–British naval rivalry of the
    years leading up to the First World War.
6   The International Order of Good Templars was one of the most
    successful temperance movements. Its first Scottish lodge was
    established in 1869.

72 Volunteering Memories

1   This previously uncollected story appeared in the *Glasgow Evening
    News* of 11th April 1908. This story marks the start of a brief
    experiment in printing Munro's comic short fiction in the Saturday
    edition of the *News* rather than in the "Looker-On" column in the
    Monday edition. Ten Erchie stories appeared in this position before
    reverting to Munro's familiar Monday setting. The change was
    announced on 30th March 1908 in a brief note which contained one
    of the very few public statements that Munro was the author of the
    Erchie and Para Handy stories — it will be recollected that the
    collections of these stories published in book form in Munro's lifetime
    were attributed to "Hugh Foulis".
2   As part of the reforms of the British army introduced by Richard
    Burton Haldane (1856-1928), Secretary of State for War in the
    Liberal Government between 1905 and 1912, the various militia and
    volunteer units were re-organised into the Territorial Force.
3   The Enfield rifle, introduced into British service in the middle of the
    nineteenth century was indeed cleaned by "skooting" water through it.
4   A district of central Glasgow lying just to the north of Sauchiehall Street.
5   Part of Glasgow Green — a public park much used for parades,
    processions, meetings and entertainments. In 1899 the Fleshers'
    Haugh was drained to form playing-fields. The name Fleshers' Haugh
    comes from the former use of this site as the location of the city's
    slaughterhouses — a flesher being the Scots term for a butcher and
    haugh being a low-lying piece of ground.
6   Scottish music hall artiste who was at the height of his fame in the
    1870s and '80s. He is best remembered for his comic song "Jock
    McGraw the stoutest man in the Forty-Twa" — the Forty-Twa being
    the 42nd Regiment of Foot — the Black Watch.
7   A superior type of tenement property where the entrance and
    common stairs were tiled, often with highly decorative patterned tiles,
    rather than, as in humbler properties, simply painted or distempered.
    As the reference to servant lassies suggests, many tenement properties
    in Glasgow were of a large size and were designed to be occupied by
    the servant-employing classes. This group of the population was vastly
    larger in the early twentieth century than in the twenty-first century.
    In "Mary Ann" (no. 18 in this edition) Erchie discusses the servant-
    problem.
8   Archibald Lauder's Wholesale and Retail Wine and Spirit Merchants,
    76-78 Sauchiehall Street — situated at the corner of Renfield Street.
9   In 1908 The Glasgow Highlanders (Honorary Colonel — The Duke
    of Argyll) formed the 9th Territorial Battalion of Glasgow's own
    infantry reigiment, the Highland Light Infantry.

10 Erchie attributes the quality of being "gallows" to the Glasgow Highlanders. This is more usually written as "gallus" and is often seen as the Glaswegian's most obvious quality. It conveys a sense of boldness, impudence or mischief and the word has also become a term of approbation of appearance or conduct. A Glasgow street song conveys both senses:
> Oh, ye're ma wee gallus bloke nae mair.
> Oh, ye're ma wee gallus bloke nae mair.
> Wi' yer bell-blue strides,
> An' yer bunnet tae the side,
> Oh, ye're ma wee gallus bloke nae mair.

11 Queen Victoria's review of volunteer forces, held in Holyrood Park, Edinburgh, on 25th August 1881 has, by reason of the remarkably inclement weather, gone down in history as the "Wet Review". Sixty years later obituaries in local newspapers could still be found reporting that Mr X was "a veteran of the 'Wet Review'".

73 Mrs Wetwhistle Provides a Text

1 This previously uncollected story appeared in the *Glasgow Evening News* of 25th April 1908.

2 Mr Grant's situation is at the Singer Sewing Machine factory at Kilbowie, Clydebank.

3 Woolwich was of course the home of the famous Royal Woolwich Arsenal.

4 The Queen's Park Locomotive Works of Henry Dübs had in 1908 just completed a major rebuilding. Dübs had amalgamated with the Springburn-based Neilson, Reid & Coy. and Sharp, Stewart & Coy. in 1903 to form the North British Locomotive Coy. Ltd.

74 Duffy at a Music-Hall

1 This previously uncollected story appeared in the *Glasgow Evening News* of 9th May 1908.

2 Whelks, the popular edible mollusc (and theatrical projectile.)

3 John Philip Sousa (1854-1932) American bandmaster and composer of such stirring favourites as "The Liberty Bell".

4 An area in the East End of Glasgow, near the Gallowgate, popular as a venue for fairs and circuses.

75 A Quiet Day Off

1 This previously uncollected story appeared in the *Glasgow Evening News* of 23rd May 1908.

2 A public holiday celebrated on or near the date of Queen Victoria's birthday, May 24th.

3 The harbour area on the north bank of the Clyde in the centre of Glasgow which had long been the traditional departure point for most sailings to the Clyde and Irish ports.

4 The paddle steamer *Bonnie Doon*, built in 1876 by T. B. Seath & Co. at Rutherglen, operated Clyde sailings between 1876 and 1880 and again from 1882 to 1886. Troubled by a series of mechanical failures she acquired the nickname of "Bonnie Breakdoon".

5 A coal depot.
6 The Anchor Line, an old-established Glasgow shipping line operated
   services to North America and India from the docks in the centre of
   Glasgow. Anchor liners like the *Columbia* (1902) which sailed to New
   York would tower above the excursion steamers.
7 Archibald Cameron Corbett (1856-1933), created 1st Baron
   Rowallan in 1911, was Liberal or Liberal Unionist Member of
   Parliament for Glasgow Tradeston from 1885 to 1911 and presented
   the Argyllshire estate of Ardgoil to the City of Glasgow in 1905.
   Announcing his gift to Lord Provost John Ure Primrose he wrote:
   "My general object is to preserve a grand rugged region for the best
   use of those who love the freedom of the mountains and wild natural
   beauty ..." The estate was used for country holidays for underprivi-
   leged children and was a popular destination for trips and excursions.
   After many years of financial loss the property was feued to the
   Forestry Commission in 1965.
8 Electric tramcars.

76 About Tips Generally

1 This previously uncollected story appeared in the *Glasgow Evening
   News* of 6th June 1908.
2 An adolescent, a half-grown person.
3 His Lordship's Larder and Hotel, 10 St Enoch Square can be traced
   in the local directories for the 1870s, '80s and '90s — but was
   presumably swept away in the extension of the Glasgow & South-
   Western Railway's St Enoch Station in between 1897 and 1902, itself
   now long gone and replaced by the massive and charmless St Enoch
   Centre.
4 A beetle.
5 A cur, a mongrel dog.
6 Herr Godenzi's Swiss Café Restaurant at 93 Sauchiehall Street was a
   feature of 1890's Glasgow — it later traded as Godenzi and Ferrari,
   Restaurateurs.
7 An ice-cream wafer.

77 The Flying Machine

1 This previously uncollected story appeared in the *Glasgow Evening
   News* of 20th June 1908.
2 The period was one of great activity in pioneering ventures in flight,
   with efforts going in to both lighter than air (balloon and dirigible)
   flights and heavier than air (aeroplane and glider) developments.
3 The period saw many prizes being offered for feats of aviation — the
   Deutsch prize of £10,000 for the first plane to fly the English Channel
   with a passenger, another prize for the first trans-channel flight before
   1910 and the prizes offered by the *Daily Mail* — such as the £10,000
   London to Manchester prize and, perhaps most famously, the
   £10,000 Channel prize, won by Bleriot with his flight of July 1909.
4 Wilbur and Orville Wright's pioneering heavier than air flight at Kitty
   Hawk in December 1903 had attracted little publicity until the
   Wrights came to Europe to promote aviation in 1908. The crash of

Percy Pilcher's "Hawk" at Market Harborough, Leicestershire, on
30th September 1899 deprived Scotland of a prior claim to aeronauti-
cal fame. Pilcher, born in Bath in 1867, had been apprenticed to
Randolph, Elder & Co., the Govan shipbuilders, and had then been
appointed an assistant lecturer at Glasgow University. He conducted a
series of successful glider experiments at Cardross, near Dumbarton.
He had produced a lightweight engine for the "Hawk" but it broke up
in mid-air and Pilcher died of his injuries two days later.

78 At the Franco-British Exhibition

1 This previously uncollected story appeared in the *Glasgow Evening
News* of 4th July 1908.

2 The Franco-British Exhibition, which ran at Shepherd's Bush,
London from May to October 1908 was designed to celebrate and
confirm the friendly relations between Britain and France. The old
enemies and rivals had established the *Entente Cordiale* reconciling
various colonial disputes. The *Entente Cordiale* was built on to develop
British, French and Russian military collaboration in the face of a
perceived German threat.

3 The central Court of Honour at the Franco-British Exhibition was
surrounded by buildings inspired by Oriental architecture. The wooden
framed structures were covered with white plaster — hence the popular
name for the exhibition — the "White City" a name which has
survived in London usage. The exhibition ran alongside the 1908
Olympic Games which were held at a nearby stadium. (See *The Age of
Sport* — no. 80 in this collection)

4 The Fairy Fountain was a much-loved feature of the 1888 Glasgow
International Exhibition in Kelvingrove Park.

5 Duffy is recalling the 1901 International Exhibition that attracted over
eleven million visitors to Kelvingrove between May and November
1901.

6 The Flip Flap was one of the great attractions of the exhibition. Two
giant arms with a passenger cabin at the end allowed spectators to get
a bird's-eye view of the site.

7 Imre Kiralfy (1845-1919) was the co-ordinator and overall designer of
the fair.

79 The Duffys Go on Holiday

1 This previously uncollected story appeared in the *Glasgow Evening
News* of 18th July 1908

2 This story was published at the Glasgow Fair Holiday weekend, when
many Glaswegians would be leaving the city for their annual holiday
"doon the watter".

3 Kilchattan (pronounced Kilcattan) is a village standing on an
attractive sandy bay in the south end of the island of Bute.

4 Erchie is probably referring to the 1901 Glasgow International
Exhibition in Kelvingrove Park — but he could also be harking back
to the 1888 Exhibition.

5 Gooseberries.

6 Erchie is perfectly correct — in the early 1800s there were 65

cowfeeders owning 586 cows producing over 1.2 million Scots pints of milk per annum — and Sauchiehall Street, now one of the principal commercial streets of the city centre was a rural backwater. The Scots pint? Almost exactly equal to 3 pints Imperial Measure.

7   A straw boater — the summer headwear of choice for the smart Edwardian.

80   The Age of Sport

1   This previously uncollected story appeared in the *Glasgow Evening News* of 1st August 1908.

2   The White City Stadium in London was built for the 1908 Olympic Games, the 4th games of the modern era.

3   The great controversy of the 1908 Games was the disqualification, in favour of an American athlete, John Hayes, of the Italian marathon runner Dorando Pietri. Pietri collapsed on the last lap around the White City track and was helped to his feet and over the line. He was later given a special gold cup by Queen Alexandra.

4   Marbles.

5   Nelson's Monument is located on Glasgow Green and was the earliest monument to the hero. The foundation stone was laid on 1st August 1806, not ten months after Nelson's death at Trafalgar.

6   *Home Chat, a weekly journal for the home* was established in 1895.

7   The St Rollox Chemical Works of Messrs Charles Tennant & Co. in the north of Glasgow boasted a "monster chimney" 455 feet in height, erected in 1843 with the intention of carrying off the gases produced by the production of sulphuric acid, bleaching powder, soda and other noxious substances. "Tennant's Stalk", as it was familiarly known, was one of the sights of the city until its demolition in 1922.

81   The Presentation Portrait

1   This previously uncollected story appeared in the *Glasgow Evening News* of 15th August 1908.

2   Kitchen sink.

3   Andrew Carnegie (1835-1919) the Dunfermline-born Scots-American railroad and iron millionaire was seldom seen selling picture-frames door to door.

4   The Skibo estate, near Dornoch, Sutherlandshire, was purchased by Andrew Carnegie in 1897.

82   Harry and the King

1   This previously uncollected story appeared in the *Glasgow Evening News* of 14th September 1908. This story marks a reversion to the traditional placing of Munro's humorous fiction in the Monday "Looker-On" column after the experiment of running the Erchie and Para Handy stories in the Saturday Supplement. Munro's fiction would continue to appear at irregular intervals in the Monday editions for the rest of his career with the *News*. A later version of this story, written after 1919, when Harry Lauder received a knighthood, appears among Munro's unpublished papers in the National Library of Scotland (MS 26915 ff133-138)

2 Harry Lauder (1870-1950) was the pre-eminent Scottish musical hall comedian of his generation. His London debut had come in 1900 and by the time this story was written he had embarked on the annual tours of the United States and the Commonwealth that were to make him an international celebrity.
3 Edward VII (1841-1910) succeeded Queen Victoria in 1901.
4 John Savile Lumley-Savile, 2nd Baron Savile (1853-1931) had worked in the Diplomatic Service before retiring aged 36. He owned 33,900 acres of land and often entertained Edward VII at his principal seat, Rufford Abbey, Nottinghamshire.

83 Erchie on Heroes
1 This previously uncollected story appeared in the *Glasgow Evening News* of 28th September 1908.
2 Andrew Carnegie, the Scottish-born millionaire philanthropist had established a hero fund in the United States in 1904 but announced the creation of a British Hero Fund Trust in a letter from his Scottish home at Skibo Castle on 21st September 1908. $1.25 million in 5% bonds, yielding £12,500 per annum was given by Carnegie to establish the fund.
3 The term lorry now suggests a motor vehicle but it originally applied to a horse drawn flat-bed goods vehicle, such as a coal-merchant might use for delivering sacks of coal.
4 The introduction of Old Age Pensions by Chancellor of the Exchequer David Lloyd George in 1908 afforded Neil Munro much material for his stories. For example, see the Para Handy stories *Pension Farms* and *Christmas on the Vital Spark* (nos 27 and 41 in the Birlinn edition).
5 The Hero Fund was close to Carnegie's heart — he wrote once: "It is emphatically my ain bairn. No one suggested it to me."
6 Erchie's assertion, subverted by Jinnet's feminist scepticism, that heroism was inevitably confined to the male "sect" was certainly not shared by Carnegie who specifically included women in the remit of his fund.
7 George Geddes II was the officer of the Glasgow Humane Society from 1889 to 1932 and won fame for the number of people he rescued from drowning in the Clyde, as well as for the number of dead bodies he recovered from the river.

84 Mrs Duffy Disappears
1 This previously uncollected story appeared in the *Glasgow Evening News* of 2nd November 1908.
2 The long campaign for votes for women had been given a new direction by the foundation of the more militant suffragette movement, the Women's Social and Political Union, by Emmeline Pankhurst (1857-1928) in 1903.
3 The "land" Duffy speaks of is not the nation but a "land of houses" — a tenement.
4 A coal depot.

85 Erchie and Carrie
1 This previously uncollected story appeared in the *Glasgow Evening News* of 14th December 1908
2 The dominance of the ice-cream trade in Glasgow by the Italian community is testified to by Erchie's reference to Quadragaheni's Ice-Cream Saloon. Its designation as the "Rale Oreeginal" is of course also a reference to Erchie himself, who described himself in these terms. Sadly there is not a Signor Quadragaheni listed in the Glasgow Post Office Directory for the period.
3 An electric (as opposed to a horse-drawn) tramcar. The electrification of Glasgow's extensive tramway system, a pioneering example of "municipal socialism" was commenced in 1898 and completed by 1901.
4 Carrie Amelia Nation (1846-1911) was an American temperance campaigner who became known for her "bar-smashing" exploits. Many temperance campaigners wore a miniature lapel badge of a hatchet in tribute to Carrie's exploits. As can be judged from this story Carrie Nation extended her activities from America to Scotland. Indeed she talked at a meeting in Glasgow's City Hall on the day this story was published. Edward Scrymgeour of Dundee, the founder of the Prohibitionist Party, a man later to find fame by unseating Winston Churchill as M.P. for Dundee in the 1922 General Election, accompanied her on the platform.

86 Duffy's Horse
1 This previously uncollected story appeared in the *Glasgow Evening News* of 20th April 1909.
2 A mare — a female horse.
3 Erchie is making sport of the distressing continental habit of eating horsemeat.
4 The continental tours organised by Thomas Cook from 1855 did much to open up foreign travel to a wider market.
5 This story appeared in a period of considerable tension between Britain and Germany as displayed in the naval construction rivalry to build ever large and more powerful battleships — the *Dreadnought* race.
6 As ever Munro is inspired by a topical reference. E. H. Bostock's "Scottish Zoo and Variety Circus", which had been established in 1897 in Glasgow's New City Road and which had combined a zoo with, at various times, a circus, a variety theatre and a roller-skating arena was forced to close down in 1909. Bostock offered his livestock to Glasgow City Council but they declined the opportunity to establish a municipal zoo. New City Road was an area well known to Munro — he had stayed in various tenement flats there in the late 1880s, before moving out to the suburban delights of Hillfoot Terrace, Bearsden.

87 Erchie the Cheer-Up Chap
1 This previously uncollected story appeared in the *Glasgow Evening News* of 14th June 1909.
2 Reluctant

3 High spirited, jocose.

4 The doctrines of Christian Science, which included the belief that healing came from the spirit rather than from orthodox medicine, were propounded by the Church's founder Mary Baker Eddy (1821-1910) in *Science and Health* published in 1875. The Christian Science movement and various controversies associated with it attracted much press coverage at this time. The first entry for a Christian Science Church in Glasgow appears in the Post Office Directory for 1907 at 141 Bath Street, not very far from one of Munro's favourite haunts — the Glasgow Art Club at 185 Bath Street.

88 Erchie and the Theatre Nursery

1 This previously uncollected story appeared in the *Glasgow Evening News* of 5th July 1909. At this time Munro was heavily engaged in the formation of a repertory theatre for Glasgow. The Scottish Playgoers Company Ltd. had issued their prospectus in March 1909, Munro being one of the Directors. In September their first season would open at the Royalty Theatre — a season which would conclude with the premiere of a new play by Munro — *MacPherson* — based on his now well-established character Erchie.

2 The Metropole Theatre in Stockwell Street was a popular music-hall venue for almost a hundred years until it was burned down in October 1961. The Metropole name lived on in the New Metropole, Jimmy Logan's unsuccessful attempt to revive a theatre at St George's Cross in 1964. This latter theatre, the West-End Playhouse had been launched as "Glasgow's Theatre of Distinction" in August 1913. Later re-named the Empress, and still later the Falcon Theatre, it, like so many of the city's theatres has now vanished.

3 One of the provisions of David Lloyd George's "People's Budget," introduced in April 1909, was the restoration of child tax allowance.

4 The provision of Old Age Pensions for all those over 70 years of age was a major plank in the Liberal Government's social plans and budget proposals.

5 Despite Glasgow's reputation for "municipal socialism" — manifested in the city's tramways, waterworks, telephone system, gas and electricity supply — there is no evidence of the city fathers taking up Erchie's suggestion of a Baby-Lending Bureau.

6 The oft-revived theatrical adaptation of Sir Walter Scott's *Rob Roy* by Isaac Pocock, first performed in 1818, was one of the great successes of the nineteenth-century Scottish theatre.

89 Duffy's Piano

1 This previously uncollected story appeared in the *Glasgow Evening News* on 23rd August 1909.

2 Tinkling.

3 The origins of one of the most famous names in piano-making came when John Broadwood (1732-1812), left home in Cockburnspath, Berwickshire and walked to London to become a cabinet-maker. He married into a family of Swiss harpsichord-makers and founded the piano-making business that bears his name in 1770. His grandson,

Henry Fowler Broadwood (1811-1893) is more likely to have been
responsible for Duffy's piano.

4 A piece of furniture, either a tall chest of drawers originally used to
hold needlework or a low open-fronted cabinet.

5 A prosperous South-side district of Glasgow.

90 Erchie Explains the Polar Situation

1 This previously uncollected story appeared in the *Glasgow Evening
News* on 4th October 1909.

2 The North Pole had been the target of many expeditions in the late
nineteenth and early twentieth centuries. An expedition in 1908/09
led by Robert Edwin Peary (1856-1920) of the US Navy claimed to
have reached the pole on 6th April 1909.

3 The Scottish shipping company of David MacBrayne had energetically promoted their steamship sailings from Glasgow to Oban as
"The Royal Route" — as their literature pointed out, "The Route has
been called the Royal Route ever since her late Majesty Queen
Victoria traversed it. She thrice visited the Highlands and twice sailed
on the Company's Steamers." There is no evidence that MacBraynes
risked their magnificent excursion steamers like the *Columba* and *Iona*
in Arctic waters!

4 Erchie's comment indicates a considerable familiarity with the story of
Arctic exploration. One of Peary's companions on his 1886 expedition
to Greenland had been Matthew Henson, a black American. Henson
(1866-1955) and four Eskimos would accompany Peary on the last
stage of his 1909 trek to the Pole. Dr Frederick A. Cook (1865-1940)
had served as a surgeon on Peary's 1891/2 expedition.

5 William Howard Taft (1857-1930) was 27th President of the United
States and served from 1909 to 1913.

6 Duffy's question is still a matter of debate. Peary claimed to have
reached the Pole on his 1909 expedition but returning to America
found that Cook was claiming to have got there independently in
April 1908. A bitter controversy resulted and the balance of opinion
eventually favoured Peary's claim and evidence from Cook's Eskimo
travelling companions suggests that he stopped far short of the Pole.
More recent studies have suggested that Peary may not have actually
reached the Pole either and that navigational errors resulted in his
thinking he had reached the Pole when he was still some 30-60 miles
short of it. Perhaps Erchie's last word on the matter hits the mark "It's
no' nearly sae ill to get to the Pole as to prove, when ye get back, that
ye were ever there."

7 A Scottish delicacy made from meat from the head of a cow or pig
boiled, finely chopped and served cold in a jelly made from the stock.
Also available: potted hough — similarly made from shin meat.

91 Erchie's Politics

1 This story, published in book form in the 1993 edition, first appeared
in the *Glasgow Evening News* on 10th January 1910.

2 A reminder that the January 1910 General Election, the first of two to

be held in that year, was being fought as this story went to press.

3 Adam Smith (1723-90) the Scottish philosopher and political economist would obviously have had very great practical difficulties in saying anything to William Ewart Gladstone (1809-98) in 1863 or any other year.

4 The British battleship H.M.S. *Dreadnought*, launched in 1906, gave its name to a new generation of capital ships. The Dreadnoughts were fast, heavily gunned and outperformed the older classes of battleship. The German Naval Act of 1906 committed Germany to matching British battleship production in number and quality, but even this commitment never quite reached Erchie's level of three a month.

5 German-British rivalry was a fairly constant feature of the first years of the century and sparked off a wide range of literature on the coming war of which Erskine Childers *The Riddle of the Sands*, published in 1903, is perhaps the best known example.

6 Jinnet had little option, women being denied the parliamentary vote until after the 1914-18 War.

92 A Menagerie Marriage
1 This story, published in book form in the 1993 edition, first appeared in the *Glasgow Evening News* on 18th April 1910.

2 Messrs Bostock & Wombwell's Menagerie, in New City Road, convenient to Erchie's home.

93 Erchie and the Earthquake
1 This story, published in book form in the 1993 edition, first appeared in the *Glasgow Evening News* on 19th December 1910.

2 The typical Glasgow tenement flat had a bed-recess in the living-room.

3 A constituency unknown to Hansard. However it is a reminder to us that this story appeared during the General Election campaign of December 1910.

4 One of the issues of the December 1910 election was the Liberal party's threat to reform the House of Lords by removing from it the power to oppose money bills and to restrict its delaying power in other matters.

94 Erchie and the census
1 This story, published in book form in the 1993 edition, first appeared in the *Glasgow Evening News* on 3rd April 1911.

2 The decennial census was underway as this story appeared.

3 Duffy is referring to one of the characteristic delights of tenement life, leaning out of the window watching the world go by and exchanging news and views with neighbours (unkindly referred to as gossiping by some mean spirited critics.).

4 Entrance hall.

5 Cupboards.

6 The Lanarkshire steel town of Wishaw, a close neighbour of Mother-well (the home town of Para Handy's engineer Macphail), lay on the Caledonian Railway route. This opened in February 1848 from

Carlisle to Carstairs with branches on from Carstairs to both Edinburgh and Glasgow, however if we accept that Duffy was born at that time this would only make him 63 rather than the 65 he claimed.

7 John Sinclair (1860-1925) Liberal politician and Secretary of State for Scotland from 1905-12. Among the tasks of this office was responsibility for the Census. There is a pleasant appropriateness in Lord Pentland's nominal involvement with this statistical undertaking as he was of the Caithness family of Sinclairs whose 18th century forebear Sir John Sinclair of Ulbster had organised the First Statistical Account of Scotland in the 1790's.

95 The MacPhersons at the "Ex"

1 This story, published in book form in the 1993 edition, first appeared in the *Glasgow Evening News* on 29th May 1911.

2 The Scottish Exhibition of National History, Art and Industry at Kelvingrove had been opened on 3rd May 1911 by the Duke and Duchess of Connaught. See also comments on Glasgow Exhibitions in the Introduction.

3 Bohea was a black Chinese tea, once highly favoured, whose name became almost synonymous with the beverage; for example in Alexander Pope's *Rape of the Lock* we are told of "distant northern lands ... where none e'er taste bohea".

4 A hard peppermint confectionary much favoured for surreptitious sucking during Church services. Also known as Imperials or granny sookers.

5 A Seidlitz powder was an effervescing mixture of sodium bicarbonate, tartaric acid and potassium tartrate once extensively used as an aperient.

6 Tickle.

7 The provision of an abundant supply of pure drinking water from Loch Katrine in the Trossachs to Glasgow by a 34 mile pipe-line was one of the great achievements of civic enterprise in the nineteenth century. The undertaking was inaugurated by Queen Victoria in October 1859.

8 One of the features of the 1911 Exhibition was An Clachan a recreated Highland village, which naturally enough had an Inn—in Gaelic, An Tigh Osda, which served such typical Highland delicacies as tea and non-alcoholic heather ale.

96 Togo

1 This story, published in book form in the 1993 edition, first appeared in the *Glasgow Evening News* on 17th July 1911.

2 Among the features of the 1911 Exhibition was a Japanese Tea Garden and in July the Exhibition was visited by Admiral Count Heihachiro Togo (1847-1934) the victor of the battle against the Russian fleet at the Battle of Tsushima in 1905 and 650 sailors from two Japanese warships.

3 One of the convivial highlights of the civic calendar was the annual inspection of municipal water undertakings; a tour of reservoirs, filter works and pumping stations during which the quality of the water

supply was tested and its purity and character, when appropriately diluted with whisky, assessed.

4 Swim, bathe.

5 Japan had fought a war against China in 1895 which resulted in Formosa and the strategic harbour of Port Arthur being ceded to Japan.

6 A passage-way providing access from one property to another; used colloquially of any busy or crowded location.

7 In the Russo-Japanese War of 1904-5 a Russian fleet sailed from the Baltic to the Far East. On their way they fired on some Hull trawlers fishing on the Dogger Bank under the somewhat strange misapprehension that they were Japanese torpedo boats. One trawler was sunk and two crew members killed.

8 Careful examination of the map fails to reveal a Yahoo in the Straits of Tsushima, between Japan and Korea. However one of the land battles of the Russo-Japanese War was the Battle of the Yalu River, fought in Korea in 1904 and Erchie may have a confused recollection of this.

9 Admiral Zinoviev Rozhestvensky was commander of the Russian Baltic fleet which sailed round the world to be defeated at the Battle of Tsushima.

10 Mikado. Clearly Erchie was not a devotee of Gilbert & Sullivan or he would not have so mishandled the former title of the Emperors of Japan. As the text indicates the British government had made an alliance with Japan, however this been signed in 1902, before the Russo-Japanese War. See also note 10 to story 1 *Introductory to an odd character*.

11 A high collar forming part of dress uniform.

12 Dundee had a large jute manufacturing industry which was being threatened by lower cost Japanese imports.

13 Two of Glasgow's leading industrial concerns—the Queen's Park Locomotive Works of Henry Dübs and the Fairfield Shipbuilding and Engineering Company in Govan.

14 Hesitating.

97 Strikes

1 This story, published in book form in the 1993 edition, first appeared in the *Glasgow Evening News* on 21st August 1911.

2 1910 and 1911 saw a considerable number of industrial disputes and in July and August 1911 the entire country was affected by a transport workers strike. Troops were called out to move supplies and serious disturbances were reported from various industrial centres.

3 The Dennistoun depot of the Glasgow Corporation Tramways Department was in Paton Street, just off Duke Street in the East End of the City.

4 In 1911 aviation was the coming thing with a Round Britain air race being held.

5 Drive them.

6 Lloyd George had become Chancellor of the Exchequer in 1908 and in the so-called "People's Budget" of 1909 had funded both re-armament and the Liberal social reform programme by increased

taxation. His range of measures included a capital gains tax, higher income tax, death duties as well as increased taxes on alcohol and tobacco.

7 A wash tub fitted with an agitator to stir or pound the dirty clothes.

98 Cinematographs

1 This story, published in book form in the 1993 edition, first appeared in the *Glasgow Evening News* on 23 October 1911.
2 Knitting needles.
3 Stockwell Street between the Clyde and Argyll Street.
4 Always a popular subject in the early years of the century and not an unlikely subject for one of the early cinema films. As the story suggests the cinema had by this date become an established, if not yet totally understood, part of Glasgow life. In 1911 there were 57 premises in the city licensed to show films. For another view of the cinema craze see the Jimmy Swan story *From Fort William* in which a Highland customer comes to Glasgow and visits the "picture-palaces".
5 A straw hat.
6 All, everyone, the totality.
7 A but-and-ben was a two-roomed house, here Jinnet is using the phrase to indicate a room behind that in which Lieutenant Rose was eating.
8 Crabs.

99 Duffy's coals

1 This story, published in book form in the 1993 edition, first appeared in the *Glasgow Evening News* on 1st April 1912.
2 A small compartment in a chest or trunk.
3 The most famous example of the India Rubber Boom was probably the Brazilian city of Manaus, situated on the Rio Negro, some 900 miles inland from the coast in Amazonas State. From 1890 onwards it experienced a remarkable prosperity due to the rubber boom and went through a vast and elaborate building programme, including a cathedral (Manaus became an episcopal see in 1892) and an opera house, the Teatro Amazonas, built in 1896.
4 A colourful description of the feminine habit of holding spare hair-pins in the mouth.
5 The Aberdeenshire seaport of Peterhead produces a red granite stone once much used in building.
6 The Glasgow ice-rink at Crossmyloof in the South Side of the city.
7 Roald Amundsen (1872-1928) was in fact Norwegian, not Swedish but had indeed got to the South Pole first; reaching there in December 1911, a month ahead of Captain Scott. The news of his triumph would have only just reached Europe as this story appeared, and obviously the tragic news of the loss of Scott's South Pole party had not yet emerged.
8 Stones.
9 A coal heap.
10 Minimum wage legislation enforced by Wages Councils had been introduced by Winston Churchill, President of the Board of Trade, in

the 1909 Trade Boards Act. In 1992 it was announced that the last vestiges of this legislation were to be dismantled.

11 Blocks of fuel consisting of coal dust bound together with pitch.

12 Glasgow's gas supply had been municipalised in 1870 and despite Duffy's professional jealousy supplied gas for street, stair and household lighting as well as for domestic heating.

13 Possibly a reference to gas-lighting in theatres.

14 "Skooshing": an onomatopoeic term, *cf* swishing. It will be recollected from earlier tales that Glasgow's electric tramcars were referred to as "skoosh-cars".

100 The Conquest of the air

1 This story, published in book form in the 1993 edition, first appeared in the *Glasgow Evening News* on 3rd March 1913.

2 The Germans, under the leadership of Count von Zepellin had been developing airships, or dirigibles, since the beginning of the century.

3 Flying a kite.

4 Evening.

5 The North Sea. For understandable reasons the expression "German Ocean" finally passed out of currency with the First World War.

6 Erchie, we feel, is letting his imagination run away with him. German airship development was primarily military and it might prove difficult to find advertisements in the German press for moonlight aerial cruises.

7 The number of Germans working as waiters was a subject of frequent comment. Jimmy Swan in *The Commercial Room*, a story published in February 1913, has an encounter with an unsympathetic German waiter and in a war-time story *Jimmy Swan's German Spy* Jimmy is told by a hotelier of "the hundreds o' German waiters I've had here, payin' them the best wages ...". Germans were a significant part of the resident alien population with 52,000 Germans being recorded in Great Britain in 1901—approximately 20% of the total alien population. Another high profile occupation for Germans was as musicians on Clyde steamers—Dougie & Sunny Jim's comments on this phenomenon may be consulted in *The Stowaway, No. 48* in the Birlinn edition of the Complete Para Handy Stories.

8 The musical Jinnet is referring to Epes Sargent's well known ballad, the opening lines of which run:
> "A life on the ocean wave
> A home on the rolling deep
> Where the scatter'd waters rave
> And the winds their revels keep ..."

9 The origins of interest in military aviation in Britain had been the formation of the Royal Naval Air Service in 1908; as a result the terminology adopted, e.g. squadron, owed much to this source. It will be noted that Farnborough's long link with aviation was early established.

10 A characteristic Scotticism replacing the English "married to".

11 The Royal Flying Corps had been formed in 1912.

12 The Reuter's News Agency had been founded in 1849, using pigeon

post, and in 1858 become a world wide organisation following the development of the electric telegraph.
13 Apron.

101 Jinnet's visitor

1 This story, published in book form in the 1993 edition, first appeared in the *Glasgow Evening News* on 12th May 1913.
2 The public health department of the City Council.
3 Vacuum cleaners, originally operated from the street, had been invented in 1901. By the time of this story smaller machines suitable for domestic use were becoming available. The manufacturers of a rival to the "Dinky", the "Hydrovakum" had as early as 1910 advertised their machines pointing out that their system involved "No noisy engines, no strange men tramping through the house. No dirt. No mess. No machinery. Your own maids do the work, and it is easier than sweeping or beating carpets, and far more thorough."
4 Used by plumbers to detect leaks.
5 Thomas Alva Edison (1841-1931) the American inventor was indeed, as Erchie hints, thrang (or busy) thinking of new inventions. With more than 1000 patents to his credit he has some claim to be considered as the world's most prolific inventor. The incandescent light bulb and the gramophone are perhaps the best known products of his genius.
6 The presence in the city of the Glasgow & West of Scotland College of Domestic Science, founded in 1875, doubtless contributed to the subject being all the rage, even if the grandly named institution was more commonly referred to as the "Dough School".

102 Black Friday

1 This story, published in book form in the 1993 edition, first appeared in the *Glasgow Evening News* on 25th May 1914.
2 For further comment on the effects of the Temperance (Scotland) Act of 1913 see note 2 to No. 128 *The Soda Fountain Future.*
3 The new legislation restricted the long established custom of morning opening.
4 Two of the great political issues of the day—Irish Home rule and the campaign to win the vote for women, the latter chiefly associated with the Pankhursts and the Women's Social and Political Union.
5 A schooner of beer was a glass containing 14 fluid ounces. The conventional Scottish bar measure of spirits was a fifth of a gill, although some hostelries prided in advertising themselves as "Quarter-Gill Shops"; in England the barely moist sixth of a gill was the favoured measure. The "wee hauf-gill" thus equates to an English treble. Such traditions have now been swept away in the interests of European standardisation and the gill and part thereof is but a fond memory — "O tempora, O mores!"
6 A morning drink.
7 The idea of summer-time or Daylight Saving had been discussed pre-war but was not introduced until 1916. Erchie is being ironic and comparing the effects of the licensing hours changes in making more

time available for productive purposes to a change in the clock.

8 A mystery. The obvious reading is a whole or round fish, such as a herring, as opposed to a filleted fish such as a kipper. However the context suggests an innovation, comparable to the advent of the tinned salmon, and the availability of kippers and other filleted and cured fish obviously predates tinned salmon.

9 An alcoholic stimulant, as opposed to the traditional accompaniment to gin.

10 The influx of Italians, from the 1890's, into the catering industry had a major impact on the eating and social habits of Glasgow and the West of Scotland.

11 One of the elite groups of the shipbuilding labour force, rivetters were, we may feel, unlikely to be seen queuing outside an ice-cream shop.

12 In front of.

13 The two commonest forms of ice-cream purveyed by the Italians were the slider—or rectangular block of ice-cream between two wafers and the pokey hat—a cone filled with a scoop or scoops of ice-cream. The latter could be converted into the ever-popular Macallum by the addition of raspberry syrup.

14 The Forbes Mackenzie Act—the Public Houses (Scotland) Act 1853 had introduced the novelty of an official closing time for pubs and forbidden Sunday opening except for the service of *bona fide* travellers.

15 Dark mornings.

103 Downhearted Duffy

1 This story, published in book form in the 1993 edition, first appeared in the *Glasgow Evening News* on 8th February 1915.

2 With the coming of war many of the Clyde steamers were commandeered for military service. The Caledonian Steam Packet Company's *Duchess of Hamilton, Duchess of Montrose & Duchess of Argyll* were taken as transports in February 1915 and many paddle-steamers were to be used as minesweepers. However the cheerful Erchie suggests that the *Fairy Queen* on the Forth & Clyde Canal was still available to maintain Britannia's claim to rule the waves. The *Fairy Queen* was a much loved pleasure craft which ran canal excursions between Glasgow and Craigmarloch. She had been built in 1897 by J. McArthur & Coy at Paisley for James Aitken & Coy of Kirkintilloch and was a single screw steamer 65' in length. So popular was she that the route she sailed was advertised as the "Fairy Queen Route" even after 1912 when she was sold off the Canal and became a ferry on the Tyne. This news seems not to have reached Erchie, though he would have doubtless been just as happy to sail on her sister ship the *Gypsy Queen*.

3 German submarine warfare against merchant shipping commenced in February 1915.

4 Admiral Sir John R. Jellicoe (1859-1935) Commander-in-Chief of the Grand Fleet. He was to lead his forces to an expensive but strategically important victory at the Battle of Jutland (May 1916) and in December 1916 became First Sea Lord.

5 Horatio Hubert Kitchener (1850-1916), a former Commander-in-Chief in India, had been appointed as Secretary of State for War in

Asquith's cabinet on the outbreak of hostilities. In 1916 he was to go on a military mission to Russia and was drowned off Orkney when the cruiser *Hampshire* struck a mine.

6 Sir John French (1852-1925) was the first Commander-in-Chief of the British Expeditionary Force, commanding what the Kaiser had referred to as "a contemptible little army" from the outbreak of war to December 1915, when he was replaced by Haig.

7 Continuously or persistently.

104 Erchie on the Egg

1 This story, published in book form in the 1993 edition, first appeared in the *Glasgow Evening News* on 15th March 1915.

2 Some of the suffragettes and other "new women" may have been slim to the point of anorexia but we suspect Erchie is thinking of emancipation rather than emaciation.

3 The Sustentation Fund of the Free Church of Scotland provided for the maintenance of clergy and churches in parishes otherwise unable to support the costs.

4 Hen roosts.

5 Ducks, being somewhat unsatisfactory parents, were frequently reared by the clutch of duck eggs being placed under a hen to incubate.

105 Erchie on Prohibition

1 This story, published in book form in the 1993 edition, first appeared in the *Glasgow Evening News* on 5th April 1915.

2 Such dramatic and draconian measures were avoided but nonetheless considerable official efforts went into reducing the consumption of alcohol in the industrial areas.

3 King George V on behalf of himself and the Royal Household renounced the use of alcoholic beverages for the duration of hostilities.

4 The Kintyre town of Campbeltown's prosperity was founded on whisky distilling. A standard work on the subject lists at least 34 distilleries operating in the town at various dates in the 19th and 20th centuries.

5 Two of the famous Glasgow tea rooms. It will be recollected that Miss Cranston's Willow Tea Rooms were visited by Erchie and Duffy in story no. 22 in this collection *Erchie in an Art Tea-Room*.

106 Duffy will buy bonds

1 This story, published in book form in the 1993 edition, first appeared in the *Glasgow Evening News* on 28th June 1915.

2 Drain.

3 As a means of financing national defence War Bonds paying $4\frac{1}{2}\%$ interest were energetically promoted and bond purchase encouraged as a patriotic duty.

4 A coal dump, a coal merchant's store.

5 Dust.

107 An Ideal Profession

1 This story, published in book form in the 1993 edition, first appeared in the *Glasgow Evening News* on 16th August 1915.

2 With all available men needed for the armed forces women came increasingly to take over what had been previously exclusively male occupations. This included the replacement of male tram-car conductors with female employees.

3 The restriction of public house opening hours in areas of importance to munitions production was not designed to provide a gentleman's life for young Johnny Duffy but was part of Lloyd George's campaign to fight the drink menace.

108 Margarine for Wartime

1 This story, published in book form in the 1993 edition, first appeared in the *Glasgow Evening News* on 6th December 1915.

2 David Lloyd George (1863-1945), Liberal politician, was Chancellor of the Exchequer at the outbreak of war but became Minister of Munitions in July 1915 and planned a major expansion of munitions production. On Kitchener's death (see above No. 102 note 5) he became Secretary of State for War and eventually in December 1916, Prime Minister.

3 A chaumer or chamber was a bothy used for the accommodation of unmarried farm workers. The moral condition of such chaumer dwellers was a cause for frequent concern and had attracted the attention of various inquiries into housing and social welfare. "Chambering" is here being used by Jinnet as a polite euphemism for sexual promiscuity.

4 To haver is to talk foolishly.

5 Reginald McKenna (1863-1943) was Lloyd George's successor as Chancellor of the Exchequer. In this role he advocated strict economy and introduced a range of new taxation measures.

109 Duffy in the Dark

1 This story, published in book form in the 1993 edition, first appeared in the *Glasgow Evening News* on 27th March 1916.

2 Well not exactly; what the poet (Richard Monckton Milnes 1809-1895) actually said in *The men of old* was:
"Great thoughts, great feelings came to him,
Like instincts, unawares."

3 As with so many of these stories a topical reference, this time to war economy measures.

110 A Bawbee on the Bobbin

1 This story, published in book form in the 1993 edition, first appeared in the *Glasgow Evening News* on 13th November 1916.

2 The Paisley firm of J & P Coats was the world's largest manufacturer of sewing thread.

3 One of the effects of war had been the increasingly rapid replacement of gold sovereigns by Treasury notes.

4 A farthing, a quarter of a penny, the smallest coin.

5 Metal tokens stamped with a church's name or a Biblical text given to

members in good standing as their proof of communicant status, thus
admitting them to the Sacrament. As they were typically made of lead
a bag of communion tokens would make a formidable weapon.
Tokens were, in the twentieth century, increasingly replaced by
printed communion cards—hence we may speculate the reason for the
ready availability of a bag of old tokens for the irate Mr
MacGallochary.
6 Gartnavel Royal Hospital, Glasgow's main psychiatric hospital.
7 A halfpenny.

111 Nationalised Eggs

1 This story, published in book form in the 1993 edition, first appeared
   in the *Glasgow Evening News* on 20th November 1916. For another
   contemporary view on the egg crisis see *Para Handy in the Egg Trade*,
   number 96 in the Birlinn edition of the Complete Para Handy Stories,
   a story originally published in October 1916.
2 The wartime coalition government had been established by Asquith in
   May 1915.
3 China eggs used to persuade hens to continue laying.
4 Winston Churchill (1874-1965) was in fact available for the Erchie-
   inspired role of National Egg Co-ordinator. He had resigned as First
   Lord of the Admiralty in May 1915 following the failure of the
   Dardanelles expedition and did not return to Government office until
   June 1917 when he became Minister of Munitions.
5 The controversial figure of Horatio Bottomley (1860-1933), financier,
   company promoter, founder of *John Bull* and bankrupt, cropped up in
   many political contexts but not so far as is known, as Minister of Hens
   and Eggs.

112 A Slump in Zepps

1 This story, published in book form in the 1993 edition, first appeared
   in the *Glasgow Evening News* on 4th December 1916.
2 A German Zeppelin or airship.
3 The Glasgow firm of Wylie and Lochhead were among the city's
   leading funeral undertakers.
4 German "frightfulness" and war atrocity stories were a commonplace
   of Allied propagandists from the earliest days of the war. Many of the
   stories were later proved to be ill-founded, however Erchie's reference
   to Zeppelin raids does reflect the fact that during the war 53 separate
   raids were carried out on British targets, including civilian centres,
   with the loss of 556 civilian lives. A small figure compared to the
   horrors of air raids in the Second World War but at the time a
   shocking extension of war to the home front.
5 A reminder that the public houses of the period were exclusively male
   domains where no respectable woman like Jinnet would be seen,
   except perhaps at the off-licence counter.

113 The New Pub

1 This story, published in book form in the 1993 edition, first appeared
   in the *Glasgow Evening News* on 25th December 1916.

2   In order to release manpower for the war effort and to concentrate transport resources many lesser-used passenger stations were closed in the third year of the War.

3   General Sir Douglas Haig (1861-1928) British Commander-in-Chief on the Western Front from December 1915. Seven days after this story appeared Haig was promoted to Field Marshal.

4   As part of the government campaign to reduce the consumption of alcohol state control of public houses was introduced into various industrial areas and measures were taken to further control opening hours. Lloyd George, the Minister of Munitions said "Drink is doing us more damage than all the German submarines put together."

114 Marriage a la mode

1   This story, published in book form in the 1993 edition, first appeared in the *Glasgow Evening News* on 1st January 1917.

2   A perceptive forecast of the post-war housing shortage and the pressure for "Homes for Heroes".

115 Bad news

1   This story, published in book form in the 1993 edition, first appeared in the *Glasgow Evening News* on 8th January 1917.

2   A Danube river port captured by the Central Powers in their successful campaign against Rumania which had entered the war on the Allied side in August 1916.

3   A less than complimentary reference to Crown Prince Wilhelm (1882-1951) who had, with little evident military experience, commanded the 5th Army on the Western Front and directed the German offensive at Verdun in February 1916. This engagement lasted until December and cost over 400,000 German and 540,00 French lives.

4   The world's first tank went into action in September 1915 during the Battle of the Somme. "Tank", it will be noted, appears in quotations in this story, a usage indicative of contemporary uncertainty about the invention. The name was given to what was officially described as a "landship" in an attempt to disguise its identity for security reasons.

5   Joseph Joffre (1852-1931) was the French field commander until the end of 1916 when the losses of Verdun and the failure to achieve a breakthrough on the Somme front resulted in his promotion to Marshal of France, appointment as President of the Supreme War Council and removal from active command.

6   Sir David Beatty (1872-1936) had just succeeded Jellicoe as Commander in Chief of the Grand Fleet. He had won national fame for his dashing command of the Battle Cruiser Squadron in the early years of the War.

116 Erchie on Allotments

1   This story, published in book form in the 1993 edition, first appeared in the *Glasgow Evening News* on 22nd January 1917.

2   As part of the nation's wartime effort to maximise food production official encouragement was given to the establishment of allotment gardens.

3   A small quantity.
4   Garden forks.

117 The Last of the Bridescakes
1   This story, published in book form in the 1993 edition, first appeared
    in the *Glasgow Evening News* on 12th February 1917.
2   The West End, or Kelvingrove Park in Glasgow was a favourite place
    of resort as well as being the venue for the city's series of International
    Exhibitions. The highly ornate Stewart Memorial Fountain was
    designed by the distinguished Glasgow architect James Sellars and
    built in 1872-3 as a tribute to Robert Stewart (Lord Provost from
    1851-4) the originator of the city's Loch Katrine water-supply scheme.
3   By this stage in the war, food shortages, especially of imported
    products such as sugar, were becoming severe. German submarines
    were to sink over 2600 Allied ships, a total of 11 million tons of
    shipping. A few weeks earlier the *News* had noted that in city tea
    rooms "... each person ordering tea is visited by a waitress, who doles
    out the sweet stuff in sparing spoonfulls." See also note 4.
4   Hudson Ewbanke Kearley (1856-1934), 1st Baron Devonport, a
    businessman and Liberal politician, was created food controller in
    November 1916 and given the remit of regulating maximum prices for
    foodstuffs and achieving economies in the use of food. He developed a
    voluntary rationing scheme and, as this story implies, was particularly
    concerned with the problem of sugar supplies, chairing a Royal
    Commission on the issue. He resigned, due to ill-health, in May 1917.
5   Flat iron pans used for cooking oatcakes or girdle scones.

118 How Erchie Spent the Fair
1   This story, published in book form in the 1993 edition, first appeared
    in the *Glasgow Evening News* on 23rd July 1917.
2   A small pocket timetable showing the times of transport connections
    from Glasgow, together with useful information on local holidays,
    weekly half-days etc.
3   James Dalrymple, C.B.E., was General Manager of the Glasgow
    Corporation Tramways from 1904.
4   Seaweed.
5   The south-west portion of the crypt of the Cathedral Church of St
    Mungo is all that remains of the Bishop Jocelyn's extension and
    remodelling of the first Cathedral building. Jocelyn's work was carried
    out in 1197, two years before the Bishop's death.
6   The *Lord of the Isles* that Erchie and Jinnet watched people missing at
    the Broomielaw (Glasgow Bridge Quay) was a magnificent paddle
    steamer built in 1891 for the Glasgow and Inveraray Steamboat Coy.
    by Messrs D. & W. Henderson at their Meadowside, Partick, yard.
    Designed to operate the daily "all the way" sailing from the centre of
    Glasgow to Inveraray, she was, from 1912 onwards in the ownership
    of Turbine Steamers Ltd. who employed her on their popular daily
    cruise from Glasgow down the Clyde and round the Island of Bute.
    During the War she remained in civilian service and was used on the
    route to Lochgoilhead.

7 Originally intended as a war-time measure the concept of "Summer Time" had been introduced in 1916.

119 Erchie's Work in Wartime

1 This story, published in book form in the 1993 edition, first appeared in the *Glasgow Evening News* on 16th May 1918.
2 Literally a pigeon's clutch or hatching of eggs.
3 The United States had declared war on Germany in April 1917 and by the time of this story the troops of the American Expeditionary Force had just fought a successful major engagement at Belleau Wood and were engaged in the Second Battle of the Marne.
4 A flat stone used in the game of hopscotch.

120 Government Milk

1 This story, published in book form in the 1993 edition, first appeared in the *Glasgow Evening News* on 2nd July 1918.
2 The Scottish delicacy of the soda-scone used buttermilk in its recipe.
3 A reminder that milk was distributed in bulk rather than in our now familiar bottles or cartons.
4 Yawning.

121 Coal Rations

1 This story, published in book form in the 1993 edition, first appeared in the *Glasgow Evening News* on 17th August 1918.
2 Coal rationing had been announced in March 1918.
3 A kitchen fireplace fabricated in cast iron and incorporating an oven and a hotplate which was typically used for both heating and cooking purposes in tenement flats of this period.
4 Another reflection on wartime steps to reduce the strength, and discourage the consumption, of alcoholic beverages.
5 Erchie was clearly living in a quite superior tenement flat in that it possessed a bath, a fairly unusual fitting in such properties at this period.
6 Glasgow city council, the "Corporation", ran a large scale municipal gas undertaking.

122 Celebrating Peace

1 This story, published in book form in the 1993 edition, first appeared in the *Glasgow Evening News* on the 30th June 1919.
2 The signature of the Peace Treaty between the Allied Powers and Germany took place at Versailles on Saturday, 28th June 1919, two days before this story appeared. Fighting had of course stopped with the Armistice on 11th November 1918.
3 The German Emperor was not in fact handed over to justice or even to the Argyll & Sutherland Highlanders. He had abdicated on 9th November 1918 and had fled to the neutral Netherlands, where he lived peacefully until his death in 1941.
4 Thomas Woodrow Wilson (1856-1924) 28th President of the United States. A Democrat, elected President in 1912 and 1916, he was a major participant in the Versailles Peace Conference and advocated the creation of the League of Nations.

123 The Coal Famine

1 This story, published in book form in the 1993 edition, first appeared in the *Glasgow Evening News* on 12th January 1920.

2 William Hesketh Lever (1851-1925) made a fortune from the manufacture of soap, founding the model industrial town of Port Sunlight on Merseyside. Involved in a wide range of philanthropic activities he received a baronetcy in 1911, became Baron Leverhulme in 1917 and was advanced to the rank of Viscount Leverhulme of the Western Isles in 1922.

3 In 1918 Leverhulme bought the Island of Lewis and in 1919 added the Harris estate to his holdings. His intention was to develop fishing and fish processing and improve the conditions of the crofting population. However the scheme was unsuccessful, in part due to problems of crofting tenure and in part to local reluctance to surrender independence in favour of a weekly wage. He ceased operations in Lewis in 1922 passing over part of his holdings to a local trust in Stornoway. Leverhulme continued to develop fisheries and fish processing in Harris, developing the port of Obbe, renamed Leverburgh. When he died in 1925 his trustees immediately halted all his Hebridean projects.

4 A deerstalker hat.

124 A Turned Suit

1 This story, published in book form in the 1993 edition, first appeared in the *Glasgow Evening News* on 1st March 1920.

2 A dashed thing.

3 Sir Arthur Conan Doyle (1859-1930), the creator of Sherlock Holmes, became fascinated by Spiritualism after the First World War and lectured and wrote on the subject.

125 Erchie on Divorce

1 This story, published in book form in the 1993 edition, first appeared in the *Glasgow Evening News* on 12th April 1920.

2 Mary Pickford (1893-1979) was a Canadian born American film actress who rose to prominence in the silent movies where she won the nickname of "The World's Sweetheart". A founding partner of United Artists Film Corporation.

3 The actor Owen Moore was the first husband of Mary Pickford, marrying her in 1911 and was divorced from her in 1919.

4 Douglas Fairbanks (1883-1939) American film star, married Mary Pickford in 1920; they divorced in 1935.

5 Charlie Chaplin (1889-1977) English born film actor and director moved to Hollywood in 1914 and played a leading part in the development of the film industry. Married to Mildred Harris in 1918, she divorced him and he married Lila Grey in 1924. Chaplin later married Paulette Goddard and Oona O'Neill, contributing to Erchie's "wave o' divorce".

6 This familiar passage of instruction from the Apostle Paul begins "Wives, submit yourselves unto your own husbands, as unto the Lord."

126 Our Mystery Millionaire

1 This story, published in book form in the 1993 edition, first appeared in the *Glasgow Evening News* on 17th May 1920.
2 Harry Duncan McGowan (1874-1961) Glasgow born businessman, started work in the Nobel Explosives Co. as an office boy and rose to prominence in business in Britain and Canada. In 1926 he was to be instrumental in bringing about the merger of British chemical firms and creating Imperial Chemical Industries; he became Chairman and Managing Director of I.C.I. in 1930. Knighted in 1918, he was created a baron in 1937.
3 The tramcar heading towards Glasgow University.
4 In 1871 Alfred Nobel, the Swedish inventor, licensed production of dynamite in the British Empire to the British Dynamite Company. This concern, with offices in Glasgow, established a factory at Ardeer in Ayrshire, and later became the Nobel Division of I.C.I.
5 Allan Glen's School was founded in 1853 and specialised in scientific and technical education.
6 A curious comment. Belvidere Hospital is in London Road, on the north bank of the Clyde, and not particularly convenient for catching millionairism in Pollokshields, which one would think would be more conveniently served by the Victoria Infirmary in Langside Road.

127 Erchie Sorts the Clock

1 This story, published in book form in the 1993 edition, first appeared in the *Glasgow Evening News* on 13th September 1920.

128 The Soda Fountain Future

1 This story, published in book form in the 1993 edition, first appeared in the *Glasgow Evening News* on 11th October 1920.
2 This story was first published in the year in which the Volstead Act had introduced Prohibition into the United States and in many circles in Britain similar sentiments were being expressed. It was possible for a local community, through the Veto Poll mechanism of the Temperance (Scotland) Act of 1913, to declare itself "dry" and to refuse to grant licenses. Because of the War the first such Veto Polls were not in fact held until 1920 and in that year several communities, such as Kirkintilloch, went "dry".

129 Reminiscences

1 This story, published in book form in the 1993 edition, first appeared in the *Glasgow Evening News* on 8th November 1920.
2 Margot Asquith neé Tennant (1865-1945) was the second wife of Henry Herbert Asquith, the Liberal Prime Minister. Her popular and colourful *Autobiography* was published in 1920 and had clearly provided the cue for Munro's writing this story.
3 Fair dealing or fair play.
4 Harum-scarum.
5 Gossip.
6 H. H. Asquith (1852-1928) (see note 2 above). As Jinnet goes on to suggest, a somewhat stuffy and reserved character, in contrast to his

ebullient and spirited wife. "Wait and see" was a phrase associated
with him and indicative of his character. Asquith had lost his East Fife
seat in the 1918 General Election in the general rout of non-Coalition
Liberals. He was elected for Paisley at a by-election in 1920 and held
this seat until created Earl of Oxford and Asquith in 1925.

7 Giddy, empty-headed.

130 Glad News

1 This story, published in book form in the 1993 edition, first appeared
in the *Glasgow Evening News* on 17th January 1921.

2 Erchie is paraphrasing the well known phrase of Lloyd George's
"What is our task? To make Britain a fit country for heroes to live in."
This phrase was used in a speech in November 1918 and became a
popular slogan for post-war reconstruction.

3 The Coats family from Paisley were the dominant force in that town's
important thread milling and textile industry.

4 Bobbin.

5 Where indeed? The Coats family were extremely keen yacht owners
and the 1910 Lloyd's Register of Yachts lists twelve sail and steam
yachts owned by the Coats clan. For another account of the Coats
yacht-owning interests see the Para Handy story *Among the Yachts* No.
41 in the Birlinn edition of the Complete Para Handy Stories.

131 The Footballer's Life

1 This story, published in book form in the 1993 edition, first appeared
in the *Glasgow Evening News* on 21st March 1921.

2 The Kilmarnock player whose high transfer fee so attracted Duffy's
comment was joining one of England's most successful football teams.
Placed 16th in the English First Division in season 1920/21 Preston
North End were also semi-finalists in the F.A. Cup. In the next season
they were again 16th in the League and were the beaten finalists in the
Cup. In 2001/02 Preston are competing one division lower.

3 A celebrated Clydesdale stallion which in 1911 had been sold for the
then world record price of £9500. On its death in 1914 the Baron was
buried but was exhumed four years later and its skeleton presented to
Glasgow's Kelvingrove Museum, where it is still a popular exhibit.

132 Celebrating the Eclipse

1 This story, published in book form in the 1993 edition, first appeared
in the *Glasgow Evening News* on 11th April 1921.

2 As usual Munro is highly topical with a reference not only to the
eclipse but to the Scotland-England match played on the Saturday
before this story appeared. The result—Scotland 3, England 0.

133 Firewood

1 This story, published in book form in the 1993 edition, first appeared
in the *Glasgow Evening News* on 9th May 1921.

2 The Royal Order of Foresters and the breakaway Ancient Order of
Foresters were popular friendly societies founded in the early
nineteenth century.

3 The gleam of a fire.

134 Duffy's Flitting

1 This story, published in book form in the 1993 edition, first appeared in the *Glasgow Evening News* on 30th May 1921.

2 A poetic term for the heavens, used by Munro both here and in his Para Handy stories, e.g. *Hurricane Jack* no. 53 in the Birlinn edition of the Complete Para Handy Stories. *cf* "This most excellent Canopy the Ayre ..." (Shakespeare *Hamlet* Act 2 Scene 2) or "Without any other cover than the cope of Heaven" (Tobias Smollett: *Humphry Clinker*)

3 As the Vulgate is the Latin translation of the Bible it is a little difficult to accept that "Duffy are you on" appears in it—through perhaps the Apocrypha ...?

4 The Royal Princess Theatre in the Gorbals (built in 1978 as Her Majesty's) is now known to Glasgow theatre-goers as the Citizen's Theatre.

5 John Clyde, a noted local actor, took the title role in the first Scottish feature film — *Rob Roy* — produced in Glasgow in 1911.

6 The reference is to the popular stage version of Walter Scott's *Rob Roy* by Isaac Pocock. This work, first produced in 1818 was for many years the most popular dramatic work in Scotland. It, like the novel, has scenes set in the Trossachs village of Aberfoyle.

7 Archibald is mis-quoting Prospero's words from *The Tempest*, Act 4, Scene 1:

"Our revels now are ended. These our actors,
As I foretold you, were all spirits and
are melted into air, into thin air:
And, like the baseless fabric of this vision
The cloud-capp'd towers, the gorgeous palaces,
The solemn temples, the great globe itself,
Yea, all which it inherit, shall dissolve,
And, like this insubstantial pageant faded,
Leave not a rack behind. ..."

135 After the Fight

1 This story, published in book form in the 1993 edition, first appeared in the *Glasgow Evening News* on July 4th 1921.

2 The reference is to the monthly magazine of the Church of Scotland—not generally considered to be a good source for up to date boxing results.

3 George Carpentier (1894-1975) French boxer who won the world light-heavyweight championship and unsuccessfully challenged Dempsey for the heavyweight title.

4 Jack "The Manassa Mauler" Dempsey (1895-1983) was world heavyweight champion between 1919 and 1926. His defence of the title which occasioned this story took place on 2nd July 1921 at Jersey City and was the first boxing match to produce a $1 million gate. Dempsey knocked out Carpentier in the fourth round.

5 An expression from the days of prize-fighting, meaning to produce a flow of blood.

6 The 18th amendment to the United States Constitution had come into force in January 1920 and introduced the Prohibition era.

7 Not a reference to hair loss but a Scottish term for parting hair.

8 Sir Philip Sassoon Bt. (1888-1939) Millionaire, Conservative

politician and art connoisseur and a close friend of the Prince of Wales (later Edward VIII).

136　Saturnalia

1　This story, published in book form in the 1993 edition, first appeared in the *Glasgow Evening News* on 23rd January 1922.
2　Plays performed by guisers at Hallowe'en.
3　The Hengler family were prominent in British entertainment from the 18th century. Among the family's enterprises were permanent circuses in London, Dublin, Hull and Glasgow. The Glasgow establishment was opened in Wellington Street by Charles Hengler in November 1885 and operated there until 1903. From the next year Hengler's Cirque performed in the Hippodrome building in Sauchiehall Street.
4　The title of the student's rag magazine and mystic cry of collectors— claimed to be derived from the exhortation "Ygorra hand over the money".
5　A higher education college for women associated with Glasgow University. The buildings are now incorporated into BBC Scotland's headquarters, Broadcasting House.
6　The name of a prominent Glasgow crammers and commercial college.

137　Keep to the Left

1　This story, published in book form in the 1993 edition, first appeared in the *Glasgow Evening News* on 27th February 1922.
2　Erchie attributes the excitement to a clash between the Glasgow Rangers F.C. and their Edinburgh rivals Heart of Midlothian.
3　An opening in a tenement building providing access to the back yard.
4　May 15th. (Whitsunday) was one of the Scottish Quarter Days on which rents etc. were payable and tenancies were renewed or surrendered.

138　Glasgow in 1942

1　This story, published in book form in the 1993 edition, first appeared in the *Glasgow Evening News* on 23rd October 1922.
2　Sir Arthur Conan Doyle (1859-1930) the historical novelist and creator of Sherlock Holmes became in later life a convert to spiritualism, writing and lecturing extensively on the subject. Another writer who looked into the future with an even larger measure of bleak pessimism than Erchie was George Orwell, author of *1984*. Attractive as it may be to draw comparisons it is unlikely that he was greatly influenced in his dystopian view of the future by Erchie's reflections. Orwell (Eric Arthur Blair) was at this time serving in Burma in the Indian Imperial Police—though in view of the significant Scottish influence in those parts it is not impossible that copies of the *Evening News* found their way to Scots engineers serving with the Irrawaddy Flotilla Company.
3　Noise or confusion.
4　The proposal to create a circus, or as we would now say, a roundabout, at the busy intersection of Argyle Street, Jamaica Street and

Union Street never came to fruition and the corner is still one of Glasgow's busiest.

5 Erchie is not, we may assume, suggesting that the "No-Accident Week" initiative would bring in visitors from The Mearns, an agricultural district in Kincardineshire. A more likely source for these timid travellers is Newton Mearns, an affluent Renfrewshire suburb of Glasgow.

6 Rubber, a corruption of caoutchouc.

139 No Accident Week

1 This story, published in book form in the 1993 edition, first appeared in the *Glasgow Evening News* on 15th January 1923.

2 A picturesque, and remarkably peaceful, village in rural Renfrewshire.

3 Many of Glasgow's policemen were traditionally recruited from the Highlands and Islands and were, in consequence, native Gaelic speakers.

4 The Glasgow Orpheus Choir was an important part of the city's cultural life for many years. Founded in 1906 by Hugh Roberton (1874-1952) it made many famous recordings. Roberton was knighted for his services to music in 1931 and continued as conductor of the Choir until 1951.

140 The Grand Old Man Comes Down

1 This story, published in book form in the 1993 edition, first appeared in the *Glasgow Evening News* on 19th March 1923.

2 William Ewart Gladstone (1809-1898) Liberal statesman and Prime Minister; frequently referred to as the "Grand Old Man". Gladstone's statue in George Square was originally sited in front of the City Chambers, where the Cenotaph now stands, and was moved, as the story indicates, to accommodate the monument to the dead of the Great War. The Cenotaph was unveiled in May 1924 by Earl Haig.

3 John Ellis, a Rochdale barber, was appointed as the public hangman in 1899 and retired from his position in March 1924 having officiated at 203 executions.

4 Gladstone's name may be associated with a design of bag or portmanteau as Erchie has it; he is much less clearly identified with *The Land o' the Leal*, a touching poem by Lady Nairne (1766-1845). The land of the leal (loyal or true-hearted) is heaven and the poem tells of a dying woman's words. The last verse gives the flavour of the piece:
    "Now fare ye weel, my ain John,
    This world's cares are vain, John,
    We'll meet, and we'll be fain,
    In the land o' the leal."

5 Many of the "Red Clydesiders" of the Independent Labour Party, such as Emmanuel Shinwell, James Maxton and David Kirkwood, elected to Parliament in 1922 had previously served on the Glasgow City Council or other public bodies such as Education Boards.

6 James Oswald (1779-1853) was a Liberal politician and active in the campaign for the 1832 Reform Bill. Oswald's statue has the reformer with his top hat in his hand—an obvious target for mischief makers of

all ages. The tale is told by George Blake that Neil Munro took the novelist Joseph Conrad across the Square to Oswald's statue after a dinner in the North British Hotel and encouraged Conrad to throw stones in the top hat and by so doing become an "honorary Glaswegian."

7   George Square does not lack a statue of a General, having monuments both to Sir John Moore (of Corunna fame) and Colin Campbell (Lord Clyde) who won renown in the Crimea and the Indian Mutiny. However Sir Robert Peel's fame was as a Tory Prime Minister and repealer of the Corn Laws. More locally he was elected Lord Rector of Glasgow University in 1836.

8   The point of this reference is that the equestrian statue of King William III, which stood until 1923 at Glasgow Cross, was removed in that year due to road alterations. It was later re-elected in Cathedral Square.

141 The Doctors' Strike

1   This story, published in book form in the 1993 edition, first appeared in the *Glasgow Evening News* on 5th November 1923.

2   As is so often the case Munro is being highly topical. A major dispute between medical practitioners and the friendly societies which administered the National Health Insurance system had broken out earlier in the year, the occasion being a proposal to reduce the capitation fee from 9/6 (47p) per head to 7/- (35p). At one stage 95% of the Glasgow doctors had withdrawn from the panel system. As may be expected the crisis provoked the standard response of a Court of Inquiry and a Royal Commission.

3   A "panel doctor" was one who treated patients under the health insurance scheme. "Graith" is a term for tools, implements, machinery required for a particular job—thus the striking doctors were picking up their tools and walking out of the quasi-state system of health care.

4   Émile Coué (1857-1926) was a French hypnotist who developed the theory of auto-suggestion. Trained as a pharmacist he became a psychotherapist and developed the doctrine of Couéism which was summed up in the mantra "Every day, in every way, I am getting better and better".

142 The Coal Crisis

1   This story, published in book form in the 1993 edition, first appeared in the *Glasgow Evening News* on 7th June 1926.

2   St Enoch's Church, at the south end of St Enoch Square had been built by the City Council in 1780 and replaced in 1827. This building was demolished in 1925, the year before this story appeared. The crisis which resulted in yet another attack on Duffy's coal quality was of course the General Strike of 4th-12th May 1926. Although the other unions returned to work after nine days the miners, a cut in whose wages was the immediate occasion for the strike, remained out until August.

3   An accurate phonetic rendering of the Dumbartonshire town of Milngavie, a noted pronunciation test for foreign visitors, English news-readers etc.

4 Butter was normally sold by the grocer or dairyman cutting a quantity off a 56lb. block and moulding it to shape with wooden handles— these frequently had a design of a thistle or other appropriate motif.